PRAISE FOR *GIRL OF*

"Nostalgia in a novel, especially in a first-pe[...]
From the opening suicide of a stuntman—"taker of all falls"—a screenwriter
recounts "the damage I caused in bygone days." This is a bildungsroman of
Hollywood dreams and cover-ups, a novel of "failure and conspiracy" on a
lavish scale. "Movies and fame: what a perfect marriage, each dependent on
projection," the young writer observes, after admitting: "I'm the sucker who
tells the story because the rest are gone." There's even a daughter named after
a movie studio, and the Communist Party is, finally, just "another dream that
had been imported to Southern California." A fast-paced novel of ambition,
deceit, and disillusionment, *Girl of My Dreams* is as thrilling as a hit movie;
yet it's also an indictment of the way the movie business works. The language
is impeccable; the architecture is so tightly constructed that the ending is
both inevitable and not what we're expecting." —John Irving, National Book
Award–winning author

"*Girl of My Dreams* is irresistible. It has been a long time since I read anything so
interesting in every way." —Joan Didion, National Book Award–winning author

"Smart, snarky, richly detailed, gossipy, hilarious and, in the end, yes, serious, Peter Davis's *Girl of My Dreams* is a thorough delight." —Richard Russo,
Pulitzer Prize–winning author of *Empire Falls*

"Thrumming with kinetic energy, *Girl of My Dreams* is a mad dash through
Hollywood in the 1930s. With insight and humor, Peter Davis explores the
magic of filmmaking, the vagaries of fame, and the lives of the many players and participants—from directors to actors to writers—who populate this
outrageous and captivating world." —Christina Baker Kline, #1 *New York
Times*-bestselling author of *Orphan Train*

"If *Girl of My Dreams* were simply a novel about Hollywood in the Golden
Age, it would qualify as superb. But it's really about America then and now—
how we love, how we cheat, what we crave, what we dread. And that's what
makes it sublime." —Beau Willimon, creator of the Emmy Award–winning
series *House of Cards* (US)

"Academy Award–winning filmmaker and acclaimed author Peter Davis is uniquely equipped to bring the glory days of Hollywood to blazing life. Young screenwriter Owen Jant gets more than he bargained for in this dark and brilliant coming-of-age novel. So does the reader. Robert Stone said a novel should be a grand slam, and Davis has knocked it out of the park. The movies have always told us who we are, giving us America writ large, and *Girl of My Dreams* is a big bonafide American classic." —Lee Smith, author of *The Last Girls*

"*Girl of My Dreams* is a vivid Hollywood romance, replete with sex, scandal, and studio intrigue, wrapped around a fierce political indictment of the violence at the heart of industrial capitalism. Peter Davis has deftly fashioned both an epic evocation of the golden age of American movies and a powerful history lesson." —Stephen Greenblatt, author of *The Swerve: How the World Became Modern*

"*Girl of My Dreams* is witty, sexy, and sharp. I loved it. Davis gives us the old, still exclusive Hollywood of the Thirties, when it had real glamour and real menace. A Hollywood that no longer exists except in this wonderful novel that is preeminently about the malleability of identity and the creation of self, both on and off the screen. Davis makes one long for the old days in all their innocent and debauched glory." —Susanna Moore, author of *In the Cut*

"Author-filmmaker Peter Davis has given us a contradiction in terms, a book about Hollywood in the Thirties that, ironically, has depth. Davis knows this turf and has populated it with richly invented characters, all striving and most failing in a place where you can't win for losing and politics divides them all. It is a wise and savvy book, with wit and pathos . . . coming soon to your screens!" —Candice Bergen, Emmy Award–winning actress

"I'm feverishly soaking up Peter Davis's marvelous novel about Hollywood, *Girl Of My Dreams*. Put it down? From these cold dead hands!" —Dick Cavett, host of *The Dick Cavett Show*

"Peter Davis has crafted a cast of characters worthy of Hollywood film in the magically sexy and inviting glory days of the 1930s. They are seemingly untouched by the Great Depression or any other form of reality except the extraordinary fantasy world created for everyone else through the sheer power and vision of the few ruthless men who trafficked in stardom. Fascinating exploration of beauty and depravity." —Christina Crawford, author of *Mommie Dearest*

"Some people write cozy tales. Academy Award winner Peter Davis has written an era—Hollywood in the Thirties—punctuated with the stench of studio politics, illicit romance, labor strife, S&M, murder, vengeance, and despair. People get rich on the whim of celluloid—and get poor just to placate whimsy. Studio tycoons, gossip columnists, gangsters, and union leaders edit the lives of those around them with impunity. And yet people sing here, sometimes in preference to talk; after all, performance is what they know. It is the world of illusion, and its players rarely discern the difference between what is real and what is imagined. Written in vivid and distinct prose, *Girl of My Dreams* is a five-star novel." —Bob Rafelson, director of *Five Easy Pieces*

"*Girl of My Dreams* is truly wonderful. Set in Hollywood during the 1930s, it's the time of my mother and father, Margaret Sullavan and Leland Hayward, who were beginning their major careers. That time is rendered precisely and winningly in all its glamour and affliction and recklessness." —Brooke Hayward, author of *Haywire*

"A young blood on the make in Hollywood, then and now, is the stuff of a great story, and Peter Davis has written a page-turning novel of the legendary Thirties starring exactly the kind of people who made that the golden age of American fantasy. Every page has its delights, its horrors, its humor, sometimes all three at once. *Girl of My Dreams* is the mirror of America in the decade that led to everything we are today." —Ben Mankiewicz, host of Turner Classic Movies (TCM)

"*Girl of My Dreams* is the enchanting tale of what would have happened if *Downton Abbey* had been made in Hollywood in the 1930s. It's the time of my parents with all that decade's bright lights and deep shadows." —Hoagy Bix Carmichael, producer of *Stardust Road the Musical*

GIRL of MY DREAMS

GIRL OF MY DREAMS

A Novel

Peter Davis

Cover design by Neil Alexander Heacox

ISBN: 978-1-4976-8228-3

Distributed by Open Road Distribution
345 Hudson Street
New York, NY 10014
www.openroadmedia.com

For Alicia

GIRL of MY DREAMS

What happens on the screen isn't quite real; it leaves open a vague cloudy space for the poor, for dreams and the dead. Hurry hurry, cram yourself full of dreams to carry you through the life that's waiting for you outside, when you leave here, to help you last a few days more in that nightmare of things and people. Among the dreams choose the ones most likely to warm your soul.

Louis-Ferdinand Céline, *Journey to the End of the Night*

1

Joey Ankles the Lot

Picture a time when left was right and right was wrong.

Picture this, a man who looks like a boy perched on a motorcycle at the top of a palisade above the ocean, his face empty as if he doesn't quite know what he is supposed to do next.

This is what happened when I was in my twenties in the Thirties, a story of wilting bloom. We came, we wished, we dined out on promise. Seeing that tumultuous dawn break over us like a great wave, who could know if we'd be borne on it toward a gleaming new world or drowned in its foaming fury? Compared to Joan Crawford or Marlene Dietrich, Palmyra Millevoix was a fresh breeze rippling through aspens. Compared to the Big Strike in San Francisco, Hollywood's guild wars were milkshakes. Compared to the Communist Party, Jubilee Pictures was anarchy itself. Compared to the Depression, our salaries were not merely astronomical but pornographic. Let's turn one of those around: compared to Palmyra Millevoix—Pammy, which she disdained but accepted—Greta Garbo was a fraud. Into the dungeon wild dropped our Pammy, sorceress of undisclosed fantasies, while I, slave to regard, was shackled to the keep's lowest rung.

Here comes Palmyra's brother-in-law, the stuntman Joey Jouet, only to be yanked off, a reminder of what could happen in that time and the cause of my being funneled into his sister-in-law's sphere. He serves, too, as a warning of Mossy's carelessness. Yes, I knew Amos Zangwill, knew him before the war. He was different then.

In those days Mossy kept a lackey he used as a hatchet wielder. Dunster Clapp was the reptile, a remittance man from the east eager to bulge his trust fund by enrolling as a toady at Jubilee. It was a fetish with him to take orders from the strong and pass them along to the weak and dependent. You could see it in his face: pampered, dishonest, cold but also scared. He was gleeful when carrying out orders.

Cutting costs, on Saturday afternoon Clapp had told Joey Jouet, a Jubilee employee and therefore supplicant in these hard times, that he was having too many accidents and had to get off the lot. Clapp fired half a dozen other studio workers that day. When Jouet was summoned he was at Victorville on location in a costume epic where he was mortally wounded in several sword duels and a fall from a castle parapet. He performed these stunts flawlessly. He had expected to be in Victorville another ten days. Stunned, he didn't feel he could go straight home with this news. He picked up his Ariel motorcycle at the studio and drove it to a motor court in Hollywood. What could he tell his wife, unable to design and decorate sets because she was home now taking care of their two small daughters? Could he go to Mossy Zangwill? What a joke!

Joey Jouet was the kind of Hollywood worker who loved every minute of his job. Loved perfecting a leap into thin air, a dueling technique, a plunge through a window so the star wouldn't be the one to get hurt. He was enthralled at the way a plot sprang to life as real actors and fake buildings were thrust into service to the story. Joey studied other jobs on the set besides his own—the grip, the gaffer, the decorator. It wasn't a matter of aspiration; remarkably for Hollywood, Joey had very little actual ambition. What this curly-haired eager young man had was love of how movies were made.

He had run off from his bad home in Shawnee Mission, Kansas, not to Hollywood but to Ringling Brothers. He joined the circus at fifteen and by paying attention to the performers when he wasn't cleaning lion and elephant cages, Joey was able to become an acrobat in three years. He was too careful to be a great acrobat, and he was also not particularly theatrical. He enjoyed the sensation of floating—just being free of his childhood home was a form of weightlessness—but he wasn't fond of repeating the same act again and again. He saw too much cruelty to the animals and too much among the people, the man who dove fifty feet into the shallow pool whipping the unicycle rider with a chain, the lion tamer running off with the wife of the fire-eater. In those days numberless kids were beaten by numberless fathers, and Joey had had his fill of brutality in Shawnee Mission. Nor was applause, which the clowns and other acrobats gulped, important to Joey. The winter he turned twenty, when the circus headed back to Sarasota, Joey went in the other direction. He found his true home and vocation in pictures.

By the time he was twenty-five, Joey was every assistant director's favorite stunt double. When I knew him he was thirty or so, regularly working with cameramen to design his own stunts. His curls were naturally blond, those of an innocent five-year-old, but he was often wigged depending on whom he had to absorb a sock in the jaw for. While Mossy Zangwill was pushing, dragging, ordaining Jubilee's rise from a Poverty Row studio to the status of what *Variety* called a Minor-Major, Joey Jouet was taking falls in some of Mossy's big action pictures. He'd done such a good job in *Fugitives from Folsom* they let Joey keep the Ariel motorcycle he'd ridden.

I saw him a few times keenly combing a set where I, a junior writer, had been dispatched to help with a few lines of dialogue. The rest comes from the police record. And Pammy.

Ever eager to please, with innocent boyish features to mock his thin mustache of a stock villain, Joey Jouet, taker of falls for everyone from Doug Fairbanks (Sr. and Jr.) to Trent Amberlyn to Jimmy Cagney, paused his Ariel on the hill at the top of Chautauqua Boulevard that bright Sunday in the spring of 1934. I suppose he readied himself. Surveyed the scene, panning in effect from the Santa Monica mountains around and down over the ocean and out to where Catalina Island lay, visible in those smogless days. I wait for him at the bottom of the hill, as if Jouet's destiny were in the future, still to be played out. As if Mossy Zangwill could change course, or Pammy Millevoix could.

Of all human faculties memory is the most insistent yet also the most fallible. Since I am not among the legions of the formerly famous,

I have neither scores to settle nor apologies to pour like syrup over the damage I caused in bygone days. Oh, I may have changed a few names of people whose grandchildren now run things and could want me for a quick rewrite. But essentially this is what happened, my stupendous renegade recollection. Let my chronicles of mortification stand. Hooray for Hollywood.

Unable to believe at first that Jubilee Pictures would let him go, Joey had called another of Mossy Zangwill's henchmen, the production chief Seaton Hackley, from the motor court where he spent Saturday night after coming in from Victorville. Hackley was known as a troubleshooter; sometimes he could modify decisions even if he couldn't reverse them, cushion blows even if he couldn't prevent them. "This must be a mistake, what Dunster Clapp told me," Joey said to Seaton Hackley. "Can't you fix it?"

"No can do, Joey," said Hackley, hanging up.

Joey fitted the goggles over his eyes, adjusted the strap around his curls and started rolling, then hurtling, down Chautauqua, a steep grade. He might have been an aviator. When he slowed at the bottom of the incline, after looking up the coast toward Malibu, he turned down toward the Pier a mile away. He was on the winding beach road, already a narrow thoroughfare that people rushed along in their roadsters, a slender hint of its later proclamation as the Pacific Coast Highway. Joey halted quickly. By the side of the road he knew someone. Mervyn Galant's Hispano Suiza had a puncture!

Joey asked the washed-up silents director if he needed help. As always, Galant hid his shame beneath a stream of words. "Bet your life I do, gave the chauffeur the day off, say I know you, didn't you handle a chariot for Freddy Niblo in *Ben Hur*, you worked in one of my pictures too, did a wingwalk for me in *Maisie Flies Over the Moon*, didn't you." It wasn't a question and by this time Joey had the Hispano Suiza jacked up. In five minutes he had replaced the wire-spoked flat tire with the spare and heard Galant—as the old hasbeen himself later reported—offer him a job. "Son, no question there's work for you on my next picture. Where you serving now, Metro?"

A loud report made Joey jump, a passing car's backfire. "No," Joey said, "I've been at Jubilee." "Jubilee?" Galant arched his famous hedgerow brows. "Heap of work on that lot, isn't there?" "Yesterday," Joey said, "was my last day." "Sorry to hear it, son. Zangwill's a viper, all right." "Yes, Mr. Galant," Joey allowed before he was off again.

In seconds he covered the mile to the Santa Monica Pier and passed under the half-moon sign offering sportfishing. I suspect Mervyn Galant's job offer was ironic to Joey but not bitterly so. I suspect he was thinking about his ten-thousand-dollar life insurance policy. Jubilee would hire someone's cheaper nephew or cousin who was agile and had been laid off by a carnival or circus. The Depression was closing marginal circuses that were unable to do enough business to feed the animals, dumping acrobats onto the tight stuntman market.

Once, on a set between takes, Joey saw a woman drawing a kitchen with two stoves. Shyly, he asked why two. She told him if he looked at the script he'd see it called for two stoves for the different dishes the cavalry would be fed when they paused at the outpost. Why not forget the stoves and have two large pots sitting over the fire in the fireplace the carpenters have already built, he suggested. The set designer took this to the producer since no one consulted directors on program Westerns, and the producer was pleased to save the money. Within days the saucy designer-decorator Elise Millevoix and the modest Joey Jouet were a sweet item on the set of *Cheyenne Sharpshooters*. Though a set designer was a number of rungs above a stuntman on the studio ladder, and Elise Millevoix had a star for a sister, Joey added a glow to any space he occupied.

No one on the Pier was disturbed when Joey rode his motorcycle the length of it, careful to dodge the Sunday strollers who came out from downtown on streetcars. A few of the vendors waved, recognizing the stuntman who had leaped from piers in several movies. "Hey Joey," the dwarf who ran the bumper cars shouted, "King Vidor send you down here to get ready for a cop chase?" The man who sold cotton candy told his customer, "They darken Joey Jouet's hair he can look like Walter Huston, Bruce Cabot, anybody, if he's going fast enough. Probably practicing for a New York shot at Coney Island. His wife does something too. Her sister's Palmyra Millevoix. Connections."

Joey pulled up at the end of the Pier as if he were reining in a horse. The cotton candy man said he saw Jouet placing something on the railing at the end of the Pier. On the cycle, Joey returned as far as the carousel, and it looked as though he were leaving the Pier. He spun around, racing the Ariel's engine before he roared out toward the end, vigilant about avoiding so many parents with their small children.

STUDIO DAREDEVIL IN FINAL STUNT was the headline in Hearst's *Examiner*. The story said that Joey Jouet, brother-in-law of Jubilee Pictures's brightest star, Palmyra Millevoix, had put up a ramp out of planks used to repair the floor of the Santa Monica Pier, then launched himself as though from a ski lift far out into the ocean, which swallowed him and his motorcycle so fast the stuntman could never have heard the throngs on the Pier begin to scream. Jouet had been driven to suicide, the *Examiner* went on to declare, by the Reds, who wouldn't let him alone after he briefly joined and then quit the Party. The *Los Angeles Times,* sounding its own alarm, claimed that Joey, newly unemployed due to belt-tightening at Jubilee Pictures, was a casualty of the Depression Franklin D. Roosevelt was making even worse with his socialistic policies. *Variety* wrote that Joseph Cayson Jouet, champion of stuntmen, was a shining example of the truism that the good die young. "A victim of Hollywood," the reporter wrote, "where 1934 is proving you're up one day and sunk low the next, Joey Jouet perished, paradoxically, mimicking one of his masterful stunts, driven into the Pacific by no one's screenplay but his own. The whole town sends sympathies to his widow and toddlers."

That was when Pammy called me. Would I compose (she used that word, as if she were asking for a song) a few lines about Joey for her to say at the funeral? We had met twice, once at a writers' cocktail party. She had listened attentively to the host; writers love that. She said now she needed to be with her sister and nieces all day and night, and she was too overcome to think. "Poor Joey, poor Elise, poor little girls never to know their generous adoring father." Shocked, I said it would be an honor to do anything to help. Was she favoring me by asking a favor because she'd heard I'd been assigned to *A Doll's House*? "You're such a consummate dear, Owen," she said, "I am so *désolée*." And so I went off those planks, too. The surf that covered Joey Jouet soaked us all.

The funeral was held on Jubilee's Stage Three, a red rose garland the size of a wheelbarrow decked in front of the casket. With a few exceptions, nobody who was anybody was there: a stuntman after all. Stuntmen themselves, technicians, and set designers were scattered in folding chairs; a sprinkling of assistant producers showed up. Mossy Zangwill gave the eulogy, blunting criticism of the studio for having laid off Joey the day before his death. He called Joey Jubilee's own daring young man on the flying trapeze. "We couldn't exist without men like Joey," he said. "You can't make pictures without excitement. You can't have excitement without stunts, and stunts can't happen without stuntmen. Joe was the best, and we'll miss him more than he'll ever know."

No one even whispered—why, if he was the best, was Joey Jouet fired?

In the front row, her tears flowing freely, Joey's widow, Elise Millevoix Jouet, held both her small daughters in her lap. The daughters dazed, the mother inconsolable. I didn't know yet how inconsolable. Palmyra was too upset to say the sentences I'd written and went right to music. Her voice cracked on the word "wretch" in *Amazing Grace*. It took less than twenty minutes to turn Stage Three back into the set for *Prelude to Murder*, for which I'd written a couple of scenes, changing the killer from the conductor to the flutist but keeping the victim in place beneath the cribbage table.

Mossy left alone everyone with the rank of assistant producer or above; all technical workers who attended Joey's funeral were docked a half day's pay.

2

The Palmyra Millevoix Booster

Years earlier, on seeing Pammy's first test, Sam Goldwyn said she couldn't act, wasn't beautiful enough, and would make people nervous. "God's sake, I've seen happier statues. Never blinks. Who the hell she think she is, Queen Victoria?" (Which Goldwyn pronounced Bictodia.) He also thought Pammy's features were too fine and too collected, like Jimmy Cagney's, toward the center of her face. Passable in Cagney, impossible in a woman. An MGM cameraman came to her rescue, discerning it was only her regal forehead that made Pammy's features seem low, and he knew how to deal with that. Actresses, especially those past thirty, like to be shot from above so audiences can't see neck wrinkles or any hint of jowls. Palmyra, still in her twenties when she first came out to be tested, was actually in need of the opposite treatment since she had no wrinkles at all. The MGM cameraman suggested, just before what was to be her second and last test, that she be shot to indulge her features from slightly below her chinline, less like a heroine, more like a goddess. In person, even with several Hollywood years behind her, Palmyra was still so unscathed by makeup and miscasting that eyes flew naturally to her as if she were a nest and the rest of us lost sparrows looking for home.

One afternoon in 1933, Mossy had called me to his office to order press releases on Pammy, the first singing star who was both composer and actress. He didn't like the valentines that Jubilee's publicity depart-

12

ment was churning out so he'd see what a junior screenwriter might come up with. When I met Miss Millevoix she wasn't in the negligee female stars affected in their bungalows. She wore a dowdy polkadot housedress and was playing checkers with her six-year-old daughter Millicent. Millie's first look at me was a scowl. Her mother glanced up and smiled.

"*Three* games of checkers, Millie!" Palmyra said. "You'll be beating me by the time you're, well, eight, no nine, when you're nine you'll be three kings up on me before I get one. You know you will." A reluctant grin sneaked onto Millie's face. "Costanza?" Palmyra summoned, and a tidy Filipina emerged from the next room. "Time to take Millie home." The frown that returned to Millie outlasted her mother's hug and almost became tears when Costanza had her out the door. She stuck her tongue out at me.

"Let's sing," were the first words Pammy spoke to me as she headed toward her piano. "I hate a white piano," she said. "It's a decoration, not a musical instrument. This one's left over from Jeanette MacDonald and I hear she didn't like it either."

"I can't," I said, "I really can't sing." "Yes you can," she said, "do you know any of mine?" "About like I kn-know the n-national anthem," I stammered. A lie: I was occupied mostly with getting decent script assignments, not memorizing songs.

"You're supposed to get to know me, Mossy says, so let's try a few bars, okay?" It was if she were coaxing a child, and I was embarrassed into joining her. "There's things I do," she sang and played while I tried to hold her tune, "And things I don't, And in words of just one syllable, There's things I will and things I won't, But can we be Jack and Jillable?" Palmyra went on, not flirting despite the lyrics, and when she sailed past "To the party you'll be bringable, If you're Crosby you can be Bingable," she swung over into a piece of another song that I stayed out of, a jazzy one. "I've got a guy, I long to be with'm, He flies higher than all of the birds; I'd give up my melody, harmony and rhythm, If I can just get him to say the right words." She included a two-measure tag that became a jazz riff at the end.

Pammy medleyed through a few of her hits, and I got the point. My press releases would write themselves after this exclusive recital—these sweet sounds from the voice of a young widowed (was she?) mother bravely carrying on. Treacle spilling from my typewriter. Listening and watching, I was in awe but not in thrall. Something remote about her, not merely professionalism though she had plenty of that, did not invite familiarity. Perhaps it was that she was foreign. A moat surrounded her.

"Negro and Irish singers both do my songs better than I do," she said. I saw why. Distance, separation, was important to her. She didn't take you into her confidence like the black and Irish singers she mentioned. I was invited to hear her sing but not into intimacy with the singer. The best of her music is bone simple, with an air of permissiveness that encourages improvisation by other musicians. Palmyra cradled a song with a voice like smoke, and in her blues and torches I heard the suggestion of pleasure with the certain expectation of pain. When her songs were appropriated by black musicians, as black music had earlier been appropriated by whites, they had more to them. Her melodies beg for the harmonies and cadences that Duke Ellington first gave them and that have been improvised by successors including the rockers.

Perhaps only Mae West, writing scripts for her own movies, was as versatile as Palmyra, a multilingual icon in the musical theaters of Paris and Berlin before she ever came to America. The first time she landed in New York, not long after the Great War, Palmyra had been taken under the wing of Eddie Marks, an old time song plugger from Tin Pan Alley. Marks brought her into the American idiom and got her singing jobs in speakeasies, yet he also weaned her toward ditties that didn't show her best side. Her novelty tunes had brief currencies, never became standards. But she was getting her American education. She wrote a little number ending with "Yes I'd like to get even, not even with Steven, I'd just like to get even … with you," a song whose melodic line is as natural as walking. She stayed in New York two years. Possibly because she needed to get away from vaudevillians like Eddie Marks, Palmyra Millevoix was one of the few creative talents who actually improved by migrating from New York to Hollywood.

But that was later. First she returned to Europe for most of the Twenties. Palmyra knew the expatriate Americans but did not belong with them. She sang in all the continental capitals, and almost as an afterthought she became a mother.

～

Finishing my private concert in her bungalow, Pammy said, affecting an all-purpose European accent, "Vair can ve go for some absinthe?" Off we went, she still in her polkadot housedress and I in my flapping wide tie and wider lapels, across Venice Boulevard from Jubilee to The Moving Picture Bar, the low-ceilinged studio hangout. We were brought double Scotch sours. Photographs of Jubilee notables, including of course La Millevoix herself, speckled the walls. "So what do you want to know?" she asked.

My eyes bulged. I wanted to know everything. "I suppose to begin at—"

"I was born at Strasbourg, I think," she laughed, "but make up whatever you like, that's what I do. Not as old as the century, two years younger than Mossy—but never mind, you'll make that up too." Listening to her I did detect some kind of accent, but I couldn't locate it. "You'll be torn between having me ten years younger than I am and needing me to be old enough to be the respectable mother of a six-year-old in this year of someone's lord 1933."

When she passed quickly over what she called a macabre Belgian convent in Ghent, followed by her finishing school in Switzerland and on to her time in a Berlin cabaret and then to the Paris stage, it occurred to me to ask about her husband.

"Husband?" She looked as though I'd struck her or perhaps used a Sanskrit word she didn't understand. "Ah, Millie's father, of course. *Tragique, mon cher, tragique.* Say what you will. I'll be amused. Try me," and she winked, "on my love for America."

Press releases tumbled from my Royal. Admittedly purple, the words were not about love but enchantment. I typed of how, for her closest friends, Palmyra Millevoix would elide from her own "inimitable" songs into Rudy Vallee's Vagabond Lover, which she sang low and a little husky, not almost falsetto and defended the way Rudy did. For the signature phrase, "I'm just a vagabond lover," she brought the words to great length and held them there, roasting her chestnuts until they were done to the crisp she wanted, before she rushed in with, "In search of a sweetheart it seems," which she sped through as one might rifle a drawer, until she reached the final syllable. She held "seems" for four created notes so listeners would be drinking from her voice as from a fountain in the village square, preparing them for the last words of the song, "The girl of my vagabond dreams." She held "dreams" until you knew it was a village square you reached after a long, parched pilgrimage, a search, home to the home of your heart.

I was so carried away I made Millicent's father a daring French aviator dying heroically in the final days of the Great War. Someone in Publicity, which had earlier maintained Millie was a little sister, pointed out that Millicent Millevoix would have to be a teenager if her father were killed in a war that ended fifteen years earlier. I made the father into an Italian nobleman who died when his Bugatti crashed at Le Mans.

What I left out of my press releases was that when Pammy made her way to Hollywood in early 1930 she had been forced to change her name. Palmyra was too ugly, Millevoix too foreign. Her acting name became Pamela Miles. She was shoveled around to several studios until an executive said she obviously couldn't act but he needed bodies, sounding like a general demanding fresh troops if only for cannon fodder. He insisted she be made a platinum blonde. Pammy herself called her hair dirty blonde, but it carried a trace of animal red; it reflected her features and expressions. Her open gait, legs a little apart—challenging as a no-nonsense honey blonde with russet tones—looked only slutty in platinum blonde. Platinum was just right for Harlow, just wrong for Millevoix. Her flashes of anger, which looked attractively subversive with a wink of humor, were mere petulance in platinum, spoiled petulance at that.

"I don't know why any of you wanted me at all," Pammy sighed to a Warner Brothers producer, "when all the studio does is alter me like a dress. They change my name, my nose, my hair, hide my ass, make my breasts look like ice cream cones. The only things you leave alone are my ears and teeth. Everything else you pad, chop or mash." "Oh no," her producer told her, "we'll get to your teeth in good time, have to close that gap between your canines and bicuspids so there's no space between them when you flash that Grand Canyon smile."

She made four pictures at Warner Brothers, one silent, three talkies, all turkeys. Then Pamela Miles, heartily sick of what she was doing, walked a picture whose director bullied his actors with bad line readings. After she told the studio the picture was arch and witless, they suspended her. Her agent warned her disobedience in this town is like poison to the Medicis. Warners had their planter call the gossip queen Louella Parsons.

In her column Louella hectored. "Kids these days always know best, but if I were young Miss Miles, fresh from what some call the seedier precincts of the Continent, I would special delivery my lucky bosom back onto the set of *Baby Can't Play* pronto if not sooner." As unjust as she felt the Warners campaign was, Pammy wouldn't budge. She was through with Pamela Miles. "If Greta Garbo can get away with a name that un-American," Pammy said, "I may as well fail as myself since I'm a complete disaster as someone else." She did what other actors and actresses only wished they could do: she went home and wrote a hit. Two actually, under her own name.

"Born Blue" was declamatory, with the tempo of speech but chanted musically, nourished by the Deep South blues she had begun to listen to on what were then called race records. After an up tempo verse that warned listeners, the sweetly mournful chorus:

> If you hear this song in a bar or a train,
> Put a nickel in the Wurlitzer and play it again:
> Born blue, born blue,
> That's me, not you,
> You can make me laugh, you can make me cry,
> Sometimes you make me want to lie down and die
> 'Cause I was born blue, it's always been true.
> No matter where I go or what I do
> It's what I know, what I've been through,
> For I was born, I was born, I was born blue.

She ripped into the last two lines with a blowtorch:

> I was born, yes I say born, my heart is torn, Mister blow it
>   on your horn—
> 'Cause I was <u>born</u> blue.

This became a signature not only for herself but for millions who had the Depression surrounding, defining their lives. Yet Pammy knew a record that was only sad would have a limited appeal to fans who also wanted to kick up their heels and simply sing. She wrote the flip side of "Born Blue" as a playful melody that could be sung anywhere at a party or by a barbershop quartet. Here's the verse to "Can Sara Wear a Pair 'a Dungarees":

> When I see a pretty girl in tights
> I wonder how she spends her days and nights;
> Though I really hate to bother
> I'll just have to ask her father
> If she can go informal
> And still be mostly normal
> At the party, it's the biggest one in town,
> On the dance floor if she doesn't wear a gown.

The crooning chorus was belted by male singers as if they owned it:

> Oh,
> Can Sara wear a pair 'a dungarees?
> I'll ask it sweetly, I'll go down upon my knees—
> Hear my prayer, Mr. McDougall, I know you're kinda frugal,
> So can Sara wear a pair 'a dungarees?
> Mr. Mac said there'll be rumors
> If she don't stay in her bloomers;
> This ain't what me and Pearl
> Had in mind for our little girl,
> So Sara wears no pair 'a dungarees.

> But Mr. Mac, when Sara's gone to college
> Where profs impart the knowledge
> And parcel out those bachelorette degrees—
> She's bound to want to wear a—
> And I'll take care of Sara
> If you'll only listen to my fervent pleas:

When she's gone off to Bryn Mawr
With Aunt Sadie's kid Lenore,
Sure then Sara wears a pair 'a dungarees.

For its time the song was slightly risqué, just edgily modern, since it did assert the right of women to wear pants. After Pammy's record came out, Eddie Cantor quickly followed with his own version (of course, he wouldn't touch "Born Blue"; Bing Crosby did but his jaunty recording didn't attempt the anguish in Pammy's) and for a while Rudy Vallee had more requests to sing about Sara in her dungarees than even "The Whiffenpoof Song," his own standard. Pammy was bringing in over sixty thousand dollars a month from both songs during their heyday.

There was a problem trying to start a motion picture career over again, but the solution became Mossy Zangwill and Jubilee Pictures, which bought her contract from Warners in late 1931.

In quick succession, the reborn Palmyra Millevoix played Mary Queen of Scots; a war-widowed singing mother struggling to make it on Broadway (art imitating life imitating art, in my attempted legend); and an English doctor trying to wipe out a plague in India where, naturally, she meets Ronald Colman.

Her star had risen. By 1934 she was who women wanted to be. And men wanted.

3

Assaulting Ibsen

Early Saturday, two weeks after the demise of Joey Jouet, I lay on my living room floor confronting the ceiling's jagged crack—sinister some mornings, today a bolt of lightning—and began the tantric exercises everyone was doing for digestion, muscle tone, eternal youth, the optimistic Southern California compound then and now. "I am monarch here," I said aloud. "No one can top or stop me because I am the march of my generation. A monarch who rules his fate."

Such a fool. I am. Better to know or not know you're a fool? I'm the sucker who tells the story because the rest are gone. Or, like Mossy, ageless, now refusing to read books, especially if they're about him. Doing the exercises I wondered if Joey, motorcycling into the Pacific, had died of fright. No, that wasn't Joey. He was dead on impact then, with a broken neck, as if he'd hanged himself? Or did he drown, like a fisherman swept off his lobster boat by a wave he hadn't seen coming?

I was catapulted into an obsession by Joey's suicide as effectively as if he'd hurled flaming branches at my walled castle, igniting every chair and curtain inside. Because Pammy asked me for a favor I surmised I had her favor. The hope that plants a seedling of itself in a young breast is as much curse as blessing since it drains every moment of contentment. Potential is always rearing its greedy portentous head.

The joke was that she hadn't even made use of the favor I did, speaking no words at the funeral.

My castle was a shack, tucked on Sumac Lane in Santa Monica Canyon. A closet of a bedroom, bathroom with a stall shower, kitchen with a card table in it, and the tiny, dark living room with two wooden chairs, an empty crate for a coffee table, and a secondhand couch I kept doilies on to avoid having to look at the stuffing that leaked from either end. It wasn't as though I had visitors. Yet when I looked out at the sycamores and eucalyptus climbing the hill to where associate producers and car dealers lived who could afford much more than my prewar forty dollars a month, I was happy.

By prewar I mean pre-prewar because in 1934 only the most prescient—Winston Churchill and a smattering of hypersensitive Jews—thought we'd ever be fighting the Germans again. The booming Twenties of my teens had passed quickly, hollow though the boom was, while the Depression Thirties were dragging ponderously. But for me at twenty-four, there was already a job in pictures, this compact shelter, and Palmyra. Mine was a love all the more precious for being unknown to its object.

Nor was it only Palmyra. It looked as though I was getting on in the world. I'd been praised for my idea about two sets of robbers coming to knock over the same bank unaware of each other; Gable and Cagney, as polar opposites, would be perfect for the two gang chiefs, or try Eddie Robinson if we couldn't get Cagney. I'd been invited to Mossy's big party, I'd had lunch with Trent Amberlyn and Fred Mac-Murray, everyone had seen Palmyra Millevoix—yes!—blow a grateful kiss to me as I left the commissary, and I'd been assigned A Doll's House, which four other writers had failed to lick.

At this time, early 1934, I was disguised as a blank page on which other people wrote orders, urgent entreaties, or merely a list of chores. A writer, yes I was that, but a derivative, complaisant sort who wanted only to oblige, not to express a self at least as hidden from me as from others. Watch what I do with my treatment for A Doll's House, I said to my estranged self, never mind Ibsen: I didn't need approval from the dead. I'll give them a Nora tougher and more lovable than he had.

The kiss from Palmyra, blown across two tables and observed by a squadron of my betters, was the result of my providing her a stanza she meant to use in a song she was writing for a picture she wasn't in and hadn't even been set to score. Jimmy McHugh and Dorothy Fields had been writing the melodies and lyrics for a musical with a kid in it who was always being teased by taller boys. The producer felt that if the kid, played by Mickey Rooney, had a song of his own it could literally beef up his character. When McHugh and Fields, who Hollywood said ripped up the Depression and threw it away with "On the Sunny Side of the Street," returned to New York for a show that meant more to them than this movie, it was natural for Palmyra Millevoix to be asked to fill in with a couple of numbers. We were kind of a family at Jubilee—larger and more loving than our original families in many cases, if also more contentious—and it was just as natural for Palmyra, who was busy starring in two other pictures, to reach down and ask a junior writer if he had any quick thoughts for a song Rooney might sing. The next morning I handed her assistant these lines: "Please don't call me Shorty anymore:/ I find it nasty and it makes me really sore;/ If you must talk about my height,/ Be prepared for me to fight/ Until the day comes when I've left you on the floor."

Why did Palmyra pick on me in the first place? Out of gratitude for my funeral oration she hadn't used? Maybe she wanted to help an eager beaver or didn't want someone more established whose work she couldn't discard. She wound up using only my first line, but when she threw the kiss at me in the commissary, I levitated. Having seen her in a couple of places, I now saw her everywhere, including all the places she wasn't. I became a fantasy factory, a miniature of Hollywood itself.

Elsewhere on the lot I looked for approval from any quarter—an illiterate producer, lazy actors, a short-order cook of a director. If the approval, in other words, came from morons, I valued it just as highly. I didn't consider the vacuum where my moral conscience was supposed to be any more than I did the desert where my creative impulses, such as they may have been, lay starved and gasping.

I will meet a girl at Mossy's party who will change my life tonight, I thought as I jounced along to work in my Essex coupe, and her attentions will entice Palmyra to take notice. This morning I'll make *A Doll's House*, my first shot at an A picture, accessible to the unwashed and, more important, acceptable to Amos Zangwill. Other writers will observe enviously when I deliver my treatment to Gershon Lidowitz, husband of the daughter of movie pioneer Abraham Fine. Mossy disdained the ungifted Lidowitz but he needed Abe Fine, still trusted in semi-retirement by the New York bankers who financed Jubilee. Mossy knew that Fine knew Gershon's limitations and was grateful he was retained as a weak-handed Jubilee producer. Lidowitz, said to be the original butt of the quip that the son-in-law also rises, was known by his many detractors as Littlewits.

We reported irritably for typewriter duty every Saturday morning at nine and tried to leave by one. The other writers on *A Doll's House* had all listened to Littlewits and like leashed dogs had Nora decide to stay with Torvald in the end, destroying the play. Mossy knew this was wrong but he didn't know how to get around the puritanical mood of the new Motion Picture Code that was beginning to be enforced. No more loose morals or broken homes. The Roaring Twenties, the Fatty Arbuckle sex scandal, onscreen flaunting of Prohibition, freewheeling lives of the stars themselves—all this offended the religious core of America, which called for theater boycotts. Hollywood trembled. Movie executives, often Jews yearning to be accepted by Christian America, decided to police their industry before the offended Bible Belt and the inflamed Catholic hierarchy declared total war on their products and, by extension, themselves.

The early screen versions of *A Doll's House* had been reasonably faithful to Ibsen, complete with the overacting that nineteenth century European theater brought into the motion picture's silent decades. I knew Nora had to leave Torvald; the story was Nora's coming of age, not her relationship with her stuffed-panda husband who deserves abandonment. Littlewits fretted a hint of divorce would annoy the censorious new Code-keepers, and he insisted the movie not end with the door shutting behind Nora. That last part had to be attacked this Saturday morning before my other triumphs could follow.

"Where you been, Ownsie?" Mr. Royal said, welcoming me just before seven, long before any other writers had pulled onto the lot. "Don't you know this third act needs more wrinkles before you can turn it in even to someone as dim as Littlewits? Can't do it all by myself much as I'd like to." "Shut your trap," I ordered, "let's see if we can light the fuse." "You think you can cold-cock this mess in a couple hours and then amscray?" That was the way even typewriters talked in those days. "Won't get the girl if I don't give her chocolates," I said. "That's all you know," said the Royal.

"Page thirty-two, third act," the Royal warned, "we need eight pages to the mark Littlewits likes to see in his treatments. What's Nora gonna do?"

4

Fame: A Lamentation

Ta-ra-ra-boom-de-yay, here comes our Joel McCrea, his star shines night and day, Ta-ra-ra-boom-de-yay!" Mossy's crier ushered special guests into the party as they descended the steps from the foyer to the long living room that had been turned into a ballroom by Jubilee's prop department. "Ta-ra-ra-boom-de-yee, let's welcome Edward G., hope he's not mad at me, 'cause if he is I'll flee." The crier, who accompanied himself on an accordion, was an assistant producer named Teet Beale. His face looked as if it had been stomped on yet he had clearly spent the afternoon in a Jubilee makeup room. High arched, plucked eyebrows, hair dyed the red of an ace of diamonds. Beale had the performed jolliness of a court jester who knows of an impending beheading that hasn't been announced yet.

This was my first big-name Hollywood festivity, the first time I'd been at Mossy's house in the three years I'd worked, off and on, for him. The word "party" applied to the evening not as a merry gathering but as an ecclesiastical chain of command from the cardinal on down. The guests were less a cast of characters in any particular production than a directory of those who had caught and held and in turn craved Mossy's attention. They looked as if they belonged on a Quattrocento canvas that included everyone who was anyone in Florence. Mossy himself had yet to put in an appearance at his own gala; he was said to be upstairs.

With no one paying attention to me, I looked around. The place was lavish, of course, Spanish colonial for a grandee at least, perhaps a prince. Yet I had the sense of rooms that were the outcome not so much of furnishing as looting. The style was imperial arriviste, with everything, from pictures to couches, appearing to have come from boxcars that had been uncrated that morning. The walls held Van Ruisdale, Giorgione, Van Gogh, Renoir, Manet, each one plaqued with the artist's name and dates as if it were in a museum but with an effect more aggressive than informative.

Guests floated by me snatching canapés from the trays of Filipino houseboys, engaged not really in conversation but in ultimatum. "You'll have to choose, Lansing, between this town and me because I can't stand it here anymore, fetch me a martini." "Get me Loretta Young and you can have anyone you want." Two men in doublebreasted suits were trading movie stars as if they were playing cards or hog futures. "I'll give you Shearer for Talmadge but you have to send her back eight weeks maximum. Thalberg will insist." A sleek high-cheekboned woman cast a frozen look at her weary ascotted watery-eyed husband whose hand was in the crotch of the scared brown boy who was passing *escargots*. "Oh Roo Roo," he said, "don't be so Oyster Bay." And the most familiar refrain: "I'll never work with either of them again and that's final."

The room was filling up with both failure and conspiracy, neither of which I could recognize on this Saturday evening in my yearning twenties. I was so surrounded by what I took for success I was blind to everything but what shone. I felt green and dumb, as if I'd been in Hollywood three days instead of three years. Guests were auditioning for other guests' opinions as well as their absent host's; here was where you found out where you stood on the weights and measures of the town, and on the scale covering the ballroom floor I weighed less than an ounce.

"Where, for God's sake, is our host with his gaze blank and pitiless as the sun?" I whirled at the basso voice to find Yancey Ballard, the writer of historical adventures like *Spanish Armada* and *Caesar's Curse*. The lanky, cheerful, cynical Yancey was known to his fellow screenwriters and even to a number of producers as Yeatsman due to his affection for, and inclination to quote, the poet himself. He'd work Yeats into any conversation, usually without attribution. Yancey was one of the literary finds B. P. Schulberg made when he raided New York and Chicago after talkies began requiring writers to have a semblance of skill with dialogue and not merely the ability to type "THE BUTLER FINDS THE MASTER IN A COMPROMISING POSITION WITH THE UPSTAIRS MAID." Originally from Alabama, Yancey worked for the *New York Herald Tribune* and had a hit novel, *The Red Cloak*, to his credit before Schulberg recruited him.

Yancey read my mood and quoted his bard. "Feeling a bit lost, chum? Forget it. Your youth's gone quickly here, leaving faith and pride to young upstanding men climbing the mountainside." When we first met at Jubilee Yancey had wished me luck and said he'd once been in Hollywood for six weeks too, adding that that had been four years and a marriage ago. "But how do you tell," I asked, surveying the ballroom, "who counts for what around here?"

"Ah, that's the trick," he said, "in Hollywood both the best *and* the worst are full of passionate intensity."

"Ta-ra-ra-boom-de-yah, comes Pammy Millevoix," bleated Teat Beale. Elegant, sultry Palmyra proceeded into our midst on the arm of the forgettable actor Rolfe Sedan. Proud, not prideful, Pammy smiled and nodded at a few familiars as she advanced into the collective consciousness of the gathering. Her mane, the shade of melted butter, hung not quite to her shoulders, and her pale green shantung gown traversed her breasts in ripples, hugging the almost African curve of her hips and thighs. As for Rolfe Sedan, he was a date arranged by the studio, where someone was hoping he would become Jubilee's answer to Ramon Novarro, who was already passé himself.

When she disengaged herself from Sedan at the foot of the stairs, light from the nearest chandelier caught the slight downturn of Pammy's eyes. This was her bone structure, really, yet it seemed a guide to what was always lurking no matter how she laughed, at herself and others. In her demeanor Pammy was an ardent child of the flapper age—excessive, elusive, playful, willful, idealistic but also skeptical. Her involvement in the songmaking repertory and the physical abandon in her singing does a hairpin turn when she appears rebellious and even scandalous one moment while in the next she becomes deeply romantic and traditional.

She was not a mingler. She swept around the room greeting, detaching, accepting a martini, pausing for a moment's intense exchange, moving on. I noticed, of all things, her eyebrows, wispy boundaries between her wide forehead and her hazel eyes. She used her brows to gesture, almost like hands. One would be up while the other was down, or they'd be spread in laughter, or they'd shade her eyes that transmitted, apparently with no reference to anything being said or enacted, the merest suggestion of cloud. Her one-sided smile curved up on the left while on the right her lips stayed closed and serious. That partially upturned smile is what never fades. Palmyra's nostrils widened slightly, even flared in key scenes, giving her face a look of desire whether it existed or not.

That was the thing about a star; she or he conveyed instantly something about themselves even if what was being conveyed, as with Trent Amberlyn, was utterly false. What made a star? Attitude and presence, an insistent energy, though what kind of energy varied from star to star. But looks. Looks are so often what we recall. Beauty, yes, yet imperfections, caricaturable badges, make as much impression as the *soi-disant* glories. Bette Davis's foggy voice, Cagney's features all gathered at the center of his face. The pouches under Bogie's eyes. Crawford's mile-wide slash of a mouth, Stanwyck's sneer, you pick it, that singular feature setting a thirty-foot image apart from all others. That is what invaded our fantasies, a minute particular that was like no one else and became the skeleton key admitting its bearer to our unconscious.

Palmyra Millevoix's singularity was a small bend in her nose that began perhaps three quarters of an inch below the bridge and made the nose slightly steeper until it reached the famous flared nostrils. This bend was too small ever to be confused with a bump, but it did give Pammy a serious mien that the perfect little button noses, so cherished at the time, did not possess. The nose was made gentler by three or four freckles that often had to disappear for scenes in which any suggestion of cuteness would be a contradiction of mood or even class. It was her eyes, set apart like two cabochons, their greenish gray accentuated by the distance between them, that heralded Palmyra's more perfect aspect. Their downturn, echoed in the sloping eyebrows, gave her even when she smiled the hint, the memory, or possibly the foretaste, of rue.

I pushed forward into a throng of young studio people as anonymous as myself; we were what the trades called hopefuls. It was true, we did live on hope, and when we were out of work it was even what we ate. I strained to hear any buzz about *A Doll's House*. Pretending to have as good a time as anyone, downing gins and tonic until the grand hall began to swirl, I was approximately a stage prop.

What does fame mean? I wondered. These people have it—Spencer Tracy, Palmyra Millevoix of course, C. B. DeMille, sometimes it's fame-by-affiliation as with Mrs. John Barrymore. A few flee from it but the rest seem to experience it as a form of immortality as well as an aid to mortal survival. Always falsity is present because they're pretending to something greater, more extended, than they could possibly be. For Trent Amberlyn fame is two-edged because he does want to be famous—it's all he has ever known he wanted—and he also wants to role-play, which is why he became an actor in the first place. But he hates being famous for what is in fact alien to him, and he hates living a lie, which makes him hate himself for not being what he is famous for being. Tonight his studio-arranged date is Palmyra's young friend, Teresa Blackburn, who will have a major part in a new Jubilee picture. Studio talk had it that Mossy played with the idea of a well photographed romance with Palmyra herself. To Trent anything is better than being Bernard Gestikker from Otumwa, Iowa, which is who and where he began—but he'd prefer not having to sneak his real self around corners. Bernard Gestikker was a misfit in Iowa; Trent Amberlyn is fine in Hollywood, but not all of him.

Shadows darted past, ignoring me. Was that Miriam Hopkins, George Arliss, Basil Rathbone? A fan might have felt he'd died and gone to Heaven; I thought I had vanished. They were not the shadows; I was.

The emergence of Hana Bliner and Wren Harbuck through the French doors leading to the Zangwill's fabled garden grabbed all eyes. They had thought to slip back into the party unnoticed, the starlet Hana and Mossy's assistant production chief Harbuck, but everyone spotted them. Hana was still fastening a strap while Wren, known for his polish and manners, was trying desperately both to knot his tie and re-part his oiled hair. He coughed explosively, as if that would disguise his recent errand from his wife and the other guests.

When the laughter and scattered applause died down, I walked over to the French doors to look at the famous garden, as brightly lit as a stage. Mossy and Esther Leah planned it after a voyage to England; they had seen the Chelsea Flower Show and then gone north to the Thane of Cawdor's lush estate in the Highlands. Peering into Mossy's garden yielded little of its rumored excesses, which were blocked by arbors and hedges, but I could tell it stretched for acres. Amos Zangwill was as particular with his plantings as with his stars. When he saw the garden and the mansion it ringed, George Bernard Shaw's comment was that he wished he could rewrite *Heartbreak House*.

Next to me, Wilma Ockenfuss of *Variety*, chubby as a strawberry, asked if I thought the Harbuck indiscretion with Hana Bliner had to be a blind item or if the presence of so many guests as witnesses made it possible to write a straight account of their emergence through the French doors and what had undoubtedly preceded it. "Heh heh," I said through all the gin I'd gulped, "shall we sally forth to see the garden's charms for ourselves?" Shrugging, she moved off in the direction of Tutor Beedleman, one of Jubilee's more genial writers but also one who disliked the press. I heard the silly woman say to Tutor, gesturing in my direction, "How can someone be so young and already out of date?" Then she asked him the question—blind item versus using names—she had asked me. "Water, Wilma, seeks its own level," Tutor said, "and so does slime."

Taking my arm, Tutor guided me to the safety of other writers. Guests clustered around the room according to hierarchy, vocation, or ideological preference, as the fugitive Alabaman Yancey Ballard described them to me. He unfurled his collective nouns as a banner of disillusion. "See the blush of Reds," he said, "hugging the bottom of the stairs to proselytize newcomers. A cloudburst of actors have spread themselves throughout, drenching us in fragile ego. Over there at the buffet table a hazard of agents gabs while across from them is a threat of producers. And wouldn't you know it, under the fanciest chandelier stands an ostentation of directors while around us, never straying from the bar, hovers the grumble of screenwriters."

The little Red cell, next to a potted palm Esther Leah had draped a pearl necklace around, had their satisfied zeal and camaraderie. "In Russia there's time only for struggle, one said, "not like this country where we waste our breath arguing over the best highway to Hell, this country where we haven't had a revolution since the eighteenth century." "It's coming soon," said another. "Then we'll see," said a third, "what people can do with their own bare hands to make the new society."

Power stalked the premises. Without bothering to waste one of his famous glares at the Reds, Edgar Globe was working the party, the burly entertainment lawyer wading into any conversation he wanted to dominate. Globe was with his slinky long-lashed Texas wife, Francesca, who swept her eyes over the important men in the room and held a director's hand a half beat too long when she shook it. The couple was up to no good.

Photographs in the Zangwill den, where I wandered alone, paired Mossy with Charles Lindbergh, with Mrs. Roosevelt, with Noël Coward, Bobby Jones, Dempsey, Tunney, Babe Ruth, Barney Baruch, and so on. These were composites tricked up for Mossy by Jubilee's art department in the early days when the studio, and Mossy, needed status by association. Years later, when he met one of these people and an actual photograph was taken, as with Lindbergh and George Bernard Shaw, Mossy replaced the earlier composites he'd had made unless he preferred the fake ones, which he often did.

I was assailed by a vision of Mossy as the Chinese emperor who, to cover his tracks, had all those killed who had built his monuments—in this case Jubilee's movies. Everyone in the photographs, at the party and in Jubilee's pictures, would be destroyed by Mossy, none left to redress his wrongs or tell his secrets. He was so far only a ghost at his own party, a commanding absence. Perhaps he planned to—

"A thousand a week for your thoughts, Wallflower," Sylvia Solomon said as she tapped me on the shoulder. The highest paid screenwriter in Hollywood had decided to spy on Mossy's den herself.

"Apparently my thoughts are worth less than a third of that," I said.

"Then for your delusions," she said. About a dozen years older than

I, Sylvia made the most of not being particularly pretty or even pretending to be. Everyone at Jubilee confided in her, and no one went far trying to get the better of her, including two refined, thirsty and constitutionally unemployed husbands who had more or less lived off her until she threw them out. Sylvia was never without a lighted cigarette in her ebony holder, which she wielded like a baton. Her hair flew as if it were wings, and a small mole by the side of her nose made her look serious even when she was joking. When she trained her owlish brown eyes at them, producers found themselves blabbering nonsense in story conferences just to avoid her look, and Sylvia could win approval for a plot point by asking, with *faux* innocence, "Can you think of a better way to do this?" riveting the executive until he stammered, "Ah, really, no, I can't."

"It's the dues of youth," Sylvia said, "that's all you're paying." I told her I'd been sure I could at least mix a little with people here, but I honestly didn't know how to be one of them. "No one," she said, "is one of them until they notice you and they don't notice you until you do something noticeable, good or bad. Just the fact you're here means Mossy has seen something about you. That's enough, Wallflower."

We both left the den and Sylvia rejoined her date, the infamous drunk and puffy braggart Jamieson McPhatter. "Thought you'd stood me up have another drink will you look at that fairy in his tights did you know Selznick wants to see me," I heard the pompous McPhatter spew as I wondered why Sylvia Solomon, engaging enough in her way, wasted her time with that bullfrog. When I knew her well enough to ask what she saw in Lord Jamieson, Sylvia said she wanted to collaborate on his next script since they wouldn't let a woman write Nelson at Trafalgar all by herself and he'd already muscled his way onto the project. She also knew McPhatter would fall into a stupor and she wouldn't have to sleep with him, only drive him home and call a taxi. But that was later. For now, I was discarded.

In the center of the room, the directors resembled a clot of playground bullies, bullies wearing gold cufflinks engraved with castles or racehorses. They told each other stories about the vanity of stars, the stupidity of producers, who they'd bring out from Broadway to be in their next picture. The more pensive ones were out-blustered by the others. Although they couldn't begin their work until we finished ours, I did not hear them mention writers. I liked pictures better before these guys became the dictators. That's why I'm an irrelevant discard.

In the midst of the clot was a tall slender man, youngish but with a creased high forehead from which close-cropped hair was beginning to recede. Nils Matheus Maynard had come to Jubilee more recently than I, but unlike me his reputation preceded him. Listening to Largo Buchalter, a particularly noisy blowhard, Nils reached into his pocket and pulled out a brass ball. Making no show—I noticed him only because the blowhard's voice attracted my attention as he broadcast his conquest of a rising actress—Nils placed the small ball between the thumb and index finger of his right hand. Without a word, as if he were fidgeting for his own amusement, he made the ball become two, three, then four balls, each held between a different pair of fingers.

"Attaboy Nils, let's see what you're up to," said handsome, dark Frank Capra, interrupting Largo Buchalter's monologue. Buchalter glowered at Capra, understood he had held the floor too long, and yielded resentfully. "Oh sure, Houdini, wow us," he said.

"No," Nils said, "I could never be confused with the incomparable escape *meister*, but once upon a time, as some of you know, I was myself the sorcerer's apprentice." As he spoke, Nils had pulled a deck of cards from his jacket pocket and had each of the other directors pick a card.

"What's the secret of magic, Nils Matheus?" someone asked Nils, who was often referred to by both his first and middle names. Others had now swelled the group.

"Stupid question," said the bloviating Largo Buchalter, unwilling to cede the floor entirely. "What he does is go around fooling people, that's all."

"Not fooling," Nils said quietly, "I hope amazing and delighting them. Same in magic as in pictures or stories. First, please them. After that, you can do anything."

"What pulled you from magic to pictures anyway?" another director asked.

Nils Matheus Maynard was an established headlining magician before he ever made movies. He began his training with Harry Houdini himself (or the rabbi's son Erich Weiss, as the cognoscenti preferred) when Houdini was in the last weary spiral of his illustrious career. He had done everything from swallowing needles to falling into Boston harbor while handcuffed and locked in a safe to an impossible jailbreak. As a boy Nils had been taken by his mother to the escapade in Boston, and he became a Houdini worshipper at that moment, the moreso because of a condition that denied Nils any hope of emulating the daring physical feats of the master.

Nils's mother Bruna was a von Bickenheim of Bavaria, with distinguished roots in universities and the discipline of mathematics. The family had been compromised, Nils told me when I got to know him, first by her emigration to America and then, more grievously, by her marriage to Nils's soft, shiftless father, Rufus Maynard, an indifferent sailor and sailmaker from Gloucester, Massachusetts. Their second son was sickly, a bleeder, and it was because of Bruna. She had an uncle with severe hemophilia, and she knew she was the source of Nils's disease.

Hemophilia, with no known cause or cure, displays itself with serious bleeding only in males yet is directly inherited only from females (in rare cases, females may have mild hemorrhages). A hemophiliac father will have no sons who bleed, but all his daughters will be carriers. A carrier mother will have half carrier daughters and half hemophiliac sons. When Nils was a boy hemophilia was still called the disease of kings, largely because it afflicted both the English and Russian royal families who, as it happened, had intermarried. In the superstition of the day, a family with a hemophiliac was sometimes thought to be in the grip of a diabolical possession. The blood transfusions Nils needed were regarded with suspicion, and his mother was ashamed whenever she had to take her son to the hospital in Boston.

Bruna von Bickenheim Maynard was so horrified by her son's condition that she fled back to Bavaria from time to time. This left Nils and his non-bleeding brother with their frequently unemployed father whose chief pleasures were Scotch whiskey and swapping tales with other old salts in the sailmaking lofts of Gloucester.

Coming and going in Nils's life, his mother was alternately overbearingly protective and a deserter. Nils obeyed her rigidly, but this had no influence on her abandonments. Joining a small group of parents with hemophiliac sons, Frau von Bickenheim Maynard encountered a woman from South Braintree, Evelina Tedeschio, whose son Mario was the same age as Nils. Nils and Mario played together during group meetings, but since South Braintree is on the other side of Boston from Gloucester they saw each other only once a month when parents gathered to discuss ways to handle their bleeding, and blood-needy, sons. Mario liked to hit his mother, knowing she couldn't hit him back. Evelina Tedeschio disclaimed any sense of guilt or anger by asserting she felt honored that God had favored her with the responsibility to make her son an inspiration for others. "Nonsense," said another mother, "my line is cursed and so is yours. All of us here gave birth to vampires."

The hostile Mario became the obedient Nils's best friend, and between their monthly visits they wrote letters. Nils told Mario he wanted to find a formula for curing hemophilia; Mario wrote back he wanted to make the whole world hemophiliac so people would know what the suffering felt like. Evelina Tedeschio made her son a virtual prisoner inside a virtual shrine to his illness, pillows and pads on every piece of furniture, high locks on the doors to prevent the boy from wandering. When he was eleven, Mario escaped from the Tedeschio home in South Braintree and made his way by trolley and bus to Gloucester. He waited until dark before tapping on Nils's window.

The two boys were missing for five days—Nils's mother was away and his father was mostly drinking—and the only person to panic was Evelina Tedeschio. This meant the police looked only on the South Shore; meanwhile Nils and Mario found their way to Lowell, well north of Boston, where they hired themselves into a shirtwaist factory and took milled cotton to the women who transformed it into cloth. If any of the thousands of needles in the factory had poked either of the boys they'd have been in serious trouble, but they were careful. Exposed gears were another hazard, and poor ventilation left the air filled with cotton fibers. Some of the workers, all women, were in the early stages of tuberculosis and often had to spit onto the floor, which endangered everyone else. Yet Nils told me he never felt healthier in his entire childhood than during those few stolen days in the textile mill when he was treated like everyone else. The jig wasn't up until a watchman found the boys sleeping in the mill. Nils wasn't allowed to see Mario again.

To Nils most of childhood was combat, and most of his bleeding was internal. His hemophilia was of a relatively moderate variety, yet when he played with other boys he was sure to come home with grossly swollen and excruciatingly painful joints. Knees, elbows, ankles, wrists were the worst. A contact sport sent him into agony as his blood flowed eagerly, inside his joints, to any bruised area. When he had to miss school because of pain, Nils read books about magic. "Anything to escape," he told me. He was better with his hands than his sailmaking father, and he could make rabbits disappear for his dazzled school chums, some of whose parents thought it was the work of Satan. Nils had no respect for his father and something approaching hatred for his mother.

In 1914, when Nils was fifteen, he won a sleight-of-hand contest that gave him six weeks as a junior assistant to Houdini. Unlike Houdini's other assistants, all older and more experienced, Nils knew he could never become an escape artist or contort his body in any fashion. He practiced with cards, birds, ribbons and scarves up to ten hours a day. He described this as a preference, never telling Houdini or the other assistants about his hemophilia, which had begun to abate but would never permit him to twist himself into the human pretzel that was routine for escape artists.

From Houdini, Nils learned to make objects disappear and reappear elsewhere, to take the audience into his confidence, give them the impression they knew a trick as well as the performer, then with a whisk and a blinding hand-eye movement leave them astounded at how utterly they had been deceived. Nils told me a magician is really an actor playing the part of a magician. He acted his apprentice part so well that at the end of six weeks Houdini asked Nils to stay on as part of his retinue. Houdini liked to say great tricks are like unsolved crimes, and now Nils was learning to commit them.

Houdini took Nils to Hollywood where the peerless magician made several silent films, all disappointments. Chaplin tried to give

Houdini suggestions to make his pictures more believable. Houdini insisted he had only to replicate what he did on a stage, but audiences did not buy this on the screen. For Nils it was all going to school.

After several years Nils felt he'd learned enough, and the master was becoming self-destructive. Houdini kept himself locked in a coffin under water for over an hour, which left him ill for days afterward, and he began doing something Nils found eerie. Some weeks Houdini would spend all his time exposing fraudulent mediums and spiritualists. "This was holy work to Houdini," Nils said, "but to me it was breaking the proscenium. I love sham. It's why I became a magician. Audiences love it. It takes them away from the deeper shams and disasters of their lives."

Within a year after going on his own, Nils was filling theaters from San Francisco to Savannah, seeing his name grow larger on posters. He could make anything vanish on one side of the stage and rematerialize on the other; he could cut one woman not into two but into six women, which brought audiences to their feet. He introduced himself theatrically, almost in a trance as he chanted his spell: "Hear me, O Spirits, in my torment. Numerals are the invisible coverings of human beings. We ask you to release us through numbers. Let every rope or strap, every knot be broken, every form of matter change its shape and location. Let identity itself multiply, for I am Nils Maynard but also Matheus von Bickenheim."

Having borrowed the name of his despised mother, Nils would begin his tricks while explaining he needed his mother's noble heritage to invoke the powerful forces that would help him perform magic. The ancient von Bickenheim attachment to mathematics at Heidelberg resurfaced in a way his forefathers wouldn't have predicted but would recognize. He would turn one dove into four, one handkerchief into ten, and again and again one woman into six. He took a few prisoners from Houdini: Nils could make a trumpet leave one table and arrive instantly on another playing "Stars and Stripes Forever," and he could throw four ringing alarm clocks into the air, make them vanish and reappear hanging from watch chains on the opposite side of the stage. When he had worked his way up to playing New York, Detroit, and Chicago in the mid 1920s, Nils was making eight thousand dollars a week and pocketing virtually all of it. He was free. He never spoke to Houdini again, nor would he see his mother, even when she tried to come backstage in Boston.

Nils tired of repeating himself. Unlike Houdini he was not a great showman craving adulation nor would his disease allow him to top himself with physical feats. But there was another form of magic Nils was certain he could do.

The magic of a magician was mundane compared with the magic of film—what is a severed rope restored to a single strand or a vanishing dove when stacked against prehistoric monsters or a leap from the wing of one airplane to another?—which is why Nils became a moviemaker. "Magicians like to believe they can defy the Creator by doing things no human has ever done," Nils said, "but a filmmaker *becomes* the Creator by constructing his own world. It just takes him a little longer. Six days becomes twelve weeks or so." Instead of imitating his former hero, Nils used the magic of the screen itself—cross-cutting, montage, close-ups, fade-ins, dissolves, special effects—to make people howl, to scare and amuse and reassure them, to make them weep over the salvation of an orphan or the redemption of a scapegrace. He began making pictures in the last days of the silents and managed a seamless transition to talkies.

After a successful adaptation of a hit play, Nils fumbled and made a few attempts at what he intended as intellectual pictures. An explorer goes to Tibet and finds his journey is philosophical rather than geographical. The dictator of a small country begins with ideals and is corrupted by power and privilege until his son, home from college in America, literally does not recognize his grossly bloated, bemedalled and brutal father. This was a decent moment but the picture itself, which Nils made for Jubilee, was a failure, stumbling over its own pretensions to political significance and moralizing. Louella Parsons, among others, brought Nils back to earth: "One of the brightest boys in our constellation of directors," she wrote, "likes to go around town proclaiming that if pictures can talk they might as well say something. Fine and dandy, but he should remember the ringing declaration from the founding fathers of filmdom—if you want to send a message, take it to Western Union." That was a message Nils heeded. A long time later Mossy told me had planted the item by calling Parsons himself. True or not, from then on Nils made entertainments.

When Nils finished disclosing his path into pictures to his fellow directors, Largo Buchalter, who hated to have anyone else hold forth, could only say, "Well la-di-da." Nils realized Buchalter was about to start a new story about himself, belittling others. "I think," Nils concluded slowly as he looked Buchalter in the eye, "that what meant the most for me in terms of freedom was to be famous and rich and still so young." The bully braggart in the director's cluster had suddenly been outbullied and outbragged. Nils wasn't quite through. "Frank," he said to Capra, "will you give me back my four of clubs?" He went around the circle naming the card each director had picked earlier. When he finished, Nils handed the deck to Largo Buchalter and told him to keep it. "Just in case you think it's marked." To me, Nils was virtuous glamour.

A royal moment. The prince of melody descended the stairs. Dapper, double breasted in blue serge, dark hair lightly brilliantined. Teet Beale was at last intimidated—no ta-ra-ra-booms for this guy, any lyric would fall dead at his feet. Beale humbly bowed and said, "It's an honor to have you here, Mr. Berlin." Irving Berlin nodded with a wisp of a smile and went to greet Palmyra. "Mr. Berlin," she said, "I wish I were your sister in song, but I'm only your fourth cousin at least twice removed." "Music is music, my dear," said Irving Berlin, "and I'm happy to have you anywhere in the family."

Blinded by my betters, I was wondering why Mossy was a phantom at his own party when suddenly I was slammed on the back. It was not Mossy, who did not do such things. Seaton Hackley, Mossy's henchman who played his part in Joey Jouet's final hours, was praising the *Doll's House* work I turned in that afternoon, which felt like the previous century. "A humdinger script," he called it, forgetting it was only a treatment. He must have received it from Gershon Lidowitz already— Littlewits himself—and shoveled it up to Mossy, from whom he may have detected a passing blink of approval. "Love the way you solved the third act. Always had a soft spot for Torvald myself. Nice to give him the drinking problem, automatically makes him more interesting and justifies the wife leaving home, even taking the kiddies to her mother's while old Torvie promises to get off the sauce. She's not really abandoning her home that way. Leaves us with morality in the saddle and the prospect of a reunited family. You think Fred MacMurray is ready for Torvie?" Maybe, but he's not ready for Garbo, I didn't dare say. Garbo was the star they wanted for Nora though I'd heard Pammy was hoping she'd get the part.

Hackley's praise made me proud, with no inkling of how much more Ibsen would hate me than the other writers who did nothing worse than change his ending while I had triumphantly destroyed everything he meant in the play. I looked around for Lidowitz. Not here. He somehow didn't rate, yet I did. My moment of strut. Woozily, I took out my car keys and jingled them. Just to make some noise.

Haloed beneath a chandelier, with the self-possession of a nested starling, Pammy greeted people alone. Her honey-gold hair was now in a twirled mound at the top of her head—she re-coiffed in the powder room?—while the green diaphanous gown was both French and ancient Greek. She was classical *and* romantic. Was it possible?—yes, she'd begun working her way toward me. She must have heard about my coup at the studio; surely Seaton Hackley wouldn't have praised me without a nod from Mossy, a nod that had made the rounds. A disobedient strand of her upswept hair, straying from the rest of her coiffure, caught more light at the back of her neck. What would she say to me? Or I to her? Why could she come to me like this but I couldn't approach her? Or could I? The way of the pecking order: a junior screenwriter speaks when spoken to, ready with a bon mot. I wasn't.

I'd say, "You're looking even more ravishing than usual." Naw, that's what a flit would tell her. Likewise I couldn't say how much I loved her in *The Many Lives of Theodosia*, a negligible effort by all concerned. Palmyra was getting nearer, greeting friends but drawing unrelentingly closer to me. How about just going with "Mossy really knows how to live, ha ha, you should see the main house." Death. I was terminally abashed. Here she is. In two seconds I'll have to say something. No, oh.

In the last tenth of an instant, like a car swerving to avoid a crash, Palmyra angled—she had almost bumped into me—to kiss and embrace Simone Swan Bluett, who did her costumes on *Autumn*

Nocturne. "Star light, star bright, first star I see tonight," said Simone to Palmyra. Had Pammy been heading for her the whole time, then, or had she changed her mind as she approached me, deciding late in her sashay that her dresser was worth her time and affection while I was not?

"I told you, it's just dues," said the reappeared Sylvia Solomon, patting my shoulder. Maternally, sisterly? I turned to her and said, "It's discouraging and I'm embarrassed that you noticed." "Look," she said, "be thankful you don't have to sleep with anyone to get around this town. It wasn't so easy for me. Though come to think of it, it wouldn't hurt if you found your way into the right bed here and there."

How do you get into the right bed anyway, I did not ask as we were joined by Yancey Ballard and other writers. The angular Yeats-man stooped to my eye level. "Feeling isolated? It's good for the soul. I myself look forward to becoming a sixty-year- old smiling public man some distant day." We screenwriters huddled, indeed grumbled, in a corner filled with a reproduction of Rodin's *Thinker* and another of a Greek god entwined around a goddess. Some of these writers were Hollywood notables making three thousand or more a week, some were notorious, some disappointed, some permanently hopeful, most suspecting they would be better people if they did something else. Novelists, playwrights, journalists: they'd all had what they now thought of as honest, if not sufficiently gainful, toil. Now they were in harness, overpaid, feeling they were debasing themselves before illiterates prior to being replaced by another of their species who would, in turn, also be replaced. Or else they were trying to be hired to be overpaid, debased, and replaced. Self-respect was not an attribute many of them had in excess.

A cocky thickset writer junior even to me, Mark Darrow, began babbling, perhaps from nervousness or drink. "I always start with a twist, a guy's told he has a fatal disease, or it's the night before a battle," he said, "then I decide who should be in that plot point—a thief, surgeon, bunch of salesmen looking for dames." Mark's wife grabbed his elbow and said, "Honey, please, these men have so much more experience." But Yeatsman said, "That's fine, fine, but I like to start with someone I'm interested in, flawed of course, I think what's improvable about him, then I go further and think only what's provable. When I get to the provable I can start to write, and things will happen to him." "No, no, no, that's entirely wrong," said Mark Darrow as if he were his famous uncle Clarence rebutting the prosecution in a courtroom. "You have to have the gimmick first," he went on, "like a coat hook so you can hang everything on it and the good guys—"

But now Yeatsman interrupted, having heard enough of Darrow's nonsense. "You know what's too bad?" he said. "What's too bad is the kids of this country being brought up by our pictures to believe crime doesn't pay or you shouldn't have sex till you're married, or—" And he was in turn interrupted by Sylvia Solomon, who said, "Now here's what we could do, folks, that the Hays Office morality police in charge of protecting youth from reality couldn't object to—we could make a picture about a hateful Hollywood executive, excuse the redundancy, who throws a party where everyone present loathes him for one reason or another and finally he is murdered while the party is still in progress—"

Yeatsman said, "And after the cheering stops, for the rest of the movie Bill Powell and Myrna Loy have to figure out who did it, and no one wants them to solve the crime."

At that very moment, cued by Sylvia and Yeatsman, Amos Zangwill descended the stairs into our midst and promenaded his ballroom. "Speaking of the unholy ghost," said Sylvia. "Cuchulain himself," said Yeatsman.

Decades later I still see him entering now in his dark suit with his half smile, regal, not arrogant. Where did that smile come from, an executioner's smile but also the grinning rictus of his dispatched victim? Trim, almost small, creating a lagoon of space one could violate only at the peril of being repelled like a clumsy pirate hurled to the sharks off a galleon. A small cortege followed as Mossy nodded to his guests.

"What a night!" Largo Buchalter bellowed as Mossy passed the directors. "We're all having the time of our lives, Mossy!" "Glad you've been elected spokesman, Largo," Mossy said as he smiled at Nils Matheus and Capra but not at Buchalter.

Mark Darrow, drunkenly on the make, broke from the writers'

kennel. His wife tried to pull him back to safety, but he elbowed her aside. He seized what he must have felt was the main chance as Mossy passed an elaborately framed Picasso drawing. In the drawing a male abstraction was inserting part of himself into an opening in a female abstraction. "What a genius he is with a phallic symbol, isn't he Mossy?" Darrow ventured. He pronounced it fay-lick. Yeatsman groaned; there was too much silence in the room and everyone had heard.

"Phallic it is," Mossy replied with the correct pronunciation, "symbol it's not."

"Oh sure, AZ," said Darrow, obviously unaware that Mossy hated being called by his initials as if he were LB Mayer. Mossy's temperature seemed to rise a little as he considered "AZ" and how he might discipline its user; we were seeing the studio head as padrone reproving one of his villagers. "I'll tell you what is a phallic symbol, Marky"— "Oh god," Sylvia whispered, "he only does that to your name if he hates you"—"when you stick your pencil in your mouth, Marky, and rotate it the way you do in story conferences so it blackens your lips and looks as if you'd really like to be sucking someone's cock instead of yessing my every belch, that is when the pencil becomes a phallic symbol. Am I right, Mel?"

This last was tossed over Mossy's shoulder to the family psychoanalyst, Melvin Baron, who followed in Mossy's train. Dr. Baron obediently nodded as fast as he could. "Yes absolutely definitely, Mossy, I couldn't have put it …" But Mossy slashed him with a gesture and moved on. Mark Darrow faded wordless into the burled woodwork, smiling bravely as he may have imagined Sydney Carton did on the steps to the guillotine.

"See?" Sylvia said leaning toward me. "At the next party you'll be welcomed by all as one of the happy band of brothers and sisters present for the execution of Mark Darrow. While young Mark himself will be lucky if he ever gets invited after this to the opening of a tin can. Did you catch the glare Marky's little wife gave him?"

By this time Mossy had again disappeared upstairs into his library with King Vidor and Nils Matheus Maynard. There had been talk that the directors might try to form a guild as the writers were doing, and we all knew Mossy would want to head off any such insubordination.

He was vaguely apolitical on the right, but many writers called him fascistic, an adjective we threw around promiscuously when discussing studio heads.

With Mossy upstairs, Palmyra reigned. The producers fell over themselves courting her for their next pictures. She was able to fly away, a brightly feathered songbird, telling them all they were too kind.

Teet Beale, the crier, announced midnight supper, "Ladies first, *s'il vous plaît.*"

As wives and actresses streamed past us toward the buffet table, a writer next to me began to swear. "Fuck it all, what I hate most here are the women's perfumes," said Poor Jim Bicker, a former hobo who sold a magazine story to Jubilee and was now on his third screenplay. He made eight hundred a week, more than twice my salary, but he still had the nickname Poor from his days riding the rails. Even tonight in his relative prosperity, he had torn cuffs, unpressed pants, and he looked as if he had just arrived from a brawl, which was a possibility. "You could use a little education," he said to me.

"Why the perfume?" I asked.

"I prefer the body stench of bathless hoboes," Poor Jim answered more to his highball glass than to me. "Yeah, a hobo's honest smell is better than these women with their artificial scents all swimming together like rare tropical fish in this dazzle of a tank. Like to take a pick-ax to the tank, let all the water run out. They couldn't survive without their privilege. Their scents and the sloppy paints on their faces cost more than I saw in a month before I was bought out and became part of this vulgarity. Some say they're Reds, can you beat that?" Poor Jim threw up his hands. "Maybe I'll fuck me one of them later." He sniffed, scorning and lusting after the extravagantly adorned women.

The Canadian director of Westerns, Walter Heatherington, was telling an ancient man with blue hair, who was addressed as Monsieur Le Comte, about the death of his best friend as they advanced along the line in France in 1918. "My mate Lorne was pushing along in the mud next to me one moment, and the next his head was at my wrist, blown clear of his trunk, and the sergeant told me to keep moving."

"Ah, *mon Dieu,*" said the very old blue-haired man, who had been involved with the Lumières in devising early film projectors and cameras, "*De temps en temps* I think all of us should have died in the trenches. In my own first war with the Bosch, in 1870, I was wounded in Alsace and they thought I would die of blood poisoning—how you say gangrene in my leg. I was evacuated to Lyon to die in hospital. A nurse was posted there, *une jeune fille, comment s'appellait-elle,* ah Danielle. I recall how she brought me around when I could lie only on my back and she came in the night to wash me again in my helplessness. Danielle's *spécialité de la maison* was the upside down backward squat, to this day there are mornings when I think of nothing but the muscles in her back as she rose and fell. Danielle broke my heart and left the nursing to become a nun. Then I wish I died in Alsace. But it never gets any easier, *relations sexuelles,* does it?"

I asked M. Le Comte what that was.

"Call it the seduction, my boy. Half the people here are working so hard hoping they will be *coucher* with the other half by two a.m., and not a few will succeed. Some of us will be dead, still aching with desire in our final breaths, dying to love a little more as we die. Meanwhile, I recollect Danielle. Long dead herself, of course, unless she is a retired mother superior. Sex and death, they play with each other, unwilling partners who always win and always lose. You think the cinema is about sex, but it is really all about death, and someday you'll see why."

I didn't, though, not for many years, until I arrived at my own version of what he was saying. All the people in the movies of his early days with the Lumières, like most of us at Mossy's party, those who wrote and directed and produced the pictures, and especially those who acted in them, are dead. Le Comte himself is of course long gone. Looking at old movies is simply looking at dead people, at death itself. The ancient French film pioneer was prophesying that motion pictures were going to last even though their makers would not. Wedded to death: what an art form.

"The shock of the war behind, the pull of a war to come," said M. Le Comte. "*Alors,* we are always between two magnets."

"Ta-ra-ra, Darryl Zanuck, He puts us in a panic, The whole town's in his box, Whether he's at Warner's or Fox."

PETER DAVIS

"Monsieur Zanuck enters the fray," said M. Le Comte, "your Napoleon I believe."

Teet Beale was quickly silenced and a clamor arose for Palmyra to sing. Mossy came out of his library to stand at the crest of the six steps leading down into his ballroom. Esther Leah Zangwill, a compact bundle of nerves who had spent much of the evening ordering around the kitchen staff, made an appearance beside her husband. Mossy was a bullet of a man with eyes that did not see so much as penetrate their object. Esther Leah fidgeted, never leaving anything—a piece of furniture, her hairdo, a child's clothing—alone. When a writer asked Mossy, "How's Fussy?" it meant he knew Esther Leah well and was in Mossy's good graces due to a script that was shootable. "She tolerates me," Mossy would answer. "No one knows why." If Esther Leah found a servant smoking in the kitchen or heard an underling criticize Mossy, although she did both of these things herself, repeatedly, the offender was banished.

Mossy did not announce that Palmyra would sing. He only moved his eyes toward the piano. If you looked away from the vacant baby grand for a moment and then looked back, you would see a studio musician had materialized at the keyboard.

Palmyra smiled her faintly one-sided smile and proceeded to the piano. At parties earlier in her career she had scandalously added blue lyrics that could never be in a movie or on a record. She'd had a hit in 1932 with a song called "Give Me a Chance," in which the last chorus had lines ending with "chance," "romance" and "passionate trance." At a party given by Marion Davies in the Oceanhouse beach mansion William Randolph Hearst had built for her, after the aged and curiously shockable publisher had gone upstairs to bed (curious since he lived openly with his mistress), Pammy stepped to the microphone and uncorked an altered last stanza:

You're here to pitch,
I'm here to catch;
Where I itch
You know how to scratch,
So honey if you'll give me a chance,

46

I'll take hold of that thing in your pants;
I'll stroke it and I'll suck it,
I'll sit on it and I'll fuck it
Till I leave you in an unaccustomed trance.

This pretty much brought down the Oceanhouse, and by noon on Monday the whole town was trying to quote Pammy's words. Unfortunately for her, the song had been recorded by a young reporter for Hearst's Los Angeles *Examiner* who wanted to curry favor with the chief. Hearst, too furious even to reprimand his mistress, had the recording sent to his friend J. Edgar Hoover with a note: "This one has Red sympathies. Let's cool her off." The head of the FBI office in Los Angeles paid a visit to Mossy at Jubilee. "Don't bother to get scratches on your record by playing it on my phonograph," Mossy told the G-man, "because I was at the party myself." But what he said to Pammy was, "They're threatening to go to the Legion of Decency with it, Walter Winchell, the churches. Bad luck, but no more union garbage and Red meetings for you, young lady, or your career will be over. They'll deport you as an alien, and they'll try to take your daughter away. They'll keep her here. They're not kidding about deportation."

"Whaaaat? Take Millie? You're joking."

"They'll claim anyone who sings songs like that is an unfit mother. Period."

For the next two years labor organizers complained they couldn't get Palmyra Millevoix at their rallies anymore. The more sophisticated among them shrugged. "She's sold out like the rest of 'em. Works for the fascist Zangwill. 'Nuff said."

Mossy's party was entering its climactic phase when Pammy reached the piano, where the accompanist from the Jubilee orchestra offered a few chords to gain silence. "I came to the California of unlimited hopes," Pammy began before the talking died completely. "Most of you have helped me and none of you have hurt me—much." Appreciative titters. Nils Matheus Maynard clinked his glass with a spoon until the room was quiet. Mossy came down all the stairs but one, which he needed to stand on in order to see above heads to Pammy; sensitive about his height—five and a half feet—he also didn't want to stay at the top of the stairs like the Pope on his balcony. Pammy smiled across the room at him. "My employer, our genial and easygoing host" (chuckles from the braver guests) "has asked me for a song. He is a skeptical optimist, while I remain a cheerful pessimist. The best we can do to keep the wolf away is have some fun and thank Amos Zangwill for the evening." Scattered applause for Mossy. "Times change, don't they?" Palmyra was keeping time now with her hips as the piano vamped a few notes. "In the Twenties we had plenty, In the Thirties it's all gone, But in the Thirties we got dirty, And we dance from dark till dawn. Oh my heart will jump for dancing, For dancing till we fall; That's when I want romancing, Please take me to the ball."

"Give us 'Lucky Rendezvous,' Pammy" someone cried. "No, 'Moon-beams,'" yelled someone else. Pammy was savoring the wait, roasting those chestnuts I'd described in my overwrought press release, until she had just the anticipation level she wanted.

"But the country around us," Pammy went on, "is not dancing because it can't even stand up. I'm not trying to raise money or plead-ing any cause. I just want to say my sense of justice, which has been asleep for several years, is awake again."

Mossy looked at his toes while the Lefties in the room clapped and everyone else waited. An odd occasion, I thought, for Palmyra to put her social conscience on exhibit, but then entertainers are exhibition-ists by nature. She had the audience she wanted, the most visible and powerful members of the industry. Sylvia Solomon poked me in the ribs. "Hooray for Millevoix," I said to her, "and watch out Hollywood." "I'd put it the other way around," she whispered, "especially watch out for the big guys on the playground."

"We are all dreamers," Pammy said to the room, "or we wouldn't be writ-ing, directing, acting, composing, or producing, would we?" (Sylvia whis-pered again, "At least one person here puts writing first.") "We dare make dreams come true. But when you gain the dream you lose the dream. The song I'm going to sing is about lovers who have to part, their *tristesse*. But it's also about my songs themselves. When I have a song in me it is a happy full feeling because it's still inside me. When I release it, I'm as empty and sad as anyone waving farewell or remembering any time past that we cherish."

The piano trilled, and here's some of what Palmyra sang:

> I can't do a thing when I have to say goodbye,
> Since the word all alone leaves a tear in my eye,
> So please don't ask if you don't want me to cry:
> I never have found where's the good in goodbye.
> I've made a sandwich ham and cheddarly
> Just for Gertrude Ederle;
> The tickle in my nose has felt
> A breeze for Franklin Roosevelt.
> You can take me way back to where time began,
> To the east of the Anglo-Egyptian Sudan;
> But search as I may and try as I try
> I just haven't noticed the good in goodbye.

Pammy had written the song for a nightclub croon in Jubilee's *Reno Weekend*, which needed to acknowledge and relieve the self-pity of its three divorcees, only one of whom had by that point in the picture found a cowboy. Years later Harold Arlen played with the same theme, and the song became "What's Good About Goodbye." I still prefer Palmyra's, but then I would. She finished with "So please don't you ask me or I'll have to lie; I never have found where's the good in goodbye."

The wanton secret of motion pictures is that everyone connected with them is a starstruck fan. Yeatsman allowed himself a whistle, as did some of the producers. Mossy was clapping from the top of the stairs, to which he had returned. A shout of *"Encore, je vous en prie"* from Tutor Beedleman brought a smile from Pammy, but she had finished singing for her supper. She was swept up by her forthcoming costar Trent Amberlyn, joined by her best friend Teresa Blackburn, who was just starting to win good parts herself, and Teresa's brother Stubby Blackburn, a shortstop for the Los Angeles Angels in the Pacific Coast League. Together they led Pammy away from the piano.

Even though some guests were going home, others were still arriving. The alert Teet Beale spotted big game. "Ta-ra-ra, Here's a neat trick, Descending now's La Dietrich, Blesses us with mirth and fun, Shines brighter than the sun." Enter Marlene grandly. "Between her usual brace of flits," said Tutor Beedleman. Dietrich's wide-eyed smile enfolded the room and no one in it. High-waisted black slacks making her legs even longer, an ivory blouse forming a V so expansive its first button was below her self-assured breasts. Boyish, womanly, naughty and haughty, freed from the rigid grip of gender. Why she lighted on me I don't know; I must have resembled the cringing courtier I was. The low voice, the open throat: "Can you take me, Darlink, to Mr. Zangvill."

Leaving all the men and half the women with their tongues hanging—though I heard one actress say to another, "I'll bet that dame poses in her sleep"—I escorted Miss D back up the stairs to the library. She took my arm. No ceremony with her host once I'd opened the library door. "Mossy, ve must talk, ve must weally sit down mit each udder." I shuffled out of the library along with Baringer Donovan, the Warner's producer. "Ten more minutes," Donovan said to me as we rejoined the rest of the party, "shit, *five* more minutes, and I've had a deal with Jubilee so I could tell Jack Warner on Monday to go hump one of Zanuck's polo ponies." "Tough luck," I said. "Nothing to do with luck," he said, "it was that hun bitch's timing. Say, who are you anyway?"

Down I went another fathom. What hopes I'd had when I'd come! How they were dashed! Pondering my exclusion from the kingdom of notability, I tried to convince myself it was temporary. I thought about the fame of a hero like Charles Lindbergh who had earned it (then paid for it so dearly with his infant son's kidnapping and death) and the residual fame of the has-beens like Anita Billow who simply moved about in her cocoon of repute. Billow, who was here at the party, had been a silent star whose Polish accent (née Bilowitsky) kept her not only from achieving talkie stardom but even from getting small parts. She was a somebody relegated to nobody status by technology. Unable to make the necessary adjustments to her thickly accented English, unlike the sultry Dietrich or the whispery Garbo, she sounded like a truck driver with a sore throat. For Anita Billow, fame was lifelong access. She simply went around looking ravishing, nursing her legend, saying she didn't miss acting. For the public, each kind of fame dissolved into each other kind, soothing them with voyeurism and wish fulfillment. In Hollywood, fame became a kind of magnetic north, and those whose fame lasted would merely be the famous who embodied the public's more transcendent hopes. The stars' glamour surfaced as the mysterious flash of lightning extended indefinitely.

The directors did their late-night hammering. "Actors are basically crazy, can't let the inmates run the asylum." "Piece of practical advice, never fuck a starlet if you can fuck a star." "Thirty-foot-high image of passion—audiences think this is reality and the world outside the theater is an illusion. Know what, they're right." "Escape, escape, escape. Eggheads knock it, I live for it." "Naw, gimme a tough guy fighting in an alley, a broad upstairs in a rooming house, they meet in a breadline and I'm cooking with gas."

I looked out the window and pictured Father Junipero Serra creating a mission on this site in the 1700s, on the ground above Beverly Hills. He would have put a holy place here. The Indians converted, farmed, carved their crosses, built a few huts around a chapel, sickened with European diseases, prayed. Father Serra made their faith his cause. The bones of the Indians and their Spanish confessors and conquistadors might be buried beneath the Zangwill palace and gardens. This vortex where I was sinking had once been a mission. A mission it was again.

"What a pleasure—Owen Jant, isn't it?" I was returned to the party by a voice followed by a hand on my arm. My hostess, Esther Leah Zangwill, gentled me back to the occasion though I realized my gin-soaked reverie had canted me somewhat and I tried to pull myself together. Before I knew anything I was saying, "Me? A pleasure? I couldn't be, I don't even know what I'm doing here, sorry." And she said, "Think I do? But that's how I am most of the time, not knowing where or why, mustn't let it worry us." She shrugged, and looking into her importuning eyes I saw I'd done something right by being mistakenly honest. "Not knowing," she said, "and being worried about that, then not caring." Esther Leah gave the impression of looking on the proceedings with an alternating current of disbelief and resignation. How many of these men owed their careers to her husband, how many of these women had he slept with? Adept at hiding both shame and love, Esther Leah was short, an oval-faced woman with large dark eyes, too prominent a chin, a warm Mediterranean complexion. "You'll get used to this," she said. "It's like what I imagine weightlessness is. Look for meaning, you'll go nuts. Look for a little pleasure, you'll find some. Soon it will be a burden to feel any other way." Esther Leah patted my shoulder and was off hostessing.

Palmyra had found her way, after many detours, back to Rolfe Sedan, the actor she'd come in with. She whispered to him. Did her lips brush his ear?

With no Mossy to thank, guests kissed or double-kissed Esther Leah on their way to the parking valets. I knew Rolfe Sedan could not be important in the life of Palmyra Millevoix—at best a cipher, not unlike me, just so she wouldn't have to show up alone—and this left me grateful. The upsweep of her hair now made her taller, more regal, than when it splashed onto her shoulders as it did in most publicity shots. Had anyone photographed her this way, and could I filch a copy? Wait, why was she patting Rolfe Sedan on the shoulder and moving toward the stairs by herself? She was going home alone too? Losses surrounded me, yet redemption was at hand. In our mutual solitude my spirit would fly to her.

I had not at first heard the low laugh coming from the open library door at the top of the stairs. In a moment Amos Zangwill and Marlene Dietrich were descending as if leading a stately procession. The low laugh again, from Marlene. "Mossy darlink, you haf giffen me eggsackly vut I need." "Well," he said, "it's a two way street, Marlene." "No, but egg*zackly!*" she said, clutching an empty martini glass like a weapon. "On vun little cocktail I am as you say loaded. Bad boy." Mossy shrugged and smiled.

From nowhere the two little chaperones Marlene came in with were alongside Pammy at the bottom of the stairs. "Boys, I see you in za morning," Dietrich said as she dismissed what Tutor Beedleman called her body doubles. "Tonight I think to speak with Mademoiselle Millevoix." She hooked her arm in Palmyra's. They had known each other in Europe, hadn't they? I hustled out of their way, leaving ahead of them.

"I assumed you must be reading every book in that library," I heard Pammy say. "Vell, you know Mossy," Marlene chuckled as they climbed the stairs she had just come down. "Und Mossy gafe you vut you vant?" Pammy asked, mimicking Marlene. "Und how, darlink." "Oh well," Pammy said, "I'm glad to know Mossy does that for somebody." They exited together, laughing.

I thought, how genteel, if baffling. In those days the word "clueless" had not entered the lexicon. Yet I was able to reflect on my grandiloquent delirium of the morning. In my self-coronation, I'd forgotten a monarch is also a butterfly that can be crushed by anyone's inadvertent heel.

But when I'd slunk to my car I had no car keys. I remembered jingling my key chain during the proud moment after hearing my *Doll's House* version praised. I crouched behind a bush until Pammy drove off in Dietrich's car. When I slunk back into the house against the tide of guests leaving Mossy's party, I tried to hide against the wall. On my hands and knees in the deserted ballroom, I searched for my key chain until a Filipino house boy reached down to tap my back. He handed me my keys.

5

The Odyssey of Poor Jim Bicker

Y ou cringe before that bitch and you know it. Let me tell you, she's out of tune in these times, never mind her singing. You know what she could do?"

Blinking, barely awake, I said I didn't know. Poor Jim Bicker was haranguing me early the next morning. He broke into my sleep by pounding so hard on my front door I leaped up certain I'd been hit in the head with a hatchet. I knew he lived in a decrepit apartment somewhere in Hollywood, and as I'd dragged myself to the door I couldn't imagine what he was doing on Sumac Lane in Santa Monica Canyon.

Freed from the dingy suit and soup-stained tie he'd worn at Mossy's party, Poor Jim was in his customary baggy pants and a striped jersey that set off his angry face with a little ring of neck hair that fringed over the collar. "You know what she could do with her fame, she and Amberlyn and a few others? They could lead this town to a revolution. If we had a revolution in the most conspicuous American business except for automobiles, we could start to save this fuckin' country, which doesn't deserve saving. So Millevoix says her conscience is awake now and then for Christ's sake sings us a romantic ballad. Drops the ball when she could be running for a touchdown, right? Am I right?"

"I really don't know," I said.

"You're a rank priv like all of them!" he shouted. "You don't even know that because you don't know this bleeding country we got on our hands. Yet you're also still a boy, and a boy can learn."

Apparently Jim Bicker had appointed himself my instructor. While I cut up two oranges and put on water for tea, he settled himself on the secondhand couch in the cramped space that passed for a living room. My little home had a steep roof that swept almost to the ground, framing two windows and the front door; the effect was of a man with a cap pulled down over his face. "You call the way I live privileged?" I asked. "Salary cuts are threatened at the studio. How privileged is that?"

"Okay, some of the privs are going to camp out in hard times for a while. The picture business is essentially thriving, people wasting their quarters to forget what things are like outside the movie houses, and the eastern banking privs, Episcopalians who don't like the Zangwill ilk anyway, are using breadlines as an excuse to rearrange their colony out here so profits will be even higher this year. Tight millionaires molding bad times into a reason for being even tighter. Blind privilege is all they know. Everything else is invisible. What these people here think they're going through is nothing but camping."

I still wasn't fully awake, and Poor Jim was ranting a sermon on injustice. Well, it was Sunday. He flew into his own version of the Depression, which had started for him in upstate New York where he was raised.

"My dad made screws," Jim Bicker said, "that's what he really did, twenty-seven years in the same factory. The Erie Metal Works. Laid off in '30, and I'm still living home eating his food in '31 because I'm using the typewriter and haven't sold a scrap. Sent out fifty, sixty stories and the magazines that bothered to answer told me I wasn't for them. By the middle of '31 my father was a shell and Erie Metal a bad memory. He didn't want to give up his party-line telephone. He gave it up. He didn't want to sell his car. He sold it. He didn't want to go on relief. He went on relief, which wasn't enough to keep the family in canned pork rinds. No jobs for me either, an unskilled complainer, or rather that was the one thing I was skilled at. I couldn't stand to watch the old man sink while my mother cried in the bedroom all day. We'd kept this letter for years from a relative in Sacramento with respectable handwriting, Bloomie Symmes. She'd written my father asking for family news, said anyone of us should come by if we ever made it that far west. I waved out of Buffalo on a June breeze."

With ten dollars in his pocket, Jim began his journey. "Jumped into a gondola car on a freight heading downstate," he said. "Hah, first and last time I rode al fresco. That night as we sped along I found out why the other 'bo's were in smelly boxcars in such fine weather. By morning when we hit New York City, my first time, I was a human icicle. Shivering so bad I couldn't protect myself and before I even got out of the freight yards two bums rolled me for my ten bucks. Couple of experienced hoboes helped me to Bellevue, where they told me I had pneumonia and kept me on sulfa for four days."

When he was released Poor Jim went uptown and camped out. One of the friendly hoboes had told him he'd be welcome in Hoover Valley. "That was in Central Park near the Obelisk the rich people stole from the Egyptians. Someone at Bellevue handed me a dollar when I left, and me and my hobo pal feasted on it, in our way, for a couple of days. Lot of rich people in the city, I didn't see anyone jumping out of skyscrapers like they were saying. But I saw more people wandering like me, beggars and apple sellers, living lines of men and some women waiting for bread around a whole city block, soup kitchens. People asking me did I have a dime because their kids at home were having boiled water with half a potato for dinner. Pretty soon I'm begging myself."

Jim Bicker talked like a tough man observing his life while he was living it. At times he became very agitated, choked with rage. That, I guessed, was the son of a ruined father. I asked him if he looked for a job while he was in New York.

"Yeah, I kind of looked for work all the time. Does this guy in the garment district need something hauled, a fish peddler want his garbage thrown out? Couple of day jobs in the flower district, then fixing tires in a repair shop. I didn't have the clothes to be a salesman or a waiter. I'd never realized you can't even apply for most jobs unless you have clean things to wear and someplace to bathe. I'd go to the public library, read till I fell asleep in the long room with the green lamps on every table. Librarians each had a different way to wake you up—

curtly, icily, apologetically, gently. 'This isn't a hotel, Mister.' Then I'd read some more—Chekov, George Eliot, Sinclair Lewis, Dos Passos. Nights I'm back at Hoover Valley."

When the police raided Hoover Valley, Jim went to a hobo jungle on the Brooklyn waterfront called Tin Mountain, where he met a woman he described as a pretty nice doll. She was on the run from a drunken father in the Long Island potato fields. I shivered—ignorant, shocked—when Jim told me about the father's abuses. "Andrea liked books herself," he said, "and we read a swiped copy of *The Possessed* together, all those passionate death-loving fanatics trying to cook up a revolution in Russia. She told me she'd like to become a Communist, which I had no idea about, but I'd met a Jewish hobo if you can imagine that, and he'd told me about Soviet poets coming to the city.

"We went to an apartment on the Lower East Side where they read their poems. There was a poster advertising the Soviets—'Friendship between the Great Experiment in Europe and the Great Depression in America.' We talked to the woman whose poems were about Mother Russia and the Revolution. Tatiana Etcherbina, a great large-eyed high cheek-boned beauty except for her teeth, which were a wreck. We told her what the Depression was doing to America. 'This is what you call poberty?'—that's how she pronounced it. 'I no believe what you call depression, your city is so rich. You don't know poberty, come to Russia I show you many million poberties, not few hundred. Socialism is big opportunity for us. I love position of artist in socialism so a man who deals in trucks don't sent here like you have big capitalists on Park Avenue, but I do sent here for read my poor poems.' When we hopped the subway back to Tin Mountain, Andrea was dead set for the Communists. Afterward I heard that when Tatiana Etcherbina got back to Russia they sent her to Siberia for being a holdover aristo."

The police raided Tin Mountain, scattered all the men and arrested the women for prostitution. Jim went with a hobo who knew where they could stay on the top floor of a movie theater in Flatbush. In the night they sneaked downstairs into the show. "I saw a nothing picture with Pamela Miles in it. What a raving pity. She wasn't acting, she was impersonating. Badly."

"She was someone else then, not herself," I defended, knowing it didn't matter.

"She's better now, okay? I want her to use that talent, that intensity, to speak and yell and sing for justice, goddammit."

"They say it's not safe. She's an alien, she could be deported."

"My heart goes out to cowards, especially rich ones. So my hobo pal finds a telephone that hasn't been disconnected on the abandoned top floor of the theater, and the operator puts me through to Buffalo. My parents' landlord had a phone. The old man was still sunk, selling used clothing on the street, but they were glad to hear I was alive. My mother sobbed and wanted me home, but they were worse off than I was. When I asked if they'd heard from any magazines, she said there was a new pile of returned manuscripts.

"I tried to find Andrea again, but I couldn't. After the janitor flushed us out of the theater, every day was keeping away from cops, hiding in Central Park, Union Square, the Library. Finding some soft place to sack was the work of the evening as getting food was the work of the morning and late afternoon. A stray dog down by the Hudson, a cute little chow, attached himself to me, and we went around together because it was easier to get a nickel or two from a passing swell if I said my dog hadn't eaten. The truth was he ate better than I did. We'd sleep in a doorway or over a subway grating, and when we woke up butchers would throw the dog cuts of meat they couldn't sell and I couldn't eat.

"My last night with the chow we spent in Central Park down near the little duck pond, and we were attacked by a rat the size of Denver. That was enough for me. The next day was very hot and the chow and I were in the zoo's outdoor cafeteria looking for throwaway food when I spotted a suit jacket a man had taken off because of the sun. The guy went to the can and I lifted his coat. No wallet in it but at least I could look respectable. I said my goodbyes to the chow as I went into the Library's main entrance on Fifth Avenue, then ducked out the side exit on Forty-second Street when I was finished with Joe Conrad a few hours later."

"You needed a suit jacket for a library?" I asked. "They kick out hoboes?"

"They don't but I was starving for better food than I could beg.

I buttoned the coat to look as good as I could and took myself to a restaurant called Joubair's in the show district. French, snooty. I came in just when their theater crowd left so they were glad to have a new customer. A piss-elegant dame at the next table with her goddam perfume made me think of Andrea, who smelled like a real woman, but before I could work myself up the perfume was overpowered by butter, fish, steak, wine, garlic, every kind of sauce you can dream of. I started with snails, which of course I'd never tasted. Ordered a bottle of Château Margaux which I'd never heard of but it was over five bucks so I figured it had to be good and it was like heaven. Then I had a veal chop swimming in cream and mushrooms and sherry. Artichoke on the side. Dessert was pastry made out of rum and chocolate. Finished the Château Margaux and realized I hadn't been so satisfied with a meal since Thanksgiving when I was a kid. The check came and I was into Joubair's for seventeen dollars they couldn't have got out of me if they squeezed my bones into powder. I asked for the headwaiter and he came over and bowed like a servile lizard, asking me if anything was wrong, monsieur. I said no, the dinner was delicious, but I can't pay for it, so can I please wash dishes. The headwaiter pulls himself up like a duke, says 'If you wish, monsieur, follow me *s'il vous plaît.*'

"He takes me back to the kitchen, turns me over to the chef, and disappears. I move to this big tub of a sink and roll up my sleeves when their real dishwasher, tattooed head to toe, takes me aside. Tells me what the headwaiter did about the last guy who thought he had dinner on the house. The dicks from the hotel next door took him into the alley back of Joubair's kitchen and when they finished with him he had no front teeth to chew with anymore and for their going away present they hit him so hard in the stomach he puked up the twelve-dollar meal he had just swallowed. I didn't need any more encouragement, so as these dicks were being led to the kitchen by the formerly cringing headwaiter I hightailed out the side door into the alley, jumped the iron fence onto the sidewalk, and mingled with the passing crowd. Within ten minutes I was back in the freight yards where I'd started four weeks earlier."

"Close call," I said, envying Jim. "Hell of an adventure. So you're back on freight cars. Nice way to see the country."

"No, no, and no!" he thundered. "Are you an educable sap or just a sap! I was rolled, remember, after my first ride. It's a vicious, dangerous, putrid way to see the country." He was spitting his words. "I wasn't back on the freights, nothing was moving in the yards that night so I made it over to Grand Central and hid in the restroom of a Chicago train until we got to Poughkeepsie where I hopped a boxcar carrying tractors and hoboes. What you call an adventure was staying just this side of the grave."

"You still had the delicious dinner inside you, and no one beat you up."

"Yeah and I had the sight and stench of rich people inside me too, infecting me like jungle rot. I hated them for the injustice of the whole thing even more than I was jealous of them. When I was jumped on the Baltimore & Ohio by two thugs, they let me go when they searched me and couldn't find a quarter. A long day and longer night and then I caught the Nickel Plate Railroad out of Altoona, the Lake Shore out of Cleveland, and a couple of toughs actually shared their meal with me, first thing I'd had to eat since I escaped from Joubair's, and I was so hungry it tasted just as good. When we finally hit the Dearborn Street Station in Chicago I saw a city even deader than New York and the cops meaner, clubbing anyone who looked like he needed a hand. I didn't last a night there but went over to the Bensenville Yards and latched onto a freight heading west. Not as much as a breadcrust among the hoboes in the boxcar."

In Iowa Poor Jim picked up some change driving a truck for a bootlegger, but the money was stolen and he was arrested for vagrancy. "That night in the jail I thought I was in heaven," he said, "a solid meal and a bunk with an actual mattress. They kick me out in the morning and I'm off on the Missouri Pacific, always in a boxcar since I learned my lesson in the gondola, and I make it all the way to the Sheffield Yards in Kansas City. A well-traveled knight of the road hooks me into a rough jungle near the Yards that's bubbling with hoboes. These places are like little towns with mayors. The mayor of this jungle knew the guy I was with and told me, 'We don't trust no strange unless he comes in with someone we know.' The whole world to them was made up of pals and what they called stranges. Knives and fights were as common as laughter. Cops came in the week before and busted heads with their billies. 'We kill one of those sumbitches and we stretch,' the mayor told me, 'but they kill us and get a pay raise.'

"Second day I'm there a bunch of the tougher ones were sitting around a fire when a sweet-looking boy maybe fourteen limped into camp. He'd hurt himself jumping off a moving freight and he was so nervous he could hardly talk. 'Hel-, uh, hello,' he said, 'I was l-looking for some-, uh, something to food.' Kid scared out of whatever wits he had. 'Wa-al lookee what my uncle's cat drug in,' one of the toughs said. 'Got a hungry walk, don't he?' another said. I'm ashamed to tell you this, Jant, but I did nothing when three of these big bastards took that kid off in the woods and had him six ways from Sunday before they'd give him anything to eat. I heard him whimper, 'Please, please let me back up, I think I'm split.' A jungle. 'Let me back up,' that's all he said."

I looked at Poor Jim Bicker and shook my head. Rape was a crime I'd scarcely heard of, an unimaginable activity. I didn't know whether he was trying to inform me or horrify me. "What happened to the kid?" I asked. "Did you take him to a doctor?"

"Sure, Owen, the place was swarming with doctors. I gave him half my dinner and led him off telling the others I was going to take my turn with him. About a mile away a church was having a social where I found a lady who could have been his grandmother, glad to take him in. I lit out on the Kansas City Southern heading for Tulsa, and it was a relief to be back on the rails. The engine broke down in a godforgotten whistlestop early the next morning. I walked around the main street looking for something to eat and saw a little closed bank. In the window there was deep brown velvet on the teller's counter, which I thought was odd. When my eyes adjusted to the bank's half-light I could see it wasn't velvet at all. It was dust. That bank had been closed long enough for it to accumulate. My first sight of the dust—and it was inside at that."

When Poor Jim Bicker first began I thought he was telling me an idea for a movie because that's what everyone did. I even wondered if he wanted me to collaborate on it. Would there be a woman's part big enough for Palmyra? By the time I realized he was venting his spleen at the inequity, and iniquity, he saw in America, I saw he believed that if he vented in my direction I'd understand something he understood.

Jim Bicker was bringing the Depression to Hollywood. Since he was hungry in his story I had the idea he might actually want breakfast, and I scrambled us some eggs while he continued.

"The train's engine still wasn't fixed so I put my sack over my shoulder to try my luck with my thumb. The wind was blowing dirt in my eyes when a man and a woman stopped for me in a rattletrap with broken windows. They looked no better than their car, all the starch gone out of them. Two squalling kids sat between them. Even from the backseat it appeared that every breath the parents took required a supreme effort. Their farm had been repossessed and they were trying to get to western Kansas where they had relatives who might take them in. The dust made the man turn on his headlights at three in the afternoon. Their car broke down in the town of Hutchinson, radiator burst. As bad off as I was I could see they were a lot worse, so I gave them a couple of quarters, which the man took hungrily, not gratefully. If he couldn't fix the car himself he might get a used fanbelt with one of the quarters, milk for his kids with the other."

"Dark in the middle of the day?" I asked Bicker.

"Darker than night," he said as he shoveled down the last of his eggs, "because you can see at night but your eyes can't get into a dirt wall though a dirt wall can get into your eyes. Like Hollywood, Jant, where the big guys get into us but we can't get anywhere with them unless they happen to need us. Shit, we're going to parties with perfume and Champagne and gold cufflinks with A and Z on them telling us Amos Zangwill encloses everything yet he don't know and you don't know what's going on out there in the planet of dust."

"Stop pummeling me, Bicker," I managed to say, using his last name as he had mine. "You're in Hutchinson, Kansas?"

"Huge grain elevators grew out of the prairie like exclamation marks, but they were empty. As wheat prices fell farmers plowed more land, planting seeds that wouldn't grow in the drought. Ranchers had cattle grazing their acres bare. When the wind came up there was nothing to hold the surface earth in place, and it was leaving. The joke in town was that crows were learning to fly backward to keep the dust out of their eyes. Farmers and workers couldn't afford each other's produce. The Hutchinson paper told about a farmer who couldn't feed his three thousand sheep and couldn't bear to watch them starve. He drove them to a cliff where he and his son, both weeping, cut all their throats and shoved them down into the canyon. The dust didn't care; it just kept blowing.

"That night my fairy godmother smiled. As I was about to start wagging my thumb on the edge of town I saw a lady in a nice hat walk in the front entrance of a small house that still had traces of a garden on the side. I went around to the back door to see if she might have any food to spare. Wouldn't you know it, she asked me to join her for dinner. Not pretty but not plain either, she had eyes that made up their mind about you fast. All her bowls were upside down to keep the dust out of them. I washed up as well as I could and put on one of my two extra shirts. Funny thing, we talked about baseball while she made dinner, she'd once seen Ty Cobb get four hits and steal four bases in a game. Meat loaf with mashed potatoes and string beans is simple as a meal gets, and it tasted better than anything back at Joubair's. She was a teacher who'd come out from Michigan when she married a professional man, an optometrist. After '29 people stopped buying new glasses, so the husband went east to Pittsburgh to work for his brother who exported steel to countries that could still afford it. She was working part-time at the library and teaching composition at the local junior college. She was supposed to close up the house and join her husband, but she'd come to like Hutchinson and didn't much miss the husband. When the wind became a scream and dust blew through a closed window like it was open, the lady asked if I wanted to stay the night.

"Even then I wasn't expecting we'd sleep together, but one thing led to another and that's what we did. We were shy, and then we weren't. After we finished, she turned the light back on to look for a tissue and I saw she was crying. Her tears were muddy. While the wind still howled outside—and not just outside—we went to sleep. In the morning the only spaces in the bed still white were the outlines of where our bodies had lain. Everything else was covered. She fed me breakfast and I asked if there was anything I could do for her, chop wood or something. 'No wood to chop, just be on your merry way,' she said, and she was smiling. Funny thing, we didn't exchange names."

As I listened to this story, I thought Poor Jim had found something pretty good in a pretty bad time. I thought I'd have wanted to stick around. "Weren't you tempted to stay there?" I asked.

"Nope, she didn't suggest it and I wasn't tempted," he said. "Hitched up with a family at a filling station—grandparents, parents, three kids. We soon hit what looked like a wall of dirt. This was known as a black blizzard and even with the windows rolled up we chewed dirt. When it let up a little, we headed for Hot Springs, Arkansas, where they said there'd be jobs at a resort. Generous folks, they shared everything. I waited on the privs for a week in Hot Springs, bringing them towels and drinks while they took the sulfur waters, everyone acting as though there was no such thing as Prohibition or the Depression. The wind died down and the dust was manageable. With tips I left Hot Springs flush, a bag of tobacco in my clothing sack and ten dollars in my pocket, another twenty in my shoe."

Some of his riches didn't last long. The driver who picked him up had a pistol and made off with ten dollars. The twenty stayed in Jim's shoe as he headed west on a boxcar out of Little Rock, enjoying the view for a precious hour before the wind came up again.

"The countryside was wounded. Thunderheads of dust left the plains bare. Nothing growing for miles. Earth's answer to greed and ignorance. Dumb suckers wanted too much from nature. Cattlemen, sheepherders, farmers, bankers, big investors, railroads striping across the prairie—they all had a hand in the ruin of the land."

Poor Jim Bicker is a sulky bastard, I thought, delivering his inverted rhapsody on America, yet he's seen things with those angry eyes. I asked how he turned his miserable journey into a job in Hollywood.

"It was anything but miserable!" he stormed. "The truth is never miserable. It's always a discovery. I wouldn't trade a minute of it."

"I mean it's so bleak. You were in danger all the time."

"That's life, my friend."

"You could have lost yours." Was I sounding like his mother?

"You don't want death, don't try life."

"Okay, I get it. America is broken, even the land is cracked. We have to fix it."

"You don't know the half of it."

"I know your family's had some hard—"

"My family, Jant, is as rotten as this whole rotten country! We're the underside of the America the big boys don't want you thinking about. How'd I get to Hollywood? How'd Hollywood get to me is the question. First of all, the Depression is nothing new to the Bickers. We've always been lowest on the totem pole, all of us lost or losing, ever since we settled in this country. Michael Martin Bircher was the first of us born in America before it was America, in Anne Arundel County, colony of Maryland, 1648. Not all the early settlers became Jeffersons or Adamses. The only thing we bottom-feeders knew was how to record our misfortunes and villainies, those we were caught for, in a musty old family Bible my parents still have."

Poor Jim ticked off the family statistics: died in prison. Ran off with a stable boy to the Louisiana Territory. Killed in a bar fight, buried in Potters Field. Hanged, put in stocks, bankrupt, wife-deserter, whore in Philadelphia, whore in Indiana, embezzler in Milwaukee. These were the entries. "So much for being scribes," he said.

I sighed. Reproached, informed, badgered, I could imagine no family tree as blighted as Jim's, yet the America he'd crisscrossed mirrored his own history.

"We are a dozen generations despoiling the countryside with our presence," he said. "Now across the ocean—which for us was Holland, Austria, and England—we'd thrived, sometimes even had our own villages. In the old country conniving and pretense and timely bootlicking flourished like they do here in Hollywood. But in the new country the colonists were making, the land of opportunity, those ruses didn't work as well at first, and most of the time, neither did the Birchers. Until one of us, on the lam for nothing nobler than forgery, found California.

"Missed the Gold Rush, of course, got here in the late 1850s, changed his name to Bicker because that's what his Mexican wife could pronounce. Two daughters and a son. Ran a dry goods business that actually drew in most of Fresno, so he planted branches of it up and down the state. His drunken brother came out to work for him, but he didn't like his sister-in-law and the feeling was mutual. The drunk either insulted or raped the Mexican wife one Saturday night while the dry goods brother was counting the week's take and stashing it in the safe. Well, Bicker shot Bircher. They let him off when he claimed his brother had attacked him, but they ran him out of the state and he took his wife and three kids back east to Buffalo and resumed the family habit of losing. Couldn't get started in dry goods, learned how to cheat at shell games and poker. His half-Mexican son became my grandfather. Providers we never have been; integrity we did not breed; almost none of us above the rank of hired hand or drifter."

"Your father in the screw factory," I said, "was an exception."

"Fat lot of good it did him. But I told you I had a relative out here in Sacramento. When I was a kid my father got that letter asking for family news, talking about a rose garden and privet hedge and a Victorian house, ending with the sign-off of Your Cousin, Bloomie Symmes. He didn't answer, but I always thought if I ever reached her precinct I'd look her up. The spelling of her last name, which must originally have been Sims, seemed to indicate someone was trying to rise, if not Bloomie herself then her husband. So from Arkansas I headed vaguely, dustily west."

Jim's journey became, if anything, even worse. He got a ride with a trucker who had scooped up a woman hugging a dead chicken she'd found on the road. She wouldn't let go of it. Jim jumped out of the truck when the radiator boiled over. "I'm thinking no one obeys any law except the one that says hunger still strikes three times a day. I wanted to show that Russian poet Tatiana Etcherbina that we have millions of our own poberties right here. That madwoman clinging to her dead chicken maybe tells the whole story."

"But you knew that wasn't true," I told Poor Jim. "You knew people would find jobs again when factories heated up to supply anything worn out, from shoes to motors. You must have known the land would be fertile again."

"I knew no such goddam thing!" Bicker yelled. "And no such goddam thing has happened. Farmers and workers are still broke, all they have from Mr. Smiling-cigarette-holder are promises, and how long do you think faith and patience will last when reality makes lies of those promises?"

Back on the rails, Jim's freight was wrecked going up a steep incline in Montana. The engineer and fireman were killed, and Jim had a sprained back and several cracked ribs. When he could travel again he caught the Northern Pacific to Spokane, where he saw he was in apple country. He found a farmer who raised both apples and sheep. "After a month picking apples and fencing sheep," he said, "I'm up forty dollars, ready for Bloomie Symmes."

For the first time he took a train as a paying passenger and the next day he was in Sacramento. "Knowing I'd need decent clothes for my passport out of the underworld," he said, "I look in the window of a store and wonder who is the bearded weatherbeaten hobo staring out. I turn to see who is next to me before I realize who the bum is. I buy the clothes and get a room in the YMCA where I can make myself presentable to Cousin Bloomie. Then I go to the address where her letter came from ten years earlier."

"At last," I said, "your appointment with destiny."

"Right," Jim said. "It's a quiet Sacramento street with trees shading the houses. There's the privet hedge, all right, in front of the gabled, many-roomed Victorian. This is going to be nice, I think. A pretty lady answers the doorbell with a bandanna around her head—she has been cleaning her house—and I think this is the answer to prayers I haven't even prayed. A beautiful second or third cousin, she's like an advertisement for something that makes your home look or smell better. Can she help me? she asks. I ask if she's Mrs. Symmes. For a moment she's puzzled, and she asks me if I have the right address. Then she remembers. I must mean old Bloomie. Well, Bloomie passed away about three years ago, and the bandanna lady and her husband bought the house from the widower Colton Symmes who himself passed on in February."

"So you're nowhere after all this time on the road," I said. I didn't see how we'd ever get to Hollywood. Yet in a way I was grateful to Jim.

"What an idiot I am," Jim said. "I go back to the YMCA and make a collect call to my parents' landlord, who surprises me by telling me to call my parents, they have a phone now. I'm even more surprised when I hear a party going on at their place. They haven't had a party since my dad was laid off from the Erie Metal Works. 'What's the occasion, Ma?' I ask. She hopes I won't be mad but they're living a lot better now. 'Of course I'm not mad, I'm overjoyed, Ma.' Then she tells me. Two months earlier she got a letter with a check from the *Police Gazette*. Seventy dollars for one of my stories. The next week comes an envelope from *Collier's* with a check for a hundred and twenty-five dollars for another story. Two weeks later a third check, a hundred and fifty dollars from the *Saturday Evening Post*. They had no idea how to reach me so they've been living off the checks. Then she says a week ago a man named Colonel DeLight called from the Jubilee Studios in Hollywood, well not exactly Hollywood but Culver City, California. Would I like to write a picture for them? Jubilee, huh. Well I was in jubilation over Jubilee. Somebody gave his studio the right name for a place I'd want to work."

Before he called Colonel DeLight, Jim found his stories in the Sacramento library. "Sure enough there's the crime-doesn't-pay yarn about a stick-up man and his moll in the *Gazette*, the *Collier's* adventure of the oil wildcatter in Alaska saving the hunter from being clawed to death by a bear even though the hunter has stolen his wife, and the *Post* tear-jerker with the parents granting their dying son his last wish, a visit to Niagara Falls, which of course I knew like the back of my hand from having grown up near there. It's the wildcatter in Alaska they want, and I tell Colonel DeLight I'll see him next week."

Jim's feet were itchy for one more ride on the iron horse. Wanting the trip to end, wanting just a little more, Jim grabbed a southbound freight from Sacramento as his farewell to the road. In addition to the usual hoboes, he shared a boxcar with a woman and a girl. "A tired dame with a face sad as an old moon is protecting this girl of maybe fifteen," he said, "from the toughs in the car. She's too pretty for her own good. The hoboes are talking about easy times in the city of angels, and I know I'm heading for the easy times they're dreaming of while they're going to be skidrow bums heaped like old boards in a new city. The tired woman is passing along her philosophy of life to the girl. 'Never go with a strange,' she says, 'because once he's dicked you he vamooses.'"

Late in the day Jim's freight passed a hobo jungle on the outskirts of Bakersfield. A few men from the jungle ran for the train as it slowed. Jim saw a boy trying for the freight too and waved at him. "This towheaded kid with a pair of quick legs, maybe the age of the girl in the car," he said, "runs alongside the train. His hair is blowing back and his eager eyes are trying to catch the freight by themselves. I'm thinking this is what I'll miss about the road. The kid is laughing—catching a train is a game with him, a new game. He reaches up for the grab iron, and he gets it but he can't hold on the right way. He tries to let go but now he's being dragged by the freight.

"I jump off to help him, and another guy jumps to yell for the engineer to stop. More hoboes pile out of the boxcar and run toward the towheaded boy. When we reach the kid I see his quick legs first. They are no longer part of his body. We pull the kid off the tracks. He has passed out and a gush of blood is pooling below the stumps where his legs have been sheared off. He comes to and smiles, asks for a cigarette, and one of the hoboes fishes out a butt to stick in the kid's mouth, tells him he'll be okay now. The kid looks up and says, 'Yeah, I reckon. I'm headed for Hollywood, you know. Them fuckin' guys can't go on forever. They're gonna need a new Sparky.'

"Actually, it's Spanky and he's too old to be one of the Our Gang rascals even if he still had his legs, but the kid says what he says. The woman and the girl are now looking at the towhead, and the girl like a tender bundle of mercy with her wheatfield hair backlit by the late afternoon sunlight kneels to ask him if he needs anything. 'No, no, no, no, I'm fine now,' the kid says, 'but gee aren't you a sweet one, for a minute there I thought I might not make it. You look no different from an angel, do you?' The kid puts up his hand to ward off something in the air. He takes a deep drag on the butt, and then he's finished. The smoke never comes back out of his lungs. The woman says to the girl, 'No use wasting tears.' The hobo who gave him the butt takes a long look down and says, 'You got to hand it to him, the kid died dead game with a hard-on.' That was the eulogy."

"Jesus," I said to Jim.

"I took a bus the rest of the way," he said, "couldn't stand to leave the woman and the girl on the freight so I paid for them too. I was being a sentimental bourgeois, but at least they wouldn't get mauled by those particular hoboes on that particular freight run.

"A carpet of beggars greeted me at the studio gates when I reported to Jubilee my first morning. Depression youth loitering with their bright hopeful eyes. Not all of them—some of them had eyes as scared as a deer's. Desperate greedy parents bring their kids to the gates like they would to school but a school that won't let them in. Nobody gets warm piss around here unless they're connected, obsessed, or cheaters."

"But wait, Jim," I objected, trying to shift gears after the story of the dead boy as fast as Bicker himself did. "You're not any of those, yet here you are at Jubilee on salary."

"The story I sold to *Collier's* connected me, and who says I'm not obsessed? I got the royal welcome at first, like all of us. Beeker Kyle takes me around, acts as if being assistant studio manager gives him permission to bust in all over the lot. Tiptoes, Kyle does, sneaking around to catch someone at something. He had me stay at his place a couple of nights until I found a room. I'm given a monk's cell off the kitchen in his Ocean Park cottage. I'm told at the studio Beeker Kyle is Jubilee's own saccharine fascist, with a semi-retarded half-brother he's generous with, while everyone else is pebbles to be walked on. In the night I hear arguments and loud swearing outside my tiny room. In the morning I see no sign anyone else has been there. When Kyle appears for breakfast he's unrested, gruff. 'My bedchamber,' he says archly as he coils his villain's mustaches, 'is the resort of infernal fiends.' Behind his back, Kyle calls Mossy ratface. On Kyle's tour I met Palmyra Millevoix. You know her?"

I sucked in my breath. "No, not really." Poor Jim asked no follow-up question as I reflected bitterly how unintentionally accurate my answer had been.

"Yeah, she doesn't do it for me. Too much a combination of innocence, which is false, with worldliness, which she uses like a shield. I sat at her table in the commissary once. She didn't eat anything but salad, which I don't trust in a woman. When Baxter Ellis Huxtable came out to write the screenplay for his unjustly famous novel, I introduced him to Pammy. Pompous ass bragged later he got into her eminent feathers and it was like being alone, bouncing around by himself."

Bicker couldn't have seen me cringe inside, hoping it wasn't true, worried it was.

"Felt like a pimp," he continued, "not exactly what I rode the rails out here to become. Kyle turned me over to Colonel DeLight, who comes on buttery in his patronizing Kentucky way. He's basically a reader but he makes writers feel he's in their fraternity. Cools off guys who get hot under the collar, warms up the ones who get frozen out. Instructs the novices in screenwriting, which he's never done himself."

Jim mimicked DeLight: "'The trick, son,' he drawled at me, 'is to make shuah you always have more than one ball in the air. Don't linger on a street lamp and its charm. Show us how the glow from the lamp looks when it comes through the windah into a room. Now you have two things, street lamp and room. From there the rest flows. The lamp throws a certain shade on objects in the room. These objects belong to Theodore, or to Theodora, and some to Theodora's daughtah, home from college to recovah from a love affair and a minor breakdown. Now we're off to the races, son, see what Ah'm drivin' at?' And that's Colonel DeLight's way of showing you how to write a screenplay. Meanwhile the son of a bitch runs a sweatshop for Mossy, the girls who sew costumes."

"I can't believe that," I said. "There are unions all over the lot."

"Not really. Mostly just union talk. Upstairs from the actresses' dressing rooms—not the stars' dressing rooms obviously, the starlets and featured girls."

"Colonel DeLight has been pretty good to me," I said. "I don't believe it."

"Surprises, that's the thing," Jim said as he put his feet on the upturned packing crate that was my coffee table and lit a cigarette. Poor Jim Bicker was spent. "You never know where you are," he concluded, "until later."

6

Sunday Could Be Grim

Dear Pammy,

Last night was a revelation. There I was at our mutual master's mansion having a perfectly decent time when suddenly something happened. You stepped to the piano ...

I had decided to write her a letter. Poor Jim Bicker emboldened me. He didn't seem to care what people thought of him; why should I? When Bicker took his leave—he was going to East Los Angeles to spend the rest of Sunday with Mexicans, helping them become as angry at gringo ways as he was—I filled my Schaffer pen and tried to be neat.

But "mutual master's mansion"? Clumsily alliterative, its true awfulness was in my presuming to identify myself with her as a fellow employee of Mossy's. She was not only a light-year from me but also far above him in the firmament, and his success depended far more on her than hers on him.

"Dear Pammy,

"After your impromptu performance last night I heard only choruses of adulation attempting to match your own matchlessness. You

72

were simply and complicatedly superb. I suppose this sounds like nothing so much as another of the countless fan letters you receive weekly, yet I have to say how wonderful you are, what a privilege it is to labor, however humbly, in the same Jubilee vineyards of which you are most deservedly queen. I was having a perfectly decent evening at Mossy's, mingling with a quorum of the town's notables, but when you materialized at the piano and put your elegant vocal instrument to work, you captivated us all, raising the party to the level of an unforgettable occasion. Forgive my intrusion, I thought I ought to tell you.

"Devotedly, Owen"

I struggled with "Devotedly," rejecting "Fondly," "Sincerely," and "Admiringly." As for my name, I considered adding Jant to the sign-off. She was unlikely to think the letter was from Owen Lashley the cutter, or from Owen Hasselbrook the timpanist, though she could conclude it came from Owen Wachtel the Jubilee assistant producer who actually was at the party. The other two weren't, but Pammy wouldn't necessarily have known that any more than she may have noticed that I was there. Oh well, be bold, be familiar, live dangerously.

I drove to Camden Drive in Beverly Hills, parking across the street from her house, where I would just slip my letter under her door. Though they'd left Mossy's party together, I didn't think she'd be spending Sunday with Marlene Dietrich, convening with the German expatriates who had begun to gather in Hollywood. She'd be with her daughter. Pammy and Millie lived in a columned white house set well back from the street. A chandelier hung over the front porch, above which was a second-floor terrace. A dozen or so fans were collected on the sidewalk. Maps of the stars' homes had recently been published; on weekends there were always gawkers. Above Sunset Boulevard the homes were defended by great hedges or tree barriers or high walls, but since Pammy lived in the more plebian flats below Sunset, her house was approachable.

Two of the fans, I saw from the window of my Essex, were no fans at all but held a sign that read SINNERS ALWAYS SUFFER LAST. The genuine fans were arguing with the sign holders. "She's gorgeous, she sings like heaven, she doesn't hurt a soul, leave her alone," said the fans. "Palmyra Millevoix is immoral and alien to Christ's teachings," said the man and woman with the placard. It wasn't clear whether they were referring to the roles she played, Millie's uncertain paternity, rumors about Pammy's personal life, or expressing general dissatisfaction with permissive popular culture.

I detoured around the demonstrators and headed for the house. Her blue La Salle was not in the driveway, so much the better. "If you have a delivery," a fan called out, "she's not here." "They say she has a place in the country," said another. "Stay clear of sinners," one of the anti-fans said helpfully. "Thank you," I said. I knelt to put my envelope through a mail slot next to the front door when a last-instant thought struck me. Almost every word in the letter was a lie except "Devotedly." I hadn't had fun at the party, I hadn't mixed well with others, I didn't hear accolades for her because I was dizzy with gin, in fact I'd had a humiliatingly terrible time at the party. Also, she really sang only one song; I'd heard much more of her music when I'd gone to her studio bungalow many months before, and I hadn't written her a letter after that, only press releases.

With my back to the sidewalk I slipped the letter under my shirt so the fans would think I'd delivered it. As I walked to my car a middle-aged man asked if I knew the star well. "Oh, just a bit," I said, "and she's as wonderful as they come." "Then why is the letter poking out of your shirt?" he asked. "I decided to deliver it to her personally," I said. As I climbed back into my car, the fans joined with the anti-fans in laughing at me.

The rest of Sunday stretched out like the Sahara, and Sunday night was always grim: the weekend was over. When I was a child that meant I'd be leaving my parents the next morning for school. Since we moved as much as we did, it was often a school where I was unsure of myself, wondering if the boys would speak to me, if the girls might notice me, who I'd play with at recess. That was when I first understood there is no such thing as a happy ending. If the weekend had been fun and adventurous, I hated to see it come to a close. If it had been boring and we'd been visiting people without children, the men smoking evil-smelling cigars and talking about the war, the women trading recipes and gossip, Sunday night was miserable in its continuation of my misery.

At home on Sumac Lane, I made myself a lunch of canned chicken noodle soup and two pieces of toast. Removing my bookmark from *Swann's Way*, I felt some relief that no one would ever ask me to adapt Proust.

The phone was ringing, but I decided not to answer it.

Backstory

My mother was the first Chinese person I ever knew. Odd how random events strike you. You may not suspect a misfortune is on its way, or that anything is going on besides a lost sled when you're a child, a car running out of gas, a wave bigger than the others. Each may seem a mere curiosity, ominous only if you have a gift for prophecy. The stain, though unsightly, did not upset me at the time.

"Little Owen come with me, Little Owen come to me, Little Owen let us see How we can spend our century." She crooned to me at bedtime. My father beamed.

Do my three syllables carry the visual resonance of something you may once have noticed, if scarcely, as you would passing a billboard or lonesome scarecrow when you were out for a drive in the country? Well after the stars, before the director. Do the syllables seem to have flashed by? A trivia question? What a fate. Yet the little trio of sounds—oh-when-jant—prove my existence.

By the same author: Gun for Hire; The Scarlet Letter; Bleak House; The Last Train; Low Sun at Durango; Richer Than Mr. Mellon; Holiday in Havana; The Sun Also Rises; Troilus and Cressida; Barchester Towers; Meet Me at the Waldorf; Playing Hooky. Lastly, my collected essays, Articles of Faith, which I hope you have seen.

You will have surmised that up through *Barchester Towers* I refer to pictures I worked on. Never mind the bastard producers didn't give me credit on all of them, or got away with an Additional Dialogue By designation that meant nada. The next two after *Barchester* are misbegotten plays. On the first of these I collaborated with George S. Kaufman while flying solo on *Playing Hooky*. They lasted a total of ninety-three performances on Broadway, ninety two of which were due to the Kaufman name.

I've been a dependent clause long enough, the occupational hazard of screenwriters, supporting players who push the action along, then wait in the wings until needed for some plotty errand.

The famous screenwriter Ben Hecht called himself a child of the century, but his claim was bogus. I was its true offspring. Though it was a decade old when I made my debut, I paralleled the century, taking personally its wins and losses as Ben never did. The Panama Canal was my first triumph, the tearing down of the Berlin Wall my last. In between came all the wars. Did a hundred million die in the most killing century in history? Christians were the champions, creating the most dead, but Communists and other religions did their share. In my view, not because I'm more sensitive than anyone else but simply because I have lived so vicariously—voyeuristically when possible, eavesdropping on history the rest of the time—I was killed a hundred million times. All the while amassing credits and debits and discredits. I collect in order to recollect.

Flashing forward, I trotted into the motion picture industry as a derivative option, doomed morally and temperamentally to live in the shadow and on the nourishment of others. Owen the parasite. Always looking to become my own self.

Between scripts I dipped my quill in thicker ink with essays on the passing scene, the motion picture business, its politics, and an occasional portrait of an obsessed filmmaker or producing tycoon. After teaching a course on writing at San Quentin during a slow period, I produced a little corsage for the *Threepenny Review* called Prose and Cons. Although a couple of the portraits found their way, as grievously abbreviated Talk pieces, into *The New Yorker*, most of my writing was for the little known *Contempo Reader*, a now-vanished quarterly that devoted itself to fiction and essays from or about the Left. When there was barely any Left left, after the blacklists of the Fifties, *Contempo Reader* began to trumpet the Thirties. I was a natural for them. I profiled some of the old Lefties—the usual suspects: McGurney Harris, Hy Soifer, Evelyn Wilberg deForest, Ripley Link, Jeremy Mah Silberman—and finally did one on Ring Lardner, Jr. for *Esquire*. This last came to the attention of an editor at the also now-defunct Summit Books, and before you knew it out came my collection, *Articles of Faith*.

I left off essays—having loved journalism a while, if only adulterously—when David Begelman hired me to do a script on the narcotics trade. Early Seventies. I knew nothing about it, went downtown to East L.A. and found some pretty strung-out kids, Cal and June. They told me they were on speed when they met. "Stopped for a week so we could ball," June said. Then they went back on. "After a bit we found horse," Cal said, "or horse found us." When they told me about this, I was curious: was the sex so inferior to the drugs that ruined them that they actually preferred the narcotics? "You don't get it," June said, "the sex was the drug and the drug was the drug but the drug was the better drug." I scratched my head and went home to work on this, and then *Panic in Needle Park* came out. Begelman dropped me as if he'd been toting a boulder.

But my childhood. When did I notice the stain, coffee or ink? It meant nothing.

"Why does the sun go to bed in one corner of the sky and get up in another?" "Mind your owen business, chuff chuff," the gruff one said out of his mustache with a twinkle when asked a question while he was busy. "Oh no, blink blink," said the gentler one. "He is his owen curious self and owenly seven years old." Nauseatingly precious, but they believed themselves lastingly blessed. My mother would call me her little magpie, tell me it was time to stop chattering and wash for supper. To which my father would gruffly reply, "I didn't think we needed a magpie around here. I thought we were rearing an eagle."

My childhood was as full of trains as other people's is of relatives, as full of trains as Poor Jim Bicker's nomadic Depression would be.

I came of age enjoying things, American bred and born, a child of western Ohio, which gave us cash registers and aviation. Cyclones of paint, congenial yet dizzying, inevitable as loose teeth in a five-year-old, lifted me off my hinges every few months, depositing me in a new spot where I'd be treated well but in essence left, as my parents said, to my owen self. We were always moving on, six or seven places every couple of years.

If my parents had been animals, my father was an amiable moose. "Chuff chuff, every boy should climb a mountain, shoot a gun, memorize the presidents, read the classics, know how to fish." While my mother leaped into and out of interests with the excited, nervous grace of a deer. Syrilla and Barnett. "Blink blink, it's time for a new city, blink blink, why don't we see what Indians are really like, surely their humble abodes need a coat or two, Barney." "Whoever heard of educating a boy, chuff chuff, without some experience of the Continent?" Syrilla, née Stedman, and Barnett Jant. With a blink and a chuff, they said in unison, "We'll try Paris as soon as the Armistice comes."

No one who was rich would have called us rich.

No one who was poor would have called us anything but rich.

Yet we didn't fit snugly in the middle either because we moved so much more than the people who came home from jobs to sit in their chain-hung rockers, swinging on their porches as they watched their generation mount the offensive called the twentieth century. The moose wasn't leisured; he was in paints, a middleman, not a manufacturer. Wherever we went people were building offices, homes, schools, bowling alleys, dance halls. When they finished building, they needed color. He gave them that. In his three-piece suit with his gold watch fob and polka-dotted bow tie and the monocle he affected, he marched over to construction sites. He'd go up to contractors in Saginaw, Omaha, Wichita, and he'd offer them colors for what they were putting up. "Here, Mr. Kenniston, chuff chuff, let me show you samples, that's the line I'm really in, the showing business, I'll show you how you can beautify this handsome structure." "Mrs. Midgley, wouldn't you like to try a muted peach in your parlor?"

Back East, he had connections with the Standard Varnish Works. "We have a painter already," the contractors would say. "Fine, let me see him." No matter where we were, Barnett Jant was able to get more paint at lower prices than the local suppliers. "It'll come right out on the same train that brought me here, be in town by Monday," and so it was that on the Union Pacific, the Northern Pacific, or the Santa Fe, the paint would flow in rivers out across the country to wherever my father found customers.

He wasn't interested in building a paint empire, only in leading the life he and my mother charted. "You can hear the air, smell the light out here," my mother said in South Dakota. A life on the move, a life of planting ourselves in a teeming little metropolis followed by transplanting out across the loamy plowland to another temporary center, a life of exploration. The moose himself hailed from Chicago while the deer started out in New York. They met at a travel agent's exhibit in Madison Square Garden.

An early mind's-eye mezzotint when we visited the deer's deer, in New York, probably around 1912, has my maternal grandmother, Ursula Stedman, herself blinking and telling my mother she was the luckiest mother alive as they bathed and powdered me. Looking down late the other afternoon at the sun striking my creased pantleg and Church's wingtip I was reminded of my paternal grandfather, Fielding Jant, the moose's moose removed from England to Chicago and to northern California by the time we visited him in 1915 or 1916. The smell of his pipe tobacco mixed with the heavy scents from his capacious box elder, which shaded us as my father and his father spoke of the war. My father said, "Do you think we should go in?" My grandfather said, "You'll have to but it's rubbish. America thinks it's under this box elder. It'll see soon." "See what, Pater?" "We're all cannibals and always will be." While my father drowsed in the garden chair I sat on my grandfather's lap and asked him to tell me anything. The sun through the box elder sprinkled us with dots of itself. Can it be the same sun on my pantleg?

"Say hello to Albuquerque, Owen, and as soon as your father fetches our things from the baggage car we'll get him to take us out to a pueblo like the one we read about."

It didn't last long. Though it is with me now in the way time has of becoming still, collapsing in defeat, admitting it is only an artifice we impose to bring form to the disorderly tumble of things that happen. Time and I have made a separate peace.

Here is the unhappy ending to my happy childhood. We were at the white wooden marvel on the beach, palatially presiding over surf and sand, my mother and I, when she went to bed early one evening with the complaint of a sharp headache. I always watched her brush her long toffee-colored hair at night, but now she couldn't stand to touch the brush to her head. My father was somewhere in the northwest with his color samples, coming to join us the next day. Disappointed at not being able to play backgammon with Mama, I wandered alone those wide corridors with their paneling and portraits of dignitaries, descending the stairs while patting the balustrade as if I owned it, seeing myself a prince entering an awaiting ballroom.

It was the prince's birthday and his young attendants and courtiers would all have to bring him presents, pricey little tributes to his highness. Midway on the staircase, as I spotted the bejeweled guests in the spacious lobby, the fantasy shifted and I became a buccaneer. The Pirate Prince del Coronado prepared the speech that would begin, "Hand over all your valuables, don't resist, and none of the ladies will be harmed."

At the foot of the stairs, though shorter than everyone in the lobby, I preened, fancying the hotel guests as my subjects. "Master Jant," said a servile concierge to me, so resplendent in white tie and green swallowtail that I welcomed him into my masquerade. "Sirrah," I said. "A wire has arrived for your mother. I shall send it right up."

Blasted from reverie, I told the man my mother was already sleeping and that I'd give her the wire at the first light of day. Tucking the telegram into the front of my herringbone jacket while regretting it wasn't brocade or at least velvet, I wheeled and made for the beach. A star-filled moonless night greeted me as I patrolled the strand. Thirsty for every star, I was proud of protecting my mother and of the telegram burning a hole in my herringbone. Cassiopeia's Chair greeted me, and the friendly Dipper, Polaris, Castor and Pollux, and my new favorite, Jupiter. As far as I was concerned, the sky was eight years old, like me, newly mapped for me by my father, expected the next evening.

My father! The telegram must be from him. Yes, the return address, visible inside the envelope window, was Coeur d'Alene. Fresh fortunes in Idaho from silver and lumber were all of a sudden generating big houses. He'd found ready buyers there a few months earlier and had returned to corral new business.

Mrs. Barnett Jant
Hotel del Coronado
Coronado, California

CHERISHED SYRILLA UNAVOIDABLY DETAINED
COEUR D'ALENE STOP EVERYONE NEEDS PAINT
STOP SHOULD ARRIVE WEEKEND STOP LOVE
TO YOU AND MONKEY STOP BARNEY

They called me monkey? That had never happened in my presence. So I thought of them as animals and they saw me that way too? But Monkey? I couldn't wait to get to the San Diego Zoo the next day, where my mother had promised we'd go. The star of the zoo was a famous female bear named Caesar, given to the city by the Navy, and I was mad to have a look at her. My mother had started me keeping a diary, and I pulled it out of its hiding place inside a sweater. She'd said to me, engraved in my memory, "We read to learn, we write to understand." I hoped she didn't look at the diary. Before sleep I wrote how happy I was to be alone with Mama, how unpleasant the discovery that my parents referred to me as Monkey. What other secrets did they have? But I also wrote how much I enjoyed her laughter, especially if I could cause it. I copied out my father's telegram and added, "I'm glad we have more days alone. Please keep this a secret."

But when I woke up the next morning the first word I heard was mercy. My mother was scarcely able to move, with pains throughout her body, a different pain for every joint. While I still slept she had called the hotel manager. "You must go immediately to Mercy," he told her while I rubbed sleep from my eyes. The car we had hired to take us to the Zoo instead brought us to the hospital run by the Sisters of Mercy in San Diego. The worst of it, for both of us, was the mystery of her pain. She was given morphine at the hospital, which relieved both of us since she slept a little and I didn't have to watch her features contorted by her pain. By the time the morphine wore off, her pain had eased. Yet as she dressed to come back to the hotel with me, a sudden stab in her stomach sent my mother reeling back onto her bed as if she'd been knocked down.

As for me, I lost my voice. For the first time in my life I had trouble catching my breath. I wheezed, gasped, and briefly felt faint. A nurse had me lie down and gave me something to inhale. "It's the shock of having your Ma take sick," she said, "a touch of asthma perhaps." I was better quickly. "Poor dear," my mother said. "Poor you," I said.

The doctors kept her overnight and a small daybed was moved into her room for me. She tried to make an adventure out of her ordeal. "Sorry you won't meet Caesar," she said, "but now you'll see the inside of a hospital instead of a zoo, with the nuns walking around like penguins." "Indubiterably," I said, trying out a word I'd heard at the hotel. Each of us, I sensed, was doing a little act to hide our fear from the other.

The next day a doctor, who thrilled me by talking about his war service in France, wanted to telegraph my father, but my mother was adamant that she didn't want to concern him while he was doing business. I butted in to ask the doctor how someone so old would get to go to war, and before my mother could chide me for impoliteness, he asked me if I could tell him how else he could get a free trip to Paris. "Doctor," my mother said, "you have four days to get me better." He smiled and sighed at the same time. "We're going to Paris after the Armistice," I told him.

My mother's appetite, always small, now disappeared. Her pains returned, localized in her mouth and stomach. "I saw a lot of this in France with soldiers who had been weeks in muddy dugouts on the front lines," the doctor told my mother, "but I don't know where you could have picked up trench mouth." He had found ulcerous sores in her throat. He thought the trench mouth was combined with severe food poisoning and gave her doses of laudanum and arsenic. The first dulled her pain while the second almost killed her. A day later her temperature rose to 105 but was controlled by aspirin and an ice bath. "You've had a bad reaction to the arsenic," the doctor said, "but it'll do the trick, scares off the poison, roots out secondary infection before it can spread." Sure enough, the third day my mother felt better, and the fourth day, Friday, we went back to the hotel. She was weak and still had no appetite but the pains and fever were gone.

My father, arriving Saturday to find our hotel rooms converted into a sick bay, looked more stricken than my mother did. "My word," he kept saying, "my word, I should have been here, why didn't you get a message to me, I'll never forgive myself, how could I not have been here?" He seemed to be talking to himself, blaming himself for my mother's illness. He couldn't do enough for her, sending out for flowers, plumping up her pillows, grabbing a tin pail of mine and rushing out to the beach, returning in a few minutes with shells for my mother to look at. Worried about my mother, I wondered if I could ever love anyone so much as I did my father. He was perfect; he'd get her better in no time. Why hadn't I brought up shells for her to see?

Over the next week, my mother slowly regained her strength. When she had some of her appetite back, we packed our luggage to leave. We were moving on to Kansas City. The morning of our departure my mother was again felled, this time by a pain so severe she couldn't move. A new doctor saw her in the hospital, a muscular younger one who was a surgeon. After he operated, which it seemed to me took about three years, he came out all in white to speak to my father. I heard two new words, "pancreas" and "tumor." I wasn't allowed to see her until the next day, and she was so pale, so white, I was reminded of all the ghost stories I'd ever heard. I was taken back to the Coronado alone, so my father could stay with my mother until dark, but I couldn't find anyone to play with. I didn't think of my parents as a moose and a deer anymore.

We stayed at the Coronado another month while my mother recovered from the surgery. The muscular surgeon came several times to see her. Once I saw him in the corridor just before he entered our rooms, and he looked solemn, but as soon as he came into my parents' presence he put on a happy face as if he'd gone onstage. My father kept very busy, bustling around my mother and, when she didn't need him, sending telegrams. The day we left my mother developed a cough.

We went up to Santa Barbara to stay with friends of my father's— the yachting Converses, who saw themselves as pioneers in the attempt to turn Santa Barbara into Newport West—and the sun shone every day. My mother was much better. She read Robin Hood to me in the afternoons, sitting in a gazebo the Converses had at the end of their high-hedged, gravel-pathed formal garden. As we roamed cheerfully through the Sherwood merriment, robbing the rich to give to the poor, chased by the evil sheriff of Nottingham, my mother's voice faltered a few times, as if she had something in her mouth that wouldn't go down, and I asked her if she had a sore throat. It was uncharacteristic of me, self-centered as I was, but I recall being anxious about her. "Oh no," she said, "it just takes time to get all well." Her soft skin felt as good as ever.

"Syrilla's a fighter," I heard my father say to Morrill Converse one morning, though that would be the last way I'd have described my mother, who could hold an opinion firmly but was gently reticent in her presentation, "and by the time you see us in the spring this will all be history." My father had gone to school in Chicago with Loretta Hibbs, who had, as people said then, married far above her station when she met Morrill Converse while he was married to his first wife and she was working as a waitress on his father's 150-foot schooner. That kind of situation could easily propel a move from Newport to Santa Barbara in those days. "I don't know why your father cultivates such a wealthy acquaintance," my mother said our last afternoon in Santa Barbara, looking up from the budding romance between Robin and Maid Marian. "He's really not himself around such a person. It may be he wants you to grow up a Republican."

It was on the train east that I saw the small stain on her cheek. A random flaw, it didn't seem possible, could she please wash it off? It was like a dark coffee stain, a little yellow around its brown, the rest of her skin the color of milk, the skin I loved to feel with my fingers and my own cheek. I wheezed once on the train when I went to bed but hid it from my parents by pulling the covers over my head. The wheeze went away. Every night coming across the country I went to sleep thinking she'd wash in the morning and the stain, the ink on her cheek below her left eye, would be gone.

In New York we stopped, as my father put it, in rooms just below one of the egg-shaped turrets of the Ansonia Hotel at Seventy-third Street and Broadway, which cost under a hundred dollars a month. We went up and up in an elevator with brass fittings and a dark mirror in back that frightened me to look into because it made faces cloudy. My grandmother came each morning to stay with my mother, and I was put into the Horace Mann School in the Bronx. When I came home my mother would be in a chaise longue the Ansonia provided us. "Tell me, my owenly boy," she would say, "the news of the rialto." A lump was found on her chest. Grover Cleveland's cancer doctor—or one of them—was still kicking and he was put on the case. He cut out the lump. I heard the word "scirrhus," and then I heard the word "malignant." Another lump was found on her thigh, and they cut again. I turned nine, and my mother insisted on taking me to the Central Park Menagerie and buying me sweaters at B. Altman. She managed this with smiles, smiles all afternoon. My father was holding her up by the time we returned to the Ansonia. I felt I'd had a birthday that wasn't a birthday though my grandmother also made a kindly fuss.

"Why doesn't your mother ever bring you up to school?" a boy at Horace Mann asked me. "Where is she?" "She's at flower," I answered and that shut him up and mystified him too, as it had me at first. I'd heard my Grandmother Stedman tell a friend that her daughter had gone to flower, and I didn't know what she meant. Then my father told me she was at the Flower Surgical Hospital.

My teacher at Horace Mann, Virginia Daniels, introduced me to *Treasure Island*. She smelled like toast with marmalade and always had a question for me—"What do you suppose the Admiral Benbow Inn looks like, or Long John Silver, or his parrot?" I think this is when I began to be interested in moving pictures, though that was hardly what Mrs. Daniels had in mind in 1918. "Adventures of the body," she said, "will lead you to adventures of the soul. In a couple of years David Copperfield and Little Nell will get hold of you." But I wasn't at Horace Mann except for the one semester.

They gave her arsenic again, and again she almost died. She had more pain in her throat. Another stain appeared on her upper leg, which I saw when she got out of bed to go to the bathroom. I stayed home from school one day and read to her and she smiled. "I remember when I first met Long John Silver myself," she said, coughing. "I never trusted him from the start." She smiled her little smile again. It was becoming difficult for her to talk. She napped. "How's Mama?" my father asked when he came back to the Ansonia in the afternoon. "Well," I said, suddenly feeling grown-up, "she's sick."

When my father and I walked to the kiosk to take the subway to the Bronx he showed me newspapers and magazines for every interest—one for sports, one for gossip, another for foreign affairs, a fourth for metropolitan scandal, and many more. "You never get tired of this city," he said, "but sometimes it won't leave you alone." Then we'd be shooting through a tunnel on our way uptown. "Think of the faces on the train," my father said, "as X-rays that lead straight into hearts if you can read then properly." We sometimes rode the subway with a scowling classmate of mine, Aidan Pugh, who was accompanied by an Irish governess. He wore knickers and a tight little bow tie while I shuffled around in short pants and a long tie that flopped from side to side when I ran the bases in ballgames. Aidan Pugh always looked as though he was finding fault, and even in sunlight his eyes were overcast.

One day he said to me just as class was starting up after lunch, "Hey Jant, I hear your mom's going to die."

"No she isn't, Pugh, damn you." Mrs. Daniels, who should have given me a demerit for profanity, instead sent Aidan Pugh to the vice-principal's office, which I took as a dark augury. But that afternoon my mother was well enough to take me to Rogers Peet to buy some knickers of my own, which gave me hope. The stain on her face was permanent now. I never asked about it. We both liked the red and tan houndstooth checks on the knickers. "I know they're a little large now," she said, "but you'll grow into them."

In two weeks my mother was back in the Flower Hospital. After school the assistant baseball coach would drop me at my grandmother's apartment on West Seventy-eighth Street, where I sat on her hearth doing homework and waited until my father picked me up after hospital visiting hours were over. I could beat my grandmother at backgammon.

Three weeks later I said to Aidan Pugh, "Pugh, see what an ass you are. I visited my mother yesterday, and she's coming home next week."

Two weeks after that my father returned from the hospital to my grandmother's and told me he had the worst news in the world. Then he mixed up his tenses. "Mama is died," he said. That was when my grandmother said, "Think of your mother, Owen, as having gone to the other side of the earth, to China. She's Chinese now."

8

New York to Hollywood

This time my wheeze continued for two days until a doctor came
to my grandmother's apartment and had me breathe from a tube. My
father, gray in the face now, carried on. He said, "We must be stoic,
Owen." I thought he meant something about a stick, we must be like
sticks. I may not have gotten that too far wrong.

Owen's father had no funeral for his mother, so Owen cannot
describe the scent of lilies and lilacs in a crowded church, the musky
perfume of maiden aunts as they dabbed their eyes, the sonorousness
of the minister, the feeling of abandonment as he stood outside the
church afterward in the new knickers his mother had bought him,
while his father let go of his hand to greet fellow mourners and thank
them for coming, telling each of them he or she had a special place in
his wife's life. Because none of that happened. What his father did do
was to put an engraving on his mother's simple stone in the old grave-
yard in Litchfield, Connecticut, which can be seen there today: "The
earth's of her, not she of it bereaved."

Observing my life now from the outside, I wrote in my diary, the
diary she had started me keeping, that I felt Owen had been taken to a
railway station by his mother—we'd traveled so much that way—only
to watch her board the train and leave without him. "I'm not little
Owen any more," I wrote three days after she died, "I'm on my Owen

89

now, my Owen self. I'm not the me I was but some other he. And the rain came crying down upon us, again."

A self-pitying attempt at lyricism by a nine year old. But what did I mean by "again"? When had it ever before rained in my life, rained in the metaphorical way young Owen was using here? Were there problems between my parents? Possibly, but he—I?—may be referring to some other problem that afflicted but did not originate within the family, related only in that both difficulties happened to Owen himself. Is there such a thing as a reverse premonition? Could he be recalling subsequent misfortunes that had not yet occurred? The "us" is ambiguous. Surely he is not using "us" as the royal we.

Yet Owen now sees himself as both I and he. He has subjectified himself, that is myself, with a new identity, a boy whose mother has died, while also objectifying himself into a character he is free to write about. "Us," then, may be his two mirrored selves. The possibility also exists that "us" is Owen and his father, two males facing an uncertain future deprived of the female they love, or even, telescoping all time into the present tense, Owen and his mother and father, the original trinity still extant though shattered by the physical if not psychological removal of the mother.

The character he was free to write about, however, lasted only a few sentences. The next entry in the diary is fairly scary, at least to the diarist. A silence lasted two weeks, two weeks when I stayed away from school, after which I dumbly scratched out:

TSO RMLA VA VA VA SHAAAH URZ VEBM SIM SIM FAK RUP RI TOT SHIGAH. TOT TOT EK EKR EKROP VA.

'RIMMA METTNUP KLIW.'

'MYAWKI NUPPA.'

SILVE MEK VA VA WIKL URZ RMLA TOT.

RAHYOZHOY!

After such silence, such sounds. Ending in the middle of a diary page. On the following page was written:

OKRABRU SULEE.

And then: "You break rules. Rules break you."

With the remark about rules, the boy has found recognizable words after weeks of nothing since the phrase about the rain crying again. He is learning speech, not a speech, speech itself, having been deprived of it for a space.

Ashamed, I couldn't show my diary to my father, nor my grandmother who had now begun to mourn the defeat of the natural order of death between her and her daughter. But I was lonely to share. One day I decided to show my diary to Mrs. Daniels, my teacher at Horace Mann. I held my breath while she read the entry about being left at the train station, then the gibberish, then the recovery of normal language. She took hold of me with a hug that smelled like warm toast. "Sometimes nonsense is the best sense," she said. "Just observe. Watch. Watch and remember. You'll be all right, Owen."

In later decades I have endured the analyst's couch for tenures approaching those of Latin American dictators, but I've never been helped more than by Mrs. Daniels's hug and her few words. She didn't understand what I wrote. She only understood me.

I recalled watching my mother as she was inching away from us day by day. After her death my mother remained present to me in certain ways for some time. I could still hear her voice singing to me in her summer sounds even as these were growing dimmer.

After the one semester at Horace Mann, we were off west, to Minnesota first, then to Chicago where the Standard Varnish Works had its headquarters, and after that down to San Antonio, which was having a little building boom. Without forming friendships in my new schools, since we rarely stayed anywhere more than half a year, I got along well enough. My father, it was clear to me, had enough grief for both of us. I didn't want to show sorrow since his own was so evident in his change from garrulousness to silence. In a certain way a silent tyrant can be tougher to live with than a loud one because he seldom lets you know what he feels or wants. You know you can't produce what he wants. I was his last connection to her, I had come from her body; therefore, I should produce her as she had once produced me. But even then, ha, I was no producer.

Barnett Jant kept an upper lip so stiff I didn't see how he ever curled it around a morsel of food. Meals were taken without the exchange of a word. A tongue spends most of its life in the dark, and Barnett would let his out, rarely, to say not what he wanted but what he thought his son ought to want. This put me in a triple bind. I would think about what my father wanted, what my dead mother might have wanted, and finally, as a muted afterthought, what I myself might conceivably want. I blundered along through the fog of what I took to be others' judgments.

One evening before we left San Antonio, Barnett let it be known that it had popped into his head he should have been a doctor. "That way, I might have saved Syrilla. With your future before you, Owen, I wonder if you might consider becoming a physician yourself." I wanted to laugh at being so thoroughly misunderstood. My father should have asked me to become a spiritual medium. It was too late for a doctor, but a medium might at least bring my mother's voice back to us. We could get up a séance. As for becoming a doctor, I hated the sight of blood, ran from needles, was repulsed by the very idea of surgery, and couldn't stand anything stronger than aspirin that came from the medical profession. Years went by.

Our journeys took us to North Dakota, down to Nevada, back east to New Hampshire, then out to Coeur d'Alene, where my father had been when my mother first became ill. We were visited by a fair-skinned woman who came to our door in a veil, which one might have seen in New York or Chicago at that time but was mystifyingly out of place in Idaho. Over her shoulders she wore a dark shawl and when she removed her accessories I saw she was quite pretty with dark eyes that took in everything. She and my father talked while I made dinner—by now I was in high school—and I heard him laugh with his whole throat for the first time since New York. I was glad. The woman laughed too, and I was less glad. After dinner my father said he would see Mrs. Roark home. Over the next few weeks my father went out several evenings, returning after I was asleep. When Mrs. Roark came over a second time there were only puzzled looks, no laughter.

We left Coeur d'Alene for Casper, Wyoming, where we stayed at a ranch for two semesters before moving on to Seattle. One night we named as many schools as we could that I'd been to and stopped counting at twenty-two. I was inhibited and dutiful in my classes but at home dreamed of adventures with presidents. Jackson and TR my standbys.

I went east for college and thought I'd stay there. Three years at

Harvard, a transfer to Yale for the writing program with George Pierce Baker, who had left Harvard in a snit of some kind. Wishing me well, Baker cracked that since I now had a Harvard education and a Yale degree, my future was assured. I didn't dare ask my father for money for the year in Paris, so I kicked around New York. The Depression had hit by then and my father was less comfortable. "The paint I sell is as wet as ever," he joked, "but the demand for it has dried up." He moved to Chicago where he could ride out the Depression in a safe office job for Standard Varnish.

I couldn't get started on a play I hoped to write, but I pinched a few stray assignments for the *New York Post* and the *Herald Tribune*. I was eating peanut butter twice a day. My Jim Bicker period, with similar aims but without Poor Jim's rail-riding moxie. Two pieces for the *American Magazine* and *McCall's*, the first an assigned article on the Kentucky Derby, which I peopled with enough of the characters I met in Louisville during race week so that the social circus became far more compelling than the matter of which horse poked its nose across the wire first. *McCall's* published my short story about a New York party where everything went so disastrously, dramatically wrong that the host couple decided to divorce and went to bed in separate rooms.

These two pieces warranted a call from Jubilee. "One hundred and seventy-five a week for ten weeks," Colonel DeLight hummed. "If things work out, young fella, you could become another Rupert Hughes or Yancey Ballard." I'd never heard of either of them, though Yancey—Yeatsman himself—became my pal and mentor.

I arrived at the wrought-iron entrance to the studio in the dismal fall of 1932, thrilled to have a job. The double gates were intimidating with their look of impregnability, as was the molded starburst at the center of each along with the giant ornate lettering: J U B I L E E. Colonel DeLight was out sick so I showed myself around the lot. The stages loomed like large warehouses for precious cargo, and I didn't have the nerve to enter any of them. The backlot intrigued me with its fake trees and lawns, housefronts and storefronts, and streets of either concrete or imitation cobblestone. The New York street looked wrong, yet also right. The great city of stone where I'd been so awed as a boy, where my mother was born and died, was here pulverized to beaverboard and *papier-mâché*. There were New England, Chicago, and New Orleans streets as well. Rome and Jerusalem were façaded for, I supposed, a historical or Biblical epic.

Although it was a sunny day, staggeringly huge lights were mounted on the outdoor sets where shooting was under way both in a French village and the exterior of an Iowa farmhouse. I recognized no actors. Neither the action nor the lines I heard were as interesting as the sets themselves.

Back among the sound stages, I made my way toward the executive offices, two-story pink buildings in unremarkable Spanish stucco with red-tiled roofs. I'd heard of Amos Zangwill, of course, and knew he was the all-powerful studio head. Yet I was unprepared for the sight— tableau really—I suddenly encountered. An imperious figure emerged from the commissary, reminding me of a king or colonial officer as he strode through a throng of menials who fawned over him. He proceeded with a gray velvet cape thrown on his shoulders, looking down upon his attendants as they pressed around him. His hair swept back in a pompadour, he affected a showy ring that I half expected one of his servitors to kiss. Each was trying to get his attention with a query, a problem, a joke. Hollywood instantly disgusted me: the potentate of a studio with an entourage he clearly required to remind him every second how wise and omnipotent he was.

"You don't have to stare," a friendly voice said to me. "He hardly needs any more of us gaping at him." It was Colonel DeLight's secretary and typist for the writers, who introduced herself as Comfort O'Hollie. With a soft Irish accent, she apologized for her boss's absence and the fact no one had been available to give me a guided tour.

I told her I'd had a fine time on my own until I came upon the emperor.

"We make allowances," she said. "This one may be riding for a fall though."

I looked at her with alarm. How dare she even whisper that? How could a mere secretary speak that way about the mighty Zangwill? "Riding for a fall?" I said. "You sound like a revolutionary." I laughed a little to let her know I was kidding.

"That's me grandmother, not me," she said. "I'll tell you sometime about the infamous Grandmother O'Hollie. People are starting to resent this man, though. Funny thing, he used to be a regular party, always liked the writers. Then these suck-ups started to treat him the way they do, and he found out he likes it. He makes four times what anyone in his department gets."

"His department? Isn't the whole studio his depar—"

"Sure, always eats lunch with the others who work for him, but he makes them draw straws to see who has to pay for him. Has the power of life and death over them."

"Over everyone, I guess." One of his retinue had just stooped to pick up the velvet cape that had fallen from the potentate's shoulders.

"Well, I mean in his department."

"His department?" I asked again.

"Oh, I forgot you don't know anyone on the lot. That strutting game-cock is Hurd Dawn, head of scenery design and set construction."

"Of course," I said.

9

Perfict Horr of Jaabalee

FADE IN: PALMYRA MILLEVOIX, a strikingly coiffed and expensively fashioned honey-blonde of twenty-six who displays certainty and a penchant for mockery, walks purposefully away from the massive carved oaken portal of a medieval pile, a pair of frolicking great danes mirrored in her sunglasses, her heels tapping across a brick courtyard to a German touring car, a Daimler, where she climbs into the uncovered front seat next to the DRIVER, who is dressed in maroon chauffeur's livery.

The castle's oaken door opens swiftly to disgorge the BARON VON DAMM, too young for his monocle but sporting the correct Heidelberg dueling scar on his right cheekbone, as he hurries uncomfortably to the touring car. His monocle, of course, falls from his eye and swings from its black cord as he rushes. He is used to summoning, not pursuing. With whatever dignity he can muster as an unaccustomed supplicant, he replaces his monocle and gestures for Palmyra to at least get into the black-roofed backseat, the proper way to ride with your driver. "Dis chust issn't done," we cannot hear him say as he replaces his monocle, "und I ibsolutely cannot allow it," he doesn't add as we don't listen to him because we're hearing instead Bach's Suite No. 43 for harpsichord, which will fade down so my own voice can be heard.

She never meant even to meet him, much less what followed,

6

Pammy assured me later about the Baron von Damm. What always fascinated me was her bravura with men. In the Baron's case, she had met him on an Alpine hunting party where she'd been taken by a Rumanian munitions manufacturer known as the Bad Boy of the Balkans, who was said to have financed both sides in the two spirited middle European skirmishes that led to Sarajevo and the Archduke, another tale she spun.

Did I have a prurient interest in her exploits? Or rather, in her *telling* me her exploits? With her knee exposed, an impudent glint in her eye. In any case I was not bothered by her little *avventuras* as she called them, and as she strides decisively away from von Damm's castle—and from the Baron himself—she slightly resembles a child leaving a birthday party she has insufficiently enjoyed. Making herself comfortable beside the chauffeur, Palmyra inserts an ivory cigarette holder between her lips.

BARON VON DAMM
You must permit me, Palmyra, at least to accompany you to the station.

PALMYRA
(her cigarette is quickly lighted by the driver)
I wouldn't dream of making you late for polo, Schotzie. *Danke* for the steam engine.

BARON VON DAMM
But there iss no ...

PALMYRA
Mach schnell, Herr Grebben! Ta-ta, Baron.

As the Daimler promptly accelerates, do we simply see the monocle drop from the Baron's eye in consternation, or shall we have him scratch his slicked Plaster-of-Paris head, turn on his smartly clicked heel, and march back into his castle? And shall we, for the sake of contrast with drowsy Southern California, as it then was, see the Daimler speeding off the courtyard bricks, wheeling over the bridge that spans what had once been the Baron's forebears' moat, rounding the turn toward the quaint Bavarian village anciently fiefed by the von Damms, heading past orderly checkerboard farmland where the train sits at the station ready to speed our Palmyra toward the frontier? Perhaps we'll leave it with the monocle dropping and try for a smirk at the socially shackled German's expense. The Teutonic manner—always ripe for a chuckle or a shudder.

(To the producer: If the steam engine reference is too close to the train we know our heroine is about to take, what other outlandish thing can Pammy thank the Baron for that he never gave her? A stuffed bear—"I so admire taxidermy," she can tell him—or a stuffed giraffe, even harder to come by; a linen press, jeweled kennel, crenelated parrot's cage, submarine, silver croquet mallet. Perhaps she always good-byes her suitors with this kind of thank-you that leaves them puzzled and feeling inadequate: she's joking but they know they should have given her something they didn't quite come up with.)

Rumor jumped the Atlantic and sped across North America faster than Pammy could. By the time she arrived in Hollywood in 1930 with her three-year-old daughter Millicent, fresh from cabaret and stage triumphs in Berlin and Paris, the talk was that she had been involved with a ruthless Great War officer who had become a follower of the fascist madman. This was denied by all her producers and by Mossy himself after he coaxed her to Jubilee, but the talk persisted. Pammy said she never spoke of her personal life because she had an innocent to protect. When the madman actually came to power in 1933, it was thought for a time Pammy had better marry Trent Amberlyn just to stanch the rumor and provide a respectable father for Millie.

"The Nazi business will ruin your career," Mossy predicted, pushing a wedding. "Even just the allegation of it. The kikes here will kill you, and if the kikes don't get you Hearst will. People are calling you a better singer and comedienne than Marion Davies, and the old man hates that. Then there's the FBI recording of your dirty song."

"Fun," Pammy said, remembering the night she brought Ocean-house down.

"What will you do?" I asked her when I found an excuse to be in her bungalow by bringing her a tiara I'd lifted from the costume department, mistakenly thinking she might like to wear it to a premiere she was going to.

"Trent's willing," she said, "but I'll be damned if I'll let gossip rule Millie's and my life to the extent of making a false marriage, moving into a false honeymoon cottage with Trent Amberlyn, and then having a false separation a few months later so we can move back to the home we love." She needn't have worried. By the spring of 1934 the ruckus over Pammy and von Damm had receded to a whisper.

As to Millie's paternity, it would remain the same kind of mystery as Pammy's own background. Baron von Damm himself? The Bad Boy of the Balkans? Was Millie's father a Frenchman named Serge, or was Serge Millevoix, who had directed Sarah Bernhardt in a number of plays, Pammy's own father? This seemed plausible and was used by several studios' publicity departments, who variously cast an American heiress, a salesgirl from Kalamazoo, an English duchess, or Bernhardt herself as Pammy's mother. Pammy could be both upper and lower class, portray irony as well as sincerity, be sexy and brainy at the same time, a little like Margaret Sullavan, with eyes that spoke sonnets and with a kinder nature than Joan Crawford. Unlike what happened with Garbo, fame was not a car crash leaving her scarred and in retreat; fame seemed only Pammy's due.

Her look was the herald of unknown treasures. In movies Pammy yielded the first kiss as one would a pawn at chess. She darted a glance at a man that said come hither but watch your step, buddy. Luminosity in the translucent flesh. The radiant heat arising from her neck and shoulders, promising everything, granting little.

The camera saw the heat, the glow, and audiences saw what the camera saw.

The account of Pammy's origins I liked best, told by her friend Teresa Blackburn, concerns a Scottish furrier, Angus Jamieson, who takes his family to Genoa shortly after the turn of the century. He has been unable to perform coitus following the birth of his fourth child. "A Scotsman," Teresa scoffed, "who can't throw the high hard one to Patricia MacBannock, his bride of twelve years." It is hoped sunny Italy will improve everyone's dour disposition. It does. Angus and Patricia leave the children with a basic nose-touching-chin crone and light out by train and carriage for the Italian countryside.

The couple reach Padua where, as Angus later puts it, after a hiatus of months they enjoy one another carnally. But that's not enough for the Scotsman. A day later, touring a church called the Capella degli Scrovegni, he spies a schoolgirl with a complexion that would bring drool to the chin of Botticelli. He gives an excuse to Patricia over lunch—he must walk and think by himself—and circles back to the school attached to the Capella where he finds the girl, who is having a singing lesson. Angus waits patiently, further entranced by this voice of an angel, and then asks the girl in his halting Italian if he can meet her father. Whatever for? she wants to know. He says because, Signorina, you are so beautiful. Then surely you wish to meet me and not my father, saith the maiden who, within the hour, is maiden no more.

The furrier hauls the girl back to Edinburgh as nanny to his children. His wife is now pregnant again and can use the help. Despite the Capella, despite the cross she wears, it soon develops young Larissa is a Northern Italian Jewess, or at least partly so, because her family back in Padua goes crazy over the breach and reads the ceremony of the dead for their lost daughter, as her sister reports in a letter to Edinburgh. Not long after this Larissa herself proves to be with child. Fearful of scandal, Angus arranges for her to leave his family's service and go to the Azores with a sea captain of his acquaintance. Larissa meets the Millevoix family there and falls into basically the same pattern as in Scotland. But Madame Millevoix, who had her own *fin de siècle* adventures, accepts with relief the situation that Patricia MacBannock would have killed Angus Jamieson for. A daughter is born, and Larissa and Serge Millevoix abscond for a time to French Equatorial Africa, where another daughter is born. The following year, all the Millevoixes are reunited in the Loire Valley in France, where, until she is packed off to the convent in Ghent to be instructed by nuns, Palmyra grows up, never certain whether her parentage is originally Millevoix or Jamieson, for Mme. Millevoix goes on having children and Palmyra is one of a spirited brood. Larissa herself eventually leaves for the chorus of the Paris Opéra and takes no child with her.

I've told how I was invaded by Poor Jim Bicker on the Sunday morning after Mossy's party. I then loopily wrote Pammy the absurd fan letter that I tried to deliver, failed, and tore to pieces. Consoling myself with lunch, I was mulling Bicker's hard-times dirge and my miscalculated letter when my phone rang. I ignored it as I slurped my salutary chicken soup, but the ringing persisted. I grabbed the receiver to hear the bark of Dunster Clapp from Jubilee, the Zangwill henchman who had contributed to Joey Jouet's death. He could fire you, as he did Joey, or he could ladle out praise from his master. In this case neither: I was to pick up a script and deliver it to Pammy. Apparently Clapp hadn't been informed of the triumphant reception of my *Doll's House* treatment. He rattled off directions to the Millevoix weekend home as if I were still a peon.

Obligingly, I drove with the script fifty or so miles east to Red Woods, as Pammy called her country retreat above Upland in the foothills of Mount Baldy. Red Woods was not only her haven but was also far enough from Beverly Hills so that she was normally unbothered on weekends by the likes of me. On the radio Pammy was singing "I never have found where's the good in goodbye." I turned it off, a reminder of Mossy's party.

I was approaching Pammy's home essentially an attendant squire. Yes, I was a writer, took myself for one, but I was also twenty-four and had in three years exactly one and one half screen credits on two movies, forgotten as soon as they were released, *The Vamp of Louisville* and *Lost Archipelago*. I'd been the first writer on no movie, and all the scripts I'd worked on had been re-assigned to other writers after me. Dunster Clapp or Seaton Hackley or Colonel DeLight, anyone in a supervisory capacity at Jubilee, could tell me to do anything and I'd do it to keep the $275 a week—a hundred a week more than when I began—flowing. A *Doll's House* would be my breakthrough, if the deconstruction of a masterpiece into a feel-good ninety minutes could be said to constitute a breakthrough. Still, I raked my work up through bloody visions as much as Ibsen did, or Brecht for that matter, soon to arrive in Hollywood himself. Feeling always an outsider, as much as any of them I plied the exile's vain trade: expectant, desperate.

Pammy was with two friends baking on the flagstones by her pool.

I wanted them to notice me, I wanted them to ignore me. The three women were so obviously enjoying themselves I felt worse than an intruder, more like a burglar of their space.

"So that left only the sister in the Alfa Romeo," one of them was saying.

"Can't believe it, honey," said one of the others. "Ah'm given to mistakes mahsef, as y'all know bitter'n innybuddy in this town, but I nevah even dreamed about doin' that."

"She never told any of that to me," said Pammy, the third sunbather. "So I guess we know who she trusts."

"And who she dudn't trust fuhther'n she kin th'ow a nekkid rhino."

Three kinds of laughter from three sylphs—throaty, giggly, almost a cackle.

Identifiable from a distance only by their manes, the three were honey-blonde, auburn, and blonder-than-blonde, more platinum than Harlow. "Race, isn't it?" I said as I approached under the canopy of wisteria vines that led to the pool, which was partially shaded by a giant cork oak. "Excuse me for the interruption, Pammy, but Dunster Clapp urgently wanted you to see a script before you go in tomorrow. Pardon me, Teresa, I'll only be a minute." If I'd thought my use of the familiar Race would somehow self-welcome me into their company, my apologetic stance immediately afterward effectively confirmed me as Messenger, Errand Boy, Stooge.

Actresses in those days were seen as sleeping beauties awakened from anonymity by the shrewdness of a male producer or director who would see their promise and mold it, bring them in from the chill of poverty that grew them. On the road from obscurity to celebrity they'd have a number of benefactors, some of whom, yes, they'd sleep with, all of whom brought them along. Essentially, they were dependent colonies of an imperial power that gradually prepared them for a degree of autonomy.

The so-called discovery of auburn-haired Teresa Blackburn did not feature her sipping a Coke in a drugstore but knocking, fairly beating, on the door of any assistant casting director who would listen to her sing, watch her dance, or sit still as she read a scene from Maxwell Anderson or Shaw. It turned out she couldn't sing a lick, but she could tear off a line of dialogue and spit it back so it rent the air. Pammy prized Teresa for having clawed her way to a level not far below where Pammy had arrived almost by accident—the European exception that proved the American rule—and she admired Teresa's Scottish class rage at people who came by their luck easily including Pammy herself. Teresa and her ballplaying brother Stubby were both outcomes of liquid evenings between feckless parents who couldn't, in the phrase of the day, rub two nickels together, and who stayed with each other only long enough to breed. In a sense Pammy and Teresa educated each other, Pammy inducting Teresa into sophistication, Teresa showing Pammy what life was like in the promised land for those who had little promise.

The third actress around the pool—described in story conferences as the slutty flirt—was Rachel Honeycut, whom I knew from her having gone around with an actor pal of mine as he was making a name for himself in gangster pictures. In any gathering of women Race, as she was called, would be the first one to be noticed. Women as well as men would gape at her almost-white hair, her breathy Hello, her mouth in a perpetual kissing contour somewhere between a pout and a pucker.

Race was from declined gentility whose principle toil was to stay on the right side of the law in Greenville, Mississippi. In her late teens she'd fled west toward anything destiny would put in her path, which was generally hard-luck men with schemes they didn't believe themselves but could sell to a Deep Southern naïf. She bounced around town for a year until she actually was discovered in a drugstore, though it was at the prescription counter. A silents producer, pushed to the sidelines less by the advent of talkies than his involvement in a horse doping scandal, had been Race's first significant Hollywood boyfriend. She was trying to buy cheap sleeping pills and he was angling for more elegant barbiturates when they no sooner met than shared chemicals. He introduced her to a cameraman and that was all it took since no one could see Race without wanting to photograph her. She had a successful test before the week was out, and in 1933 signed with Jubilee to play a party girl in a New Orleans saloon.

While her spirit soared—she had two photographs above her bed in her little Hollywood apartment, Andrew Jackson and Marie Curie, the southern populist and the female scientist—her flesh had another agenda. Race was soon sniffing, swallowing, and injecting her boyfriend's pharmacopoeia, and the boyfriend was shortly after that hitting her for real and imagined offenses against what might generously be termed their relationship. Making a picture with Race at Jubilee, Pammy and Teresa rescued her, but a pattern was established.

They had warned Race not even to have dinner with the songwriter Cyrus Henscher, who was scoring her current picture. Henscher's penchant was to charm and then brutalize women. Race went along to dinner with him anyway after he waddled up to her one day and told her he couldn't get her out of his mind. He waddled not because he was obese—he was only paunchy—but because his feet splayed out like a duck's. Race justified the date by saying she could help the songsmith reform, exactly what Cy Henscher had no interest in doing. A squat middleweight, Henscher caromed from one studio to another writing songs and mistreating women.

Henscher sang Race a tune over dessert, ending with, "I promise you my banger/ Reposes in its hangar/ Until summoned by the loveliest of humans;/ I'm just a lonely lover/ As I hope you will discover/ Though I wish I were a song by Vincent Youmans."

Race yielded. Henscher was sweet to her, even sexually considerate, the first evening. Naturally, Race saw him again. This time he took her to a hotel in downtown Los Angeles. It would be more romantic, he told her. When they were upstairs in their room, Henscher produced from his suitcase a three-foot length of hose. Before Race could react the brute had bolted the door. In the taxi she took to Pammy's home afterward, Race had to balance on her knees since she could neither sit down nor lean against the seat. As Pammy applied cold cream to her body, Race told her Henscher had warbled a macabre ditty about welts and bruises as he lashed her, then chortled.

"Son of a bitch won't get away with this," Pammy vowed. But she knew the police were thoroughly uninterested in domestic affairs where there were no witnesses, and Henscher was soon off to Paramount, out of whatever reach Pammy had at Jubilee. Of course, I didn't know any of this then.

The women by the pool were not exactly pining for a male presence that Sunday. Men don't get it, especially well behaved young men as I was, men whose presence normally elicits a smile, that women do not necessarily require our company. It had been only a few weeks since the Henscher assault, of which I remained cheerfully ignorant. As I stood trying not to gape at Pammy's and Teresa's skimpy two-piece bathing suits that had reached Hollywood from the south of France, wondering why Race, not known for her modesty, was wearing a suit that fully covered her, I assumed I'd drop the script I'd arrived with and withdraw quickly. The fact that the actresses were polite relaxed me more than it should have. Pammy was cordial enough on the hot afternoon to ask me if I'd care to swim, and like the fool I was I said, "Sure, that'd be swell."

"Race and I have to get back to town," Teresa said before I could alter my course, and the two melted away.

Reading the script Dunster Clapp had sent while I swam guiltily, Pammy sat on a lounge chair under an umbrella. She had put on reading glasses but didn't look all that interested, skipping pages, doubling back, chuckling a couple of times though altogether her focus was desultory. "They want to make fun of the Depression and rich people at the same time," she said as I dried off. "Mr. Capra and Mr. Riskin know how to do that, but Benges and Spighorr shouldn't be left in the same room with typewriters."

"I'll take it right back with me," I offered, "and give it to Dunster in the morning.

"That would be nice, Owen. I'll have to skim the rest I guess."

I kept silent but looked at her, the legendary thirty-ish woman (thirty-two to be exact) of experience with the kid who would have tripped over his shoelaces any minute except he was barefoot. I did not look at Palmyra Millevoix with lust, only awe.

"You're basically an interrogator aren't you, Owen," she said without looking up. "I trust you though."

I stammered. "I-I haven't asked you anything, have I?"

"No, but it's all there. You're a pack rat with other people's lives. I remember you in my bungalow to do publicity. Your questions were not professional as much as they were constitutional. Curiosity is your natural posture, isn't it?"

"I always want to know more than I do, if that's what you mean."

Without another word, Pammy moved off her chaise and was in the swimming pool before I could breathe again. She disappeared beneath the surface, invisible because of the sunlight flaring off the pool into my eyes. I supposed I wouldn't see her again. She'd never been more than a fantasy anyway, a figment of the collective imagination. When she reappeared at the deep end, she threw her head back and smiled. I didn't see her take a breath before she plunged again, but what was mere air to her? She swam back and forth a few more times, now submerged, now planing the surface. When she climbed out and wrapped herself in a towel, I felt I should have held it for her, but that would have been both too subservient and too familiar.

"We have to help Race," Pammy said when she sat down again. "She's out of luck. If you have a chance to do something for her, do it. If it's a bit part, make it bigger. If you see her in the commissary trapped by some pig, butt in and be your awkward self until she can escape. We need to guard her a little." She didn't say why; I didn't dare ask.

"Sure," I said. Even if she was only using me, her saying We made my pulse skip.

"Sit down. Hollywood's even crazier than the rest of the world thinks, isn't it."

It wasn't a question so I didn't answer.

"Not that the rest of the world is sane. Italy and Germany are two countries I love, and they're out of their minds." Pammy had the morning paper in front of her, but she wasn't so much reading it as bouncing off it. "Oh, this is fine for Europeans, who have warfare and disputed borders in their veins, but hamburger Americans … what will happen to us—I'm almost one of us now—when we get vacuumed into all this?"

She seemed to have accepted my presence in a way, and in another way was talking to herself. Something had shifted when she looked at the newspaper.

I glanced at her and she was again famous to me. When she said she trusted me she meant that she knew I'd do her bidding. I was a capon, and I hoped it was only a disguise. Hardly auditioning for Prince

Charming, I was an attendant the court had sent to badger her on her one day off. She was complaining about international affairs to me, but I could have been her hairdresser or Millie's nursemaid, Costanza. She had been so personal, so at home and at ease with Teresa and Race; now she was famous again, as she had been at Mossy's party.

"Play tag, Uncle Owen?" Finished with her nap, Millie had come down to the pool. She'd seen me a few times at the studio, where she resented my intrusions on her time with her mother, but on her own ground I was accorded the status of a familiar. Play tag was the last thing I wanted to do, but I began chasing the seven-year-old miniature of her mother around the pool. That was part of her mother's fame, too: you had to do what her kid wanted because she was Palmyra Millevoix. I was rescued from this chore by the announcement from Costanza that Bruce Sanders had dropped in.

"Help me," Pammy said. "Stay right here, close." Sanders had been a beau of Pammy's briefly during her Pamela Miles period. I didn't like the grasping fellow, a middling actor who worked sporadically in pictures about armies or athletes. With this new social assignment I understood I was still a capon, only now I was to be part of the shield Pammy held up to ward off the unwelcome swain. Costanza scooped up Millie.

Pammy pulled her lounge chair so close to me it appeared we were in an intense private conversation that would render any third party an intruder. If only.

Sanders was a cocky guy, his hair peroxided to help him play half-backs and doughboys when he was a decade and a half too old for those parts. He made a jaunty approach under the wisteria canopy, yawing his head from side to side as he sailed toward us. When he padded across the flagstones, accompanied by a haughty salivating pointer, Pammy was leaning toward me with her throaty chuckle sharing a presumed intimacy though in fact what she had just said, looking at a headline, was that Mussolini was a pretty fair showman but he was in danger of forgetting he was only in a show.

Pammy did not rise to greet the visitor. His self-righteous pointer made things worse for Bruce Sanders by starting to drink out of the pool. "Unless your dog's stomach is made out of glass," Pammy said, "the chlorine in there will eat right through it."

"Heel, Brutus!" Sanders yelled, and after he repeated his order several times and swatted the dog, Brutus reluctantly gave up the pool. "He's not half the canine his father was," Sanders said, and then, attempting a little historical familiarity, the actor added, "You remember Brutus's father, Pam?"

"I recall you had a big spiteful dog." Pammy wrinkled her nose as she said this.

Brushing off the remark, Sanders squinted at me. "Jant, isn't it? Still doing heavy lifting for Zangwill?"

"Something like that."

"Actually," Pammy said, "he's too modest to say so, but Owen will be writing the next Garbo picture as soon as Mossy can spring her from Metro."

"Oh, uh, LB will never let go of her." Sanders had not stopped cocking his head from side to side as if this gave him both stature and credibility. "I'm starting at Warners myself in a couple of weeks. Dieterle wants me at eight hundred per."

Which, even in the Thirties, was birdseed for a Hollywood actor, and Pammy tore right into it. "Wow," she said, "no telling what you can do with that, Bruce."

"After the first picture my agent tells me it can be tripled."

Still birdseed to a star like Pammy. She raised her eyebrows so they formed little arcs above her reading glasses, which she had kept on. She affected a kind of thoughtful calculation. "That would be wonderful, Bruce. Of course, with twenty-five hundred a week your hands are sort of tied, aren't they?"

"What do you mean?" Sanders stumbled gullibly onward.

"Well, you can do some things, but you can't do others. I mean, you could have a little plane, or you could have a big boat, but not both, right?"

Sanders was miserable. He didn't yet have the eight hundred a week, maybe he was blowing smoke anyway about Bill Dieterle, and here was his former girlfriend, now a movie star, telling him that even if he makes three times what he does not yet make, he's still below the level of her eyesight. Not quite defeated, he tried advancing again into the historical familiar. "Speaking of boats, we had one helluva sweet time going over to Catalina on that Coast Guard launch, didn't we? How about doing that again, Pam?"

Pammy winced at the memory and thrust back her own historical unfamiliar. "Bruce, you went around for a short while with a bland studio creation named Pamela Miles, someone invented to feed candy to audiences with a sweet tooth for the unreal. You did not go out with, or even know, Palmyra Millevoix. Let's leave it at that."

"I, uh, guess I shouldn't have dropped in. We were on our way to Alta Loma, Brutus and I, female show dog there ready to be bred, and we thought, or I mean I—"

"Take care of yourself, Bruce."

The belittled actor and his slobbering dog slunk away to do their reproducing in a more hospitable meadow.

Pammy took off her reading glasses. "I know I was awful to him, I'll get Mossy or Harry Cohn or someone to give him a couple of weeks' work."

"Pretty nervy of him, coming by without—"

"You know, it was the publicists at Warners who not only hung the name Miles around my neck but also concocted the glorious tale of my father dying heroically in the World War, my mother moving to America in search of democracy."

"I thought your family was … I don't know … your career in Paris—"

"Oh that was later, darling, and anyway don't believe everything you hear, even if it's from me. Well, I got my name back and I kept my pokey nose." She laughed, recalling her nose had been called too conspicuous and was a candidate for cute-button surgery until she'd declared her name and her nose were who she was and that would be that. "Miss Millevoix," she went on in quotational mode, "who acted for a time under the studio soubriquet of Pamela Miles, was briefly squired by the consummate boor and untalented gentleman caller Bruce Sanders before she came to her senses."

"But if you knew that about Sanders, why—"

"A slow week, darling, and I'd never been to San Simeon."

She laughed again while I, unable to shed solemnity, pondered her double identity, her use of "darling," her many voices. "Well anyway," I said, "here you are at your beloved Red Woods."

"I should never have called it that, should I? Another target for the reactionaries." Pammy put down the script, stood up and began to walk me around the acreage of Red Woods, where she had managed a cornucopia of trees, flowers, fruit and vegetables. From the wisteria arbor that led to the pool, we crossed beneath huge cork oaks that appeared as parasols to the shrubs beneath them, and then we were in a lane of tall cypresses, followed by a small field with a dozen or so rows of corn. A file of persimmon bushes abutted the cornfield, and on the other side of the persimmons were rows of all kinds of berries. A patch of strawberries nestled by staked vines of loganberries, raspberries, blackberries, elderberries, and on the far side of the berries tomato vines were hanging from trellises. A small orange grove occupied perhaps half an acre. The ranch house itself, rambling and unpretentious, was set off by a semicircle of lawn and protected from the road by a line of alternating date palms and camphor trees. On the seven acres surrounding the house, Red Woods featured a creek running through an unexpected stand of bamboo, low cedar hedges arranged in a maze of gravel paths around a gazebo, two coops for chickens and pheasants, and the inevitable wild growth of California redwoods. It was an endlessly provocative reach for a child to be a child. "Millie's in her Eden here," Pammy said as we reached the bamboo.

"I've stayed hiddenly religious all my life," she said. "I was brought up with the Gospel, rejected it, yet who can avoid feeling evangelical as a Red? And I still believe Jesus feels your sin, you know."

As she paused, my heart sank into my shoes. I'm dealing with a nut here, just like all actors, what a letdown, a zealot after all. She smiled and I saw she read me, was laughing at me. I made the further mistake of thinking she didn't believe, not really, what she had just said. We were making our way along the creek that led to the larger redwoods. It was hardly a forest—we could see the road in one direction, the pool-house in another—yet it served, as did all her acreage, as sanctuary.

"No," she went on, "I'm neither in a state of faith nor joking about it. I'm noting it, that's all. Jesus: he remains. All of us knew from the time we were in trees and swamps that when we've done wrong we can be redeemed only by a Jesus who dies for us. You get out of Catholicism, but it refuses to get out of you."

"How did you get out of it?"

She eyed me. Her tone became confidential, not confessional. "The convent in Ghent. Eleven or twelve I guess I was. It's the Church that lets you out of the Church. When the nuns were holding me down, rather when one of them held me so the other could do what she did, and then they traded places, I still knew Jesus was with me even if the Church wasn't. When I went to the priest, Father Montaillou, and he told me he'd hear no more of this, even then I knew Jesus was in me. I somehow conceived the notion that Sister Jeanmaire and Sister Maria Christina and Father Montaillou were Antichrists. The Church was full of Antichrists. About Sister Jacqueline I felt different because she was younger and didn't force me as much and had a sugary mouth, but they all of them made me feel like a piece of clothing, a chemise, that is being worn too much and needs laundering. I began to see myself at the age of twelve as Saint Joan, a martyr, only unlike her I had to keep quiet so no one would burn me. I was a martyr to sex. At the time I didn't even know that it was sex, it was being touched and touched very unpleasantly by these two malodorous monster nuns. But I still had Jesus. I prayed to him and to God I could be left alone, and when I wasn't left alone I thought I am not praying correctly so I prayed many different ways. Nothing worked. I began to wonder if I could still believe."

"How could you stay a believer after that convent?" I asked.

"The war. I helped out, you know, in a blood bank. We were told to pray continually for God's help. Sometimes it seemed to work. Boys recovered who looked as though everything had been shot away. Perhaps Jesus was in the blood we poured into the wounded. One sees unbelievable things. I remember thinking how could both sides pray to the same God and then kill each other? But still, I came out of it only confused.

"I did not lose Jesus until I went to the Sorbonne and was talked out of him by the philosophy professor who spoke about Ypres and Verdun where perhaps a million died. He said if God exists and lets such things happen I don't want to know him. If God is good he wouldn't let this slaughter occur, and if God is bad I want nothing to do with him anyway. He told us to watch the unequal contest of labor and capital as France settled down again after the war. It was all around me—the selfishness, class boundaries, inequality in the land of *égalité*, the way the rich took one look at the poor and sneered. The poor had really saved the rich in the war—and for what? To return to the same arrangement, the same fixed order. Sister Jeanmaire and Sister Maria Christina were my Ypres and Verdun. It was a narrow view but I bought it, you might say I succumbed to it. This left a hole in me where God had been. I had hated the nuns, but now I pitied them and envied them too, for their certainty. In Paris I read the *Manifesto* and as much of *Das Kapital* as I could get through. Profit and exploitation. Workers in chains. Surplus value. Infinite wealth accumulation. Time started over again, the way time started over with Christ. The year zero. Nothing is left, nothing but music and martyrdom and the year zero. When I met Marx I thought, ah, the hole is filled."

I said nothing.

Pammy was in Hollywood when the wave of disillusionment with capitalism became intense after the market crash in 1929. She had seen class disparity in Europe, but in the picture business the outsized salaries of the few at the top, overlording the many low-wage toilers, were baffling. When she found herself making huge money in bad movies, she thought surely a socialist country would have better art, a more equal distribution of capital. Hollywood people have too much time and money on their hands, a Red organizer telegraphed the functionary who had sent him west. We'll give them something to do with both, the New York commissar wired back.

We had returned to the pool, to some Chassagne-Montrachet that had been placed there in an ice bucket while we walked, and to the script Dunster Clapp had sent me out to Red Woods with. She frowned at the script. Distractedly, she poured the golden wine into two goblets. As soon as I felt I was with the real Palmyra, she slipped away. I was convinced that even if I had the courage to touch her, my hands would feel nothing and I'd hear her tittering at me impishly from the other side of the pool, a mermaid's ghost.

Again her mood shifted. She focused sternly, her lower lip over her upper, her brows knitted. "What do you think of Mossy?" she asked, still looking at the script. "I mean really think of him as a person."

I didn't know him as a person. I only knew him as lord and master. I managed to stammer that he had so much power I hoped he used it wisely.

"The hardest part for me," she said looking at her wine, "is to figure out his intentions so I can resist them." She returned to the script and flipped the pages with curiosity but with none of the scrutiny of an actor considering a possible role.

What was she seeing in the script? In the stories we wrote we needed to make life bearable both for ourselves and our audiences. We worked from some controlled recess of what we were pleased to call imagination to make the palatable fate—it was Hollywood after all—unconfused, triumphant, mostly happy.

Pammy slammed down the script on the flagstones. Her face was like gristle. I had never seen her ugly before. Could you take a picture, I briefly wondered, of the mood in her face? Her eyes were cold, her mouth hard. "You don't much care for it?" I said.

"It's only a little stupider than the last one they sent. What makes me furious is he thinks he can do whatever he wants with any of us. Power is his life. Go here to this restaurant with this escort, don't go to that opening, make this picture, don't be seen with that actor. Well, he knows what he can do with his power." Pammy gulped the last of her Montrachet, and I thought for an instant she was going to spit it out.

I was helpless to help her. Still it seemed cruel not to try. But before I'd uttered a whole sentence—"Why don't you let me talk to someone in the story dep ..." she came down on me like rain. "You men! One of you talks to another and figures out how you can control some woman. You're all alike!"

I apologized, scurrying out of her path. This was the tyranny of weakness; the person with the complaint, the grief, the illness, has to be attended. Don't argue. But there was also the tyranny of strength, of the person who can do to you whatever he likes because he holds the cards. Just now Pammy had the former, Mossy the latter. In service to both, I was vassal to each of their tyrannies. Her look was tough as a boot.

Abruptly, the pendulum swung back again. "Let's sing," she said.

"I may be with song." She pulled out a folded page and made some scribbles. I've heard pretentious writers, usually men, compare their inspirations to pregnancy; with Pammy, who had actually borne a child, this seemed a comparison she'd earned. I saw some words, a musical measure, then a burst of more words. I looked away, not daring to move. When she stopped scribbling, she asked kindly, "Would you like to hear?"

I said sure, anything she wanted to sing. She apparently was able to get herself out of gloom or anger—and she'd just been possessed by both—by impregnating herself with music. If she'd signaled a gestation period, I was in the delivery room.

No fool like a young fool; I was back to wishing I could be her cocker spaniel.

"This one's not quite ready. I fooled with it this morning. It would be better if I played the piano but I don't want to go up to the house, so we'll just try it here." In those days most songs had verses before their choruses; I regret their passing.

"Ever since you went away," she began in a key lower than I'd heard her before,

> I've waited to hold you again,
> Now the train whispers along the nighttime track
> Bringing my faraway honey back
> Back to me where you belong,
> Where I can sing my nighttime song.
> I'll sing to you and hold you tight
> And won't let go the whole dark night.

She paused, "Okay, okay, I need some dibbling in the whisper line, but here's the up-tempo chorus:

> Oh I've been brokenhearted
> Since the last time we parted,
> I've been brokenhearted 'cause of how much we started—
> How I wish you'd see to

The matter of loving me, too,
You'll never know how much I care
No matter when or where.
Oh I'll be brokenhearted till the next time I kiss you,
I'll be brokenhearted 'cause of how much I miss you—
I'll be brokenhearted till the next time we kiss,
I'll be brokenhearted—it started when we parted—
I'll be brokenhearted ... like this.

She held the last word to become thiii-iiisss. "What do you think? Is it stillborn?"

"It'll be all over the radio," I said.

Millie ran down to join us at the pool. "Are you still reading the screamplay?" she asked. She had been calling scripts that since she was three.

"Shhh," Pammy said, "don't you know Owen's a screamwriter?"

"Hopes he is," I said.

Costanza appeared through the wisteria with a package. "Oooh, look at the present for me," Millie said.

The package, large enough for a football, was elaborately wrapped in purple tissue paper with gold stars on it, tied in a pink ribbon. "For you, Mrs. Pammy," Costanza said. She called Pammy Mrs. as if to confer more respectability on her unmarried motherhood. "I know this address is a big secret, but it was outside the front door."

Pammy said she wished fans could understand how desperately performers needed their small portion of privacy. It wasn't fair, not on a Sunday, way out in the country like this. Millie said, "Come on, maybe it's a toy for your adorable daughter."

Idly, Pammy unwrapped the package. When she had the outer paper off, the box indeed appeared to hold a piece of sporting goods, some kind of ball. "Yay," Millie said, doing a little dance, "It'll be something for me." I was sitting very near Pammy, and I thought an odd essence came from the box. Pammy opened it. More tissue paper. She plunged ahead until she beheld the gift, in the center at the bottom of the box, and gasped. It was a lengthy, perhaps nine- or ten-inch, gray penis, the gray of a storm cloud, fishbelly gray. Underneath it, on a greeting card that had a color picture of a clown in a wide-mouthed laugh, was scrawled in what looked and smelled like feces, "For the Perfict Horr of Jaabalee—use as nieded."

I jumped up and clapped the box shut, I hoped before Millie had seen it.

"Can I play with it?" Millie asked. Then she hadn't seen. Had she?

Pammy was the color of the gift. "What the hell else do they want?" she said.

10

The Rite Spot

Driving home across the dusty wastes of the parasitic outskirts and finally the nowhere downtown, I thought I might propose a little charter revision to the city council. Add one letter to the first word of your city and rename it Lost Angeles. A city with the dwindles. By this time my shock over Pammy's grisly present had waned into the usual late Sunday drear. I wished I could repair the damage, protect Millie.

In an alley off skidrow I heaved the package into a garbage can. We had first thought I should take it to the police; then we thought about my turning it over to studio security. We finally decided anything I did would be sure to leak either to *Variety*, the *Examiner*, or the *Times*, so I simply threw it away. Destroying fingerprint possibilities, of course, but the lowlife probably wore gloves.

Reaching Beverly Hills, I was momentarily startled by the gaudy combination of Tudor, French provincial, Spanish colonial, tropical, antebellum, glass and wood modern, and English manor architecture. For the stars and other movie creators, these were the most luxurious slave quarters in the world, the people in them manacled not only to their studios but to their fans. Anyone could have a run of flops, anyone could be fired. Pammy might get two thousand roses and ten thousand fan letters a week, but she also attracted the rage and craziness crammed into the package I'd just thrown away.

By the time I'd gone out Sunset and followed Amalfi Drive down its curves to Sumac Lane, I was hungry. I parked in front of my little house but didn't go inside. I walked to the mouth of Santa Monica Canyon where I knew I could get something quick and filling at Sam's Rite Spot, a dark dive across the road from the beach, red and white checked oilcloths covering the dozen tables. A couple with two toddlers were the only other diners I saw, and I saw them only because the children were noisy.

I was halfway through a chili size and sucking on my root beer when I noticed, or didn't quite notice, a shadow gesture in my direction from two tables away. She asked me the time, the clock in the place being broken at a quarter to twelve; it was always deep in the eleventh hour at Sam's Rite Spot. A plea was just visible in her eyes, as if some dire consequence such as a scheduled execution might be disclosed by what time it turned out to be. When I said six she was relieved. "Thank goodness it's only that," she said, "because I have to drive all the way to Arcadia." She had an hour to travel across the same broad expanse of municipal basin I had just driven.

"I was afraid it was later," she said. "Do you have as far to go as I do?"

"About a block and a half," I said. The woman was eating fried oysters and I thought about ordering some for myself. She was skinny, with an athlete's body. Little bumplets showed on her chest beneath a light blue closefitting jersey. Her hair was sandy, a little stringy from the ocean. When she smiled I saw a small gap between her two front teeth, a space that would never be permitted by a studio but was not unpleasing to look at. Same with her jaw: too elongated for a cinematographer yet it was faun-like.

"Lucky you," she said. "My mother's watching my little girl while I came down for a swim." She was almost boyish. I didn't see how she could have a baby. Besides the light blue jersey, she wore a dark blue cotton skirt with little white musical staves on it.

"So early in the season," I said. "The ocean must be freezing." It was barely April, warm enough for an inland pool such as Pammy's but not for the chilly Pacific.

"Not to me," she said. "I'm warm-blooded, and the water makes me feel so alive."

Her flesh, what little there was of it, did actually look warm. Her arms glowed with the sun they'd had. She was not what producers called pretty, but she was appealing, and her manner, once she had relaxed about the time, was engaging.

"Excuse me for asking," she said, "but do you really live only a block away?"

"Yeah, a little more." As I answered I saw her more attractive aspects. Her face was not boyish as I'd thought, merely thin like the rest of her. Her body at first looked to be that of a teenager, but her hips were a woman's. Her nose had an almost imperceptible (though not to a camera) hook in it yet in an agreeable way so that she might have been a schoolteacher the kids made fun of but also really liked. Her eyes, nearly round, were swampy green and gave onto crinkly laugh lines at the corners. Her legs were long and tightly muscled. Probably an excellent swimmer. The bumplets under her jersey actually resembled, I saw as she savored her last oyster, small pieces of fruit, not kumquats after all but possibly damson plums with baby mulberries perched on top of them. Though she'd looked thin as an X-ray, the transparency was filled out with more flesh than I'd first perceived in the Rite Spot's shadows. Until it wasn't transparent anymore. She was squinting at me now, appraising me.

"I'm very salty from the ocean and I have this long drive. Would it be awfully forward of me to ask if I could wash up at your place?"

A man named Willard at Jubilee, a junior writer like me but a lot bolder, had sent Valentine cards to good-looking women around the studio—stenographers, women in makeup, in the sound department, even a couple of actresses. He may have sent a dozen. On each card he wrote that he had been a secret admirer for months and hoped they could soon get to know one another. Willard was able to date five of these women, an unjustifiably high batting average in my opinion. What would he do here?

"That would be okay," I said. Her car was even rattier than mine, a Model A from the twenties. An empty baby bottle was in the passenger seat when I climbed in for the short drive to Sumac Lane.

"Looks like where Hansel and Gretel lived," she said.

Inside, I asked her if she wanted anything to drink and hoped I had a Coca-Cola or some beer though I was doubtful.

"Water, that would be nice."

She sat down, and I guessed she wasn't in too much of a hurry to get back to Arcadia. Reading my thoughts, she said, "My little girl will be asleep before I get back anyway. She's only one and a half. My name is Jasmine."

To come up with that name, someone must have been reaching for something in her family. I didn't know where to go after I said it was good she had parents who were so understanding and watched her baby on a Sunday. But I was wondering where her husband was. Again anticipating me, she said, "My baby's father and I are separated."

"Oh, I'm sorry."

"I'm not and he's not either. What do you do?"

"I write pictures."

She laughed. "That's impossible. Are you kidding? You can't write a picture any more than I can paint a symphony."

"I write scripts for the movies."

"I don't go to them, but that's nice."

"Why don't you go?"

"I used to. It was all either bang bang, ha ha, or kiss kiss." She sipped her water.

Hearing my entire profession reduced to this predictable set of triplets, I recalled my father's warning when I told him I was going out to Hollywood. "Corn flakes manufactured by short order cooks pretending they're chefs," he said. "Nothing but bluffers. Underneath your bashfulness, you may be one too." The problem was I respected my father and was afraid he was right. All of us just bluffers.

I answered my guest lamely, downcast at the memory of my father's words. "Maybe that's true," I said, "but themes do have all kinds of variations. Uh, like in music or literature. I suppose you don't work yourself."

"Heaven help the working girl," she said, "because no one else will. I'm a secretary for a lawyer in Pasadena. A regular career girl." She sat up and jutted her jaw assertively. She was so thin I thought her ribs must feel like a washboard.

"I guess that's interesting work," I said.

"It is. He represents all kinds, bankrobbers to illegal Mexicans to old ladies swindled out of their savings. He keeps his hands to himself."

Where was this heading? If she was telling me the lawyer didn't make advances, surely that was a not-very-veiled hint that I shouldn't either. Not that I had any idea in that direction. Still, why did she keep talking instead of just washing up and leaving? The little gap between her two front teeth was interesting, promising.

"Well, that's good," I said. "At the studios some of the supervisors try—"

"I've heard about casting couches," she said. "My mother can't wait for every new *Photoplay*, and she reads Louella Parsons like the Bible. You're a strange one for working in pictures, though, aren't you?"

She seemed to be sizing me up. I said, "I don't know what you mean."

She said, "You're not so cocky as I think of picture people, and you're not trying to sell me anything. Are you sure you're in the movie business?" She was smiling.

"What would I be trying to sell you anyway?" I felt I was being tested.

Then she floored me. Her voice went up a couple of notes and sounded almost like a jittery bird. "Do you want to make me?" she asked sweetly.

Make me was what she'd said. I misunderstood utterly. This was the come-on phrase of the day, well known to everyone, even to me. Usually uttered by a man, as in Christ, wouldn't I like to make that dame. Yet somehow I mistook it and immediately thought, make her what? A ham sandwich? A drink? Despite the currency of the words—*make me*—I was as unaccustomed to the question as to the act it implied. Let's not count a couple of fumblings in college. All this I revolved inwardly, as Homer liked to put it, while pondering an answer.

"I'm sorry," she said, "I shouldn't even mention—"

"No, no," I interrupted, finally awake to the prospect here. "Actually, I'd like that so much." I went over to her chair and took her head in my hands because I couldn't think of what else to do.

Her kisses were good and a little salty, and I reflected she'd been swimming all afternoon though I further reflected that shouldn't turn her mouth into the ocean. With her tongue she began to explore my teeth and lips, and she no sooner finished the inside of my mouth than she began on my chin and then ears. Ears! At that still-for-me-tender age I had no idea ears were used for anything but listening. When she stood up, my arms around her touched my own shoulders, she was that thin. Her body didn't feel like a teenager's after all; she felt, as she tasted, like a hungry woman. From the sea.

Undressing, I began to shake. She must have seen what she was dealing with. "Relax, Owen," she said. Before my nerves had a chance to take over completely, something else was happening. Aaaah.

What a surprise! It is maintained by some evolutionists that opposable thumbs are what set us apart from dolphins and other brainy organisms unable to use tools. Moralists say our conscience is what defines us as human and superior. These people are forgetting the blow job. What other beast of any genus or phylum has devised such a way of being pleased and pleasing others? Orangutans? Forget it. We have no way of knowing whether the original discoverer—let's just see what happens if I place this hole in my face over that thing sticking out of his crotch and give it a good suck—was a man or woman, and given what we do know about the ancient Greeks we have to conclude it's a toss-up. Fellatio, the very signature of gratificatio. For this moment, the gravid glorious oral moment, the tongue and lips and warm wetness were all; the person who administers this favor of favors dispenses joy, and a man is blessed to be the recipient. Jasmine was my initiation, and she spun my head off. Sing hey nonnie nonnie and a posthumous Nobel for the inventor of this wonder.

Then I was inside her and we were on my single bed though I had no idea how we arrived there. Her ribs touched mine, and her breasts, bursting with energy, ground into my chest. Her slenderness felt, to my feverish embrace, like the tines of a fork covered with the peel of a juicy grape.

Jasmine moved with the skill and knowingness of an athlete. Her legs traveled from my hips to my back and moved up almost around my shoulders, pulling me to her faster than I imagined even when I had previously tried to imagine what full sex really consisted of. I understood Jasmine was aiming for something, and what she was aiming for was her own pleasure, not mine, which increased mine by powers. Not long after that realization I slipped my mooring utterly.

She was still moving, more quietly now, having arrived at her own moment just before I had at mine.

Then I was bathing us both in sweat, a young buck issuing forth his liquids. I felt like an entire irrigation system.

When I could say anything, it was an apology. "I'm sorry, I know I've gotten you all wet. I hope …"

"Don't hope and don't sorry," she said. "Hope is for what hasn't happened. This has happened quite well, thank you so much."

She showered while I heated her some mushroom soup, the only can I could find in the only cabinet in my kitchen, such as it was.

She came out of the shower with one towel around her waist, another turbaning her hair. That left me staring at her uncovered chest. I tried to look away, to busy myself pouring her soup from saucepan to bowl. But no matter where I turned I couldn't avoid her small, upwardly tilted breasts with nipples like the eyes in Renaissance paintings that follow you wherever you are. As she ate her soup I again felt the push of my desire. I was embarrassed for what was going on just below my T-shirt and underpants.

"I'm suddenly starved," she said, "and this soup tastes better than it has any right to. Do you have any bread?"

I made her some toast and took a slice for myself.

"Mmmm," she said. "Dunk yours in my soup."

I did that and fished out a mushroom. "Just like a bachelor," she said. "You have almost nothing to eat, yet the one thing you do have is delicious. Know anyone famous?"

"I see them around," I told her. "They don't know me, so no I don't, not really."

"Someday," she said, "they'll know you. My mother likes Wally Beery."

I had edited out the afternoon as well as Mossy's party the previous night and told her something more honest, by accident, than if I'd given her an account of the great names of Hollywood gathered one evening earlier. I thought of Pammy and Mossy now, and I added, "Even if one or two said they know my name, none really know me. Maybe one. Do you know who Amos Zangwill is?"

"Who's that?"

"He's head of the studio I work for, he keeps behind the scenes, Jasmine."

"I don't really follow pictures. My mother and father go to any-thing Wally Beery is in. I'd like to tell you my name is not really Jasmine. It's Janice."

"That's all right. You have to protect yourself."

"It wasn't that. Jasmine sounds better. I was trying to get your interest with an exotic name. Janice, ugh."

"It's fine. Don't worry." I was glad we'd both been square with each other. I could easily have recited a list of famous people, but I'd already achieved whatever such a recital might have been thought to be worth. I barely suppressed a smile of self-satisfaction. Don't be so smug, I scolded myself, she doesn't give a damn.

Jasmine-Janice had finished our soup, still bare-chested and turbaned.

I felt I should say something. "You look pretty terrific that way," I said.

Before I could finish reaching for her hand she was in my lap. This time her kiss tasted of the mushroom soup, yet still a little briny. She had parted the towel and already had me inside her as I hoisted her to the bed. I don't know how I navigated.

It was better this time because I wasn't so nervous and she wasn't so needy. We were here for the sheer delight of it. As we proceeded, I also understood how much we were strangers, nothing in common but our desire. People married for this and then regretted it their whole lives, didn't they?

Janice stopped moving. "Do you think it would be all right if I turned over?"

I had as much idea of what she was suggesting as if she'd asked whether I'd mind her speaking Telugu. But I said, "Please do what you want."

Janice rolled and thrust her bum skyward. She had me re-enter. Her vagina felt tighter from behind, more supple and arrangeable for her own pleasure. We resumed moving. She whirred and churned as if she were a mixing bowl and I her humble spoon. "Shoot it up to my shoulder blades," she said. "Unnnnh," I said if I said anything. We remained this way, upping and downing, for longer than I'd have thought possible, my hands on her hips, her head buried in my pillow. I was in a rodeo of ecstasy. At length she began to make little feral sounds, and I realized she was concluding. I charged now toward my own conclusion. She became more urgent, female, biological. I flew.

Resting my head on her upper back, I wondered when I'd see her next because now I wanted to. Surely I'd see Jasmine or Janice, whoever she wanted to be, again. Would she come back to the ocean next Sunday? "Oh gee," I began, "I really hope we—"

Reading my thoughts one more time, she said, still facing my pillow, "Oh dear, how swell this has been. We'll just keep it that way and not burden it with a future."

"But," I began again, "I was kind of thinking—"

She disengaged so abruptly when she turned to face me that I felt just as abruptly deprived. "Don't," she said, and kissed me on the chin. She added, with some emphasis, "Mustn't try to repeat perfection."

Yet that itself sounded repeated. She chuckled, then was serious. "You wouldn't like one thing about my life, and I couldn't adjust to yours."

She was up and dressed quickly. "No shower," she said. "I want to keep you on me for the drive home."

We'd each had something from the other, something pleasurable, for me immensely pleasurable, and then, like snails, were receding back into our own shells.

"Thank you," she said, kissing me on the cheek, which I thought both odd and right. "You're a good man, Owen." Then quickly put her lips on mine without parting them. And was gone.

It occurred to me that no one—in my personal life or in my career as errand-runner, junior writer, general factotum—had ever before called me a man.

I fell on my bed and slept, a leaden drunk on the steps of a church.

11

A Life in the Day
PART I: MORNING

Question: Where is God when you need him?

The next morning, Mossy's secretary Elena Frye told me later, the boss's office was an early hive of dispute. Nils Maynard charged in at seven o'clock because he had to be on his own set by eight. As much as he admired Pammy, he thought she'd be wrong in his next picture, a brittle satire on an upperclass marriage in which the husband's fortune plummets along with the stock market, whereupon his scheming wife dumps him in favor of a mortgage-foreclosing banker. The picture would belong to the two men; the fickle wife was only a lever setting up the antagonism between them. Nils said Pammy had the flesh of a hot water bottle, looking as though she might be running a slight fever, her eyes dark and bright at the same time. No camera could hide that. Mossy was insistent, and the former magician could find no rabbit in his hat either to charm or dissuade the studio chief. Mossy promised to have his ace construction man, Tutor Beedleman, warm up the wife's part to please Nils by the time shooting started. "But Millevoix does your picture," he said. Nils said, "I don't think so," and left for his set.

Elena told me that whenever Mossy referred to Pammy by her last name he was doing one of two things. Either he was disguising his own interest in her, or he was considering her as something between valued property and an artist, both of which, by studio standards, she was. I believed she'd be the perfect Nora in *A Doll's House*.

Driving to work that Monday morning, I was queasy about my visit to Pammy's Red Woods. I'd intruded, then failed her in a way I couldn't define but that was somehow tied to the ghastly package she received. The interlude with Jasmine/Janice redeemed my day with pleasure and confirmation. Though she was real enough to have left a lipstick, which I had no way of returning to her, she also had the quality of a phantom. I might pine for Palmyra—I often called her by her full name in reveries—but that didn't prevent me from being a twenty-four-year-old longing for a touch. The alternating current between dreams and reality in Hollywood during the Great Depression yielded such high voltage that the contradictory flows of energy made you dizzy. Almost every movie was in some way a denial of the Depression itself. The more famous a star, the more impossible it was to imagine the star affected by the Depression, even if he or she played the part of a pauper.

Movies and fame: what a perfect marriage, each dependent on projection. In the search for identity that was my Grail over these teeming months, I attributed divine powers to those whose prominence endowed them with a magical existence. What was a star's glamour anyway? Glamour was no less than the radiant moment extended and absorbed into personality. It became a defiance of inevitability, of time and death. It made up for something that wasn't there or that had been but had vanished. My wait for a portion of this existence, I assured myself as I approached the studio gates, was over. *A Doll's House* would attach me at least to a screenwriter's renown.

A vast moan arose from the waiting mass as I steered my roadster toward the guard booth at Jubilee. Hopeful and hopeless, patient and impatient, the dispossessed bunched around my car. Even more than with the stars, who they didn't dare bother, they implored anonymities like me to get them inside for a day's work. I had learned to ignore them, real people wishing only to become part of the fakery.

From Jubilee's gates, the studio looked like a dozen airplane hangars in a well-guarded penitentiary for high-risk repeat offenders. Inside was a miniature civilization with a caste system both rigid where authority was concerned and flexible when talent showed itself. A factory town with each filmmaking task having its own little company. I hurried to the green stucco building where non-starring actresses reported at 6:30 for makeup and costuming, 5:30 if they were going on location. Looking for the costume sweatshop Jim Bicker had described, I went to the top floor.

In a crowded cavern above the actresses' dressing rooms I counted twenty-eight coffee-skinned women, about half hunched over their Singers, the other half stitching by hand. One of them got up to see what I wanted. She was short and had the flat-nosed impassive features of Mayan sculpture. Her Spanish accent was so heavy I had to ask her to repeat several things. She said there were thirty-five sewing *muchachas* and some weren't in yet. They worked twelve hours a day and were paid forty cents an hour. They were not allowed out of the building or even downstairs. If anyone saw them they were told to say they were studio maids. "We send most what we make home," the woman said, meaning Mexico. "To get enough to eat we need night jobs too, or husbands, but most husbands are on the other side. Some wait for us in Tijuana on Sunday."

I'd heard of the women in the nineteenth century coming off farms to work as virtual serfs in the New England mills (the mills Nils Maynard and his boyhood friend had briefly run away to), and everyone learned in school about the Triangle Shirtwaist Factory fire of 1911 in New York, but this hot room was a page out of a history I thought was past. I judged the workers here to range in age from about thirteen to forty looking like sixty. "Our fingers fly all day," my informal guide told me, "or we be fire. Fire by the Colonel." They brought their lunches in the little brown bags I saw by each machine, and if they forgot or didn't have a nickel for a couple of tortillas, the Colonel would have leftovers sent in from the commissary, accompanied by a dock in the women's pay.

So this was another of Colonel DeLight's jobs, getting the Mexican women's fingers to fly the way he did with the writers, who also did piecework and could be bounced off the lot if their fingers didn't fly fast enough. But don't go too far with that one, I reminded myself, because all the writers have cars and some have pools and servants who are probably sisters of these women.

The women sewed all the actresses' clothing that wasn't bought or rented from Western Costume. Since Jubilee was lightly sprinkled with union sympathizers, Reds and Red-leaners in 1934, Mossy wanted this covey of serfs kept invisible. I wondered how Elena Frye felt about these women, if she even knew they were on the lot. And Pammy. Pammy couldn't have known because she'd have nailed Mossy if she had. The stars were dressed in their bungalows and seldom came to the wardrobe building.

"Looking for something, Sonny?" I turned and saw Colonel DeLight twitching his mustache at me from the top of the stairs. "Wandered a bit off course here, haven't we?" Slapping his pantleg, the Colonel beckoned me as he would a sheepdog and, like one of those loyally trainable creatures, I trotted over to his side. "Private quarters, Owen my boy," he said, "no one comes up here without my say-so."

Large boom-voiced courtly southern Colonel Ambrose DeLight was often playful in his husbandry of writers and liked to joke he was really only in charge of keeping them sober. "Ah'm jes' a towel boy in a whorehouse, gents," he'd say as he walked down the hall. "Now you boys have all the fun you want, but no drinkin' around the typewriters between lunch and five-thirty, hear?" He'd be answered by a chorus of "Whatever you say, Massa," which would set the typewriters to clacking furiously, and the Colonel would call out, "That's what I like—a good bunch of liars. Haw!" Or else, on a bad day when one writer's ego had been lanced by Mossy, two more had been fired, three others replaced, he'd yell, "Awright boys, enough gloom, le's have us some fun, what's post time for the first race at Santa Anita?" And off several of us would go, piling into the Colonel's ancient Hudson. "A heart has been located in his anatomy," said his fellow southerner Yancey Ballard, "but it's fashioned from buffed ivory."

I followed the Colonel down the stairs without looking back at the woman in the sewing cavern who'd been speaking to me. "Look, Colonel," I said in the stairwell, "This is plain slave labor and you know it."

As soon as I said slave I remembered where the Colonel was from; he might not regard slavery unbenignly. He probably had a granddaddy who owned dozens of people. I added didactically, "These conditions are not what America tolerates in the twentieth century."

"Wrong all day long, Sonny," he said, draping a proprietary arm around my shoulder, "They ain't complaining, are they? And they ain't starving, are they? Which is what a lot of other wetbacks are doing in this year of Our Lord. So let it rest."

"But this studio is rich, there are people here who take home thousands a week. The way you keep these women is cruel, and you and Mossy know that. It's not human."

"Wrong again. That's just what it is. Human. Been some that has and most that hasn't since dawn broke over Noah's Ark. Now I'm heading back upstairs, you run along into the costumery here and see if you can get yourself a date for tonight. What you need is to have your ashes hauled, boy."

Furious, helpless, I scuttled to my office to begin work on an original and wait for Mossy's triumphant summons on *A Doll's House.*

The morning was heating up in the throne room. Mossy began so calmly with his supervisors and flunkies they all thought it was going to be only a Monday morning preview of the week's work. Perhaps one of them, the conniving production chief Seaton Hackley, suspected a storm was percolating beneath the calm. Others present, the lineup of fugitive grotesques it took to run a studio, were the deceptively genteel assistant production head Wren Harbuck; the hatchet man Dunster Clapp, who had fired the gentle Joey Jouet; suave overeducated nasal-accented British turncoat Percy Shumway; Curtt Weigerer, the chunky head production manager, his jaw hanging like a clothes iron, a side of beef with the demeanor of a storm trooper; Goddard Minghoff, Mossy's amiable yet icy chief of staff; the yes-men Oddly Tumarkin and Dexter Twitchell; and Beeker Kyle, the villainous assistant studio manager who had been host to Jim Bicker when he first encountered Jubilee. These functionaries were a palace guard, variously capable of acting as modest ambassadors, jocular persuaders, or ruthless enforcers depending on what roles their maestro felt the situation required.

When Seaton Hackley fired anyone his voice was like an oceanliner blowing a basso horn in a fog-shrouded harbor, while Wren Harbuck would steer someone off the lot sounding like an apologetic piccolo.

"Fine weekend everyone?" Mossy asked as he casually leafed a script.

"A little fun, a little work," said Tumarkin. "Very little fun, whole lot of work," said the suck-up Weigerer. It was Weigerer who kept the inventory on his office wall headed Rag Daze, a special calendar for charting the menstrual cycles of the important actresses on the lot; directors were warned not to make harsh demands, don't have them swim if they don't want to, during their periods. "As for me," said the momentarily courageous Hackley, "enjoyed some time with the fam."

"Whilst I," said Percy Shumway, betook myself to Arrowh—"

"Good," Mossy cut in, "and did anyone chance to hear from Bernard Gestikker?"

"Bernard Gestikker?" said Wren Harbuck. "Who in the world …?"

"Gestikker?" said Dexter Twitchell. "Bernard?" said Oddly Tumarkin, whose first name Grszoddl no one, including he, ever used.

"Oh sure, Chief," said Hackley, "that's Trent Amberlyn's real name before you changed it."

"That's nice, Shmuel, you win the quiz," said Mossy to his head of production, who had been born Shmuel Himmelfarb not far from Mossy himself in the Bronx. Seaton Hackley knew a hurricane was about to hit when Mossy used his original name. "All right," Mossy continued. "Let's start over. Has anyone heard from Trent Amberlyn?"

Head shaking all around. "Not me, Boss." "Nor I." "Saw him at your colossal splash Saturday night," said Wren Harbuck, proud of his own little splash when he waltzed in from the garden with the starlet Hana Bliner. "Haven't seen him since." "Not a peep." "Me either," rounded out the chorus of yes-men saying, for a change, no.

"How happy, how blessed, for all of you." Mossy paused, then let the storm break. "Trent God Damn Amberlyn is in the Hollywood lockup!"

"Whaaaaat?" Unbelief all around, insincere unbelief acted with as much flatulent insincerity as these bottom-feeders could muster.

"Soliciting a minor," Mossy went on. "Who was no doubt soliciting him and who Trent probably thought was eighteen or so but turned out to be only fifteen. A parking lot off Hollywood Boulevard on Las Palmas up near Franklin, cops happened to be patrolling it same time Trent was, ect ect ect, goddam treacherous little pansy ain't dried shit without Jubilee, how could he do this to me!"

This was not about Trent then. It was Mossy whose dignity was affronted. Mossy purposely used street grammar when he was upset, and ect was et cetera.

Open season on Trent. Dunster Clapp and Curtt Weigerer set the tone when they both said "vicious little cocksucking queer" at the same time. The rest chimed in with their poofs, flounces, wrists, any slurs they could come up with to condemn Trent. "Someone that light in his loafers should know his way around," said Goddard Minghoff, Mossy's gatekeeper and the gentlest of his executioners. It was quipped around Jubilee that you had to go through God to get to Mossy; a producer wishing to gain favor at the studio tried to get God on his side first. In the present crisis, God added helpfully that he would look into the morals clause in Trent's contract, shouldn't be difficult to fire him.

"I see," said Mossy. "So you all agree it's capital punishment for Trent?"

"Any queer has it coming to him," said the malevolent Curtt Weigerer, his face the blunt side of an ax. "Tar and feather the little fairy."

"Is that so, Curtt?" said Mossy. "And just what does Jubilee have coming? Trent Amberlyn has millions of fans and is worth more millions to this studio. You're all so far off the point. The point is how dare not a single one of you know where our stars are?"

"Boss, it was a weekend—"

"Oh, that's right, scandals don't happen on weekends. Remember Fatty Arbuckle? Blockheads! I expect you to know where our talent is at all times. Now Trent is still down there when he should have been bailed within two hours of his arrest. He's been there all night, and we can be sure someone from the *Times*, the *Examiner* or *Variety* will be at the jail within half an hour, maybe all three plus the *Reporter*. Weigerer, you have cop friends, Shmuel you know the detectives, get to them right away. And the rest of you—I don't want any of you overpriced baboons *ever* not to know where our stars are. If somebody does land in a lockup, you get them out of there within an hour, *half* an hour. Always have cash ready for bail even on weekends, *especially* on weekends. Does any of you dopes not get this straight?"

"We all get it, Boss," said production chief Hackley, suddenly a spokesman for the chastened chamberlains. We let you down, and—"

"It *never* happens again!" said Mossy. "You can all be replaced, replaceable parts if I say the word. "This *never. Happens. Again!*"

"Never," said the production chief, blinking, reduced almost to tears.

"Never," said Dunster Clapp.

"But what do we do about Trent?" asked Beeker Kyle.

"I wondered when anybody would ask," said Mossy. Oliver Culp is on his way to bail him, and Esther Leah is going along to be the weeping aunt, Mrs. Gestikker.

"But Oliver," Seaton Hackley began, "Oliver is just a fairy himself."

"True, Seaton," Mossy said, and Hackley was relieved his boss was back to using his social name. "But Oliver don't pick up boys to split their ass that I know of, and that's who Trent called, and Oliver called me."

Oliver Culp was the librarian at Jubilee.

"Do you think this was a setup, Boss?" Curtt Weigerer asked, playing to the Zangwill paranoia that could surface at a critical moment. Jubilee was the newest of the majors, and sometimes the big studios played dirty tricks on each other. Mossy himself had used both Dunster Clapp and Curtt Weigerer to foster discontent at other studios among the craft unions starting up around Hollywood. Weigerer, a born enforcer, knew the notorious labor racketeer Willie Bioff from Capone days in Chicago. Bioff could make phone calls to start blue-collar trouble anywhere in the country. Weigerer himself, often called a fascist by free-spirited writers and actors, flourished in an atmosphere where fear and discipline were essential tools for controlling creative people whose habitual social state was anarchy.

"What do you mean a setup?" Mossy asked.

"I mean LB or Jack," Weigerer said.

Mossy was capable of suspecting rival studio chiefs of sabotaging his product. They could have a star like Amberlyn followed, knowing he was looking for other men, and they could tip the vice squad, always eager for headlines, when cruising was going on. The studio or the police themselves could easily plant a cute boy in a parking lot.

"I don't frankly think Jack Warner or LB Mayer would stoop that low."

Curtt Weigerer had worked for Harry Cohn at Columbia, had moved on for special assignments at Metro; he knew stooping. But he said, "Whatever you say, Boss."

"What I say is I want you bastards I pay obscenely high salaries to be on sentry duty with my stars, and I don't want no actor or actress to be fifteen minutes in a lockup before one of you is on the case. Am I understood?"

Mossy saw pleaders all morning as kings in earlier times received underlings and favor seekers. Their ambition, greed, cunning was overmatched by his own. Mossy's system was simplicity itself. Loyalty was all he demanded, not agreement, only loyalty.

His office was crafted to intimidate. At the end of a private corridor, the seat of power was huge, an emblem of his necessities—the need always to be a step ahead of his visitor, to have a story people wanted, to show money when that helped and to conceal it when crying for economy, most of all to express domination in every gesture and design. A reflecting pool on one side of the room was a grandiose distraction. As were Monet's water lilies hanging above it. Strong men slumped in their seats, which was hard not to do because of the way Mossy had the chairs tilted backward on the supplicants' side of his desk. An aggressive wash of light shone on whoever sat across from Mossy; the person was virtually Klieged by a ceiling spot and a light from below, both of which Mossy controlled from his desk. The desk itself was massive, often bare, platformed like Mussolini's. When anyone objected to the harsh lighting, Mossy's excuse was that he talked to a lot of aspiring actors and actresses; he needed to be able to see how they'd show up on film.

But Mossy had another lighting idiosyncrasy. One side of his face was lit, while the other dipped into shadow. Disconcerting first-time visitors, Mossy became both sinister and cherubic because if he leaned one way the light on his head would tend to halate while his face looked like Beelzebub himself. This added to his mystery, and he often used the shadowy face when greeting a writer and again when firing him. One feature of Mossy's turn in this darker direction was that, at thirty-four, as old and as young as the century, he was beginning to lose a small amount of his dark russet-tinged hair from the top of his head, and the halo would often be highlighting a tiny bald spot on his crown. With his little tonsure, Mossy could resemble a medieval monk gravely purposed to sentence a dozen suspected heretics to a session on the rack prior to their execution. Perhaps all he actually said was, "Manny, I'm afraid we've decided to go in another direction," but the effect was as if he'd told Manny his testicles were to be snipped and fried in whale oil.

In the long corridor leading to his office, one wall held photographs (some real, some composite fakes) of Mossy with stars and potentates, while the other was lined with a one-way mirror enabling Mossy to see into his waiting room—who was nervous, apprehensive, hopeful, annoyed. People had been known to cross themselves when the nod finally came from Elena Frye to proceed into the sovereign's presence.

At the very end of the corridor, just before the main chamber, you were flanked by two mirrors, a flat one opposite the one-way. If you looked in either of them you saw a great many frightened reflections of yourself. When Mossy deemed you important enough to rise from his desk and come across the room to greet you, what he saw was what he loved, an infinity of Zangwills. The most treacherous mirror was behind Mossy's desk, concealing a private door; actors were so inhibited by being made self-consciously aware of how they looked that they were disabled from conferring about anything more significant than a fresh wrinkle.

Mossy himself was the best actor on his own lot. Dressed as fastidiously as a gangster, he could charm, berate, mother, father, rage as he did with his toughs-in-waiting over Trent Amberlyn, cajole, play the fool when he had nothing to lose, become a tragedian with everything to gain—all better than anyone he hired. He could withhold approval, vengefully suspend an actor for refusing a bad picture and then, when he heard the actor was about to sign with Paramount, offer him the role of his career opposite Joan Crawford or Palmyra Millevoix. "A superprecautious son of a bitch," the labor racketeer Willie Bioff once described Mossy, "with a pair of mountains for balls."

His constitutional discontent seldom permitted Mossy, even on social occasions, not to be working. When I got to know her better I asked Esther Leah if Mossy ever slept. "And how," she said. "You should see him, always on his back, with those long eyelashes at last closed, a smile on his face, as serene and guiltless as an angel."

"But with the heart of a devil," I was cheeky enough to say.

"Not really," she said. "Just the brains of a devil, the heart of a hungry child."

"Who can never have enough."

"Who can never have enough."

After Elena had shooed the chastened executives who had not been alert to the Trent Amberlyn arrest, she led in a petitioner that Monday morning, Willow Blatchley, the old silents tycoon. A man given to apoplectic rages, Blatchley had a stroke that left him speechless. The stroke occurred in 1927 after he had taken his new wife, Renata, half his age and looking for fame and fortune herself, to a screening of *The Jazz Singer* at Warner Brothers. Blatchley went into a tirade against sound on film, clutched at his throat, flailed his arms, and fell down a flight of stairs, a scene he had filmed many times in his pictures. Mossy had been given his first job in Hollywood by Blatchley and had learned moviemaking at his feet. Literally. On one occasion, before a premiere, he had made Mossy shine his shoes. Errands and dirty work, often followed by harsh reprimands, were Mossy's diet with the temperamental tycoon. Mossy had gone over to Metro in 1925, signaling, though neither of them knew it, his own sure rise and, even before sound, Willow Blatchley's sunset. When he was told the circumstances of Blatchley's stroke, Mossy had shrugged, "Melodrama is so old-fashioned."

Yet Mossy granted the movie pioneer a brief appointment, and he was wheeled in by Renata, who serviced his needs and hadn't figured out how to leave her helpless husband. Blatchley could walk only jerkily, sixteen frames per second like his old two reelers, he scribbled ruefully to Mossy, so he needed the wheelchair.

Blatchley had a book in his lap. "He wants to produce for you," Renata began. "He has a property he knows he can develop if you'll buy it. A bitter romance, a rich man, his unhappy wife, their lovers. We can work well together."

"I'm sure you can, Renata," Mossy said. "You're looking tip top, old man," he added. "How's he holding up?"

"Doctors say he'll talk again soon."

"Well then," Mossy said with a smile, "I'm so glad you came in now." He chuckled and Renata tried to. "Tell me, what's the property."

"Willow wants you to know he has mellowed. He's a much easier, kinder man than when you knew him. In his stroke he has found humility."

"That's nice, darling. I can't say I envy you. What's the property?"

With trembling hands, Blatchley lifted the book off his lap. "D-d-d-d-d," he tried, but as he held the book he seemed to be shaking it at Mossy rather than offering it to him.

Renata took the book from her husband. "It's by Sinclair Lewis, *Dodsworth*," she said. "We think Walter Huston would be perfect. He's cold lately, he'll come cheap."

"I know the book and I saw the play. Keep your copy. It's a downer, people don't want that now. Huston's washed up. Glad you came in, keep your chin up old man."

Elena hustled them out, wheelchair and wife, almost before they saw how much Mossy had enjoyed turning his old mentor, and tormentor, down. Mossy didn't want *Dodsworth* at Jubilee, but he owed a small favor to Sam Goldwyn and he suggested the book to him, with Walter Huston's name attached. Goldwyn got Willie Wyler to direct Huston in the part. When he heard about it, Blatchley had another stroke, this one fatal.

In came a clown, down on his luck. He'd made the silent-to-talkie transition, had a contract at Jubilee, but lately his comedy wasn't getting laughs. With a face like putty, he could make his features resemble a rooster, a spastic taxi driver, a jackhammer. Mossy admired him.

"Nobody likes my material any more," he complained. "You ought to let me out of my contract. I'll go back to where I started, play county fairs, birthdays."

Mossy saw the man was not just the traditional sad clown but acutely discouraged, and he tried to cheer him up. "That's an idea for a picture right there," he said. "I'll get Maurice Sugarman on this, he's always spouting ideas, he'll like thinking about a county fair and a comic who's been laying eggs."

"Jokes, though, I need jokes and business," said the inconsolable clown.

"Sugarman will come in on it. He's full of jokes."

"The worst of it is, I can't tell you."

Mossy became more interested. He'd been suspicious when the comic asked out of his contract. Maybe Columbia or somebody was making him a better offer. Now he saw the man was in real pain. "What's so awful you can't tell."

"I'm dead in my pants."

"It happens," said Mossy. "So I've heard." He turned away from the sad comic.

"My wife is patient, but it's been weeks. I hate to admit it, I tried another woman."

"I'm shocked."

"It was worse. I don't know what to do."

"This too shall pass," Mossy intoned Biblically. He thought of something. "Hey, what about bringing your wife over to Catalina on my boat. Tell her you're going to star in a new picture and the chief insisted you steal his yacht for a few days. The sea air, the birds, the island itself. Go crazy."

"Gee, the worst it could do is cheer me up. You know I dreamed I was on a boat, scared, we were going through the Panama Canal and everybody wanted to dunk me."

"You flunk geography—it's the Equator where they dunk you. Panama Canal, you're home free."

"So that's what it means."

"Dr. Freud tells you what they mean. I put them on the screen. A county fair and the Panama Canal, a comic who needs a break. Sugarman's meat and potatoes. I'll send a car for you and the little lady to take you to my boat in Long Beach. Get out of here."

Not that this was all generosity on Mossy's part. If he thought someone was what he called an official talent, he'd do anything not only to hang on but also to put the talent so heavily in his debt that when the Columbias and Foxes came around they had no one to talk to.

Writers slouched in. As MGM was known for being a producers' studio, Jubilee prized writers. "In the beginning was the word," Mossy repeated to his salaried dreamers, "and in the end is my word. If you guys don't do your job, no one else has a job." That didn't mean writers were happy; always disgruntled, they had to sit still for being condescended to by everyone else in the food chain. Ordered to appease church attacks on Hollywood, four writers were working on the story of Job, complaining they were in as much pain as Job himself. Mossy told them it would be spectacular when the Red Sea parted. They said that wasn't the Job story; a good man lost his family, property, and was struck with sores on his body, all because God and Satan were arguing over him. Mossy thought for a moment. "The story is God and Satan, Job is the field they play on. Walter Pidgeon and Lionel Barrymore fight over Trent Amberlyn. Get going, children, type me some good and evil." The fun we had.

A red-maned actress, Brenda De Baule, had two minutes to convince Mossy she was right for a gangster moll after he had lost faith in the producer's ability to cast his own picture. "The part is important," Mossy told her, "because if we don't believe she has a mind of her own we won't care when the heavy pushes her into a wall." Declaiming a line from the script, the actress said, "This broad don't take no guff from nobody, and that means you, Mr. Big Nobody!" Mossy liked that. When they stood to shake hands, the actress stared at Mossy's fly before fixing on his eyes, keeping hold of his hand. She waved her hair off her face but it settled right back over one eye as she smiled goodbye. "Elena," Mossy said to his secretary after the actress had gone, "find out if Miss De Baule is free for lunch tomorrow. Maybe today."

Mossy's next meeting was a ream. Poor Jim Bicker was in to hear instructions on the adaptation of a novel he'd taken over from another writer. Bicker was difficult and surly. He and Mossy were like animals genetically programmed to fight, but Mossy knew Jim gave his scripts an edge that made gritty pictures. He was stuck with Poor Jim anyway because of his two-year contract.

"Story has no charm," Bicker said.

As if you have, Mossy wanted to say but held back because he needed the work out of Jim. "Charm's not what it needs. It needs pace, action, toughness."

"This picture and I can't find each other."

"Good," Mossy said, "keep looking. That'll make whatever you do find better. The novel's okay, for a novel anyway. I bought it for the characters, the ex-con, his wife and daughter, the detective, the teacher who drinks, the crooked lawyer, the bowling alley guy. Now we're going to have those people do what it makes sense for them to do in a motion picture. They're no longer going to be staring at each other while they think and we read what they're thinking. They're going to be doing, playing, fighting. They need visible energy. The characters are still the meat, but we need gravy badly, and mashed potatoes, beans, then ice cream. Gravy comes from what's already inside them, like a turkey's gravy from giblets—heart, gizzard, liver. Part of this gravy is the ex-con maybe wants to prove he was innocent in the first place. Shut up for a minute. I know in the novel he *is* guilty, but the people who go to pictures really like a man who's been, pardon my French, butt fucked, so we watch him come back against the odds and right the wrong. We don't know that at first, everyone just assumes he's guilty, his wife and daughter included, but he wants to clear his name, so naturally he has to find out who actually pulled off the robbery he did time for. See?"

Mossy and Poor Jim were mirrors of each other. Though inherently hostile, both believed in happy endings. One saw Shirley Temple's smile in every sunrise, the other the destruction of the old order, replaced by the new order where greed was abolished. One saw everyone saluting the flag, studio profitability, and the pure virtue of American life. The other saw a tomorrow with a motto: to each according to his needs, from each according to his ability. No one was selfish in this vision, not really.

"But you've stuck me on a story without a heart," Jim Bicker said.

"Not every story needs a heart, goddammit," Mossy said. "This one has *kishkas*. All you have to do is push the bittersweet relationship, more bitter if you want, give me some mystery about why the detective hates the ex-con so much—are they long lost brothers? Or did the detective see someone who looks like the ex-con kill his mother? Gimme a chase, underground maybe, in the sewers, I don't know, then punch up the ending. Meeting over."

For a later draft of the same screenplay, Mossy would tell another writer to give the story heart, but heart happened not to be what he valued in Poor Jim Bicker.

Mossy left his office by his private door to go across the building and give a confidential instruction to Dunster Clapp, no doubt a threat only Clapp could deliver with the menace his boss wanted. Then he stopped in the design room to see what Hurd Dawn, the head set designer, had on his easel. He told Dawn to change a living room into a dining room so the characters would have something to do while they argued.

Meanwhile, Elena ushered in a small squad of writers with their flustered director. The mirrored corridor stretching from the outer office to the inner sanctum gave pleaders time to become even more nervous, and when they achieved the sanctum itself they might be trembling. Finding Mossy gone, one of the writers said it was like a reprieve from the governor just before an electrocution. In this case, the meeting was with all the writers who had worked on a script along with the bewildered director who was trying to turn their work into ninety minutes that would hold together. A week of shooting had produced an indecipherable mess.

The first writer, a former reporter, had been brought in to adapt a current novel. Writer number two came for scene construction and continuity. Writer number three, a playwright, was enlisted to brighten dialogue. Writer number four added physical and visual tension, screen pacing. Writer number five came for gags, despite the fact that the story was fairly serious. Then writer three had returned to touch up the dialogue just before shooting, after which number two came back to tighten the structure. Before all this happened, a reader had synopsized the novel, giving it three pages plus a recommendation, which was don't touch it. It got touched anyway because Dick Powell loved it, or said he did, or someone said he did.

As the writers fidgeted, a door slammed in the outer office as Mossy returned from his errand and charged down his corridor. He began speaking while no one in his inner office could yet see him. "Over and done with, cut our losses, this is a baby only a mother could love, and I'm no mother. Picture's canceled."

They still couldn't see him and he'd already executed them, especially the director. The writers looked at each other, then at the director, who had his head down, making sounds—*"Wha, wah, whaaa"*—and nobody knew whether he was starting to cry or trying to say something but couldn't push out his words.

At last Mossy was visible—double-breasted and gold cuff-linked, dark reddish hair shining, nose pointing like the prow of a ship—in the office itself. One of the writers, who had been in the Army, stood as though an officer had entered.

Another writer thought hopefully, desperately, perhaps Mossy was referring to a different project. "What's that you're talking about, Chief?" he asked.

"This picture's finished," Mossy said. "The dailies are dreck."

Trying to come to the director's aid, a third writer said, "We've just been clearing our throats so far. The best stuff starts getting into the can tomorrow."

"No, not tomorrow, not ever. Picture's done."

"We can fix it, Boss, fix it fast," said the youngest writer in the room, who happened to be number four.

Now Mossy had heard something he could pounce on. "Tell me, tell me right this minute. And a minute is just what you have."

This writer, whose ideas had been routinely rejected by his senior colleagues, asserted himself. "The pilot," he said, "shouldn't be a pilot but the captain of a cargo ship that's being taken away from him unjustly after he's rammed by a Coast Guard cutter driven by a man who hates him for having won the girl they were both in love with."

At the word "love," Mossy's ears almost literally pricked up. He leaned forward, saying nothing, always the sign for a writer to continue.

"Meanwhile, the girl herself, a morsel everyone wants but only the captain has, is being blackmailed by another guy she rejected who happens to know her father was also once involved in a shipping scandal of his own. The father—I'm thinking of Walter Connolly, maybe Roscoe Karns—did smuggle arms to the English when they were first in the war and we weren't, but it was a good cause. His daughter—a Bebe Daniels kind of woman, sympathetic but put upon, married to the disgraced captain—wants to save the two men she loves, her husband and her father, but doesn't have the money the blackmailer demands to keep quiet about the father, who's also running for mayor …"

"Stop!" Mossy yelled.

Something had happened to change the room from a funeral parlor to the starting gate at a race track.

"I can get Connolly, rest of the cast stays as is," said Mossy. "Stop shooting. Have the new script by Friday, do you understand? Do all of you understand?"

Eagerness is a poor word to describe the joy, gratitude, alacrity and enthusiasm with which the entire room leaped to "Yes!" their chief.

"One more thing," said the chief. "I'm not in the complicated-picture business on this one, I'm in the love business. The father, the captain, the guy in the boat, the blackmailer, they all love the girl. Go type me some love."

Before they had even retreated to the other end of Mossy's corridor, the director was kissing the young writer. "Salvation," he cooed. "It's a different picture, but you saved it and I owe you my firstborn."

Control was not only Mossy's goal but his gift. He could smell when a picture was going bad, and this was most often because he could smell the people on it losing confidence. He didn't so much understand films as he did filmmakers: writers, directors, producers, stars. Not that he didn't know what he liked and, with even greater decisiveness, what he disliked; but his gift was in knowing who to hire and when to fire. If a writer groused to Mossy about being made to write a script that was only a reworking of a standard formula, Mossy would say, "Formula! Formula? Do you know what formula is? It's what works, what will work. Okay, I'm a baby and I'm crying, so go out and make me some formula. But make it new and fresh, the stale stuff gives me indigestion."

Loving his pictures and the audiences he made them for, Mossy also loved having power over his audiences. Once we walked together into a theater playing a Jubilee movie. "Look at this," he said as the opening credits finished. "In four minutes I will cause the people in this theater to laugh. In twenty-two minutes they will be scared out of their wits, and in thirty-seven minutes I will make them cry." And so it came to pass.

It was Yeatsman, Mossy's favorite writer, who best characterized the birth and death of a project at Jubilee. "Ponder the temperament of a bubble," he told me. "A bubble is bewitching as it floats upward, catching the sunlight, displaying the rainbow on its surface, appearing both two and three dimensional, membrane-thin yet spherical, and it rotates exquisitely on some hidden axis, full of promise of other bubbles as well. Then, with no warning, it pops. You don't ask why."

Yeatsman could go toe to toe on scripts with Mossy, one of the few who dared confront the boss. Towering over Mossy, Yeatsman, with Princeton and early service on the *New York Herald Tribune* behind him, could fight bare-knuckled, using no educational advantage but referring only to pictures or stories that worked. When Yeatsman wanted to pitch a story he sometimes needed a few paragraphs about characters and plot wrinkles, but that morning he needed only four words to convince Mossy. "Madame Bovary. Palmyra Millevoix."

"Jesus Christ! That'll be our biggest picture in 1935. Maybe '36. It'll take time."

When Yeatsman was talking to young writers like me, he would tell us he preferred originals, but he knew his three thousand a week salary wasn't supported by screenplays he dreamed up. "I'll do a rewrite if I need to buy a car or put in a new kitchen," he said, "while an original will only pay for swimming pool repairs or minor renovations. A new house or a divorce requires the adaptation of a best seller." In a puckish mood he could twit his Irish idol, whose lines he'd garble. Yeats wouldn't have been amused, but Yancey once finished a drink in the commissary and said, "I must arise and go now, and go to the industry, the labile industry, a small garden of words to tend there as I type alone in the fee-loud glade."

Late morning, when two more writers burst in, it was because Colonel DeLight had been unable to pacify them. After weeks of struggle, separately, on two problematic scripts for which neither could find a solution, Sid Croft and Reggie Chatwynd had just discovered Mossy had put them both on the same story to see what each could make of it independently. Sid, a bluff Midwesterner, had written silents and their title cards, while Reggie was a radio playwright brought over from England because of what was supposedly a demand for literacy in talkies.

"So what's on your mind, gents?" Mossy said pleasantly.

"You know good and goddam well what's on our minds," said Sid.

"I asked Sid's help this morning with a plot point," Reggie said, "he asked my help with an enigmatic character, and we discovered—*mirabile dictu*—that you have us working on the same blasted script."

"Ah, this kind of thing happens," Mossy said as though consoling one for having fallen off a ladder, the other for a broken romance.

"It's not exactly a freak of nature," Reggie said. "You had a few names and details changed, gave us the same picture to write. Utterly dishonorable."

"You're a deceptive bastard," said Sid.

"Now wait a minute, boys. I thought I'd shorten the process, that's all. Sid, you're in the construction business, none better. Reggie, your dialogue's razor-sharp. You both like to work alone. Thought I'd take the best of what you both turn in and maybe have Jamie McPhatter touch it up."

"Keep that illiterate drunk off my work," Sid said. "Reggie, us together maybe?"

"Don't mind if I do, old boy."

Mossy smiled. "I'll never lie to you, boys," he lied, which he knew they knew. He'd deceived them, been found out, and talked his way around it until he got what he wanted in the first place. "Give me a weeper. Think of a rickety ladder—he climbs, he falls, he climbs back up—only this is about a girl who has to support her family. She—"

"She's a hooker," Sid interrupted.

"Don't interrupt me when I'm interrupting myself," Mossy said. "Actually, a hooker would have been fine before the Code. No, she's a, a, an assistant curator at a museum, everything's swell, she gets a promotion. Then she gets blinded in the accident, and I don't like the car crash so give me something else, I like fires. Life is hard but she's plucky. She lands a job—"

"As a radio announcer," Reggie broke in, remembering his earlier career.

"That's right," Mossy said. "They give her stuff in Braille, you'll figure it out. Loretta Young will be perfect. And the radio station owner falls in love with her."

The writers left, not only pacified but pleased. "He climbs, he falls, he climbs back up," Mossy said to Elena. "I'm never more truthful than when I'm lying."

In these salad days, Mossy would rule by force, by truth, by guile, by lies, whatever weapon was at hand. Though he manipulated, he was not as manipulative as he was instinctual. Others planned their moves rigorously. Mossy simply, naturally moved and lured and struck by pure instinct, the hunter-gatherer-warrior habit. He seemed to be without intent, operating by reflex. His reflexes were as full of decision and direction as the deliberations of the most devious and sinister general or archbishop or foreign minister, each of whom he could impersonate depending on what the moment called for. Yet Mossy himself was not sinister unless we say that specialty is what evolution provided a bee. He stung or provided nutrition, but he acted without malice, from involuntary hunch, to protect Jubilee, promote his interests, to escape when he had to, win when he had any kind of advantage and often when he had none.

Enter the fair Palmyra herself, answering a summons. "Ah, this is Adrian at his best," Mossy complimented the reigning Hollywood dress designer rather than Pammy herself as he greeted his biggest female star. "Casual in the crushed velvet slacks, yet seductive above in the V-neck."

"Flattery will get you anywhere and no doubt does," Pammy said, refusing to sit down. "Leave Brenda De Baule alone. She's a nice kid."

"A nice kid she's not. I only called her for lunch. See if I could do something."

"You already have. What do you want now?"

Photoplay had a contest, and Pammy, with her electric compound of sexiness and wholesomeness was voted the star men most desired and women most admired in 1933. Her attributes projected well onto Mossy this morning, and he had trouble staying on his side of the desk. For her part, as she confided to Teresa Blackburn, Pammy wanted to stay as far as possible from Mossy and was ready to uppercut him if he put a hand on her blouse's sleeve that she already resented his having identified as one of Adrian's.

"I can get Cukor for exactly two days to reshoot a couple of sequences," Mossy said. "Don't argue. When you do your first cute meet with Freddy March, it's too much. The two of you look like you're ready to jump each other. You're scheming and he's scheming, fine, but you're also suspicious. You need to do that suspicious look you do so well you should get a patent on it."

"You're too kind," Pammy said, emphasizing her mock by blinking her lashes rapidly, "but I never allow my producers to get personal. Mr. Cukor and I will work it out, thank you." She whirled, gave a slight wiggle at Mossy, and clicked her heels.

Mossy called after her. "Hold on, I got a problem."

Without waiting for Pammy to turn around, Mossy described a conflict with Orville Wright. "He don't want a girlfriend," Mossy said, descending into his Bronx vernacular. "He gave us permission to do the picture, now he's balking. The script and I say he's gotta have a girlfriend waiting for him to make the first flight and come down safe. He says no, and he won't let Wilbur have one either. Wilbur's dead over twenty years and his brother still won't let him have a girl. Will you talk to him when he comes out tomorrow, turn on some charm, tell him how honored you are to meet him, ect ect."

"He's obviously too smart to fall for a petticoat display. It's an insult to his dignity. And mine. I have to get back to the set. Go fish."

The two henchmen Seaton Hackley and Curtt Weigerer were in with the news that an actor had died on Stage 11 while the camera was rolling. A character actor with a genius for gesture who had once been prominent on the stage, Burns McElroy, was shooting a scene when he collapsed. "It's a great scene," said Hackley. "Imagine the publicity," said Weigerer.

"Imagine nothing, you heartless punks," Mossy said. "Realism yes, reality no. Nobody wants to see actual death. Don't develop the film or someone will pass it around as a stunt. Studio pays for the funeral, send Addie McElroy flowers. Have Owen Jant compose a note. What else?"

"Boyd Drasnin lost twenty two thousand last night," Hackley said, "playing poker with some sharpie down from Seattle. Boyd wants an advance."

"We don't give advances to producers. And hush this. Public don't want to hear about big Jew producers so rich they can drop that kind of dough and not feel it."

"Boyd feels it. He's over in his office throwing up," Curtt Weigerer said.

"Probably a hangover. He lost my sympathy when he left his wife who's worth ten of Drasnin who made us that turkey about southern belles in the foreign legion."

By now Felix Le Beau, a short director with a long cigar, had rushed in from Stage 11. He'd been directing the scene when Burns McElroy died. "Doc Lewiston pronounces him dead," Le Beau said, "and I figure there's nothing to do until the mortuary guys arrive so we shoot the rest of the scene, where Burns has no lines but he's still on camera in his chair. We prop him up and his eyes are still open and we finish the scene where his son-in-law tells him he's got to change his will. We're on a two shot favoring McElroy see, and suddenly his left eye closes—not a wink but a dismissal, he's completely shutting out his son-in-law, even better than we had it in the script. I can't believe my luck and yell Cut! at the top of my lungs which is hardly necessary but I'm so thrilled to see Burns has upstaged the villainous son-in-law."

"Dead, Burns McElroy steals his last scene. Is that what you're telling me?"

"Exactly," Felix Le Beau said. "It'll cut like butter."

"You win the compassion Oscar, Liebowitz. Get back to your set."

When Le Beau, who hadn't been Liebowitz since high school, had gone, Hackley reminded Mossy that he said he couldn't use the death on camera.

"A good scene's a good scene," Mossy said.

Petitioners arrived and departed like trains. But not me: I waited fussily in the writers building. The morning had begun irritatingly in the brutal sewing machine room, yet the day was full of promise in terms of my *Dolls House* treatment. I'd be knighted or maybe just patted on the back. I was tired of being patronized.

"I'm labor," Mossy told a director he had just replaced before the director had shot a single scene. "New York is capital. I'm with you guys, never forget it." A writer begged Mossy for a chance to direct, have control over his material as it jumped off the page into the camera. "You're already an architect," Mossy told him, "why the hell would you want to become a carpenter?"

Mossy told a producer bragging about his film that what Jubilee turned out was no less a team effort than the temples of India or the cathedrals of France. If the earliest motion pictures were projections of the filmer's dreams, by 1934 most of the dreams were shadows not of individual imagination but of institutional fantasy, shadows of the country's wishes and fears. The studio did not have the final cut; it *was* the final cut.

At almost noon that morning Mossy issued what became known as the Santa Barbara Proclamation. He was occupied firing the immense Luther Chambliss, a two thousand a week writer whose weight was said to be about one third his salary and a man given to bombast. "You knew there was a problem in the first draft, Luther," Mossy said.

"Oh but that's what I've clearly solved," Luther said. "When I changed the—"

"Oh but you clearly haven't," Mossy told him. "It's as plain to anyone in the story department as it is to me. We'll solve it in the next draft, writers tell me. We go through other drafts, two more sets of writers, the problem still exists. No one really likes the lead or in this case believes he has the balls to get rid of the crime syndicate running your small town. We make him police chief, or the D.A., we still don't believe him. We give him a girlfriend, but that doesn't help either. So we say—and I've traveled this road before—we'll solve this when we have a director. He sees the problem, too, but he wants to get going and he says we'll solve that on the set. The star says his character is weak, but we only have him six weeks and he tells me we'll solve that in rehearsal, the other actors will help. Then we say we'll solve it in production itself, the shooting will iron that out. We see the problem again in the rushes, and it's like a toothache, but we say, okay, that's what editing is for, we'll kill this shit-covered beast in the cutting room. Yeah. Next fucking thing you know, we're in a first preview in Santa Barbara, and there it is maybe thirty feet wide now and twenty feet high, bigger than any living thing, the same problem, tapping you on the shoulder saying, Hey, remember me, I'm still here. So, Luther, take your lard ass off my lot and into a steam room, you're done at Jubilee. I'm going to solve this problem or I'm not going to make the picture."

"But why," Luther Chambliss stammered, "why, why—"

Mossy silenced him with a look of contempt, his eyes shining as if through the visor of a helmet. "Why? Because it rhymes with I. Meeting over."

Simple enough, if savage, when he held all the cards, though even when he didn't Mossy could still prevail.

When confronted, having run out of lies and strategy, he would equate the studio with himself. "Jubilee, c'est moi," he had said when Pammy cornered him with a ruse he pulled on Teresa Blackburn, sending her on loan to Paramount to duck a promise to cast her as Joan of Arc because he had decided he'd try to pry Irene Dunne from Columbia instead. "This is better for Jubilee, which is better for me," he told Pammy, "which in the end is better for everyone who works here including Teresa herself."

At the stroke of noon, Nils Maynard leaned in indignantly to say that April Devereau had stormed off his set screaming that Mossy had ruined her marriage and she'd be damned if she'd make another picture for him. Nils blamed Mossy for this because he'd seduced Devereau while she was, all Hollywood thought, relatively happily married to the publicist Tam Kilpatrick. Devereau had been the fourth most popular female star, according to *Photoplay*, for two years in a row, and getting her in a picture was a coup for Jubilee. "More important than adding a notch to your gun," Nils fumed at Mossy. Mossy's eyes shone more brightly as he opened the visor a half inch and prepared his counter. "Calm down," he said to his director, "this is trivial." He buzzed Elena. "Get me Miss Devereau in her bungalow." Mossy took the offensive immediately. "April, damnit honey, you have a problem you come to me with it, you know you can. Remember the head waiter in Monterey when your veal chop was overdone? 'Ennysing za matter mam'selle, I weel take care.' Heh heh, we fixed that, didn't we? Don't close down a whole set, honey … yes, he's here, he's wild about your performance, we all are, but you're keeping forty-two people from doing their jobs right now … I'll be over to see you after lunch … There's a good trooper." He hung up. "*Voilà, monsieur,*" said Nils. "Your words, not mine," said Mossy. Nils vanished back to his set.

At last, just past noon, Comfort O'Hollie, secretary for writers who didn't rate individual secretaries, came in with my summons to the front office. Be there in ten minutes. I started to shake. By this time I was truly uneasy—I seldom had the confidence nature gave a titmouse—and Comfort gave me the locker-room pep talk. "The more challenge, the more courage," she told me. "As me grandmother, the infamous rabble-rouser says, believe it and you can achieve it." I tried to compose myself. She socked my shoulder. "Get a grip."

I looked at her, wishing I were her male equivalent. Comfort sparkled, with black eyes and red hair both glowing, so young, only about eighteen, that writers' protective instincts generally eclipsed their lust. "What makes you so brave?" I asked.

"Me Da was in the Irish Republican forces"—newly arrived, Comfort said *farces*—"when the Troubles began in '16, at which point in history me Ma was preggers to burst. The bloody British trapped me Da in a barn with his little band of fighters. They'd been delivering leaflets mostly, complaining about the treatment of the Irish, except for one little explosion at a train station that harmed nobody, so the story went. 'Everyone out!' the English lieutenant yelled, 'Everyone out and no one gets hurt.' No one moved a hair. The bastards threw in gas and the fighters began to choke. They put wet socks over their mouths and didn't budge. 'Out, out!' the lieutenant yelled again, 'and no one will be molested.' The British knew me Da was the leader of his brave boys. Finally, the lieutenant shouted into the barn, 'Come forth, O'Hollie, and the rest of your lads can go home. Come forth O'Hollie, come forth now!' So me trusting Da, wanting his boys to return to their loved ones, did come forth, or come fort' as we say. They blasted him to Heaven right there. 'Come fort' O'Hollie' became a rallying cry, and they even yelled it at the funeral. The patriot who cut the throat of the lieutenant outside a pub yelled it again. I'm born three weeks later. Never had a father, but I did get me name from him."

Comfort's grandmother, emboldened by her son's martyrdom, had emigrated to Vancouver and ranged the Pacific northwest as a labor organizer, trying to unionize everyone who turned a screw or lifted a bale. An uncle was a grip on Westerns and had sent for Comfort. Grandmother O'Hollie became a legend among workers, and Comfort was trying to get her to come to Hollywood. "Buck up at battalion headquarters, Corporal Jant," she said to me now. "Not an inch, don't give an inch." She socked my shoulder again and saluted.

Bolstered, I almost danced through the lot to the executive building. I'd landed my first big fish after three years, and all I had to do was reel it in. *A Doll's House* was to be *my* house. "Hey kid," I heard myself called across the company street, "got me a part?" I looked up and saw someone who was all grin and ears, recognizing the wispy mustache and laughing eyes of Clark Gable, strolling from his set with gruff distinguished Walter Pidgeon, who nodded to me as though I weren't quite invisible.

"Sure, Clark, have it this afternoon," I managed. He'd be awful as Torvald, no one would believe a woman could leave him, and he'd be playing a stuffed shirt for laughs. Pidgeon, though, was too stiff; a shirt can be *too* stuffed. Well, maybe Pidgeon. The two were on brief loan from Metro, and Gable had just finished another loan to Columbia where he had shot *It Happened One Night* with Capra. No one in town was hotter than Gable, whom I'd met for a moment in the commissary the week before. Had he heard I was hot, too? Visions of glory clouded my eyesight.

The sight of Percy Shumway was never a consoling one to a writer approaching an audience with his majesty. Shumway was known for battering screenwriters with glib analogies to English novelists or playwrights solely for the purpose of putting them down. He always found a corner to sit in, an apparition wearing his permanent look of derision. Still, I thought possibly Shumway had been in Mossy's previous appointment and was just leaving or even that he might have a helpful pointer or two about Ibsen. He had, after all, read literature at Oxford with I. A. Richards. So he claimed.

The other person in the office was Jack Grader, a former football player, friendly in his way, but his job was basically to evaluate everything at the studio, including scripts, actors, performances, previews, directors, set decoration, budgets, cutters and cutting machines, virtually every element that went into the making of movies, including the finished pictures themselves. He substituted ranking for all other relationships to people and objects. That is only a fourth-rate gambler, he would say of a character on a Mississippi riverboat, where we need at least a second-rater. And the change would be made. What I saw when I entered the throne room, then, was the king with two of his more efficient hangmen.

I decided to maintain my optimism with a breezy "Hi Chief," and a cheerful "Glad to see you, Percy, Jack," trying to look confident and ready for my *Doll's House* praise. I'd thought I might even get to be assistant producer on the picture. At Mossy's first words, my young face must have exhibited the look you have when your elbow has accidentally hit hard against a piece of metal or concrete and before the full pain has shot through your arm but you know it's on its way.

"Don't trust your instincts." That was what I heard first, or thought I did, but I later decided that what Mossy may have said was, "You don't trust your instincts, only approval." And then he said, "So trust mine." He didn't say whether he meant his instincts or his approval, but they amounted to the same thing.

"You're off *A Doll's House*," he said next.

"But how ... everyone said I did a fine ... I don't understand." Mossy's words so bewildered me I had no idea where to go.

"To begin with, I hate the new title," he said. "*She's a Doll*. It disgusts me."

"Title is Lidowitz," I tattled, not daring to call him Littlewits.

"I don't load my mind with details," Mossy said. "The story has lost its bite, meanders toward a hopefulness that hasn't earned its keep."

"I thought you wanted an up-ending. Why did Seaton Hackley praise—?

"It's not just the ending. Look, I make pictures with intelligence and taste, but it don't hurt if there's a booby or two in them. Nora's got negative sex appeal here."

"Our GBS did all this so much more strikingly well," Percy Shumway butted in to support his boss, "if what one wants is sort of Woman Independent, you know."

"I'm afraid," said Jack Grader, a mannerly hangman, "that what we have is a fifth-rate husband when what we need is solid third- or perhaps even second-rate."

Shumway enlightened me further. "Now don't you see what Shaw gave us in *Man and Superman* was an absolutely spot-on Life Force in Ann Whitefield, while Jack Tanner essentially doesn't know what hit him."

"Nora's quandary seems second-rate, Owen," said Grader, piling on after the whistle had blown. "We need a first-rate dilemma to get a top-rank actress opposite a Torvald, or Tom as we call him, who's worthy of both her affection and desertion."

"You have contempt for Lidowitz, you think he's a subnormal," said Mossy and I winced. How could he tell? I thought Lidowitz a fumbling imbecile. "I want Lidowitz supervising the picture so I'm putting Gravier and Stallworth on the script."

Hacks! I didn't dare say because I wanted a job and because, after all, what was I in training to become myself? Hacks! (I didn't dare repeat.) Who can barely spell their goddamn names much less write a drama much less lick Ibsen's boots. "Good luck to the Bobs," I finally said weakly, since my replacements had one first name between them. (Question: since Gravier and Stallworth quickly turned the screenplay into a comedy, *The Doll Gets the House*, who did Ibsen hate most as he writhed in his grave—Gravier and Stallworth because they guillotined *A Doll's House*, or me because I had it rolling on the tumbrels?) I was crushed, and I guess it showed on my face.

"Now never mind this, young fellow," said Mossy, who had never called me that before. "This is nothing in the long run."

"I eat in the short run," I said, drowning in self-pity.

"Oh for Christ's sake, Owen, I'm not canning you off the lot, just off the picture. My audience in Squirtville's gotta love my pictures, and they're not gonna love this one the way you outlined it, that's all. I have something else for you, much bigger, I'll tell you about it later. For now, get over to publicity. Stanny needs help."

As I was leaving, sentenced to menial press agentry, my last glimpse of my firing squad a mezzotint of their death masks, Elena came in with an elegant bouquet that she carried like a baby. "Here they are,

Mr. Z," she said with more formality than I'd ever heard her use. "Fit for a king, or at least a prince. Empress Joséphine roses." She placed the aristocrats on Mossy's desk.

Hitting the company street, I imagined my life unhappening, unspooling backward in the projector all the way to my mother, trying to find where, had I turned in the other direction, this disaster wouldn't have happened. *My* audience in Squirtville? An audience he had decided he owned and I couldn't reach. Stung badly, I wondered what might have become of me if Mossy had loved my treatment. But he hadn't; I was the subnormal now, not Littlewits, who was only playing the game he'd been taught.

If Gable saw me now, just minutes since we'd passed on the lot before my garroting by Mossy and his accomplices, would he already know to ignore me, intuiting through the ether that I was no longer the fair-haired boy but back to being the office boy? I'd lost altitude so fast I was without hope of the fame or glamour, granted that screenwriters shared only derivatively in these, that sustained the town. Cheerless, I mused.

"Don't meddle with Mossy on a bad day," Yeatsman was fond of saying, "because he'll make yours worse." He made me feel I'd let him, the studio, the entire cinesphere, down. The contradiction was he could be gentle, though when he was I always suspected a purpose. On the rare occasions when he was in a true panic—a picture was going down the chute to oblivion, an actor he needed was stolen by Mayer or Harry Cohn, New York was advancing on him like Birnam Wood to Dunsinane—I found him nimble. He called New York Bigtime when it loved him, Ostrichtown when it didn't.

The essence of Mossy and the other studio heads was they were able to put their ideas into forms as communicable as diseases. Once the audience caught the illness—sex, crime, romance, comedy, ridiculing the rich, sinners seeking redemption—there was no cure. No cow would ever be sacred anymore. In the Hollywood mirror every image cracked, every precept taught by the schoolmaster and the parson was twisted into a laugh, a pant or a scream. The actors and their environment generally sold beauty and perfection. When the audience left the theater, Poor Jim Bicker lectured me, they'd have surface satisfaction but deeper discontent. From the discontent, according to Bicker, would grow and spring and march a country so aggressive that nothing short of planetary dominion could satisfy its masses.

As for what animated Mossy and the other bosses, they were suing for damages. Most of the early tycoons had cruel, unsuccessful, weak fathers. In the Zangwill family, the tyrannical yet irresponsible father ran off when Mossy was eleven. They never heard from him. Mossy blamed his father but also hungered after him, finding his mother a negligible person who was both pathetic and deserving of her abandonment.

Craving salvation through power, Mossy created an institution in which everyone else was stacked, ascending blocks in a pyramid, to support the great stone at the top. In this structure it was not uncommon for a writer's ideas to strike Mossy as his own. That was what I'd been vainly hoping for myself in *A Doll's House*; he'd like my take on the classic so much he'd think it was his own. Fundamentally, our ideas were his not only in the sense that he owned what was done at his studio but also in the more psychologically compromised sense that writers spent their time and brain muscle in attempts to mimic his taste and sensibility, to become Mossy himself, internalizing him in order to sell him their version of a picture they hoped he wanted made. The effect this had on a writer was that he was invited to negate his identity, a recipe for developing terminal contempt for oneself. A few resisted. Yeatsman would fight with Mossy; weaker souls plunged into despair for hanging on to a salary they had become addicted to.

As though they existed in a pre-Copernican universe that revolved around them, Hollywood executives turned distortions into new realities. Mossy once asked Yeatsman and Tutor Beedleman for a suspenseful thriller that was also a goofball comedy with heartless villains. Miraculously, they complied. This became *The Producer's Party*, about Hollywood itself, and the portrait of executives made all the studio heads in town squirm until they heard the audience roaring. They knew they were being wickedly ridiculed, but it was happening entertainingly, profitably, and since they were all such narcissists anyway they were happy to see the reflection of themselves no matter how absurd, even loathsome. Ridiculous men the lot of them, but they knew what they wanted.

While I, demonstrably, did not. Slouching toward exile in publicity, I wandered the lot miserably. Somewhere two roads had diverged, and I'd taken the wrong fork.

With admirable timing, Frederic March strolled by me in the company street, chatting amiably with the writer Edwin Justis Mayer, another of the rare breed who would stand up to Mossy. Not a wave or nod from either one of them. Had Mossy sent telegrams to everyone on the lot to ignore me? It was in the air: I was a nobody again.

12

Purgatory

F airy tales, that's the business I'm in," said Stanny Poule, head of the department, when I reported to Publicity. He was middle-aged, grew a brush mustache, and with his green eyeshade and black cord above the elbow on his striped shirt, he could have been an editor on any big-city daily. He liked to remind newcomers, and himself, he'd had a life prior to Jubilee. "I was an honest reporter once, St. Louis, and now I've graduated to being Hans Christian Andersen. If I see a star who isn't leading a storybook life, I give him one, or make her sound like a novitiate in a convent when in reality—which we don't like around here—she's just had an abortion."

The Publicity Department was a long low-slung building conveniently next to the commissary, which made it easy for press agents to take stars to lunch with outside reporters as a way of keeping the reporters off the sets, where they might see something unpleasant. The department was run like a newspaper, with its own reporters, copy editors, and a virtual city room. But it was also not like a newspaper because the only job of anyone there was to put the best face on everything and to tell no truth unless it happened to produce higher wattage for a given star or the studio itself.

"What I need you to do, Owen," Stanny Poule told me, "is to write me quick bios of Amy Blaine and Billy Steerforth. I got no one to put on this so I asked the boss for help, hope you don't mind."

Of course, I did mind a lot, but it wasn't Stanny's fault. Blaine and Steerforth were young contract actors Mossy hoped would become first leads. They were both pretty boring, and I thought maybe I could confect a romance.

Those who worked in Publicity tended to know a good deal of studio dirt, star dirt (as opposed to the more sanguine star dust), because they were so often called on to hide the truth and had to know what they were disguising. Stargazers themselves, they tried to remain intimates of the stars, which they could do so long as they knew their place as satellites. In the case of Blaine and Steerforth, they were so ordinary there wasn't even dirt on them.

Another publicist, Ned Thoms, a gentle idealist on the tortuous path to becoming a moody cynic, came in with a problem. Ned was the eleventh in a family of eleven, taught from an early age that his own life was of no interest to anyone, so it came naturally to him to publicize the lives of others. "Hugh Astor wants to quit," he said.

Astor was no star but a reliable leading man with his own fan club. He'd been a North Dakota boy whose name was changed from Borko Lukenbrot. He'd never been comfortable with his new identity. "What picture does he want out of?" I asked.

"No, I mean walk off the lot, out of the industry," Ned said. "Go back home."

Hugh Astor was running into the wall many actors hit. What hurt them most was the impersonalization of their personalities. For those who had thought they might have stage careers, the parts they were asked to play in pictures seemed silly to them. Instead of walking through these roles, adding just the right eyebrow arch here and smirk there, they began to overact, to trust neither the camera nor the director. In such cases the camera became their stalker instead of their partner. Very occasionally one would say Goodbye Hollywood, I'm gone. And actually become Borko Lukenbrot again.

Most stuck around town complaining. "What Jubilee wants me to do is not what I became an actor to do," they'd say. One day an actor would realize it had been months since he was offered a picture, a year and a half since his last choice role, and he saw they were no longer tailoring material to his strengths. Publicity was still sending over fan letters, getting his name into columns, having him cut ribbons at supermarket openings. He'd wind up his ego and go see Mossy. If Mossy wanted the actor he would plead, even go down on one knee (he hadn't an ounce of pride if he wanted someone) as if he were proposing, which in a way he was. If he didn't want you he'd say, "Gee we're going to miss you" when what you'd counted on was, "I can't live without you." After that an actor couldn't get an appointment with Ned Thoms, much less Stanny Poule.

"Get a delegation from Astor's fan club to come tell him how much they need him," Stanny told Ned. "They plead with him to stay in pictures. That should do it."

Mossy kept an occasional derelict in Publicity like Mickey Siskind, who had written title cards for silent movies and was a charming raconteur until he was too drunk. Mickey had once saved Mossy from being fired for going overbudget at a Poverty Row studio by writing an amusing short that made use of Mossy's outtakes in another picture. After Mickey began conversations with reporters by calling promiscuous leading ladies sluts and their male counterparts whoremongers, Stanny wanted to fire him. He knew Mossy wouldn't allow it, so he reduced the old screenwriter to a planter. Planters would call up select reporters and columnists and try to get them to print mere items, not even stories. Columnists remembered when he had been the high-priced Mickey Siskind ten years earlier and would often print the squib for old time's sake. Things like it's William Powell's anniversary and his wife wants everyone to know their union is stronger than ever. This after he'd been seen three nights in a row at the Cocoanut Grove with Jean Harlow. Mickey could still do that pretty well in 1934.

If a subtler plant were called for, Stanny would do it himself. He called Louella, for instance, when Jubilee wanted to discipline Pammy for trying to have *Mind Your Own Business* rewritten after shooting had begun. This led to a blind-item warning in the Parsons column that a certain female star was getting too big for her bodice at Jubilee and had best mind her p's and q's or else she could find herself back in Hitlerland. A cunning reminder that Pammy might have a checkered past available for exploitation by an unfriendly columnist. In this case it didn't work, and Mossy ordered a rewrite when Pammy threatened to call Louella herself and invite her to the *Mind Your Own Business* set, which was in complete disarray with a first-time director from the New York theater.

The powerful columnists, especially Louella and Hedda Hopper, were regarded with a mixture of shrewdness, fear, and hate; like the gods, they had to be propitiated. The columnists, as representatives of the public, fawned on the idols, and then hacked away at their feet to find out if they were clay—and if the feet were flesh, this naturally hurt. They always blamed their readers when talking to the stars: I hate to ask you this, Hedda would say, but your millions of fans are dying to know—are you leaving your husband/wife? Is it true you've been seeing Tracy/Stanwyck? Did you check into that desert clinic for a touchy operation/drying out/nervous breakdown? The stars were allowed to be beautiful and rich as long as they said they wished they could lead lives just like the miserable rest of us, thereby mollifying their fans' jealousy and eerie rage.

The cooperative stars were all seen to be leading their fairy tale lives, courtesy of Publicity, even in the face of tragedy. When Loretta Young's aunt lost the baby Loretta wanted for her own she was so brave she took a day off to fly east for the funeral even though she herself was deathly afraid of airplanes. Thus spake Hedda Hopper. Babies die, favorite uncles are killed by trains, parents separate, if nothing else is going on a beloved schnauzer goes off to the kennel in the sky, while the star remains steadfast.

In a publicity gimmick, Mossy was photographed handing the keys to a new Cadillac to Venetia Stackpole as the starlet's birthday present from her generous studio. It was Stanny Poule, asserting the Adamic prerogative that Mossy occasionally yielded, who came up with the starlet's name, which had originally been Bronislawa Klenkowski. "Your new name preserves your family's roots," Stanny told her without explanation. As soon as the press had its story, a studio guard whisked the Cadillac away from Venetia. Since the studio had paid both for Venetia's abortion and for a genuinely for-keeps car to give the gas station attendant who had caused the pregnancy (only a Pontiac though), Venetia felt she was in handcuffs. She complained to Mossy when Stanny had her anointed Miss Dam Site and arranged for her to open the sluice gates at an Oregon waterway.

"Here's what we do around here, Miss Stackpole," Mossy told her. "We make a Who? into a Wow! Any complaints?"

"No, sir."

"Then don't let me hear any beefs about how we do it. Now get." Mossy treated the Polish girl the way Germans treated Poles in those days.

"So the whole thing is a business of falseness?" Venetia asked the considerably more studio-wise Pammy.

"And of truth," Pammy replied, "sometimes definitely a business of truth."

The publicity for a new star was so blatant that at first everyone laughed about it, including the rising star. After that the star became aw-shucks modest, but he saw how the public adored him and began to think there might be something to it. Next he saw people at the studio and around town in awe of him, and finally he became so impossible no one could approach him without praise. Or her. Worse, the publicity departments, which had started the whole ball rolling, ended by believing their own words. Mossy made a specialty of knowing how to deal with stars, but even he admitted the publicity apparatus reminded him of Victor Frankenstein's laboratory. "The story of the stars," he said, "is one third soap opera, one third Greek tragedy, and one third madcap comedy."

One fan worked an entire year on a dollhouse for Pammy's putative little sister. Some of the press guessed that Millie was Pammy's daughter, but Stanny Poule had kept the fiction that Millie Millevoix was a sister. With the public becoming more suspicious, that was the story I'd changed the year before, the last time Mossy had ordered me into Publicity, by confecting the tale of a race car driver dying in his Bugatti at Le Mans, leaving his distraught widow and infant child.

As innocent as he wanted Pammy in life, Mossy had still put her into an early Jezebel role, a scheming housewife, almost Bovary-like but living in Indiana. "SHE'S A TWELVE O'CLOCK WOMAN IN A NINE O'CLOCK TOWN," the poster blared, and everyone went to the picture, which was called *Fallen Grace*. The poster showed Pammy's negligee coming down off her shoulder, a scene not actually in the movie but carefully retouched into something risqué by the advertising department. This couldn't have been done in the Code-run prudish world that 1934 ushered in, but it had been just the ticket in 1932.

"All right," Stanny Poule said to me. "Go see Blaine and Steerforth and write me quick cock-and-bulls of glory about the would-be somebodies so I can pitch blurbs to AP, UP, Reuters. "They'll like you because you show interest in the humdrum lives of the proletariat before they come here to have us make monsters of them."

The department lush Mickey Siskind ambled over to me, his eyes not yet rheumy as they'd be in the late afternoon, though he hadn't bothered to shave. "You can make Blaine and Steerforth into Pickford and Fairbanks," he said, a little wobbly and with his sour breath sweetened by rum. I nodded unenthusiastically and began to move off. "No, listen." He grabbed my tie. "A city built on fantasy is where everything is true, nothing is factual, see? Today's hero is tomorrow's figure of scorn. In Hollywood every worm turns. You're crazy about someone or something? Wait and worry. They'll collapse on you. Only thing you can do is put whatever you love or fear into a picture. At least you'll have a record of that."

"Then you have some records of your own, Mickey," I said to cheer him up.

"The hell with you," he said and shuffled off.

When he was still sober part of the time, Mickey Siskind had been assigned the original publicity of how Palmyra Millevoix came to Jubilee. Mr. Zangwill, so the press release went, was in a story conference in 1931 trying to move a writer and producer off dead center on a script about a pair of doctors married to each other, treating malaria in the tropics where there was also a smuggler the wife becomes involved with. Seaton Hackley was in the room too. "But who will we get to play the woman?" Zangwill said, according to Mickey Siskind's release. "I like that kid Bette Davis. She's got spunk."

"Laemmle won't let her go," the producer said.

"Crawford then."

"Same with Mayer."

"Stanwyck."

"After *Ladies of Leisure*, Columbia won't let anyone else touch her."

"All right, geniuses," said Zangwill, throwing up his arms, "now I know who I can't get. Who can I get who will lift this part from notable to unforgettable?"

The screenwriter spoke up. "Chief, you know who's a little like Davis but sexier, something like Stanwyck but not so nasty, a little like Garbo but less foreign yet still Continental, tough like Kate Hepburn but smoother, sultry like Harlow but smarter?"

"Stop being a press agent," said Zangwill. "Who are you talking about?"

"Palmyra Millevoix."

"Who? Change her name."

"Already been tried," said the producer. "She won't."

"What I'm saying," the writer continued, "is she's got everything those others have, only more because she's got her own charge of electricity."

"Let me meet her," said the studio chief. "Palmyra Millevoix."

When he saw her early rushes, Zangwill said it was beginning to look as though the screenwriter had a point.

This was the gist of the press release the studio sent out when Pammy's first Jubilee picture opened. Nowhere did Siskind mention that the screenwriter in the meeting was Yancey Ballard. Yeatsman didn't mind. He said the planets exist only to make the sun brighter anyway, and his magnitude compared to Mossy's was approximately that of Pluto.

Stanny Poule's phone rang. It was Mossy telling him about Trent Amberlyn's arrest. Stanny took a couple of notes and said, "Huh, I guess I shouldn't be surprised." Then he swung right into Mossy's own Bronx patter. "Got it. It don't happen till I say it happened, and when I say it happened it ain't ever gonna happen again." He changed his vocal pitch. "Mr. Amberlyn, who was doing research for a part in a picture, is shocked at the invasion of privacy but will decline to sue the

Los Angeles Police Department on the grounds that these brave men risk their lives every day for the sake of the community ... No? Okay, Mossy, I won't put out anything at this point."

Ned Thoms picked up his phone and listened. It was Pammy. She had apparently decided to complain about the gruesome package we had opened at Red Woods. This was too hot for Ned and he handed the phone to Stanny. "That's awful, dear, just awful," Stanny said, "You can't even count the freaks out there ... You want me to do what? For-get about that, Pam, even if I'd issue such a press release asking the public to leave you and Millie alone Mr. Zangwill would kill it ... No, you're a very fortunate woman but you have to pay some costs. I'm surprised someone as smart as you thinks you can clamp down ... No, you're *not* entitled. Listen to me, Miss Millevoix, you're a piece of property everyone likes to look at and you're fricasseed chicken if you start to think otherwise."

On the way to the commissary I had to detour to deliver a publicity release to a big star on loan to Jubilee. I heard music from inside her trailer, which seemed to be moving a little, oddly rocking. When I knocked and heard no answer I decided she was in the shower, so I carefully let myself into the trailer to drop off the release for her approval. A curtain separated the entrance from the trailer's main room. The record was piping a song from *No No Nanette*—"Tea for Two," I think—and I could see on the other side of the curtain that someone was on top of the star, who was naked. When he turned his head to the side, I saw he was an equally big star. I can't mention their names even today because of course they left the relationship, if it was that, out of their decorous autobiographies, and one of them has a prominent grandson who runs a studio. But what a fuck they were having. Olympian. The room was steamy, sweat flew from the little day-bed. Laughter, panting, shrieks. I didn't want to hear; I heard. I didn't want to peek; I peeked. Her nipples were the size of thimbles. I remembered someone in Publicity saying she had the boobs that launched a thousand quips. I turned away. At last she lay there, as he did, spent. I didn't know what to do—leave the press release and run, sneak out with the pages and pretend I was never there, go out and knock again? The record was still playing loudly. I crouched like an idiot behind the curtain, an idiot whose career was about to end before it had gone anywhere. At length the man spoke. "Oh my lord," he said, "but that was a good take." "Uh huh," the woman said, "one more time for the close-up." As they began again and trumpets announced Helen Gallagher singing "Too Many Rings Around Rosie" from *No, No Nanette*, I stealthily slipped out the door and shoved the press release underneath. The trailer was rocking again.

I ran to the commissary.

The atmosphere there was jovial, a little compound of high-style cafeteria and grandstand where you stared at the Thoroughbreds. At a producers' table the conversation veered to the pluck of one man who had a property all the others admired. "Yes," the man said, "but I don't know what to do with the heroine's best friend because in the book she's a lesbian." "Oh, that's no problem," said one of the others. "In the picture just make her an Austrian."

Sitting next to me at the writers' table, Yeatsman overheard this exchange and muttered to me, "Hearts will be broken with solutions like that, and they won't be the hearts of producers. It was easier out here when writers could just compose title cards like 'She was cool in a crisis and warm in a taxi.'"

As I was leaving the commissary I bumped into the actor and actress from the trailer. They entered laughing. No touching now, just a conspiratorial glance between them. I stood at the cash register paying for my lunch as the two stars paused to bask in the recognition they were receiving from the rest of the diners who mostly pretended not to notice them and raised their voices to prove it. The man had outfitted himself in a double breasted powder blue silk shantung jacket and ascot, checked slacks, and brown and white shoes. The woman was costumed in an ecru suit and matching little ecru felt beret, with a playful stem sticking up about as much as, twenty or so minutes earlier, her nipples had stood out from her chest. Carrying a doeskin purse with a gold clasp, she was all lady. Her shoes almost matched his, brown and white pumps. She said to him while they waited for the hostess to seat them, "For a fellow you have the best ass."

Colonel DeLight wanted a junior writer to test typewriters and make a selection among the Royals and Coronas and Underwoods so

GIRL of MY DREAMS

he could give all his charges new tools to work with. It was humiliating but since I'd just been fired off a script, which he obviously knew—"If you ain't too busy, boy, I'd like to have your opinion on some typing machines over to the stationers"—I didn't see I had any choice.

As I drove off the lot the crowd of seekers was as large as ever. Extras were milling nervously. To get through the dispossessed throng I had to crawl slowly in my car. "I have an act George Jessel loved." "Don't they have anything for twins?" "I been building muscles down at the beach, I know I can do one of the Apeman's pals." Nobodies from Moline come west to make their last stand with their backs to the ocean. One of the scrawny kids ventured to my window, "Hey mister, are you somebody?"

"No," I said and sped away.

13

A Life in the Day
PART II: AFTERNOON

Answer: God remains on location.

A little after two o'clock, Yeatsman sat in Mossy's easy chair, deep leather with bronze studs, mulling what he was going to do with *Madame Bovary*. Mossy was not yet back from lunch with Brenda De Baule. When the studio head was out, his office was the quietest spot on the lot, far more private than Yeatsman's own office in the teeming writers building among his harried colleagues always looking for advice or solace.

As a familiar, perhaps the only familiar in Mossy's employ, Yeatsman could use the space for contemplation that many others regarded as a potential torture chamber. In order for it to be transposed to film, any novel had to be stripped, flayed to its bones. Yeatsman wanted to leave out the Bovary background and begin in the convent.

The young farm girl Emma, instead of having her world squelched by life in a nunnery, has her horizons broadened by reading. Millevoix was said not to have liked her own convent, Yeatsman thinks, but she'll love this one, plus looking like a teenager again. Emma devours *La*

Chanson de Roland, Ivanhoe, Joan of Arc. She is chastised, the books confiscated, all but the Bible, where she finds the perfect romance of Adam and Eve. The heroic Crusades and great love stories animate the young girl so much the Mother Superior has her removed from the convent. Back on the farm milking cows, caring for her invalid father, every chore dreary yet enlivened by Emma's yearning: Yeatsman knew he had to show boredom without being boring.

The young doctor, Charles Bovary, arrives. He cures Emma's father and is a little on the earnest side—Brian Aherne?—but good looking and living in a town; he personifies salvation. The wedding is hurried, cheap, not what Emma planned, but at least she's off the farm. Charles adores her; she finds him tedious, his affections bothersome. Tasting Champagne, and the high life, at an aristocrat's provincial ball, Emma gets a whiff of what her life could be. Gossip surrounds her in the little town—we'll skip the move to another town, Yeatsman suggests to himself, which adds little to her character—especially from the meddlesome druggist and his wife. The druggist, however, has potions Emma uses to escape her doldrums, as well as a young boarder who becomes infatuated with her. She resists the boarder and he runs away to study law, leaving her sick and regretful. Why didn't she yield?

Emma's daughter is born, and the more the baby clings to her mother, the more Emma sends her off to a wet nurse. Charles is a proud father, Emma an unwilling mother. Now comes the suave, stylish Rodolphe—Adolphe Menjou, Yeatsman thought, possibly Charles Boyer—to have one of his servants cured by Charles. Emma takes up with him, is soon running out of the town at dawn for trysts at Rodolphe's castle. The Code Nazis will hate this, Yeatsman knows, but we'll make the wages of sin just what they want, as Flaubert did. Rodolphe is so elegant; Emma must live up to his luxury, and the druggist introduces her to a conniving merchant who is soon selling her clothes far beyond her husband's means. And then furniture to fit out the home not of a provincial doctor's wife but of a duchess. She and Rodolphe exchange passionate letters. Her smothering domestic life, made even worse by the townspeople's gossip and intrusions, contrasts with the joyous transports of her affair with Rodolphe. Emma pleads with Rodolphe to take her away; we can tell even as he agrees that he's planning his own escape.

Rejected on the very night Rodolphe was to spirit her to Venice, Emma takes to her bed, sick with lost love, recoiling from her husband and daughter. She dresses her daughter in fancy clothes the Bovarys can't afford, tells her romantic stories of the rich life in Paris—stories she is really telling herself—but avoids any real affection. Emma is plunging deeper into debt, and the conniving merchant is taking most of Charles Bovary's income. Recovered from her illness, Emma goes to the larger town where the druggist's former boarder is now a young lawyer. Gary Cooper? Yeatsman wonders; we don't need another Frenchman. He becomes her lover, she brings him expensive presents, draining the last of her gullible husband's money. More passionate letters between the lovers, read over Emma's humdrum housewife existence. Charles is patient, naïve; he wants Emma to have anything she wants even if he is ruined.

When the conniving merchant finally demands full payment of all Emma owes him, she has a tantrum. She returns humbly to the wealthy Rodolphe to beg for a loan. He refuses and when Emma has an even more violent tantrum—Millevoix will love this, Yeatsman thinks—Rodolphe has his servant throw her out. She runs through the rain across fields and stumbles several times. The music is building. Reaching the druggist's house in the middle of the night, she searches for the key to his pharmacy, finds it, and in a fury of self-pity and self-hatred—Bernhardt would have been superb in a silent version of this, Yeatsman is thinking—she swallows several mouthfuls of arsenic.

As Madame Bovary lies in bed, poisoned, her bewildered husband and weeping daughter plead with her to remain with them. A priest comes. Dissolve to a month later as the grieving Charles goes through Emma's belongings. He finds the letters from her lovers. He collapses on the spot. In the final scene, Madame Bovary's daughter is in the convent where her mother discovered her own yearnings, and she is reading *Ivanhoe*.

"As much as a dollar for your thoughts," Mossy said smiling wanly as he dragged his deboned wasted drained body into his office and, unable to stagger as far as his desk, plunged backward into his favorite chair as his favorite writer reluctantly vacated it.

"'Tread softly because you tread on my dreams,'" Yeatsman quoted his master.

So normally abnormally active, hopping with such agility from place to place and subject to subject, so filled with nervous energy that even his hands couldn't stay still, Mossy was hard to envisage in his present enervated state. The image itself would not form. Yet Brenda De Baule had apparently left him, for once, slack. He could not even open a note Elena had handed him.

Mossy's exhaustion derived from lunching at the Brown Derby with Brenda De Baule, brought over from France, sort of, by way of Brooklyn to become Jubilee's answer to Greta Garbo. This was not a fixed destiny since, Mossy confided to Yeatsman, she was worth couching but not casting. Mossy's eastern scouts had found Bogdana Deccabalu in the kickline at the Brooklyn Paramount, given her half a day to say good-bye to her family in Flatbush—she hated her milkman father for abusing her in the predawn before his delivery route, hated her mother for letting this occur, promised to send for one younger sister before the same thing happened to her—and shipped her to Paris for six months. In Paris Jubilee's representative arranged for her to have French lessons and, more importantly, French *accent* lessons, while he went about officially changing her name and acquiring a French passport for her. Jubilee then re-immigrated her to the United States and had photographers and columnists waiting on the West Thirty-ninth Street pier when she voyaged in on the Île de France. She was a Continental starlet.

The only trouble was the former Bogdana Deccabalu could not act. She couldn't even act Brenda De Baule. Her French accent had too little Left Bank, too much Sheepshead Bay. She was, however, adept at Mossy's luncheon plans, and then some. Fatigued from his postprandial labors, the poor man had to give a rude précis before proceeding to something he wanted to ask from Yeatsman. The drawback of using the studio head's office for study and reflection was he made himself handy for favors.

"Mouth like a Hoover," Mossy said as he free-associated and gradually regained strength. "The woman could suck a basketball through a straw, dancer's ass twisting on you, she pants like a starved dog I find it adds to the whole event don't you, Packard's getting messy though, listen I got a miserable third act on *Escapade in Acapulco* out of Benges and Spighorr who must be drunk all day, you did the treatment, fix it by Friday so we can shoot Monday I'll let you have anything you want next, I need less talktalk, more on the jewel robbery and castanet girls, put in a fatal accident at the mine, coupla three yuks then the kid winds up with the *other* guy's girl like I told Spighorr who paid no attention, which was what everybody in the seats wants and we all go home happy, New York included, once more with Brenda De Baule I'm turning her over to Dunster Clapp if you don't exercise your option, any skirt on this lot is yours if I get my script Friday."

"You know, Mossy, you give responsible infidelity a bad name. You're a setback for all us occasionals."

"I got to have these other jobs, my wife doesn't understand my needs." When he said "my wife" instead of "Esther Leah," Mossy was always a little ashamed.

"I'll warrant," said Yeatsman affecting Edwardian propriety, "that precisely what Esther Leah does understand are your needs. Only too well."

"Friday then on the script so I can tell my director what I want on Saturday and he can shoot it Monday."

"Just a goddam minute, will you, or as my bard put it, 'The stallion Eternity Mounted the mare of Time, 'Gat the foal of the world.'"

"So he must have, Yeatsman, and that mare says we have a script Friday."

"Don't expect too much here, Mossy. Death and sex and money are all any sane audience has a right to."

"Even in Mexico, no horses for the chase. I don't want no Western."

Mossy ordered Chinese tea as a restorative and cancelled his afternoon fellatio as well as his shoeshine. No calls, he told Elena. He stayed by himself and, with rare quiet descending on him, gave consideration to what he needed to do. Idly, he opened the note he had been holding since Elena handed it to him. "Tell this to Orville," Pammy had scribbled, "maybe he'll bend a little. Imagination is not real, Mr. Wright, yet surely its fruits are. The romance of flying was possibly all you needed, but the audience needs the other kind too. Let us celebrate you with both kinds." Underneath that she wrote:

The brothers Wright
Thought about flight,
Thought about it day and night;
Dreamin', buildin', cogitatin'
In the garage they had in Dayton.
They had nothing but an image;
This wasn't the game, just a scrimmage—
Until they saw the contraption working
The brothers stayed at it, never shirking.
Neighbors came to gape and gawk:
Next thing you knew was Kitty Hawk.

Mossy stared at the note for a moment. Hmp, maybe after all, he said to himself.

He returned to his own plight. All his work was merely a way of going down into the town and seeking forgiveness—forgiveness for sin original only in that it belonged to him alone and he both valued and apprehended its persistence. On Sunday mornings as a boy he would head out to the open spaces of the Grand Concourse holding his mother's hand. They would survey the wider world. On their way to Mossy's grandmother, which was the only reason his mother would have him wearing a yarmulke, they looked at all creation. "Things you don't know about yet," she often said to him, "those things you can see here, a bigger map for you, Mossy darling, that has Italians, Irish, Armenians, Germans, Poles, the Coloreds in it, Chinese too, with problems like we got and some of their own. A world you'll live in one day when you finish with your old bubbe, sweet as she is, and your schnorrer of a papa, unbearable as he can be. Me, too, Mossala, though I hope wherever you land you'll send for your tender loving Ma, eh?"

Mossy regarded her in a quizzical manner that suggested he would not be sending for anybody, especially not anybody who leaned on her perception of herself as helpless. "But you may, Amos," she added, reading his determined little eight-year-old squint. "You don't know yet what you'll do when you get out there, but whatever it is, you're going." She was not giving her son a philosophy, only a direction, and the direction was: out-of-the-Bronx. Horace Greeley couldn't have put it better.

His goddamned father. The brutal rage of the unprovoked tyrant who knows he's weak. Mossy's father inherited a small hat business and ran it straight into the ground and forever after blamed all those near him, blamed his smart son and his dumb one, his daughter, his wife and her sister and their mother, blamed the Slovak super downstairs, blamed the plumber, the butcher, even the teacher at Mossy's school when she said the ingredients in America's melting pot didn't all melt. That was Moe Zangwill, hot and cold at the same time, boiling and frozen. Short and squat, muscled with anger, raging around the apartment in undershirt and suspenders, topping himself with one of the derbies he couldn't sell.

If life in these circumstances taught Mossy any lesson it was that humankind is only walking distance from Hell. People eventually will burn up. All that will be left, he was sure, will be pictures and words, musical notes for sounds the earth won't even remember. What he had known as a boy and carried with him at Jubilee was the simple notion that he should expand the walking distance as far as he could and let Hell take care of itself.

When he was alone Mossy did not dream movies; he dreamed moviemakers. If one of his dreams floated by in the form of a star, a director, a writer, sometimes a composer, Mossy would yell to himself, That's It! The logjam was broken and soon there would be a theme, script, cast, production. The old man, as he was called by employees twice his age, put together the collection of gifts he wanted in order to make a love story, a comedy, a drama, an adventure, a spectacle.

In a story conference he paid less attention to the details of the story than to the storyteller. If he believed the teller he believed the tale. He'd help you pick up the thread of a story if you lost it. What he wanted was your desire. While his assistants were already smirking at your stumbles, he'd be steering you back onto your own track. A slicko storyteller didn't necessarily get Mossy's green lights. Someone he believed got them. And for a generation, America believed Mossy.

Which didn't mean he was not a son of a bitch, double crosser, diabolical seducer, and all the rest of the constellation of vice. It only meant he had an accurate stethoscope. When he heard murmurs of the heart, he responded to them.

Carelessly, unknowingly, Mossy had played a leading role in the stunt-man Joey Jouet's motorcycle plunge off the Santa Monica Pier into the Pacific. Joey's wife, the set designer Elise Millevoix Jouet, was at home in a duet with Mossy that Sunday. She had dark hair over willing features centered around her button nose that was not as prominent as her sister's yet capable of making its own little statements. When the nostrils distended slightly the man looking at her could assume she found him attractive. Finding Mossy attractive had been easy. Part of his charm was power, part was his being a distillation of want, but the compelling part was that Elise felt Joey's career remained completely safe in this time of cutbacks if she were sleeping with the head of their studio. She was so discreet even Pammy had no suspicion. Joey died of a misunderstanding.

Elise, who knew nothing about Joey's having been fired by Jubilee the day before, found herself wondering, as her visitor rose and fell on top of her, how Mossy rejected people. On this day, this unexceptional Sunday of Mossy's first—and as it turned out only—call at the Jouet home, the two little girls were with their cousin Millie at Red Woods while Joey, as far as Elise knew, was off doing his stunts in Victorville. She hoped her playful daughters weren't exhausting their Aunt Pammy.

Mossy ground his way toward the inevitable. Until he began his charge he was warmly attentive to Elise's desires, but then, abruptly he was only about himself, turning the act into a collision of flesh. She heard a propeller overhead, a Sunday pilot out for a spin. Did Mossy execute people himself or did someone else draw and quarter the victim? Elise's reverie was interrupted by a closer sound, something downstairs. Just the Persian. If Mossy were a racehorse, he was charging down the homestretch. No, a cat wouldn't close a door. Pammy brought the children home early! One of them must have been naughty or become sick. But no, it wasn't that either. Elise heard a tread heavier than Pammy's. Oh Christ! But Joey was safely in Victorville on location. Wasn't he? Must be a delivery, sometimes they were made on Sunday. A sound by a window.

The Jouet home, a modest two-story Spanish tiled stucco, was perched on one of the cluttered Santa Monica streets just off Wilshire, well back from the pricier ocean villas. Downstairs, Joey looked out the window and saw Mossy Zangwill's Packard touring car on the street. Why hadn't he noticed it as he coasted his motorcycle into the driveway? He had so much on his mind. He put his hand on the banister. Hearing a sound of coupled pleasure upstairs, he took his hand away. Well, he was a stuntman, he knew how to take a fall.

Nom de dieu, what could Elise say if the intruder was Joey? What should she whisper to Mossy right now? What was there to say to anyone? How could she ever make this up to Joey, sweet Joey, a dreamy husband who wouldn't hurt a termite if it was eating down the house. Mossy, damn him, was at the finish line. Elise heard the side door open softly while Mossy concluded noisily, his face almost battering her into the headboard. Hoping it wasn't Joey, wondering desperately how to make Joey understand, how to use Mossy to Joey's advantage without Joey's knowing it, Elise heard the door click shut. No slam, still soft. It was the last sound she ever heard her husband make.

She didn't know when she could call Joey or for that matter where. Maybe it wasn't Joey. Would he go to Pammy and confide in his sister-in-law, who adored him? Pammy would be indignant, even horrified, on Joey's behalf. But later, on Elise's behalf, the incident would be safely, Europeanly, ignored.

Wheeling his motorcycle out of the driveway, Joey knew where to go, and where to go first. He headed up toward Chautauqua for the view. Then he would fly.

Mossy tunneled darkly in his leather chair. He felt a pang and didn't know where it came from. That had been a good job at lunchtime but no one to put into *Escapade in Acapulco*. The part was too small for Teresa Blackburn, but Spitz Toogan said Maria Trilby would be right for it. A slim blonde with a chin a cameraman could do interesting work with. Get her. Hire Cyrus Henscher to score it. Though he heard rumors Henscher was bad with women, all Mossy wanted was a sprightly Mexican score. Henscher would be the ticket. But something was wrong.

Elena buzzed. She was sorry, knew he wasn't to be disturbed, but Arthur Brisbane was on the line from New York, the third time he had called in twenty minutes. Brisbane was a premier columnist for Hearst and at times ran down a rumor for the press lord. "All right, what can I do for you, Arthur?"

"One of our boys at the Examiner out there says Trent Amberlyn is in the pansy pen downtown. The chief wants to know if we go with this."

Mossy bought time with a laugh. Evidently he did not have every single cop paid off because the *Los Angeles Examiner*, may it burn in Hell, now wanted to print Amberlyn's—and therefore Jubilee's—mortification. Hearst hated the way Palmyra Millevoix was being described as a bigger star than Marion Davies had ever been, and he'd love to stick it to Mossy, or at least withhold sticking it in such a way that Mossy owed him a huge favor. "Why, I have no idea what you're talking about, Arthur, or Mr. Hearst either," Mossy said. "Amberlyn is on his way in from location out in the Valley and should be back on Stage Seven by five o'clock or so. Shall I have him call you?"

Five o'clock being eight in New York, well past the time Brisbane wanted to wait in his office. Columnists loved to exercise their sadism, expose the clay feet that would appeal to Bible Belt morality and everyone else's voyeurism, but they were lazy. Mossy treated the press with diplomatic disdain.

"That won't be necessary," Brisbane said. "Our tips aren't always airtight. The chief sends his regards. Good luck handling the new Puritan movie Code."

Mossy wondered briefly why Hearst hadn't had Louella Parsons make the call since this was her territory and it was probably she who had the tipster downtown. But Brisbane was closer to the throne. Hearst might suppose Brisbane scared Mossy more than Parsons because a call from him meant the rumor had already spanned the continent.

The coming of the Code. Mossy considered what the new Motion Picture Code would do to his business. The Code was intended to soothe wary investors and stave off the Protestant Bible Belt and their Catholic counterparts, who wanted actual censorship of movies. A Catholic bishop had issued an edict that no picture shall be produced which will lower the moral standards of those who see it. Among images banned from the screen were depictions of what was called sex perversion, illegal drug traffic, white slavery (though not black), miscegenation, sex hygiene, indecent or undue exposure, excessive kissing, lustful embraces, suggestive postures and gestures, and even surgical operations. As he thought about all this, Mossy, who hadn't patterned his movies after his personal life but pretended to pattern his personal life after the movies, shuddered. He couldn't live the Code, and the Code could ruin him. Already, Mossy was witnessing the occasional mysterious disappearance of his erections.

Who stole my boners? Mossy wondered. And his simple answer was the goddamned Code. The Motion Picture Code stole his hard-ons and gave them to priests in Chicago and Boston, who aren't even supposed to have them. And to evangelists in Memphis and Dallas. He had two producers he suspected of being currently impotent since he was paying their mistresses to give him performance reports. The strange case of the missing hard-ons. It might be contagious. They could make a picture about this in defiance of the goddamn Code. Brenda De Baule, firebrand that she was, had cured the problem for the time being, but you never knew when it might crop up again. He'd better keep her around for a while.

Elena buzzed him that two writers, a director, and a producer had been waiting half an hour. Mossy fairly dreamed through their story conference. "Tell me what you want to do," he began.

"----------------," the producer declared.

"-------------------------------," one of the writers agreed.

The other writer demurred. "------------------------------------?" he asked.

"------------------------------------!" the director emphasized, and the producer was with him. "--------------------," he said, and repeated himself. "--------------------."

The second writer still wasn't sure. "------------------------------ ---," he worried.

The first writer was reassuring. "---------------------------------," he said, not wanting to discuss this now and trying with a hand signal to indicate to his collaborator they would solve that problem on their own, in private.

Mossy's hands got busy. He gesticulated. "-------------------!" he said, meaning they shouldn't bother him again until they knew. "--," the producer explained levelly, furious at the second writer for expressing his doubts publicly.

Now the director wasn't satisfied. "------------------------------------?" he asked.

That was not for him to worry about. "-----------------------------------," Mossy said impatiently, silencing the director.

The producer began to sum up. "--------------------- ..."

Mossy said, "Don't insult us by telling us what we already know. Meeting over."

Alone again, the studio head began to dive into a state of extreme anxiety. He worried about the whole schedule of Jubilee Pictures. What was in production was too light and insubstantial, what was planned too larded and solemn.

Who should intrude upon our Mossy in this solitary state but the Prince of Wales? That was what the Empress Joséphine roses were about that Elena had brought in while I was being evicted from *A Doll's House*. The Prince had spent time in America ten years earlier, enjoying himself especially in California, and he was eager to feel free again, which he could never do while on duty in his own country or the Empire. No one outside his immediate retinue, including his family, yet knew about the twice-divorced American, Mrs. Wallis Warfield Simpson, whom the Prince had met several years before and who, several years later, would cost him the throne he had waited for so patiently. With his retainers in the outer office, Edward P., as he was referred to behind his back, strode loftily into Mossy's office with a single companion, the English lickspittle Percy Shumway, who had so adroitly aided in my execution that morning.

Shumway opened the bidding by telling Mossy His Royal Highness was having a champion visit to Hollywood and would like to see a movie set. The Prince himself was admiring the Empress's delicate petals whose stems Elena had swaddled like an infant when she placed them on Mossy's desk. "'Orchid,' you know, comes from the Greek word for testicle," said His Royal Highness chuckling just a little, "yet the perfect rose has no par in beauty or elegance. One knows the exquisite rose by her dusty pink, deep veined slightly wavy petals. You're to be congratulated. Would these be Empress Joséphines?"

"In the flesh, Your Highness," Mossy said, forgetting the Royal. "I knew they had many charms, but your description makes me wish you were writing screenplays here. I do raise orchids as well, since you mentioned them."

"But they're parasites," the Prince shot back. "Orchids are often parasitic."

"Not the species I cultivate," Mossy said. "I favor ones that originate in Hawaii and are pollinated by butterflies, the Phalaenopsis semi-alba."

In the manner of earlier Hollywood executives sporting ostentatious cars and later production chiefs obsessing over art, Mossy had his gorgeous flowers. Rembrandt and Van Gogh were mandatory for a studio head, and Mossy dutifully hung them, but it was his garden that most enticed and reflected him. He loved the seedlings and buds and mature flowers, he learned the stamens and pistils and stigmas and pollinia. He even cherished the dying plants completing their cycle, dropping seeds to carry on their line. The Empress Joséphines remained the most honest organic matter in the room, their long-stemmed delicacy present to deflect Mossy's origins and the Prince's well-known aversion to Jews, as if no Jew could have a flower so absurdly upper class on his desk, named for Napoleon's wife, a gentile production if ever there was one.

"Proust overdid the Cattleyas," said Shumway, straining to flatter his boss and impress his future sovereign simultaneously, "you're much better off with Phalaenopsis."

Mossy paid no attention to him. "It happens, Your Highness, we have several pictures shooting this afternoon, and I'd be delighted to take you around to any of them."

"What's so extraordinary," the Prince said, "is that with your Fairbanks and Chaplins and Pickfords, and now your Ronald Colmans and Joan Crawfords, you've achieved a pantheon of royalty in a few years that took us ten centuries to incubate."

"We're mostly ordinary people," Mossy said, "who the public happens to smile on for a precious few moments, but stars can fall fast if they make a few lousy pictures."

"But tell me, old chap," the Prince went on, "what does Jean Harlot's bosom really look like?"

"Oh, that's quite funny, Your Highness, heh heh. Miss Harlow's measurements are classic, almost as perfect as a rose. I wish we had her here at Jubilee, but she spends most of her time at Metro-Goldwyn-Mayer Studios."

"Yes, of course," said the Prince to the monarch, "but tell me, really, how does one manage to live with all the Mayers and Cohns and Goldwyns and whatnot?"

Ah, thought Mossy, the disquisition on the Jews. A Jewish orchid, he inferred, would be a parasite species, wouldn't it? Shumway squirmed, realizing the Prince of Wales had either not heard his introduction to Mossy or had not understood the likely background of a person called Zangwill. One of the whatnots was sitting right there in his royal presence, and Shumway's job might be on the line. Which way would Mossy go, defiant indignation or subservient submission to Edward P.?

"Well, now, you become accustomed," Mossy said. "The gentlemen I do business with are filled with imagination and positive energy, honorable people as long as they don't try to affect the airs of a true aristocrat such as Your Highness."

"Ah, quite right, quite right," said the Prince.

But Mossy wasn't dropping the subject. "Do you know any Jewish people yourself, sir?"

"Well, there's old, ah, soanso, something-berg or -stein. I forget his name, good man though in the War, capital. But one hears they're full of push, you know."

"Push, if I may say so, Your Royal Highness, is what built the British Empire."

The Prince of Wales blinked, focusing directly at Mossy for the first time and possibly understanding he might well be talking to a whatnot. He hadn't quite caught the name, though it sounded German. "Quite so," he said. "What kind of picture are you making today?"

When I heard about this, I thought at first the Prince of Wales had confused the name Zangwill with Zanuck. Since Zanuck wasn't Jewish, Edward P. could have thought he was speaking to a fellow Christian. On the other hand, why would an aristocratic Englishman, much less heir to the throne, ever have heard of him or, if he had, have any idea whether Darryl Zanuck was anything at all? The Prince of Wales would neither know nor care whether an obscure (to him) motion picture maker called Darryl Zanuck was or was not a Jew. Mossy had installed his Empress Joséphines to angle the P of W away from his own origins and then, provoked, led the discussion right into the Prince's teeth, attempting to blunt, if not convert, the Nazi-sympathizer's anti-Semitism.

The typewriter errand over, another was begun. I wended my way across the lot to Nils Maynard's set with a publicity release I drummed out for Stanny Poule. I was to wait until the director wasn't shooting, give the release to an actor, wait for his comments, then rush it back to Poule. Would I be doing this ten years from now, twenty? The mask of servility loomed as my life's prospect. I'd been a star in the ascendant that morning. Now I was a factotum, no more, perhaps less. Invisible. My head whirled.

Shorter than the Prince and trim, Mossy led him and Percy Shumway around the lot to the same sound stage where I was heading. "Jolly," the Prince was saying, "jolly indeed to be putting all this imagination onto cinema screens round the globe. Must take rather a good deal of effort."

"It does," Mossy said, "rather a very great deal of effort, Your Highness."

"And a world of bother."

"But it's all worthwhile when you enter a crowded theater a thousand miles away and you join hundreds of people in the dark, all looking at what you've done."

In those days Mossy didn't normally patrol the Jubilee lot. It scared people. Some of the fear came from the Depression itself, which increased anxiety everywhere, but mostly it was the way he squinted at his workers. With Mossy in charge of each line that was spoken, every blade of painted grass on every artificial lawn, he was seen to be swaggering around his domain even if he was only sauntering. Since Mossy's hand was in everything, he didn't need to show himself. He preferred to be everywhere present, nowhere visible, as Flaubert instructed for an author, comparing him to God in the universe. Mossy was the author of Jubilee.

"That street mise en scene you showed me," said the Prince of Wales as they strolled through the backlot, "quite like Covent Garden, you know, yet not."

Father Junipero Serra was said by Yeatsman to have sanctified the Jubilee backlot, as he may have the Zangwill estate a few miles inland, with a mission as he marched north from San Diego to Carmel. Before that, before the Europeans, the land had been contended for by the Chumash and Cahuilla peoples, later by the Mojaves and the Yokuts. Now it was Mossy Zangwill's mission, to be defended against any invaders.

From Yeatsman, a memorandum typed by Comfort O'Hollie: "Chief Seathl to Governor, Oregon Territory, 1855: 'To us the ashes of our ancestors are sacred and their resting place is hallowed ground. You wander far from the graves of your ancestors and seemingly without regret. And when the last Red Man shall have perished, and the memory of my tribe shall have become a myth among the White Men, these shores will swarm with the invisible dead of my tribe, and when your children's children think themselves alone in the field, the store, the ship, upon the highway, or in the silence of the pathless woods, they will not be alone. At night when the streets of your cities and villages are silent and you think them deserted, they will throng with the returning hosts that once filled them and still love this beautiful land. The White Man will never be alone.'"

"Stage Eight we're heading for," said Percy Shumway, "just round the corner."

I had already delivered the publicity release to the actor when Mossy came onto the hangar-like sound stage and introduced the Prince of Wales to Nils Maynard, who was waiting for a small fill light to be set so he could shoot his film's final scenes. Nils's first question, after bowing, was whether the Prince had been afflicted with the hemophilia that ran in his family. Shumway, toady more to the crown suddenly than to the studio, criticized Nils for asking an appalling question. Mossy stiffened and glanced across the sound stage to the small exit door he had just entered, preparing to swiftly escort the Prince off the set. Nils explained that he himself had hemophilia, that his pain and bleeding had markedly lessened since he became an adult, and that he was hoping to make a picture about Queen Victoria, some of whose heirs had the disease.

"Never bothered by it," said the Prince. "Several great uncles were, as you say, afflicted." Mossy was distracted by an actress going by in a hoop skirt.

"The royal disease," Mossy said, returning to his duties. "Our Nils here should be at least a duke himself, shouldn't he?"

Edward P., to everyone's relief, was amused.

Nils ran his fingers through his hair. He knew better than to think hemophilia struck only royalty, and he had no interest in small talk. "This picture is called *The Boy from Boise*, sir, and I'm afraid we have to shoot, film a scene. Please excuse me."

"I already have," said the Prince with a smile. When Nils had hurried over to his cameraman, the Prince added, "Good chap, very fine chap."

The Prince watched the lighting, which interested him more than the actors. The scene was a tense dinner with a nineteenth-century banker, his wife, and their son, who wanted to move farther west against his parents' wishes. After the first take, the Prince, naturally enough, expected to see the following scene. Shumway explained the scene had to be shot again until the director, Nils, was satisfied, and that even then they would push on to another scene using the same set but not the scene that would actually follow in the finished movie. The Prince seemed moderately annoyed by that, and then visibly lost interest when the same scene was filmed again. For the third take, the lighting was changed slightly to favor an actress's eyes, and this revived Edward P.'s interest, but only momentarily. Mossy, Shumway, and the Prince of Wales left quickly after the fourth take. Despite his denials of hemophilia himself, the Prince may have been afraid that he was a carrier of the sick gene; he never permitted himself an heir.

Nils's next scene was a large family gathering where an argument would take place. Never a commander, Nils was more of an usher, letting the actors know where he wanted them to move and doing it in a way that also let them know the mood he wanted, which in turn gave the actors the idea of how to say their lines. Whenever tension did arise he could always disarm everyone with a sleight-of-hand or two. Everyone but the cameraman. Cameramen were not diverted by Nils's tricks and tried to take advantage of him by lighting scenes either their own way or the way a certain actress wanted so she would request them on her next picture.

As Nils gathered his cast together before they had their final makeup touches, he told the actors to shake all the friendliness out of their systems now because in a few minutes they had to loathe each other. Over the years, Nils had developed if not a philosophy at least an antihero patter he would deliver to actors, who found the message reassuring. "A director is a necessary evil," Nils intoned, "sometimes more necessary, sometimes more evil. Get it right the first time and you won't have to see my diabolical side. I have two and only two functions. I serve the actors, and I serve the story. So tell me, my darlings, how can I help?"

No director today could say what Nils said because the Directors Guild virtually has the word "vision" as a membership prerequisite. Nils would have to start with, "My vision of this film has less in common with Kurosawa than with Steven." If anyone had to ask who Steven was, he'd be off the picture. The director is frequently such a rooster he confuses vision with strategy with ambition with grosses with points in his contract as he looks down at his tailored scruffy corduroys. Mr. Spielberg, you have a lot to answer for; you have entertained us vastly, but you have infected a generation of your fraternity with so much advanced narcissism you can't escape a just cinematic god somewhere.

We can still look at Nils's best wartime pictures, *Angels with Broken Wings*, for instance, or *Seven Came Home*, with no embarrassment at all. Nominated several times, he never took home the chicken, as he called it, until finally the Academy threw the Hersholt Oscar at him. The French accorded him Chevalier thises and thats, but he knew these were consolation prizes in his dotage. Nils confessed to me, "I once left a heavier footprint in this town. There were consequences, real or feared, for not returning my calls." By the Eighties the people who returned his calls, if they were returned at all, were secretaries whose twenty-seven-year-old bosses were always at lunch. At least the old magician meant what he said, serving the actors and the story, and in his way in his day, which I was present for as the sun rose, he made pictures that moved and delighted.

Nils had a sly contempt for actors who were more photogenic than talented, but when he had to use them he tried to make them into graven images of themselves. "I'll let her just be a statue," he said to me about April Devereau, the actress who had stalked off his set in the morning and had to be talked back by Mossy, "and have her do a slight grimace, that'll be okay in a close-up. As little talk as possible, no moving, no having to relate to the other actors. Even with the good ones I tell them don't act, just think and feel. The camera will do the rest. With a real movie actor like Gary Cooper, he uses his eyes like swords. The closer the camera is, the smaller the performance needs to be. The camera sees all, knows all, and, unfortunately for some actors, tells all."

Unlike some European directors who made fierce, asphyxiating class distinctions, Nils was collegial on his sets. It happened that his director of photography on *The Boy from Boise*, Dirk Straker, was more at home with tyrannical directors, and when he wasn't given explicit orders did things to irritate Nils. Shouting at the camera operator while being overly fawning to Nils himself, Straker said, "I'll let you know where to move the camera, Barney, as soon as the maestro informs me what the hell he wants from this scene!" Nils got around him by doing a rope trick—he cut a rope four times into small pieces, then pulled it whole again out of his pants—that so awed the entire company the DP simply shut up for the rest of the day.

Nils tried to avoid being one of the directors who cravenly treated a star like a cross between a priceless jewel and a retarded child. Directors could forget to take their sons on promised fishing trips if a star wanted them at a meaningless photo session; they could leave their wives for them, try to gain control of them, and have tantrums when a star left them or preferred another director. The stars had their own tantrums of abandonment if they weren't cast in something they felt they deserved. The whole community could enter a state of rejection. A writer was replaced, a director put in a vise between the star and the producer, the star not wanted for the next picture after her grosses sank on the last one even if it had been a picture the studio forced her into against her will. Fear stalked the town like a gargoyle who knew everyone's address.

"Never show the panic you feel," Nils told me as he waited for the next setup and I waited for the actor to return his marked-up copy of the press release I'd brought, "or else chaos reigns. Make a decision even if it's the wrong one and the actors are confused and the DP smirks, damn him, but you go with that until you think of the right way to do the scene, which you won't necessarily know until you've shot it the wrong way. Actors can go dead unless the director sparks them. Just waiting for a lighting change actors have told me they're wasting their lives. I'll do my magic tricks, and the actors are like children, but if you do that too much they can become passive. They need you to stimulate them but not spoon-feed them."

Straker, the surly DP, barked out his lighting and camera position orders, then changed them. Nils and I watched a carpenter—an ugly man with a disfigured eye—hammer a broken chair together, tear it apart, then hammer it whole again. He was enforcing a little slowdown of his own. He dared Nils with his one good eye to try to do anything about it. Nils shrugged. At last the brutes were blazing, blinding, and with the other lights combined to turn everything hot as a furnace. Makeup ran and had to be redaubed before every take. Between setups rumors blew a stiff breeze around the sound stage. Who was too drunk to get in front of the camera so the studio let it be known he had the flu. Who was pregnant without a ring on her finger. Who had joined the Communist Party. Who was a secret fairy. Who was going to take over What Picture when Who Else was fired off it. Who was skipping to Fox for a better contract.

Nils still hoped for a master before they broke for the day, but Straker was having his lights and camera moved in slow motion. The set had turned somnolent. When I asked him why everything was so slow, Nils mused that this was frustrating but the worst was yet to come. He leaned back in the canvas chair that said MISS DEVEREAU on it.

"You don't like your rushes?" I asked.

He stared at me for a moment, a conjurer deciding whether to let a novice in on one of his tricks. "No, the scenes look all right in the dailies. The temperamental April Devereau, who ran off this morning in tears, is now waiting patiently in her dressing room after Mossy sent her about a thousand orchids and a fully stocked aquarium for her kid. So you have a highball in your hand and watch the dailies at the end of the next day's work, and you're relieved. The star, in this case Devereau, hits her marks, it's all in focus God willing, the line stumbles actually look more spontaneous so you plan to use takes you'd thought contained mistakes. You're a magician again."

Nils leaped up and jumped over a cable as he strode toward the set with its baronial furniture. He made a circuit as if he were the camera shooting the scene with all the actors in place. "Directing," he continued, "can be better than sex. It can *be* sex. When it's going well, a director can feel like the guest of honor at an orgy. The actors give you something you didn't even know they had or that you were getting when you were shooting. Suddenly you're a genius. You realize everything you have ever learned from others has merely stood in your way, and your way is going swimmingly. You're tempted to call up that smart-ass writer and tell him the movie didn't get written on his typewriter after all, it's getting written in the camera. The set is a dictatorship yet it's also strangely egalitarian, a little family is created on the set, and you're the good father the others never had. The collaboration is alive, but now the producer and the writer are gone and what happens is between the director and the actors, the director and the cameraman. Soon it will be between the director and his cutter. And it's so personal, the director brags to himself, it's so *me*."

"What's it like having that much control?"

"Only a fool calls it control, and there are plenty of fools. It's more like warfare, every shot a tactic to seduce the audience. You build your shots around the campaign of seduction you're waging, but it's still warfare."

"Who's the enemy?"

"God. Dullness. God can be very dull in his stillness and majesty. He doesn't like anyone else to be the creator but himself. He thinks he's the only artist, and the rest of us are impostors. His creations are always nobler than ours, but we stave him off and once in a while we do what he meant to do but hasn't actually gotten around to doing yet. On rare occasions he might even help us. In the film of Queen Victoria, if we get to make it, I need to show her at her coronation ball not only as the young dazzler she was that night but as messenger of an age. You think I don't need God for that?"

The contrast between what Nils was telling me and what I could see was stark. The crew was moving listlessly around the set, actors were slumped in their canvas chairs doing crossword puzzles or complaining to each other. "And today?" I asked.

"Today is bat crap," Nils said, sighing, his entire frame sagging. "But I think it will hold your attention if we can show how tense things are between the prodigal son and his parents at this big family get-together where they want him to pledge his obedience and he wants to declare his independence by running off with, God help us, Devereau, who's too old for the part, but that we can handle. Dialogue is the least of it here—it's all in looks and shrugs and a camera that notices a napkin being twisted by the mother, a look the father shoots at his son, a note the son keeps folding and unfolding beneath the table, concern for the son on the features of the maiden aunt."

"You'll get all that this afternoon?"

"No. We'll get the master, and that will tell me what I need in the two-shots, the close-ups, if Straker doesn't make everything too unbearable. You want so bad for it to be good, not to have endless takes. Even at an orgy you can get tired of repetition."

"You edit the film and you feel better," I offered.

"Hardly. That's when Hell hits. You see a rough cut, just you and the cutter. It's ghastly. The minister resists temptation in too many scenes and you're sick of him. The girl is sexy where you don't want her to be, yet she's a lump where you want her to be a morsel. No mirth where there's supposed to be a laugh, no fear in a horror scene. Nothing works. Even the villain—juiciest part of the script—isn't believable. You wonder where you can get some of the hemlock Socrates drank. There are those pills you bite down on. Self-immolation is good, you're shrieking in agony as the flames eat you just before you lose consciousness, and that agony is joy compared to what you feel now. Plus you know you'll never work again. Just impale yourself on the Moviola and have done with it.

"The cutter tells you to hold off, she hasn't been editing pictures fifteen years for nothing, in the silents cutting was a real art, how about you go away till Wednesday and she'll show you some stuff, maybe she'll want you to reshoot a scene or two and this time give her a little coverage, maybe there won't be too much egg on your face.

"So you stumble away, embarrassed, humiliated. You've let your underling, your cutter, who probably makes about a tenth of your salary, throw you off your own picture. You steer clear of the studio, go to Santa Anita, the beach, take your kid to the mountains. Wasting time, waiting for the hangman."

"You've hated your films that much?" I asked. "And yourself?"

"Much more. But then you come back and have a look at the cutter's new cut. Moves better, not so bad, she has minimized places where the picture drags and motivation is unclear, cut the talky exposition, punched up the good action you do have, the dramatic moments you haven't quite ruined. Maybe you're not dead yet. You jump over your producer's head and ask Mossy's permission to reshoot to make the villain more treacherous, the main actors are still on the lot, the sets you need luckily haven't been struck yet because they're being reused.

"You tell Mossy you're on the verge of something fantastic, never been done, you just need three more days' shooting. He says 'pipe down with the bullshit, I already know you're in trouble, my spies are everywhere as you should know, frankly I sneaked a look at the last third of the picture last night, it's my studio don't look so injured, and it is my considered opinion'—he says to you as you recontemplate suicide only this time it's murder-suicide because you're taking Mossy with you—'that you may not be in as bad a fix as you think. Reshoot two days, tell Straker to get his ass in gear or he's at Republic doing Westerns next month, and while you're at it reshoot your star with her father and dress her differently, the audience won't know how to react if she's showing cleavage in that scene, we want brains and the audience doesn't think the two can ever be found together, so put her glasses back on while you're disguising her bazooms."

"As it turns out," Nils concluded, "Mossy is just a little bit right, even if not the way he thinks he is, you get a couple of ideas of your own, and you're not dead yet and don't have to kill him, and that's how pictures get made."

At last the director's forces were arrayed for battle. He yelled, "Action!" and the camera moved smoothly on its tracks around the living room as the family argued about what was to become of their prodigal son. Though the actors barely saw him, Nils moved his hands as if he were conducting an orchestra. The take proceeded majestically as no fewer than five actors spoke, each one hitting his or her point, two of them interrupting each other to perfection. The camera came to rest on the son, whose eyes gave both his parents exactly the right degree of love and rebellion. "That's all I'm going to listen to from either of you," he said. "Please try to remember whose life this is." He sighed. The master shot was over, and though I knew he would make them do it again, Nils was pleased. Everyone was. He shot his arms out, and a pair of white lovebirds flew from each sleeve. The four birds circled the set and came to perch on Nils's shoulders as the cast and crew applauded. "Okay," he said, "next we shoot *Secret Shikse Rituals.*"

The look on Dirk Straker's face said he didn't know who he hated more, his delighted crew or Nils Matheus Maynard with his dazzling legerdemain. I was left to wonder how long those birds would have waited patiently until Nils had a take he liked.

The actor playing the prodigal son handed me back the press release. "I'm from Butte, not Bozeman," he said, "and my old man's a grocer not a high powered land speculator, whatever that is. Other than that, it's okay, I guess."

Errand over. I was on my way off the sound stage when Nils summoned me. I walked obediently to his canvas chair with the block letters MAGICIAN on it. "Hey Jant, don't you like the take?"

"Everyone else has already told you. You don't need to ask me."

"I need to make it unanimous," he said.

"Thanks, it was great. If you do it again, maybe the father could look more stern."

"Right, glad to hear it. Now cheer yourself, Owen. You're too upright, dogged, gray. You're already clean, innocent, aiming to please. Give yourself a break and Mossy will too. Cut loose. You've been wanted and found trying. That's enough."

As I left the stage I didn't know whether to feel found out or complimented.

Mossy had been having his own exertions far more complex than mine and of course having far more effect on an entire population. He was like the Russian landowners whose estates were measured not in hectares but in how many serfs they had, whom they described as souls. Counting extras, Mossy had twenty-two hundred souls in his domain that week in early 1934.

The child star Skip Teeter was in Mossy's office with his parents, a pair of drunks everyone wanted to kick off the lot. They'd come out from Kentucky with Skip to escape bill collectors and had their son cadging for dimes on La Brea when he was spotted by the statesman-like Hurd Dawn, then the new head of scenic design at Jubilee. Hurd either wanted to pick the boy up or thought he'd be perfect as Becky Thatcher's brother in the first talkie version of *Tom Sawyer* that Jubilee was making. Skip soon became the adorable bucktoothed towheaded mischievous hero of a series of highly profitable B movies enjoyed by both parents and children. Skip and Company. Skip's parents had been told by an executive at a rival studio that Jubilee was getting a bargain on Skip's services for a mere three thousand dollars a week.

When Skip forgot a line that morning, Pa Teeter had hit him right there on the set. He hit his son hard enough to raise a lump on his forehead. "You smeared his makeup, you idiot!" Ma Teeter had yelled. The director had the parents thrown off the set while the script girl applied ice to Skip's forehead. After three years, Skip was becoming somewhat ungainly, almost adolescent at twelve. He was bowlegged, his ears were growing outwards, and he had developed several moles on his cheeks that makeup turned into bumps rather than camouflaging. One of his shoulders slumped down awkwardly.

Mossy knew Pa Teeter was talking to another studio. "Three thousand dollars a week is a good deal of money for a twelve year old," Mossy said to the Teeter family.

"It sure is, Mr. Zangwill," Skip said, "but my old man is a selfish—"

"Shut your face, young fella," said his father, "or I'll shut it for you good."

"Now, now," said Mossy, "I understand you've hit the boy today. That's not how we treat people at Jubilee."

"You're making millions off our son," said Skip's mother, "and we been told Skip could get five thousand a week at Fox or Warners, maybe more."

"Hell, I could produce his pictures myself," said Pa Teeter. Skip rolled his eyes.

"We have a contract with Skip signed by both of you," Mossy said calmly. "It's not in anyone's best interests if Skip gets a reputation for walking out on agreements."

"We didn't say nothing about walking out," Pa Teeter said, "but we oughta get what our boy is worth."

"I don't care about any of that, Mr. Zangwill," Skip said, "but I'd sure like to get my puppy back I had to leave with my uncle in Kentucky. He's grown up by now."

"We'll send for your pet right away," said Mossy.

"I'm talkin' do re mi," said Pa Teeter, imitating a B movie he'd seen.

"I'm not deaf," said Mossy. "Tell you what I'll do. We'll give Skip a bonus of a thousand dollars a week, but I want something in return. Two things."

"That'll be hunky doodle," said Pa Teeter. "What kin we do ya for, Mr. Mossy?"

"First, I want the two of you to stay off Skip's sets. Directors and producers have complained, and Skip is a precious asset Jubilee wants to protect."

Skip looked triumphant and managed to hold his tongue.

The parents were sheepish, possibly hurt. Then Ma Teeter spoke up. "We ain't gonna make trouble, sir, and if you don't want us there we'll stay away."

"Good," Mossy said, scowling at Pa Teeter until he nodded glumly.

"Now the second point is Skip is getting on to adolescence fast. He's almost at that awkward age. We want to correct his bowlegged walk, get his shoulders evened up, skim off those moles on his face, fix those floppy ears."

Skip was stunned. He didn't understand exactly what Mossy meant, but he knew pain when he saw it coming. "Mr. Zangwill," he began, "I don't have to be in pictures. I can go back to school, sir."

"Hey," said Pa Teeter, brightening, "you mean you're gonna fit Skip out so he can be a star when he grows up, too?"

"That's exactly what I mean, Pa."

"Well, hunky doodle," said both parents at once.

"That's not for me," Skip said. "I like being the way I am. No fixing up for me."

"I understand, Skip," said Mossy as understandingly as he could muster. "But you're a very valuable property. I don't mean just to the studio. You're valuable to your parents and yourself. You'll have money for college, for cars, you'll be able to support a wife very well someday, and your parents in their old age."

"Or right now," Pa Teeter laughed. Ma Teeter laughed too.

Skip set his jaw. "No!" he said.

"You'll do what the man said," Ma Teeter told her son, "or your pa and I will know the reason why."

"I'll handle this, Ma," Mossy said. "Skip, when you finish the picture you're on at the end of the week, you're going to get a vacation. Let Jubilee handle this. You won't have to work at all while you're healing. From the surgery. The result will be perfection."

"Healing?" yelled Skip. "Surgery? I'll run away, I swear."

"Wouldn't do any good, Skip," said Mossy. "You're too well known, you'd be recognized everywhere. Look, the operations won't take more than a few weeks, and you'll have three months off. Full pay."

"No!" Skip thundered, but he was beginning to cry.

Mossy came around his desk. He gave Skip a fatherly pat on the shoulder and tousled his hair. "Hey champ," he said, "I meant it when I said perfection." Skip cringed from his boss' touch. "Someday you'll thank me for all this. I promise."

The Teeter parents proudly led their son from the office, delighted at the thousand dollar a week raise. Skip was stumbling and weeping.

Skip Teeter never did get around to thanking Mossy. His career nosedived as an adolescent. The plastic surgeons and dermatologists left him looking more like a laboratory creation than a teenager. His smile, which had been so infectious, was destroyed into a leer. By the end of the decade he was as drunk as his parents, who by that time had spent all their son's money anyway. He was a bitter young man, and he told people his life had been stolen from him. Right after Pearl Harbor Skip enlisted in the Navy and was killed—gladly, gratefully, I've always thought—at Guadalcanal. His obituary said Amos Zangwill had been his benefactor.

Mossy played us all as if we were instruments in his mighty orchestra. If an instrument was broken, it could be replaced. We were the Jubilee Philharmonic, conducted by Maestro Amos Zangwill, with the whole country for our audience plus wherever on the rest of the planet someone had a projector and a screen.

When the contrite Trent Amberlyn was pulled in late that afternoon, his look alternated between defeat and desperation. He was brought in by Curtt Weigerer, to whose brawny frame Trent seemed almost to be handcuffed. But he had a friend with him as well, a bit player named Boyard Boulton, a small pudgy man who had clearly never been in the office of a studio head before. His eyes flicked around the room like a lizard's tongue, with his own little mixture of intimidation and contempt. Boy Boulton, as he was called, was known in a certain circle as Trent's lady-in-waiting.

Mossy was frighteningly silent as Trent awaited his beheading. Curtt Weigerer knew he wasn't supposed to speak either. Trent refused a chair and shifted his feet, a prisoner in the dock charged with conduct unbecoming a Jubilee star: picking up a fifteen-year-old to pay him for sex. "Mossy," Trent offered when he could find words, "all I can say is I was sure the kid was at least nineteen or twenty. I'm so sorry." He ran his fingers through his dirty unpresentable dyed blond hair. "I'm a wreck."

"I swear, Mr. Zangwill," Boy Boulton said, his eyes darting everywhere in the room but at Mossy, "some of these minors are unbeliev-ably seductive little bastards if you know what I mean."

"I can't say I do, Boy," said Mossy gently.

Curtt Weigerer snickered. Mossy gave a nodding cue. "Mr. Zang-will," the henchman said, "wants only Jubilee employees present. This is Jubilee business now."

"Excuse me," Boy Boulton said, "I was only trying to help my friend."

"We'll help your friend," Mossy said.

"I can't tell you how ashamed I am," Trent said when Boy Boulton had left.

"Your career could easily be over," Mossy said.

"A blessing."

"Self-pity won't help."

"It may make this bearable."

"The scandal could be unbearable."

"I know only too well," Trent said.

"But that wouldn't be any better for Jubilee than it would be for you." Mossy's voice began to rise. "We can handle what happened," he went on, "but you have to do what I tell you to do, which is to keep completely silent about this, to everyone including all your friends, which means you have to control that little shitheel who just minced out of here with his furtive fairy eyes. I don't trust him."

"He'll do what I tell him to."

"And you'll do what I tell you to do, Trent," said Mossy. "You need to work with someone smarter than you, and right now that's me. Understand?"

"I understand."

"You're going to be married."

"I'm what?"

"I'll let you know when I decide who the lucky girl is."

This was too much for the man about town who had been called by *Photoplay*, in a story I helped with, Hollywood's most eligible bach-elor. Trent was passing quickly from sniveling to defiant, as if some-thing had actually changed in his position, which it assuredly had not. "God, in case you haven't heard," said Trent, "is dead, and you have not been chosen to succeed him."

"Know anyone who can play the role better?" Mossy asked. "Besides, God is not dead, he's on location. I'm filling in for him until he comes back, and you're getting married. Remember, you're an actor, so go ahead and act like the man you're supposed to be, who your adoring fans believe you are."

"I have to be who I have to be on the screen. In my private life I can be myself."

"In your private life, yes, but being off camera doesn't mean private, and when you're off camera but in public you're still who I say you are. Trent Amberlyn, heartthrob to five million teenage girls, twenty million bored housewives, twenty or thirty million wishful middle-aged and old ladies. I gave you your name, Mr. Bernard Gestikker, and I can take it away. Right now I'm telling you who Trent Amberlyn is."

"I guess you can do that," said Trent, abjectly folding his hand. But he was still a star, clearly wanting to remain one, if chastised, and he shook his head at his putative maker. Like everyone else at Jubilee, he could be both dazzled and mystified by the boss. "What drives you, Mossy?" he said. "What makes you make decisions like this?"

"I do what I do because that's what I do when I do it," Mossy said. Turning to Curtt Weigerer, he added, "Go find that fifteen-year-old kid. Give him a present, ten thousand dollars cash, and tell him and his parents they should make themselves a new start with your gift. Also tell them that it wasn't Trent Amberlyn but his double that their kid met, only we don't want any false rumors flying around so we'd appreciate their silence. One last thing—they're probably a family on the south side of the law in a few other ways, so tell them any loose talk and we tell the police they're blackmailers."

Trent smiled a little, shaking his head. "All right," he said, "we'll all play the game just the way you do."

"I don't play the game," Mossy said, "I am the game."

When Trent Amberlyn and Curtt Weigerer had left, Elena brought in a pot of tea and two delicate porcelain cups. This was for Louella Parsons, portly, bossy, all-knowing even if much of what she knew wasn't true. She followed Elena into Mossy's office, sailing in like a cruise ship tooting her horn with three big hello's to the studio chief. The problem with Louella was that some of what she knew actually was true. "Didn't I see Trent Amberlyn outside?" was Louella's opening gambit. "Is he in trouble again?"

"He sure is," Mossy said, ignoring the 'again' and pouring tea for Louella, who had built her career not on talent but access and built her access on the almost infinite power of her employer, Mr. Hearst. Mossy sat the gossipist at a little round table well away from his desk, indicating this was a social moment, though of course neither of them was going to let his or her guard down. "Yes, Louella," Mossy continued, "this is a state secret I'm letting you in on, completely off the record until we release it. Trent was in to announce his engagement, and I'm begging him to hold off until we release his next picture. He may lose the heart of his fan base, which as you know is mostly women."

"Why I never," said Louella. "I couldn't be more surprised. Is it an actress?"

Mossy knew she was already thinking this might be a dodge. "You know I'd love to tell you, Lolly, but Trent swore me to secrecy. I promise you'll be the first to know."

Louella wasn't buying. "It's around town," she said, "that he picks up sailors and even got caught with a kid over the weekend."

"That's the most absurd thing I've ever heard," Mossy laughed.

"Well, if Hedda prints it and I don't, Mr. Hearst will want to know what's holding me up. Who's the girl, Mossy?"

Mossy shook his head, smiling. She had him. If he didn't tell her, she'd print the rumor about Trent being arrested, which wasn't a rumor anyway but simple fact. His mind whirred, all gears spinning. "Lolly," he said, "this is an exclusive, and Trent will kill me. I didn't know myself who the girl was until just now. You can't print it. Trent told me when he was in the office. It's Thelma Thacker."

Thelma Thacker was a plucky actress who came out from Minneapolis to play best-friend parts, and a couple of times she'd been the wife to bad husbands who left her, but she found her niche, really, in Westerns at other studios. Although Jubilee still held her contract, Mossy had been putting her on loan to Republic and Anchor Bay, a little company where she had graduated into becoming the first female gunslinger by helping Tom Mix chase down some outlaws. Mossy got four times her salary through the loan-out, which was for a serial with fifteen episodes. There was one problem with Thelma Thacker as far as marriage was concerned. Everyone knew she was a lesbian. As soon as he said her name Mossy realized he must have been thinking about homosexuals and he'd come up with perhaps the least likely candidate he could have mentioned.

"People say Thelma Thacker likes women," Louella said.

"If I had a buck for all the things people say," Mossy told her, pouring her a second cup of tea, "I'd buy Jubilee back from the bankers and make only pictures that uplift the social standards of American civilization." Mossy knew, of course, that he'd have to call Trent and Thelma as soon as he was rid of Miss Parsons. "Lolly you can't print this yet. Promise me."

"Well, live and learn," Louella said. "You know, Amos, I had lunch today with Rabbi Magnin."

Mossy couldn't have cared less about this, but he amused himself by envisioning the invincibly gentile Louella Parsons breaking bread with the self-appointed guardian and spiritual guide to the Jews of Hollywood. "And how is Edgar?" Mossy asked with no interest whatsoever.

"I bring word from Rabbi Magnin that you shouldn't make *Mad Dog of Europe*."

The property, which Mossy found both funny and horrifying, was a satire on Hitler by the screenwriter Herman Mankiewicz, and Mossy knew he could make it cheaply. "The good rabbi has my phone number," Mossy said.

"Yes, but he knows you don't like him. He thinks the movie will bring unwanted attention to members of the Jewish faith."

Apparently the lady couldn't say Jews or even Jewish people. "He does, does he?" Mossy replied.

"Frankly, Amos, I've had my doubts about the project myself. The rabbi said in no uncertain terms that such a picture could only inflame opinion against members of his faith. It will only increase the, uh, problem."

"You mean the Jewish problem, Lolly?"

"That's exactly what Rabbi Magnin means, and I have to say I agree with him."

"There are days, dear, when I almost wish I were a believer.

Please don't write that down. I was joking. That's as off the record as Thelma Thacker."

Elena buzzed Mossy, and he picked up his phone with annoyance. "Elena, you know perfectly well when Miss Parsons is here I don't—oh yes, all right, put him on." He looked at Louella and said, "Sorry Lolly, it's a friend of mine on the Jubilee board in New York. Hello Whitney, you're at your desk pretty late there, aren't you?"

Mossy listened, set his chin, knew he should have gotten Louella Parsons out of the office, and shook his head at himself. "Now Whitney," he said, "I'll have to see about that. I'm awfully glad you called … Me? No, I'm not worried at all, not concerned, I simply disagree, and I won't accept it, I won't be able to accept it, grateful as I am … ha ha … Sure I'm grateful, why wouldn't I be? Now I'm holding up your dinner, I know. I'll call you back tomorrow, Whitney. Thanks."

Mossy was at his peak here, like one of those creatures—rattler? buzzard? stag?—that does everything without intent, operating solely on reflex. He darts or springs. He swoops. He bites, chews, swallows. What came across as murderous impetuosity was only Mossy's being in tight communion with impulse. Even when, like a chess player who devises a dozen moves ahead, he seemed to be plotting, he was really only driving intuitively toward his target. The fight-or-flight synapses in Mossy were like tuning forks that, placed properly, can make an entire structure shudder with their vibrations. His impulses were as joined to his acts as a trigger on a pistol is to its hammer.

Shaking his head again, this time at Louella, Mossy smiled. "They want to increase my salary, can you imagine that? At this time, in this year? The board wants me to accept … Ouch! Ow!" Suddenly Mossy doubled over in pain.

Louella hurried around the little table. Mossy was growing pale. He crumpled to the floor, writhing. "What can I do, Amos?" Louella asked.

Mossy pushed out his words. "So sorry, Lolly. It's my ulcers. Again. This time it's, oh God, worse. Anyway, you won't find me taking a raise when the Depression is forcing me, ow, to cut people every month. Will you excuse me, Lolly, and please don't write anything about this, promise me, but I'll have to go into Cedars, I'm afraid."

Louella Parsons rushed out and Elena rushed in. Mossy straightened up and resumed his chair. "I'm going to have to lie low at damn Cedars for a few days, maybe a week," he said. "Elena, the sons of bitches in New York want to fire me."

"They what?" Elena said. "They can't do that."

"Greedy pissants, they say I lost too much money in 1933. The truth is, Jubilee was ahead last year while Fox was going bankrupt and the others were hurting. It's their goddamn theater chain that's losing by booking dogshit stinkers from other studios."

"That's enough to put anyone in the hospital," Elena said.

"Get me Dr. Kleinhans, we'll have to book a room at Cedars while I figure this out. They can't fire a man who's in the hospital. After that, get me young Jant, he could use a piece of candy. First, Winchell. He won't be at the Stork Club yet."

Elena got Walter Winchell on the phone, and Mossy leaked the exclusive that Jubilee's financiers in New York wanted to install one of their own—which meant an old-line moneyed Episcopalian like themselves—as head of the studio so they could control him. All the premier newspaper columnist in America needed was a veiled hint of anti-Semitism to run with a scorching unsourced item, leaving Mossy in the clear and, since Winchell was in New York, giving the impression to the Jubilee board that it was one of their own members who had sprung the leak. Mossy asked the columnist to wait a day before writing the story because he was going into the hospital for painful ulcers and wanted the bastards on Wall Street to know what they'd done to him. By the time Winchell's story appeared in the *New York Daily Mirror* two days later Mossy was safely ensconced in the Cedars of Lebanon Hospital.

Winchell wrote that the Jubilee board of directors had driven Amos Zangwill to have an ulcer attack, and it wasn't certain the doctors would be able to save his stomach. The phenomenally successful studio chief and exuberant picture maker might be on a bland diet for the remainder of his short life. The board ought to be ashamed of itself, especially if its nefarious plan to unseat Zangwill had anything to do with the prejudices that had landed Germany in its fascist sinkhole and were threatening to make their way across the ocean. The columnist listed Mossy's successes and achievements in molding great stars such as Palmyra Millevoix and Trent Amberlyn. If the big boys on Wall Street intended to shoehorn one of their own into the leadership of a Hollywood studio they'd find out what a sham and shame it was to sell short on Amos Zangwill.

Cowering before the onslaught of Mossy's ulcer attack and Winchell's condemnation, the board of directors immediately denied the rumor, producing a contract extension and, eventually, the very raise Mossy had lied to Louella Parsons about. For her part, Louella had the exclusive on being present at the ulcer attack itself as well as announcing the impending engagement of one of Hollywood's shiniest stars, whom she was not yet at liberty to name.

Mossy was so preoccupied with outwitting his New York bankers that he never came close to making *The Mad Dog of Europe*, leaving the anti-Hitler field to the more artistic hands of Charlie Chaplin. Years later Mossy told me he'd been a fool to pay any attention to Rabbi Magnin or his shikse representative. "A helluva mistake not to produce that picture," Mossy said. "Can you imagine—a rabbi telling a Christian to tell a Jew not to make a movie criticizing the biggest anti-Semite in history?" But what even Mossy didn't know and Louella Parsons had labored to forget was that, though she'd been a Catholic for as long as she cared to recall, she was born a Jew.

Mossy's summons for me that afternoon was to tell me to get out of town. When Comfort O'Hollie came for me I was so excited the boss wanted to see me again that I ran from the writers building to the executive offices two studio blocks away. Maybe Mossy had had second thoughts about taking me off *A Doll's House* and was now relenting, seeing that while changes were needed I was the one to make them. But maybe his second thoughts were about letting me stay at Jubilee in any capacity at all. With tremors of both hope and fear, I sidled past Elena into the throne room. Mossy, however, was not given to second thoughts; they were not in his nature.

"Take the Lark." That was all he said at first. A lark was what I wanted. I deserved a little fun after what I'd been through that day. "Get yourself out of town," he went on. "Wha, what do you mean?"

I stammered. He was kicking me off the lot for good. "Get up to San Francisco," he said, "I like the overnight train, the Lark."

He wanted to make a movie about the earthquake of 1906, but he had no story. He wanted me to talk to survivors for a few days. "Get me some idea of what they went through," he told me, "who were the heroes, the cowards, what about the police and fire departments? Come back with four or five characters we can play with." Mossy didn't like the books he'd seen about the earthquake, or had his readers read, because they all blamed the earthquake and fire damage on divine vengeance or poor architecture. Bad city planning and construction. The people's own fault, not the San Andreas Fault or any other California tectonic plates shifting their weight around. Zeus hurled a thunderbolt of caprice. Sinners were being punished; a decadent way of life in the wickedest city since Sodom was being wiped out. Instead, Mossy wanted people's own stories. "Take a thousand from Curtt Weigerer," he said, "spread it around to people you talk to, treat yourself to some high class pussy, bring me back a treatment for a picture."

I was thrilled yet daunted. I was sure I couldn't do what he wanted alone. "Jim Bicker is a fine judge of down-to-earth people," I told Mossy, realizing it was a mistake as soon as the words were out of my mouth, but I blundered on. "Maybe Poor Jim should go with me, we'll see twice as many people in half the time."

Mossy looked at me as if I were a gnat he'd somehow misjudged for a butterfly. "Jant, do you want to be a writer or do you want to be an assistant Communist?"

"Of course," I said weakly, "I'm a writer. I simply thought—"

"You goddamn didn't think at all! You guys would just hunt up the most bedraggled survivor and find out he lived in a house cheaply built by some capitalist greedmonger, and the whole natural disaster of the earthquake is reduced to a fat wad of injustice. You're so impressionable, Jant, and Bicker will wrap you around his finger and then wrap a red flag around you. If that's what you want, go work somewhere else."

I understood he was offering me a little plum to offset my demoralizing experience of being kicked off a script. I understood he didn't ordinarily do that with writers he canned. I understood I'd been a fool. I understood it might be too late. "Sorry," I said. "Bad idea."

"I've had some myself. Often wrong, never in doubt. Relax, Owen. There's only the one tale, how we suffer and how we're delighted. Go tell it. Bring forth what's in you, and it will save you. If you don't, it will destroy you—or else I will, take your choice. Bring me some good stories, I'll let you work on the script with Jamie McPhatter. Not Bicker, for Christ's sake. Get out of here! You waiting for a chauffeur?"

Jamieson McPhatter was the inflated blimp who had been with Sylvia Solomon at Mossy's party. He was capable of blowing his own horn until everyone had left any room he was in. But he had worked on DeMille's *Ben Hur*, the silent one, and on an early version of *The Last Days of Pompeii*. It was widely assumed by producers he could do catastrophes and natural disasters better than anyone since Noah got flooded in Genesis.

As I went to my Essex to drive home, I saw police cars roar onto the lot, followed by an ambulance. They squealed up to the executive building. A moment later Mossy was carried out on a stretcher, accompanied by two grave-looking doctors in full hospital white, stethoscopes at the ready. Alarmed, I saw Mossy loaded gently into the rear of the ambulance. I hurried back to the writers building to call Elena. She said our chief had had a sudden severe attack of ulcers, possibly complicated by a strangulated hernia, but I shouldn't worry. He was going into Cedars for a few days. It was a precaution. "Don't worry," Elena repeated, her tone confidential, a tone I didn't understand as I also couldn't understand why I shouldn't worry. "Keep going on whatever he told you to do," said Elena, hanging up. A moment later I heard the police and ambulance sirens screaming as the chief was borne off the lot, screaming, I realized years later, Mossy Zangwill's Bronx cheer to the rubes on Wall Street who had thought, only an hour earlier, that they had his number.

It was a precaution all right. In my head as I drove home, I drafted the get well note to my boss. Would it look too presumptuous if I sent flowers too?

14

Recoveries

Reassured by Elena that the boss was going to be all right, I danced back to Jubilee the next day to prepare my assault on San Francisco. Mossy had beaten New York so badly that it raised his salary from ten thousand a week to twelve thousand, not petty cash in those days. "Too muchee," said Pammy when she heard about this. "He's making and taking too much, and I'm going to get him to put the raise into a fund for actors he treats like slaves." "Good luckee," said Trent Amberlyn, who hadn't yet been informed about the identity of his fiancée, Thelma Thacker, whom he had never met. "An arranged marriage like in India where the bride and groom meet on their wedding day."

Yet it was fun, even on a diet of daily anxiety. Was it an accident the studios had been built on the Tehachapi fault line, site of a women's penitentiary and—fate was laughing—source of our periodic earthquakes? When earthquakes struck while a scene was being shot, actors ran to stand under the set's door frames, supposedly the strongest part of a room, though the door frames were false. At times the fear itself could be fun.

Only Wordsworth accurately described Hollywood in the Thirties: "Bliss was it in that dawn to be alive,/ But to be young was very heaven." The solidest flesh belonged to Amos Zangwill, who wasn't the usual kind of idealist at all. "Only the paranoid survive," said Mossy.

In his insouciance and his focus he was a bridge, last of the old-time studio chiefs who ruled by decree, first of the modern executives with their committees and foot soldiers all over town.

When I went to Curtt Weigerer to collect my expenses for the San Francisco trip, he tried, true to his scorpion nature, to cut the sum in half, insisting with some reason that a few days in San Francisco was worth two hundred dollars maximum—I should be paying Jubilee for the privilege—but he'd make it five hundred, an extravagance far beyond my station or desserts. What he actually said was, "Take five C's and beat it." I stiffened. Unexpectedly, I found a trace of spine, and said, "Okay, why don't we have Elena call Mossy at the hospital and see if five hundred is what he meant." He looked ready to sledgehammer me with his thick head. Possibly Mossy himself, in the act of conferring the assignment, had managed to ossify my customarily invertebrate posture. Curtt Weigerer glared at me from his desk; surely he was about to heave a lamp, perhaps he'd strangle me with his bare hands. What he did was whip open his top drawer, grab a wad of bills, and throw ten hundreds at me. "I want to know," he barked, "where every cocksucking penny goes, receipts for everything, even newspapers and shoeshines." "Whatever Mossy wants," I said, and scurried from the odious, irritable presence of the production manager–executioner. Even the playground bully didn't win every time.

Before heading north I had to see Pogo. His office reflected the man: it was receptive. Unlike the Viennese contingent in Hollywood, who patronized the occupants of their couches with references, possibly fictional, to the time they'd spent with Freud, Dr. Leszek Pogorzelski, from Cracow by way of Lisbon, with only a brief pilgrimage to Vienna, mostly listened. After the initial session in a chair, I had lain on his couch feeling he was looking either at me or at the notepad where he occasionally jotted something. Yancey Ballard had suggested him when I complained of having serious doubts about my worth in the picture industry or anywhere else. "Stick around Pogo for a while," Yeatsman had said, "and let Pogo stick around you." When I groaned at his miserable word choice, he added apologetically, "Puns are close to the heart of psychoanalysis, you know."

Curtains with waltzing couples on them were always drawn over the windows, separating Pogo's consulting room from the outside world, Wilshire Boulevard to be precise, speeding automobiles and ambition. His pictures were in pastels—three women at a sidewalk café, the reproduction of a Juan Gris cubist still life of musical instruments, a few others. At times I would turn to the Gris to speculate whether one of the instruments was a guitar or cello. The couch was a concession to the founder; it was covered in a flowery tapestry like the photographs of Freud's own study at Berggasse 19.

The doctor was blessed with a broad mouth that curved naturally into a smile, a round face with curious owl eyes, and tousled brown hair beginning to have a fringe of gray. No beard. I felt comfortable looking at him though normally my eyes were trained on his walls or on a Florida-shaped crack in his ceiling. He reminded me of no one but himself, with qualities of a genial college professor and a well-informed tour guide.

I told him I'd miss a few sessions while I was in San Francisco; it would be helpful for me, he said, to go forth and be with real people so different from my normal environment where unreality was the objective. I launched into a plaint about the unknown effect of having had an abbreviated childhood. Was it only self-pity? I mused about my mother gone so early, how her loss might have affected me. I recalled searching the face of every woman I met, the features and particularly the eyes, for some sign of motherhood. I was still, fifteen years later, doing this one way or another. Kindly eyes in Louisa Pemberton and Sylvia Solomon, the forty-year-old writers at Jubilee. "They look at me with something beyond interest and edging toward worry," I said, "at least that's how I read them. Their age the age my mother was when she ..."

I was silent. Pogo was silent.

"... stopped having age," I went on. Now I lurched forward, trying to bootstrap myself into the present, telling Pogo of brown-eyed Yvonne, the aging Jubilee script girl (as she was still called at fifty). I couldn't tell if she was condescending to me or flirting. Motherhood slips into girlhood, longing toward lust. I'd been reading Pirandello, pondering the quest for identity in his plays, and I said, "Listen, perhaps it's not a mother or girl or woman of any kind I'm looking for, perhaps this is about my writing. Unlike Pirandello with his characters in search of an author, I am an author in search of his characters." I stopped, craving a response. How smart I thought I was.

"Not so fast," Dr. Pogorzelski said. "To find your characters you must first find your own character, which has so far been hiding rather successfully from its presumed author."

I winced. I thought about telling him okay, I'll see you after San Francisco.

Luckily I'd had a dream, two really, both sexual. "In the first," I said, "Mossy and Nils Maynard are in Mossy's office. They're over by the reflecting pool measuring penises. They look like statues instead of men, and each points proudly to the tip of his penis. Though they don't notice me—in fact I don't really seem to be there—I see their reflections in the pool and the elongated reflections of their penises. There is no talk. Was this a contest? A light shines suddenly in the window and the dream ends. What I think about this is—"

"What's the second dream?" Dr. Pogo wanted to know.

"As full of talk as the first one was silent," I said. "I'm in the noisy commissary with Palmyra. Which would never happen, at least I'd never be there alone with her."

"In dreams anything can happen, like movies."

"Not movies under the new prude code."

"The Motion Picture Code hasn't reached into our dreamtime." Chuckle. "Yet."

Sometimes, I thought, he thinks he's funnier than I do. Apparently he wanted to remind me of the junction between my work and my sleeping fantasies.

"We're surrounded by tables full of faces," I continued, "though I don't recognize them. They're, well, extras in my dream, everyone jabbering. Pammy laughs heartily in a way I've never heard, and she says, 'Do you ever wonder how many people in the world, at any given time, are fucking?' I'm shocked at her word. We do some figuring on populations, and she says, 'Not everyone screws every day.' At this I notice how shy I am—she has said both 'fucking' and 'screws' while I've made no reference to sex. But I say, 'I guess a lot of people are, uh, in bed.' She laughs again, and others around us also laugh, distracting me. Writing numbers on a piece of paper I have with me, we come up with a total. I write something on the paper even though I can't see what it is, and she says, 'Yes that's it, a normal figure, many millions the world around.' I say, 'It could be a conservative figure.' 'Oh yes,' she says, 'then let's be liberal. At any moment there must simply be oceans of people fucking, whole oceans.' More laughter, and it seems the entire commissary of extras is laughing though I can't understand how they heard what Pammy was saying. At this the waiter brings me the check to pay and the dream ends."

"So, what to think?" Pogo asked.

"It all shows how inhibited I am," I said disconsolately. "In the first dream two guys are measuring their pricks and I'm not only not in the contest, I'm not in the room at all. Invisible in my own dream for Christ's sake. These two guys are my superiors, almost my kings. To them I'm a serf."

"And they are Narcissus, gazing at their images in a pool. You're in awe of them, but you may also look on them as men who cannot see beyond their own reflections."

"Which doesn't help me in the second dream, where this beautiful woman is talking about sex but I know I can't have it with her even though people all over the world are having it, and others are laughing at me. I'm ashamed to use the words she uses, even in a dream. Shamed. If I think about my parents in connection with this dream ..." I paused.

Pogo was silent. But I paused too long. Psychoanalysis is a bitch mistress, insatiable, sucking the air out of your lungs until you can say no more. Finally I said, "I don't know why I brought up my parents."

"Shame," Dr. Pogorzelski said, and for an instant I thought he was shaming me. "You used the word 'shame' just before you mentioned your parents, the very people who shame us when we venture out sexually. No reason Miss Millevoix and you shouldn't be having a cheery cackle over the sexual calculations you're making. You do the writing, as you do in a script, and she talks it the same as she would in reading lines you've written. She's the one who says millions, but you're the one writing it down. Politics sneaks in, too. You say 'conservative,' she says 'liberal,' you're protective, she's bold."

"You mean sexually or politically?"

"There's a difference?" He chuckled again. I didn't want him enjoying himself. "No," he said, serious now, "for our purposes here it's a question of being open or closed. We all need to say stop and we all need to say go. Perhaps in your fantasy she is on one side of you, your fears on the other."

"Okay, good. You think my parents made me ashamed about sex?"

"They didn't have to. Your mother died too early for her to have had a conscious effect on your later sexual habits, but not too early for you to have desired her, not too early for you to have felt guilty about desiring your father's woman, your very strong father at that. So you have the guilt and the fear both. How old were you—seven?"

"Nine. I was nine."

"Same as Lincoln, no? The perfect age for you to have felt some desire, aimed at your mother in particular. You didn't know many girls because your parents and you traveled so much. And she dies just at that moment when you are beginning to feel desire and before you have transferred it to girls your own age."

"The guilt wouldn't shame me from even expressing desire in a dream, would it?"

"Unless something else is happening."

"Like what? What could that be?"

"What could that be," he repeated without making it a question. I knew he wanted me to keep going.

"Not long before she got sick," I said, "I remember running into my parents' bedroom early in the morning. I had to tell them something, I forget what. My mother sprang up from the bed, I don't know if she was wearing her nightgown, and she dashed to the bathroom. My father glanced at me with a strange look on his face. Maybe he shook his head. I don't remember anything being said."

"You believe you disturbed them at coitus?"

"I don't know. Possibly. Soon after that my mother went into the hospital."

"What do you think was going on—for you?"

I was silent as I tried to remember more. Then I thought remembering was beside the point. Then I worried I'd never know anything. Then suddenly without my being aware of any thought at all, I heard myself blurt, "I stopped my parents from having intercourse? I desired my mother for myself and then she got sick so my own desire killed her. Is that what you mean?"

"I don't mean anything. You just said it. Is that what *you* mean?"

"I don't know—so the mere having of desire awakens an old guilt?"

"If you think so. We need to know more."

"I am doomed to walk the earth searching for a woman, feeling I don't deserve her when I do find her?"

"It's not so simple, not so final, dear Owen. In the first dream you said you were the serf of your bosses, yes?"

I was touched he called me dear. "Something like that," I said. "A serf is what I said I was to those two men at the studio. I can see them right now, as if I'm having the dream while I'm awake, comparing penises over that reflecting pool with Monet's lilies hovering over it." I swiveled on the couch to look up at Dr. Pogo. He wasn't looking at me but off to his right at a picture on his wall of a tree whose branches, scrutinized closely, became human forms. "I'm not dreaming now, am I, doctor?" I asked. "That would mean I'm going mad."

"Madness is having dreams while you're awake, and not knowing they're dreams," he said. "You're neither dreaming nor mad."

"Unless I'm mad at you for not getting Mossy out of my dreams."

Dr. Pogo was not interested now in kidding around. He said, "And in the second dream Palmyra Millevoix tells you oceans of people are fucking."

"Yes, but—"

"What about the mermaid?"

"Who? What mermaid?"

"The woman who came from the ocean that you had the fling with recently?"

"Well, she was hardly a mermaid."

"Pardon me for remembering, but you said she tasted salty."

"I see. And Pammy swam, too, that afternoon before I met the woman you call a mermaid. She even vanished, Pammy did, in her pool. The sun blinded me."

"And in the first dream, which ends when the light shines into Zangwill's window, you call yourself a serf."

"Right, but—"

"No buts. Serf is also the surf of the ocean, and if you're part of that perhaps even at some distance you're allowing yourself to desire it and plan for the eventuality of sex with a woman you want most. You'll be in the surf, Owen, we don't know with whom, not only with the woman from Arcadia who was almost anonymous with her two names. Remember she herself was just out of the surf. Your first dream is silent, like the old pictures, while the second is a talkie. Pictures growing up, you too. Palmyra says oceans of people fucking. Remember, too, you took charge, paid the check. You had intercourse with someone from the ocean, your own mermaid, yes? Be patient."

"I'll have to dream more."

"You'll have to live more."

15

Overnight

Downtown I booked the sleeper to San Francisco. The old station was dingy, dark with misfits and bums, hungry Mexican kids offering shoeshines for two cents. To bolster myself against Curtt Weigerer, I picked a high-end shoeshine from a toothless man who might have been forty and looked seventy. That shaved a nickel off my thousand dollars, but I gravely handed him a quarter, keep the change. The aroma of a Mexican spice garden, enticing, made me hungry, but it mingled with ancient piss. A guitar player in a food-stained serape serenaded passengers boarding the Lark with "Cielito Lindo," and I tossed him another quarter. Defying Weigerer. The assignment excited and menaced me.

The Lark took you from the western anarchy of Los Angeles to the formality of San Francisco with its eastern ways, perched improbably on the Pacific. Like my session with Dr. Pogo, both an ascent and a descent. A stranger among strangers, I avoided the other passengers, disdaining the hoi polloi as if their souls were unworthy of attention, knowing that by any studio standard I belonged among them.

I couldn't sleep in my compartment. The story in San Francisco would be the dying framing the living in today's Sodom. Turned into pillars of saltpeter. Would survivors remember what it felt and looked and sounded like when the earthquake struck almost thirty years ago, when the fire took over after the quake? Municipal vengeance.

My compartment was closing in on me, and I went out into the coach among the other travelers. Wanderers, near-vagrants, pilgrims, commuters. All looked green-gray, ghosts of the Depression, alive by virtue of not having quite stopped breathing. A solemn sad-eyed woman held a baby, even the baby didn't squall but lay slackly in its mother's slack arms. Two people across the aisle from one another spoke in murmurs. A man sat bolt upright in seeming rigor mortis, not moving a muscle or even, when I watched him, blinking. Four men in derbies played cards, silent, grim-faced, almost in slow motion. Two women knitted, wordless, possibly mother and daughter, appearing to add no rows to their patterns. Everyone awake, vigilant against something that could sweep them all away if they dared close their eyes and lose consciousness. I sat down in the empty seat next to the upright man.

We raced the night through the Mojave desert. The people in the coach sat motionless, faces now purple, night shadows from the moon ducking in and out of clouds, faces flickering as if a projector were running too slow. Entropy's tableaux.

I drifted back to my analyst's office. But it wasn't Pogo. I was telling a dream to someone else. As soon as I saw the studio I was afraid, but I couldn't avoid going through the iron gate, the J U B I L E E letters waving to warn me away, the apparition of a studio cop jerking his arm at me to enter. In Mossy's office, which was tubular like the inside of a submarine, I confronted his back, swiveled away from me so I could see only his shiny hair, which had lost its reddish tinge and was jet black. It was clear we were submerged deep below the ocean's surface. I wanted to leave and couldn't.

Mossy turned slowly in his chair until he was in profile and I could see malevolence in his one visible eye with long dark red lashes. His feldspar chin underneath a mirthless smile signaled danger. He turned back to face the knobs and gauges, instruments that were the command controls of this submarine. A flash of light, from undersea lightning or a giant flashbulb, obliterated everything, and Mossy was gone from his chair where an open crate of walnuts had taken his place. The nuts began to shake until their shells cracked and birds flew out, a flight of larks I thought. They swooped and flapped their wings to stay in place the way hummingbirds do. I told them I knew why they were larks and they didn't fool me.

Continuing to dream, I was reporting the dream to the Viennese analyst who had taken Pogo's place, and I worried that Pogo had become ill. "So, ve haf here an exaltation of larks, no?" the Viennese man said as I noted I'd fallen into the hands of one of the very doctors I was trying to avoid. "No," I said, resenting him for showing off his English to prove he knows a collective noun, "ve haf no exaltation, ve haf only ze larks zat seem to be Mossy transformed, I dunt know vy." The doctor did not see I was mocking him and rattled right on to the position of birds in Freud's thinking. "Zay are zeggzhual players, like za nuts." He dragged out his pronunciation of sexual and went into Jung's view of birds as spirits, which led him to Shelley's "To a Skylark." "Ve are egglectic, no? Ve can be picky and choosy." He played with lark, both bird and train—"You're on za Lark, heffing a lark, a liddle spree, larking about." Then his words became the birds and they darkened ominously into shadows that were all over the room. Though he wasn't present I feared Mossy. He flies, he's here, he's gone, he's there, he's everywhere.

The train jolted as though it might have run over a small animal. I pulled myself up from the dream within my dream. The man next to me was still upright, his eyes now shut as if someone had put pennies on them. He bounced stiffly at the jolt yet his eyes did not open. When I looked at him his lips curled into an admonitory smile. Did he see me through his lids, was he dreaming himself?

We were lumbering into San Francisco.

It was after dawn. I was not aware of sunlight. Clack-clack, clack-clack, outside the train the figures were dim, bustling. The faces inside the car arose. The train had stopped. I hurried to my compartment for my suitcase, and when I returned to the coach the souls were moving in the aisle. I stood behind the card players, still in their derbies, looking like four bowling balls in a row. Behind me the sad-eyed mother carried her baby, and the others appeared to have no luggage, only their underslung dismal air. I walked out of the train, out of the station, into the wall of fog.

16

Festival of Resistance

Y ou don't know what it is to be killed until you are brutally, abruptly, surprisingly killed—by someone you thought friendly, a comrade—and after that you will know, it hardly needs declaring, nothing at all. You will presently be extinct. Your knowledge shrinks as you watch your life shrink, watch the knife with the blade eight, ten inches long, make its unstoppable way toward you. Ashes to ashes and nothing to nothing.

The knife was at my arm, held by the enemy I'd thought a friend. Why my arm? He only wants to scare me, I was thinking hopefully as I tried to retreat. At the same time I could see the knife headed north toward my neck.

As a child I saw chickens killed that would flap around after their heads were neatly hatcheted off. One managed a circuit of my grandfather's barn, 360 degrees, coming neatly, amazingly to rest at his feet while he still held the gleaming though stained instrument of its beheading. He laughed. "Will you look at that, Owen? The creature doesn't know it's dead." It was doubtful I'd make it around the barn.

I held the knife back, that is I held the wrist holding the knife, trying to push it away, but this bulging arm against my own, though twice the age of my arm, was pure brawn, muscled and sinewed and bicepped from thousands of jobs of dockwork, from its hefting and hauling, probably from numberless fights in waterfront bars, until my arm was no match for it despite the doubling, trebling, of my strength through fear.

But was it only fear, fear and desperation, I was feeling? Was there not also the sense that at last, like San Francisco itself, this was something real? And was there not the further sense that my enemy, who had earlier been chummy if not my chum, was in some schoolish way making a mistake that, if only one of our teachers were present, she would have quickly rectified? "No, Steve" (which name I'll temporarily donate to this stevedore), "Owen is your friend, or at least ally, and you remember we had 'ally' in vocabulary last week and it meant someone on your side who is joined with you in a common purpose, so please, Steven, let Owen go, and Owen, you let Steve loose too or I'll have to keep you both in detention after class and send you to the vice principal who is not stingy with his ruler. No fighting on the playground. Now, Steve, right now!"

But there was no time, no playground to be rescued from by the benevolent teacher, because time was about to stop, four, three, two, and I could hear my breaths as I wondered, since they were surely to be my last, if I had ever heard my own breaths before. How did they smell. The trivia of the condemned facing his executioner.

Mossy had said he thought people would like to see a disaster worse than the Depression. New techniques in miniature and special effects would let him show, convincingly, an earthquake as it destroyed block after block of the great metropolis. "Tell me," he had said, "exactly what people were doing before the quake struck, what their brothers and mothers-in-law were doing, the way the woman next door was pulverized. Give me details, what happened every second of the quake. How did they survive? Even better, how did those who died die? And then the fire. The fire that follows will be the gravy on the roast beef."

Now I was the beef about to be carved, the disaster worse than the Depression. Except no one would ever know. Mossy would miss the picture I didn't bring back more than he would me, and Curtt Weigerer would wonder where the rest of his thousand dollars was.

When I arrived in the city, San Francisco not only felt bracing but was also visible to me. I saw through the fog to a place I could understand, or thought I could. Pure and knowable, apparent and transparent—this was the steep-hilled, sea-girt city I entered. One knew where one stood in San Francisco even when the place swam in fog. In Los Angeles, some of the poor and the working class were religious or political freaks, enthusiastically in favor of beating up a labor organizer; some of the rich, on the other hand, were Communists. They may have been the most casual, careless Communists, with butlers, pools, Japanese yard men, may have been cheerfully, hypocritically unaware of the disconnect between their behavior and their ideology, yet they colored themselves Red and called for the abolition of private property, called for the overthrow of the existing structures of state and capital. In San Francisco the poor, the workers, a slice of intelligentsia were where Reds were found if Reds there were at all, and the rich gazed out of the windows of their clubs with horror at any sign of unions. What a relief!

The papers had done interviews on the twenty-fifth anniversary of the quake in 1931, and that's where I started. At the doughty *Call-Bulletin* I bumped into a half sober reporter his colleagues called Roughride Reynolds because he'd actually been with Teddy Roosevelt more or less charging up San Juan Hill in the Spanish American War. Ruddy, big-bellied, laughing in every sentence as he swilled his beer. He told me the whole charge was a sham, that the troops had simply walked up an undefended rise and that he, Reynolds, had staged the photograph that ultimately put the first Roosevelt in the White House. After the war he'd come west and landed on the old *Evening Bulletin*, covering the earthquake when it struck. "Ought-six," he said, "not one of us thought we'd get out alive. First the quake scared us half to death, then the fire ate up the city."

I read a few interviews Roughride had done with earthquake survivors for the 1931 series, but he'd lost their addresses. "Fact is, Sonny," he said to me, "I made up a lot of this, haw haw. Go down into the Tenderloin, or Fisherman's Wharf, old-timers will talk to you. Making a picture, eh? Better have a gentleman of the Fourth Estate in it. Haw."

At Hearst's *Examiner*, I saw a newsman named Hoover Townsend, a ramrod in pinstripes and a vest. It was hard to imagine him as anything but a banker. I asked what drew him into this line of work. "Someone has to uphold community standards," he said. His only interviews were with Nob Hill crusties who had their servants tell them what damage the quake and fire were doing.

Better luck at the *Chronicle*, where a reporter named Jack Quin sent me to his cousin Mike who had not only done interviews but also published a pamphlet on the earthquake, *A Celestial Joke*, a bitter screed on the class distinctions present even in a natural disaster. "Oh sure," Quin told me, shooing his unruly red hair off his freckled Irish face, "everyone pulls together, everyone's in the same boat, the quake reduces everyone to the same level of horror—for all of an hour, two at most. After that the swells take over. 'Dora, would you make certain there's marmalade for the mister's toast, Bannister will bring round the brougham so Lavinia and myself can survey the destruction downtown. Marquez, do give last night's leftovers to the Ladies Aid but be back to have supper on the table by eight. We'll be wanting the lamb shank this evening.'" Poor Jim Bicker—Mossy was right—would have loved this guy.

Mike Quin slipped his voice back out of his impression of a prissy Nob Hill bluenose. "Christ on a crutch but I'd like to have seen some of them go without their damn lamb shank for one bloody evening!"

I told him I wanted to meet waterfront people who had been around since the turn of the century—gamblers, lowlifes, barkeeps, prostitutes. "You're the boss," he said, and sent me off to what was left of the old Barbary Coast. Waterfront dives were new to me, but it wasn't hard to get people talking. "What were you doing at the time of the earthquake?" I'd ask, buying someone a beer or a shot. "About what I'm doing now," they'd all start, and then the tales would pour.

The Barbary Coast had mostly been destroyed in the earthquake and fire, but the grizzled barflies rebuilt the taverns, opium dens, gambling houses, flophouses, and whorehouses for me as if they were all still around the corner. As I listened I saw the henchmen at the studio as neighborhood enforcers with Mossy as their double-breasted head gangster. Pammy would be a singer in a posh gaming house Mossy had in a shakedown vise until the detectives Nils Maynard and Yeatsman foiled him and his crooked cohorts. I myself was the enterprising reporter who exposed the whole scheme.

A one-legged bartender told me he saw three men trapped on the roof of a burning building. "Must have been two thousand people down in the street, stopping to watch as they ran from the flames a block away. A company of soldiers were trying to keep order. The three men on the roof were screaming for help as the fire climbed closer and the roof began to cave in. The Army captain ordered his sharpshooters to aim at the men on the roof so they wouldn't burn. Boom. Boom. Boom. The soldiers shot the three men to kingdom come but at least they weren't roasted alive."

An old lady with dyed blonde hair rasped that she'd been a madam and her establishment escaped the flames. "No ya wasn't no madam, Minnie," one of the workmen brayed at her, "Ya was a workin' girl in the old Ruby House, ya know ya was." The woman joined the laughter and went on. "Ordered all my girls," she said, "to give it away to any cop or fireman. Saving the city, they were, deserved a little relaxation."

(Pretty quickly it was obvious that oral history is, in practice if not by definition, nostalgic calisthenics, subject to contamination from what happened later as well as the usual discrepancies imposed by nostalgia itself.)

After the first day Mike Quin met me for a drink, excited about what he claimed was a far better story than the earthquake. "It's happening today right under your nose," he said. I said I didn't know what he was talking about. "Nevermind, Skinny, make your goddamn moving picture."

The next morning I went on hearing about such things as the stampede of cows up Market Street bellowing and wild with fright. "The street opened up in the aftershock," an elderly man in Union Square told me as I tried to visualize how special effects would handle this, "and swallowed all the cattle into its chasm, all but a baby calf who wandered over to me as I crouched by a swaying building that somehow didn't fall. It was ridiculous but I started petting the calf. A Catholic priest came by and said we had to get the ferry to Oakland, and he led us down to the ferry, the calf following me like I was its mother. Ten thousand people were trying to catch that ferry, and we waited five hours.

"People huddled together here in Union Square," the old man went on, "as the fire lit up the night sky. One group was praying loud when a crazy man came by and screamed the Lord had sent this to them so they shouldn't pray to him any more. A great roar shook everyone, and it was an eight-story building collapsing like a crushed biscuit. I was walking behind a fellow swinging his lunch pail as he tried to report for work. A cornice from a bank broke off and flattened him. The Army dynamited buildings to deprive the fire of nourishment, whole blocks of buildings. Wagons with horses still harnessed, drivers in their buckboards lay dead in the streets."

"The unbelievable worst I saw," a bartender told me on my third day, "was I came on a man trapped in the burning wreckage of a grocery store. Meat was cooking around him, chops and steaks from the butcher's counter barbecuing. The man lay silent, pinned under two huge wooden beams. A rookie cop ran up and got a bunch of us to try to move the beams. We couldn't budge them. The man didn't begin to scream until one of the beams was on fire at his legs. He begged the young cop to shoot him. The cop kept pulling on him while the man pleaded to be shot. No one could move the poor fellow. Finally the policeman asked the man his name and address. The man shouted it out. 'Phineas Mulford!' he yelled, a name I'll take to my own grave. The rookie took the address, and he crossed himself before he shot the man square in the head. But he couldn't stand what he did, and he ran around the corner and shot himself."

A woman at Fisherman's Wharf was the first person who let me know what Mike Quin was referring to when he said something else was happening in San Francisco. "What's going on right now, Sonny, in this year of Our Lord 1934, is going to make or break this city. Never you mind God's little hiccup back in Oh Six." She pointed to a group of men marching picket across the street. They shouted and held signs.

Squat, indefatigable Mike Quin was on me every evening after I finished my day's quotient of survivors. Wanting to know what I'd done, nudging me to do something else while I shut him up with earthquake lore. I was buying the drinks; he probably figured let the skinny make his own mistakes. I might have seen an item in the morning paper, but I was so intent on finding the story Mossy wanted, figuring out his movie, that the occasion in San Francisco, heating up in front of my eyes, had eluded me.

The morning after I saw the marching pickets I let Quin take me down to the Matson docks. The SS *Lurline* was parked there, sleek, shining, a Thoroughbred of the sea. I looked at the *Lurline*, luxury on the waves, wishing I were on it. I saw Pammy's eyebrows, each really the watercolor of an eyebrow, and imagined how she'd look on the deck at sunset. I didn't hear Quin. "Paralyze the docks with their strike," Quin was telling me, probably for the third time. "The *Lurline* doesn't look as though she'll ever sail to Honolulu again, does she? Not a soul aboard. Then they'll paralyze the city itself, maybe the whole coast. You hear me, Skinny?" He called me that, I knew, not because I was particularly thin but as a way of whittling me down to the size of an apprentice.

Quin would get a kick out of writing my little obit after the stevedore finished me off with six or seven thrusts of his blade. Skinny got in over his head. A featherweight going in against that big lunk Primo Carnera. Who's to blame, the featherweight for being brazen or the Dago for doing what comes naturally? "Ya wanna see us working for pennies like Coolie labor, dontcha?" the huge stevedore yelled at me. "No, no," I gasped as I ducked away, "I don't, I don't." He dealt me a clean slice in my leg as I kangaroo hopped away from him. "Lay off, ya big Kraut," another stevedore yelled, "He's like the rest of us only been to school." But this guy ran off, and my tormentor wasn't buying. "He's nothin' but a Hearstie is what he is," he sputtered. He had me against a storefront, and he smelled blood. Facing death, I understood for a tenth of a second how he was right in a way. I might as well work for Hearst since I was a voyeur here, hoping to profit in my own way from the striking longshoremen's grief and pain.

After we left the Matson docks Quin had taken me around the Embarcadero to the dockworkers' headquarters a few blocks from where the foundation was being laid for the bridge to Oakland. Alleys and small streets chopped into the Embarcadero all along the waterfront. This was where the Barbary Coast had once darkened and enlivened the neighborhood before the earthquake and fire destroyed much of it.

Quin was introducing me to the city he had a lover's quarrel with. "Six hundred thousand of us here, Skinny," he said, "fifty percent white collar, fifty percent laborers. Blessed with harbors and panoramas. From the heights you look out over blue waters to the rolling Marin hills and the mountain peaks beyond. At night the cities across the Bay—Oakland, Berkeley, Alameda—sparkle with a million lights, and if a moon makes its appearance the waters present a level meadow of silver. A young Italian, big, broad-shouldered, graceful, echoes the elegance of the city. Center fielder for the Seals, boy from Fisherman's Wharf swings his bat like an eagle spreading its wings.

"Through the heart of San Francisco cleaves the wide Market Street," Quin said, "backbone of the city. The groove down the center of Market holds the cable for cable cars and we call it the slot. If you're north of the slot, you're prosperous, at least a merchant. South of the slot you're a laborer, you're in the Irish stronghold, you're a Catholic. If you have a little store you're paying protection to the Muldoon brothers, as sorry an excuse for Irishmen as ever disgraced the shamrock. The Muldoons run half the cops and three quarters of the whorehouses of which there are well over a hundred. More tentacles than an octopus, more poisonous than a nest of rattlesnakes.

"The residential sections reach out from Market Street over all the hills of the city—here are the Italians, over there the Chinese, down there the Negroes, up there the swells, each district as sharply defined and controlled as an autonomous republic. But the key to everything in San Francisco is the little knot of shipowners and dock owners, often the same people of course."

"Why is one small group," I asked, "the key to so much else?"

Quin patrolled his subject like a cop on the beat he knew better than anyone else. Which didn't prevent him from additional roles as a teacher and a preacher. "Because, Skinny," he said, "cargo is the word that drives this town. Before we're anything we're a seaport. Most of us, one way or another, get our income from the transactions that surround the movement of cargoes. Insurance companies, banks, real estate brokers, wholesale firms, shops, hospitals, schools, restaurants, theaters, hotels— all exist for the service or entertainment of a community devoted to the constant flow of boxes, barrels, bales, the tonnage that feeds or clothes or houses distant populations and brings back raw materials and cash. Yet the men who lay hands on this cargo and keep the living pulse of the community beating basically derive no share in its returns. And the seamen who bring in the cargo, whose hazardous work is the cornerstone of the city's prosperity, are looked down on as one of the lowest forms of existence. The straw bosses do the hiring, and they belong to the owners. A longshoreman gets up before dawn, trudges dock to dock. Often he finds no job at all and when he does he has to pay a piece to the straw bosses, which keeps the longshoremen in competition with each other and drives wages down. Company unions, sure, but no organization workers can call their own. Corruption rules the system, and the owners, who seldom even lay eyes on the cargo, much less lift it, rule the corruption. That's our city, and that's what the strike is about."

I said I could see why the longshoremen and the seamen had their backs up.

"Nothing makes a capitalist madder," Quin said, "than the existence of something he can't buy with his money, confuse with his lies, or scare with his threats."

Conditions on the waterfront had turned the stevedores into dry leaves awaiting a spark to ignite them. The spark was both desperation and hope, the desperation brought about by the Depression, and the faint hope sent from FDR's Washington that it was permissible for working people to organize themselves. Once lighted, the flames were fanned by the Reds, who saw every strike as a small revolution that could lead to a large one. In Quin's opinion, the Reds were useful catalysts, not causes, in the strike.

"Young Skinny," Quin said, though he looked no more than a few hard-living years older than I was, "San Francisco is shaking more now than it did during the Quake." As he led me around the Embarcadero we passed pickets at most of the docks. Quin shouted encouragement to them. "Twice as many longshoremen as there are jobs on the waterfront," Quin told me. I said that was pretty much the situation among writers in Hollywood. "There you go," he said, and I knew he wasn't taking me seriously. "You got a union?" he asked. Maybe he was taking me seriously a little bit. "Yes," I said. "Well no. We're trying to have one." "Get going," he said.

It was late May. The longshoremen's strike had begun a few weeks earlier, essentially with the workers themselves—Quin called them the good old rank and file—defying their own leaders, who were afraid of the owners and didn't want to rock, literally, the boats in San Francisco harbor. "Fellows bringing home only fifteen, twenty a week," Quin said, "want maybe a buck an hour. That and a union shop with a union dispatcher. No more straw bosses. That's the part drives the owners crazy."

Upstairs in the International Longshoreman's Association headquarters just off the Embarcadero, Quin introduced me to men waiting to go on picket lines. Tough-looking guys, eating sandwiches in a single bite, soup in a swallow. Peopling the place with actors, I thought Victor McLaglen or Wally Beery would have been at home. Two men named Cromartie and Widdelstaedt, two sides of beef, each looked as though he could grapple an ox to the ground or perhaps just throw one into the hold of a ship. "Hey Nickie, me and the Crow could use six, seven more sammitches," Widdelstaedt yelled to the back of the room. In a minute a composed, slender fellow came forward with two bowls of soup. "Soup!" Widdelstaedt barked. "Did I say soup? Crow, did I say soup, we don't need no more fuckin' soup, we'll have to piss all afternoon, I said sammitches."

"Sorry boys," the slender fellow said, "I've already served you more than the Strike committee says. Everyone gets one, two at the most, you guys each had four." He turned to Quin and me. "Mike, you want their soup? And your pal?"

I was introduced to the cook, Nick Bordoise, as he handed me a steaming bowl of potato soup with carrots, onions, and chunks of brisket in it. Bordoise wasn't in the ILA but in the cooks' union, and he'd had a recent appendectomy that kept him off his regular job in a downtown restaurant. He was from Crete and had been to sea as a cook on a freighter; he was helping the ILA while he recuperated. He was marked by his Greek accent and his outspoken sympathies. His name, Quin told me, had been Counderakis, but he changed it to his wife's name to keep out of range of the immigration authorities. Bordoise looked vulnerable, and Quin asked him how he was after his surgery. "Still redder than your hair, Mike," Bordoise said quietly. "The

Reds are for what I'm for, workers' rights and we own the fruits of our labors. *Kali orexi*. Eat up."

Bordoise spoke like someone being recorded, yet he had a sweetness in his voice I didn't hear among the barrel-chested stevedores.

"Don't need fuckin' Communists," Widdelstaedt said. "Yer as bad as the finks."

"The Reds are supportin' us," another longshoreman said. "More than I can say for the papers, the cops, the damn city government. Did ya see the *Examiner*?"

I actually had seen the *Examiner* the day before. Hearst's paper said Moscow was using the waterfront strike to seize San Francisco as a colonial possession.

"You know I feed you good, right?" Bordoise said and was answered with a small cheer. "Okay then, but five million Americans are swallowing poison every day, not with their mouths but their eyes. The five million readers of Hearst papers."

The union members banged their tables and said Nick should be an honorary member of the ILA. Widdelstaedt said any union member reading a Hearst paper should be beat up good, an ominous threat I didn't sufficiently recognize.

Bordoise was a gentle fellow, a little like the younger scenic designers at Jubilee, the designers who hadn't yet become prima donnas. Whenever I was in the ILA hall, Bordoise was as eager to give the longshoremen a satisfying meal as fancier chefs are to know how a patron likes their bouillabaisse or veal Marengo. The others, even the toughs like Widdelstaedt and Cromartie, also struck me as honest guys trying to do a job and be paid fairly for it. At the moment I fancied myself more like a stevedore than a studio hack, more at home in the union hall than at Jubilee where I was trying to worm my way into acceptance. What a fool I was, I suddenly thought the following day as my attacker slashed the air with his knife and lunged at me when I'd temporarily broken his hold. I felt accepted up there in the union hall, yet I was only being measured. In a moment he had me pinned against a parked car. Here came the blade again.

Outside the hall a day earlier, the afternoon atmosphere along the

Embarcadero was of a battlefield where combat had not begun. The police lined up to protect the docks while the strikers marched on the landward side of the street shouting and shaking their picket signs. "It's not the cops they're shouting at so much," Quin said. "It's the scabs."

The nonunion workers, the scabs, were returning to work from lunch. Some were thickset football players from the University of California at Berkeley; their coach had told them strikebreaking was a healthy form of spring practice. Some were hoboes who needed any kind of work during the Depression; some had been imported from other cities along the coast, like Los Angeles, where strikebreaking was essentially a profession. A few were blacks whose only chance to work on the docks was as strikebreakers. In the years he himself had spent at sea before becoming a journalist and pamphleteer, Quin noted that the only blacks among the seamen were ones hired as stewards. "But it'll change if the strike wins," he said. "The Seamen will stay out in support of the Longshoremen, and both unions will bring Negroes aboard if they won't work as scabs anymore. But first these owners need to be taught a lesson they won't forget."

I never asked Quin if he was a Communist; I assumed it.

As a landlubber, I did ask what was the attraction of the job for seamen. They were routinely mistreated by captains and first mates, underpaid, often robbed and beaten when they went ashore. Aboard ship, they were held almost like prisoners.

"Yes," Quin said, "and the cruelty at sea is matched by the cruelty of the sea."

"Then why ship out in the first place?"

"It's a job when you can get one. And have you ever stood at the railing with spray in your eyes at sunrise, come through a storm that tested every fiber of your body and brain, felt your ship roll under you like it was a woman, breathed with it as it plowed furrows in the fickle currents, or tangoed into a distant port with all that fun and possibility and strangeness ahead of you?"

That shut me up.

In addition to police on foot along the Embarcadero, guarding the docks as though they were working for shipowners, which in a sense they were, other police cruised the waterfront in radio patrol cars, on motorcycles and on horseback. The cavalry were everywhere. Quin pointed to police lookouts on top of the Ferry Building.

"Pressure is mounting, Skinny," he said.

That night Quin took me to a workers' meeting in Dreamland Auditorium. Four or five thousand Longshoremen, Teamsters and Seamen were packed in, many with their families. Curious San Franciscans also showed up, some no doubt hoping to see a fight, many interested in the strike that was paralyzing their city. A stout Teamster told me they called the hall Dreamland because it was used for boxing matches, and many of the fighters left the building unconscious. He horselaughed.

The great cavern of Dreamland could have been a studio sound stage with seats. The various unions—most had already joined the strike, some hadn't—were convened as if for a pep rally before a big game. Mike Quin said it was much more. It was the outpouring of a century of frustration, of overwork and underpayment, of earlier strikes that had failed, of a kind of barbarism where human beings were treated as beasts of burden. "The working men," he said, "have now come together to claim their own."

Most of the huge crowd were not sitting but milling, greeting friends, shouting encouragement. Quin mingled. Small groups were singing labor songs. Nick Bordoise, the cook in the Longshoremen's headquarters, was passing out sandwiches. He sang a Greek accented "Solidarity Forever": "You can't fooling me I'm stuck to the union." In some parts of the auditorium there were arguments—whether the unions should all make common cause or hold to their separate crafts, whether a union shop was a necessity, whether Communists were helpful or bad for the labor movement, whether union members with families could hold out as long as single men.

A bell sounded, the chiming kind used to signal the start of a prize fight. Lights dimmed and a spotlight coned the stage, where a microphone stood. As I looked for a seat I spotted a tall elderly lady, a white-haired woman in a long, rather foreign dress buttoned to her neck. She held her chin high as though she were under some kind of siege and needed to keep all her dignity about her for the sake of some principle. Peering at her, I was shocked to see Yancey Ballard escorting her, deferring to her. What the hell was Yeatsman doing here? Who was the old lady? Mike Quin reappeared as the bell was rung several more times, and we wedged ourselves into seats next to two large union men. "The Longshoremen's national leader, Joe Ryan, is here," Quin said, "and he's sent around a deal to the local committees that he's negotiated by himself."

"Boys, gentlemen, and ladies," said a man in a business suit who had stepped to the microphone at the center of the stage, "I bring you greetings from the president of the United States." This received conditional applause, some boos. In back of me someone said that if Roosevelt was on their side the best thing he could do was stay out of their way. The man on the stage introduced himself as Edward McGrady, the Assistant Secretary of Labor. "This strike," McGrady said, "can be settled as all issues are, through compromise, and you men can be back at work with pay raises if you just won't let the radicals and frankly the Red element control what you're doing." This was greeted by a shout from the rear of the auditorium: "No one controls what we're doing but us!" Cheers. "All right," McGrady continued, "what I mean is President Roosevelt, the most pro-labor president in our history, fully supports your right to collective bargaining, but he believes the continuation of the strike can only hurt everyone out here on the Coast, all the working people and honest businessmen alike. So it's time to go back."

This line of reasoning was going nowhere. The general sentiment was, We've been pushed around enough. Chants erupted: "Support the strike! Support the strike!"

A gaunt man of perhaps eighty shuffled to the microphone to respectful applause. "The old man of the sea," Quin said. "Andrew Furuseth has worked for seamen's rights since the last century, believes labor is holy and wages are like divine grace."

"The anger of early days," Andrew Furuseth said, "the denial of our rights has led us to where we are. But the owners now offer us most of what we want. We can settle this far better when you're back at work." A few clapped; everyone else was silent. No one would boo someone regarded as a union saint, but they wouldn't do his bidding either. "To work," Furuseth went on, "is to pray. Your labor is your sacred possession. I want to say to our brothers who are former seamen come ashore to start your families and become longshoremen, it is time after three weeks to return to our tasks. As sons of God everything we want can be achieved, can be settled, and can be settled by arbitration."

As Furuseth ambled off to far less applause than greeted his entrance, Quin told me arbitration would not win the one point longshoremen care most about, the union shop. "Old Andy's day is done, and at this point he merely clutters up the scene."

The strikers wanted their pep rally and were being told to end their strike. The next two speakers came to the stage together—Mike Casey, San Francisco's International Brotherhood of Teamsters leader, and Joe Ryan, International Longshoremen's head, whom Quin told me had made his own deal with the dock owners. Casey, who had once been so tough he was known as Bloody Mike, tried to shoo his men back to work and was met with boos. He left quickly.

The dignified elderly woman with Yeatsman as her escort rose from her seat several rows behind Quin and me and began making her measured way to the front. She leaned on her cane as well as on the arm of a young woman I recognized with disbelief. It was Comfort O'Hollie from Jubilee. Yeatsman cleared the aisle in front of them.

Joe Ryan strutted to the microphone. He had risen from poverty, but Quin told me he was now more comfortable with politicians, racketeers and even business leaders than with his own longshoremen. He was wearing a double-breasted suit, splashy cufflinks, a diamond stickpin in his ostentatiously handpainted tie, and a huge ruby ring on his pinkie. "You men have made your point," Ryan began, "You've made it loud and clear, as your brothers have up and down the Coast. I salute you."

Scattered applause. But it was provisional; essentially the union members were applauding Ryan for applauding his longshoremen. "I'm here to announce very excellent news," Ryan went on. "I've arrived at an agreement with the major industrialists here. We have the best offer we can get, and it will bring better offers in every new contract."

"It won't bring us a union shop!" a man shouted from behind Quin and me.

"High time to get the Bolshies off our backs!" Ryan shouted right back. "And high time for San Francisco to lead everyone on the Coast back to work!"

"You're leading us straight to Hell, Joe!" from another corner of the auditorium.

"I've negotiated fair terms," Ryan tried again, but this was met with guffaws.

A beefy man next to Quin said, "I've been to fixed fights here before. This is nothing new for Dreamland."

Joe Ryan, a famous labor leader unused to opposition, made one more try, but he was angry at his own rank and file. "Now listen to me, all of you, I was on the Chelsea docks in Noo Yawk loading pig iron before most of you were born. I've fought for fair deals all my life, and this is the fairest deal I've ever made—it's a gentleman's agreement, raises for every dockworker, no scabs, no overtime without extra pay, no more kickbacks at the shape up ..."

And that was as far as Joe Ryan could go. At the phrase "shape up," which meant continued control of hiring on the docks by straw bosses working for the owners, Dreamland exploded in a thunder of boos and nos and catcalls.

A longshoreman with an eyepatch, a former brawling seaman known as Pirate Larsen, ran to the stage and hurled himself onto it. "It's unanimous, King Joe!" he shouted. "You're a fink yourself and you're trying to make finks of all of us! No to your shape up, no to the owners, and no to making separate sweetheart deals up and down the coast with any owner who pays for your next holiday in Europe!" Cheers.

"And I say," Ryan bawled, "no to your radicals and no to the Communist line!"

"The only line I follow is the picket line, King Joe!" To the accompaniment of wild cheers, Ryan evaporated from the stage, taking a seat in the front row. Boxing had returned to Dreamland, and Pirate Larsen knocked out Joe Ryan in one round.

Comfort O'Hollie was now helping the old lady up the steps of the stage while Yeatsman waited below. Had he come along as Hibernophile and chaperone for Comfort, or were he and Comfort ...? I didn't dare finish my own thought. "Is this a union meeting or a vaudeville show?" I asked Quin. "You might call it a resistance festival," Quin said.

Pirate Larsen was speaking again, and there seemed to be a program for the evening's events after all. "Before we turn the proceedings over to the man who's really representing us in the strike," Larsen said, "meet a true worker's hero, heroine rather, the courageous woman who not only stood on the barricades in Dublin against the might of the British Empire, who fought alongside the Irish Revolutionary Army after her brave son was martyred in the cause of Irish liberty, but who also happens to be the aunt of our own working-class martyr, Tom Mooney. Say hello to Patricia Mooney O'Hollie, best known as Grandmother O'Hollie!"

Accompanying her grandmother, Comfort O'Hollie was paying her debt to the father she'd never known, who had been ambushed by the British in 1916. "What do the Irish have to do with this?" I asked Mike Quin. "Your guess equals mine," he said. "I'd heard an old Irish firebrand came down from Vancouver to plead with the governor for her nephew's release, but I didn't know she'd be in the hall tonight." On the stage, Pirate Larsen had taken the arm of Grandmother O'Hollie. Tom Mooney was a radical who had been arrested in San Francisco almost twenty years earlier when a bomb went off, killing ten people, during a World War Preparedness Day parade. Although the district attorney's case against him was based on perjury and the jury was tainted, Mooney was sentenced to death, which was later commuted to life imprisonment. His name became a rallying cry for the Left. Union members often chanted "Free Tom Mooney," and that was what they did now as Grandmother O'Hollie hobbled on her cane to the microphone.

She was brief. "The greetings I bring you from my nephew Tom are clear," Grandmother O'Hollie said, her brogue quavering but stronger with each syllable. "Make the owners hear you, make them listen to your needs, never you mind the social theories, stick to the real problems the strike has to solve. And no matter what anyone tells you, stay out until your just needs are met. So says Tom Mooney from his prison cell!"

This was easy for everyone to applaud because her dismissal

of social theories was a signal not to pay attention to Communist proselytizing.

"I promise you as sure as I stand here," she went on, "to continue the struggle wherever working people are oppressed to the appointed end of my days." Grandmother O'Hollie paused as more chants of "Free Tom Mooney" filled the hall. For a moment she looked to be swallowed by her memories, but then she held up her hand for silence. "When this too short earthly span is over," she said, her Irish voice rising now, "and others have taken up the causes we've all lived for and a few have died for and more of us will *have* to die for, when my hour comes round I promise to pass out leaflets on the number of hours a day Saint Peter can require wings to be worn while I organize the angels!" The cheering started, but this time she held up her cane and shook the hall to silence. "To those who think I'll be traveling the other direction, send word to the Devil he'll have his hands full and more with Grandmother O'Hollie! God bless this strike!"

She was performing for the very ovation she now received. I preferred her no-nonsense granddaughter, which was why I was suddenly so jealous of Yeatsman as he disappeared out of the auditorium with Comfort and her grandmother. But Mrs. O'Hollie had neatly caught the sentiments of the Dreamland crowd, many of whom had been brought up on Communion wafers with the certain promises and threats of an afterlife.

In contrast, the overgrown pixie with the hook nose who now took the stage had neither an air of elegance nor an aura of destiny about him. Looking haggard, he wore a dark cardigan sweater over an open-collared shirt. "I'm Harry Bridges of the Strike Committee, International Longshoreman's Association Local 38–79," he said prosaically. All the others had been opening acts; though he was only beginning to be well-known, Bridges was the main event. Lean and a little bent even in his early thirties, he was a former Australian seaman who jumped ship in San Francisco to become a longshoreman. Bridges had taken over the strike strategy when the union leadership had essentially backed away from the men on the picket lines. Applause for Bridges was enthusiastic but stopped quickly when he began to speak again without even holding up his hand. "Bridges represents labor," Quin said, "but he's all business."

"Dollar an hour for us longshoremen," Bridges said in his Down Under accent, "dollar and a half when we work over thirty hours a week, a hiring hall we control and no more company union. Goodbye to the straw bosses and their wretched kickbacks. We don't think that'll bring down the republic. We're the refuse and the rejects, we dockmen and seamen, let's see them refuse and reject these entirely reasonable demands."

Dreamland was silent, attentive.

"To those of you who may be tempted either by empty cupboards or the owners' paltry offers," Bridges resumed, "I tell you this. You can separate a dog from its leash but not from its hunger. Now we've slipped the leash, but until we find enough to feed our families we have to keep hunting and barking."

"That's it, Harry," a few shouted as Bridges warmed to his task.

"The history of maritime labor in San Francisco is a tale of heroism and injustice," he said. "We've been beaten, shanghaied, drugged, shot, stabbed, kicked, swindled, and exploited. We're controlled by men who brag they want our blood spilled. This afternoon the owner of the American Hawaiian Steamship Company said, 'We can cure this best by bloodshed. We have to have bloodshed to stop the strike.' What's our answer?" Bridges was cascaded by boos and curses.

"Our relationship with men like that," Bridges spoke calmly into the microphone, "is not one of employer and employee, is it? It's one of master and slave. You know it, they know it. The Embarcadero itself is known as a slave market. Yet you've heard the gentleman from Washington say don't strike. That's the *Labor* Department which is supposed to look out for our interests, and *they're* saying put your tails between your legs and go back on those docks so you can be treated like scum, go back on those ships where you're nothing but deck slime. Do you want to go back under those conditions?"

A chorus of nos boomed through Dreamland.

"Our president, Mr. Roosevelt, offers us hope, then he snatches it away. It's all right to organize, his people tell us, but don't you dare strike. It's all right to chew but you're not allowed to have teeth. Well, strike we have and strike we must."

Bridges was interrupted by chants of "Strike, strike, strike!"

"Now then, Mr. Ryan," Bridges said looking down at the national union's leader who was still sitting in front after being booed off the stage, "you call your sweetheart deal with the shipowners a gentleman's agreement. But Mr. Ryan, why didn't you consult the Strike Committee or the membership at large before making an agreement in our names, finding out what we all think"—and Bridges swept his hand over the hall—"instead of signing an agreement over all our heads?"

Now Joe Ryan shouted up from the auditorium, "You're acting for the Bolsheviks! You don't want the strike settled!"

"Oh," Bridges said, "well then, may I ask everyone here, are the Communists leading this strike, are they telling you what to do?"

Nos again rocketed around the auditorium.

"Who's leading this strike anyway?" Bridges lofted his words.

"We are! The longshoremen! The seamen! The teamsters!" The cries came from every corner of Dreamland. "We are! We are!"

Joe Ryan, trying to hold on to some semblance of his leadership, shouted up one more time. "All right, men! I didn't know there was so much unity."

At this Ryan was called every insulting name in the vocabularies of several languages. "No backroom sweetheart deal," Bridges said. "Any agreement anyone makes in your name comes back to you, not to Joe Ryan, not to me, not to the Strike Committee, but to you, the rank and file and sinew and muscle of the unions. We'll go back, all right, we'll go back when you tell us and vote to accept an agreement, not a half-minute before. I make a motion that the salaried union officials be severed from the negotiations and you put the strike settlement in the hands of the Strike Committee, which will consult you—or I'm not standing here in front of you—always and on every detail before agreeing to anything." Several dozen longshoremen and seamen seconded the motion. "All in favor," Bridges said, "Say aye!" He was drowned in ayes.

$\sim$

In the morning Quin had me on the docks early. Some of the pickets were wearing their Sunday best, suits and ties and fedoras, as they marched along the Embarcadero. Others, the younger ones, wore striped jerseys and T-shirts. Mounted police separated the pickets from the piers across the street. A number of strikers hoisted signs: FULL RECOGNITION was block-printed on one, with others urging SUPPORT THE ILA, DON'T SCAB, LONGSHOREMEN AND SEAMEN STAND TOGETHER. The festive mood was sustained for the time being, with Army veterans singing "Mademoiselle from Armentières." The rhythm suited the march as it had all those years before in France. I didn't see Harry Bridges, but he could have been anywhere on the Embarcadero. *Hinky, dinky, parley-voo* bounced off brick walls across from the docks.

When a work crew of strikebreakers was herded onto one of the docks, a striker in a jersey yelled, "Let's stop them!" Policemen reined their horses closer to the marchers. The younger pickets looked ready for anything, but an older fellow in a dark suit and bowler yelled back, "No! If they don't start nothin' we won't either." The work crew was allowed to pass, not without glaring and grumbling, strikers and strikebreakers swearing at each other. Mounted police looked menacing, but I wasn't sure how effective they'd be if the pickets managed to get between the horses and the docks. The sentiment percolating through the strikers' ranks was they'd missed doing something brave and declarative when they let the strikebreakers through to the dock. "Closing this port," one of the younger pickets shouted, "means closing the port! I say let's block the docks!" An older man answered, "Mates, the time has come. We block the docks." Then the yell went up, "BLOCK THE DOCKS!"

Surely there must have been plans for this, but what it looked like was spontaneous energy bursting into a strategy, rippling through the striking longshoremen like a single blow to a line of balls that causes all the others to vibrate. Very quickly, columns of picketers all along the Embarcadero were shouting for the docks to be closed off. The chant became a roar. "BLOCK THE DOCKS! BLOCK THE DOCKS!"

As if this were a signal, which it may well have been, hundreds more strikers poured out of side streets, especially from Mission Street in the direction of union headquarters, onto the Embarcadero. The police themselves were now reinforced by squad cars and paddy wagons that dumped out scores, maybe hundreds, of police on foot, most carrying billy clubs. The Embarcadero became a turbulent sea of human agitation.

Mike Quin pulled out a camera and began taking pictures. "Quite a party, isn't it?" he said. I was too frightened to say anything except, "Do you think we're safe?" To which Quin replied, "Don't worry, Skinny, you're not on one side or the other, are you? Stay on your fence and enjoy the fun." I didn't feel like I was on the fence.

A policeman climbed on top of a squad car with a bullhorn. "Clear the lanes to the docks!" he yelled to both pickets and police. "This is private property, you strikers know that. We can allow a peaceful march, but there will be no disruption of private property!"

A picket yelled, "Protecting the big guys like always, eh, Captain?"

The police captain answered through his bullhorn. "We're protecting private property, same as if your home is broken into and you want us catching the burglar."

This brought derisive laughter from the strikers. They yelled back that the cops would never come to their homes anyway, only to the nabobs on Nob Hill.

A yellow schoolbus pulled up to a pier about a hundred yards from where Quin and I stood. He said we ought to move closer, and we trotted along the sidewalk. At that moment a few dozen more mounted police cantered down Folsom Street onto the Embarcadero. A squadron of bruisers, young bruisers, came off the bus and made for the docks. "It's the football team again," Quin said, "come over from the U of Cal to scab." It looked like there were about fifty of them. A striker shouted to them they should have brought their shoulder pads and helmets. A wedge of policemen formed to run interference for the football players as they tried to get onto a pier. Strikers closed in, enveloping the wedge, and more policemen hemmed in the strikers.

The captain balancing on the roof of the squad car bullhorned for the strikers to disperse immediately. The strikers yelled back they were going nowhere until the football players headed back to their classrooms. Concentric circles had now formed: the football team surrounded by police who were surrounded by strikers who were surrounded by mounted police who had an entire circle of pickets around them. "You want a moving picture, Skinny?" Quin said. "Wouldn't Busby Berkeley like to see this from overhead?"

The only direction the strikers would let the rich boys—as they called the players—go was toward their bus. "This is your final warning!" the captain shouted. Some players looked longingly toward their schoolbus; others were ready to fight. A striker yelled, "Don't send a boy to do a man's work!"

The football players were impatient, or panicked, or both. The dance began, but it was more a *danse macabre* than anything Busby Berkeley staged. The players stampeded through the police circle formed to protect them and rushed toward the dock, but no one was running interference for them anymore. A few broken field runners actually did make it past the pickets, but the longshoremen stopped most of them and were shoving them toward their bus. Players and strikers got into fist fights, and I saw teeth spat out, pounded eyes that were going to turn purple, bloodied noses. The battle cry was from all three sides because the police were now engaged as well as the strikers and football players. The shouts back and forth, the billy clubs and fists, reminded me of clanging swords and cannon balls in sequences pitting pirates against merchant sailors, with the British Navy steaming in to enforce order along the Spanish Main.

When most of the football players had been terrified back onto their bus, the mounted police charged the strikers with tear gas canisters. Similar skirmishes were going on up and down the Embaracadero as police, strikers, and strikebreakers all joined in small battles. To get away from the fumes, Quin and I retreated up Mission Street with handkerchiefs over our faces. The occasion became legible when I stopped seeing it as a movie scene and began to be very scared. Hundreds of strikers were all around Quin and me, but those coming behind us up Mission, running to get away from the tear gas, were less scared than mad. New pickets appeared from union headquarters at the corner of Mission and Steuart, many wielding broom handles while a few had baseball bats.

In the midst of this melee, Nick Bordoise, the union's cook, was handing out sandwiches to strikers as they came off the Embarcadero, like a waterboy at a football game, running onto the field during a time-out. Nick had slung a huge sack over his shoulder and was hauling out sandwiches to give passing strikers as they came up Mission Street. His calmness made it easier for a policeman to arrest him. "What for?" this incongruous Gunga Din asked. "Aiding an illegal strike," the policeman said, and jerked Nick toward a squad car. Fortunately for the Greek cook with his immigration problems, the policeman was distracted by a violent attack across the street, and Bordoise ran to the safety of the union headquarters.

The police were hurling tear gas canisters as they advanced up Mission Street. Strikers with broom handles and bats stood in front of the rest of us. They hit the canisters back at the police as though they were batting baseballs. This had an immediate effect since most of the police were not wearing gas masks. A cheer went up from the strikers as they saw policemen choking on their own poison. Yet the police kept coming.

Several blocks up the hill from the Embarcadero, the strikers made a stand at a vacant lot, an abandoned construction site filled with loose bricks. The captain with the bullhorn, now on foot, apparently identified with Teddy Roosevelt and began yelling, "Charge!" at his men. The police were met with a shower of bricks. One hit the bullhorn and temporarily silenced the police captain, but he was quickly up again yelling, "Use your weapons!" Most of the police didn't seem to like this order because they fired into the air, but at the sound of gunfire I was scared again and talked Quin into coming inside a Chinese dry cleaners. An obliging proprietor named Wun Chew allowed us to go upstairs where his family lived. We watched the action while Wun Chew's wife and children stared at us, then giggled.

The police captain was running back down to the Embarcadero, which made his men pause in their own march up Mission Street. The strikers cheered what they saw as a retreat. They began to advance back down the street, throwing bricks and shielding themselves from billy clubs with garbage can tops. "Like boys playing," Quin said, "just boys.

Both sides, boys." Several police were knocked down. Wun Chew ran upstairs to hide with us when gunfire raked the street. "This not your country," he said as he knelt beside Quin and me, "this not my country, this country belong to crazy."

At the bottom of the street the captain now ordered his cavalry into action. The mounted police trotted in formation up Mission Street toward the dockworkers making their stand. "Jesus living Christ!" yelled a striker who saw the mounted brigade advancing up the street. "Aren't all of us Americans?" The captain, who was not on a horse himself, fired a short-barreled shotgun at the man, who fell in the street. Two friends helped him to the sidewalk, where he slumped against a shop window.

Several dozen strikers apparently anticipated the cavalry charge, because their tactic now took the kind of ingenuity that can't be spontaneous. Some reached into their pockets while others stuck their hands into a sack being passed around. In the next instant the strikers were throwing handfuls of marbles down Mission Street at the horses. The lead horses began to slip on the marbles. Once the front line stumbled, the horses in back of them panicked. They literally turned tail and galloped back down Mission Street.

The strikers whooped like cowboys. But it was all over very quickly after that. Sirens shrieked and squad cars closed in on the vacant lot from all directions, each filled with police firing wildly. Strikers ran for their lives.

"Barbarian bastards," Quin said furiously. "The Third Reich has come to San Francisco."

I didn't say anything to contradict him, and by now I was wholeheartedly on the union's side, though it did seem to me the pickets had transformed themselves into an army ready to fight. Maybe the massiveness of the forces arrayed against them demanded that. I felt sorry for the horses. As for the police using firearms, it didn't appear to me they were aiming to kill so much as to scare the pickets into retreat.

"Pretty fair motion picture here, wouldn't you say, Skinny?" Quin had recovered a little from his anger.

"They don't make movies about labor strife," I said. "Too political."

"Then they're bigger idiots than I thought."

Violence itself was so far from what I knew that before I'd become frightened it had indeed been a movie to me, like a clamorous dream where I felt present but not really engaged or endangered, almost in the posture of an anthropologist. Here are the oppressors and their helpers, here are the aggrieved and their sympathizers: see police battle strikers while you hold on to your detachment and safety as participant/observer. Mostly observer. You will report your findings, as Margaret Mead did, to Franz Boas at the Museum of Natural History. You're in a little danger but not much, especially after you and Quin perch upstairs with the Chinese family, who are also participant/observers with better detachment credentials. When the squad cars drove away and the wounded strikers were loaded into paddy wagons, Wun Chew led us downstairs.

All this could be reported to Dr. Pogo, my Franz Boas who wished me well on my field study among the natives; he could analyze it as a dream. I wasn't entirely sure the battle had an existence outside my imagination of it.

Dreamland Auditorium the night before had been more real. I'd been to contentious studio meetings as well as gatherings where the writers were trying to form a guild. Yancey Ballard, before he ever heard of Grandmother O'Hollie, had helped form the first Screen Writers Guild. I understood meetings. Violence was something else. I'd never seen any violence at all outside of movies. Yet this had happened and I could even read about it in tomorrow's papers. When I thought I had a tomorrow. Before the fracas with the stevedore that was shortly to end my life. My killing: my erasure: hardly worth an oratorio but perhaps a little fugue from Mike Quin.

I was trying to grasp the novelty of violence when Quin said he was off to write about what we'd witnessed, and he'd see me later. Foolishly, I decided to go over to the union hall to see how the members were doing after their pitched battle.

So many longshoremen were milling around the entrance I didn't go upstairs. The acrid tear gas had not yet completely blown away. It was still early afternoon, but outside union headquarters it felt as though the battle had raged all day long. One man was unscuffed and wore a spotless suit with a well-blocked fedora. He was across the street from most of the strikers. They looked so upset I didn't want to bother them. Since the unscuffed man looked like what I thought of as respectable, I went up to him and asked how the men were holding up. The innocent, ignorant mistake that costs a life.

"No damage to them they didn't bring on themselves," he said, which shocked me because I'd thought he was a union man himself or at least a sympathizer. "No one hurt bad," he added, "more's the pity." He scrawled a few words on a piece of paper and asked who I was. "Well, just a bystander," I said. "You ought to go bystand yourself somewhere else," he said. Then he disappeared. I crossed back over to the union side and saw Widdelstaedt and Cromartie, the two men Quin and I had talked to the day before in the union hall. Widdelstaedt had only a small cut on his forehead, but Cromartie could barely stand, a rivulet of blood came from his nose, and one of his eyes was swollen shut.

I was about to ask if I could help when Widdelstaedt swung backhanded at me and knocked me down. I was more amazed than hurt. "You're with the cop snoop," he accused, "and I saw you upstairs in headquarters yesterday, spying on us."

"No, no," I said, getting up, "I was just asking how you guys are. Today was awful. I saw a lot of it with Mike Quin."

"Quin, hah! He can be a dupe too. That guy across the street was a dick, and you were giving him info." He knocked me down again.

"No, I wasn't," I said as I brushed myself off. How foolish to try to reason with someone in a rage. The stevedore—it was Widdelstaedt but I'd forgotten his name in my fright—came at me and I saw a knife flash out of his pocket. He backed me against a car. Pinned there, I saw my death in his dim bloodshot eyes. He raised the knife and I caught his arm, but he was far stronger. I ducked. I ran. He caught me. That's when he sliced my leg. I hopped away. He lumbered after me as the men at the union hall laughed at both of us, no doubt their first laugh of the day. I turned a corner and saw a narrow alley. I'd lose him in there. But he followed me down the alley. It led nowhere, a dead end. I jumped for a fire escape ladder but couldn't quite reach it. Several garbage cans were lined up, and I wanted to stand on one to reach the ladder, but their tops were all gone, used as shields, I supposed, by the union men. Nothing to stand on: the story of my life.

Steve was upon me. The hulking Widdelstaedt. He lunged and gashed my arm. He was in the power of his anger, and once he had dealt me the slice in my leg, his anger became hunger. The very blood running down my pantleg and spilling on the ground enhanced his lust—like a shark, like Ajax—for my extinction.

Every discovery at twenty-four is intense and fragile. By sight, by habit, by experience, new things become known, fresh material is fed into the psychic oven to be baked until risen to the level of wisdom. Now I'd never have that. Here he came, knife pointing at my eyes.

He trapped me against a brick wall under the fire escape ladder. Raised his arm to deliver the death blow. I grabbed his wrist and kicked him in the knee, which made him yelp but that was all it did. His eyes were full of a bright dullness. I was the target of the rock bottom truths in this man's life. Not only his eyes but his whole face was an accumulation of logical, everlasting, conclusive hopelessness. He had identified the enemy, and I was it. I saw his point: privilege versus penury. I wanted to live anyway. When I couldn't hold his wrist any longer I squirmed away. He moved nimbly for a big man and quickly had me against another wall.

Four, three, two, one, and it would be over. He lunged, I darted. Each time he missed he backed right up so I couldn't dash for the alley's open end. I was wearing down, and he was playing with me, dog and cat, cat and mouse, bird and worm. He didn't mind if it took him five minutes or half an hour to carve me; he knew he had me trapped against the literally dead end alley and the garbage cans. I'd be his revenge for every deprivation he'd endured in four decades or so, the stand-in for all the forces ranged against him. My tongue was sour felt. I heard rapid breathing and a cry of Help! Someone yelled Help again. I barely recognized the cries as my own. The giant stevedore was measuring me now as I backed into a garbage can. He took his time. Two frozen images: my mother gleamed up behind him, Mossy was a ghost behind her. I looked at the garbage can—Christ! Why hadn't I thought of this before. All my training had been to clean up messes, not make them. I was almost too tidy to save my own skin.

What would Dr. Pogo think—this raced through me again. The abbreviated childhood I'd moaned over was about to become a far more abbreviated adulthood.

But here was my life preserver, the garbage can. Faster than I'd ever moved, I upended the can, jumped on its bottom and reached the fire escape. Banana peels and coffee grounds and fish bones and a cat corpse scattered in the alley. As soon as I'd climbed to the second floor I pulled the ladder up, though it didn't make much difference. Widdelstaedt wasn't interested in the effort. He stood beneath the fire escape bellowing and threatening while I climbed up one more story and found an open window, disappearing from his attention.

I ran for the hotel, home base in this hide and seek contest of unequals. It might have been ten blocks away or thirty, but I was there before I knew where I'd been. My jacket was soaked with my exerted, scared, determined, panicked but finally preserved sweat.

Quin was waiting in the lobby, wondering what had happened to me. He told me many strikers were in the hospital, many in jail, and thanked a whimsical god no one was killed. He looked at my leg, bloody, gashed. I was panting too hard to make much headway in my story when he said, "Movie Mogul, why don't you get your eager but inconsequential ass out of this town before your luck runs dry."

17

Mossy Swims

His first day out of the hospital, Mossy, ever wily, invited Nils Maynard to his home for a swim after the day's shooting was over. He still wanted Nils to use Pammy in the picture they had argued about. Nils didn't want to swim, didn't want to go up Coldwater Canyon to the Zangwill manse, didn't want to discuss the Pammy issue any more. But he also didn't want to be unfriendly to the presumably convalescent Mossy. He had never been at Mossy's home as the only guest. The lavish garden itself intimidated Nils, a feast of nature, overdone, aspiring to encompass the entire plant kingdom, defying compliment. Mossy greeted Nils at the door and shrugged off solicitude about his health. "Damned painful at first," he said, "but in the end it was all precautionary."

Mossy told Nils he thought the script for his next picture needed tightening and he wanted the two of them to agree on changes before bringing back the screenwriter. Relieved not to be talking about Pammy, who he still firmly thought would be miscast in his film, Nils said sure. Maybe he wouldn't have to swim and could simply leave when they finished a brief talk about the screenplay. He was still suspicious.

They agreed to remove a talky scene between the husband and an old doctor who treats what he refers to as the wife's vapors. A description of the wife's behavior was far less dramatic than the behavior itself. Mossy said, "As Shakespeare put it, show don't tell." "By all means," Nils agreed. They cut an ugly scene where the wife coldly sends her stepdaughter off to boarding school. The scene is a good one, Nils thought, but he's still trying to make the wife more palatable so I'll agree to take Millevoix, who's exactly wrong for this. All right, for the sake of getting out of here. He told Mossy cutting the scene was fine, expecting the boss to bring up Pammy again.

"Fine yourself," said Mossy. "Let's refresh ourselves with a dip."

"Are you sure the doctors want you to exert yourself this much?" Nils asked.

"Absolutely. Exercise is the best thing for what ailed me."

Nils remembered he hadn't brought a bathing suit. Freudian slip, he told himself.

"Doesn't matter," Mossy said. "Gable left his a couple of Sundays ago."

As he related this to Tutor Beedleman and me later, Nils put on Clark Gable's suit, a very slight piece of material, and prepared to swim. Mossy emerged from the bathhouse in a bright zebra-striped suit. This was silly, embarrassing. Nils felt exposed in Gable's fig-leaf suit, but they plunged in. The water was bracing and Nils enjoyed himself at first. He swam up and down, a little breaststroke, a little Australian crawl. Nils had always been an excellent swimmer, swimming being one of the few vigorous activities that his mother had allowed her hemophiliac son. Perhaps, Nils thought, he could impress the boss with his physical prowess, so he swam faster and faster. But he was wondering why Gable had been there. That was exactly what Mossy wanted him to do. He wouldn't ask. Had Gable even been there? Nils swam as fast as he could.

Mossy did a swan dive off his springboard, just missing Nils as he was moving toward the deep end of the pear-shaped pool. There was no talk, which unsettled Nils, but he didn't know what to say to break the silence. Mossy treaded water after his dive. Surely he was about to say something. He said nothing.

"Dumbly," Nils told us, "I swam underwater. When I came up, Mossy had swum to the shallow end and was lounging against the steps that led up to the flagstones surrounding the pool. Ah, I thought, the swim is over, and I can leave. I went under one last time. As I blinked through the chlorinated water, I became aware of Mossy sitting on the steps at the far end, doing something because his legs were moving even though he stayed in the same place. When I surfaced, I saw he was taking off his trunks. Oh Jesus."

When Nils described this scene I was confused, uncertain what the point was.

"Mossy proceeded," Nils said, "to dive in from the shallow end and swim languorously up and down his pool, not exhibiting himself particularly, just naked. A frog stroke, a surface dive, a slither past me where I treaded water not knowing what to do. I couldn't look at him, I couldn't look anywhere else. We'd each been trying to upstage the other, Mossy with his silence, I with my speedy swimming. But he trumped me when he took off his bathing suit. Flashing by me, slicing through the water like a barracuda. His torso a compact missile, limbs like knives."

"So Mossy's a secret fruit cup?" Tutor Beedleman offered.

"Hardly," Nils said. "Mossy just naturally wants to own the other guy. He takes all the space. I know this as a magician. Doing a magic act means you take the stage and hold it, like a commanding actor. On my sets, as a director, I'm in charge. I know how to do this. But Mossy, everywhere he goes is his own set. He wants to invade you until you say I give, I cave, what do you want me to do? He won't stop until he has you."

"That's not one man raping another?" I asked.

"Yeah, fucking his mind," Nils said. "Mossy doesn't bother with your body. He skips right over that and leaps into your mind."

18

Re-Entry to the Kingdom

Sunlight glinted off the fronds of the palm trees and the hood ornaments of the other cars, especially the expensive ones. Relieved to be safe at home, I'd awakened very early on Sumac Lane and even with my bandaged leg did a kind of hopping run down to the ocean to make sure it was there. I was still so anchored to what had happened—and almost happened—in San Francisco it was a happy surprise to see the Pacific rolling, boiling, slapping away at the sand. Southern California was the Kingdom of Heaven.

Driving to the studio, I felt I'd been in a fierce wind that left me wrong in the head. What was Mike Quin doing on that sidewalk? Was that Widdelstaedt himself driving the car next to mine? It wouldn't have shocked me if the stevedore had jumped out at a stop sign and broken my windshield. Yet I was free of all that now; the owners and longshoremen could fight until the redemptive sun turned to ice. I drove along Sunset, uncrowded at that early hour, cranky little cars putt-putting along, beeping cheerily at each other occasionally, gardeners hosing the bougainvillea and chrysanthemums, sprinkling the lawns because it would likely be a scorcher.

Passing the pink stucco Beverly Hills Hotel and turning down through the *allée* of palms on Canon Drive, I fancied myself in Jerusalem. Ideas churned on how to do what the studio wanted and also convince them to do what I wanted. I was taking the long way to work to assure myself of the glories of this Eden. This presumed Eden, as Yeatsman never failed to remind me. Reaching Olympic Boulevard, I remembered I had an appointment with Dr. Pogorzelski and doubled back a few blocks. Trapped in the alley the day before, I'd assumed Widdelstaedt's carving knife would cause Pogo's couch to lie bare this morning. When he summoned me from the waiting room, I settled in by saying how glad I was to see him though I wasn't really seeing him but staring at the Florida-shaped crack in his ceiling. I spilled it all out. As the huge longshoreman pursued me, I told Pogo I felt I was looking straight into the next world. I gave a blow-by-blow of Widdelstaedt chasing, slashing at me until I finally leaped out of his grasp onto the fire escape. Dr. Pogo was silent, waiting for me to continue. Finally, I said, "That's it, that's the whole thing."

"Umm," he said. "What do you think it means?"

"What do I think what means?"

"What do you think your fantasy means?"

This is what always puzzled me about psychoanalysis: tension between reality and the imagination. Perhaps it is the same tension that exists in writing. How much are we mining, how much are we making up? Dr. Pogorzelski was certainly a good and compassionate doctor. Though he'd gone from Cracow to study with the master in Vienna, he never pulled apostolic succession on me nor, I gathered, on his less fortunate colleagues. Unslavish about psychoanalytic dogma, he was secularly open to whatever varying interpretations or theories I would bring him. Early on, in the first or second session, he had said our analysis (and he did say "our," impressing me with the collaborative nature of my treatment) would consist eclectically of present concerns, memories of the distant past, dreams, fantasies, word associations, and the relationship between the two of us. Our twin goals would be to try to untie inhibitors preventing full expression of what I wanted to be and do and say and write, and to retrace the beginnings of neurotic behavior so that it need no longer be repeated.

So far so good. But I was never too sure how Pogo—or other members of his profession—dealt with reality. In-your-face occurrences. Here I'd just told him of a narrow escape from death in my encounter with the distressingly real would-be killer Widdelstaedt, and his response was to ask me what the fantasy meant.

I swiveled on the couch and looked at him where he sat, his knees possibly eighteen inches from my head. I was like a small gun going off. "Are you n …? Doctor, every word I've just told you is exactly what happened to me in San Francisco! *Exactly!* Please! Not a shred of it was my imagination!" I swiveled back into my usual supine position, jerking my head and folding my arms over my chest as if to say, Take that.

"Oh, of course, sorry," Dr. Pogo said. "I hear so much of people's violent dreams and fantasies I'm afraid I lost myself. It's a staggering experience. Are you all right?"

"I'm all right. The guy cut my leg. Other than that, okay."

"Did this terrible incident remind you of anything?"

"It reminded me I want to stay on this planet for a while. It reminded me I'm glad I'm not a stevedore. It reminded me how oppressed workers are by owners. It reminded me of what scapegoat means. That guy would kill someone who's not even close to being his true enemy. It reminded me of what your profession means by displacement!"

I was still hot. But then, taking my own cue, I remembered two real dreams I'd had the night before. (Real? But then what was San Francisco? Provisional? Dreamlike but not as real as a dream?) In the first, I met a doctor in the street, much older than Pogo. I knew he was a doctor because he carried a black bag. He asked what I wanted. I was unable to answer. I only looked at his gray hair and clean-shaven face, which was kindly but also judgmental. I noticed his blue tie hung down from an old-fashioned curved collar. The dream ended.

"What do you think of that?" Pogo asked.

"I guess it meant I was on my way to see you, a doctor who tries to help though I can't always say what I want to. I wanted to get to you after San Francisco."

"Mmm-hmm," he said. "And the tie?"

"Sometimes you wear an all-blue tie, don't you?"

"Actually, I don't, but that doesn't matter. Any other thought?"

"I think the dream means that I've been rescued from this awful thing that almost happened to me, and I'm glad to be safe again."

"Mmm-hmm. I don't think so."

"You don't? What then?"

"It's not that you're not relieved to be rescued, or to be home, or seeing me again. Incidentally, you were not rescued. You rescued yourself, you absolutely saved yourself, and no one is responsible for your being alive and on this couch except you yourself."

"What do you think, then, about the dream?"

"The man in the old-fashioned collar is not me but the doctor from long ago, the doctor of your mother. Not perhaps her actual doctor but the composite of the doctors who treated your mother in her illness. You want him to cure her, to change the past, and you don't dare say so because she has sacrificed herself for you, and if you undid that you might have to die instead of her. Not a real sacrifice, one created in your unconscious."

"It's that depressing?" I couldn't imagine a sacrifice that guilt-producing.

"I don't know that's depressing," Pogo said. "Perhaps it's bringing forward a part of you that doesn't accept what happened to her but senses, irrationally, that it could have happened on your own behalf. This can create similarly irrational guilt, which we can deal with, but can also help you bring all of yourself into the present, helping you understand her illness and death, that she cannot be cured or returned to you. Acceptance is not necessarily depressing. Perhaps it is only"— and he paused—"growth."

"You mean I've delayed my grief all this time?"

"Not entirely. Surely you were sad when she died. Also you couldn't write in your diary, remember? You were mute, as in the dream. But then you got up and went on. Except not all of you went on. Part of you stayed behind, in denial. What is the blue tie?"

I chuckled. "Well, Doctor, if I can paraphrase Freud on his beloved cigars, sometimes a blue tie is just a blue tie."

"And sometimes blue means sad. The doctor cannot cure your mother."

"If I were a safecracker, tumblers would be falling into place. "Born Blue" is Palmyra Millevoix's song. Yes. I had another dream too. More falling. I dreamed I fell out of bed actually. I startled myself. Possibly I even woke up, I don't recall, to reassure myself I was still in bed and hadn't really fallen. And then I fell right back to sleep. Still falling, heh heh. But this is just the classic dream of being born, isn't it? I'm reborn after my terrifying brush with death in San Francisco."

"And?"

"Isn't it enough to be reborn?"

"I don't think so."

That was Pogo's usual way of letting me know he thought there was more to whatever I'd said or interpreted. "What then?"

"This is my own fantasy," he said. "Use it if you wish. Do you remember your dream of Ulysses? Odysseus?"

Months earlier I'd told him of a dream about Odysseus in which I imagined the hero of the *Odyssey* outwitting a group of players on a football field, running around them toward the goal line, then diving for a touchdown. At the time I'd gone no further than to interpret the dream as my hope of eventually outsmarting the old-timers at the studio and becoming a Jubilee champion writer. Pogo had supported that.

But now, he said, "I think your falling is like your diving, diving means going down, going under. In the earlier dream a touch*down*. You descend in the dream to the underworld, like Odysseus, like the descent to Nighttown in Joyce's *Ulysses*. Odysseus speaks to his mother. You are going to the underworld to retrieve your mother. You are also re-enacting her death even while you, as yourself, join her in the underworld. But you cannot bring her back, and you don't really want to be in the underworld—yet—so you awaken yourself for reassurance. San Francisco shook some apples out of the tree, yes?"

"Ah, so I'm doomed," I said, "to walk the earth forever, like a Greek unhero, or perhaps like Oedipus himself, looking for the woman who is my mother."

"But unlike Oedipus, you'll never be able to marry your mother."

I laughed. "We'll see about that."

Pogo said, with just a trace of triumph, "An element of a movie plot's what-if is in the dream. What if you hadn't saved yourself in San Francisco, what if you had indeed dropped, fallen, off the fire escape into the not-so-tender mercies of the stevedore Widdelstaedt. What if he became your executioner and sent you to the underworld?"

"Oh." I was a little dazed. I'd never catch up with this guy.

"Till next time, then."

"No goddammit." I was still angry at Pogo's initial failure to see my San Francisco experience as reality. I wanted my parting shot. "Of course," I said, "if I'd been an Army veteran telling wartime battle experience you'd have had an institutional framework—ah, a soldier at war, he may have shell shock, a terrible revisiting of comrades being bayoneted in the trenches of France. But here's a simple peacetime occurrence where I almost lose my life and your first instinct is to call it fantasy."

"Your point," Dr. Pogorzelski said, "is well taken."

As I entered the studio, the early sun disappeared in mist, leaving a silken sky. The action at Jubilee was not just on the sound stages. Mossy had flown to New York to mend fences. Goddard Minghoff was in charge and ordered a speed-up of all work, including scripts, to let any New York spies on the lot know the boss's absence wasn't hindering production. Having had my confidence shaken by my close call in San Francisco, I consulted Yeatsman on how to write my earthquake treatment. While I was telling him I also had to write something about the strike, he interrupted to tell me Pammy was moping. Minghoff was threatening her with suspension. She was on the lot but hadn't shown up on the set where she was shooting; since she was fond of me I should go cheer her, get her quickly over to her set. My skin, like the peel of a grape about to burst, felt tight, not ample for this labor. I thought, never send a boy to do a man's ... but I stopped myself from that kind of thinking.

Pammy answered the door to her bungalow in her robe. To my amazement she kissed me on both cheeks. A strand of her hair, wispy, brushed my chin as she drew back, and I thought I might run a fever. I held my breath, thrilled. I'd never noticed her eyelids, but as she turned aside, blinking, her eyelids, translucent, had the character of thoughtful concern and ... alabaster. Having escaped death so recently, I could have died at that moment to preserve the perfection of my bliss. She said she wanted to let me in on a secret no one knew. "I need," she said, "a confidant. I believe I can trust you." At this I was, if possible, even more thrilled. I was suddenly an intimate. Speaking or singing, Pammy had a voice like Champagne. Could I take her in my arms? Don't be ridiculous.

Sweeping back her honeyed hair, Pammy said, "Look, I have to tell someone. Teresa would talk her head off if I told her. Plus, she'd criticize me."

"Thanks," I said. "If nothing else I can be depended on to keep quiet." I was fishing, hoping she'd spell out some virtue of mine other than silence. She wasn't biting and simply ignored what I'd said.

"The Commies are after me. Again."

"What does that mean?" I asked, not knowing whether they were attacking her for being a capitalist or trying to woo her back to her old outspoken sympathies.

"The thing is," she said, "I agree with them, but I don't want to be with them."

"Why not?"

"They're humorless, dogmatic, and they suck the life out of you. Aside from that, I love them."

"What do they want you to do?"

"Address a meeting at the Shrine Auditorium. Introduce the ambassador."

Mike Quin had told me Alexander Troyanovsky, the new Soviet ambassador to the United States, was coming west to look at the country he was now accredited to. American Reds were giving FDR unusual praise for recognizing the USSR though they heaped most of the credit on Maxim Litvinov, Stalin's foreign minister, who negotiated the exchange of ambassadors. "So tell them you're busy that night," I offered.

"Except I want to help them. What they're saying about the capitalist system and its holding down the working class is right. Look at this Depression. It's not the capitalists on the bread lines. The industrialists hurt a little, but the big thing hard times do for owners is drive down wages, force the unions either to make bad deals or give up jobs to scabs who gobble up the dregs from the troughs of the rich guys."

"You can give the speech you're giving me and then say here's the ambassador."

"Don't be naïve, Owen. Hollywood's part of the system too, and my appearance at what will be seen as a Communist rally will enrage all the studio heads, which will in turn hurt every union and guild in this town. 'Get the Reds out of the picture business'— can't you just hear Louie B. Mayer and the rest singing that song in unison?"

She did have a problem. I saw a sheet of yellow paper on her piano, filled with block printing, the unlined kind of paper used by Western Union to give a copy of sent messages to the sender. "All right," I said, "send them a telegram of support they can read at the rally, and tell a couple of your friends to send their own telegrams—Frederic March likes the Reds, doesn't he?—which will take the sting off the whole business, and you won't have to go."

"That just might do it," she said, "and I'll think about it while I'm dressing. Excuse me. I want you to tell me about San Francisco—a lot of Reds up there, too, no?"

While she was in the next room I couldn't resist looking at the yellow sheet of paper I'd spotted. The printing spread over four of the little half pages Western Union favored. Must have cost a fortune, I thought. I read:

Mr. Amos Zangwill
Waldorf Astoria
New York City

 Coming together,
 Transcontinental medley,
 A portal opens,
 Hotel door,
 Eyes on eyes,
 Lips to lips,
 Wordless.
 Hands, mouths,

Swirl of fingers, hungry lips:
Not so fast:
Pace
Proportion,
Going down,
Now ungowned,
Ancient, Grecian, deliberate
Abandon.
Tongue—
Probing recesses,
Recess, process, possess,
Pause, full stop—
Slow, fast, slowly, faster, finding
Scent beneath smell,
Desire's scent.
Then the form,
An unfamiliar, familiar shape
Moving, tangle of legs,
Moving, almost combative,
Afraid to move,
Softness, hardness mingled,
Venting dew,
Mingling wet sweetness,
Moving, moving, moving
In harmony
Until, until, until
One gives over
Now now now now now,
One part of the form
As the other looses torrent,
Clasped,
Fresh,
Old, new,
Transcontinental medley,
Coming together.

At the bottom she added, "Sleep deeply, dream sweetly, Your P."

My turn to mope. Just a subaltern, that's all I was. As my head lolled to my chest, I heard her behind me. Startled, I straightened to military attention, guilty, dejected.

"You're awfully nosy, Owen," Pammy said, but she said it kindly, regretfully.

And you're a fucking Communist who doesn't have the courage to admit it! is what I wanted to say but didn't.

"I know I'm horrid, beastly," she went on Britishly, "but when I'm not mad at him I'm mad for him, which is madness itself. Son of a bitch that he can be, yearning, craving, in his way a bighearted son of a bitch though. The world sees a schemer, the studio sees a tyrant. But inside the tyrant is a willing boy and inside the boy is an artist aching for approval."

"Gee, you could print that in *Photoplay*," I said, wanting to hurt her back.

"Sorry," she said, shrugging off my insult. "I should have put the damn thing away. I should have known about you. I did know. In my selfishness I forgot. But Owen, dear Owen, don't you see? Your little crush ..."

Little? Crush? Suddenly, for the second time that morning, I was furious, far more than I had been at Dr. Pogo.

"Your crush will subside, soon, you'll see, you'll find a girl more your ..."

She paused. More my what? Style? Speed? Type? Age? Class? What horror was she about to utter? Again I was proving my facility for staying silent, passive. How sweet to be prized for a quality I hated, tongue-tied frozen fearful silence.

"You know," she continued, "more the kind of girl you should be with. Maybe a young starlet, you could almost have your pick you're such a dear, or a junior writer like yourself, or someone completely, mercifully out of the business, free of all of us."

What do you say when you've been knocked down, knocked that flat? "Thank you, Pammy," was all I could think of. Thank you for decking me.

"I know. You came to coax me onto the set. They're doing a shot that doesn't need me anyway, but they want me over there and ready. Tell them I'm on my way. *Merci beaucoup* for the idea about the Reds. We'll always be friends, won't we?"

She hugged me. No kiss on the cheek now. I breathed her, lavender and almond, my anger wilting like lettuce. Hopeless.

19

Treatment

Greatness," Yeatsman was saying to me, "once resided in the throne, the church, the academy, the sword. Now it lives in the flashbulb. The flashbulb and the movie camera make hostages of us all, destroying identity and replacing it with celebrity. That's the machine that cranks and hums here, and we're the oil for it."

Yancey Ballard was from a family of Alabama dairy farmers who had devised a way to mass produce and preserve butter in the nineteenth century. Ballard's Better Butter began to be sold in Chicago not long after Mrs. O'Leary's cow kicked over the lantern in 1871, and Ballard's soon started its own sales fire. By the time Yancey was born in 1895, the family was as rich as the Alabama plantation owners. The boy grew into lanky southern ease, effortlessly becoming a squash champion in prep school, someone who succeeded too handily, whom others tried hard to emulate, and the too-hard trying was already their failure. He was sent north to college and missed being a classmate of Scott Fitzgerald's at Princeton only because he enlisted early in the war, going overseas with the Canadians. In 1915 he was in the battle of Neuve Chapelle when the Canadians were ordered to make a feinting maneuver to draw the attention of the Germans away from the principal battle zone, where the British were attacking.

"That's always been my trouble," Yancey drawled, "I'm diversionary, can't help it, can't be the main event to save my soul. I was lucky though. Fella next to me was hit in the head by shell, had his brains land next to my feet. Looked like salmon roe. All I had was shrapnel in my shoulder." That was enough to keep Yancey out of further combat, and he spent the rest of the war writing battle reports for the First Canadian Division. He didn't come home until 1920.

"I had my Paris," he told me, "right after the Armistice, and it was angrier and less drunk than it became in the Twenties." He worked on the Paris edition of the *Herald Tribune*, and what he fell in love with was not Paris but Yeats. A trip to Ireland was futile, netting him no admission to the poet's presence but only a dose of gonorrhea in Sligo. When he sailed home, Yeatsman finished his Princeton time and then gravitated to Hollywood in pursuit of an actress he'd met years earlier in Paris. The career choice of Hollywood pretty much cost Yancey Ballard his family, who regarded Jews, along with leprosy, as two of mankind's incurable afflictions. He sold a story to the newly formed United Artists, assuming it would be a ticket to the actress's affections. But she had already been in Hollywood a month, which was time enough. "Only the most *stupide* girls here have a *liaison avec l'écrivain*," she told him, adding dismissively, "*Jamais. Pour moi, je cherche le cinéaste! Bonne chance, mon cher.* See you around, as they say." She helped along Yeatsman's education.

A decade later, most of it spent at Jubilee, Yeatsman thought of Mossy alternately as his champion and his nemesis. "'Some violent and bitter man, some powerful man,'" he told me, echoing his bard, "'Called architect and artist in, that they, Bitter and violent men, might rear in stone The sweetness that all longed for night and day, The gentleness none there had ever known.' Wasn't old Ghostie thinking of Mossy and the rest of us when he wrote that?"

"He has his visions," I said, "and I guess we're supposed to accommodate them."

"'I am worn out with dreams,'" Yeatsman quoted, "'and yet, and yet, Is this my dream, or the truth? O would that we had met When I had my burning youth!'"

"Yeatsman, uh Yancey, I need your help."

"We all need help," Yeatsman said, warming up. "As we pace the corridor of life, people keep coming out of little doors, and each one hands us a piece of our destiny. Here's your driver's license. Here's your degree. Here's your first job, oops you're fired, you're not ready for this. Here's your wife, here are your kids, and if you write some scripts that actually get made here's your next wife, your new kids, your pool, the maid, the houseboy, don't trust him. Here are your kids as they get older and betray you. Here are your ulcers, a gift from Mossy or some producer. But here's your mistress. The doors along the corridor keep opening and the faceless people hand you more small portions of your fate. Here are some screen credits, here's a sweet holiday in Tuscany, here's your psychoanalyst, here's your reconciliation, more travel, your retirement, your heart attack, cancer, thrombosis, shingles. Here's your death, weren't quite ready wcre you? Here's your ... forget it because you're already forgotten." He took a deep breath, lit a Pall Mall.

All I wanted was to bring him around to suggesting how I could complete my San Francisco assignment so the studio would be pleased. "Meaning Mossy," he said, and I nodded. I was too much in awe of Yeatsman, but he was tender with me, affectionate in the way of a big brother who cautions you away from the precipice he himself has plunged over even while knowing your momentum is already going to carry you over it as well. Fifteen or so years older than I, with good screen credits—*Forgotten Hero, Manhattan Matinee* and the first *Count of Monte Cristo*—he was both a princely paragon and, as he tried to tell me, a warning. A complicated gifted guy, jealous and insecure, demanding and reticent, unafraid of the bosses yet unable to resist their blandishments and raises, squeezing his life into manageable proportions from the wonder of what it might be, all the more admirable to me if not to himself because he had managed to fit snugly into the Jubilee cocoon. I saw him as a marvel of energy and lassitude, inspiration and doggedness. "So what have you got?" he asked.

When I finished telling him I had material on the earthquake but wanted to write the strike story, he sighed. "Forget the earthquake," he said.

"What do you mean? That's the whole reason Mossy sent me up there."

"I mean plot your characters first, not your plot. Forget there ever was an earthquake. When you have the people you want to write about, write them against type. A good man does a bad thing. A fearful fellow does a brave thing. A fallen woman does something virtuous, and so on. Figure those people out, then sneak the earthquake into their lives. Or smash them with the earthquake. Since motion pictures are the medium of the obvious, you'll be smashing them anyway within half a minute of the first wineglass shattering as it falls off the first table. But before anything, figure out who they are."

"I feel like breaking the laws of history anyway."

"Attaboy. Other places you can't break the law, you can't rob a person or a bank. In Hollywood we do nothing but rob, we break the law all the time. It's only the lore here, not the law, you mustn't break. If you're a lore breaker we send you back east."

"You want me to forget the strike too."

"That's different. You'll never get away with a picture about a strike anyway, so it becomes the horse in the bathtub. You don't mention it, you don't look for it, don't even go in the bathroom, which creates problems. But all the time the horse is upstairs in the tub, everyone knows it. You not only have to forget it, you have to drown it."

"You know I can't do that."

"Okay, but that's the principle."

Dutifully, I ordered my Royal to attack 1906. The social classes in San Francisco were much more defined than in Los Angeles, but I rejected the rich-boy–poor-girl obviousness and decided to write about two equally obvious working-class families. The seedy family of the nurse doesn't like the rookie cop's family because they're Irish and because they're cops. The cop's family says the nurse's family has never added up to anything but trouble. One of the nurse's aunts, whom she lives with, runs a house of ill repute and pays off crooked cops. But the two kids love each other and as soon as he gets his patrolman's badge and she gets her RN they'll marry.

A member of the cop family arrests a member of the seedy family and a fight breaks out. The young cop and the nurse decide to elope and are on their way to the train station to head for Reno when the street opens up in front of them. They're nearly crushed in the furious first tremor. Buildings topple. Each knows his duty—the nurse makes her way past scenes of agony to the hospital, while the rookie cop reports to his stationhouse. That night, the after-quake fire begins to spread across the city, and the cop helps firemen save families. Down in the Tenderloin the madam—the nurse's aunt—is helping her girls and customers escape when she gets a phone call. She can barely speak when she hangs up; she gives her assistant instructions and sinks into a chair, virtually in shock.

The cop is all over the city, leading children to safety, carrying old people downstairs into basements. Making his way to the Tenderloin, he goes into the aunt's brothel to see if he can help customers get away from the fire. Everyone has left except the aunt, who as flames grope the house is simply staring at the wall. As he leads her outside she tells him her family's home is destroyed. No survivors have been found.

The young policeman is undone, but he knows he has to get to his fiancée's house to see if she is still alive. Reaching a shabby neighborhood, the aunt and the cop see that the entire block is flattened. Only the family's dog howls his sorrow into the night.

Mad with grief, the policeman rejoins his squad and in a distracted way helps quake and fire victims where he can. All the policemen fan out to keep order, and our young cop hears cries of pain coming from a man trapped under a part of a collapsed building. As the fire draws closer, the cop tries to pull the man free, almost does, but no one else is around to help, and he can't do it by himself. When the flames begin to burn the man, he gives his name and address, begs the rookie to shoot him and tell his wife he loved her. After an agonizing soul-search punctuated by screams and pleas from the burning man, the policeman pulls his pistol out and shoots the fire victim. Unlike the story I was told in San Francisco—realism, I remembered, is fine in movies, but hold off on reality—our young cop does not then shoot himself. What happens is almost more unbearable. A patrol wagon pulls up and six policemen jump out. They could have lifted the masonry off the victim and saved him. A patrolman from his own precinct tells the rookie there's an urgent message for him to go to the makeshift field hospital set up at the Army's Presidio fort.

At the Presidio, the rookie sees what looks like an acre of cots with wounded victims lying on them, moaning and screaming. It's reminiscent of a war scene that could have been painted by Goya or photographed by Mathew Brady. Nurses and doctors are doing triage, saving who they can, trying to make the others comfortable. The rookie sees the back of a nurse he recognizes as his girlfriend. Thank God she's alive and has summoned him! He runs past rows of cots and takes the nurse in his arms. It's not his fiancée. Her aunt now materializes, also summoned to the Presidio, and the nurse leads them to the cot where the girlfriend lies. Pallid, bandaged, laboring to breathe, she is clearly dying. The duty nurse tells the policeman and aunt that the girlfriend had been pulling victims from a burning building downtown when a beam fell on her. She looks up at her aunt and boyfriend, smiles wanly. She gasps out a question about her family, and before the policeman can say anything the aunt says they're shaken and hurt but they'll be all right. She asks how the policeman is, and he takes his cue from the aunt: just another day at the stationhouse, he smiles. He takes his fiancée in his arms, and she dies. A high shot shows the aunt and the policeman walking off together past the acre of cots, heading downtown where each is part of the city that is beautiful and corrupt, vital and decaying, destroyed and ready to be rebuilt. FADE OUT.

Yeatsman grimaced at me, and Comfort O'Hollie flatly refused to type the last page. "Look," I said to them, "that's life and death in the earthquake of ought-six."

"Too bloody morbid," said Comfort, full of proud independence now that she had unregretfully packed her impossible grandmother with her Hibernian righteousness off to Vancouver. "I'll be drawn and quartered before I'll type the end of this treatment."

"Not a studio in Hollywood will make that picture," Yeatsman said, "certainly not one that calls itself Jubilee."

I changed the ending so the policeman, hugely relieved, finds the nurse at the Presidio as she helps earthquake victims. The policeman's own father, also a cop, is on one of the cots, a cornice having crushed his spine. The nurse/girlfriend has been tending to him, and the father has changed his mind about her, ready to admit that even a rotten barrel can contain one unspoiled apple if you take it out of the barrel soon enough. The father draws his last breath, and the family will have to be supported now by the rookie himself. In the final scene, the eager young cop and his beloved nurse walk past the acre of cots, heading downtown where each is

"And so on," said Comfort.

"Slightly more palatable," said Yeatsman.

The bounding main. A freighter rolls and pitches in late afternoon seas as it plies the Honolulu–San Francisco route. One young deckhand, rangy and handsome, is plainly doing more than his share, helping others lift, swab, handle lines. A nasty captain, barking commands, orders that two squabbling sailors be whipped. Our young deckhand watches the flogging, administered by a hulking seaman with a horse-whip. When one of the two sailors being beaten faints, our handsome deckhand protests. Enough is enough—this is the twentieth century. The captain barks that if the deckhand weren't engaged to the ship-owner's daughter, he'd be getting his own taste of the lash.

Making port the following day, the captain finds a line of ste-vedores picketing to prevent his ship from being unloaded. Afraid his cargo of pineapples, mangos and papayas will spoil, the captain orders his seamen to unload the ship themselves. Led by the young deckhand, they refuse. The shipowner shows up, furious, and when the captain points to the deckhand as the source of the trouble, the owner explodes.

The owner's daughter comes to plead with her boyfriend to unload the cargo. He says the seamen will stand by longshoremen; her father should settle with his workmen on the dock. Torn, but proud of her boyfriend's defiance, she invites the deckhand to dinner with her par-ents, where they can have a reasonable discussion.

Servants, silver trays with cocktail glasses, wall portraits of pow-erful men greet the deckhand in the shipowner's Pacific Heights mansion. The young man is something of a catch at the party, and a prosperous guest offers him a job bossing a construction crew. His company has just landed one of the contracts to build the new Golden Gate Bridge. The host is impressed that his daughter's boyfriend is holding his own. Throwing an arm over the young man's shoulder, the shipowner admits he hadn't approved of the relationship between his daughter and one of his deckhands, but he's come around. How would the young man like to be in the front office as assistant manager of the whole shipping fleet? The daughter is delighted. Flattered, her fiancé promises to think it over.

Next morning, the stevedores on the dock remain adamant. A labor agitator we immediately spot as a crook is egging on the strikers with promises and threats. The deckhand is undecided. A more honest Harry Bridges–like organizer shows up to tell the dockworkers their hopes for a fair shake are to stick with the seamen so they can present the owner with a united front. The deckhand's girlfriend arrives in a fancy convertible, and the longshoremen jeer him as a traitor when he goes off with her for lunch.

Later, a fresh crew of longshoremen is hired to unload the ship. When the young deckhand returns to the dock, the picketing workers tell him the new stevedores are scabs undercutting their own ability to bargain with the skinflint owner for a decent wage. Police are called to break up a fight between the new hires and the pickets. One of the strikebreakers, a middle-aged man, is badly hurt, and the deckhand takes him home. The older man hasn't had a regular job since hard times started, and as much as he hates to scab it was the only way to put dinner on the table. His daughter thanks the deckhand for bringing her banged-up father home. She's a no-nonsense department store clerk hoping to go to college, which was why her widowed father was down at the docks in the first place. The deckhand, of course, likes her. She clearly likes him too.

Now he's really confused. What kind of woman to love, what kind of work to do.

Naïve as well as ambitious, the young man makes the wrong choice and takes the shipowner's job offer. His delighted fiancée starts planning the wedding. His fellow seamen and the longshoremen are disgusted. When he looks in on the injured widower, the department store girl says she hopes he's happy with his decision.

The new assistant manager is told to fire the seamen on his old ship and hire a new crew that aren't troublemakers. Be a man, the shipowner tells him when the former deckhand hesitates, it's just business.

His fiancée tells him not to worry. He does everything he's told to do, hates it, and is hated by his former shipmates. At a party with his fiancée's rich friends—scions of Nob Hill—he has an argument with her, stalks out.

Wanting to make up with his fiancée, the young man goes to the department store for a present. He is waited on by the injured worker's daughter, who helps him pick out a bracelet he could never have afforded before. She tries it on and he sees how beautiful it is on her. He frowns and she thinks it's because of something she said. No, no, it's not that, won't she have a bite with him when she gets off? At a coffee shop, he pours out his troubles with his new job and his girlfriend. The department store girl shares her own worries. Her father may never work again, and she won't be able to go to college.

Our young man walks her home and—surprise!—they kiss. He insists she take the bracelet he bought for his fiancée.

The rich fiancée phones the former deckhand at work. She forgives him for the spat the other night and tells him he must be at her place right after work to plan the engagement party her father wants to give them. Her tone tells the young man he works not only for her father but for her as well. He sees the crooked labor agitator mumbling privately to his fiancée's father, begins to put two and two together.

The department store girl shows up at the office and gives him back the bracelet. She doesn't want to play second fiddle to a Pacific Heights snob.

Down at the dock things are worse than ever. The ship is supposed to leave for Hawaii, but the new seamen don't want to cross the longshoremen's picket line either. The crooked union organizer throws a brick through the shipowner's office window. Ordered to fire everyone on the picket line, the young man tells the shipowner what he can do with his job and walks off the dock. The pickets give him a cheer.

His fiancée blows up at him and then, when she sees she's losing him, tries to be conciliatory. He can get his job back if he apologizes to her father. No dice.

The young man goes to the department store, and the nice girl thinks he has come to get his money back for the bracelet. Miss Pacific Heights won't have him either, is that it? No, the young man wants her to take the bracelet for herself. He's finished with the job and with Pacific Heights. How's he going to eat? she asks. The young man laughs. He wants to go to college too—meanwhile he knows where he can get a job building a bridge. And the department store girl knows where the young man can get at least one free meal this very evening if he doesn't mind sharing it with her father. How does he feel about meatloaf? He gives her the bracelet as we FADE OUT.

Yeatsman had me add another sequence at sea. He wanted my hero to go out on a big fishing boat for a few days after he quits the shipowner's desk job and before he breaks up with his rich girlfriend. No one knows where he has gone, and the two girls and even their fathers worry, especially when there's a storm at sea, but this is where our boy figures out who and what he wants to be. Yeatsman also told me to have the department store girl refuse the bracelet at the end and insist on giving the hero his money back, the signal to the audience she is not thinking like a girlfriend but like a future wife.

"You might just possibly get away with this," Yeatsman said, "if you keep the labor strife in the background to the love triangle, and it's okay to have a son of a bitch shipowner with that shithead captain whose part you can beef up, but not a single scene more with the pickets, and cut all speeches about bargaining power or workers' rights."

I turned in both treatments and waited.

SCABS TOY WITH MOUNTAIN CONGESTED CARGO STOP CAN'T YOU JUST SMELL IT ROTTING STOP REGARDS QUIN

The laws of nature are simple and beautiful. Here life was imitating my sorry little treatment just as my treatment had been aimed at imitating life. Mike Quin's telegram was his try at keeping me up to date, but all he did was make me feel inferior to reality. Art attempting to imitate life, regardless of how close it comes to its model, is still not life. Is it then the opposite? A lie?

"Why are we here?" I asked Yeatsman.

"Because we're not all there," he responded tartly.

20

Cuts

Mossy charged home from New York with murder in his heart. He called a meeting of everyone at Jubilee on the largest sound stage, where the interior and part of the exterior of a mansion had been constructed to service a comedy featuring the idle rich of Newport and the daughter of one of their butlers. The set was littered with faux-mink stoles, horse trophies, Persian rugs, crystal chandeliers, and even two authentic Bentleys in an adjacent garage where both a romantic scene and a little class-war showdown were to be shot. Yeatsman and Elena Frye gave me details of this meeting, not because I wasn't invited—we all were press-ganged—but because they knew things I didn't. Elena said she'd never seen her boss in a worse mood.

Folding chairs had been arranged to accommodate several hundred Jubilee personnel. The studio workers did not arrange themselves hierarchically—actors in front, then producers, on and on—but simply and democratically according to who arrived first at the sound stage. Cy Henscher, who had so abused the starlet Race Honeycut, was at Jubilee to see about a job. He seated himself next to Teresa Blackburn, who immediately moved elsewhere. I happened to be near Trent Amberlyn, whose star continued to rise after his quashed arrest, and between us were two set builders and a secretary. Pammy was with Simone Bluett, her costume designer. That couldn't have happened, I reflected patriotically, at General Motors or, for that matter, at MGM. This was the Jubilee atmosphere either because Mossy set a tone of relative equality among people who worked on his pictures or because he regarded everyone who was not him a trained seal, which amounted to the same thing. I considered sitting next to Pammy. I didn't dare.

It had just occurred to me to consult Yeatsman on my cowardice when Goddard Minghoff arose to call the assemblage to order. On his way to the podium he stopped to whisper to Mossy and Edgar Globe, Jubilee's lawyer. A plan or a plot?

Yeatsman was preoccupied. I saw him trying to be casual as he edged over to the busty script girl, Binney Deems, whom he had seen laughing with some grips. Binney, a devotee of peroxide and dime novels, had a racy book open on her lap. Yeatsman read over her shoulder. He saw one line, "Can we be sure no one else is at your place? Rod panted. Meg put her hand on ..." That's all Yeatsman saw when Binney looked up to ask how she could help him. The grips moved off to flirt elsewhere. "All the girls in the writers building are tied up," Yeatsman said, "and I was wondering if you could type some pages for me by tomorrow morning. I can stay late and decipher my scribbled changes for you. Bernie Sugarman wants ..."

"Oh poor Bernie," Binney said with a gravelly chuckle as if the producer were an intimate. "Bernie thinks he has Mossy's and Eddie Globe's balls in his pocket just because he knows someone's phone number in New York. She shifted her legs and Yeatsman saw the flex of a smooth calf while she gave her foot a little shake as if to rid it of pins and needles.

"Can I count on you for the pages then?"

She ignored the question, noticing Yeatsman noticing her calf. "Bet you've seen your fill of pussy, Yancey."

Yeatsman gulped. Two, he reasoned, could play this crude game. "Well, Binney, I suppose a fair share of pork has passed your way."

"Some. I happen to prefer pork that thinks."

"Ah, one order of brainy pork then." Yeatsman was in uncharted waters.

"We'll just see, won't we? After I type the pages of course."

Was this what Yeatsman meant by responsible infidelity?

Binney wasn't through. She was going to make Yeatsman pay. "I'd hate to be married to a writer," she said.

Already feeling guilty, the very married Yeatsman asked why.

"Half the time he's writing and he's miserable," she said. "The other half he's not writing and miserable because he's not, and half of both those times he's chasing tail. You're the wife, you get the rest. No thanks."

Goddard Minghoff was at the podium. A stately man with the bearing of a senator, the loyalty of a satrap and the principles of a hangman, Minghoff was called upon to deliver bad news in the most diplomatic fashion. Since he was no hatchet man for Mossy—that was Dunster Clapp or Seaton Hackley—he could be even more sinister in the way of a courtier who has the king's ear and a ring through everyone else's nose.

"As you're all well aware," Minghoff cleared his throat, "the Jubilee family has been experiencing exceedingly tough times along with so much of the country."

As Minghoff knew, everyone was *not* well aware of anything of the sort. Jubilee movies had been successful even during the Depression, and salaries had been climbing (including Mossy's though that was secret). Recently, Teresa Blackburn had her salary doubled for her first starring role, and Mossy had more or less raided Fox for both a director and a star, each of whom was handsomely rewarded. But Minghoff went on.

"Mr. Zangwill has a few words to say about what I can only call our sour pickle, but before he does I want to let all of you know we in the front office are doing everything we can to keep hard times away from the gates of Jubilee. We're going to need your help, but we ourselves are not asleep at the switch. This week, in the face of declining grosses in Minneapolis and Detroit, we're putting five theaters up for sale in those two cities. That's to keep the cameras rolling here on the lot. Sacrifices are painful but essential. Furthermore …"

"That'll do, God, I'll take it from here," Mossy said, rising from his chair to stride to the podium, humbling his lieutenant. God Minghoff was not popular at Jubilee (though not as hated as his brother, the infamous union buster and strikebreaker Boris Minghoff), and Mossy would know that as he had just used Minghoff to soften us all up, he had also used him to curry favor with the masses. The king overruling his nobles to commune directly with his grateful peasantry.

"Certainly, oh, the floor is yours, Boss, along with everything else, heh heh," said the startled Minghoff, trying to salvage a scintilla of dignity. "Take it away, Mr. Z."

Or had they planned it, Mossy driving the unloved yes-man from the stage?

"Thank you, God," Mossy repeated as he looked over at Minghoff, never tiring of the pun and basking in his own positon as superior even to the almighty. Mossy's eyes could have been onyx, disclosing nothing of his mood, indicating only that he was impenetrable. "But the last thing I want to do," he said, "is take it away, not any of it. What I want most, what we all want I'm sure, is to keep the Jubilee family together, all of us. To get to the point, as I want us to do in our pictures, does anyone here have an idea of what the national unemployment rate is?"

Silence. Actors and directors were scratching their heads. I looked around and writers were scowling. Jubilee's screenwriters: some were notable, some notorious, some permanently disappointed, others permanently hopeful, most with a suspicion they'd be better people if they were doing something else. Directors were itchy, irritable, wanted the meeting to be over so they could get back to their sets or sessions with their cutters or at least their mistresses. Over a dozen pictures were currently being shot at Jubilee. Producers were eager to be helpful, as if their jobs depended on this, which they might have. "Hmmm," said Gershon Lidowitz, "must be around ten percent now, isn't it?"

"Wouldn't that just be wonderful, Gershon?" said Mossy. Littlewits was a straight man here, whether he was conscious of that or only willing to play the role. "No," Mossy said, "try twenty-five percent. One out of every four working people isn't working. And in factory towns it's often half or even more who have no jobs. We're a factory town ourselves, aren't we folks? You all do know that MGM and Warners have made mandatory cuts, Paramount's worried about receivership, Fox is frightened of bankruptcy, and those are the majors. The little guys are long gone in this Depression. I knew things were serious but

I didn't know how serious until I reached New York last week. Jubilee's board of directors wants a fifty percent pay cut—for everyone."

An avalanche of groaning rolled over the sound stage. Pammy booed loudly.

"I said nothing doing," Mossy went on, ignoring Pammy. "They could have my head first, that's what I told them. But we have to do something, and I'm asking for half of what the board wanted, and I'm asking it only for salaries above a comfortable living wage. Twenty-five percent for everyone making over $150 a week."

Deeply pulmonary sighs from the secretaries and office boys. Since none of them made anywhere near $150, none would be cut.

Everyone else was silent. Then the grumbles started, especially among the writers. "Why should we bail out Jubilee?" Poor Jim Bicker wanted to know.

Mossy furrowed his brow and nodded his head. His lips tightened.

Largo Buchalter to the rescue, a director who was also a producer. "Because, Bicker, we don't want to chop off the head of the goose that lays the golden egg."

Buchalter was such a known ass-kisser that no one fell in line behind him.

"Sounds like the goose is goosing us," said Tutor Beedleman, unable to resist a chance to get a crowd's chuckle, which was all he got. Pammy's silence was audible.

"What about our contracts?" several people said. "We have contracts, you know."

More silence, especially from Mossy, as people all waited for someone with authority to respond. After the longest, quietest minute I ever spent in the midst of several hundred people, Trent Amberlyn walked up to the podium where Mossy stood waiting. "Gimme the goddamn cut, Chief," Trent said. "What helps you helps us all."

The applause rippled from the back of the audience and worked its way forward. Shouts: "All right, Trent!" "You're the man, Amberlyn!" "That's what makes a star a star!"—by the time the yelling reached the actor he was in Mossy's grateful arms.

Trent Amberlyn was still under a cloud, of course, following his arrest for picking up the boy, about which most of the studio knew nothing. This was how he repaid Mossy for keeping him on, keeping him out of jail, keeping him rich, keeping him a star. Possibly he also hoped he could get Mossy to countermand the order that he get married.

What else we didn't know, which Elena Frye didn't tell me until much later, was that the board of directors did indeed ask Mossy to prune the studio budget, but their memos to him showed an entirely different set of priorities. They meant production and front office costs. They wanted Mossy to have pictures shot in fewer days, use the same sets for three or four films, and cut down on crowd scenes so the studio wouldn't have to pay so many extras. The front office cuts they wanted had to do with executives and their assistants. Millions of dollars could be saved. Like all studios, Jubilee was top heavy. The board of directors was not thinking about cutting talent salaries. Several of Mossy's executives hadn't supervised a production for months; they played pinochle in the morning and were on the golf course or at the race track after lunch. But since the executives and their assistants were like household help to service the master's whims, as opposed to the field hands who planted and harvested the produce but were less controllable, Mossy cut salaries instead.

Mossy did one other thing in New York. He warned his board they'd have to raise him to twelve thousand a week or else he'd go run Fox whose own board was at the moment disenchanted with their choice of Darryl Zanuck. His daring *coup de chutzpah*—as he described it to Elena—resulted from the backing he knew he had from Walter Winchell combined with the board's gratitude for Jubilee's immediate capitulation to the new Motion Picture Code. He was the first studio chief to officially and fussily bar anything resembling sex or profanity from his productions. Mossy came home with his twelve thousand a week and his determination to cut almost everyone else. To keep his raise quiet so that even studio accountants didn't know, he delayed taking it for ten weeks, then had it paid to him as a lump sum for a script he hadn't written and hadn't sold to his story department. He titled the imaginary project *All This Is Mine.*

Where in this was Pammy with Mossy? She certainly hadn't joined the cheers for Trent Amberlyn. She'd hissed the big cut. But she also fell before Mossy's charm, as she'd admitted to me. Was it professional with her, or personal? Was there a difference?

"Not enough gas, boy," Colonel DeLight told me about my earthquake treatment. "This here earthquake feels too much like a deus ex to the fellas upstairs. We're shelving it for now, but Littlewits and Sugarman both like it and want to work with you."

Was that supposed to be a compliment? It didn't matter. The earthquake was somewhere in the Hollywood ozone because a couple of years later Anita Loos wrote *San Francisco* as a musical melodrama for MGM. Loos smartly kept virtuous motivation out of her script and set it in the old Barbary Coast with Gable as a rowdy saloon keeper who thumbs his nose at the city's bluebloods until the quake more or less levels everyone.

My strike treatment went as far as Janny van Moylan, a new producer whose family was actually part of the San Francisco establishment but who had rebelled against them. "We have something here," he said, thrilling me with his use of the first-person plural, indicating he wanted this property. "But we need more conflict and more resolution. I mean, there's a strike going on, isn't there? Fine, give me a Harry Bridges type but a homegrown American, very anti-Red, in fact let's have no Reds except a nasty European agitator who runs back and forth between the fat cats and the union guys, sowing trouble everywhere—he may be Red or fascist, all we know is he's foreign and bad. So what happens? I'd love to infuriate my family. Do the guys win anything or are they crushed, or let's leave it up in the air as the former deckhand and the department store girl go off into the sunset. As long as love wins, the rest doesn't matter." My sentiments precisely.

It was a good question as to what was going to happen. Another telegram.

MEETING OF BIGGIES, MAYOR, TEAMSTER HEAD, BRIDGES STOP RUMORS FLY BRIDGES LIFE IN DANGER STOP REGARDS QUIN

How sweet Mike Quin should pester me just when I was trying to give some shape to the shapeless. I struggled on, sneaked in a little more labor-management strife van Moylan wanted though nothing that would make Clifford Odets jealous. Van Moylan liked it even better with his mark on it. He took it to Goddard Minghoff who killed it outright. "A strike by any other name still smells as rotten as Red politics. *Verboten,*" he told Janny. Janny said he was sorry he made me put in more strike. I was just telling him to forget it, this is part of my education, when we heard someone scream, "FIRE!"

We all ran outside and at first saw nothing. When word was passed to Musso & Frank's restaurant, the legendary Hollywood watering hole, that part of the Jubilee studio was on fire, Jack Gilbert, the great silents star whose high-pitched voice ruined his career by disqualifying him from talkies, squeaked into his martini he hoped it was a sound stage that was burning. It was no sound stage. Alas, it was New York.

Everyone rushed to the back lot, where two fire trucks were already on the scene. They were too late. New York Street, as it was known, was burning up fast. The brownstone façades, the corner deli, the cigar store, the stoops where so many kids had played jacks and marbles, so many ingénues had been kissed good night by so many ardent leading men, the nightclub entrance with neon lights that had, depending on the production, blazed Delmonico's, Stork Club, or El Morocco, the Wall Street brokerage, the church steeple, orphanage, row of elegant town houses—all these were shooting flames, and the flames ate more ravenously because their nourishment, after all, was not marble and concrete or even solid wood but mostly *papier-mâché* and beaverboard.

"Cott! Superbe! I loff eet! Vut ve got makes me zo heppy! How do you doing, I'm Josef von Sternberg." This was Largo Buchalter entertaining his actors and crew who had raced off their own set to watch the end of New York Street. Von Sternberg, who had brought over Marlene Dietrich from Germany and been quickly eclipsed by his protégé, was reduced to bragging about past glories in Europe and begging for work in what he called Hollehvood. He was the butt of jokes from those who exulted in schadenfreude.

Tutor Beedleman, who had written the script Buchalter was shooting, strolled up to Buchalter's team to ask how things were going on the set. Instead of introducing him to the cast, most of whom didn't know the writers on the lot, Largo made Tutor the butt of his next crack. "Would you believe it?" he crowed as flames licked into the New York Stock Exchange. "This man could have been the most distinguished rabbi in America if avarice and alcohol plus an insatiable need for hookers hadn't blurred his vision?"

Curtt Weigerer came over to tell Buchalter to get his crew back to work. "Here he is," Largo said, "only child of a loveless match between a meat cleaver and a fly swatter."

He had something there, I thought.

Spotting me on the fringes of Largo's group, Weigerer reminded me he still hadn't received my expense account for San Francisco. "Most of it was stolen by scabs working on the waterfront where I was doing research," I said, "right before one of them stabbed me." Weigerer could see I was still walking with an obvious limp. The head production manager steamed. I had no idea where my remark about theft came from. But as we watched a bowling alley and automat condense to cinders, I knew that suddenly and unexpectedly, I had learned how to lie. "Welcome to Hollywood," Largo said as a police station keeled over while the row of town houses tottered.

"Oh no," I heard a middle-aged woman say to her husband, "you don't suppose it'll spread to Colonial Street, do you Dwight?" The two were visitors on the lot and might have been relatives of construction workers or minor players. The husband shrugged. "Well, Ruth Ann, I just hope the wind don't spread it over to Tombstone." His wife was starting to sob. "They're robbing our history, Dwight, it's who we are as Americans. There goes New York. Please Jesus don't let them take Colonial Street."

Goddard Minghoff and Dunster Clapp were huddled near one of the fire trucks. Minghoff was being practical. "We'll have to suspend on two pictures with New York exteriors," he said. Clapp was in the mood for vengeance. "I'll get the bastard that did this," he said, "string him up by his balls." They didn't notice Mossy, who had joined them. "I wonder if we'll ever know," he mused to his minions, "much more than we know right now. New York burned us, and someone decided to burn it right back."

The flames leaped toward a Chinese laundry and a pool hall as the fire department began to control it. They were able to confine the conflagration to New York after all; Paris, London, China were all spared, as well as the rest of the United States. Dwight and Ruth Ann could reassure their friends in Muncie or Cedar Rapids. A row of tenements collapsed, but Fifth Avenue apartment façades, with canopies supported by brass poles, were unscathed. Across New York Street, the tenements shriveled to ashes, confirming that the poor suffer most in disasters.

"Palmyra Millevoix skipped the fire," Tutor Beedleman said as we walked back to the writers building. As if I hadn't noticed her absence. She stayed in the dressing room on her set when everyone else ran out to see the show. Achilles sulking in the tent? Or was she, as she liked to put it, found in thought? A sucker for punishment, I went to her set because I hadn't seen her since the day I'd spied the dreadful telegram to Mossy and she told me to get lost, or that's how I came to see it. Millie and Millie's nursemaid Costanza were just leaving after a visit; Pammy hadn't dashed out because she didn't want Millie to see the fire and be frightened into nightmares.

Mother and daughter were finishing a book together, each reciting successive sentences. "When the fisherman put his little boat away at sunset," Millie read, "he noticed his tar-tar-tarp?"—"tarpaulin," Pammy prompted—"was neatly folded." "He knew," Pammy read, "that he hadn't left it that way in the morning, so he raced home to his cottage not letting himself even hope who he would find there." "In less time than it takes for a fish to jump out of the sea," Millie read, "the lonely fisherman was lonely no more, for the girl of his dreams had returned from the faraway mountain and was lighting the wood in his stove for their dinner."

Millie looked up at me strangely. "I don't know you. You're not my father."

"Oh," I said and began to back out the dressing room door. What misery had led the girl to that statement? Anything I'd done? Quick as I was to blame myself, I didn't think I was the cause. What, then, had led this unfrightened normally happy little girl to say that? But she saw me retreating and before her mother could jump in with a reprimand to her or an apology to me, Millie said, "Uncle O, when did you come in?"

From what mountain of her own had she returned? "Your reading is getting so good," I said, "I'd come from a faraway mountain myself just to hear you read."

"Mrs. Pammy," Costanza said, "if we gonna pick out a present for Millie to bring to the birthday party, we better vamoose." As a Filipina, Costanza was a favorite of Pammy's both for her loyalty and as someone with whom she could speak Spanish. Unlike the starched, white-uniformed nannies then popular among successful movie people, Costanza carried within her an exotic flavor that mixed Asia with Europe, serenity with impulse. When Millie almost hugged me but kept her distance, I tried to avoid making a little count of the reasons I wished I really were her father.

"Almost eight," Pammy said to me when they'd left. "All I remember is her clinging to my breasts like a bumblebee. I respected her for how much she wanted to live off me, but she stung me down to my toes. Do I sound okay? I had polyps taken out of my nose yesterday and I can't tell if I still have a voice?"

I said she sounded fine. Actually, she seemed a trifle hoarse, like a torch singer, which I found sexy. Perhaps today her voice was merely sparkling wine. She wore a pearl-colored silk dressing gown that crossed just above her breasts, revealing more than I dared look at. "But it's too soon after surgery for you to try," I said.

"Hush," she said, "Let's sing." She said that when she wanted to break a mood.

She went over to the little upright she had in the dressing room. Pammy's contract stipulated there had to be a piano anyplace the studio put her, even in a small dressing room on a sound stage. "RCA wants a new recording of 'Born Blue,'" she said. "With a fresh chorus to add to the old. The album is ready and waiting except for this song. There are some new notes in this version. I want to kick it a bit."

"But then won't it be more Hollywood than blues?"

"Thanks. Don't apologize, I probably needed to hear that. My excuse is times are changing and this isn't 1931 anymore. Times are a little more up-tempo. Why shouldn't my song keep up with that? Anyway, have a look at the lyrics."

"I don't think I want to," I said.

Pammy put the sheet music over her mouth. "I forgot about the telegram. I'm so sorry I put you through that, Owen." She laid a hand—a condescending hand, but I treasured the touch—on my arm. She chuckled. "Don't worry, this isn't a love song, it's still a sad one. Anyway, I'm furious at Mossy over the pay cuts, which I can't believe he needed. I'm breaking it off with him. He's a scoundrel and he can go chase a starlet or slink home to poor Esther Leah if she'll have him. She's taken the children to Baltimore to visit her family, and I'm absolutely flushing the bastard out of my life next weekend. Take a look while I try out my pipes."

She put the sheet music in front of me, handwritten with her notes penciled and her lyrics in ink. "Brand new 'Born Blue,'" I said.

"Warners couldn't resculpt Rin Tin Tin," she said, "but they could do it to me. I was mad after their goddamned plastic surgery, and sad. I was suspended, my new country was in the dumps. That led to 'Born Blue' originally, down below your ankles blues. I've been fiddling, so here goes. Do you think these stanzas might help?"

Pammy wasn't normally pretentious. I found it curious—annoying even—that she said stanzas and not verses or chorus.

She played and sang:

The gay things I recall—
Late spring and early fall—
Gave me joy and joyful clues,
Gave me all that I could choose.

Singing to the sunrise, to the sunset too,
Singing to a chorus of people just like you.
But my happiness is followed,
Yes it always has been hollowed,
By the can't-quite-prophesy-it, wish-that-I-knew-why-it blues.

Shows up like a singer or an actor on cue,
I never can forget it,
It's hardly to my credit,
For I was born, my heart is torn—
Yes I say, born, born, born—
Blue, blue blue.

She played the final chord and sat back, clearly waiting, as clearly as if she'd cocked her head at me, which she was too proud to do.

What could I say to Pammy? It was still blue, but she'd lightened it by injecting a note of self-rebuke that made it seem as if the person singing was an oddball for being melancholy since the acceptable way to be was happy. I didn't like that suggestion, yet I didn't want to discourage her and I was also afraid to tell her and risk evaporating what I flattered myself was our friendship.

I didn't have to tell her.

"You hate it," she said.

"Well, no," I began, "I could never hate anything that came from you. It's just that this is kind of …" I stammered. "Kind of, maybe, dry. I don't know."

"Dry," she said.

"As if there's something wrong with someone who doesn't think happy days are here again."

"Dry," she repeated. "Yes, I haven't got the new version right yet, it hasn't come together, and I have to make it fit with the old version that I'll be rerecording. I'll tickle it at home tonight. It needs some torch. Then I'll know how to sell it."

By sell I knew she meant putting the song across when she sang it, not sell as in market. Though I reflected possibly they were the same thing.

She started scribbling changes on her score in a frenzy, but she looked up once and said, "Please don't go yet."

The rhyme scheme of the stanzas, as she referred to them, was rather complex. Aa, bb, cc, dd, b, which contained an interior rhyme, followed by c, ee, ff, c. I suppose "Born Blue" has proved to be outside the canon of either blues or popular music, living a kind of autonomous life in the musical ether, somewhat like Porter's later "Begin the Beguine," which blends classical and popular elements, or the earlier Berlin standard, "Alexander's Ragtime Band," which has no ragtime in it whatsoever and is wonderful.

Many of the women who wrote hit songs in those days are no longer names we recognize, and the main reason we know Palmyra Millevoix is that she was also an actress. But we do still have some of the other women's songs, as we have Pammy's. "Fine and Dandy" by Kay Swift is still played, and so are "Willow Weep for Me" by Ann Ronnell and "Close Your Eyes" by Bernice Petkere. The female songwriter we know best from that era is Dorothy Fields, who was responsible, with her collaborator Jimmy McHugh, for "I Can't Give You Anything But Love, Baby," "Exactly Like You," and "I'm in the Mood for Love." With her occasional collaborator Jerome Kern, Fields wrote "The Way You Look Tonight," for which the pair won Academy Awards. With McHugh she wrote "Blue Again," a fine song though it never pushed into the category of Pammy's "Born Blue." When Palmyra Millevoix saw Dorothy Fields at a movie premiere, Fields told her she wished she'd written "Where's the Good in Goodbye," to which my Pammy (*my*—what a laugh on me, but let it stand) replied she'd give anything except her daughter to have written "On the Sunny Side of the Street." "How I'd like to leave my worries on the doorstep," Pammy quoted as flashbulbs popped and she gave Dorothy a hug.

After she stopped scribbling her changes for "Born Blue," which she would keep changing until the moment she rerecorded it, Pammy turned to me and said, "Since you've midwifed my song, could you do something else?"

She knew I'd jump off Pike's Peak for her. "Why not?" I said.

She handed me a slip of paper. "Call this number and ask how late someone will be there today?"

A raspy-voiced woman answered the phone and I said I was calling for Palmyra Millevoix. Pammy shook her head vigorously; she'd meant the call to be anonymous. I blundered on, having no idea whom I'd reached. I asked how long the woman's office would be open today. "My office? Is that what she calls it?" The voice sounded like a sneer. "Well, you can inform Miss Millevoix, *s'il vous plaît*, that someone or other will be right here at, ah, West Coast Headquarters, until seven this evening."

"The Communists keep pestering me," Pammy said when I hung up, "and I want to help them but keep them away. I have an old Plymouth I never use any more. It's on the lot next to my LaSalle. Could you be a perfect dear and deliver it to them? If I show up myself they'll take pictures or at least call every reporter they know."

"But if I take it to them," I said, "they'll still know it's yours. Won't they gab?" Gab: my stab at gangster lingo since we were engaged in an undercover operation.

She rubbed her chin thoughtfully. "Yes and no, because it'll be yours. Watch."

Pammy pulled out the pink slip California issued car owners. In the space for purchaser she wrote Owen Jant; the previous owner was listed as Pamela Miles, her old pseudonym. Defying logic, the pink slip had a line for who was actually selling the car, as though it could be someone besides the owner. "This should give anyone a double take," she said, "who might be trying to make sense of the transaction." With a smile, she designated the seller as Goddard Minghoff. "That will mess up the chain of title enough to bewilder any Red Squad," she said puckishly.

Like so many blessings, the car was to come from God. She warned me to take all other identifying material out of the glove compartment so that anyone using it would simply be driving a 1929 Plymouth and not a car that had belonged to a movie star. On the piece of paper she'd given me with the phone number was an address in Venice. The car itself, when I saw it, had no rear bumper, a broken taillight and a dented front fender.

The short drive from the Jubilee lot in Culver City to Venice took me from a real place devoted to the imaginary to an imagined district that had been forced to accept reality. The dreamer who plotted the Southern California version of Venice, a tobacco tycoon, excavated his own Grand Canal around which he built homes for motion picture royalty. He dug his ditches and flooded them to provide side-street canals, along which he put luxury homes and tropical flowers. Gambling casinos sprouted on the boardwalk, along with an amusement park on a pier that hung out over the Pacific. By the time the tobacco baron succumbed to his occupational hazard—lung cancer—the silent star Francis X. Bushman was having parties for Rudolph Valentino on the Grand Canal.

But one day, according to the controlling real estate legend, bubbles appeared in one of the subsidiary canals. And then a kind of rainbow in the water, and after that an unsightly slick. The Venetian dream did an about-face. Goodbye to movie star mansions, hello to ugly oil derricks whose pumps looked like praying mantises, hello to a narcissistic slum and eventually to a throbbing little bohemia. The villas under construction became broken phantoms of themselves, ruins before they were even finished. Oil wells turned the precinct into a noisy, smelly, contaminated skid row. Along one of the streets servicing a minor canal in 1934 was an office, or outpost, or subdivision, or just hangout, of another dream that had been imported to Southern California: the Communist Party.

As I pulled up at the hut that served as Venice HQ for the Reds, I was not exactly greeted but challenged—as if she were a sentry—by the sour woman I'd spoken to when Pammy asked me to make the phone call. "So you're the one running errands for Miss Millevoix?" This was less a question than an insult. The woman seemed to be composed of blocks, as burly as she was surly, a rectangular block for her legs, a chunky block for her torso, and an almost perfectly cubic block for her head, a block with a sneer. The woman pronounced Pammy's name in a tone mocking radio announcers on gossip shows about the stars. "You mean to tell me," she went on, "that this wreck is what the great Palmyra Millevoix drives herself around in? Hee hee."

"I called you," I said, "but I only used her name so you wouldn't hang up. This Plymouth is mine. I took your number from someone at the studio."

"Be that as it may." She looked at me skeptically. "Palmyra agrees with us like a comrade and she's also afraid of us. Not that we care, as long as we have wheels so we can get around to recruit and organize. You're at Jubilee too? Hee hee hee." Her laughter suggested she'd caught me committing a minor felony. She advanced—menacingly I thought—to take the keys and snatch the pink slip out of my hand.

"Sometimes I'm there," I said, trying to be a little cagey to protect Pammy and some figment I was forming of myself as secret courier.

"All right, Mr. Jant." She glanced at the pink slip. "The Party is much obliged."

"Thank you, Miss ... I don't know your name."

"And you don't need to. I suppose you need a lift somewhere."

Those were the last words she spoke to me. She gave me a ride back to Jubilee in the Plymouth but said nothing the whole time. I looked at the little cube that was her head, aptly topped with red hair, trying to think of something to say, but her adamant profile itself was a vow of silence as stern as a nun's. Irked she was, and—despite the gift of a car that would help her make more Reds—irked she stayed. When she dropped me back at the gates of Jubilee, she barely slowed down. I thanked her, but she had already ground the gears of the Plymouth into low and was speeding off.

Returning to my office, I found the telegram Comfort had placed on my Royal. OWNERS THREATENING TO OPEN PORT BY FORCE STOP THIS WILL MEAN WAR STOP REGARDS, QUIN

21

Forward and Backward

Nils Maynard asked me to come to his cutting room that Sunday so I could be a guinea pig when he ran a sequence of a new picture he was shooting. Sundays were lonely days I didn't like or that didn't like me. My idyll with Jasmine/Janice, a tumble of delight even if it led nowhere, had been the exception proving the rule. I was glad to have somewhere to go.

Especially after the night before. Esther Leah was still away with the children, and Mossy had thrown an almost-stag party—almost meant a few men brought dates or wives they thought would impress the host. I was invited at the last minute to fill out the stag part, and I suggested to Mossy I bring a tennis pro I'd met because I knew he'd like the jock aspect and tennis lessons were fashionable at the time. "Perfect idea, kid," said Mossy, "just what will spice up the premises. I'll let everyone know."

The night was a disaster. By the time I picked him up at his apartment in Hollywood, the tennis pro was already reeking of Scotch. Though he'd looked elegantly presentable on the court in his long white pants and slicked hair that was never mussed even after a difficult point, Ansel—I remember only his first name—was socially impossible. "Will there be babes there?" was the first thing he said as he settled into my car. I couldn't *not* bring Ansel because he was now advertised to the

287

other guests by Mossy as someone who would cure their backhands. "What's the chances of a piece of ass?" Ansel asked. I told him we were going to the home of a big studio head, my boss, and I hoped he'd meet some nice people who would want lessons from him. "No need to worry about me," he said, "because I'll fuck a starlet as soon as a star."

This stag party was worse than most because the couple of dozen men were inhibited around the four or five women, and there seemed little to do but drink. Ansel led the way with Scotch highballs, and he made a clumsy, pawing move at a maid serving canapés. I saw Mossy flush with anger, but his lawyer Edgar Globe's flirtatious wife, Francesca, did ask Ansel about lessons. As he finished demonstrating his spin serve, the drunken pro brought his hand down slowly across her chest, and Francesca giggled as Edgar Globe pushed Ansel away. "What do you all do here for relaxation," the pro asked a group of men that included the dignified actor Edward Everett Horton, "screw each other's wives?" When Horton glowered at him, Ansel said, "Oops, attempted overhead goes into the net." He made passes at two of the women, whose husbands were unamused. The women had no trouble swatting him away. "Aw, double fault," said Ansel. Just before dinner was served he peed into a small palm tree encased in a porcelain vase finished in cloisonné enamel. Francesca Globe joked that Ansel was more potted than the palm.

I tried to drag my mistake away, but Mossy insisted we stay for dinner. Why did he keep us there? Did he think this was in some buffoonish way funny, or was he piling up offenses? The pro sat at the table ossified, silent, foodless. I thought his head would fall forward into his untouched soup, but instead he slumped sideways into the lap of a producer's wife. Only then was I permitted to take the useless drunk home. "Lost in straight sets," said the producer, who harvested a laugh at Ansel's expense.

Ansel bristled, straightened his shoulders. "Who in hell wants to spend an evening with a bunch of rich yids anyway?"

When I tried to apologize to Mossy he waved me off with a pasted smile. It wasn't my fault. Maybe I wouldn't be blamed. I pushed Ansel out the front door.

Nils's cutting room was humming Sunday morning, cheering me, and I almost forgot about the tennis pro. Racks of film lined two walls, shelves for sound tracks a third, and the fourth held a poster of Rudolph Valentino looking as though he would kill or seduce with equal panache. Fortunately, Nils had not been at the ghastly party the night before so we didn't have to discuss that.

The sequence he wanted to play for me began with a scene in a diner between Constance Bennett and Joel McCrea. The movie was called *In Love Again*, and Mossy wanted it to repeat an earlier success the two stars had in a World War drama called *Born to Love*. Gershon Lidowitz was the producer and had, in a coup, been responsible for getting McCrea away from RKO to do the picture. In the diner McCrea is trying to lure Bennett into leaving her husband. He makes his case as a lawyer would in a courtroom. Cut to an office where three minor actors ask each other where the missing McCrea is; they hope he's staying away from that married hussy. In the following scene the two stars walk on a beach together as waves crash behind them. Bennett tells McCrea she loves to look at the ocean, and we see the ocean roaring toward the illicit couple. The two decide to run off to Hawaii together and are on the sand kissing when Bennett's husband, played by Guy Kibbee, stumbles upon them and yells that his cheating wife will never see her children again. The scene ends with Bennett, in soap opera fashion, springing away from McCrea and hiding her eyes as if to make the entire situation disappear.

What did I think? Nils asked. I thought the diner scene was too long since after a shot of her misty eyes no one would doubt Bennett was ready to follow McCrea to the North Pole. But what was Kibbee doing on the beach? At this the cutter, a crafty film-smitten old-timer named Billie Bonsignori who had worked with both von Stroheim and Mack Sennett in the silent days as well as with her phantom hero Valentino, began to nod vigorously. Nils looked at her and shrugged. "I told you we needed the suspense, maestro," Billie said. Nils said, "Okay, okay, let's be obvious." Billie went to find two shots—McCrea and Bennett in a car, and Kibbee following in his own car.

Nils ran the beach scene in reverse on the Moviola. We watched as Kibbee bounded backward out of view, and Bennett kissed McCrea passionately as they rolled on the sand. Instead of surf rolling in on them, the ocean retreated, and Bennett unloosed herself from McCrea; the two then popped up into standing positions as two puppets might. The water slithered away and reformed itself into waves. Run backward, the dialogue McCrea and Bennett spoke sounded as if they were Swedes. (I heard Garbo speaking her native tongue once and wondered if, run backward, it would sound like English.) As Bennett and McCrea jabbered away in Swedish, Nils said, "We don't need much of this either. Let's kill most of the dialogue. All we want is suspense."

While Billie was looking for and intercutting the car scenes into the sequence, Nils swore at Bennett and McCrea. I'd heard they were relatively easy to work with, but each had come separately to Nils and asked for more close-ups. "Will you look where we've arrived?" Nils said. "Frankenstein made his monster, and we've made ours. We're nothing but toys for the stars to play with."

I only nodded. As always, I had already transposed Pammy into the scene. Did she demand close-ups from her directors? I didn't think so, but stardom was an infectious disease; once bitten by the rat of renown, the victim would generally squirm and wretch with vanity. Nils had already shifted gears. His wife had made two announcements to him that morning. First, she was leaving him; second, she was pregnant. "In that order?" I asked. "She told you in that order?"

"The pregnancy was a business decision," he said. "I respect that."

He didn't want to pursue the subject. Everyone knew Nils's wife, Fiona, was cold in public. What he'd just said confirmed that this quality—or lack of quality—carried into their private life. Her pregnancy was essentially a contract insuring her income for the next eighteen years. I was beginning to learn about Hollywood marriages.

Nils glanced at Billie, who was thrashing around in her trim bin. Her assistant cutter was off on Sunday and she was having trouble locating the shot of Guy Kibbee in the car pursuing Bennett and McCrea. Fifteen years earlier, the director told me, he'd have been afraid to come into a cutting room. Any intense gesture at the Moviola, or having film wind through his fingers too vigorously, could have caused a bruise or even a bleed. But his hemophilia, with maturity, had receded from a constant menace to an occasional nuisance. "I sometimes have bleeds at the beginning of a picture," he said. "Pure nerves. My fingertips themselves may seep blood. After that, the bleeding stops and won't happen again until I start another picture. My best friend wasn't so lucky."

"Your best friend?" I asked. Then I recalled the story about Nils and his hemophiliac friend running away to a shirtwaist factory in Massachusetts where wires and gears and needles were a threat to make the young boys bleed.

"We do all we can to manage our destinies, Owen," he said coyly, "yet we don't have the control we think we have. We worship reason at our peril. Even the supreme rationalist Isaac Newton postulated a certain subtle spirit, as he called it, that pervaded all matter including the human body. Most scientists remain aloof behind their cloak of pompous reason. Unreasonable reason only impedes the perception of deeper reality."

As he spoke Nils had removed a handkerchief from his pocket and twirled it, demonstrating its emptiness. Billie stopped hunting for trims to watch him; this was why she liked working with Nils. He passed the handkerchief from his right hand to his left, still twirling it. As he passed it back into his right hand, the handkerchief disappeared and four shiny little metal balls dropped to the floor, bounding up so Nils could scoop three of them. "Missed one," he said. "Billie dear, could you catch it for me?"

"You son of a bitch," she said as she stooped to pick up the fourth ball and it became powder in her hands. "What did you just do?"

"A good trick is like an unsolved crime, isn't it?" he said. "That's why I had to go into pictures—I didn't want to be a criminal forever. Do you have those shots?"

"Christ, in a minute," Billie said, reluctantly going back to the trim bin. "Okay, maybe five minutes."

"Rationality itself is the biggest trick of all," Nils said, turning back to me, "because it makes us think we have power when we don't. Instead, we must pay attention to our visions, no matter how fiery, dangerous or painful. Keep your pain. As long as you suffer you live. The lesson of hemophilia. If the world is a miracle, which I believe, then the history of life is a mysterious dream. Hegel himself, a logician par excellence, told us all history is a river of dreams, and if we could merely collect the dreams people had dreamed during a given period, the true picture of an age would emerge."

"What do you mean your best friend wasn't as lucky as you?" I asked. He looked at me sharply and for a moment I thought he was about to tell me to get out of his cutting room for being insufficiently appreciative of his trance on mystery and reality.

"Yes, my best friend was unable to perceive the miracle of the mystery and remained chained to reason, a black kind. Mario Tedeschio was as attracted to risk as I was to magic, but he thought his risks were logical. Perhaps in a way they were. After we ran away together to a Lowell mill, risking our lives or at least our easily bled bodies among the looms and whirring machinery, we weren't allowed to see each other. But the bond between us remained, and several years later I found out where he was through another hemophiliac. I was in New York still working for Houdini. Mario had become like these guys out here at Muscle Beach, a fitness fiend. He had me come up to Harlem to the old Stillman's Gym one day, and what I saw was alarming. Mario was working out wearing boxing gloves. I told him he was nuts to endanger himself. He said he only shadow-boxed. The other fighters were swinging away at each other or hitting punching bags. Little guys in vests and derbies with cigar stubs in their mouths were throwing medicine balls into big guys' bellies. But Mario used huge oversized gloves. Though he hit a punching bag once or twice, mostly he was taking swipes at himself in a mirror. I thought it was stupid, but he didn't seem to be hurting himself."

"So his own bleeding had receded too," I said.

"No, that was the thing, it hadn't. Just from wearing the gloves and mostly punching air he had bruises on his hands. He winced when he hit a punching bag. He shrugged that off and lifted weights too. Mario's mother, Evalina, had driven him crazy with her overprotectiveness, and now he was driving her crazy because she didn't even know where he was. Since only a mother can pass the gene for hemophilia along to a son, insane as it was, Mario had never forgiven Evalina. If Evalina could have kept him in a padded cage, she would have. I started to feel I was the lucky one for having a mother who pretty much deserted me. When we were together in New York, Mario couldn't stop looking over his shoulder, even on crowded sidewalks. He was afraid his mother had hired private detectives to find him. I was pretty sure she didn't have the money for that. He said he was making plans to go to Tahiti, where he would fish and start a resort."

"Oh no," I said. "Doesn't a hemophiliac need to be near a blood supply?"

"Mario said he'd be fine once he was far enough away from his mother. Tahiti would do that. My last morning in New York before Houdini was moving on to Detroit, Mario told me to meet him at Stillman's, ten sharp. On the subway to Harlem I was thinking why is Mario doing this. Tahiti? A resort? Training as a boxer? I was leafing through the *Herald Tribune* and reached the sports section at Eighty-sixth Street. Jack Dempsey was in town training for his championship fight with the Argentinian bull, Luis Firpo. He was going to box a number of sparring partners that morning at Stillman's. Jesus, I thought, I'll never get near the place it'll be so packed. Neither will Mario, even if they do know him from working out there. Well, we'll meet outside Stillman's. As the subway stopped at Ninety-sixth Street, it hit me, and I gasped for breath."

"What hit you? What are you talking about?"

"I almost jumped off the subway to run the last thirty blocks, but I realized the train was a lot faster than I'd be, probably faster than a taxi. There was no Tahiti. The only resort was the last one. I ran to Stillman's from the 125th Street stop.

"The mob outside the gym made me feel helpless. I ducked into a stationery store and bought a large envelope, stuffed a piece of the newspaper into it to make it look thick and important, and quickly lettered on the outside: FOR JACK DEMPSEY FROM TEX RICKARD— URGENT. Rickard more or less owned Dempsey and was promoting the fight, but I gambled he wouldn't bother coming to a sparring session. Stillman's bouncers saw the envelope and hustled me upstairs into the crowded gym, where you could hardly breathe for the cigars and sweat. I headed toward the ring, shoving and pushing and waving my envelope, yelling 'Urgent for Mr. Dempsey.' I made it almost to ringside, as far as Doc Kearns, the champ's trainer and manager, who was screaming at a spy from the Firpo camp to get the hell out of his fighter's training facility. But I was too late."

"What do you mean too late?" I asked.

"What was going on, maestro?" Billie said to Nils.

"Mario Tedeschio was already in the ring, and I saw him bounce a punch right off Dempsey's chin. It wouldn't hurt the champ, of course; people said Dempsey chewed on pine to make his jaw stronger. But it would get his attention, it would get the champ going, which was exactly what Mario wanted. I screamed to Doc Kearns that Dempsey's sparring partner was a hemophililac. Kearns said, 'What's that, did he do time for it?' I screamed back, 'No no, the guy's a bleeder, he can bleed to death from a cut!'

"That's not true, of course, a single cut wouldn't kill Mario, but I had to get Doc Kearns, who was as much a doc as Al Capone, to stop the session. By the time I was able to make Kearns understand that this kind of bleeder had a terrible disease and was in mortal danger from injuries of any kind, Dempsey was whaling away at Mario. They were wearing headgear, but the champ was mostly working on body punches that day. A left to the midsection, one to the chest, a right to the stomach, a left to the eye, another right to the solar plexus, a straight left to the nose. Then a shower of blows I couldn't count, mostly to the chest and stomach. Mario wouldn't go down. He had trained himself pretty well and blocked about one of every two punches, skipping away from the champ. I saw his face starting to swell under the headgear. The Mauler got Mario against the ropes and hit him with everything he had. By now I was screaming and Kearns was yelling— 'Stop hitting, cut it out Champ, ring the goddam bell for Christ's sakes.' But the fans, who'd all paid Stillman a buck apiece to get in, they were yelling too, and Dempsey was pounding Mario into a pulp, literally slugging the life out of my chum.

"When the bell finally rang to end the round, Kearns jumped into the ring, with me right behind. But Kearns's concern was not Mario, it was for his meal ticket. He was telling the Mauler to get up off his stool, they had to beat it out of Stillman's fast. I ran to Mario, slouched on the stool in his corner as he began to swell up and get as dark as a thundercloud. His stomach was already purple from internal bleeding. His blue head wobbled, puffing up everywhere, even the ears. Cranial bleeding can destroy brain cells. The only red blood was from his nose and eyes, which were streaming. Yet Mario himself was smiling. The smile of a wounded, triumphant ghost.

"By the time the ambulance arrived and attendants lifted Mario onto a stretcher, Kearns had cleared Dempsey out of Stillman's and most of the crowd was gone. Mario looked up at me from the stretcher. 'I landed a couple of pretty good ones, didn't I?'

"'Why, Mario?' I asked my friend when I saw his eyes rolling back and he was about to lose consciousness.

"'Tell my mother,' he said, 'I did it for her. Aw, why bother? Anyhow, this is the quickest way to Tahiti, isn't it?'

"Those were his last words. He vomited a dark pool on the stretcher. Bled to death internally, his body a cavity of blood by the time we got to the hospital. I said I was next of kin because I knew Mario wouldn't want his body sent back home for his mother to make a shrine in a cemetery. He's buried in Queens not far from where my boss Houdini was stuck a few years later. Mario had tricked Jack Dempsey into killing him."

"How terrible you had to be a witness," I said.

"Mario wanted a pal to see him through, that's not so bad. One paper ran an item about the sparring session, the *New York Evening Graphic*. Mario had talked some idiot at Stillman's into taking his word that he could mimic Firpo's bulling-forward style for a couple of rounds. Walter Winchell was still after the Champ for ducking service in the World War, so he wrote that Dempsey didn't mind killing in the ring even though he never took his chances in the trenches of France. Tex Rickard issued a statement that Dempsey was heartbroken at what happened to Mario and he'd suspend training for the rest of the week. Regardless, the Mauler finished off Firpo in two rounds."

"Did you ever get in touch with Mario's mother?" I asked.

"Never. For all I know, she thinks he's alive and in Australia or something."

"Or Tahiti," said Billie Bonsignori, who at last had the new shots in. "I can't even imagine what it would be like to have hemophilia."

"Oh, a bleeder is like everyone else," Nils said rather breezily, "only more so."

We watched the car pursuit, Constance Bennett and Joel McCrea in a Ford on their way to their rendezvous on the beach, with Guy Kibbee following in a Hudson. Nils thought the shots were okay. "But the suspense is already there," he said.

"The suspense is never already there, honey," Billie said. "You have to build it like you were building with blocks."

"Time is not linear," Nils said. "We can speed it up, slow it down, reverse it. A Moviola can play with time as much as memory does. We don't have to be literal."

Nils looked at me. "I think you need the cars," I said. "I wonder if you also have an anguished close-up of Kibbee." That was me, all right, indentifying with the cuckold.

"As it just so happens, young man," said Billie, "I do have that shot."

"Great," said Nils, "let's see if we can hit the nail even harder on its head with Kibbee listening to a song on his car radio about his sweetheart in someone else's arms."

"Careful, maestro," said Billie, "or I'll tell that to Littlewits, and he'll make us do it." In order to include the close-up I'd suggested, she ran the shots in reverse. McCrea appeared to be backing his car into Kibbee's. As Billie reeled her Moviola backward, I saw a little note tucked in Nils's copy of the script. I knew the handwriting:

> Your hands are cut
> And they bleed.
> I guess that's what
> They think they need.
> I look at you
> And see you suffer;
> I know my cue—
> To be your buffer.

Pammy was going to be in Nils's next picture whether he liked it or not, apparently, and had already begun her campaign. Nils looked at me looking at the note.

"You know she's a switch-hitter," he said.

I knew nothing, said nothing.

"She was in Mexico last weekend with Elsbeth Hammond."

Hammond was a casting director known as a shrewd judge of budding talent. She gave useful tips to young actors, principally toning them down, nudging them not to try so hard, be the way they were at home. She was wiry-haired and attractive in an athletic way, her firm arms and breasts appearing to be extensions of her will, like racquets are for tennis players. "Write me a part for a little Deanna Durbin type I want to put in a comedy," she once told me, "and then go bulk yourself up a bit. You're much too spindly." Since Pammy was a big star, I was surprised she even knew a casting director, stunned that she actually desired a woman. I'd thought the night of Mossy's party when she waltzed off with Marlene Dietrich was a joke, not a sexual frolic. When I was allowed years later to go through Pammy's journals, I did come upon the escapade Nils referred to. Setting up the weekend, Pammy had written Hammond, keeping a carbon:

> Beth, Beth I'm scared to death
> I can't say no, you won't say yeth;
> Write quick, till then I hold my breath.
> I won't believe if I hear *nada*,
> We can go where they make *pina colada*—
> My devious plot is Ensenada.

Hollywood was a compact town on weekdays, but on weekends it stretched from Santa Barbara to Ensenada as people decamped for holidays, assignations, playtime. East to Palm Springs, which was barely getting started, west to Catalina Island. That was the geography of Hollywood in 1934. Beth Hammond, trying to mimic Pammy, wrote back:

> Pam, Pam I don't give a damn
> If the whole world knows just what I am—
> Meet me at Musso's, we'll go on the lam.

To which Pammy replied:

> No: you come to my verandah,
> We'll say mean things, even slandah,
> While we head for the border in the south
> Where I'll give you my nipples, I'll give you my mouth,
> And what I want is what you got;
> What I don't need is what you're not
> Tomorrow in the commissary
> I'll be nibbling the Jubilee Cherry;
> If we're on just pass and give me a winka,
> We'll drive to Mexico, find us a finca.
> Though I'm just a cut above a slut
> You make me feel quite dreamy,
> When we have lunch I have a hunch
> You'll get me wet and steamy.
> I'll end this doggerel with my own coda:
> We won't stop till you're in my pagoda.

Paperclipped to the page was Louella's item, which I had missed: "Palmyra Millevoix was spotted in Ensenada over the weekend with the energetic" (Louella didn't dare say mannish) "Jubilee casting director Elsbeth Hammond. Where were the toreadors? Girls' night out, I guess."

The cutting room was beginning to feel claustrophobic. I didn't like hearing about Pammy, I thought Nils's movie with her was going to be fine, taut—and I knew it was beyond what the studio would let me work on. For his current film, Billie had the close-up of Guy Kibbee from the trim bin. Cuckolded husband looking bilious, undone, deceived. As unstoppable as a careening trolley, the film ran forward again.

When the phone in the cutting room rang, it was almost noon.

The Summons.

22

Annals of Mortification

I squealed to a stop in Mossy's driveway.

A car I'd never seen, a Buick with Illinois plates, was parked in front of the massive door next to a DeSoto coupe. A man in a tan fedora came out of the house. "You Jant?" he asked. I nodded. "He wants you to wait in the garden," he said, and sped off down Coldwater in the Buick.

I went into the garden, which began on the right of the house—mansion, to be accurate—and continued to the horizon. Aimlessly, I started down a path lined with white lilies, perky orange pistils poking up from their asymetrical centers. The vast cultivation with all its plantings made me feel invisible; perhaps I could vanish into a hedge like a rabbit, down a hole like Alice. I was such a contented subordinate, a footman grateful for leavings from the banquet table. Why had I strayed into bravado and piped myself into a pathetic fool's paradise with the notion that I could please Mossy by bringing the tennis pro to his party? Because I was in fact not a happy serf at all; I was a ruthless conniver, and the tennis pro idea happened to blow up in my face. The servile version of myself was actually my chief enemy in my desire to rise. Fear was my primal emotion. It occurred to me that it might also be Mossy's. But he clothed himself in aggressiveness and snarls while I was only an inept show-off, parading my fear in sycophancy and self-degrading complaisance.

"Bit of a reprieve here, eh?" a voice squeaked behind me. A gnome emerged from behind a potting shed, an elderly Cockney gnome, almost bald, carrying a trowel, wearing gardening clothes topped by a green vest that resembled a jerkin.

How could this little guy know what his—and my—master had in store for me? "Oh hello?" I asked, as though it were a question he could answer.

"Yes, I'd say we've had a stay of execution. Was supposed to start at noon, but if we're lucky the rain won't be here till nightfall. Good news for my roses. They love the sunshine, but they need the rain. They'll be grateful it won't arrive till after dark. Show you around, young duck?"

I was grateful he didn't call me guvnor. "Anything you like," I said. My little tour did, in a different way than the gnome meant, postpone the inevitable.

Obediah Joyful, as he introduced himself, told me to call him Obie since everyone did. He explained that Mr. and Mrs. Zangwill had found him on a trip to England. "They'd gone to my employer, the great landscape designer Gertrude Jekyll, and invited her to California to paint them a garden. That was her attitude, each plant was only a single brush stroke to her. But the poor thing was much too old, almost blind, so she gave me her benediction. Off I went in harness to Mr. and Mrs. Z."

Unlike the other Hollywood moguls, the Zangwills would not allow the pool or the tennis court to be focal points. They decreed an English garden but a magnified, overwrought one, excessive yet delicately planted with variegated beauty on all sides. Obie had worked with the Zangwill's decorator to make the interiors and exteriors extensions of one another. Red velvet in the dining room led to red celosias and scarlet sage, blue chintz in the conservatory gave, through leaded windows, onto lapis lazuli azaleas. The achievement of such a mature garden in a few years was the result of Obie's worldwide transplanting. Archways and hedges appeared to stretch for a mile.

A series of curved and circular spaces blunted any sharp angularity while ensuring that anyone peering from the living room would have an intriguing glimpse through floral vistas with colors only Monet or Turner could envision. Obie led me to a clearing between two semicircular ponds featuring goldfish and frogs; one was fed from above by a Venus statue whose nipples flowed with water, the other by a marble Cupid whose erect penis gushed into his pond. "The master insisted," Obie said with embarrassment, "but when I sent the garden photographs back to Auntie Jekyll, I left out these statues. Auntie wouldn't have approved, may she rest in peace." We walked on into the maze.

"I'm not so young myself," Obie said. "My last birthday I was eighty and the madame started calling me an ottogeranium."

"Octogenarian?" I asked.

"That's what I said."

Rose-clad arches led the way through the garden, each trellis topped with ball finials. With Obie naming names of breeds and hybrids, we passed Sarah Bernhardt peonies, gentle tulips, lacecap hydrangeas, and entered a little orchid lagoon of cattleyas, Appalachian sunsets the color of areolas and gold coins, phalaenopsis Aphrodite white and purple orchids, and a canopy of Seaforth Highlanders with long violet petals fading to white at the base. Each floral carpet was a source of fascination yet Obediah Joyful propelled me onward to discover more. Here were dahlias and lupins, cactus with white hair, bleeding heart verbena sporing white petals with tiny sensual red tips, all arrayed like an army ordered by their commander to conquer the world by glorifying it.

Dazzled, I could find no superlative worthy of what I was seeing. Obie did it for me. "The rose, you see," he said, "is a universal signal of beauty, romance, love and even perfection, and the garden is a grand teacher. It teaches patience, watchfulness, industry, and it teaches trust. Trust your vision, trust the rose to match it and surprise you."

The roses, the garden itself, seemed continuous to infinity, but Obie said, "What is it you see there, young duck?"

"More garden," I said. "Garden on and on."

"Walk over here," he said, leading me to a path where I suddenly saw a small figure, no, two of them. So we weren't alone. Then I saw we were. I'd seen Obie in miniature, and myself tootling after the little man. We were approaching a wondrous, gigantic mirror. It was flanked by other mirrors almost as large. "This was no scheme of mine," Obie said hastily. Mossy had wanted his garden to give the illusion of going on forever, endless. Only slowly, hesitantly, had I recognized I was part of the illusion.

In my own reflection I saw the sniveling, grateful apprentice as well as the ruthless conniver. This was a mirror not of nature but of wishes, vanity, fears and artifice. I remembered the little sign outside Mossy's door, "Don't come in if you want to keep your ideas to yourself." Each of us who approached Mossy to promote anything tried to become him, use his language, his taste, internalize him to sell him some part of ourselves-made-himself, so that we no longer were our own proprietors. Mirror me, he demanded. The writer's ideas would strike Mossy as his own, and he had no trouble later in recalling them *as* his own, because they had been crafted to become exactly that, figments of the Zangwillian imagination.

Thinking to myself upon what meat doth this our Caesar feed, I asked Obie what Mossy was like to work for. "The master is good to me, amuses himself with me and thinks I don't see that though I do. Gardens teach the art of observation, you know. Mr. Z can be intense at times, grim, not as patient as he should be with his garden."

A stocky man with a jellied eye ran up to us, breathless, asking if I was Jant. I could imagine Mossy telling him to fetch me, amputating half my name just as the man in the fedora had. Because of the ugly blind eye I recognized him as a carpenter who built sets at Jubilee; he'd been on Nils's set the day I was there. "Mr. Amos Zangwill is waiting for you!" he yelled and turned to trot back toward the house. Obie wished me luck and I told him I needed more than that. "Keep your city wits about you, young duck," he said. I started to walk away from the giant mirror, but then, though I was embarrassed to be so in thrall to the man Obie called the master, I set off running. By the time I reached the driveway the one-eyed carpenter had driven off in his DeSoto coupe.

Mortification of the flesh. I remembered what he'd done to an old character actor with a reputation as a bully, Humphreys Fulton, who came in for a part, any part in any picture, one day while I happened to be in the office. Mossy had made him shine my shoes. I was as embarrassed as Fulton was, and all the mortification got him was an appointment with Largo Buchalter, who was looking for a butler, perhaps two days' work. Buchalter didn't cast Humphreys Fulton. At humiliation, it turned out, Mossy wasn't especially creative, only exacting. Approaching the house at a canter, I glanced at a pair of French windows on the second floor. As I looked up, a face pulled back quickly behind the gauzy curtain. I didn't care she'd been sweet to me, it was all deigning. What I imagined behind the curtain was a hard mouth, cold eyes. This was already worse than I expected.

Mossy didn't play around with a calm voice before the storm. The hurricane struck the instant he opened the door. "A lesson, Jant! Do you know what a lesson is?"

I said I thought so. I said I was deeply sorry for what I'd done. I said bringing the drunken uncouth tennis pro into his home was a terrible thing to do.

His smile made me shudder. "This calls for a memory lesson, Jant! Do you know what memory is?" His voice was staccato, precise.

"I hope I do."

"And you know what a lesson is."

"That too." Though at the moment I was wishing I were dead with no memory and no knowledge of what a lesson was, no knowledge of any kind.

"You're going to receive a memory lesson. The yardman is off today so you're going to clean my pool. You're going to get a pair of my pants pressed at the one cleaner in Hollywood who stays open on Sunday. Plus whatever else I can think of. But first, up the stairs you go. Now!" Mossy gestured to the grand staircase.

I saw myself as a Chinese coolie drawing a rickshaw along, a rickshaw loaded with three fat actors comically stuffed into its small seat: Oliver Hardy, Sidney Greenstreet and Lionel Barrymore. Each had a bulging suitcase holding burglar tools and crowbars and gold ingots, anything to make the load heavier. I had to pull against the rickshaw's great weight along a rutted road while each bellowed at me to go faster.

Zangwill the Vengeful directed me into an antechamber off the master suite. Through a door I heard water running; evidently a bathroom separated me from the master bedroom. I saw an antique cobbler's bench, a child's rocking horse that had come apart and several pairs of shoes. Mossy's voice was lower here. "Take this glue," he said, "and put the horse back together. When you've done that, shine the shoes. I have polish for each—black, cordovan, tan. Get it right. Then you'll run an errand while you have my pants pressed. You have the soul of a valet, Jant, now you can be one."

Errand? He was gone before I could even ask what errand. Brutalized as if I were being beaten, I went about my menial tasks with alacrity, a born serf. Yet a serf not devoid of aspiration and therefore filled with a coward's contrition. Who didn't even have the pride to quit on the spot. Tell the bastard to go to Hell. I toiled at the cobbler's bench—why not?—and heard the shower come on in the bathroom. Laughter, then a serious question. "You weren't mean to him, were you? He's young and innocent."

"Not innocent. I gave him a dressing down, which he damn well deserved, and sent him on his way." The shower was on, spattering her. I envisaged the water splashing from her hair to shoulders I'd never see. The shower hitting her shoulders: I couldn't even imagine lower than her shoulders.

Polishing the cordovans, I wondered what would happen if I burst through the bathroom door and threw the broken rocking horse at the two of them.

A few bars of a nonsense shower jingle drifted out. "In the kingdom of soap, the soapless lose hope, So get me the soap or I'll go into a mope and fetch me a rope, Don't you dare grope till you hand me the soap because I'm soaplessly in love … but not with you-hoo-hoo-hoo." Listening, or rather unable not to listen, I tried to console myself by recalling that Cole Porter was said to have said she was good only for ditties.

I finished my tasks swiftly and was downstairs waiting for the next labor—would there be stables to shovel clean?—before Mossy pranced down in a change of clothes, twill slacks and a green shirt resembling Obie Joyful's buskin. The squire descends. And condescends: he was in a better mood. Did he know I'd overheard them, and was that part of his pleasure? He handed me a rumpled pair of pants and a section of a script.

I looked at him, a despot, and tried to imagine her upstairs, tried to imagine lower than her shoulders. The two of them together. I couldn't. "After you have the pants done, Owen, take these pages to Sylvia Solomon's house," he said, "and wait while she reads them and dictates changes. Then bring them here so I'll have them for tomorrow morning. And a boutonniere for my lapel. Chung's florist on Santa Monica Boulevard. They have a blue cornflower I like. Get going."

He was much calmer though he clearly wanted me out of there before she came downstairs. Maybe he had forgotten about the pool. Surely he had little flowers in his garden that would have sufficed for his lapel. But that wasn't what this was about. I saw the pages were from *A Doll's House*, from which Gravier and Stallworth, the writers who replaced me, had now apparently been dismissed. The despot continued: "Another part of your lesson, Owen." (At least he was now using my first name.) "Will you tell me why I'm calling this picture *She's A Doll*? I'll tell you why—because Nora herself, after a big struggle at last realizes that is exactly who she wants to be. She wants to have his pipe and slippers ready for him when he comes home, she wants to show other women this is how to be fulfilled and happy, she wants to tease him, ever so gently, about his golf game, and most of all she wants to be kept barefoot, maternal and in front of the stove."

I dared to add gamely, "In front of the stove with a bun in her oven he put there."

He snickered. "Tell Sylvia to look at my notes on the zoo scene and also the leaving home. Now beat it."

I drove back and forth between Hollywood and Beverly Hills to complete my labors, wondering if I could put some kind of poison in the blue cornflower. I'd shined the shoes to make them look like mirrors. The way officers in the Army made their butt boys do. I did it. Lord, I did it, despising myself more than him. He'd returned to Lidowitz's and my early title—*She's A Doll*—that he'd rejected so convincingly I'd come to hate it myself. Did he remember it had been the title on my treatment?

Sylvia Solomon lived in the flats of Beverly Hills, still elegant, beyond anything I could even wish for, but below Sunset Boulevard. In her ultramodern house, a Richard Neutra, she warmed up the cool stark lines with deep pile carpets and furniture upholstered in colorful Italian designs, almost baroque in their lushness, that Neutra would abhor. Sylvia was the first screenwriter, male or female, to take home four thousand dollars a week. She waved me in with her cigarette, wary because she knew who had sent me, but she was friendly. She offered me a smoke and a drink, which I turned down, and she could see I was essentially hovering to get her to work. "How dare his royal Mossiness interrupt my Sunday afternoon Schubert"—a statement, not a question, delivered in a husky voice tinctured with cigarettes and gin— "I'm giving him nothing until tomorrow noon, if then." Reluctantly, she plucked the needle from her phonograph.

"He doesn't want much," I said, "just your take on a couple of scenes he has already made notes on." I hoped she didn't know I'd worked on the script myself.

"Do you realize what he's doing with *A Doll's House*? And what I'm collaborating in? Jubilee Pictures is repealing the declaration of independence for women, written to our shame by a man, and turning the great Ibsen into a shill for traditional subjugated domesticity. Shit."

This was her warmup, the warmup of self-contempt I saw many writers perform before plunging their talents into an assignment that made them drink more and think even less of themselves. She looked at the pages. "Ah well," she said, "at least Mossy isn't quite as loathsome as Gravier and Stallworth. Those two buffoons should be battered to death with their own typewriters by the even more loathsome Colonel DeLight." I said I thought Colonel DeLight was sort of the advocate for writers at Jubilee, someone who stuck up for us against the bullying of the executives. I didn't mention I'd been suspicious of him myself since he hustled me out of the room filled with the Mexican seamstresses.

"Colonel DeLight," she mumbled, not looking up from the script, "wishes he could fire the writers and have monkeys write the scripts. Count your fingers after you shake his hand."

She was silent for a minute as she studied the pages. "No," she said, "Mossy's not as bad as Gravier and Stallworth. You ready to write, Owen?"

"Pencil poised, legal pad balanced on my knee."

"All right, the zoo. We're sketching scenes, not rewriting the damn script."

Zoo? I wondered. I hadn't even had a zoo in my version.

"A horrible scene in a dinky little smalltown excuse for a zoo," she went on. "No, the hell with that, it's the god damn circus. This town wouldn't even have a zoo, but a traveling circus they could have. Mossy will just have to spend a dime and get more extras along with a few more animals in cages. Put in the circus. The family is coming out of the big tent, two parents, two excited kids. Nora is bored. Tom—we're still calling Torvald that, aren't we?—is herding everyone to the car and home where he wants Nora to make dinner for some of his golfing pals. She's disgusted. The kids want to see the bear in his cage. The bear is being fed after performing and as the family watches, the bear swats his trainer and piles out of the cage toward the kids. Nora sweeps her children out of the way while Tom pushes a vendor's stand in front of the bear. It's an ineffective gesture. The bear overturns the stand and lumbers toward Nora and the kids. Nora takes an iron pipe that had held up the canopy over the vendor's stand, and she hits the bear as hard as she can on the nose. The bear is stunned and in pain, and by now the animal keepers and trainers have surrounded it. In the car Tom says his little birdie Nora was a very good birdie but he's proud he pushed the vendor's stand in front of the bear since it saved them all. Close-up on Nora with a men-are-idiots look on her face. Hah! End of scene." Sylvia was temporarily appeased by her modest rebellion.

"Gravier," she said, "had Nora cowering with the children while Tom battled the bear. Who's the driver in this picture anyway? Not goddam Tom, for Christ's sake. Nora's the driver. The way they wrote it even my aunt wouldn't have agreed to play Nora. The husband should never push the action, it's really almost a minor part, a foil. Nora's much too passive in the earlier script. Claudette Colbert wouldn't touch it, Joan Crawford would spit at it. Did you get my take on this, Owen?"

"I think so," I said, still scribbling.

"Good. Let's head for the finish line. Nora leaves home. Cut Torvald's promise to make things better for her—I mean Tom—and have him just ask if she knows what she's doing. She knows, all right. She's leaving this dumpy Wisconsin backwater and her dinners for people he's about to have his bank foreclose on, and she's heading for Chicago to work in an advertising agency, no, to do publicity for an American tour by Gertrude Stein, a free woman if ever there was one. Take that, Gravier and Stallworth. Tom is furious, insisting her home and her duties are in Wisconsin, but she is even more furious. 'I don't hold,' Nora says coldly, 'to your concept of duty, either yours or mine.' Tom is speechless with rage and disbelief, but it is the rage of a weakened man who can't control anything in his life anymore, especially his wife. Nora remains firm. Mossy's right to cross out Gravier's ridiculous moment of having her begin to melt. She never wavers here. Seeing that his fury has no effect, Tom slows down and tries his sweet little birdie approach the way he used to, the way she used to like. Nora no like anymore. The scene ends with Nora slamming the door and heading with a single bag for the bus that will take her to the big city. Put a note at the top. We're changing the title. From now on it's She's NOT a Doll, put NOT in caps. Let Mossy choke on that one. I bet you aren't used to taking dictation, Owen."

"No." But I'd come to expect anything today.

"Not the way it usually is, is it? An older woman giving dictation to a younger man. Usually just the opposite, and when they're all through the older man chases the young thing around his desk, ha ha. Sure you won't have a drink, Owen?"

I was still catching up to her scene dictation.

"But," Sylvia continued, "but the sequence doesn't quite end there, unfortunately, because I have to add the part I'll hate myself for in the morning but that hints at last-reel redemption for Tom. He follows her out with the two children in hand, and we see Tom, a saddened and remorseful Tom, watching Nora leave, and we feel a twinge of sympathy for a chastened man who is burdened with the chores and the children as well as his job, and who may just have learned a bit of a lesson. Scene: she'll arrive in Chicago. But that's enough. My typewriter's over there, Owen, blank pages on the left."

As I typed fast and Sylvia went through two more cigarettes accompanied by gin, she became enthusiastic. "I know what we'll do with her in Chicago," she said. "Nora's going to be just fine—for a while anyway, sending a little subversive signal to the ladies out there." She laughed at herself. "Now rush this over to Mossy, will you honey?"

Honey, I thought to myself. What does that mean? We're social friends now? You're a nice kid, don't let Mossy beat you up too much? Run along little boy?

I was gathering the pages and proofing my typing when Sylvia spoke again.

"How would you like to go to a party tonight, Owen …?"

I interrupted her with a question of my own. "Did you say publicity or agent for Gertrude Stein?" But I had also heard her question. She wanted me to go with her to a Hollywood party. Then all Mossy's humilation was almost worthwhile because now this rich prominent Hollywood writer was taking me seriously. Anyplace she went would be touched with gold. Maybe Fairbanks would be there. Pickford. A young star like Cary Grant or a king like Chaplin himself. This was my chance that came about because I did something stupid with the drunken tennis pro. Sylvia herself was pretty, I was beginning to see, not exactly pretty but sexy, a lower lip that beckoned when it didn't have the cigarette resting on it, a nose that pointed with possibility, eyes that asked a question.

"I meant publicity," she said, "but if it came out agent don't worry about it. Hurry, will you, honey? I was asking if you'd like to come to a Party meeting tonight. You can make it if you drive fast and make short work of old Mossy."

"He has things he wants me to do."

Predictably, Sylvia was indignant. "On a Sunday! How can you let him treat you this way?" She seemed to feel it was an insult to her that Mossy made me an errand boy. And she didn't even know about the shoes, the pants, the boutonniere.

"This is how I'm learning the business, I guess."

"It's no business," she said. "It's handcuffs made of platinum."

"Yours maybe," I said. "Mine are just steel like regular handcuffs."

"Well, hurry," she said, and then she added, "Please."

A Party meeting, I thought. That meant Party with a capital P which meant only one thing in this town, and no way to get out of it. I was not an equal to Sylvia Solomon, certainly not a date. I was merely a potential recruit.

Mossy was pleased with the changes. "Count on old Sylvia to come up with something I can use and an audience can eat. This will turn into a script I can show Stanwyck. I've decided I want to wear gray shoes tonight after all. Shine them up."

"I thought I'd done my penance," I said.

"Not yet. The gray shoes and polish are here in the butler's pantry."

"I ... I have an appointment. I'll be late."

"Sylvia hitting on your bones already?"

"No."

"Sure she is. What I said is go shine my shoes. Now. Maybe we'll forget about the pool today. But this is a memory lesson, young fellow. Get cracking."

Which I did. My final labor for the day. Degradation complete. If I were in something like *Pilgrim's Progress*, I was about to be released from the Vale of Shame.

Why did he treat me, or anyone, like this? A better question, I knew, was why did I let him? The answer to the second question was simple. If I craved preferment—and I did—where else could I make $275 a week in 1934?

At my house, where I quickly changed into clean clothes for Sylvia, a telegram awaited: GENERAL STRIKE MENTIONED STOP WHEN WILL FANTASY PEDDLERS DROP GILDED GUARD AND BE SOCKED BY REALITY STOP QUIN

23

On the Night in Question

Did I even know how to dress for a Communist Party party? I was too young not to wear a tie. When I called for Sylvia she looked better—slinky—and didn't smell of cigarettes or gin. Catching my glance, she said, "A nap and a bath still work wonders on an old dame, don't they?" Her perfume was faintly verbena, alluring if not exactly seductive.

The gathering of the faithful was in Santa Monica on La Mesa Drive at a large white stucco house with a red-tiled Spanish roof. The back of the house overlooked the Riviera golf course and great sward of polo field in Mandeville Canyon, divided by a hill from where my Sumac Lane shanty squatted in Santa Monica Canyon. So many cars were lined up on La Mesa that two uniformed Mexicans were running back and forth parking them. "That's a hoot," said Sylvia as we pulled up in her Chrysler, "valets at a Red rally." I saw some Chevys but they were outnumbered by Pierce-Arrows, Lincolns, Cadillacs. Two couples arrived in chauffeur-driven limousines. They were a hoot too.

Inquisitive energy hummed above the voices raised in greeting. Strangely, this was the one Party party I was ever asked about when the Fifties rolled around. The party's nominal purpose was to raise money for the defense of the Scottsboro Boys, nine young black Alabamans accused of raping two white women in a boxcar. All the meetings I went to, all the demonstrations, this is the only one they seemed to have a record of, and of course the FBI agents expected total recall of an event that occurred twenty years earlier. For once, thanks to my diary (which I never told them about), they were right. The FBI haunted all of us who were present for this occasion.

We were shown in by a kind of usher who looked disconcertingly like me—short hair, neatly combed, an earnest, unforgiving expression, eager both to please and to be superior. He was carefully dressed down in overalls and a work shirt. We moved past banners saying FREE THE BOYS and STAND FOR SOMETHING OR YOU'LL FALL FOR ANYTHING toward a silver hors d'ouvres tray featuring crudite and oysters. The tray was being passed formally by a butler—tall, dark and handsome—who wore black trousers, a white waistcoat, black bow tie and starched white shirt. "Working-class chic is apparently only for white people," Sylvia murmured, her lips almost touching my ear.

"Darling Sylvia, thank God, at last a friendly face." Our hostess, known on both coasts as the widow Flower, waved at Sylvia with her mother-of-pearl cigarette holder. For an instant as they hugged I was afraid the cigarette itself would light my improbable date's hair on fire. "My precious," the widow Flower continued, "what an extraordinarily fresh young face you've contrived to bring with you." The word *young*, I surmised, was as far as she'd go toward an accusation of cradle-robbery.

Sylvia introduced me to Gloriana Onslow Flower, an unrepentant snob out of her time and place. "Bertrand," she called out to the tray-bearing butler, "make sure our dear friends have all the oysters in the sea." Our hostess, Sylvia whispered, belonged not at a party promoting revolution but in pre-Revolutionary Paris vying with Marie Antoinette and Madame de Staël for the best salons and lovers.

She had begun, Sylvia went on, as Gloriana Onslow of the ancient but fallen Onslows of Massachusetts, related to Cabots, Lowells and Peabodys. At twenty-two she became an O'Brian, of the construction O'Brians, six or eight steps down socially but representing an enormous coup economically. This meant she had the wherewithal to live as an Onslow should but hadn't been able to do since the middle of the nineteenth century when alcohol, improvidence and rash marriages had drained the family substance.

It was said no nail was pounded between Hartford and Portland that was not hauled from Boston and hammered by an O'Brian carpenter. Eugene O'Brian was only Anglo-Irish, not fully leprechaun Irish, which meant that a few homes in Louisburg Square did not close their doors to Gloriana and her husband. Eugene knew he had married status if not frugality, and it pleased him to think his sons might one day be admitted to St. Paul's. Gloriana said she could tell when anyone pronounced O'Brian with an *e* instead of the *a*. If she spent money too frivolously Eugene became upset not over extravagance but waste. It was unseemly for his wife to own twenty-eight ball gowns. "Now dear," she'd say, "time to give your silly Celtic thrift a rest."

Gloriana admitted she was an unlikely candidate to have become, in what she called her frisky forties, a Communist. She liked to repeat, however, that she knew something about widows and orphans because ever since poor Eugene fell into a cement mixer while inspecting a construction site in Worcester she had had to fend for herself and her two sons. She didn't add that the thirty-two million dollars she inherited from poor Eugene, three generations removed from the Potato Famine that had sent the first O'Brian packing, made the fending tolerable.

"After two years," Gloriana liked to recall, "I Flowered." When it became likely that Prohibition would eventually be repealed, the owner of Flower Ales in Manchester, Bernard Flower, sailed to New York, where the widow O'Brian had sheltered her penury on Park Avenue, to position his English beer for conquest in the New World. The brewer picked up Gloriana at a performance of the Ziegfeld Follies where she had been dragged by a sister from Boston who wanted to do something wicked. Bernard Flower promptly forgot the first Mrs. Flower back in Manchester. Gloriana told of her initial tryst with Bernard following which, in deference to his nationality, she had said, "There now, feeling better, Mr. Flower?" Her remarriage ensued.

Even while it was still illegal his ale was unpopular, but Bernard Flower proved to have a knack for snapping up land bargains. Soon he owned a sturdy portion of western Long Island or, as he put it, a great deal of Great Neck. After providing Gloriana with a daughter on whom she doted, the ale and land baron was thrown from his polo pony, shattering his skull, during a match against a team of Argentinians. It was thus, at the end of the Twenties and her own thirties, that twice-widowed Gloriana found herself, as she put it, abruptly de-Flowered may the dear fellow rest in peace. With a dozen more millions from English ale and Long Island real estate, plus her two O'Brian teenage males and little female Flower child, the briefly grieving Gloriana betook herself and her brood in a private railroad car across the country in the depths of the Depression to settle in the West in 1932. Having a few contacts in Santa Barbara, she gave the Eastern enclave a try but wrote her sister that she found it conversationally arid and too much like Boston without the culture that is Boston's only excuse.

Eschewing Beverly Hills, Gloriana was a snob to the snobs and chose Santa Monica for its coastal access. She liked proximity to the motion picture industry, where she found social inspiration and concupiscent sodality. In her pantheon was only talent, but it had to be a particular talent she herself happened to appreciate. She disdained Dietrich, loved Ronald Colman, indulged Gable but wanted him to play only comedy, couldn't stand the likable Jimmy Stewart, loathed Garbo but approved of Crawford and Stanwyck. She pitied Jack Gilbert and thought it unfair that his squeaky voice killed him in talkies. In this private aristocracy she adored George Cukor, didn't warm to Frank Capra, loved David Selznick for his excesses, disapproved of Darryl Zanuck or at least didn't trust him. Where Mossy was concerned Gloriana was alternately petulant and tolerant; when she entered her Red period she told friends he was her favorite fascist because he was at heart a *farceur*. She knew Pammy only in passing, and she didn't think Pammy had the courage of what Gloriana referred to as her *soi-disant* politics. "Career, career, career," she said. "Like all the stars, she doesn't want to come out of the trees and risk her salary, or in Palmyra's case the approval of her boss. Meow."

In lovers, Gloriana favored writers for their tormented souls, though she found young actors irresistible. Her first Hollywood conquest of consequence was Gary Cooper, who had just made the earliest film version of *A Farewell to Arms*. She thought him elegant, handsome beyond description and, unlike his screen persona, articulate. Her complaint was simple: "This man," she confided to Sylvia, "has the most divine équipage I should hope to find in California but absolutely no *derrière* with which to push it."

Gloriana snapped up Poor Jim Bicker, wallowing with him in his misery, as ravenous for his rages against society as for his animal passion. The day soon came, however, when Poor Jim had the misjudgment to introduce Gloriana to an unkempt Communist professor out from CCNY, a man whose cheekbones and goatee—his only neatly groomed feature—were Lenin's while his piercing eyes and tousled hair belonged to Trotsky, enabling him to look like both Revolutionary heroes at the same time. Gloriana swallowed him whole and joined the Party. Her sons, of course, hated Professor Bruno Leonard, but he took care to charm Gloriana's daughter with sweets and Winnie-the-Pooh books. The professor was the guest of honor at Gloriana's soiree and was caroming around the room from cluster to cluster.

Before Gloriana pushed off from Sylvia and me she advertised that Professor Leonard would be addressing the assemblage as the climax of the evening. Sylvia said, "They harangue us, it's true, but honey, we live in such a goldfish bowl out here, so remote from the real ocean with real fish in it, that we can stand a little haranguing."

There it was again. Honey.

"Mossy had his turn around the floor with Gloriana, you know," Sylvia said.

"No I didn't," I said, adding blindly, "she's older than he is, isn't she?" Immediately I wished I could bite my tongue off. "Not that it matters," I stammered.

Sylvia was forgiving. "That's right, Owen. Not that it matters."

Poor Jim Bicker walked by. "You smell them?" he asked.

"What are you talking about?" Sylvia asked back.

"The perfumes of the rich women all swimming together while they do their incantations about the poor. I may be sick."

He walked away. Sylvia shrugged. "I like Jim well enough," she said, "and he's a tough writer, but really no one put a gun to his head to come here."

As Gloriana sailed around her party, Sylvia added a postscript to her story about our hostess. "When Gloriana did her little two-step with Mossy," Sylvia said, "he had his man Obie Joyful fix her the most gorgeous stunning bouquet. His message was, 'To My Wild Flower, From the Moss you have gathered so wickedly—and winningly.' On and on it went, he had Tutor Beedleman write it for him and I helped Tutor."

A Jubilee executive named Abner Prettyman came by, quietly letting Sylvia know he was there. Although Prettyman was one of Mossy's bailiffs, I'd never met him. "Time to rally the masses against the classes," he said. "And which are you, Abner?" Sylvia asked. "I'm with the people, always have been," he said over his shoulder as he moved on. "*Which* people?" I mumbled. "Exactly," said Sylvia, "he's obviously spying."

I drifted to the canapé table as Sylvia spoke to a short older woman with a diamond necklace and an upswept pompadour that made her taller but ludicrous. Threading my way through strangers, I was blockaded by two unbudgeable women who apparently had the same name. "The problem, Roxanne," said the first, shortwaisted and buxom, "is that the working class wants raises more than changes, and the middle class craves its privileges more than it dares the risk of revolution."

"That, Roxanne," said the second, slender and bony, "is precisely why we have to radicalize the workers."

"The out-of-workers, Roxanne, because everyone's unemployed now."

"The meek will inherit the earth all right, but only if we fight for them."

"Still, what if they don't want the kind of earth we deliver them?"

"We educate them to like it, Roxanne. That's what study groups are for—getting the working class to see itself *as* a class."

"Which leaves us where with the middle ... I mean bourgeoisie?"

The second Roxanne tittered. "Like Comrade Stalin, Roxanne, we may have to crack a few heads to make our omelet."

Electing not to tell them they meant eggs not heads because I figured they really did mean heads, I slithered around the Roxannes and darted for the canapés. I collided clumsily with a squat red-haired woman I'd seen somewhere. "I know you," she interrupted my apology. "You're Eleanor's kid, Davey, aren't you?"

I explained I didn't even know any Eleanor. I was offended to be called a kid by someone who couldn't have been more than a couple of years older than I was, but she was filled with both wrath and a worldweariness that gave her the demeanor of age. She identified herself as Katinka the Red. With her hot-coal eyes, ruddy complexion, arms bared as if for combat, shoulders coming at me, Katinka was like a whole squadron. I felt surrounded. "Okay," I said, "I've seen you at Jubilee."

"Not any more," she said in a rasp, proceeding with one of those cocktail party—in this case Party—tales that unpopular guests subject their cornered prey to. "I began as a moony little Wobbly," she said, "a naïve Iowa farmgirl with thoughts of reform. I passed into my Bolshie phase early in the Depression, and I can see nothing ahead now, no cure, but total revolution, where I hope to be a foot soldier."

While I swallowed that along with a smoked scallop, pugnacious Katinka the Red, oozing hatred, gave a rueful laugh. Wolfing down snacks herself, she said Stalin was too gentle with the kulaks. "Just exterminate them, hee hee," was how she put it. As a little contest with myself, I tried to tease out something nondoctrinaire, but she held to her belligerence as if it were a life preserver. If I said the market may go down again, she snickered not for the big boys it won't. If I said at least Mossy wants a picture with some realism in it, she snorted that his merchandised realism was only a matter of form, hardly the content most Americans live with. If I said the whole society seems upside down, heh heh, even the Yankees can't win a World Series these days, she sniffed that it was only musical chairs and the fat wallets in St. Louis or Detroit or Chicago were having a turn with their own crib toys. Everything to Katinka was economics, conspiracy and ruthlessness as she fused Marx with Darwin and wound up irate at what she called the way of the world, a world she couldn't wait to destroy even as she inhaled its canapés. "When they get tired of the Depression," she said, "the bankers will start the World War all over again, same teams, different players, there's profit in death, don't you see that, Owen, hee hee hee hee."

Katinka's mirthless laugh curdled in my ears but reminded me where I'd seen her. She was the woman I'd given Pammy's Plymouth to at the Communist office in Venice, talkative now, lubricated by her surroundings and drink. Almost at the same moment she remembered who I was. "Oh sure, you're the guy who runs errands for the great Palmyra Millevoix. I drove you to Jubilee after you delivered her car."

Two nobodies, I was thinking. Of course we didn't recognize each other. Neither of us is anyone.

"It wasn't her car," I lied. "When I told you I was calling on her behalf I was lying," I lied again. "I hardly know her myself," I said, managing a sliver of truth.

"The high and mighty don't want to be seen with us—not yet."

If she didn't exactly soften when she realized we'd already been through a transaction together, her hostility lightened. Her name was originally Oriole, she told me, but she hated birds and changed it as soon as she heard the first Red speak Russian. She had been a script girl at Jubilee until she was fired for trying to organize the other script girls, stand-ins and body doubles into a union. "A union of underlings, practically throwaways," she said. "That's what they really couldn't stand, so they canned me." It occurred to me Katinka might be a psychological body double for Mossy. Each of them lived in certainty. "I tell you, Owen," she said, "there's no help for it but destruction. What will we replace banks or studios or even the government with? We start over. We can't know what to build until we see the shape of the vacant lot. Then we'll figure out what to put there. First we have to make the lot vacant."

Behind us a producer said to a director, "Six months ago I bought a Mozart letter for a thousand dollars. You won't believe what it's already worth. Take a guess."

"There will be casualties," Katinka said.

My rescue was provided by an unlikely source. "My boy, you look bewildered," a voice boomed at me. I turned from Katinka the Red to the owlish gaze of Professor Bruno Leonard himself. The stout pipe-smoking professor was upon me to ask a favor. He was going to speak to the assembled troops in Gloriana's long narrow lanai room. Would I help him arrange chairs in the lanai so they all faced in the same direction? As Gloriana's lover du jour he knew both his entitlements and his limits. He put his arm around my shoulder and led me to the lanai, where the two of us set about turning the room into a miniature auditorium. "Young America, what aileth thee?" he asked, placing his pipe on an end table. "Even the most convinced of us have our doubts. I know I do." Then this late-fortyish fugitive from upper Manhattan intelligentsia fixed me with perhaps his second-best Kremlinological stare and raised his brow expectantly.

"I'm confused," I said, "irritated listening to zealots or even worse, to the rich talking about the poor as adorable pets who need better care." I looked out the lanai's glass doors into the canyon below, a canyon away from my waiting shack, where I wished I were.

"I don't know that's quite what they're doing," he said. "The Bible exalts the poor but it doesn't say they're the only repositories of virtue." He put his arm around my shoulder again, a teacher having found his pupil. Or was it something else? Bruno Leonard was comfortable relaxing into the role of didact. He was not rigid, in fact he was Socratic, but he was eager for the play of pedagogical grilling, the Q and A that led eventually to a thesis that seemed, at least for one class section, sound. Bruno was like a career military officer who leaves the service but never quite looks right in civilian clothes; however pleasurable his frolic in Hollywood, he looked as if he belonged on campus. "Movie people out here," he said, "suddenly find themselves richer than they ever dreamed. Is it so bad if some of them decide to help a good cause instead of buying a string of racehorses or building more swimming pools?"

"But these rich don't really want to share with the poor, only to say they feel bad about them while using them as an excuse for their politics. Isn't it hypocrit—"

"No, no" he pre-empted me, "this isn't hypocrisy at all." He seemed to have been waiting for that word and when he heard it coming he crushed it like a gnat. "Weakness is all it is," he said, "weakness many of them feel guilty about, as they do the amount of money they make for turning out pablum. It would be hypocritical if they were advocating revolution while secretly plotting against it. To promote a revolt but not quite be able to pull it off in your own life is only frailty, not hypocrisy. The churches are full of frail sinners, not necessarily hypocrites."

"That doesn't bring me any closer to knowing what I ought to do."

"About what, Young America?" The professor had found a nickname he stuck on me like a postage stamp.

"About the Party, I guess."

"Uncertain in the precinct of certainty? All the Katinkas?"

"I suppose. How long are you staying out here, Professor?"

"Bruno, please. Until the fall term begins. Or maybe this is the love of my life. Let us not discount that possibility."

I wasn't sure if he was referring to California, Hollywood, or Gloriana herself. If it was the latter, I thought I already could guess enough about our hostess to assume the professor would be discarded when whatever defined his season drew to a close. "Tell me," he said, "how long have you been in durance vile?"

"At the studio? At Jubilee? About three years off and on."

"Do you like it?"

"I do and I don't. I like working on a script I think can make a good picture."

"Your boss was once at CCNY, where I teach."

"I've heard he went there."

"I wasn't a professor yet, only a section teacher. I hadn't figured out what I was going to be, if I ever have, but your Amos Zangwill stood out by being, even at eighteen, a young man in a hurry. As faculty adviser to the newspaper, where he wrote little melting-pot stories about how happy the immigrants were to become Americans, I found him a rank sentimentalist with an eye for nothing but the obvious."

Thinking about my humiliation at Mossy's hands that afternoon, I said I didn't find him particularly sentimental.

"Then you don't go to see Jubilee pictures," he said. But he returned to the evening's theme, trying to draw me into his orbit. "I have my own ambivalence, Owen."

"You? Who are trying to shepherd the rest of us into the fold?"

"We'll see who I bring into what fold, Young America." Bruno Leonard's laugh was a smothered chuckle in which he did not open his mouth—"hmm, hmm, hmm, hmm." Picking up his pipe, he sucked on it, relighted it. He fixed me with his teacherly gaze, but I stayed a few chairs away. I didn't want the arm around my shoulder again.

"You don't exactly sound like a Doubting Thomas," I said.

"But I am," he said. "Pros and cons—the Left sees the inherent contradictions of capitalism, how it leads to an ever-growing chasm between rich and poor, rewards the selfish at the expense of the generous, denies laborers the fruits of their labor. Isn't it an insanity of our age that workers often can't afford to buy the products they make? The Communists are trying to offer goods and services to the masses they can never have in a capitalist society. Communists are in the vanguard of talking about race prejudice, all the prejudices that mock our democratic ideals. We are not created equal here; we are created by the capitalist system as atoms of greed, and soon we'll become more imperial than any society since ancient Rome. Only the Communists are willing to talk about class, the dirty unspoken secret of America, where the upper class pretends to be free of class bias while barricading themselves behind their mountains of money. Avarice is a sacrament in our economic system. Communism is the future of the world, Young America, preceded by socialism, succeeded by the withering away of the state."

"I don't hear much doubt there, or any cons," I said.

"Oh yes. What if there is no freedom and democracy under Marxism? Marxists claim to elevate the masses, but it may be that masses will have to just be masses under Communism—mobs almost—and not individuals at all. The people here tonight who have been to Russia, they've seen busy collective farms and happy factories, but these are stage sets like what you have in your studios. A colleague at CCNY has letters from Russian relatives who describe anything but a workers'—or for that matter a thinkers'—paradise. There is the unbridled power of the Party. Those who disagree with Stalin are repressed with great fervor. Capitalism could prove to be more flexible than I imagine. Sometimes I see FDR as a showboat who postures for the workers while saving the asses of the very industrialists and bankers who hate him, but it's possible his reforms will work well enough to prop up the system. In the Soviet Union, most people were happy to see the czars go, but perhaps Stalin is a czar himself. I don't know how it will turn out."

"So which way," I asked, "are you going to nudge this crowd tonight?"

"Come to class, Young America," the professor said as we finished with the last of the chairs. "Oh God, here comes ABC."

"The troops are becoming uneasy, Professor." Bruno Leonard was being accosted by the short woman with the high pompadour and diamond necklace. Sylvia, watching me like a mother hen or bird of prey, had led her officious companion into the lanai.

"I quite agree," said Bruno, "but Gloriana will be calling us all together."

"Precisely my point," said the pompadour woman. The professor introduced me to ABC, Augusta Byron Caramanlios, and told her it was, after all, Gloriana's party and she'd decide when to have him speak.

"More's the pity," said ABC, revolving and pointing her cylindrical tower in the direction of the living room.

"Augusta Byron Caramanlios has her hates," said Sylvia, "among whom is our hostess. Old ABC is the doyenne of the Left, or possibly the goyenne."

Gloriana Onslow O'Brian Flower was not ready to call her meeting to order. She was celebrating her status as queen bee too joyously to want to cede attention to any drone. Like a searchlight, she flashed her authoritative sensuality around her Party party. Her nemesis, Augusta Byron Caramanlios, tried to break Gloriana's spell. The two of them were similars repelling, with the cordial perseverance of old prize fighters who have met numerous times and know one another's moves. Bruno Leonard had said ABC had to be invited because of the loyalty of her troops. She claimed they would march, strike, give money or sign petitions whenever she gave the signal.

I spied Yeatsman, a port in a storm, but he'd been collected by ABC too. "Young man," she said to me, "you should know Yancey Ballard."

"Know him and love him," Yeatsman said, possibly on his third cocktail.

"Well then, Yancey," the dowager ABC resumed, "what do you honestly make of all this self-righteous convention of insincere radicals?"

"Oh I think they've very sincere, Gussie," Yeatsman said. "They're sincerely drawn to free booze and caviar doled out by Our Lady of the Perpetual Lusts."

"You're wicked, Yancey," said the far wickeder ABC, gesticulating with her foot-high hair, "but you know she's much worse because she corrupts anyone she touches, an indefatigable destroyer. This evil woman must be stopped before she destroys all Reds."

At that instant the hostess herself swooped upon Yeatsman and ABC as if she'd heard every word. I was certain she was about to ruin her own party. How little I knew.

"Why Augusta darling," said Gloriana, hugging her to her bosom and avoiding the Caramanlios pompadour as best she could, "you mustn't fill poor Yeatsman's ears with bile about me. Don't protest, you know you can't help it, my dear scorpion. But he might put it in a script or worse, get it into Louella's column, and then I'd have to sue your diamonds right off your lizardy neck, my dearest."

"Oh Flower," said ABC, using Gloriana's last name as if she were wielding a barbell. "Don't you know it's all about love, good and bad love to be sure, but all love."

"Why yes," Gloriana said, "in a lifetime of hearing the word *love* tossed hither and yon on the waves of rhetoric, and especially in Hollywood hearing it applied to everything from unreadable scripts to unwatchable motion pictures, I think for sheer sanctimony and linguistic perversion of the noble word *love*, you win, Augusta."

She had sailed away before Augusta could find breath to hiss, "Serpent!"

Retreating, I bumped, literally, into the bulky screenwriter Mitch Altschuler, a true believer, jabbering to greenhorn mascot Comfort O'Hollie, who had shown up at the party out of curiosity. "I want to see what my writers are yelling about," she told me. "I have absolutely no intention of joining you lot of screaming mee-mies shouting your rubbish at each other. If I wanted that I could have stayed in Dublin where the screamers already outnumber the talkers. Outdrink them too."

But she was willing to listen to Mitch Altschuler, with dreams in his eyes, hauling as much of the Volga as he could carry to the Pacific. Just back from Moscow, he had been calling people *Tovaritch*—Comrade—at the party, especially the servants. The curly-haired Mitch, writer of detective stories for Warners, was determined to redden his movies. Turning to me, he said, "We need to write a picture, Owen, about the Russian workers, their fight against injustice—oh yes, there's still injustice in Mother Russia. The priests and the Cossacks are holding out. In the picture we'll show the conspirators, wedded to the old ways, failing to stop the new man and new woman emerging triumphant in their factories. Hollywood likes happy endings, we'll give them one."

"One they can choke on," Comfort said.

"No," Mitch said, "they'll love it because good beats evil, that's all they really care about. First we make our progressive pictures, then we strike the studios."

"Do you need saving?" said Sylvia who had made her way to us.

"Not a bit," said Comfort, "I can listen to twaddle equally well at work or play." She was lightly flirting with Mitch as she made fun of him.

We were joined by Mitch's literal fellow traveler, Gifford Wilsey, from Terre Haute, where he had been raised a strict Methodist. Though the two had gone together to the Soviet Union and Mitch's mother had bragged about it all over Crown Heights, not a soul in Gifford's hometown knew where he had gone. His parents were so ashamed that his father told the family's minister to consider his son deceased. Gifford was a man on stilts with rimless glasses; he had been a basketball player at Purdue, majoring in American history and becoming a devotee of Eugene Debs and Robert La Follette. He wrote movies with homespun themes—JackandJills the executives called them—but the Depression turned him from a theoretical into a practicing radical.

The bulky Altschuler and the string bean Wilsey were a kind of Mutt and Jeff act. "How'd you get here tonight, *Tovaritch*?" Mitch Altschuler asked.

"Steamed out Sunset *Bulvar*," Gifford Wilsey said. "You?"

"Took the direct route straight down Wilshire *Prospekt*," Mitch said.

"So boys," Sylvia said, "tell us about the promised land."

"Giff finally lost God in the Soviet Union," Mitch said.

"Russia was like our old silent pictures," Gifford said, "because all you could understand were the gestures people made. Nothing prepared me for Red Square and the clash of cultures there. Saint Basil's with the onion domes and the elegance slays you with its beauty until you reflect on your bourgeois concept of what is beautiful. The purpose of Saint Basil's was oppression, convincing serfs they belonged where they were, on their knees, while the high priests and ignoble nobles kept control of them. Then you turn around and see the Kremlin itself, Lenin's tomb with lines of ordinary citizens patiently, reverently waiting hours to pay tribute. Lenin liberated them from the bishops and the Czar who worked hand in glove to oppress them. A solemn recognition in the majesty of Red Square. When you finally see Lenin you see the implacable face of wisdom itself."

"Our silent movie tour," Mitch said, "then took us to the Soviet Union of today."

"Sure, we saw what they wanted us to see," Gifford said, "but there was no faking the new experiments with production and distribution, no acting when workers told us that at last they're making things for themselves. Hopeful, productive patriots."

"Including," Mitch said, "a farmer's daughter Giff fell for on a collective where they grow some awful wheat they call bulgur. I couldn't wait to get back to Moscow, but Giff didn't care what they fed us as long as he could make the daughter. I got him out of there just before the farmer stuck a pitchfork in him. That's when he really gave up God."

"It's just this," Gifford said, shrugging off Mitch. "No God I can imagine would let a great country like Russia suffer as it did under the czars, no more than he would let a great country like ours suffer as it does in the Depression and our rotten system with all the war profiteers who sent us off to France in 1917 while they raked it in over here. Not to mention how a God can leave Hitler alone with what he plans to do to the Jews."

That was too much for Mitch Altschuler. "Let's not overdo it," he said.

"No, Hitler means it, Mitch," said Gifford.

"Half a million Jews in Germany, for Christ's sake, Giff. Some are my relatives. Five hundred thousand Jews. You think he thinks he can kill them all? Don't be silly."

No one said anything to that.

"What about Jews in the Soviet Union?" Sylvia asked.

"Stalin loves Jews," Mitch said.

"Loves?" Sylvia repeated.

"He takes Jews into his high councils. Look at Lazar Kaganovich, Zinoviev, Lev Kamenev. His most trusted foreign policy adviser, Maxim Litvinov, is a Jew."

I ventured a meek question. "Even if you liked it there, admired the Soviet Union and its new society, why should American Communists take orders from Moscow?"

"Why do Catholics take orders from Rome?" Mitch answered, followed by a long laugh from this short man. "'Nuff said."

"No, it's a good question," Gifford said. "We don't take orders, we do take guidance—the USSR is the most advanced in both thinking and development. There has to be a solid front against the capitalists and their greed."

"We're among friends, Giff," Mitch said, "So I think I can tell them."

"We're not supposed to," said Gifford, "but okay, if you like."

"One of us," Mitch said conspiratorially, dropping his voice, "may be selected for full time P work, which will be terribly S and we may have to disappear. For a while."

"Pardon me," Sylvia said, "but it seems to me your initials may succeed in puzzling your friends yet will be as loud and clear as a star's ego to any Red Squad detective. Want to tell us what the hell you're talking about?"

"Suppleness is crucial," Mitch said, "so if the P line changes we change with it."

Gifford Wilsey nodded, but I didn't understand how his completely inelastic, rigid friend could be talking about suppleness. "Excuse me," I said, "I don't get it."

"We may be going underground to do P for *Party* work," Mitch said, "which will be highly S for *secret* in nature. Which means don't ask. P work, which will be called subversive by capitalist toadies, is probably the most patriotic thing an American can do right now. I'll be doing whatever I can to turn fascistic America toward Communism."

"I would like to tell you gently," Sylvia said, "you're being a silly ass with your cloak-and-dagger dialogue out of a B, which stands for *bad*, movie I hope any of us would be ashamed to write. I'm for the Communists because I think they describe us so accurately, but doing secret work for them is coming close to treason."

"Are you sure?" Mitch said earnestly, stunned because he respected Sylvia, who had been his mentor when he first came West. "I don't think so, Sylvia."

"The thing is," said Gifford, more modest than Mitch Altschuler but also more convinced since he had essentially traded in one faith for another, "the powers-that-be in our society know perfectly well what is happening and what is going to happen."

"And what's that?" Sylvia asked.

"FDR knows it," Gifford said. "The smarter men around him like Tugwell and Baruch know it, quite obviously Wall Street shivers over it. Simply put: the dispossessed of the world are about to embrace socialism. Hitler and Mussolini are the death throes of extreme capitalism, and when they're gone, the world will make way for the means of production to be controlled by those who work them."

Bertrand the butler came by bearing his silver tray in the center of which was now heaped at least two pounds of fresh caviar. Toast points surrounded the caviar and we all liberally mounded it on them. Mitch took more. "Ah good," he said as he crunched the tiny black eggs. "Not exactly what we had in Moscow, eggs not quite gray enough, a touch too small, but damn good." Turning to the uniformed Bertrand, he said, "*Spasibo, Tovaritch.* Know what that means? No, of course not. Thank you, Comrade. And now, *do svidania, Tovaritch.* Goodbye. Say, wait a minute."

"Sir?" said Bertrand. Ever since the Scottsboro Boys had been falsely—it soon developed—accused of rape and then convicted by an all-white jury, the Party had been eager to promote black membership. Though Gloriana's gathering was nominally to support the Scottsboro Boys' legal appeal—surely an inoffensive cause anywhere outside the old Confederacy—all the guests knew this was actually a Party party.

"What's your last name?" Mitch asked the butler.

"Munson, sir."

"Bertrand Munson, you're who we need, you're who all our organizing is for."

The butler looked puzzled, possibly nervous.

"It's all right, Bertrand," said Sylvia, who knew him from previous occasions.

"Your people stand to gain the most from the victory of socialism on our American shores," Mitch said. "Believe me, the serfs in Russia were as badly treated as slaves, and they weren't free until about the same time you colored folks were. Now they're rising to the top. Will you give us a try?"

"Give you a try, sir?" Bertrand Munson, resplendent in his formal butler's uniform, watched Mitch Altschuler help himself to a sizable dollop of caviar.

"Join us, Bertrand, join the Communist Party. I'm sure Gloriana would be proud to have one of her serv—or rather a member of her househo—someone who works for her become a Communist, come to our meetings, join the struggle. Legal slavery was ended but we have to end economic slavery. I know Gloriana would be happy to give you evenings off for our meetings. Occasionally. The Party is for the Negro, I promise you."

Bertrand Munson appeared to be relieved to have a tray in his hands, obligations besides listening to Mitch Altschuler. "I have to refill my serving platter, sir."

"*Do svidania*, Bertrand Munson," Mitch said.

"More shrimp, Bertrand," Gloriana called from across the room.

And he was off to the kitchen.

Old ABC, using her pompadour as a pointer, was herding a splinter group of her loyalists into the dining room, exhorting and shoving, until she had what she considered a quorum of perhaps a dozen. I came along to see what she was doing. A brawny knuckle of a man was already in the dining room, looking uncomfortable in an easy chair alongside Gloriana's mahogany buffet. A schism was afoot, the dowager Caramanlios's counterparty within the larger Party party. "If our hostess won't call us together," ABC said to her rump delegates, "I want at least my dearest allies in our battle to hear from a real man of the people. I should have said he *is* the people. He comes to us from the Teamsters strike in Minneapolis and the strike against Buick—the colossus of General Motors no less—in Detroit. Will everyone welcome Comrade Al Sill."

A few people said welcome to the stranger but no one clapped. Mitch Altschuler and Sylvia were curious enough to look in on the dining room faction. I was interested, too, and almost bumped into Edward G. Robinson as I crowded into the dining room. "Please excuse me," he said, genial though not without his trademark scowl, "I thought something less Hollywood might be happening in here."

It was. Al Sill was a working class legend. Born Arvin Sillenborgen to immigrant Swedish farmers, he left high school to roam the country as an itinerant worker. Angry at how he and his fellow laborers were treated, he became a union organizer after the World War and at the end of the Twenties a Communist. He was sent to the Lenin Institute in Moscow and when he came home found the country deep in the Depression. This made Party recruiting easier but fomenting strikes harder since those who still did have jobs were desperate to keep them. Now, as he arose awkwardly from his chair, Sill looked like a barrel, with the hands of a lumberjack and biceps of a steelworker.

"The fight we're in," rock-jawed Al Sill said, leaning on Gloriana's buffet, "is the fight between those whose labor creates the wealth and those who own the wealth. This contradiction is the flaw at the heart of capitalism that will help us build socialism."

"Oh Jesus," Mitch Altschuler whispered to Sylvia and me, "either this guy takes us all for idiots or he's dumber than the dumbest producer."

"Maybe," Edward G. Robinson whispered to Mitch, "but he's real."

Al Sill had little more to say. He could tell he was in an alien environment. "Those who control the wealth aren't those who make it with their hands and backs," he went on huskily. "Out here it's with your typewriters. That's why this country needs a revolution. The janitors in Philadelphia know it, the men on the assembly lines in Detroit know it, the fruit pickers right here in the Imperial Valley are finding it out. Those who resist us the fiercest are those who stand to lose, and that's just a few people, my friends, just the bosses and their stooges. What I hear, studio heads like Louis Mayer and Mossy Zangwill, treating you like canaries in your gold cages, they make Reds a lot better than I do. We mobilize to let them know our numbers have more strength than their dollars. Numbers beat dollars. I don't have anything more to say except Solidarity Forever."

Sill sat down again, still looking uncomfortable, to scattered clapping that died almost before he could hear it. In these surroundings, Augusta Byron Caramanlios surely might have warned him there would be far more dollars than numbers. At the rallies he normally addressed, songs were sung and slogans were chanted, but in Gloriana's dining room Al Sill wasn't even the night's main event. The room emptied fast.

Back in the living room two strangers moved toward Yancey Ballard, who was in the process of deciding on Party membership. They looked as unsavory as they were unfamiliar. Greta Kimple and Mort Leech were Party functionaries who handled new recruits, cross-examining them. The compact Kimple asked Yancey why Communism was necessary, while Leech, a bully as red in the face as in his politics, taunted him. "Why would you want to give up your independence of thought, you an intellectual, to take orders from Moscow?"

Sensing he was being tested, Yancey said, "The Party isn't a debating society. When my friends say I'd sacrifice intellectual freedom by joining, I tell them if you're going to have an organization that gets anything done, whether it's a factory or a studio, you need discipline. Mossy Zangwill doesn't have votes on whether to make a picture or fire an actor, does he? You're not back at Princeton making a gentlemanly choice on what to spike the punch with on Saturday night, no sir, you have to have someone in charge who makes a decision and everyone else, like in the Army, carries it out."

"Do you agree with Communist policy then?" Mort Leech asked.

"Look, dammit, I don't even know what every Party policy is." Yeatsman was on a tear. "Did we agree with orders to charge at Neuve Chapelle when we knew the Germans had artillery cover and more troops? Hell no! But we charged into that goddam forest and made kindling of a lot of it, and when we captured some of the Germans they said we must be drunk or crazy to fight the way we did. Maybe all we were was more scared than they were of dying, and maybe we believed just a little more than they did in what we were fighting for. We got control of the sector. That's what we're going to need here. The world isn't going to color itself red because Uncle Joe Stalin tells it to. All of us will have to pull and keep pulling until this town and this country understand that workers have to control what they work on, bankers can't kick people out of their homes and off their farms, industrialists can't act like slave-drivers. We have to do it because we know it's right and it can return justice to America."

"And tomorrow the world?" asked Greta Kimple.

"One sector at a time, we said in the Army, then we catch our breath." Yancey was aware he was being kidded by someone who had no sense of humor. "As the poet said," he added, "'Too long a sacrifice can make a stone of the heart.'" That was his only reference to Yeats, and Greta Kimple, stony-hearted already and as interested in poetry as a toad is in a telephone, let it fly by her. Yancey was not the supercilious skeptic of Jubilee here, the courtly southern agnostic. This was a believer, and on his face passion had replaced doubt, which had abandoned him. He said he wanted to keep the land true to its promises, recalling Jefferson's ideal of a revolution to clean things up every generation. "I am certainly not radical enough," Yancey concluded, this time quoting Lenin in Zurich before he embarked on his sealed train to the Finland Station in Russia.

"One can never be radical enough," said Greta Kimple. "That is, one must try always to be as radical as reality."

"At last I see," said Mort Leech portentously, "that my war at Belleau Wood and the war you fought at Neuve Chapelle, Yancey Ballard, was only about a slaveholder called Germany, who owns a hundred slaves, fighting other slaveholders led by Britain and France, who own a thousand slaves, for a more equal distribution of slaves."

"We now have in our possession," Greta Kimple said, "nothing less than the skeleton key to unlock the mystery of human existence. Communism can do what five thousand years of history haven't accomplished." She was becoming scriptural.

"But what about human nature, Yancey?" Mort Leech persisted, playing the shill with a trick question. "Surely you can't change human nature."

"What is human nature?" Yancey answered. "Is it human nature to have kings and peons, masters and slaves? That's what the power brokers always say. That's what the plantation owners said where I come from in Alabama. No. There is no human nature that is unchangeable as the capitalists claim."

"Good," said Greta Kimple. Apparently Yancey had passed. "Technology and reason," Kimple went on, "will produce the idea, the ideology, that we can be scientifically liberated and transformed. There is only science and progress, and Communism can direct both of them for the greater good of mankind. Human nature will be the result of evolving human effort."

Now someone else objected. It was Poor Jim Bicker, possibly because he'd been cast off by our hostess, the widow Flower, in favor of the professor. "The Communist goals are an improvement on what we have," he said, "but you can't reduce all human color and hope and endeavor to a monochromatic machine-made man."

"Did I say that?" Greta Kimple replied. "Did anyone hear me say I want the gray individual? No, Comrades, I want to see human potential expanded because that's the only way to redden the planet. Already one sixth of the world's landmass is Red. That leaves five sixths. Can we do it, Comrades? I think we can."

"Which," Mort Leech carried on, "will permit life to be organized into a single model, subject to central planning. Man himself will be remade." Leech now seemed to expand his girth as he drew deeply on his cigarette and pulled himself up to his full bulldozing altitude. "On to the other five sixths!" he shouted, having now reverted to his position of Party stalwart. He and Kimple picked up some applause in the room as if accepting bouquets. "Onward to the new man," Leech finished his catechism.

"And woman," Kimple said.

"Yes," Sylvia agreed, "on to the other five sixths. But I don't want to be dictated to. I want the Party to be democratic, the vanguard of the working class, sure, but within a system that embraces other parties as well."

"Nope," Mort Leech said, his neck bulging out of his shirt collar. "What you call the democratic system is nothing but a shell game the capitalists play to keep everyone in line. Democracy has had its day, too bad it doesn't work. Class oppressors get a stranglehold on it, finance a smokescreen of lies, and only hide behind them. When you've found the truth, what's the point of permitting error? Would you let astronomers teach that the moon is made of green cheese?"

"The Dionne quintuplets," Sylvia said, "have as much chance of convincing Americans to give up the ballot as Moscow does."

"No, Moscow won't do it," Greta Kimple said as if she'd been appointed to quell any disturbances from the one other woman in the conversation. "This will happen by our own strength as a Party within the United States. Stalin himself has said nothing important is decided by the soviets and other mass organizations, but by the Party alone."

"But not by the Party in Moscow?" I asked, tentative as ever, my only contribution to the dialogue. Taking in this heady scene of my superiors, I was nervous, smothered, elated, a teenager at a dance with an erection he can't subdue.

"Moscow has almost twenty years' experience," Mort Leech said, reclaiming the floor to put down a potentially unruly conscript, if that's what I was becoming. "Once they have laid down general guidelines, we Americans will take it from there."

Sylvia pulled me toward the canapé spread. "Where coal miners and garment workers are concerned I'm redder than they are," she said, "but I'm becoming afraid we may have to save Communism from the Communists. Another drink, Sweetie?"

Sweetie? I thought as I headed for the bar. I passed a tall man with brilliantined hair wearing a double-breasted suit, looking gloomy and out of place. It was Hurd Dawn, the head scene designer at Jubilee. I was surprised to see him at a Party gathering; he'd always looked like the essence of acquisitive capitalism to me, cocky and well satisfied with himself. Dawn was asking a woman if he could see her the following evening. This revealed a truth about the Party to me; it was also a singles market where you could go to a meeting one night and find a date for the next. "I thought we could have some fun," Dawn said to the woman. "Well then, I suppose we don't always have to be so serious," she said, "so why not?" "Good," he said, "I need something to look forward to. Just lost my job as head scene designer at Jubilee."

I was amazed, remembering Hurd Dawn strutting so proudly around the Jubilee lot that I had thought he was Mossy Zangwill himself when I first came to work there.

Tutor Beedleman, smiling and familiar, suddenly popped up like a tin face in a shooting gallery. Dapper, short, scrappy, eager. Always faintly amused. "Owen, my dear man," said Tutor, "so invigorating to find you at the circus. Can anyone tell me what we're all doing here? What is the goddam balance between liberty and compulsion anyway? If everything is provided by the state, what's the incentive to work? Yet if everything is privately owned there's no incentive to better yourself because the rich have it all locked up and bettering yourself is impossible. Reds or Republicans, what'll it be?"

"You're leaving out a big category," I said.

"Oh, I hate the Democrats," he said. "I want to wipe that jut-jawed smile off FDR's smug sunny face. I'll go for an extreme solution, Big Business and Wall Street, or Workers of the World Unite. Nothing in between."

"You're pulling my leg," I said.

"Now that you mention it, wouldn't that be fun? We should try it sometime."

"Was Hurd Dawn fired?" I asked. "Is that possible?"

"Too big for his britches is what Dunster Clapp said. Mossy went along with it because he wants to show New York he can trim staff. The younger boys in set design make about a quarter of Hurd's salary, and they can do the job. Go find your girlfriend."

Tutor's wild, mild eye began to rove like the glance of a wallflower desperately searching, imploring faces to ask her for the next dance.

Wandering among the faithful with a drink in each hand, I had a flash of what had really brought me to Gloriana Onslow Flower's house. It wasn't Sylvia's invitation alone, nor even her rescuing me from Mossy's vengefulness. No, what had truly propelled me to the party was the affair between Amos Zangwill and Palmyra Millevoix. I said their full names to myself as a distancing tactic. It didn't work. They hovered more closely than ever. Pammy would be an even bigger star here than on the Jubilee lot, Mossy an even bigger threat. Thank God they weren't at the party. I worked, slaved when ordered, for one, and was in love, infatuated certainly, obsessed I suppose, with the other. But in my mind they were to stay separate. I hated picturing them even in the same room.

Instead, they had united. I couldn't help feeling the union—parental? I quivered—was against me. I knew how irrational this was, but that was the nature of obsession. My sense was of being helpless before conquering powers. I was here looking for help among those who represented the helpless. The hostile forces of the nation personalized themselves into Mossy, with Pammy as his moll. I despised him, scorned her. Not daring to confront my boss, I could enlist in the fight against bossism, capitalism itself. I was suddenly furious at Mossy, a delayed reaction to his brutal treatment that afternoon, with an anger so strong it surfaced as a kind of dilating righteousness.

I reverse zoomed my anger, went wide with it, and saw the whole world as vassal to self-anointed, capricious power. I was famished for a philosophy, a faith. And my hunger zoomed in now on the Party, the Party that would rid the world of itself. Reader, I became a Red that night.

I almost tripped over Sylvia. She was talking to Bruno Leonard, who looked like he was trying to become an ex-professor, a new Hollywood native. I felt a stab when I saw them together, almost nose to nose. As Mossy had taken my love, this CCNY refugee would now steal my date. Sylvia noticed and with two deft motions took her gimlet with one hand and slipped the other under my elbow.

"You thought I was horning in on your girl," Bruno said. "Oh no, don't object, I saw. We are territorial souls all of us. I'm a senior figure, Sylvia herself may have a month or so on you. We transfer everything, Owen, can't help ourselves. Just because I've gone over to Marx doesn't mean I've forgotten what I learned from Freud. I believe the widow de-Flowered will presently want me to sing for my supper—and much more."

"I wasn't jealous," I lied as soon as Bruno left us.

"I'm flattered," Sylvia said. "To Bruno, all his friends are intimates. But they change. Purposes, decisions, ambitions, sweethearts all exist to be changed. Life is a party Bruno gives, and if you don't keep showing up he feels betrayed. Since he's become an appendage of our hostess, I see him less now than when he first came west and was snapped up as an exotic creature who could actually talk ideas and tell us about the radicals on the East Coast."

Gloriana herself, treasuring every second and all insults to her class, at last cruised to the center of her gathering. Gently tinkling her Champagne glass with a silver spoon to command attention,

Gloriana crooned to the room at large. "Comes the revolution," she said in a voice whose bluster would have offended her Bostonian relatives even more than her words, "the man we're about to listen to will be honored as our homegrown American prophet. We're all red, white and blue patriots here, are we not?" A couple of hisses and an amiable boo interrupted the hostess. "No, really we are—red for our politics, white for the motion picture screens, blue for our country in the Depression. The Depression that progressive thought and policies can lift us out of. Our guest this evening is a man whose visions can forge a new reality, and if you don't mind being herded into the lanai I think you'll agree that Professor Bruno Leonard makes both common and uncommon sense."

Bertrand the butler had set up a humidor for use as a podium, and the professor began with modesty, however posed, as he drew us into his orbit. If you had photographed him that night you'd have said, yes, this exile from the East has miraculously managed it, he looks like both of them, this is the perfect marriage of Lenin and Trotsky. "I'm Professor Bruno Leonard from the City College of New York," he began, "and I count for nothing in our mutual struggle. At CCNY I teach history and government, hoping my humble efforts can help change the first and overthrow the second."

A fat character actor of no note, Gates Billings, applauded and was immediately stared down. If Edward G. Robinson had done the same thing the whole room would have joined him. But Robinson was far too courteous and too good a listener.

"Revolution is an art," Leonard continued, "and I am not an artist. Many of you are, however, which is why the revolution comes looking for you. In your motion picture art, timing is everything. So is it with revolution. Like a captain when a turbulent wind howls, the revolutionist trims his sail when he must. Other times, when the day is fair and the breeze blows in the right direction, the sails are billowed for full speed ahead. This is where we are today as we face a worldwide depression whose causes and cures are social, economic and political. Our sails catch the wind in 1934."

"'Thou, too, sail on, O Ship of State.'" Too many cocktails had regressed Yeatsman to a schoolboy Longfellow quoter. Bruno Leonard drew his mouth into the unsteady grin of someone who isn't sure whether he's receiving ridicule or approval.

"Roosevelt and his crowd look at the world through a straw," the professor continued. "From their high perches they peer down and see only tiny pieces of the picture. We Reds see the picture whole. Why? because we look from the bottom up, without straws, we see the expanse of class injury, the enhanced eyesight centuries of pain have conferred on the workers, the dispossessed and the disenfranchised."

Coming down a notable notch and several octaves, Bruno wooed the fearful among us. "Boys and girls, here's what I say. Most of what you read and hear about Russia are Hearst's lies and in Los Angeles it is especially the Chandlers' rot. Remember how they helped frame Tom Mooney. But some of what they say is true. The Soviet Union is not summer camp. It can't afford to play softball with the rest of the world hating it, plotting against it, led by the industrialists and the fascists."

"Is there a difference?" Hurd Dawn piped up, wanting to participate from his new and unfamiliar posture of outcast.

"There are plenty of differences," Bruno said, "but in this fight there are no distinctions. Big business and big fascism are in bed together, and we know what happens when people who like each other get into bed."

Appreciative titters from women and guffaws from the men who hoped to sleep with them later.

"No, they can't play softball with the hostility of the fascist and capitalist systems surrounding them, with fifth columnists swarming among their own population. Uncle Joe Stalin gives a choice to the peasants—we're trying something new here. If you join our collectives, stop fighting each other, great, welcome to the new Russia, but if you won't we can't help you, sorry. Progressives understand most countries and their institutions are against us. Read the Chandlers' *Los Angeles Times* dispatches making the Soviet Union look like a giant slave colony. The whole world will someday soon be divided between the U.S. and the S.U., and we have to be ready, folks, we have to be ready to make our stand, we have to arm ourselves first with revolutionary ideas and ideals, and then with a plan to undermine the capitalist bosses and their sycophants."

"But it's not only idiots," Tutor Beedleman interrupted, "who say labor in the USSR *is* the equivalent of slave labor, not just the Hearst and Chandler newspapers. Are their any real choices of leaders there or even of the kind of work you go into?" Tutor was silenced by catcalls. I couldn't tell if his question was a plant or genuine skepticism.

"No, don't boo," Bruno Leonard went on from his humidor at the front of the lanai. "It's a good question. There is no Jeffersonovich in Russian history, no Voltairovich. All they had were czars running a police state with savage pogroms and suppressions of any uprising where people tried for a more equitable arrangement between rulers and the ruled. We here have our traditional Bill of Rights liberties, the ideal of equality even if we're far from living up to it. We have democracy at the ballot box, but it's been taken over by parasites to the powerful. In the South colored people aren't even allowed the dubious privilege of voting for parasites. But our revolution will bring no dictator to America, not even a benign representative of the proletariat. It will not be easy. We can never be dictated to here even by the proletariat. Marx himself said the revolution will be toughest here, the hardest to implement, because capitalism is so cemented into our way of living and thinking. It will take enormous effort to break up the reinforced concrete of American capitalism. That's why the Party needs not only money but ideas and work, work, work!"

"Yea Bruno!" shouted Poor Jim Bicker. Whether he was being mocked or admired, Bruno accepted the cheer as flattery. He was contradicting the doctrinaire Greta Kimple and Mort Leech, who said they'd suppress freedom in favor of revealed truth, but he was challenging his audience to take up the socialist project with fervor.

"Wait!" Bruno said. "I can assure you socialism here will have a human face. Make no mistake, there will be a workers' party worthy of the name. We intellectuals must form a durable and lasting alliance with labor unions. This is happening in Europe already and we must make it happen here. We must not fail anymore. Failure is guilt's brother, and we have no time for either. We cannot feel guilty or apologetic about doing what must be done to establish a people's socialism in America with the great Russian Revolution itself as our guide!"

Interrupted by cheers, Bruno Leonard nodded his agreement with the audience. That is, he was agreeing he'd just said something wonderful and that the audience's approval was precisely what he himself approved of. He was giving a B plus to a group of bright but not wholly informed undergraduates who were readying themselves to repeat on a midterm what he'd just said. Bruno was overdoing his case, of course. That's what we did; we overdid.

"Joe Stalin asks us to prepare for a great undertaking," Bruno said, leaning on his humidor. "Exploitation in this country is as American as apple pie and Mom. You have plenty of apple pie and Mom in your pictures, why not exploitation too?"

Cheers for Bruno were blended with the no-count actor Gates Billings bawling, "Yeah, let's show America to the Americans the way it really is!" Did he really think he could get a part this way?

"What are we to make," Bruno asked rhetorically, "of what I call the crisis of simultaneity? If Rockefeller rakes in millions while a hobo starves while FDR grins propping up the capitalists while they curse him while Hitler plots death while Stalin builds collectives—can we say all this simultaneity adds up to an alarm bell for action?"

An assistant director, wishing he were on a set, yelled, "Camera, speed, action!"

Gates Billings bleated, "Act now!" Others chimed in but Bruno quieted the room.

I, however, was stuck, lost in the crisis of simultaneity. If everything Bruno Leonard had rattled off—Rockefeller, FDR, Hitler, Stalin—was happening at the same time, time itself being an artificial construct for measuring existence and experience, why couldn't we bring the past forward and shrink the future backward, thereby having everything present in the present? No time like this time.

"Are you taking all this in?" Sylvia, at my elbow, nudged me to her own present.

"Sure am," I said.

Stout, impassioned, declamatory Bruno Leonard, doubts vanquished, shed all traces of academic restraint now and wound himself up to hortatory incitement.

"What do you do with all the contending information that cascades upon you? I'll tell you what: you let thought become words and words lead to deeds. For once in our lives we do not criticize, we do not complain, we ACT! We don't let the top dogs treat us like trees to lift their legs on. We don't let intellectuals spray perfume on the dung heap of capitalism, we intellectuals and artists for once in our lives ACT. Don't just think, DO. Don't make your peace with the fascists. OVERTHROW THEM!"

Bruno let the shouts and cheers break over him. He held up both hands.

"Those of you who took the advice of Horace Greeley and came west know you didn't find the promised land. But you did find a land of promise, of possibility. We're in the welcoming West, not the hidebound East. Then let us begin tonight, in Santa Monica, on La Mesa Drive in the home of Gloriana Onslow Flower, and let us begin with resolve, determination, open hearts, and, lest we forget, open wallets. This way to the revolution!"

During the extended applause Bertrand the butler reappeared to pass the silver tray around again. Still respectful, but was he also a trifle jaunty? No caviar on his tray now. It was empty until people began placing checks and cash on it. When the tray filled up and there was the threat of money spilling off it, Katinka the Red was right behind Bertrand with a canvas sack she raked the contributions into. Many people were already standing since there hadn't been nearly enough chairs, milling their goodnights to each other, as the tray made its way around the lanai and on into the living room to which most of the conversational revolutionists had adjourned.

I found myself next to Yeatsman, who was writing a check for a thousand dollars, and Mitch Altschuler, who bellowed across the entire house, "Get low, everyone, down where the sharecroppers and factory hands are, get low into your pockets and write high—write the highest check you can afford and then double that!"

Bertrand Munson shoveled his silver tray among the guests with the same combination of propriety and coercion that an elder uses passing a collection plate through the pews after a sermon. So we were led, led ourselves really, into a new kind of sacramental servitude to an institution as insistent on doctrine as the medieval church and no less inquisitorial toward its dissenters. Whoever was naïve enough not to have brought a check, or canny enough not to want to be traced, threw cash onto the tray, usually hundred dollar bills.

As the tray approached me, Mitch Altschuler again solicited the butler, plucking him by his starched white sleeve. "Are you with us, Bertrand?"

"Sir?"

"The Negro is at the heart of our program, Bertrand."

"Good to hear that, sir."

"I know Gloriana will be tickled to give you the night off when we have our meetings. We need you, sure, but you need us, too. Can we count on your coming to our unit membership meeting next Thursday?"

"Thursday is my day off, sir."

"Oh, ah, yes, of course. Good. And no more sir stuff, Bertrand. I'm Mitch. You won't even have to ask Gloriana for the night off. See you Thursday then." Mitch Altschuler, as the saying went, had bagged his first Negro. He smiled but he was really smiling at himself. His whole unit would be thrilled, proud, envious. "Good to know we can count on you, Bertrand."

"Thank you, Mr. Mitch," Bertrand Munson said. "Seeing that there's still going to be a few people who tell the others what to do and all the others will still have to do it, I expect I'll be taking my chances with Mr. Franklin D." Mitch gaped. To everyone's surprise, Bertrand Munson was declining the honor of joining the chattering insurgency. "Excuse me, Mr. Mitch," he said. With that, leaving the abruptly crest-fallen and bewildered Mitch Altschuler, who might have just seen his chances of doing important P work diminished ever so slightly, the insouciant butler thrust his tray in my direction.

I placed a fifty dollar check on the tray, aware I was at the extreme low end of eleemosynary zeal, but then I was also only a rookie writer. Sylvia wrote a check for ten times that, made out to the Scottsboro Defense Committee as we'd been instructed. I was told later that Gloriana's party had raised just over $62,000, all for the ostensible defense of the Scottsboro Boys—boys, not men, not even young men—who were never mentioned at the Party party. With Sylvia's check at the top of the pile on his silver tray, Bertrand nodded—a hieroglyph of amusement, reserve, bitterness and hauteur—and tilted his head sideways as he made for the next clutch of cheerful contributors.

"I believe we are, *enfin*, excused," Sylvia said.

Outside, she tried to hand me a dollar from her purse for the still-running Mexican valet who brought around her Chrysler, but I motioned away the bill and pulled out my own. To my chagrin, I had only a ten in my wallet, so that's what the valet got. I hoped Sylvia hadn't seen the ten though we both saw the valet's broad smile revealing his gold front tooth shining in the Chrysler's headlights. "*Muchas muchas gracias, señor!*" annihilated any confidentiality he and I had.

Awkwardly, Sylvia asked me if I'd like to come in when we reached her house. Awkwardly, I accepted. Quickly, she made us two stiff gins and tonic. Quickly, we drank them. The talking was the easy part because there had been so much at the party to gossip about—the people, the cause, what we'd heard. Sylvia seemed to know both who the studio spies were and who was sleeping with whom. "Not that it matters," she said, taking my hand as she finished her drink.

In her bed, we were unfamiliar, then familiar.

24

Pogo Regnant

After she invited me to stay the night, I could tell Sylvia was grateful when I said I needed to go.

At my Royal the next morning, staring wordblocked at the platen and then at the blank page I rolled onto it, I mooned not about Sylvia but Pammy. I'd be faithful to the shadow that had no substance. Disdainful of others, I'd been impotent in a venture the previous week with a reader from Paramount. Sylvia, bless her, banished that demon.

The night after the night of Gloriana's party, I dreamed a whole row of dreams. In one I'm kicking a rat. I'm on a dark sidewalk and the rat, huge, runs toward me. I kick it like a soccer ball. It flies through the air, lands, runs around and pitches itself toward us again. Us? I don't recognize who I'm with but it's a woman. I kick at the rat and miss. It passes us and turns around to run at us three more times, and then I connect again with a kick that hurls it away and the dream ends. In another dream I say a chaste goodbye to Esther Leah Zangwill and arrive at Pammy's house in the dawn. Then I see the sunrise, but I'm not with Pammy. I ring her doorbell to tell her about the blossoming sunrise. I'm told by Millie her mother's still asleep, don't bother her. I show the sunrise to Millie.

In a third dream I'm having lunch on a train with Sylvia and no less than Franklin D. Roosevelt. I can't believe I'm with FDR himself. I call him Mr. President but Sylvia is more familiar and calls him Franklin, which he appreciates. We talk about strikes, and he says he doesn't like them even though he knows the laboring classes have a point. I think: Laboring Classes? Why is he being so British? The waiter, a black man in a white jacket, brings the bill and FDR reaches into his coat pocket. I say No let me pay for it, Franklin. Oh, now it's Franklin, is it? he says. I say, Well, I mean Mr. President. He reaches again for his wallet, now in a pants pocket below the table. I reach for mine as well.

A rash of staccato dreams follows, images like flash frames, of sunrises. I see Pammy's honey-gold hair with the rising sun backlighting it. I am not with her but see her from a distance. In another flash, I telephone to alert Pammy to the sun. I ask the maid, whose name cornily is Rose, to tell Miss Millevoix the sun is rising. Rose quickly says she won't wake Miss Palmyra, and that flash ends miserably. On its heels is a vision of the two of us on the beach in front of her house, which actually is nowhere near the beach, and we see the sun peek through the dawn and come up a glowing disk over the ocean. Pammy wears a long white robe and holds a flower; the flower has wilted petals. I am wearing a turtleneck sweater over bathing trunks. We walk into the water toward the sunrise, and she vanishes in the waves still holding the flower with the wilted petals.

"Why is the sun coming up over the water?" Dr. Pogorzelski asked in our next session. I'd told him about the crazy weekend, with its pain, its lunatic and incandescent moments, and then the dreams. Since the position of the sun was the most trivial thing in any of the dreams, I scoffed at his being a geographic stickler. "But really," he persisted, "the sun doesn't rise over the ocean in California, it only sets in the Pacific."

"You think I transported us to the East Coast?" I asked.

"No, you were in front of Palmyra's house. I think you may be on guard against the sun setting. The sun rising is sexual and hopeful. The setting sun is the opposite."

"The sun is setting on capitalism," I offered. "That was the message of the party."

"I see."

"The Communists will resolve the future into triumph. It looks like only a dream now, but it can come true. A solution to a number of life's problems, isn't it?"

"Well, yes, it is. It is life itself." He paused. "For children."

"What."

"We might call it pre-rational life, the life of fables and fairy tales, the life that faith attempts to explain, make bearable."

"The Reds don't want to make life only bearable, they want to transform it."

"It's a potent faith."

"But look at Russia. The faith is revealing itself as a true guide."

"We'll see. I am from Poland. One man's revelation is another's fantasy is another's hell. Tell me about the rat in your dream."

"Fear. I'm afraid of rats."

"Why?"

"Being bitten. Injury."

"Bitten, yes, where?"

"Ah, castration? I'm afraid of being castrated?"

"That's easy, but what is a rat in your life?"

"Oh, a producer. There's a joke at the studios that an associate producer is the only person who will associate with the producer while an assistant producer is a mouse in training to become a rat. But Mossy isn't exactly a producer."

"Of course he is. He is *the* producer. And his humiliation of you for your innocent gaffe with the drunken tennis player is truly dastardly. You want to kick him for that. Or at any rate resign your position."

"I couldn't do that."

"Why? You need the money?"

"Sure, but that's not it. I could work somewhere else, write for the magazines, teach. But I want the movies. Motion pictures are the most exciting art on earth. Jubilee is the studio I know best. I don't like having Mossy Zangwill as a god."

"God, yes. God is …"

"God is not Mr. Amos Zangwill, I can assure you. A devil, yes, not a god."

"Scripture aside, I'm not sure there's much difference between them in our fantasy lives, each so powerful and terrifying. Zangwill is no worse than any other figure you might choose to explain the unexplainable in nature. The idea of God is the intuitive perception of the power of the unconscious. The devil is his brother."

"I'll think about that. Meanwhile, Mossy haunts me like a ghost."

"It's up to you whether you take his brutal treatment or reject it. In here we can only try to get you to understand the choice. A rat can be many things—penis, money, power, monstrous—not only something you fear, perhaps something you desire."

"The last thing I want to be is a rat," I said heatedly. "They're fearsome to me."

"An object of fear isn't only what harms us but what fascinates us because we wish to possess its powers, to be able, literally, to frighten others. Particularly after being humiliated. In recounting a dream, pride can have more power than memory. We don't want to admit wishing to be what we hate. The rat suggests many things for both of us to consider. Ambivalence may be the only handle to hang on to, and it is slippery. We can offer merely crumbs of insight, as Freud happens to have said himself. The whole cake eludes us for some time. This FDR dream, what were you doing with him?"

I paused. Dr. Pogo was doing far more guiding than usual, and I thought he might be impatient with me, which seemed unfair. At the time I knew nothing of Freud's famous Rat Man, who had been both terrified by his own rat fantasies and obsessed with them. If Freud was a spider and I a fly, I had stumbled into his parlor.

"I told you," I said a little testily, "I was having lunch and then we were wondering who would pay the bill."

"But you were on a train, no?"

"Oh yes, that's some sexual reference, don't tell me. And Sylvia was there, who I went to bed with. So I'm presenting my sexual conquest to the president. In the dream Sylvia already knows him. She's more sexually experienced than I am."

"I don't think so."

"Sure she is, she's older, she's been around, she's—"

"That's not what I mean. I don't think you're presenting Sylvia to FDR. In the map of your unconscious you have drawn for me, I don't see Sylvia anywhere. We're surveyors here, with our transit and compass measuring the boundaries of your land."

"My perceptions?"

"Just so. Who I see in the subconscious is Palmyra Millevoix and Amos Zangwill. Tormenting you, attracting you. Sylvia in the dream is a stand-in for the star, who is Palmyra and who you don't dare approach even in a dream. In the sunrise dreams you're not with her until the very last one and even then she disappears. With FDR you have converted the bad father, Zangwill, into a benign figure, the devil into a god. The good father. Even more benign because President Roosevelt is a cripple, isn't he? You have a power, a potency, he does not possess. He is no threat. This converted Zangwill, who Palmyra is already on familiar terms with, is who you wish you could win her from. Almost it is like asking her father for her hand. And so you wish to pay for the meal—money is an emblem of your power and generosity. You didn't say who finally paid."

"I'm not certain."

"Yes, perhaps we can't know that yet. The letters FDR are initials as well for Freud, DR, or Dr. Freud."

"I suppose Freud hovers over anyone in analysis. Over you, too."

"Mmmmm."

"Maybe my dreams are having dreams of their own. They keep doing this until …" I paused lengthily, unsure where to go.

Finally Pogo said, "Until?"

"Until at last I am awake," I said.

"What is conscious is transient," he said. "The unconscious is what endures—until we make it conscious, and then the unconscious gets a little smaller. With Shakespeare and Mozart, for example, they seem to have been able to make their entire unconscious expressible. Tell me the last sunrise dream again, the one on the beach."

I did this, giving him the same details about Pammy vanishing into the sea.

"I don't understand something," Dr. Pogo said. "You described her as holding a flower, an obvious symbol of sexuality, yes?"

"I guess so. What don't you understand?"

"The flower had sick petals."

347

"Wilted petals, yes, that's what I said."

"What about flowers?"

"Mossy Zangwill has an enormous garden, flowers blooming all over it. Gloriana Flower, the widow Flower as she's called, gave the party I was at with the Communists."

"Living flowers in Zangwill's garden, and Gloriana is notoriously alive, though her name might have planted, one might say, the word in your consciousness from which it could descend into your dreamlife. In the earlier dream the maid is named Rose."

"Not Pammy's maid's name in real life," I said.

"Yes. You said sick flower, wilted petals. Do you remember anything about flowers in your childhood?"

"No. Sure. Not much. I mean we did have flowers around sometimes, and my grandmother, she liked to have a bouquet in her apartment. That was in New York."

When I said the words *New York*, it was as though another light had been turned on in Pogo's office. Holding my father's hand, which I did not normally do, I saw us returning on Broadway to the Ansonia Hotel from my grandmother's apartment, where he had told me. "Oh, New York," I repeated.

"What about New York?" Dr. Pogorzelski asked.

"My mother died at Flower Hospital in New York. And on the East Coast the sun comes up over the ocean."

"So."

"Oh."

"See you next time."

25

Jubilee Regnant

Master Youncey," read the scrawled letter that Yeatsman thrust at me as soon as I reached the studio from Pogrezelski's office, "Newman wouldn't keep off Sugarlee so I shot him 7 times and he ran plum to gin and died off. I in seres trouble. High Sherf took me to gale and juge send to pen for life. I tole juge you in Hollywud was my boss and wooden put up with no nigger of yrs in pen for life but so plese tell juge I'm yo ol nigger. I holp you Master Youncey and yr ol miss is well and fine. I am well and fine and in seres trouble. Sir do something. Yore ol Willie Waddy." The envelope's return address was Wetumpka, Alabama, home of the state penitentiary. I shook my head.

"Look at them," Yeatsman said, pointing to the writers gathered in the rotunda of the building in which we all worked. The writers building was low-slung, two-storied, as undistinguished as an Army barracks. Near the center of the ground floor was a large circular room off of which were several writers' offices. In the middle of this space was a typewriter on a pedestal. This was in honor of a boyhood friend of Mossy's who had hoped to become a novelist. Mossy had talked his pal into forgetting novels and coming west to try his luck in pictures. As Mossy described the journey, the two of them lit out for the territory in 1921 driving an aging Stutz Bearcat that had belonged to the friend's rich uncle. Mossy's face would cloud as he told of the friend's death in an accident at the Grand Canyon. When he created his own studio, Mossy had his friend's old Underwood bronzed and mounted on a pedestal in the writers building.

Around this typewriter about twenty writers were now huddled, like gulls gathering at a lighthouse before a storm. They were murmuring about a strike. Several had looked up when I walked in, reassuring themselves that I was not their keeper, Colonel DeLight, whom they didn't trust.

The Screen Writers Guild had been formed the year before by hardier souls than I. Eventually I did join. The producers hated it, tried to splinter it by promoting a company union, the Screen Playwrights. These were two more groups I could feel inferior to. Eventually the Guild won and prospered, saved all our asses, but at this early point in my career I judged the few Guild members were on a futile errand, more articulate than I but just as ineffective. Who wanted to be numbered in the company of losers?

"Just look at them," Yeatsman repeated, having descended from his theological podium at the Party party to his more characteristic skepticism, "over there planning our little strike, or whatever it is. Work stoppage for a writer is an occupational disease anyway. Now they want to institutionalize writer's block to see if they can get the fifteen hundred a week writers up to two thousand and so on up and down the line. I'm supposed to be shop steward, but I'm leery of so-called creative people getting themselves into so-called unions. Meanwhile, this good old sot, Willie Waddy, with a better soul than mine, who once dragged me out of a swimming hole when I should have drowned and years later poured me into bed first time I was drunk so my father wouldn't find me passed out on the side porch, who never saw twenty dollars in a month, is moldering in the state pen for killing someone who probably deserved to die. What do I do?"

I looked at Yeatsman and shook my head again. "Can you help him some way?"

"I can't spring him from the pen. I'll send him a few hundred and ask my old uncle, who still goes to his law office in Montgomery, to see if he can make the right phone calls to get Willie work in a prison cotton mill instead of a chain gang. 'I carry from my mother's womb a fanatic heart,'" Yeatsman quoted from his hero, "so I'll pay off this black fellow, with whom I probably share a great-grandfather, and I'll go on being white and as red as I dare while making sure I can pay for a new swimming pool, eh, how's that? Don't you dare call me a cynic. I'm a regional realist."

Half a dozen rough-looking, muscular men in overalls and work shirts marched into the rotunda. They'll break up the writers' grumble session quickly enough, I thought; Mossy figures he'll scare the writers back to their typewriters by having some toughs threaten to beat them up. I was wrong. These men were the Jubilee carpenters who constructed the sets on all the sound stages. I'd seen some of them before.

The carpenters were coming to join the writers, making common cause against Jubilee. They'd been approached by Yancey himself, whom they knew by his given, screen credit name. He put away the letter from the black prisoner and greeted the carpenters. Sylvia Solomon waved her cigarette holder at me from the other side of the pedestaled typewriter. It was going on thirty-six hours since I'd shared her bed. She may have winked at me, and I may have wondered whether that token of familiarity was a gesture of intimacy or a friendly brush-off.

A strange moment followed. The writers and carpenters appeared to have nothing to say to each other. Everyone was getting nervous. Though his squad was outnumbered three or four to one, the head carpenter, a straightforward man named Bill Wilkins, chopped through the ice. "Look," he said, "between us we make this studio run. You guys furnish the blueprints, we build the scenery. That's all movies are, stories and places where they happen. The actors and directors are nowhere without you and us. We stand together is how I see it. What do you say, Yancey?"

"That's exactly how I see it," Yeatsman said, "and I couldn't say it half as well without taking twice as long."

"At least," Tutor Beedleman said. Other writers piped in their agreements.

"But this isn't mainly about money," Sylvia said. "It's about respect and acknowledgment of the importance of the work we do."

This was met by complete silence until a carpenter spoke up whom I recognized as the man with the jellied eye who had summoned me from the garden to Mossy's house on the day of my atonement. His name was Hop Daigle. "If you'll pardon me, ma'am, for us it is about money."

The other carpenters quickly said Daigle was right.

"They can shove their respect," Bill Wilkins said, asserting his authority by being more emphatic than Hop Daigle. "What we want is decent pay for the decent job we do, overtime for the emergency schedules they're always piling on us."

Yeatsman saw the only way to have the carpenters and writers link arms was to forget about screen credits, which the carpenters didn't get anyway, and professional massaging of the writers' allergic egos, from which the carpenters were blessedly free, and go forward on salaries. "Okay, we're looking at wages here," he said as decisively as he could. "All we have to do is set a date for the walkout and calculate what we ask for, how much notice they have to give us when they want to can us. Tutor and I will meet you to decide these points at six o'clock tonight"—he turned to Bill Wilkins—"across the street at the Mopic," which is what everyone called The Moving Picture Bar. That was where I'd fallen under Pammy's spell when I interviewed her for the press releases I wrote to enhance her fame.

As the carpenters trooped out, Comfort O'Hollie emerged from the secretaries' room with a message for me. Mossy wanted me in his office right away.

"Not a word about any of this, kid," Larry Spighorr said to me, assuming a right of condescension since he was one of the writers who'd replaced me on the Ibsen script.

"Can't you think up a more original insult?" Tutor said. Good old Tutor.

A new assignment? A raise? Invitation to a screening where my opinion would be valued? Another humbling? In which latter case I hoped I'd have the guts to tell him to fuck himself, which I should have done two days earlier on Mortification Sunday.

Mossy was already talking as I scampered down the corridor into the royal presence. "Great day, Jant, great day for Jubilee and you. Don't expect any favors."

Sir? I wanted to say but didn't; that kind of formal servility had always been unfashionable in Hollywood, probably because it was so blatantly honest. Warning me not to expect favors, of course, was his way of saying he wouldn't apologize.

Mossy's swept-back dark hair, with that russet tinge, was a little tousled today. "How are you, Owen?" Once he could see me in the throne room I was permitted a first name. He was less troubled than on the day he took me off *A Doll's House*, less intense than he'd been during my humiliations. He was jaunty, like a bettor whose horse has finished first in an early race, offering hope for the rest of the program. The blue cornflower I'd fetched for him on Sunday mocked me from his lapel.

As I mumbled that I was okay, I understood he'd make no reference to Sunday's mistreatment. Never apologize, never explain. Just move forward.

"I want to prepare a special script for a special star, Owen, and you may be right for this. I'll be producing this one myself, Nils Maynard will direct. You know him?"

"Sure," I said eagerly. "What's the property?"

"The property, eh. Do you happen to know Palmyra Millevoix?"

Was he kidding? Not really, I wanted to say, though I couldn't help hearing her singing in the shower with you the other day. "Just casually," I said.

"You're going to know her much better. Fascinating background— a star in Europe, America, the songs, the pictures, the family, her little girl, her struggle to make it here after crossing the Atlantic. I don't know yet what we'll call it, but I want you to write it, get the juice of her life from her and distill it into a great story, which she herself can star in. A fabulous picture with a fabulous star starring as herself. Think about that."

Was he crazy? Joking? Duping me? After Sunday I hated them both. Yet this was a dream assignment. Was I the one who was crazy? He'd apparently forgotten that a year earlier he'd had me write publicity about her. "Well, this sounds very promising," I finally said, then realizing how lame that was I added, "Best idea I ever heard."

Meanwhile I was thinking, so Pammy's the property. How am I going to go out on strike against this lord who has just asked me to walk through the gates of heaven? But wait, I do still hate him and hate the object of his affection.

"All right, that's done. Get going." I'd started out of his office when he said, as if it was an afterthought, "Ah, one more thing, Owen. Sit down."

"Sure." Oh God, now he was going to tell me about his affair with Pammy, draw me somehow into his subterfuges and duplicity. Poor Esther Leah. She was becoming, this bright woman who could have run a studio herself, a figure of sympathy all over town; Esther Leah hated the inferiors who pitied her so openly. "Poor" was her name's prefix whenever she was mentioned.

"That party you were at Sunday night," Mossy said. "Interesting, wasn't it?"

Christ! Now he wanted to know about me and Sylvia. The hell with him. It was none of his goddamn business. Did this mean Sylvia herself was one of his innumerable conquests? He wanted to have a locker room talk about how I'd liked her in bed. Screw the bastard. "Yes," I said, volunteering nothing.

"I know a lot of people went. Couldn't make it over to Gloriana's myself, but she's one of our great hostesses. Wonder if you could tell me who all was there?"

So he was invited himself? Why does he want to know who the people are he didn't spend the evening with? Because he wasn't invited at all, the son of a bitch, and he wants to know who the Jubilee Red sympathizers are. To my surprise, I said, "Uh, so many people were there I really don't remember. Lot of drinking. Whoever told you I was there can tell you who else."

"Yeah, but I need the names of all the guests you can remember. You know we're being attacked, don't you, Owen?"

"No, I don't know about that. People from Jubilee who know everyone on the lot were there. I was told a couple of them spied for you."

"Abner Prettyman is an idiot!" he said, referring to one of his more obvious plants. "Yeah there were people from Jubilee who work for me, like you yourself do, but Prettyman doesn't know half the people here and he doesn't know anyone from other studios. I'd like to have a big picture of the lineup, that's all."

"I'm not the right person."

"Sure you are, Jant. Goddammit, you're the best person because everyone knows you're on the square. In fact, you're the square root of square. I said we're under attack. People who favor the Soviet Union are trying to undermine our system, turn us all into collective farmers with fat wives and no property of our own."

"That's not what they say, but I'm in no position to argue with you."

"Damn straight you're not, Jant. You can be shitcanned off this lot as fast as I can look at you." He glared at me. He'd brought me in here to sweeten me up with a plum, then threaten to snatch it away if I wouldn't be a stool pigeon.

"I guess that's true," I said.

"Hurd Dawn was shitcanned off this lot, you know that?"

"Someone told me," I said.

"Thought he was bigger than the studio, bigger than the pictures he worked on, a big artist. Around here the studio is the artist, Owen, do you see that?"

At least he was back to using my first name. "I think I do," I said. Of course, what I'd been told was that Hurd Dawn was fired because he'd managed to get himself the salary of a director though he was a set designer. Jubilee could get half a dozen set designers—one of whom was Elise Millevoix, Joey Jouet's widow and Mossy's former mistress though I didn't know that yet—almost as good as Hurd for the amount they were paying him.

"I know Hurd Dawn was at Gloriana's," Mossy said. "Did you see him there?"

So that was it. Mossy would start small, very small, get me to affirm something he knew already, and it wouldn't hurt the already dead Hurd Dawn. Yet by admitting I'd seen him at Gloriana's I'd pound one more nail in his coffin. I wouldn't do it, but I wanted to avoid a confrontation if I could. "I didn't see him there," I lied.

"Uh huh. Now I know perfectly well someone who was there who you have to have seen because I'm told he was the god damn master of sinister ceremonies. Don't worry, I'm not going to ask you, I'll tell you. Professor Bruno Leonard."

"You're playing a game with me," I said.

"No, Owen. I *am* the game. Bruno Leonard was at Gloriana's."

It was not a question. He liked that refrain about being the game. I thought it was safe to volunteer now. "Yes," I said, "Professor Leonard spoke at the party."

"Yeah, fifteen or so years ago I was a student at City College and he was just starting out as a wiseacre teacher. Spouting his adolescent pony shit all over campus about Marx and Lenin and how big things were happening in Russia where about half my old neighborhood came from and those big things were going to spread through all of Europe where the other half of my neighborhood came from. Years go by and he's grown up and the big things haven't spread but he's still spouting only now it's grown-up horseshit. I had no use for the man then and even less now."

"He's a talker all right," I said, wondering how much Bruno Leonard's disapproval of Mossy's college newspaper stories found its way into Mossy's hostility. "Some of what he said seems informed," I added, "some maybe off base."

"Off base, is it? It's pure horseshit. Now tell me, Owen, I just want to know who was in his audience. Who besides you was listening to the old wiseacre Sunday night?"

"Sorry, Mossy, when people are on their own time, I think it's their business."

"You won't tell me then?"

"No."

As he stared at me across his desk, Mossy stood, then apparently thought better of the declarative move, which made me expect he was throwing me out of his office, and sat down again. He shook his head. I wondered where my wormy little suggestion of a vertebra had come from. Sylvia? The general solidarity of Gloriana's party? Mossy's old nemesis, Bruno Leonard? Possibly from Mossy himself, abusing me so crudely the other day and now badgering me for names. Even a mule refuses to jump off a cliff when it's being whipped. Perhaps I saw a chasm too deep for me to jump into and survive.

"You're all nuts," Mossy said. "This country's return to prosperity is your best hope, not some cockamamie theory about taking ownership from people who know how to be owners and giving it to a bunch of saps who have no idea what to do with anything they own bigger than a kitchen table or maybe an automobile. You Reds are all nuts."

"I never said I was a Red."

Mossy drew himself up into sermon posture. "Let me tell you something," he said. "I don't know about molecules or airplanes or governments, but pictures I know. Pictures are made by studios, and studios are run by people who know how to make pictures. Actors, directors, cameramen, writers, many people help make motion pictures, but the producer pulls it all together and he represents the studio. The animals don't run the zoo no matter how pretty they are or talented; the zookeeper runs the zoo no matter how big a son of a bitch he is, and I'm the zookeeper of this zoo. You understand?"

"Of course I do. I just don't want to be a ferret or a trained seal either."

Mossy ignored me. "If this ever changes," Mossy said, "the picture business as we know and love it is destroyed, boom, like that. It so happens that at Jubilee and on some of the other lots around town, the animals are getting ideas they can run the zoo. We call it a Red plot, which in a way it is, but in another way it has nothing to do with the Reds, it's just egos, animals thinking they're bigger than the zoo. The Reds are using them, and they're using the Reds. Studio heads need to know who these people are that are trying to ruin our picture-making factories, worshipping false idols with their red smoke. The first thing we agreed on was the need for loyalty. Are you loyal to Jubilee, Owen?"

"I am, yes. If I'm treated fairly I'm very loyal to whoever treats me fairly."

That stopped him for a moment; perhaps he recalled my Sunday scourging. He nodded. "I'm bringing you along here, Owen, that's why I'm handing you the Millevoix script. Is it safe to say you want to see Jubilee continue to make good pictures?"

"Yes, definitely."

"Then, Owen, you should want to help us root out the bad influences all over town who want to stop us from making our pictures." Mossy rose from his chair and walked around to my side of his desk. "That's why," he said, "you must tell me who was at Gloriana Flow-

er's home Sunday night. The producers association wants to know. A
bunch of writers are in this nutty guild, as if you could unionize creative work, as if writers were no more than assembly line workers in
Detroit. Ridiculous, isn't it?"

He raised his eyebrows and looked at me fondly. Why not tell him
the names of the people I knew the names of? He knew most of them
anyway. He was asking mostly to test my loyalty, wasn't he? He said,
"Look, we don't want to hurt anyone, but we don't want to get hurt
either. The producers association wants to try to help these people see
our point of view, what's in all of our best interests as studio employees."

Oh, so we were all in the same boat, all studio employees, including him. That sounded sweetly reasonable. Talk to the people who
disagree with you, come to some agreement. On the other hand, if
I started telling Mossy names, I might get someone fired. "The other
studio heads might not be as easy to talk to as you," I said. What the
hell was I saying that for? They were all tyrants, like Mossy. And we
were on assembly lines, weren't we, not so different after all from people making Fords and toothpaste.

"The Reds, the union and guild bastards are accusing us of everything from cradle robbing to stealing their paychecks," Mossy said.
"Don't we have the right to face our accusers? In order to face them we
have to know who they are, don't we?"

"I can't tell you names of people who might get hurt because of
what I say."

The gently reasoning Mossy promptly vanished. "Don't push me!"
he yelled. "You claim to be loyal and you won't even let me know who
my accusers are! I can take the Millevoix assignment away as quick as
I gave it to you."

Another threat. He'd already said he could get rid of me; now he
made that concrete by telling me he could take away the Pammy plum.
"I know that," I said.

"Then make it easy on all of us. Help this studio function as it should."

"I'll do everything I can to make Jubilee even better, but I, I can't
tell on people for going to a party." I was stammering a little, but I
didn't budge.

"God damn it!" Mossy's face was hot now, and he paced away from his desk. Then he turned back toward me. "No, God damn *you!* All I ask is a little loyalty from you. I need to know who I can trust. Tell me who was at the party and tell me *now.*"

He pounded his desk. Three times, bam, bam, bam. This was frightening, yes, but strange too. Why did he need to do this? He could easily find out most of the names from others. Why was he testing me this way? I said only one word. "No."

Mossy boiled over. As he yelled, frothy flecks appeared around his lips like volcanic ash. "Listen to me! I can fire you not only from Jubilee, kid, but from every lot in town! You know that? No one who belongs to the producers association will hire you. You can go teach kindergarten in Oshkosh for all I care. You won't work again, my boy, at any studio in Hollywood. Take my certain word on that!"

My boy might have been the most accurate thing Mossy had ever said to me. I was in so many ways his boy, coming and going at his whim, working on this script, fired off that one. I was even his bootblack when he told me to be. Yet I mulishly balked. I was his toady, but I wouldn't also become his stoolie. "I don't doubt your word," I said, though his word was precisely what I did doubt, "but I won't tattle."

Where had I found such a schoolboy word? Whatever its source, it seemed to calm the Grand Inquisitor. As he walked over to Monet's water lilies hanging above his reflecting pool, I saw him visibly deflating, gas let out of a dirigible so it could land. I began to understand something. One threat was scary; a second froze me in my shoes. But three, four, five threats meant nothing was going to happen. He wouldn't even pull the Millevoix plum out of my mouth.

This was a lesson I learned about Mossy. The really bad things that happened usually sneaked up on you with no threats at all. A single threat might still be carried out and was therefore to be taken seriously. An armada of threats was, paradoxically, unarmed, even toothless. If the threatener failed, he went on to other matters, conceivably with a scintilla more respect for you.

"You know New York, Owen my boy?" He was still standing with his back to me, looking at the lilies, appearing to study them as if some truth embedded by Monet might pop out of them, perhaps the names of all the guests at Gloriana's party.

Remembering my brief stint there when I really was a boy, I said yes. "You know Morrisania, Crotona Park?"

"Is it like Central Park?"

"Hah," he said, striding back toward me but looking up at the chandelier over his desk as if it contained an audience. "The boy wants to know if it's like Central Park. Yes, Owen, Central Park is like Crotona Park the way Garbo is like Marie Dressler. No, Owen, Crotona Park is in the Bronnix, as some in my neighborhood used to call it. That's where I was brought up, in the Morrisania section of the Bronx, near Crotona Park, Franklin Avenue and 169ᵗʰ Street. My father was a hatter and always mad. Made and sold hats, had a nice shop the swells came to over on the Grand Concourse." Mossy preened a little, putting on mock airs as he imitated his father.

"But," he continued, "Pa ruined it with his temper, and then he did us the favor of squeezing the last pennies out of his failed business and escaping with his bookkeeper to St. Joe, Missouri, leaving us to the tender mercies of my uncle Abe, God bless him. But before Pa deserted my brother and sister, my mother and me, he'd lash out in his lumbering way, and when he took off his belt everyone knew to hide. The apartment was two bedrooms and when I couldn't stand my brother and sister I'd sleep in the living room. He threw water on me once to wake me up so he could beat me. Never dared hit my mother, who was taller and smarter than he was. What he went for were his two sons, his daughter, the family dog, and one night he strangled our pet canary that didn't know enough to shut up when he wanted quiet."

"What a brute," I said. The truth was I couldn't even imagine a father like his.

"The escape for me was outside into Morrisania and Crotona Park, where I'd go to play marbles. I owned it, you understand, I *owned* that part of the city. From a hill in Crotona Park—we called it a hill because you could sled down it—you could see the Jersey Palisades to the west and all the way down to the Brooklyn Bridge if you looked south. But I never wanted to go anywhere because right here, Morrisania, this was not just my world, it was my possession. Marbles was my game and I'd play it every day after school. I got good at it. You know what chalcedony is?"

"No, I don't." His whole childhood was a foreign country to me.

"It's a beautiful stone, with stripes and lines going through it, and it can hold the colors of the rainbow. You can see into it like you're looking into someone's eyes. One of its varieties is agate, only semi-precious in the gem business but to me the most valuable thing in the world. The best marbles are made from it, aggies. We'd pitch our marbles into a circle and aim at them with our best shooters, using your thumb against your forefinger like the hammer of a pistol. Bing, bing, bing."

Mossy demonstrated with his thumb. It looked like the hammer of a pistol poised to fire its lethal aggie. What I visualized was Mossy in San Francisco using his aggie expertise to help the longshoremen as they aimed marbles at the charging horses. I also reflected that of course he'd have been on the owners' side.

"At the end of the afternoon," Mossy said, "I generally won the most aggies by hitting the other boys' marbles. We hardly ever talked about it, but all of us were Jewish. Most of us not religious, just Jewish. My teachers, except maybe phys ed, they were Jewish too. Everyone I knew was Jewish or if they weren't I didn't know it. If anyone had asked I'd probably have told them even my marbles, down to the last precious aggie, were also Jewish. You know why I'm telling you this, Owen?"

I said I did not know. What I figured was he was leading to some incident where he lost some of his prized aggies, or some Christian took them, and he forced someone else to tell him where they were. I still wasn't going to buy tattling.

"So one day I had to go out of this world," Mossy said, "where the marbles and everything I saw was mine. I was nine. You ever been to the place called nine, Owen?"

I laughed. I said I remembered it well, thinking age was one thing my childhood had in common with his. It didn't seem like the moment to say that was when I lived in New York myself, when my mother was dying. Mossy was back in his own nine now.

"What happened," he said, "was my great aunt died and I had to go to her funeral with my mother. A sunny Sunday in the spring. The funeral was not in Morrisania. Oh, it was still in the Bronx, the damn

Bronx was the entire known and unknown universe, but the funeral was in a synagogue down on Willis Avenue in the Mott Haven section. Maybe only a mile or so away, which in California is nothing though in the Bronx it was a light-year. A kid in a city knows his neighborhood like he knows the freckles on his sister's forehead. But Mott Haven I did not know."

Mossy walked around his office as if he were surveying his old precinct. I wondered where he was going, either in the Bronx or in this terrain he now ruled. He came to a spot above where I sat.

"I don't remember the funeral except I had to put on a skullcap, a yarmulke, before my mother and I entered the synagogue. I hated that. My older sister and younger brother and my father went somewhere else that Sunday, a Nickelodeon show I think. I was furious they got out of going to the funeral. I hated listening to some intoning rabbinical voice bidding old Tante Clothilde goodbye and another voice, the cantor I guess, singing and chanting. Then it was over."

I assumed this was his first contact with death. "A terrible experience," I said.

"No, no, it was what it was, but I'm not there yet," he said. "My mother and I walked over to a place called the Hub, a kind of Times Square of the Bronx, the intersection of Willis Avenue, 149th Street and Third Avenue. Big shopping area. All the hot shot stores, crowds of people in them. My mother thought she'd buy me a nice pair of pants as a reward for the funeral—short pants, of course, which I couldn't stand. She'd get herself a flowery blouse. Must have been around noon, churches had let out their Christians, people were strolling, but at this point I still thought everyone was Jewish."

I found this hard to believe. "You'd never heard of Methodists and Presbyterians and Catholics?" I asked.

"I'd heard of the Pope, and I knew he didn't belong to us. I'd seen churches, but I hadn't put anything together. I knew there were Irish and Italians in the Bronx, but I'd never met them and for all I knew they were a different kind of Jew. I assumed Lincoln was Jewish because his first name was the same as my uncle Abe. Anyway, we're walking along 149th Street, big thoroughfare, came out of one shop and we're about to go into the place where my mother thought she'd get me a pair of pants I didn't want.

"So I'm looking around, confused, I never saw such a crush of people. Another kid about my age is walking toward us with his mother as I'm coming down the sidewalk with mine. 'What's that, Ma?' the kid says pointing at a vendor. 'He's selling kielbasa, Billy, that's a Polish sausage,' says the mother. 'Over there, what's making that noise?' And the kid looks at a police ambulance going by. 'That's a claxon horn, it's for letting people know they should get out of the way,' says the mother. Now he points at me, at my head, which I've forgotten to take the yarmulke off. He looks up at his mother and asks her, 'What's that funny thing on his head, Ma?' She laughs and says to him, 'Oh my goodness, it's nothing, they wear those caps. That's just a little Jew, Billy.'"

Mossy paused, shaking his head. I didn't get what I was supposed to get, but I knew enough to shake my head too.

"The other kid doesn't understand," Mossy said, "so he asks something like what does that mean. His mother says, 'I already told you, never mind. It's nothing. That's just a little Jew, Billy. Pay no attention.'"

Now I got it. But he went on.

"That's right, Owen, my first shot at people who thought me unworthy or different or dismissible. I was so ashamed of my yarmulke I wanted to snatch it off, but I couldn't because that would hurt my mother, who was embarrassed herself. She held my hand tighter, and I sensed her own shame and fury. And her helplessness to do anything that would make a difference, either to me or to the other kid or to his mother. For me it wasn't just the yarmulke either, or my mother's total weakness. It was me that something was wrong with. I didn't have to hear about my people killing their Savior, in fact I didn't hear that until I was in high school, by which time I was armed against such nonsense."

I didn't know what reaction he expected, so I was mute.

"All I had to hear, Owen, was what I heard—I wasn't a boy, I was only a that or an it. Never mind, she said, and pay no attention, she said, and it's nothing, she said, nothing. Have you ever been a nothing?" (Well, yes, I thought, and at your hands, Mossy, but I didn't dare interrupt.) "She didn't even call me a he, all she said was *that is a little Jew, Billy*. Well, Billy, wherever you are now, if you're not in prison you're probably a cop or a clerk, or maybe you made it into vaudeville, but this here little Jew, Billy, is now head of a studio making moving pictures for all the squirts in Squirtville, for people like you, Billy, and people *are* goddammit paying attention and around here they *are* if they know what's good for them *minding* what I say. Jew-Billy Pictures, is not, I swear on my life, going to be taken away from me by unions, guilds, the New York bloodsuckers, or the sonofabitching Reds. Do you understand that, Owen Jant?"

I understood.

"Then go," he said.

Back in the writers building, my betters were again huddled, circling the bronzed typewriter of Mossy's dead friend. They still looked like gulls around a lighthouse but now, from the way their heads were all down it was clear the storm had hit. If they could have stored their heads under their wings the way gulls do, they would have. No one was talking. Yancey saw me come in.

"How'd it go?" he asked.

"I don't know," I said. "He's a tough man."

"Let me tell you how tough," Yancey said. "One of the carpenters came back ten minutes ago. Zangwill bought them off with a raise the size of a split pea and the promise none of them would be let go for at least six months. In case anyone didn't get the hint, he's posted a platoon of scabs at the studio gate, all of them carrying toolboxes. They may not even be real carpenters but only extras Mossy hired to stand there. The carpenters' defection leaves us alone—we can't go out without them. He doesn't need to put unemployed extras lugging typewriters outside the gate. He knows we know how many unemployed writers there are. The strike is off. Zangwill wins."

I said I was so sorry, and I was. The writers were as deep in gloom as the orphaned gulls after a storm has razed everything but their lighthouse itself, which provides no real comfort or protection but simply stands there as a remnant. Yeats crept back into Yancey. Bleakly, he recited: "'A shape with a lion body and the head of a man, A gaze blank and pitiless as the sun, Is moving its slow thighs, while all about it Reel shadows of the indignant desert birds. The darkness drops again.'"

26

Biopic

Zurich, Cairo, Marrakesh, Montreux, Bordighera, the Île St. Louis, Inverness, Hamburg, Palma, Tin Pan Alley and the Brill Building, Lucca, Salerno, Edinburgh, Cap d'Antibes, Russelsheim Am Main, Malta, Bruges, Lyons, the Brighton Pavilion, the Plaza Athénée, Sintra, the Parthenon, Olympia, Odessa, Leningrad, the Connaught, Chicago, the blood bank at Verdun, Barcelona, Gare du Nord, Gare de l'Est, Bucharest, Bad Nauheim, Cologne, Leipzig, Prague, Bordeaux, Linz, Schoneberg.

Gerhardt, Henriette, Giovanini, Sir George, Laurence, Gilles, Dominique, Etienne, Golo, Wolfgang, Achim, Amalfreida, Marcelle and Marcel (sister and brother), Edeltraut, Aloys, Ernst, Veronique, Max, Charlot, Julien, Paola, Gerda, Auguste, Honore, Sebastien, Beckenbauer, Theophile, Claude, Paul-Henri, Amaury, Ted, Bruce, Jonathan, Anabel, Marie-Claire, Rex, Douglass.

Places and names Palmyra Millevoix dropped from her first thirty years when I went to her studio bungalow for my initial talk with her that could lead to a biographical screenplay. She was serious, almost morose. She was utterly different from the playful gamin who had lofted material to me for press releases on the earlier occasion a year before when I'd been sent to her bungalow and she had played songs for me.

She was very precise about the type of wound she saw when, at seventeen, she worked as a nurse's aide in the blood bank just off the Verdun battlefield. Spend the time you need with her to get the juice of her life: Mossy's instructions. I wasn't going on strike and I wasn't fired, so I was collecting material for this best, most painful assignment. Pammy herself was enthusiastic about Yeatsman's desire to write his Madame Bovary script for her; she had been brought up on Emma Bovary. But she was against this biographical project. "Silly man," she said. "Silly *men*," she corrected herself. "How vain. They want to put in marble, and now in film, the women who interest them. It makes no difference at all to our true identities, yet they will start the Trojan War or write a symphony because of what they call love but is actually their own vanity."

She didn't seem to include me in the category of *they* and *them* who kept being wrong about women. Was I exempt, then, from her designation of gender? A compliment or an insult that she neutered me?

Pammy did not quiver when she described the scene at Verdun—blood flowing out of and into the wounded soldiers at the blood bank—but she did sob twice in her accounts of the places and people she had known. The first time was with the mention of the names Gerda and Achim, which she breathed as though these old friends from a previous life were now in danger, and the second was when she was telling a story about Bucharest. That time I pulled a handkerchief from my pocket and offered it to her. While she blew her nose she looked at me as if she had just noticed I was there.

27

A Revel

It came to pass as Mossy had ordained that the day rolled around for the wedding of Trent Amberlyn and Thelma Thacker. Weeks earlier, Trent stood sheepishly in Mossy's hospital room at Cedars when Thelma Thacker strode in, hips first, and immediately had to stop herself from asking the boss why she'd been summoned. The man who owned her contract and had her on loan to other studios for four times what he paid her was, after all, in a hospital, possibly gravely ill. Mossy greeted her from an armchair where he sat wearing a white silk bathrobe over black silk pajamas. As much as she resented her owner, everyone in Hollywood knew he had keeled over in his office, and some of the flying rumors had him in a coma close to death. "I'm so sorry you're ill, Mossy. I'd have sent flowers, but I was afraid—"

"Don't worry about it," Mossy stopped her. "I'm much better."

"What a relief," Thelma said. The fact was she wasn't close to Mossy, had never been invited to his home, and she knew as well as he did she wasn't headed for stardom even in the Westerns she made with Tom Mix, who himself was fading. The summons to Cedars was a surprise and a mystery to her. And was that Trent Amberlyn across the room? What was he doing there?

"Thelma, say a nice hello to Trent Amberlyn," Mossy said.

The two actors shook hands awkwardly. As they exchanged the requisite pleasantries, Mossy noticed gratefully that Thelma was only about three inches taller than his bantam-sized star. Thelma had strawberry hair that was beginning to be called dirty blonde, and no one bothered to dye it because her parts as a cowgirl in black and white B pictures didn't require much in the way of glamour. She was ahead of her time in wearing blue jeans around the house she shared with Matt Sampson, the horse trainer she'd met at Republic when Mossy first had her out on loan a couple of years earlier.

Thelma was the sweet one; Matt, like any horse trainer, had a sharp tongue and could be unexpectedly gruff, especially with humans. Matt lifted the vagrant profession of Hollywood horse trainer into one that demanded skills as exacting as those needed to train Thoroughbreds for the Kentucky Derby. Born in west Texas, named Mathilda by her parents, Matt became the partner and authority figure in Thelma's life. Thelma and Matt were a fixture in the subset of the Hollywood social scene that featured lesbians. Parties in their Tarzana home were lively, musical, and were attended by women far weightier on the scale of motion picture prestige.

As a star who commanded the screen, Trent was surrounded by a magnetic field even in a hospital room, but Mossy was pleased to see that Thelma herself had an appeal that would fit well in this match. A strong chin, softened by a natural smile and eager eyes reminded Mossy why he'd signed her in the first place. She had square shoulders, nice tidy breasts maybe a half-size too small, and an outdoors body, which was precisely why she made her living where she did and not in Jubilee's dramas or comedies. An attractive girl, Mossy told himself, this may work out just fine.

"No reason to mince words or beat around the bush," Mossy said to his two properties, one of them still ignorant that she was about to be made adjacent to the other. Mossy immediately regretted his figures of speech but understood where they'd come from. "You two nice kids are going to be married soon. To each other."

Trent, who already knew his fate, hung his head in embarrassment. Thelma thought the boss must be teasing. "Mr. Zangwill," she said, "I didn't know you went in for practical jokes, but this is a good one. You must be feeling lots better."

Mossy didn't have to say anything more. Trent's posture told Thelma all she needed to know. When she glanced at her intended—intended, that is, by the patient in the silk bathrobe looking contented with himself—Trent was shaking his head.

"This is silly, this is ridiculous," Thelma complained. "Trent and I don't even know each other and anyway people say he's …" She caught herself. "And you know Matt Sampson and I, we're, uh, very devoted to each other. I can't marry anyone."

"It'll be good for both of you," Mossy said. "I'm a happy matchmaker." He didn't add that he'd told Louella Parsons, who was ready to break the news in her column.

"Isn't there some other way, Boss?" Trent asked with a forlorn look that Mossy would never allow to be captured on camera because it was such a drastic contradiction of the swaggering he-man parts Amberlyn played.

"Yeah, Trent, there's always another way," the studio chief said. Thelma looked hopefully at Mossy, who now arose from his chair. "The other way, Trent, is for me to let you be exposed as a fairy, which half the reporters in town are dying to do anyway. That slime Billy Wilkerson already ran a blind item about you, and Lolly Parsons saw you with that hangdog expression outside my office the day we sprung you from jail for picking up a fifteen-year-old and you came to my office with that cheese-ass Boy Boulton who I never want to see on my lot again."

Trent Amberlyn looked even more embarrassed for being described this way in front of the woman he had to regard as his fiancée.

"All right, you want to save Trent's career," Thelma said, "but why me? No one cares if two women share a house, and I don't get parts that need me to have a public boyfriend anyway, much less a"—and she spat out the word with disgust—"HUZZ-BANNED, for God's sake." Thelma dragged the two syllables into an alien curse.

"I have plans for you, my dear Thelma," Mossy said, improvising. "I've been thinking for some time it would be nice to bring you back over to Jubilee and put you in some parts where you can actually act instead of doing calisthenics with horses."

The appeal to her vanity didn't work. "I'm happy where I am," Thelma said, "though I wish I got half the salary other studios pay you for my services."

Mossy caught himself flaring up. No need for this, he quickly realized. "Listen to me," he said calmly, "both of you. Thelma, your salary is doubled as of your wedding day. Trent, your Spanish colonial has extra rooms up on Mulholland, doesn't it?"

"It does," Trent said. "But I like to keep them for ..."

"I don't really care what you like right now," Mossy said, turning to Thelma. "Mulholland, my dear, faces two ways, like you two lovebirds will soon be doing. You can look out at Beverly Hills and Hollywood, or you can look over at the Valley where Tarzana is. Matt Sampson will soon have a room at Trent's mansion, and no one will stop you from sledding down the hill to Tarzana for a little privacy now and then."

"This can't happen," Thelma said, looking for support at her fiancé, who himself saw a thin slice of possibility where he'd make common cause with his designated bride.

"Mossy, there must be a choice besides sacking me. I quite agree with Thelma." Trent's six months at acting school in London had left him occasionally anglicized.

"That's good," Mossy said. "I'm glad to see the two of you agreeing. It'll help your relationship, just the way it does for any of us happily married Americans."

Mossy stepped between his two pieces of property and held each of their hands. "It happens," he said, "I've told Louella Parsons about your engagement. She's holding the news till I release it. You'll be married in my garden. Now go have a drink with each other, make your wedding lists. Young Jant will spruce up your bio's. Meeting over."

Appropriately, especially for Hollywood, the wedding was in June. The nuptials were celebrated under a spreading live oak in Mossy's garden. Mossy himself was safely away at Lake Arrowhead for the weekend, immune to any slipups that might mar the occasion he had dictated to the reluctant bride and groom.

There were no slipups. *Photoplay* had the exclusive on the wedding and sent a photographer and writer who covered the ceremony well enough while cordially hating one another. The reporter was shy and liked to speak softly to her subjects. The photographer barged his bulky six-six frame into every conversation, flash-bulbing away any possibility of spontaneity or intimacy. Nor did he recognize well-known personalities. "Say fellow," he said to the especially handsome best man who was pouring Champagne for guests before the ceremony, "mind telling me your moniker?"

"Randolph Scott," said the amused pal of Trent's.

He was a good best man, a dashing romantic actor who would look respectable in *Photoplay*. With possibly the strongest chin and most chiseled features in town, Randolph Scott was more handsome than John Wayne, though he didn't have the Duke's disdainful squint or cocky swagger. Randy's own housemate, Cary Grant, whose star was just beginning to rise, prudently skipped the wedding. Thelma's Matt Sampson was at first indignant, threatening a boycott, but Thelma finally convinced her to be maid of honor.

When she heard that *Photoplay* would be in attendance, Louella Parsons ran off in a huff to Palm Springs for the weekend with the Louis B. Mayers. She had broken the original story, improvised to her in Mossy's office the day he (sort of) collapsed, but he wanted the wedding to be a pictorial event in the premier fan magazine. Mossy promised Louella an exclusive interview as soon as the newlyweds returned from their honeymoon, for which he had paid all expenses, in Acapulco.

Many of the three dozen guests were friends of Trent's, hangers-on along with his agents and their wives. Jubilee's publicity head attended, Stanny Poule, who kept revising my proffered Amberlyn bio to make it clear this man-about-town was the catch of the decade for Thelma Thacker. Stanny was the former newsman from St. Louis who rued the day he'd signed on to become a pale imitation of Hans Christian Andersen in Hollywood. "At least this time," he muttered to me, "we really do have a fairy tale."

Boy Boulton hovered on the edge of the small crowd, rigid with unaccustomed decorum, afraid to indulge his trademark cackles,

GIRL of MY DREAMS

knowing the owner of the garden would have him executed if he
were noticed by *Photoplay* or gave offense to anyone. I did hear him
snicker to a friend about a slender young man who had just offered
a platter of crab louie, "No use for the kid's crabs, but I'd plonk his
derrière anytime."

One guest at the wedding happened to know both bride and
groom. He was a stately, handsome black man, a consummate actor
named Burle Kince who did an Othello in San Diego in 1930, unforgettable to all who saw it. Thelma, then an aspiring stage actress, was
Desdemona. Trent came down with Boy Boulton to see the performance and was effusive backstage. (So effusive about Burle Kince he
met no other members of the cast, neither Iago, who was played by the
emerging Franchot Tone, nor his own future wife, Thelma herself.)
Trent told Burle Kince he had to come to Hollywood, had to come
to the studio—Trent was then at Fox—to make his mark in movies.
Trent was being sweetly naïve. Kince came up to Fox and was offered
nothing but servant and handyman roles, which he refused to play. He
got one part as a lacrosse player (there were no black lacrosse players
but it didn't matter), another as an attendant in a gas station, and then
returned to the theater, where he had only a few more roles before
becoming an acting teacher at San Diego State. At the wedding he was
as striking as Randolph Scott. No one in Hollywood ever saw Burle
Kince again.

Thelma's small support group was fierce. Her woman friends
wanted to make sure she'd be well-treated and not simply displayed
as a mannequin for a star who needed what one of them referred to
as a cunty cover. The only toast at the wedding, given just before the
ceremony, was by a tall willowy writer from Toronto, Charlotte Gelfano. She had graduated from title-writing for silents to slick dramas
in the talkie era. They were marketed as women's movies, disdained
as soap operas by male critics, but they had recognizable women in
them facing realistic crises. "Raise a glass," Charlotte Gelfano said,
"to a fine woman and, from what I can see, a good man. I've known
Thelma five years, and as good an actress as she is, she's an even better
friend because her greatest talent is listening. My fondest wish for this
union, this surprising but hopeful union, is that you, Trent, will prove

as adept at listening as Thelma. Then your worries will be temporary and your pleasures lasting. To Thelma and Trent."

"Hear, hear," said Randolph Scott, "and listen, listen."

The unlikely couple stood next to the justice of peace under the live oak, while the guests sat in a semicircle in folding chairs. Thelma held a bouquet of *flocon de neige* roses—whiter than snow, really, whiter than white—provided her by Mossy's gardening wizard, Obie Joyful. Obie himself, wearing his customary green leather jacket, stood at the edge of the wedding party, looking as pleased as if he'd just stumbled upon woodland nymphs in his bower. When the justice, a bewhiskered gentleman of the old school, came to the part where the groom said, "I, Trent, take thee, Thelma," for some reason he couldn't express, Trent knelt. Perhaps he had done this in a movie. Touched by the gesture and thinking well, that's what you do, Thelma did the same. Obie Joyful put two fingers in his mouth and piped out a soft whistle. Cued, the wedding guests sucked in their collective breaths and found themselves clapping. The nuptials finished quickly.

The half-minute kiss at the end of the ceremony was duly captured from several angles by the *Photoplay* photographer, who sneered as he shot. He cracked to Trent's agent that this would surely be the first and last time this couple ever touched each other. Champagne flowed for an obligatory hour, in the service of form and *Photoplay*, before the guests tired of felicitations and movie chat and scattered, including me.

The real reception was at Trent's Mulholland mansion, where a party lasted, according to my pleased informants who eventually included Thelma herself, for a good six hours. Boy Boulton, released from his manacles of public behavior in Mossy's garden, became a kind of emcee as the celebration—minus Randolph Scott, minus the agents and their wives, but plus several more of Thelma's friends—resounded through Trent's many rooms. A half dozen young men of Hollywood, considered too *louche*, or too flaming, to be invited to the nuptials themselves, joined the festivities. "Pansies arise," Boy Boulton announced as he stood under the arch that led to the two-story living room in Trent's Spanish colonial, "you have nothing to lose but your brains."

"Then I have nothing to lose anyway," said a tattooed motorcyclist. "Oh Grandma, what tight pants you have," said Boy Boulton.

Thelma poured herself a straight Scotch. She expected everyone, including Matt Sampson, to be gone soon. Then she and Trent would sit down and devise the plan for how to live together for the shortest possible time. She watched a pair of women who had played a mother and daughter in her last Western dancing together, shortly joined by two male couples. She saw a romp developing, and she wasn't thrilled. She felt like a stranger among the men who began dancing to a Rudy Vallee record. Vagabond lovers. "Don't you hate queers?" Matt whispered to her as she poured her own drink, a tumbler of bourbon. "Congratulations, baby," Matt said as she and Thelma clinked glasses.

To my naïve surprise when the evening was described to me, Tutor Beedleman bounced in, Jubilee's cheery writer who managed to stay on the right side of Mossy even on bad days. He made a courtly gesture toward Trent and went to greet Thelma. "Hello, I'm Shirley Temple's mother," Tutor said, breaking whatever ice had accumulated between the men and women in the room. "So happy to see our sisters well represented," he went on, kissing Thelma on the cheek. "Congratulations to the blushing bride. You're getting an ace of hearts in every way." Thelma smiled, and Tutor bowed low before he crossed to the other side of the room where the men and drinks were.

Following the proclamation of their banns in Mossy's hospital room at Cedars, the bride and groom had met only once more before the wedding itself. Deciding they needed to be seen in public, they swept into the Brown Derby for lunch one day. Conversation didn't come easy. They fell back on professional comparisons of actors and directors, but they scarcely knew any in common. It was like a blind date that wasn't going too well. Trent gallantly asked what Thelma would like to have in the house for breakfast. This suddenly depressed Thelma, and she could barely say she didn't care before she began to cry. When Trent patted her elbow and thoughtfully produced a monogrammed handkerchief, she was touched enough to put her hand on his.

After lunch they went across the street to Laikin's Jewelry store in the Beverly Wilshire Hotel. They quickly picked out a wedding ring for Thelma, a simple gold band, and were on the point of leaving, Max Laikin having already had his picture taken with the most talked about affianced couple in town, when Thelma was struck by an idea. "Hey Sweetie," she said bravely, "what about an engagement ring?" The jeweler was overjoyed as he quickly led them to the gemstone case. When he asked what she had in mind, Thelma said, "Something really flashy." She laughed. Trent frowned, but then he laughed too. He was suddenly both resentful and proud. Could this woman be taking him?—a thought immediately followed by his realization that he was finally doing something in real life that the hearty males he played in movies did. His betrothed selected a diamond the size of a grape ringed by a quincunx of emeralds, and they waltzed out of Laikin's with Trent gratefully poorer by twelve thousand dollars.

The next time they saw each other was in Mossy's garden, their wedding a semi-public event, and now in Trent's house they were supposed to be alone together, in private Thelma had thought, only they were not. Trent was sipping Champagne with Boy Boulton and Tutor and another man Thelma recognized as a slick character actor, often a gambler or thug, in crime films. A foggy-voiced lounge singer was with them. Other men had begun to leave the dance floor and wander elsewhere in the big house.

"I don't know what I'm supposed to do," Thelma said. She drank quickly, poured herself another Scotch, and drank that too.

"I do," said Matt, and she guided Thelma to the stairs. Trent, who had one arm around Boy Boulton and was ruffling the hair of the slick racketeer with the other, let go of Boy and raised a glass to his wife as he said, "Turn right at the top, lovey, I think you'll like the second room on the left."

Thelma was warmer after the Scotches, but she still felt a stranger. She liked the chintz on the bed, two Swedish-looking chairs, curtains with nymphs and shepherds on them, windows overlooking the Valley. She drifted to the window in search of anything familiar, but Tarzana was too far to the west.

"We christen this bed," Matt said.

"Matt," Thelma started to laugh, "This is my wedding night. I don't even—"

"I said now," Matt said.

Downstairs, the music was louder, jazzy, and the dancing faster, almost frenzied. Three couples and a single—Boy Boulton—were whirling around the floor. The men paused only to drink, and a few of them used straws poking at hand mirrors; cocaine had recently blazed its powdery trail to Hollywood. Trent had gone outside with someone.

By the time Thelma and Matt descended the stairs, few were dancing. The men were mostly on the floor. The lounge singer and the movie thug were entangled with Boy Boulton, and Trent joined them when he came inside with the motorcyclist. The mother and daughter from the cowboy film, hardy frontier survivors of an Indian raid, were spread-eagled on a couch the size of a small boat and covered in mink. Thelma recognized Fernald Gespours, from eastern wealth, on top of Tutor Beedleman on a Persian carpet. "A tight little squadron of lesbos," Matt said as she and Thelma dove toward the mink couch. People were laughing. Legs and thighs everywhere. Men caressing and drilling, women tonguing and caressing. The air was moist enough to have signaled rain.

Sometime later Thelma heard a man say Trent was in his steam-bath with two cowboys. She was unsure what was meant by cowboys. By and by a waltz was on the phonograph, and when she looked up Thelma saw her husband in a latticework of figures on the carpet, each man submissive to Trent as if waiting for the star to declare his pleasure. Tutor Beedleman was part of this knot, eager, ardent.

Could Eden have been like this? Thelma wondered. What if Eden wasn't just one couple but a small community, which was actually more probable. An amazing wedding night, she thought, genders observing preferential segregation, but sex everywhere.

Arising at last, Trent cleared his throat to address the congregation. From somewhere he found a huge bath towel and with his characteristic élan draped it over his shoulders. Trent had a natural tendency to graciousness onscreen, toward both men and women. In time the tendency became a conviction with him, which in turn became an ideal, and then an obsession until at last he came to engage in caricatures of grace. As often happens in Hollywood, it was decades after his best work, in self-parody as a supporting actor, that Trent won his Oscar.

"Ladies and gents, boys and girls," Trent said, "Our revels now are ended. The cavort is over."

It was as if a bell had rung in the school playground marking the end of recess. Thelma watched as everyone pulled on clothing and began to clear out, including—to her grateful amazement—Matt herself. "Call me, baby," was all Matt said, almost as a plea, as she made her exit.

"I came in as Shirley Temple's mother," Tutor said cheerfully to the bride and groom, "but I'm going out as Joan Crawford. Don't call me." He swept his head upward with Crawfordian hauteur and spun on his heel as he went for the door.

The others disappeared with equal dispatch except for Boy Boulton, who clearly expected to spend the night. Trent rendered him a wordless wave. Boy's face underwent the metamorphoses that kept getting him little spot jobs in films. In perhaps seven seconds the Boulton visage went from hopeful to disbelief to shock to downturned mouth to defiance to resignation. Thelma watched with awe as Trent asserted his authority.

"'My gracious lord I am glad it contents you so well,'" Boy squeaked out. Boyard Boulton would never be asked to play Faustus himself, but he knew Trent Amberlyn had, and he hoped his parting shot would be over the bride's head. Thelma, however, knew a concession of defeat when she heard one. Trent stuck with Prospero: "'These our actors,'" he declaimed, "'As I foretold you, were all spirits, and Are melted into air, into thin air.'" With his last phrase Trent swept his hand toward the exit. Boy was already in the doorway. He managed to say over his shoulder, "A night to remember, honey."

Thelma was surprised she was still there herself, still there in a pair of panties but no bra. Modestly, she crossed her arms over her breasts. Trent behaved as if her presence were as natural as the moon. "Your room all right, love?" he asked.

"Oh sure, it's simply grand," Thelma heard herself say, uncertain as to where *grand* had arrived from.

"Well, the boy dancers and girl riding instructors have fled," Trent said. "The reception went well then, didn't it?"

"Who could ask for anything more?" Thelma said, smiling, quoting. The newlyweds were on the point of shaking hands when suddenly they began to laugh. In a moment they fell into each other's arms. Thelma was unexpectedly comfortable. It was temporary.

"Well, then, after you," said her husband, gesturing toward the staircase. Strangers, they said good night and went in opposite directions at the top of the stairs.

When she had showered, Thelma wanted nothing so much as a cup of tea. She padded downstairs in a yellow negligee that Charlotte Gelfano—who had made the toast about the couple listening to one another—had given her as a wedding present. The water had almost boiled when who should appear after his own shower but her bathrobed groom. He made the tea. "A funny night, wasn't it?" he said. "Fun and funny," she said. "I didn't want it to end, yet I did." "My own sentiments," Trent said, "precisely."

As they reached the top of the stairs and his wife turned right to head off to her own room, the room she had frolicked in with Matt, Trent turned left and said, "If you'd like to see the master suite, love, come right this way."

She didn't know what she wanted, other than to sleep, but Thelma followed Trent through a dressing room that seemed to hold a hundred suits and two hundred pairs of shoes, on into an expanse featuring windows on three sides, a chaise longue that overlooked the pool and beyond it the twinkling lights of Beverly Hills, and a vast bed covered in white fur.

"Ermine," Trent said, noticing Thelma's gaze of disbelief. "Touch it." It made the mink on the couch downstairs feel like sandpaper.

"The bed has room," Trent said. "Would you like to sleep over?"

Thelma imagined Trent having orgies in the bed, which made her feel misplaced, but then she imagined herself there, under the ermine, queenly. "Uh, thank you."

To Thelma's dismay, Trent removed the ermine. "We'd bake," he said, putting on a cotton blanket and climbing in beside her. "Bed is big enough, isn't it?"

"About the size of Montana," Thelma said, "but the sheets are cold."

She had never slept in silk before.

"I'll warm them," Trent said, rubbing his hand back and forth on the bottom sheet. Static electricity shot in Thelma's direction; she shrank away yet felt nothing. "There," Trent said, "move over a little onto this patch of warm territory."

As she moved in the direction of Trent, Thelma brushed his leg with her own. It was a strong leg, muscled differently from Matt's, not unpleasant. "Oh sorry," she said.

"No," he said, "it's perfectly all right."

She moved a little more. There was his leg again. Or thigh. He chuckled.

"Oh," she said. "Well, we are married." She found the pillow and lay her head upon it, not daring to ask who had painted the fluorescent stag on the ceiling. Trent was getting settled too, wasn't he? She raised up to lean over Trent to see what time the clock read on the bed table on his side. The clock was turned the wrong way and as she reached toward it Thelma's hair fell across Trent's ribs. Trent stopped chuckling as Thelma's nipple just brushed his chest. Thelma fell back; it was almost four o'clock.

Trent rolled toward Thelma, then away. Rolling back again, he rested his head on Thelma's shoulder. "I can't believe this," he said.

"Can't believe what?" she said.

"I think I'm actually becoming a bit stiff."

"You are?"

"God save me but I am."

Thelma felt better now, not at home, but better. "Well," she said, giggling a little and reaching for her first male since she was a teenager, "waste not, want not."

The coupling was sweet, a dessert made with the wrong ingredients but still tasty.

There would be no Acapulco. In the morning Thelma and Trent were strangers again, awkward, unsure, apprehensive. Friendly strangers but strangers all the same. They both knew they had to get out of town for a couple of weeks. Thelma decided to go to Gallup, New Mexico with Matt, while Trent said he was off to Reno with Boy Boulton and the man who played in crime movies and really did like to gamble. "You'll be recognized before you can lay down your first chip in a big place like that," Thelma said, "and everyone will think you're there for a divorce. What about someplace like Elko? I did a picture there, and they have a couple of casinos. You wear a beard and sunglasses, no one will know you." "What a helpful idea," Trent said. "After all," Thelma said, "I'm supposed to be your helpmeet." Trent was out of the house in less than half an hour.

In the way of the flesh, nine months later a child was born to the shocked Thelma. By that time she and Trent had been officially separated for two months, which Mossy permitted because of Thelma's pregnancy and its happy, presumed proof of heterosexuality. The only casualty in Thelma's life was Matt, who couldn't bear Thelma anymore as soon as she began to show. When the baby was born and named Lee Jubil after the studio that had spawned her, all Hollywood, led by Louella, roared its approval as Thelma and her daughter moved back to Trent's house. Trent beamed paternally in the *Photoplay* pictures of the couple by the kidney-shaped pool with their baby. Matt came more or less crawling back to Thelma a few months later, but by that time the willowy Charlotte Gelfano, expanding her wedding toast to include herself as a listener, had moved into Trent's house. Trent's own fellows came and went, changed and returned, and stayed awhile before they drifted off again. Trent was always delighted when a new man arrived, never sorry when he departed. Boy was the most frequent returnee, kind of a patient footman. Trent enjoyed being a father, at least intermittently, and the marriage lasted five years, a sterling record by community standards. Thelma and Charlotte moved with the daughter of Thelma and Trent to Santa Monica, and Trent visited. He would stay overnight when Lee Jubil was having a birthday party or on other special occasions like Halloween. But Lee Jubil's parents never slept together again.

28

Henscher Gets His

When I went to Pammy's bungalow for the second biopic session, she was so angry she had tried to call me to cancel the appointment. I asked what she was upset about. "Him," she said, "who else?" I asked what for, and she said, "What *not* for?" Then she asked if I'd been upstairs in Mossy's house the day she was there. Mortification Sunday. She knew I'd been downstairs. "No," I said.

"Are you lying?" she asked.

"I don't want to talk about that day," I said.

"That bastard. He's absolutely sodden with treachery. You know my sister?"

I knew her a little. Pammy announced that Elise had had an affair with Mossy. I immediately assumed the sisters were jealous of each other. She saw that and broke into my thoughts. "This has nothing to do with anything between Elise and me," she said. "Under some circumstances I'd have thought it was funny. I hadn't known about the affair until Elise broke down and told me yesterday. You remember Joey Jouet?"

Of course I remembered the great stuntman, Elise's husband, who drove his motorcycle off the Santa Monica Pier after being fired from Jubilee. "How's your sister doing?" I asked.

"Not so well, but her daughters are slowly pulling her along. Children don't stop, you know, just because a parent dies."

"I've heard that," I said.

Pammy went on to tell me that Elise also carried a terrible guilt. The day Joey died, Mossy had been with her. Already ashamed, Elise had told him she couldn't see him anymore. Mossy said he needed to talk to her about Joey's work at Jubilee. Horrified that her husband was about to be fired, Elise agreed to see Mossy and arranged for Pammy herself to take her daughters for the afternoon. When he arrived at her home, Mossy asked if Elise would mind having Joey do some dangerous stunts in a circus epic Jubilee was planning; after all, Joey himself had been in the circus before coming to Hollywood. Touched at being asked, Elise said she knew Joey could take care of himself. Only later did she understand Mossy's question about the circus picture was emotional blackmail to earn himself some Sunday brunch sex. Upstairs, they had made enough noise so Elise wasn't sure what caused the sound downstairs. She'd thought—hoped—it might be the cat. After they finished, Mossy told Elise he knew he shouldn't be with her, but Joey's job was safe forever at Jubilee.

When Elise went downstairs after Mossy left, she found the saddlebag from Joey's motorcycle. Her husband had come in, no doubt started upstairs eagerly to surprise her with his early arrival home from location, then hearing the sounds she and Mossy were making, he backed downstairs again, forgetting the saddlebag with his clothes in it as he crept out the kitchen door. As he was leaving, Joey had probably also noticed the Packard touring car with the license plate AZ parked outside.

Elise ran back upstairs and threw herself on the bed in tears. She must have lain there an hour, feverishly wondering if she could possibly mend her marriage. How would she explain to Joey? What would she tell him? How could she ever make it up to him?

Two phone calls blasted her thoughts about reparation. The first was from one of Joey's pals at the location in Victorville, calling to say how awful he felt that Joey had been fired. In shock, Elise mumbled she knew Joey would be grateful for the sympathy. The next phone call, from the police, interrupted her waking nightmare with a worse one. When Elise pieced together the firing with the early arrival home with the call from the police, she understood how hellish her husband's last moments were.

Then the police were at her door with more information. Sweet Joey kindly stopped to fix a flat tire for Mervyn Galant, a has-been, as Joey knew. There was no advantage for Joey. He helped out a broken down director while he was on his way to kill himself. As Elise conceived of her husband's death, Joey drove off the pier convinced that Mossy had fired him to get rid of him, probably with Elise's collusion, so that he and Elise could run away together. Their little girls would be rich. By the time Pammy brought her daughters home, Elise understood that while there could never be redemption for her she would devote herself to the girls for the rest of her life.

A few days later Elise, furious, guilty, grieving, demanded that Mossy tell her why he'd had Joey fired. Mossy denied doing any such thing. He said that Dunster Clapp, who had done the firing, wielded the hatchet on his own. This was probably true since Mossy would be unlikely to fire—or as he liked to put it, shitcan off the lot—someone whose wife he was in bed with, at least while he was still in bed with her. He admitted to Elise that he'd told Dunster Clapp Jubilee had to cut costs to please New York, and a good place to start would be with workers being paid more than others who essentially did the same job. This was what led to the firing of Hurd Dawn, Jubilee's prima donna set designer. Likewise, Joey Jouet—experienced, skillful and with a Ringling Brothers pedigree—was the highest paid stuntman at Jubilee. Dunster Clapp took it upon himself to chop Joey from the payroll.

Pammy hadn't suspected Elise's affair with Mossy, which her sister was ashamed of anyway and infinitely more ashamed after Joey's death, until Elise shrieked it all out in Pammy's bungalow. "He was probably confident," Pammy told me, "that Elise wouldn't reveal anything to me out of simple guilt. The bastard has no regard for anyone beyond satisfying his own appetites."

"That may be true," I said, "but both of us still work for him, at different ends of the totem pole, of course."

"Don't be so sure we're at different ends. Everyone's a peon to Mossy. He'll do more for those who make him richer, but everyone's still a peon."

Pammy had also discovered the seamstresses upstairs from the contract actresses' dressing room, the women Colonel DeLight had shooed me away from. "What does he pay these Mexican women?" Pammy wondered, "ten cents an hour, or is it fifteen?"

She knew about the writers calling off their strike when the carpenters were bought off by Mossy. "It isn't just Amos Zangwill," she said, "it's the whole damn country. But maybe we start with what's in front of us."

That was when she told me about Cy Henscher and his brutal mistreatment of Rachel Honeycut. He had beaten the young actress so badly that the day I'd seen her at Pammy's Red Woods home Race had screamed when Teresa Blackburn mischievously shoved her into the pool before I arrived. I'd wondered why Race wore such a full body-covering suit while Pammy and Teresa were in skimpy two-piece suits. Race had gone to Pammy's Beverly Hills home the night of the beating, but she'd made Pammy promise not to tell anyone about Henscher's abuse. After climbing out of Pammy's pool a week later, Race had shown Teresa the welts and cuts on her back and buttocks. Henscher had tied her to a bed and hit her until he became aroused and then raped her.

"Rape is the crime I understand least," I said, "and murder of a rapist the one I understand best."

"What a virtuous sentiment, Owen. How noble. How inconvenient that this is not an occasion for virtue or nobility."

I felt as stupid as she'd intended. "What do you mean?" I asked.

She explained that Henscher was just hired by Mossy to score a picture about a romantic couple in Atlantic City. Mossy loved the picture's beginning, but the middle was weak and the ending fell off the table. Henscher had made suggestions Mossy liked, and he offered the composer-lyricist extra money and the additional credit of associate producer. The schedule was so tight Mossy had Henscher start work on the score even before the reshooting was complete. He'd already promised exhibitors they'd have the Atlantic City love story in two months. He put a fresh writer on the picture to make the changes Henscher wanted.

Taking advantage of her temporarily preferred position with respect to Mossy, Pammy had rushed to his office and told him that Cy

Henscher was a sadistic brute and that he had mistreated Race Honeycut in particular, a contract player for Jubilee. Mossy said, "Okay, Cy Henscher is a shit with women, but Race is not in the Atlantic City picture anyway." "You don't get this, do you Mossy?" Pammy had said, trying not to explode. "You have to fire Cy Henscher." "If I did," Mossy said, "I'd have to settle his contract since I've already agreed to pay him for this picture and three more. Then we'd fall even further behind schedule and I couldn't deliver the Atlantic City picture in time. Tell you what, Pammy, I won't hire him again if that will make you happy." "Happy?!" Pammy did explode now. "No, it will not make me happy. You have to get rid of this monster now, today." Mossy had refused and that was where things stood.

"Amos Zangwill is right now a total shit heel," Pammy said to me. "Henscher should be in jail, and we can't do that, but we can do something. Will you help?"

Even while I was nodding my foolish head—Sure I'll help—I was intrigued by the politics of the situation. I was, as usual, cast as a flunky, but now I was her flunky instead of his. Furthermore, I'd be a foot soldier in a battle she was waging against him. She who was not only his employee, like me, but also his lover. I supposed she was on her way to being his former lover. "I don't want to be used," I said, "in some kind of romantic spat between you and him."

Which made Pammy angry. "This is no romance, not anymore," she said with heat. "It's mean of you to bring that up, Owen. I thought you were a friend."

"I'm sorry," I said quickly, "so sorry." And I was thinking, Oh Jesus, she's pretty cunning herself. While she was having her rendezvous with him upstairs in his house, I was a wretched few feet away shining his shoes. Of course, that part she doesn't know. And the part I don't know is if anything he says is true. Still, why her injured innocence? Twenty-four I was, and I'd never had a real girlfriend for any length of time, for any of the complexity of a relationship to show up, for any of the manipulations on both sides that can make an endless circle of coupling. "Please," I said, "Let's just go on."

"Nothing about Mossy, not his charm, not his problems as a kid, certainly not his position as head of the studio, excuses his rotten behavior. Running a sweatshop with the Mexican women sewing costumes, screwing the writers, hiring a musician who beats women, all the rest of it—the man has to be stopped, at least taught a damn good lesson."

"But how will hurting Cy Henscher hurt Mossy Zangwill, who probably doesn't even like the guy?"

"He's depending on Henscher to score his stupid picture. If Henscher doesn't do it that will hurt Mossy. Anything that hurts Mossy teaches him a lesson, and he's a man desperately in need of a lesson. Will you help Elise and me?"

"I told you I would." Another lesson, like the one Mossy doled out to me.

"I knew I could count on you, Owen." She came toward me to give me a quick kiss and a strange thing happened. I went for her right cheek, but she was going for my left cheek, and we wound up with each other's lips. She started to laugh and at that instant our teeth clicked together accidentally. Her lavender breath.

As if beckoned, Millie suddenly came in from her nap, still rubbing her eyes. Some days she was allowed to nap in her mother's bungalow at the studio. Costanza traipsed behind her. "I hope is okay, missus," she said.

"Of course it's okay, Costanza."

"Uncle Owen, did you see the picture I drew."

"A picture with a story," I said. I'd seen the picture pinned to the wall when I walked in. A bear was climbing a thick tree toward a beehive.

"The bear's going for honey to feed her children," Millie said. "She'll get stung a lot, but she'll get the honey. Then they'll all go to sleep for the whole entire winter."

"Millikins, Millikins, let's be sillikins," said her mother. "First, let's sing."

Pammy started "Mary Had a Little Lamb." We sang it as a round. Millie joined in several bars later, and I brought up the rear. Awkwardly. Millie looked directly into my eyes and smiled as she sang. Pammy looked at me plaintively. I wanted to get out, couldn't, and we sang several verses, Costanza joining me with her eager but toneless Spanish accent. At last the fleece had been white as snow for a third time, and Millie jumped into my lap. "Uncle Owen, are you my best friend?"

Before I could answer and while I was pondering how many best friends she might have, Pammy said, "Uncle Owen is certainly our very good friend." To which Millie said, "Isn't he cute?" To which Pammy answered, "He's cute and he's loyal." To which Millie asked, "What's loyal?" To which Pammy said, "You can count on him."

Loyalty again. Owen the Loyal, just the way Mossy wanted me to be. Did anyone ever ask whether loyalty was a synonym for submission?

As I left, I saw them pretending to be a mother bear and her cub, getting set to hibernate after they find a beehive filled with honeycomb in the woods.

I considered Mossy. His early search for a vague equilibrium between art, women, and ideas had been bent by Hollywood and his own weaknesses into the chase for money, sex, and power. But what a showman. He would put on a show for me when he wanted something out of me, for Pammy when he wanted her, probably at home when he wanted Esther Leah and his children to see a devoted husband and father, and he put on a show for the whole world in his pictures. His moods might begin as roles he was playing, but they became biting realities for those he victimized. His showmanship was fate for those he fired during hard times or years later cast into the erupting blacklist volcano. In each case he would promise someone that he wouldn't let temporary advantage, fashion, or the political moment dictate to him, and then—intermission over—he would resume his role.

Yet even a master showman sometimes forgets it's a show, as Pammy had said of Mussolini. Mossy could overestimate his power, underestimate the impact of his whims on others, think himself above the law, more important than presidents or kings or his New York financiers. He was capable of forgetting he was doing a show, of briefly believing he had divine powers. Then he would stumble. The other moguls themselves all found out, now and then, that their powers were not quite divine. At various times and for different reasons Mossy tried to ruin Darryl Zanuck, Clark Gable, Cecil B. DeMille, Sam Goldwyn, and Joan Crawford. He failed, just as Jubilee occasionally turned out flops. Mossy had the quality, though, of a rubber ball. Throw him down, he pops back up.

But now Pammy wanted to teach Mossy a lesson in knowing when an experience was a show and when it wasn't. Whether her motives included anger, jealousy, or moral conviction, Pammy was determined to bring Mossy out from behind the roles he played. The purposed downfall of Cy Henscher would be the occasion.

Manipulative as he was, Mossy wouldn't have admitted to any specific motive at all. Elusiveness was a major feature of Mossy's life as well as an almost insurmountable obstacle to his understanding it. Yes, he was driven but only by simple hunger: I want, therefore I am. I will possess, I will fuck, I hire-fire, I control. That was Mossy.

I, on the other hand, was so full of motive as to be owned by it. Yet I pointed myself in opposite directions. I wanted to be the best toady and to be patted on the head for this as if I were a Labrador retriever, but I also wanted to mount the hierarchy, to rise, to rise riskless, inoffensive, approved of, as though I were the Gilbert and Sullivan office boy who never went to sea yet rose to rule the British Navy. Breaking the laws of physics, I was without mass, without velocity, yet so desperate to please as to be full of energy. Thereby defying Einstein, newly arrived in the United States and all the rage; children were labeled little Einsteins if they could multiply seven times eight. As for Mossy, still a young man but with an old man's eyes, his unleashed destructiveness was no less wanton than electrons released from bondage, as indiscriminate and unsparing of the innocent as of the guilty. His formula was simpler than Einstein's $E=MC^2$: I do what I do because that's what I do when I do it. He was direct while I was indirect.

Yet Mossy and I had one ineradicable passion in common. We both loved the same woman. He had her, or had had her; I didn't, couldn't. She left him, or swore off him the way a drunk swears off rum, and she might return the way the same drunk falls off the wagon. "My damned addiction," she confided to Teresa, cursing herself for making Esther Leah's life all the more difficult. No one ever knew how much Esther Leah knew, but the Zangwill children now and then would find their father on the couch in his den early in the morning. If they asked why, he would tell them he'd been so restless in the night their mother had asked him to leave the master bedroom.

When he was in a political mood Mossy would say that if America is ever defeated it wouldn't be by the Hitlers but by our own amnesia. We'd forget what was best about us. On that he and I could agree. But then we'd disagree on what it was that was best. Mossy liked the cowboy's America. If someone—Indians or sheepherders or squatters—was where you wanted to be, sweep them out of there no matter what you have to do. God anointed us the nation of destiny. That was where Mossy and I would part company. I would incline to the Jeffersonian view of America as experiment. Just because it cured you once didn't mean the same medicine was good for every illness. If something wasn't working don't throw good lives after lost ones, good dollars after bad. Try something else. Keep on changing, improving, experimenting. Mossy would take chances in his personal and professional life, but he didn't believe in political risk. I was the opposite, afraid of my shadow in a personal encounter, numb to the perils of ideology.

Leaving the Millevoix bungalow, I was buoyed like a teenager by the teeth kiss. She did like me, or she needed me, needed me for something, knowing I'd do anything. The next day Pammy called me in the writers building and put her sister Elise on the line. Elise asked if I'd meet her in the commissary for lunch. Fine, I said, and we met over sandwiches. It was an odious plan she presented to me. I said I couldn't go through with it. Elise smiled and told me okay, I should take care of my career. They'd get someone else who really did care about the mistreatment of women and about Mossy's arbitrary high-handedness. "All right, all right," I said, "I'll do it."

Elise Millevoix Jouet wanted to do anything to hurt Mossy, and as a friend of Race Honeycut's she was horrified at what Cyrus Henscher had done to her. Elise had arranged to be assigned as set decorator for the new scenes in the Atlantic City romance Cy Henscher was making story changes and composing music for. She had called the brutal songster, welcoming him back to Jubilee and expressing delight that she'd be working on the same picture he was scoring. She added that she'd always hoped she could get to know him better. Boldly, she then walked into Henscher's office and perched herself at his piano, her neckline loose and low so that when she bent over to touch the keys Henscher could see her breasts curving toward her just-concealed nipples. Elise's looks were more conventional in their appeal than Pammy's—a high forehead over opal-colored eyes that changed with the light, peaches and cream complexion, a small nose over full lips. Henscher was paunchy, waddling as he walked; he had a sensual mouth and a jolly, occasionally wheezing laugh. Elise had met him a few times in the past, saw mayhem in his eyes, and had stayed clear of him. When he asked her to lunch, she knew she had him.

In the commissary Henscher didn't even express sympathy for Elise's recent widowhood. His first question when they'd been seated was, "Do you swallow?" The conversation went downhill from there. Elise said she'd heard he liked to play rough. Henscher was suspicious— "Oh I don't know," he said—until Elise reassured him that was exactly what she craved. She told him she was like a panther that wouldn't behave until she'd tasted the lash. Before lunch ended they'd made a date to spend a night together. Elise called Henscher every other day, purring the cruelties she would endure, tantalizing him with details she and Pammy had combed from the Marquis de Sade.

It was at this point I was given my instructions. I went to the Beverly Wilshire Hotel and reserved a suite for one night the following week, saying I was Cyrus Henscher's assistant. I paid for the suite with money Pammy had given me. Then I went to a moving company and bought a large crate which I strapped to the roof of my Essex.

As we drove downtown on the appointed morning, Elise told me about Mossy's early days in Hollywood to distract me from our bleak errand. He hired people, he had laughingly told her, to come up to him outside premieres, or in restaurants or at parties or even on a sidewalk in front of a studio. They'd ask him for jobs, tell him he was a great producer and they'd do anything to work on his next picture. At the time he hadn't made any pictures at all. They'd beg him to look at their portfolios if they were pretending to be actors, or at least let them come and read for him. Of course, they were unemployed themselves, just down-and-outs who had washed up on the West Coast and would do anything for a couple of dollars. "Wait a minute," the street bums would say to Mossy, "aren't you Amos Zangwill the producer?" "Why yes, actually I am," Mossy would say, or, "Well, that's what my wife calls me." These were the come-ons from the nobodies to the nobody that were supposed to get the attention of somebody.

A more successful gambit of Mossy's, Elise told me, was wheedling himself into the presence of stars as big as Mary Pickford and Buster Keaton. Playing on their vanity, he'd ask if he could film them at home for their private amusement. They'd let Mossy and a cameraman into their homes on weekend afternoons, and Mossy filmed them in their pools or playing with their children or their Irish setters. This meant Mossy now knew these stars and could approach them later with an actual property they might like. If they let him sell the shorts to theaters he made a little money and if they didn't at least the stars had far better home movies than they would have made themselves.

Parking a block from the Los Angeles morgue, Elise and I got ourselves into the disguises she had picked up from Jubilee's costume department—long red hair and an outrageously large hat and bosom for her, a beard and crutches for me along with a train engineer's cap. The crutches were a favor to me Pammy had thought up; they made it impossible for me to have to carry our passenger. Katinka the Red drove a rented panel truck to the morgue in return for a five hundred dollar cash contribution to the Party from Pammy. Katinka's own disguise was a nurse's uniform, also provided by Jubilee's costumers. Her name tag read Nancy Bukharin, a tribute to the Bolshevik theorist. "Let the morgue do what they will with that," Katinka said. She had switched the license plates on the truck with those from an abandoned car she'd found in Venice.

Weeping, Elise led me into the morgue where she, sadly, knew her way around, having had to claim Joey's body there so recently. The tears, however, were not for Joey, or possibly in part they were. We were a brother and sister, Elise sobbed to the assistant supervisor at the morgue, who needed to find the body of our dear aunt. She had descended to hard times, barely eking out her living on the streets, and we had grounds for believing the poor thing might have passed on.

We were led into a vast refrigerated room where we were almost overcome by the reek of formaldehyde as we passed from slab to slab.

Since we needed a cadaver with a shape and size reasonably similar to Elise's we had to view several unidentified bodies until we found the right one, a middle-aged woman ravaged, from her forlorn and sunken look of despair, less by death than by life. Elise collapsed in my arms. "Oh heavenly days, Aunt Cornelia!" she blurted through her tears.

When the morgue officials asked for our identification as we were claiming the body, Elise wept uncontrollably. "Our poor auntie, gone to glory," she managed to sob until she was too overcome to continue. They were eager to be rid of us. "I really have to get my sister out of here," I said to the assistant supervisor as I handed him a couple of Pammy's hundred dollar bills. By this time we had been joined by Katinka in her nurse's uniform with the name tag Nancy Bukharin, duly jotted down by the morgue receptionist. She held up Elise as I hobbled along on my crutches and the morgue attendants carried the shrouded body to Katinka's panel truck. I signed for the cadaver, giving the name Cornelia Henscher and designating myself as Brutus Henscher.

"Let's see the old balladeer sing himself out of this one," Elise said once we were alone, "and how the emperor of Jubilee handles it." In the panel truck I shuddered as we lifted the body into the crate I'd bought, then padded it with many blankets and pillows so it wouldn't move. "This is a new depth in capitalist decadence," said Katinka the Red with righteous assurance. "You won't find anyone in the Kremlin mucking around with a corpse." Elise and I led the little cortege in my Essex while Katinka drove what had now become the hearse.

At the Beverly Wilshire I commandeered porters and checked into the Henscher suite. The crate was labeled MUSICAL INSTRUMENT— VERY FRAGILE—HANDLE WITH EXTREME CARE. PROPERTY OF CYRUS HENSCHER. Katinka refused to enter the Beverly Wilshire. "Kid," she said to me, "You're not really Red after all, are you? No self-respecting Communist would go in a dump like this, built on the backs of the exploited masses." She drove off as soon as the porters had the crate out of her van. To disguise the odor of formaldehyde that was beginning to seep from the crate, Elise and I smoked like incinerators as the four unwitting pallbearers hauled what we told them was a spinet up to the Henscher suite. Since I was on crutches Elise carried the suitcase.

Once we were in the suite, we wore surgical gloves and worked as fast as possible. I almost vomited as we unwrapped Aunt Cornelia from her shroud and hoisted her into the bed. "Think of it as a trout you caught or a duck you shot," Elise said. "I don't hunt or fish," I said. "All right," she said, "the carcass of a turkey at Thanksgiving." Everything she said made it worse. "Let's just hurry," was all I could say.

We stuck the crate into a living room closet and covered it with the bedspread to contain the odor. From the suitcase Elise unpacked whips, chains, a pair of handcuffs, a padlock, a huge bottle of perfume and a wig. She virtually soaked the bed in perfume and fitted the wig, identical to her own hair, onto the corpse, which lay facedown. We covered Aunt Cornelia with blankets, leaving only a wisp of hair showing.

"Okay, please, let's get out of here," I said.

Elise savored the moment. "A bad man goes down," she said.

"For something he didn't do," I said. "It's not fair."

"No," she said, "It's only just."

"It can't be," I said.

"Justice, like dresses, comes in different colors," she said.

She printed a note and stuck it on the table in the suite's foyer. "Hon," it read, "I fell asleep, but I've left some toys on the chair for us to play with. Give me a good swat or two, the harder the better, and I'll wake up and screw your pants off. Your Panther."

We hurried out, still in our disguises, careful to place a Do Not Disturb sign on the double doors to the suite.

It took almost two years for Cyrus Henscher to complete the process that began in the suite at the Beverly Wilshire. Elise called him before lunch, gave him the suite number, and said she'd be there by eight o'clock. She knew Henscher was invited to a sneak preview by Mossy that evening. He apologized to Elise that he'd be late. "That will not be a problem," she told him.

The concierge at the Beverly Wilshire remembered Henscher waddling to the registration desk for his key around ten o'clock. He brought Champagne to the suite and uncorked it in the bedroom after reading Elise's note. As the police reconstructed what happened next from his fingerprints and what he stammered to them, he picked up a whip and laid it across the corpse. When nothing happened he repeatedly struck the presumed torso of Elise Millevoix with a chain. Apparently he was so worked up with lust that at length he pulled back the covers to apply the chain directly to his date's buttocks. That was when he recognized what he was dealing with. He shrieked. His scream was loud and long enough to alarm other guests in the hall, who summoned help from the lobby.

By the time the hotel management burst into the suite, Henscher had had a mild heart attack and was rolling on the floor, still bellowing. Police found him babbling, and they booked him downtown, turning him over to the vice squad. After they held him overnight he made bail and was permitted to check into the Good Samaritan Hospital with what was was generously termed nervous exhaustion as well as his heart condition.

Chastened by the fright they'd had when Trent Amberlyn was arrested picking up a boy, Jubilee executives now had excellent paid contacts at the Los Angeles Police Department. The next morning Dunster Clapp alertly called attention to the morals clause contained in all Jubilee contracts. The composer was not only charged with half a dozen crimes, including the desecration of a corpse, but also fired from Jubilee for extreme turpitude and depravity as well as bringing disgrace upon the institution that had placed such trust in him. His salary ended immediately and he was forced to fight his medical and legal battles on his own, battles that kept columnists and photographers happy for many months. When he reached Elise on the phone she told him she had no idea what he was talking about and hung up. By 1936 Cyrus Henscher was working again, playing in a piano bar in Fort Worth.

29

Mossy Schemes, Pammy Walks

IF YOU'RE WAITING FOR THE APOCALYPSE IT'S AL-
MOST HERE STOP COME SEE THE SHOW STOP QUIN

The telegram peeked out from under my door on Sumac Lane. The end of June had arrived, and it was as though a roller coaster had reached the top of its tracks. My view momentarily was of every-thing—the motion picture business, strikes, plots, the Communists, the wider confused country, my lonely heart floating on the breeze. Shortly the ride would dip and curve and plummet. But for an instant the world's breath was held.

At the studio, Mossy was furious, though not as furious as he soon would be. He had to stop the troubled picture Cyrus Henscher had been working on, pay off the actors and crew, renege on his obligations to theaters around the country waiting for the Atlantic City romance, and swallow a huge loss. He cast wary looks in all directions, on and off the lot, suspecting that someone from Jubilee had set up Henscher but not knowing who. If he thought the Millevoix sisters were behind what newspapers were calling the Aunt Cornelia caper, or that I was their accomplice, he gave no sign.

Labor strife was everywhere. Secretaries and elevator operators, even manicurists, were walking out. The West Coast seethed, with shut downs and dock violence from Seattle to San Diego. At the studio Pammy was trying to help the Mexican seamstresses get organized. The stagily affable Colonel DeLight, who remained in charge of the sewing brigade, dropped his charm and told Pammy to get off his plantation. "I always knew he was overseer material," Yeatsman said, "a southerner all other southerners despise. Scrapped his insincere charm and now shows us what he's made of."

Pammy thought injustice at the studio was everyone's business and said so to Colonel DeLight. Like bears emerging from hibernation, Jubilee people were blinking their eyes and stretching. Wilkins, the senior carpenter, had lost control of the set-builders and came over to the writers building to tell Yeatsman he realized they'd been bought off cheaply. Writers themselves—I along with them—poked their heads out of their holes and began to fuss, more noisily every day. Everyone was restless.

Everyone also knew the studio was under pressure from New York to make more cuts. The amiable dunce among Mossy's entourage, Goddard Minghoff, was told to start saving money fast. Pammy was shooting scenes on a picture called *Love Is for Strangers* when the blue-eyed, silver-haired yes-man Minghoff, looking like a senator, came to the set and told her grievously untalented director, Wick Fairless, that he'd have to lay off one of the camera assistants, a set decorator, the assistant sound man, and a grip. Fairless did this with barely a wave of his hand, but Pammy was enraged.

With the encouragement of set decorators and designers, her sister among them, Pammy complained bitterly to Mossy about the crew layoffs and brought up the issue of the Mexican seamstresses. Mossy told her he didn't give her advice on how to act and he'd appreciate her not telling him how to run his studio. The next day she didn't report to work. Wick Fairless shot around her but called her to say she had to come in the following day. She didn't. Mossy simmered, held his fire, but told the suave, overeducated Englishman, Percy Shumway, to let it be known around town that disobedience at Jubilee would not be tolerated. Of all Mossy's retinue, Shumway was the most delicate at running indelicate errands.

The following day Louella wrote in the *Examiner*, "A certain Miss who oughta be a Mrs. is acting like she owns her studio instead of being lucky enough to work there. The ungrateful girl is making demands when she should be making a picture, causing scenes when she should be filming them. She seems to be under the influence of foreign ideas that are no good where they came from and worse here. Let's hope she comes to her senses and trundles her shapely *derrière* back onto the lot as fast as it can wiggle."

The planted item infuriated Pammy and she quit her picture outright. Mossy summoned her. Elena Frye, with her hypersensitive secretarial ears, heard him remind her she was under contract. She reminded him he'd promised her her pick of pictures, and she was stuck with a terrible script, a nearsighted tin-eared director, and a drunk costar. She also reminded him he was responsible for Joey Jouet's death in more ways than one, and that planted items in gossip columns could cut both ways. "Oh shit, Pammy," Mossy said, "what do you want me to do?"

"Pay people what they're worth, right down to the bottom of the ladder."

"I do better than other studio heads."

"That's like telling me Mussolini is better than Hitler. You have to recognize the right of everyone here to bargain collectively like people in any factory."

"We're *not* a factory, dammit. Look, you know I want to make a picture about your own life, the Palmyra Millevoix story. It'll be a smash. Let's get back to work so we can do that. No more factory talk."

"Oh but we *are* a factory," she shot at Mossy. "You've said so yourself. That's what we are, factory workers, so treat us like factory workers and recognize our unions. Bank tellers, grocery clerks are joining unions. Pretty soon no one will be able to die and be buried, for Christ's sake, unless the gravediggers have a contract with the cemeteries."

"You can't unionize artists," Mossy said a bit lamely.

"Oh yes you can if you put them on an assembly line, and pictures are made on assembly lines. We're all on one, even you, our foreman."

"Aw, come on, Pammy dear," Mossy said, trying to tap a bank account that was already overdrawn.

"Aw, come on, Mossy dear," she said, uncharmed.

"You know I can't break with all the other studios even if I wanted to, which I don't. We're getting nowhere."

"That's right," Pammy said on her way out. "But we'll get somewhere soon."

She drove off the lot right after paying a call to her set and informing Wick Fairless, who she didn't think could direct traffic anyway, that she would not be returning to *Love Is for Strangers*. From what he'd seen of the dailies, Mossy knew he had a dog on his hands and considered canceling the film. But he couldn't take the assault to his authority, the precedent it could set, and suspended his star.

Two mornings later Jubilee directors reported for work to find that three of their sets on as many sound stages had been broken into splinters overnight. Apparently the carpenters were restive, though it could have been teamsters, janitors, anyone. Mossy sent out the hatchet men Curtt Weigerer and Dunster Clapp to discover what was going on, but everyone hated them and no one talked. The police filed their reports, snooped around the lot, coming up with nothing. That night four more sets were destroyed. An ornate living room, a banquet hall with faux crystal chandeliers, a Chinese opium den, even the interior of a police station—all reduced to rubble. The sets looked as if they'd been bombed, walls imploded on themselves, doors blown off their hinges, lights and lamps and tables shattered. All the structures were fake, of course—the walls themselves were beaverboard or *papier-mâché*—yet you could imagine actual people dead underneath them, war victims. Mossy hired more security guards, but no one trusted them either.

The next morning the notorious fixer and labor racketeer Willie Bioff, who had begun his union career running a stagehands' local in Chicago, appeared in Mossy's office. The jowly cigar-chomping Bioff, with more connections to organized crime than to organized labor, was accompanied by Hop Daigle, the jelly-eyed carpenter. Bioff loved his work; he lived to shake down bosses, which he managed with a dash of humor.

According to Elena Frye, the meeting was punctuated with Mossy's shouts and curses. For a big man Bioff had a high-pitched, foggy voice which he never raised. "This damage to your studio property, Mr. Zangwill," Bioff said, "it's so sad. You have my deepest sympathies."

Hop Daigle didn't speak. He looked at the ceiling, which created a strange effect because only one of his eyes shot upward; the other one focused its jelly on Mossy. This was momentarily disconcerting, but Mossy quickly looked away from Daigle and focused his rage on Bioff.

"All right, *Mr.* Bioff, what do you want to stop this criminal vandalism?"

"Oh, I want what you want, Mr. Zangwill. I want the destruction of your property to come to an end."

"Let's cut to the cash register. How much will it cost?"

"Not so much, Mr. Zangwill. Fifty thousand dollars should solve this problem."

That's when Mossy screamed. "FIFTY THOUSAND DOLLARS WILL BREAK THIS STUDIO!"

"I like to stay calm, Mr. Z. If that will kill grandma, then grandma must die."

"You know this is extortion. You're nothing but a fucking chiseler! Blackmailer! I can call the police and have you arrested!"

Bioff chuckled. Daigle looked at him but didn't cut a smile. "I don't call you no names, Mr. Zangwill. Seems the police haven't really solved your problem, have they?"

Hop Daigle spoke only once. "We didn't do this, Mr. Zangwill. I know Willie Bioff here, from Chicago, but it wasn't your carpenters who broke up their own work."

"Sure, Daigle, goddammit," Mossy said, without indicating that he believed one word the carpenter had spoken. He turned back to Bioff and shouted. "My next phone call is to Edgar Globe! You know who he is, Bioff?"

Edgar Globe, the most important entertainment lawyer in Hollywood, represented Mossy and came to his parties. I'd seen his wife, Francesca, flirting with directors, holding off the tennis pro at the *soirée* that led to my humbling degradation. The mere mention of Globe's name was a potent threat. It was said Globe could make a tree grow downward into the ground if he felt like it.

"Yes, sure," Willie Bioff said, "I know him, an honorable personage Edgar Globe is."

An honorable personage? Shit, Mossy reflected. Globe was from Chicago too. Would Edgar know Bioff's superiors? Would he have mob connections himself? All right, he'd have to muscle this on his own.

"What you're talking about," Mossy yelled, "Is completely impossible! I don't pay bribes. GET OUT!"

Without moving, Willie Bioff tilted his head from side to side. "I never used the word *bribe*, sir. Money is paid in exchange for a service, a service both sides need."

Mossy came down from a yell to a modified bellow. "Your demand is outrageous. And Daigle, you're shitcanned off this lot immediately."

"Oh, but it's Hop Daigle who brought us together, Mr. Zangwill," Willie Bioff said. We both need him and the goodwill of the carpenters and the other workers at the studio, from set decorators to lighting people to sound engineers to drivers."

"Are you threatening to put your union into every corner of this studio?" Mossy was incredulous.

"No threat, no threat. I'm just interested in all your many employees, Mr. Zangwill. I've only ever been interested in the plight of the workingman."

Mossy's fury melted into worry. "Fifty thousand dollars is an outrage and it will destroy my studio. The bankers in New York are already screaming at me to cut costs."

"Well, the motion picture industry is based on negotiation, isn't it? Why don't we negotiate?"

"I'll give you ten."

"Then it's settled at twenty-five, Mr. Zangwill. Very good indeed. Everyone will work hard and your sets will be back up by Monday."

"Shit!" Mossy said.

As nearly as anyone was able to find out, Bioff paid ten thousand to his mob handlers back in Chicago, kept ten for himself, and spread five among the Jubilee carpenters. It was his way of slicing the pie. When he was finally arrested years later, he claimed to be a labor peacemaker. He shook down virtually all the studio chiefs, often returning a few months later with another peace offering. The price of peace was as high as a hundred thousand dollars per shakedown for 20th Century

Fox, whose chairman, Joe Schenck, lied about his payoffs and went to prison, serving four months of a three-year sentence before, it was assumed, buying his way to a presidential pardon.

All the studio heads naturally wanted their own way. Mossy's way was to stonewall the unions where he could, subvert them where he couldn't, and make sweetheart deals where he had to. Willie Bioff was the perfect partner, a subverting co-conspirator and a sweetheart.

The Jubilee sets were rebuilt over the weekend. Everyone on the lot was frightened, depressed. What had happened could happen again. Cameras were rolling, but the studio was a hive of nerves. The whole town had the jitters, the other studios as well. The trade papers said Pammy had walked off the lot. She refused to return. "Everything at Jubilee stinks, there's a stench throughout the studio," she told me when I called to see how she was. "I'm for the workers, all of them, but does anybody have a chance?"

I read her the latest telegram from Mike Quin. OWNERS WANT CONFRONTATION STOP WORKERS PLAN GENERAL STRIKE STOP QUIN.

"Tell me about San Francisco," Pammy said.

30

On Location

I squared my shoulders, shifted my weight, raised my eyebrows like someone who has the right idea, and nodded decisively with what I took to be directorial authority. "Ladies," I said, "come with me." I'd installed the delegation at the Fairmont on Nob Hill, and I bundled us into a taxi, telling the driver our first stop was City Hall. It was Independence Day. I'd come up the day before on the train, while Pammy, Teresa Blackburn, and Race Honeycut had just arrived at the presumed revolution in Largo Buchalter's private biplane. Knowing of her break with Jubilee—and Mossy—Buchalter was hoping to lure her to Fox, where he was negotiating for a big picture; he'd lent her his pilot and plane. Mike Quin had dropped off a note at the hotel: "Welcome to San Francisco, tense and sea-girt, tense and waiting, where the only instruction that can be made with confidence and intelligence is to expect the unexpected. Dust-up at mayor's office. See you somewhere. Quin."

It had been the "Tell me" in Pammy's "Tell me about San Francisco" that got me. It meant I was not a handyman but an expert. On Pammy's road to activism, I was the tour guide to the potential as well as the challenges of the labor movement. Our futures were at stake; either we could make a difference in the picture business, or we could not. The idea was to find out in San Francisco. When they peppered me with questions—Race's was typical: "Tell me, Heartthrob, what do you-all want us to be lookin' at up here?"—I recognized that what these actresses, even Pammy, wanted was a director.

We were met at City Hall by little rivers of marchers and counter-marchers. I asked the cabdriver to wait. The Industrial Association, representing the businesses of San Francisco and especially the ship-owners, had marchers demanding the mayor open the port and get the city going again. Placards were lettered in paint slashes: CALL IN THE MARINES; HIRE NEW WORKERS; REDS—KEEP OUT THIS IS THE USA. Two signs had big swastikas on them; one carried the caption, THE GERMANS DO IT RIGHT, and the other blared, SIEG HEIL—BEFORE SF BECOMES MOSCOW. The opposition, mostly the wives of dockworkers and seamen, along with some radical sympathizers, marched with placards that said, MAYOR PLEASE—COLLECTIVE BARGAINING IS A RIGHT NOT A CRIME; SUPPORT THE ILA (International Longshoremen's Association); THE NEW DEAL STARTS ON THE DOCKS, and FAIR PLAY FAIR PAY FOR WORKING ALL DAY.

"It's not a set, is it?" Teresa said. It was the swastikas that caught Pammy. "I can't believe I'm looking at that in America," she said. One of the men carrying a swastika brought his placard down on the head of a man holding a HELP THE SEAMEN sign. In an instant both sides were on each other. Police, acting like referees, separated the two lines of marchers, who resumed their circling on the City Hall Plaza.

Teresa wanted to go into the mayor's office and assured Pammy that she'd be able to see him. "What for?" Pammy said. "He'd have his picture taken with me and then tell us we didn't know what we were doing. True enough. Anyway, it's July Fourth and he's probably giving a speech at some picnic."

"Now we go where the strike is," I said.

As I herded them back into the taxi, the driver did a double take. "Ma'am," he said to Pammy. "If I didn't know better I'd think you were Palmyra Millevoix."

"People tell me that," she said.

As we arrived at ILA union headquarters just off the waterfront, I caught a nervous glimpse of the alley where I'd almost been stabbed to death a few weeks earlier. No trucks or freight cars were operating on the holiday, but hundreds of pickets marched. I steered my charges toward a picket line of perhaps thirty men. They were standing guard around a pile of crates to make sure no scabs moved them to a warehouse or a ship.

"Hey, it's Palmyra Millevoix," said a man with a placard that read, WE WANT FULL RECOGNITION—ILA. "Are you slumming, ma'am, or are you with us?"

"I came to see for myself," Pammy said. "No place with working men and women is a slum to me. My friends and I are here to support what you're doing." She and Teresa and Race were surrounded by strikers who were both curious and awed.

It quickly developed that Race and Teresa didn't belong on this picket line. The strikers saw them merely as pretty girls with a movie star for a friend. I was accepted as a chaperone. A couple of pickets whistled at Race, and one asked Teresa if she'd like to come up to his place later and hear all about the strike. That drew a brief horselaugh. Out of their element, the two actresses saw they had no real role since the pickets only wanted to talk to the star. "I'd really like to see my brother," Teresa said.

Teresa's brother, Stubby Blackburn, had been sold by the Los Angeles Angels to the Sacramento Solons of the Pacific Coast League, which meant she seldom saw him, and the Solons were in town to play the San Francisco Seals in a holiday doubleheader. "Heartthrob's gonna take good care of you, honey," Race said to Pammy, "Me and Teresa's gonna take care of each other." They found a taxi and headed to the ballpark.

"How are your families doing?" Pammy asked the pickets nearest her. "The strike's already two months old, isn't it?"

"We're on wartime rations like I had in France, ma'am," a bearded longshoreman said, "but it's worth it if we get our union recognized. Wife and kids say the same."

"Trouble is, the employers have the full pockets," a shy young picket said, "and they can last out so much longer than we can."

"Yah, but they're losing *millions*," the bearded man said. "That's the part I like. Lot of dead whales in the harbor."

Completely misunderstanding him, I asked, "What's killing them?"

"I'm talking about the commercial ships—they're out there floating but they're not moving, and their cargo's going nowhere."

"The bosses treat us like dirt," another marcher said. "They set all the work rules, the penalties, enforcement, wages of course. Working men have no say at all."

"Except they don't call us men," said a burly older man with graying hair. He was carrying the American flag. "All the men on the docks is called boys. End of every day, Miss Millevoix, we're out of work. Have to hope we get picked the next day by the company's little duke, a straw boss who does the hiring. You don't bring a bottle to one of the little dukes, or kick back to him, you don't get hired."

"We ain't Reds, ma'am, but the times is drastic," said the man who had asked Pammy if she were slumming, "and people are looking for drastic solutions."

"Some are Reds," the burly man said, "but we don't need them to tell us we're working under desperate conditions for slave wages or that the owners are selfish."

The bearded man again: "They're hiring rich white boys and poor black men to scab and break the strike, and they're using cops paid for by all of us to protect their side alone. The bosses want to destroy the union, and they don't mind losing money to do it."

"They'd bottle up the sun if they could," the shy young picket said, stuttering a little, "and make us pay for it. The strike's our only weapon to make them give an inch."

"I wish I could help," Pammy said.

"Cheer for us, Miss Millevoix," said the young man, "and let your friends know."

"Yah, can you sing us a song?" the bearded man asked.

"You know 'Solidarity Forever'?" Pammy asked them.

"Sure," said several of the strikers.

"Here's a verse just for you. I'll start and you join me after you've heard the verse." She stood on a packing crate. "Let's sing," she said.

> The longshoremen, the seamen and at last the teamsters too—
> We are fighting for their rights and that means me and that
>   means you;

We won't stop till San Francisco sees the unions get their due,
And the bosses know that's true.

Solidarity forever,
Solidarity forever,
Solidarity forever,
And the bosses know that's true.

How the hell she came up with that I wasn't going to ask, but they all joined her for two more repetitions of her riff on the old Wobbly song of solidarity taken from the even older Civil War "Battle Hymn of the Republic." We spent the rest of the afternoon walking along the waterfront, talking to groups of picketers, Pammy singing when asked. Whenever I was alone with her my talk was stilted, like an inexperienced schoolteacher. I was grateful when the dockworkers invited us to dinner in their union hall.

As we climbed the stairs to the ILA headquarters I shivered at the memory of the knife attack by that big side of beef Widdelstaedt. If he recognized me he might want to finish the dark work he'd begun before. I looked around furtively, relieved not to see him or his buddy Cromartie. The person who did remember me was Nick Bordoise, the Greek chef. "If you're back here," he said, "it means we'll have some action, yes?"

When I introduced him to Pammy, he didn't recognize her but since the dockworkers did, he understood she must be special. Nick stammered an unnecessary apology. "The food here, I'm sorry, miss, it's not what you're used to." Pammy said she was starved, and he brought us bowls of chili with cornbread and iced tea. "But this is delicious," Pammy said. "Do you have enough for two friends of mine?"

While Pammy was on the phone to the hotel, Mike Quin showed up. Racing around town, he'd found out shipowners were planning a forcible opening of the port, and he'd heard businessmen in a club telling each other that machine gunning the strikers was the best way to preserve the sanctity of private property except for stringing up Harry Bridges on a lamppost. Quin had seen Bridges himself coming out of a meeting with federal officials, complaining that President Roosevelt gives with one hand and takes away with the other. The governor was threatening to call in the National Guard to patrol the docks for the shipowners. I told Quin I couldn't believe the National Guard would protect only one side in a dispute. "Ah, Skinny, stick around," Quin said. "The stage is set for a showdown between all the forces that have been aching to collide for two months, or maybe twenty years."

Pammy returned to the long table where we sat with several dock-workers and said Teresa and Race wouldn't be joining us. They'd gotten Teresa's brother Stubby Blackburn to snag the Seals' center fielder, who'd hit three homeruns in the doubleheader, for a fancy dinner at the Fairmont with the two actresses. "'Let's us little chickens have us a night off,'" Pammy mimicked Race's southern accent when she described the call, "'me and Teresa, we're gonna fight over Mr. DiMaggio. Y'all win the strike.'"

Mike Quin was impressed to meet Pammy and immediately said, "Ah, now that you're on location maybe we can get a picture going that Skinny here doesn't seem to be able to pull off at your studio." "Between the two of us," Pammy corrected Quin, "I doubt we could get a pencil sharpened at Jubilee right now."

Nick Bordoise's wife, Julia, arrived to pick him up. Her hands were chapped and the color of beets. She saw me noticing them and explained she worked in a laundry. Nick brought her a bowl of chili and sat down with us. Pammy wanted to know if he was a member of the Greek Orthodox Church. Not anymore, he explained. He was a member of the Communist Party because they were fighting for what he believed in. Shyly, possibly trying to win support in a family argument, Julia Bordoise asked Pammy if she thought it was wrong for Nick to be a Communist. "In Russia maybe," Pammy said, "not in America."

One of the longshoreman began to strum a guitar and sing, almost to himself at first, "O Susanna." By the time he was through, the room was listening, and another longshoreman asked Pammy if she'd sing something. I wouldn't believe this except I was there— she had something of her own ready. She didn't know she'd have an accompanist, and she went over to the guitar player and asked him

---

for a couple of chords. While they were working this out, Harry Bridges came up the stairs.

He was thinner than when I'd seen him a month earlier, and haggard, his hawk's nose more prominent, but his eyes were intense and everyone wanted to hear what he had to say. The Industrial Association was so hostile to him that some of their members were trying to have him deported back to Australia. He was polite to Pammy when Mike Quin introduced them, but I couldn't tell if he had any idea who she was. "What's the good word tonight, Harry?" one of the longshoremen asked. "Looks like you're about to have some entertainment, mates," Bridges said, the last word an Australian *mites*. "There isn't much to tell you, so why don't we have the music first." He looked grim.

"Can we have harmony?" Pammy asked.

"Eventually," Bridges said, smiling, "not yet. Right now we sing in unison."

Pammy pursed her lips, but Quin nodded at her to go ahead. "It's just a strike ditty," Pammy said, "and please join me the second time through. Okay? Let's sing."

The guitarist gave her two chords, and then she sang:

When the bosses cut our losses
And be fair,
When the bosses cut our losses
Everywhere,
When the masses beat the classes
And we knock them on their asses,
When the workers take control
We will roll, roll, roll.

When they give back what they stole
We'll be there,
When the workers reach their goal
We will share,
When the workers take control
Then we'll make this country whole,

When the workers take control
We'll be there, there, there.

The second time through, even Harry Bridges joined in with his high, reedy Down Under tones. So did Nick Bordoise in his Greek modulation, though his wife Julia was silent, nodding to herself. The room quieted uncertainly when the singing ended.

Quin asked if we outsiders should leave before Bridges addressed his troops.

"Mates," Bridges said, "I wish I had something to tell everyone that everyone doesn't already know. Basically, we've made no progress downtown, none at all. The ship owners have the city leaders and other businessmen on their side, nothing new, but now they're bound and determined to open the port of San Francisco by force. Tomorrow." Bridges sighed. "And they have the force in their pocket. All of it."

"Where's the federal government in this, where's the president?" The man who asked this, standing with one foot on a bench, looked ready to chew nails.

"You'll like this one, boys. While we're busy closing down shipping here President Roosevelt is on the high seas, on a yacht having himself a holiday."

Someone said he'd better not try docking in San Francisco. That raised a guffaw.

"Well, the president has a lot of things to think about," Bridges said, "and the city fathers downtown hate him as much or more than they hate us. The point is, we don't want any violence. They're armed, and they're ready to go for us at any provocation. We're petitioning the powers, we send a message by our very presence along the Embarcadero. The more of us the louder the message, the more signatures on our petition. But anyone who doesn't want to march in the picket line tomorrow, especially anyone with children, I understand. It could get ugly."

"It's been ugly for months, Harry," said the man with the foot on the bench. "We'll all be there in the morning."

We left with Nick and Julia Bordoise. Downstairs, I asked if we could give them a ride in our taxi. I think Julia was about to tell us that would be very nice, but Nick said no, they lived nearby, and they headed up Mission Street.

At the hotel things were awkward. It was still early, but we both fumbled for anything to talk about. "What do you think is going to happen tomorrow?" "I wish I could tell you." Pammy said Millie was waiting at home for her call, the perfect excuse to get away from me. I said I hoped Teresa and Race were having a good evening. "I've heard ballplayers are as bad as actors when it comes to mischief," she said.

The telegram was under my door. YOU'RE ALL BEING FOOLISH STOP I WON'T SPEAK TO HER BUT YOU CAN STOP REMEMBER THAT EVEN WHEN THE DANCE IS OVER ITS NOT HARD TO TELL THE WALLFLOWERS FROM THOSE WHO WALTZED STOP WISE UP AZ

31

Bloody Thursday

T hursday, July 5. I saw dark skies, no rain. The sun started to rise, then seemed to change its mind; not the usual fog but a deep gray washed the city. Two men in suits—pleasant looking fellows who could have been second leads in a Jubilee picture—were conversing in the lobby. "This strike isn't between management and labor," one said. "It's between American principles and un-American radicalism. We've reached a crisis."

"It's that simple," the other said, gesturing with his briefcase. "Yesterday, for the first time in fifty years, not a single vessel sailed into the port of San Francisco. Any cargo waiting to be loaded is rotting on the docks."

"Paper says the Archbishop wants to mediate and asks for more time."

"Too much time and money are already down the drain. Time's up, Your Grace."

Mike Quin, his eyes as red as his hair from attending strike committee meetings all night and perhaps from what he'd lubricated himself with, greeted us with the same words the two men in suits had agreed on. "We've reached a crisis," Quin said as he marched into the lobby to take us to the waterfront. It was just after seven. Pammy had her hair in a bun and wore a no-nonsense shift, buttoned from its hem to her neck. Quin explained to the three actresses, as a warning, that this was the day the shipowners vowed to open the port by force. The unions all vowed to keep the port closed.

The streets feeding the Embarcadero were already full of police and pickets. The police patrolled the dockside while the strikers moved along the land side, two armies, but only one was armed. Across from the Ferry Building, longshoremen paraded two abreast, with the American flag in front and the ILA flag carried behind it.

Four trucks, driven by strikebreakers, rumbled ominously down the Embarcadero. They drew shouts about scabs and finks. No one made a move to block the trucks. Vendors went around with candy, gum, cigarettes. A young boy made a dash from the lines of pickets across the Embarcadero to where the police were, ducking past them and leaping into the arms of a woman. Hundreds more strikers arrived on buses.

"The Longshoremen aren't alone here," Quin told us. "Seamen and Teamsters, the Sailors' Union, Marine Firemen, Oilers, Watertenders and Wipers, Marine Cooks and Stewards have struck, then the Ferrymen's Union, the Masters, Mates and Pilots and the Marine Engineers—all of them are out. The other side blames it all on Bridges."

As the clock on the Ferry Building chimed eight—apparently a planned signal—the police charged the picket line, breaking its ranks, driving strikers up the streets that led away from the Embarcadero. The police were using clubs and tear gas. Led by Quin, we retreated up Rincon Hill with the strikers, who shouted at us to get out of the way. We did. Teresa yelled we were crazy to come here. Pammy said no, it's good to see what America's face looks like today. Escape was impossible anyway.

We ducked into the same Chinese laundry where I'd been weeks earlier on my first trip. The proprietor, Wun Chew, recognized me as the stupid fellow he'd sheltered before. Obligingly, Wun Chew took us upstairs. His family spoke no English, and we joined them watching out the windows. "This is not real," Teresa said, bowing as Mrs. Wun Chew poured tea for us. Down below was fighting, shouting, then a lull.

Mike Quin and I made a brief reconnoiter into the streets around the waterfront. The clashes were less chaotic and more tactical than those I'd seen weeks earlier. At first the police were simply trying to drive the pickets away from the waterfront, not to overwhelm them. The strikers had immobilized the railroad tracks that serviced the docks by parking cars across them. Trucks were harder to stop and some got through to the docks. Up from the Embarcadero, a few fires had started on a hillside covered with dry grass. Quin said these were caused by tear gas shells, but the strikers were also trying to slow the march of policemen up the hill and might have ignited the grass. The fire trucks that rolled up turned their hoses on both the flames and the picketing union members.

I had just rejoined my group at Wun Chew's when we heard firing downstairs. Looking out the window, we saw pickets vomiting. Along with tear gas the police were now using nausea gas. When we looked down the street we saw several fallen and wretching strikers. We could see a few blocks in either direction, and the fighting seemed to be resolving itself not into a single battle but a dozen skirmishes. Charging in their gas masks, the police hurling the canisters looked like undersea monsters. Other police had riot guns and wooden cudgels they used to club strikers to the ground.

"Who actually is doing the rioting," Pammy said, and it was not a question.

A combination of gas and gunfire drove the weaponless strikers and their sympathizers well up Rincon Hill away from the waterfront and the Embarcadero. The Wun Chew family—five children and their mother upstairs—had stopped looking out the window, apparently having decided that the city had gone mad and was no longer worth their attention. They accepted us as friendly intruders; the kids went on with their playing, the mother with her cooking, offering us tasty little pot stickers. At noon the action on the street stopped and everyone seemed to break for lunch.

Mike Quin fetched us as if he were picking us up from school. "Armies of extras from one of your movie lots," he said, "couldn't observe their lunch hour with more precision." Leading us to union headquarters, he told us the spectators on Rincon Hill outnumbered both strikers and police. "They're like the people who went out from Washington to watch the First Battle of Bull Run," he said. He was sure he spotted some other people up from Hollywood for the festivities. Maybe Frederic March, he thought.

I asked why the strikers weren't armed at least with bricks and stones, or the horse-foiling marbles they'd had when I'd seen them on my first trip. Quin said their whole plan had been to avoid combat now, to resist the owners peacefully. "But I'm disgusted that San Francisco cops," he said, "who come from the same neighborhoods as the workers, even the same families, would turn on men who ought to be their comrades."

"That's their role," Pammy said. "Follow orders, the role they've memorized."

"I guess so," Quin said, "but it's against their interests."

"In this Depression," Teresa said, "their interest is to feed their families."

"Lucky to have a job keeping the peace is probably how they feel," Race said.

"They're not peacekeepers today," Quin said. "They might as well be the shipowners' hired army to break the union, and when the National Guard gets here, the state and property owners will be identical. It's a lesson plan older than Caesar."

Nick Bordoise greeted us at the ILA hall, oddly cheery, ready to serve lunch. "Welcome to the International Longshoremen's Association *deluxe table d'hôte*," he said, putting out salami sandwiches and apple cider. The slender Greek was going back to his restaurant the following week. "I won't forget my comrades here," he said, "but I have to sling what you say a better grade of hash, make some moolah. Remember Napoleon declares an army marches on its stomach so *kali orexi, pedhia*, eat up, my hearties." Nick's English was correct enough, but it could veer off a few decades, as if he'd learned the language from Jack London.

Seated on benches at big picnic tables, union members were downcast, looking at their sandwiches as if to find solace in them or the paper plates. It didn't seem possible to maintain a picket line in the face of gunfire and gas, and it was fruitless to try. At least inside their headquarters they were safe in what had been observed as a neutral zone.

That last certainty disappeared just after one o'clock when, lunch break over, the police assaulted the ILA union hall itself. They didn't bother to come up the stairs but shot gas canisters through the windows. Most of the union members, coughing and with their eyes tearing, poured down the stairs into the street. Quin dashed out with them. Pammy and Teresa and Race and I covered our faces with napkins and handkerchiefs. Nick Bordoise threw us dish towels he'd soaked in water, which gave us more protection. Nick put one over his own face and chased down the stairs. "*Bastardi!*" he shouted. "The bastards can't do this! *Christe! Christe!* The workers are rising, equality is on the march!" What he said sounded so European. They may have been Nick's final words.

Just then the telephone rang. A longshoreman still upstairs choked out a hello as he answered. A moment later he said, "Fuck you!" and slammed down the receiver. "Son of a bitch wanted to know if we were ready to surrender," he said.

I remembered there were stairs up as well as down, and I led my charges—all of us choking and coughing—to the roof. On the sidewalks below we saw pandemonium. Teresa said, "This is not happening."

"Believe your eyes," Pammy said. "This is what war is. It's to be expected."

Down on the street events shifted, collapsed their normal sequence, each scene partitioning itself into a splinter of time. Along the Embarcadero strikers try to put another car across the railroad tracks. The undersea monsters in their gas masks charge with canisters and drive them off. Even their horses are fitted with outsized goggles to protect them from their riders' tear gas; the horses look like sea creatures too, enslaved ones. Canisters wing through the air, land, emit their white puffs of gas. Union men wipe their eyes, cough, vomit up their lunches. Screams, low boom of gas guns. The police advance along the Embarcadero and the streets that meet it. The splinter that defines the day: a squad car, with slow deliberation as though it has its own will, turns off the Embarcadero onto Mission Street. It travels one block. At the corner of Steuart, directly below us, the car halts. Two men climb out, one in uniform, one not. The plainclothesman draws a pistol, while the uniformed officer brings a riot gun up to his shoulder.

They aim first at the southwest corner and fire into the file of strikers, then turn to each of the northern corners. They swivel to the southeast corner, still firing. They climb back into the squad car and drive away. Next to me, Race begins to scream.

On the sidewalk below us a man has pitched over and is coughing up blood. He stops moving. Other strikers have fallen and are bleeding. "Oh my God!" we hear shouted from the street. What Race sees before the rest of us is Nick Bordoise. She has one hand over her mouth, stopping her scream, and points to Nick with the other. He is down, shot, writhing as blood spills from his chest. He tries to rise, falls back, and gets up again. He leans against a shop window, smearing his blood on it. Race says, "I'm going to that poor boy," and starts to run for the stairs. Pammy and I grab her. We see Nick hold his side as he drags himself away from the union headquarters, up Mission Street. He heads, as he had with his wife less than twenty-four hours ago, for home. He staggers perhaps fifty yards up the block before he sinks to the sidewalk and is still.

It is over.

Calm descended as fast as, moments earlier, the clamor of combat had resounded.

The police, ordered back down to the Embarcadero, withdrew. Screaming squad car sirens went away, replaced by the howling of ambulance sirens. We walked downstairs to the union hall where we'd had Nick's salami sandwiches—when? Three quarters of an hour earlier? Fifteen minutes? A large emergency room was being set up, men lying on the floor or splayed out on the picnic tables. Pammy bustled about, knowing what to do as if she were in her old nurse's uniform at the front in France. She showed the rest of us how to make tourniquets and delicately wash wounds.

Race insisted on going to the street, and I went with her. Nick Bordoise lay where he had fallen. "He's gone, isn't he?" Race said. "I think so," I said, remembering the Los Angeles morgue, a comic scene, almost a wax museum, compared to this rude nightmare. I saw Nick as a baby in his mother's arms on Crete, as a boy in a cap running toward a stream, at a steamship railing with his parents, his face beneath a chef's hat in the kitchen of a fancy restaurant, serving us dinner last night, lunch today, now crumpled like a rag at our feet. The former Nick Bordoise. An ambulance pulled up, loaded him in, and drove off. "God damn hell," said a striker next to us whose arm had been twisted out of its socket by two policemen, "Hitler is more alive in San Francisco than Berlin." We helped him back to the ILA hall.

When we returned upstairs to what was now a field hospital, we pitched in as well as we could. Pammy, with her war experience, seemed to be in authority, not precisely bossing anyone but suggesting firmly that this man ought to lie still, that one should try to stand, another should see if he could move his leg, a fourth needed his wound washed again to stave off infection. Recalling her experience at the blood bank in France, she said she thought a few of the men would need transfusions. Men who had taken gas in their eyes couldn't see properly. One man wouldn't stop screaming; a mounted policeman had jumped down from his horse after the man was knocked down, then had clubbed his leg so many times it appeared to be a hundred shards of bone when Pammy got his pants off. Several men had their heads lacerated from being clubbed, one with a compound fracture of his skull.

A photographer arrived to take pictures of the wounded. He focused especially on a group of six men in a corner of the hall, four of whom had their heads swathed in white cloth, with blood still flowing from under the bandages. The other two had cut legs bleeding abundantly and one of these had his arm in a sling. I didn't recall any of us tending to this group; they seemed simply to have materialized as the photographer did. Race went over to them and asked if she could help, then quickly ran back to where the rest of us were. "They smell like hamburgers over there," she said, "and when I got real close to them I saw it was because they're all made up." I asked what she meant. "I mean," she said, "that's ketchup drooling out of their bandaged heads. Things aren't bad enough, these guys have to put on makeup?"

"That's a few Red radicals, not longshoremen," said a voice from the floor. I looked down and saw the older man we'd talked to on the picket line the day before. His gray hair was matted with his own blood, which oozed from a crack in his skull. "They're on our side, but they want to look hurt more than be hurt," the man said, wincing as Pammy sponged water onto his head. "Never mind them."

We didn't. Pammy went right on showing us how to make the injured and wounded more comfortable, propping up a head here, putting a broken leg onto a pillow there, applying a tourniquet above the gash in a man's leg that was spouting blood. Three doctors arrived, carrying bags and flanked by nurses. They were strike sympathizers. One of them did a double take when he saw Pammy, then went right to work on a man lying on the floor bleeding from his abdomen. It was time for us to leave.

On the Embarcadero, where taxis cruised as they would after any performance, a newsboy was already hawking an extra edition and shouting, "Read all about it—pickets murdered! Bloody Thursday! Slaughter on the waterfront!"

32

Finalement

Rumors met us at the hotel. Twelve people had been killed including four cops. No. Twenty had died, seven of them in a two-car crash as they raced to escape the war-torn city. No. The police are killing every picketer they can find. It's a massacre. A message from Mike Quin said he wouldn't be seeing us since he was writing an account of the day for the longshoremen's newspaper. The desk clerk said he assumed we'd be leaving San Francisco immediately and asked if we wanted our bill.

"You should leave town, Miss Millevoix," a bankerly looking man said to Pammy in the Fairmont's lobby. "This will only be the beginning. A lot more of these radicals have to get their heads broken before the wretches know who's boss."

"Thank you," Pammy said, trying to stay out of trouble.

"For your own good, Miss M," the pin-striped man pursued. "The only way to solve this is by bloodshed. Violence is the language they understand. I'd turn machine guns on these lowlifes and mow them down like wheat."

"That does sound extreme," Pammy said, still holding herself in check, but she ventured a little further. "Don't you think, sir, that the dockmen and the seamen and the others have a right to organize for better pay?"

The man puffed himself up and threw out his chin, fingering the gold watch chain draped across his girth. He may have stepped out of a cartoon labeled Big Capital. "You're not one of those Hollywood bleeding hearts, are you?" he asked. "You look much too sensible. No, Miss Millevoix, if I'm hiring someone I hire him for what he'll work for, not for what he and his cronies can extort from me by banding together into a so-called union that is in reality nothing more than a conspiracy against honest businessmen and private property. It's my property, my business, and I'll decide how often, how long, when and where a man I hire will work. When the gang of them strike and picket my property, that's an instrument of violence itself, completely un-American. It's pure Bolshevism. Not on these shores, thank you very much."

We made our way into the bar. One of the bartender's brothers was a longshoreman and the other was a policeman. He'd been on the phone with both, and he gave us the definitive word. Only two people had died—the unlucky Nick Bordoise and a longshoreman named Howard Sperry. Other longshoremen had been seriously wounded, but no policemen were badly hurt. Over a hundred union members had been taken to hospitals, but most of the wounded had straggled to their homes for fear of being arrested if they went to a hospital. "It's a miracle more weren't killed," the bartender said.

Race and Teresa found us in the bar and said they were leaving. They thought all of us should get back to Los Angeles as fast as possible. "Anything we can learn to help us organize in Hollywood," Teresa said, "we've already learned." "In spades," Race said. At that moment a messenger came for Pammy. He handed her a note. "We'll be having a memorial on Monday for our fallen comrades," the note read, "and we'd be honored by your presence. Will you stand with us? Perhaps a visit to the wounded over the weekend." The note was signed, "Bridges of the Strike Committee."

"Will you give Pammy some time to think about this?" I asked Teresa and Race.

"I don't need any time," Pammy said. "I'll stand with the longshoremen."

Teresa and Race were taking the night train to Los Angeles. "Y'all got her into this," Race told me. "Now y'all better bodyguard her like she was the Queen of Sheba."

"You don't have to stay," Pammy said.

That hurt my feelings, but I quickly said, "Nothing for me to do at the studio."

Teresa, sensing I had just hurt Pammy's feelings in return, said, "Owen, is that as gallant as you can be to my best friend? Pammy darling, I don't think you should stay. This city is the most dangerous place on the continent."

Pammy laughed for the first time all day. "Don't worry, girls, Owen will be my chaperone and my life preserver."

We had dinner in the hotel after Teresa and Race left, not talking much, not eating much. I suppose we were in shock. The conversation, if it can be called that, was artificial. "Will you have another glass of wine?" "No, thank you." "Dessert?" "No."

In the bar before Teresa and Race had left, all four of us had already shuddered at the horror we'd witnessed, already compared our afternoon certainties that we would be engulfed and unable to escape, already pitied those who didn't escape, especially the tender, fervent Nick Bordoise, already sworn at the brutality of the police and the powers who sent them, already asked what were we doing at this luxury hotel while the strikers were wondering if they'd even have enough to eat for the next week, already vowed to donate to the strike fund, already debated how to use in Hollywood what we saw here. Now, alone with Pammy, my energy searched for an outlet and could find none.

She was uneasy too. She missed Millie yet she didn't want Costanza to bring Millie up to a San Francisco in such upheaval. Weighing every word, praying for dinner to be over, I said staying in the city could hurt her in Hollywood where they hated Reds, particularly—I couldn't say Mossy's name—the, ah, studio heads. "That's the last goddamned thing I care about," she said.

Mercifully, the check arrived. We went to our separate rooms. She had a suite on the twelfth floor, I was in a single on the third.

I remembered I hadn't asked her what time she wanted to get started in the morning. What did I mean by get started anyway? It wasn't as if my services as an emissary to the strike were any longer needed. It was only Thursday night and we had nothing to do until the memorial service Harry Bridges had asked her to stay for on Monday.

She'd visit the wounded as he asked, some combination of Florence Nightingale and Lady Bountiful. So we'd each go our separate ways in the morning? I'll just call her room, I said to my brash self, and offer her the same kind of tour Mike Quin had given me on my earlier trip, the highs and lows of a great, majestic, elegant, corrupt, decadent city now in turmoil, kind of a fairy princess with syphilis.

Her line was busy. I read the papers about the strike. Almost all the stories were favorable to the group of businessmen calling themselves the Industrial Association, and unfavorable to the longshoremen, the seamen, and to a lesser degree the teamsters. Like the paperboy on the Embarcadero, the press was already calling this Bloody Thursday. "Blood ran red in the streets of San Francisco," the *Chronicle* reporter began, calling this "the darkest day this city has known since the Earthquake of 1906 ... a Gettysburg in the miniature. WAR IN SAN FRANCISCO!"

Fifteen hundred National Guard soldiers dispatched by the governor were patrolling the city, with five thousand more on the way. The commanding officer of the 250th Coast Artillery announced the occupation of the waterfront and issued a warning: "In view of the fact that we are equipped with rifles, bayonets, automatic rifles and machine guns, which are all high-powered weapons, the Embarcadero will not be a safe place for persons whose reasons for being there are not sufficient to run the risk of serious injury." The commander was quoted as saying his troops would show no mercy and he warned his own men that if any of them fired into the air instead of shooting to kill they would be court-martialed. Leafing through the paper, I thought, So the rebellion is over and the powerful have, no surprise, won. It was Jubilee Pictures writ large.

I called Pammy's room again. Still busy. More accounts of the confrontation between strikers and police described the union members as attackers and rioters, the police as embattled peacekeepers. Once more I tried her line. Busy. I was sick of reading what other people wrote about where I'd been all day, and since she was on the phone I wouldn't be waking her up by knocking on her door. Should I put my suit jacket on and be formal? Or would that be like an invitation to come back out again for a walk or drink? An invitation she'd be sure to

turn down before I even issued it, humiliating me. I left my jacket off
and put on a sweater. Trying to look relaxed.

The door swung open before I finished knocking. She was wearing
a kimono, China red with blue flowers on it, that came to her knees.
"Sorry," I said, "your line was busy"—and now I began stammering—
"I only came up to see what, I mean if you'd like tomorrow, in the
morning I mean."

"*Enfin!*" she said. "I thought I'd have to call you myself as soon as
I'd said goodnight to Millie. What are you doing standing out there?"

My legs had gone into her suite and my arms had found their way
to her shoulders, more or less by themselves. I was aware of no voli-
tion. She pulled me to her and faced me not with a smile but a look
of necessity, inevitability. The kiss was warm, hungry. More—a new
kiss, heart-stopping for me, heart-racing, heart-full. We were then
on the couch. Then then then. Her kimono was coming off, her arms
and shoulders, bare, appeared to radiate desire. Perhaps it was only
desirability. I was clumsy but it didn't matter. She was active, then she
waited, pausing for me to take the lead, unaccustomed as I was. I took
the lead, somehow I did that. Then she was aggressive, yet paused
again as I went forward. I tore at the sweater I'd put on minutes earlier
in my room, all unknowing. Always unknowing. I was thrusting. She
was thrusting. We rolled off the couch, acrobatically, without becoming disengaged, and she laughed. We pumped and wrapped ourselves
around each other until I forgot there were two of us.

Back on the couch, she said, "*Finalement*, one and one make one."

"That's my line," I said.

"I was reading your mind."

"I guess it's a little too legible, isn't it?"

"Around us the city is burning, and here we are fiddling."

I was elated, helpless, guilty. Pammy put her head on my chest and
breathed easily. How I envied, treasured, that breathing. I couldn't
think yet, but when I did I was thinking how could two people, not
insensitive to their surroundings, have seen the terror, violence and
pain of this day and then combine with passion so complete they were
transformed into a new being with its own will and urgency and force?

"It happened in the war like this, too," she said, and as I exhaled she quickly amended. "I mean not like *this* this, my Owen, but an elation of survival. You have been through a day when you feared, you expected really, to die and then you didn't die, someone else died instead, like a sacrifice, and when the sun goes down you're all of a sudden more alive, alert, and awake to the possibilities than you've ever been. Whether you're sharing an apple stolen from an officer, a dark joke or a bed almost doesn't matter. You're connecting again with life, with the fact you didn't die."

"We should be with the wounded, or at least I should," I said.

"There's not much we can do. In France when I was at the blood bank, I knew what I was supposed to do, but there's not that need here. The hospitals have the help they want, and not so many people are wounded as in war, in their bodies anyway."

"I remember the blood bank, your mention of it. That must have been gruesome."

"Less gruesome than San Francisco, actually. The poor damaged boys would be carried into our field hospital, gaping wounds, eyes full of fright, legs, arms and flesh torn, and we'd reassure them as much as possible while we transfused them, then we'd send them to real hospitals in the rear. A girl who worked with me kissed them all goodbye as we packed them off to safer places, so I started doing that too, usually a mother's kiss on the forehead. They seemed to like that. San Francisco is worse in a way because even though it's like a war only one side has an army."

"It's more serious now than when I was here a few weeks ago. The pickets then seemed to be letting off steam, and the owners were responding with violence but also jockeying for position. Now it's war, civil war, class war, I don't know."

"No one would make a movie of this," she said, "because the strikers would be heroes, the owners bad guys like the stripe suit in the lobby who wanted more workers killed. Any film would be too Red. The day can't be shown to anyone who wasn't here."

This lighted moment was a release for me after the day of terror, after so much longing for her. Yet I thought or hoped it was a release for her too, revisiting the front to discharge it forever, where French boys, and then English ones, had been borne to her with blown off limbs, peeled away faces, geysering forth their life's fluid as fast as she could replace it with transfusion.

We went to bed naturally, unspokenly, without my saying I wanted to spend the night in her room, without her inviting me. Without my willing it to happen, the circumference of my perception compressed to the room I was in. The only thing in my universe, I was thinking, is what Palmyra Millevoix and I together are, what we do, make, murmur, have. Nothing is between us, neither space nor time. Outside the world is falling apart. Inside, my world has shrunk to a point, a dot, where I have no thoughts or opinions or feelings beyond the sensation of light, and lightness.

This began a weekend I'll remember after I'm dead. We made love again, and again, and somewhere fell asleep. We were beyond meaning, having entered the realm of being. I dreamed I was where I was.

In the morning I was more eager than ever, a terrible thirst beginning at last to be slaked. Yet it was Pammy who awoke to pounce on me, throbbing gaily, avidly, ardently with her thighs. She made cloudy sighs three or four times. She sank down on me. "Oh my," she finally said.

"I'm trying hard not to say I love you," I said.

"Keep trying," she said, and when I looked forlorn, she added, "But so am I." She gave a little laugh. "How many people, the world over, are, you know, unionizing at any one time?"

That struck me as a somewhat impersonal way of putting it. Were we, then, part of the labor movement? But then what struck me much harder was the recollection of the dream in which she had asked me this same question, only she'd said fucking instead of unionizing. I became dizzy with the thought that I was now living my dream.

We made some absurd calculations, national habits and frequency of sex, where it was night and where day, and where in between so people were waking up or not yet asleep. Deductions for night watchmen and workers on the lobster shift. The total was close to one hundred and fifty million who might be unionizing. "Then we're not so special," Pammy said, "since at any given moment oceans of people are doing this."

Oceans! The same word she had used in my dream. Oceans of fucking couples.

"Uh huh," I said as casually as possible, but what I was thinking was, ah, at long last part of the ocean.

"A first kiss lasts forever, doesn't it?" she said. "Would you go so far as to say I'm really good in bed?"

Not wanting her to know how skimpy were my possibilities for comparison, I said, "If you insist, I guess I might admit that."

"I'm spirited, cheerful, responsive, brisk, varied, and humorous."

"I'm passionate," I said, "and that's all I can claim."

"We're working on that."

I got up first while she hugged the pillow where I'd lain and closed her eyes.

The question of desire and desirability, which men jumble so enthusiastically, seized me. It is the way of most female stars that their desirability runs ahead of their desire. They look like they want you, are schooled to look that way, when most of the time they want to be left alone or to read a book or check their nail polish or play with their cat or curl up with a warm, but not hot and writhing, body. In this charged moment, I was the beneficiary of a lover whose desire equaled her desirability. Or appeared to.

I noticed now, for the first time, Pammy's imperfections. She had a little notch at the top of her left ear, one eyebrow was lower than the other, her jaw—no getting around it—was too leonine. A tiny mole beneath her chin could be called a beauty mark, but it could also be called a flaw. I gazed at her and understood that in another woman to whom I'd made love, these observations could be the start of my stepping off the boat. How had I not seen these defects before, either when I sat next to her in her dressing room at the studio or at dinner, or when she swam in her pool, or on any of the limited, prized occasions when I'd been in her presence? Or, for God's sake, when her face was twenty feet high in a close-up on the screen? Where were her ear, her overhanging upper lip, the little mark between her eyes then? Makeup, a great cameraman, my own blindness? Yet no one else, no executive or reviewer or reporter, had ever made a critical observation about her face that I knew of. Had she bewitched us all?

And—you will have guessed—I loved her more for these imperfections, if that's what they were.

My eye and my heart pitched their own battle. My eye said it admired her the most and was the most discerning; my heart argued that it was the center and source of all feeling, and my eye would simply have to be quiet and follow my heart's lead. To which my eye said you'd know nothing if I didn't show all this to you. With that the two organs made peace, the one supplying sight, the other vision. I wished only for more flaws, anything to make the world think less of her so I could have her entirely to myself.

When, a little later, she came out of the shower, a towel around her hair and another sheathing her body, her face could have been her daughter's, at most that of an older sister of Millie's. She was still wet, girlish, smooth-cheeked, with unjaded sparkling eyes, curious. All there was was in front of her, of us.

I looked at her and turned away. I felt fright and hope. What about our predicament in San Francisco? She could be a target, or even I might be. Beyond that, what if I was just a fling for La Millevoix? That was something to be afraid of more than getting shot at the strike. But then hope—this is the beginning of the love of my life—filled me like a deep breath. My brain refused to let me relax.

She sang to me. A sad song relieved with a little folky cheer. It had been turned down by her publishers as well as the studio for a kind of archaism—hymnal affectation her recording company called it—and her dip into incest. They refused to let her record it and wouldn't even allow it to be released as sheet music. But she sang it to me.

> When I was young, so young and green
> I lost my loves ere I was weaned,
> My Pa to war, my Mum to drink,
> My brother shut up in the county clink.
>
> *(and the refrain:)*
> > All my life
> > I've seen strife

Strife and tears
Through all the years.

An uncle made his ward and then
Made me his woman when I was four and ten,
Four and ten no matter when,
I flew away from other men.

(the refrain again)

But then at length of twenty seasons
One love came who gave me reasons
To trust again, to soar aloft
On caresses and kisses that are so soft.

Now at last I've finally found
The love that makes my world go 'round.
With a child of joy we soon are blessed,
We give thanks for our treasure, for our gentle guest.

(a changed refrain:)

All my life
No more strife,
Strife and tears
Disappear from our years.

I had just a flyspeck of enough sense not to ask if there was anything autobiographical in what she had sung to me. A maudlin version of "Born Blue."

Pammy received a message that Harry Bridges hoped she could appear at a rally Saturday and go to church on Sunday with Howard Sperry's widow. The memorial parade for the two dead men, Sperry and Nick Bordoise, would be Monday morning. San Francisco was buzzing with talk that the port was indeed open—like an open wound, Pammy said. There were stirrings that the united labor movement was planning a general strike to shut down not merely the waterfront but the entire city.

What mattered to me was that except for Pammy's brief services to the union and a couple of excursions I took with Mike Quin to deliver food to the longshoremen, she and I were left to ourselves. Quin scoffed at me, "If you can't get a screen story out of what's taken place here you can't count your fingers." I told him politics is death in Hollywood movies. "So it's a love story between a striker and the daughter of a big shipowner. Romeo and Juliet still sells, no?" I said I'd already tried something like that. I did not add that it was a different love story that utterly consumed me.

It was not that I forgot the seriousness of the moment outside Pammy and me. I continued to have blasts of conscience all weekend at the pleasure I was taking while the city and the longshoremen suffered. My own turbulence, though, was that of selfish passion, unaccustomed passion that turned me into a fountain.

When I took food to the union men, I was surprised to see they were in a moment of what I can only recall as revolutionary joy. A sufficiently large number of them were galvanized by the shape their lives had been given not only by their own cause but also by the opposition itself. Even as they mourned the two dead men they were gaining force. I had no place among them. When I took a basket of food and supplies to Julia Bordoise, who lived in a rundown apartment, the widow was surrounded by her friends and neighbors. She was weeping softly, and two women had their arms around her. I left almost immediately, an unbidden outsider. When Pammy returned from the small missions the union leadership asked of her, she said anything happening in terms of negotiating or planning was happening very privately. "Anger is there," she said, "but profound exhilaration is also there. Everyone now knows his part."

At Mike Quin's request, we had tea with Howard Pease, who had shipped out himself before he wrote novels for boys about the nautical adventures of his most famous character, Tod Moran. He was with the strikers all the way. "Greed is the only word in the shipowners' dictionary," he said.

With Chinatown just down the hill from the Fairmont, we made a foray to nibble and look, and then, spotting a naked woman and man carved in ivory, coupling, made an about-face to the hotel. "Feral creatures, we come out of our hole and blink, then quickly scamper back to unionize," Pammy said as we were peeling off clothes before we'd even reached her suite. Kneeling, she began her ministrations while, with a free hand, she swung the door closed. We went to the aquarium, where the sea creatures in their form and motion appeared to me as wondrously diverse reproductive organs. Zipping back to the Fairmont where, with her hand on the back of my neck she guided me to the discovery of her moisture.

In sunglasses and a scarf that hid her head and chin, Pammy ventured into the city almost as disguised as a woman of Arabia, unrecognized as we climbed Filbert Street to Telegraph Hill and Coit Tower, poking skywards in the shape of a firehose nozzle. "*Quelle érection*," Pammy said, smiling, and in those green days of mine it was easy for me to smile back. Artists were finishing the politically charged murals so controversial that parts of them were painted over before the public was allowed inside. A bribe to a guard let us see the Rivera-like socialist realism scenes. A meat-packing plant, factory workers, a desperate man with a pistol holding up a blue-blood, a lunch counter as sad as a soup kitchen, a newsstand featuring *The Daily Worker*. "Could this country have as much class hatred as Europe?" I asked Pammy. "I think no," she said, "not while the bosses have so many nuggets to throw the workers, which is why the word 'peasant' is such an insult here."

Fisherman's Wharf, with crab pots stacked by the hundreds and sidewalk vendors peddling their oysters and marinating ceviche, appeared to be a bridge to the nineteenth century. Puffing steam tugs stood off the Wharf looking like hippos, and a thousand fantail fishing boats bobbed in the harbor along with a few sampans the Chinese fishermen used. As we stood by the bow of a gillnetter that had come in with salmon, I handed my camera to a sailor who was happy to oblige for a dollar. Though he said she could almost be a movie star, he did not recognize Pammy. I looked at that photograph the other day and didn't recognize either of us.

The bridge to the twentieth century was just being built. The tower on the northern, or Marin County, side had already gone up. Pammy called it a mighty beacon beckoning us toward the future unknowable;

she made the two words into a subjunctive speculation. The Golden Gate waterway was still unspanned, the crossing road itself a phantom, a figment of design. Construction on our side yielded only a giant column of concrete anchorage reaching deep for its relentless grip into the underwater floor of the southern shore of San Francisco Bay. The tower across the way in Marin proclaimed recovery; the lonely girders and half-built pylons on our side mumbled exhaustion, illustrating the Depression's chokehold. This was simply weekend idleness at the southern tower, which was being built second, but to our eyes the site signified the struggle between rebirth and decay. We gazed, wondered, didn't stay long.

At fine restaurants we sat in darkened corners, Pammy in a brimmed hat that shielded her features. Yet when we had lunch one day in a sunny cafeteria off Union Square, she was perfectly relaxed. Several poor people were getting free meals, and Pammy had me slip the manager fifty dollars. "Hard times make hard folks," he said, "but I'll feed a few dozen more thanks to you and your friend." For just a moment he glanced suspiciously over at Pammy, who had stayed seated. As we ate our custard, Pammy said Millie would love San Francisco, especially Coit Tower and this cafeteria with its bright paintings of waterscapes surrounding the city. She would bring her here soon; she said she'd never been away from Millie for more than two days.

Pammy was in full disguise, her face veiled, as she placed a wreath of red roses at the sidewalk shrine to the martyred union members in front of ILA headquarters. "POLICE MURDER" was chalked in large letters on each side of smaller lettering that read, "2 Union Men Killed—Shot in the Back." The memorial was ringed with flowers and guarded by longshoremen, one of whom was Widdelstaedt, the would-be executioner of my earlier visit to the strike. I looked at him in fear and had to stifle an impulse to run from this tattooed beef with eyes and a long knife who had tried to kill me. He remembered my face though he couldn't place it and said, "How ya doin' pal? Thanks for you and the missus payin' tribute. Good to see ya again."

Lighting a candle for her parents in the Episcopal Grace Cathedral on Nob Hill, Pammy was recognized for the only time. A fashionably dressed woman in a dark gauzy veil of her own said to Pammy in a

French accent, "*Alors, Mam'sell Millevoix*, I heard you were in town. Please be careful. Both sides are wrong, as always."

Our talk spun through the universe. Doctors in Europe and the United States. The moral superiority and insufferability of vegetarians. Politics, of course: what you could have in a socialist state, what you'd give up. Hitler, Stalin, FDR. How Millie called the Nazis Nasties. The progress of the strike. Longshoremen were lucky to see $40 a week; Pammy made over a hundred times more. What kind of society organizes itself that way? Love: the love of the ethereal, such as God or an idea, love in friendship, love between a man and woman, between women, between men, the love of parent for child, the love of money and power and whether that was a base form of love, not really love at all, or simply, in the Freudian sense, a substitution for other forms of love that had been withheld. Millie: should she be encouraged to go into show business as she already wanted to do, or forbidden and made to go straight? George Sand, Fitzgerald, Dos Passos, Hemingway, Huxley, Gertrude Stein, Katherine Mansfield. She'd had dinner with Malraux in Paris; he'd invited her to go to Indochina but she hadn't. Writing versus painting versus composing. Everything but Mossy and the future; both of us stayed scrupulously away from those twin subjects that were both unrelated and related.

The night before the memorial parade, Sunday night, was sad in our unspoken knowledge we'd soon not be alone. Our lovemaking was careful, in some way valedictory. I didn't fall asleep though I heard her breathing softly, like a child. Once, also like a child, she whimpered. She stopped before I could put my arm around her.

In the morning at ILA headquarters, a long line of men and women, many with small children clinging to them, filed past the two coffins, both open. Many made the sign of the cross as they looked at the waxy, still faces in the coffins. Pammy did not. Her bearing was stately, public as she nodded at the figures in the caskets, her private communion with the labor martyrs. I felt like her consort. As they passed their dead comrades, a number of the ILA men raised one fist in a workers' salute. Many left small bunches of flowers. Uniformed sentries guarded the coffin of Howard Sperry, who was a World War veteran.

The coffins were carried down the stairway and placed on flatbed trucks. Three additional trucks followed bearing flowers. The dockworkers' own union band began the measured cadence of Beethoven's funeral march, not so much played as moaned.

As we formed up for the march, Mike Quin accompanied Pammy and me. He was turning the pages of the *San Francisco Examiner*, the Hearst paper that union members had more or less been forbidden to read. Quin was snickering. "Look at this, the dame's on some other planet, isn't she?" he said as he showed us what he meant. The long arm of Hollywood had reached up the coast. Louella Parsons was clucking at Pammy for her presence in San Francisco as much as for her absence from Jubilee: "The film colony's small but arrogant contingent at the Bay Area's criminal dock strike ought to have faces as red as their politics. Unfortunately, they're defiant and ungrateful for the fact they live in the greatest country in the world. Miss Millevoix—or should I call her Comrade?—remains on suspension at Jubilee, which is right where she belongs. Kudos to the execs on the Zangwill lot." Pammy's face was stony. "Kudos wrapped in dollars," she said.

I have never to this day seen anything like the funeral procession. The trucks moved slowly out onto San Francisco's main artery, Market Street. Forty thousand marchers followed. People moved in such dignified order it was as if lava were flowing and the wide boulevard were a canyon. No shouting, no horns blaring. We were in the presence of a booming silence. Many more thousands of spectators lined the sidewalks, but they weren't making noise either. "In life," Mike Quin murmured to Pammy and me, "Nick Bordoise and Howard Sperry wouldn't have been given a second glance on the sidewalks of San Francisco, but in death they're borne the length of Market Street in a reverent procession that would have been inconceivable to either of them." Then Mike himself was silent. I began to hear, as the march progressed, a pitch arising from the throng that reminded me of a wordless hymn, without octave or tone, that was almost like humming.

"Now we know the sound," Mike Quin said, "of one hand clapping."

Pammy had been asked if she'd like to ride with the widows. She said this was their day, not hers, and she'd stay with the union members. Few marchers paid any attention to her. When I asked Quin about the absence of police and the regulation of the many thousands on the street and sidewalks by a few hundred dockworkers with no experience in traffic or crowd control, he looked at me as if I were a child. "Skinny," he said, reverting to my earlier nickname, "the police aren't here because the longshoremen are policing themselves and everyone else. If any police were around you'd need a whole other police force to police *them*. Labor is burying its own today."

We strode up Market Street a few more blocks before Quin told me a general strike was in the air. Bridges and the other union leaders planned a strike that would immobilize all workers and businesses in San Francisco and Oakland. I thought this was a crazy, quixotic idea that had no chance. Couldn't these fools see defeat when it was right in front of them, lying in the caskets they marched behind? The port would now be open to all ships; the longshoremen and seamen would have no choice but to return to work or lose their jobs for good. Unemployed strong-bodied men were about two dollars a dozen and easy to find in the midst of the Depression. "No," Mike Quin said, "this parade is an entreaty, silently delivered, silently received. The long quiet march confirms the solid strength of the unions. The labor movement is resolved now, and resolve leads to resolution." He walked on ahead to speak to an officer of the Teamsters.

By the time Pammy and I returned to the Fairmont Hotel, the incongruity of its juxtaposition with where we had been and what we had seen left both of us almost without air in our lungs. We sat in her suite with our thoughts, saying nothing, looking at each other, at the furniture, out the window. Pammy closed her eyes and leaned back in her chair. Whatever she was thinking, I was thinking about loss. The strike was lost. With the National Guard patrolling the waterfront alongside the police, it was clear the shipowners and dockowners—capital, in other words—had won. The woman across from me, the woman I loved, would go back to her own life the next day as a mother and a star, and she'd be lost to me as well. Absent without leave, I'd probably lose my job too. After a long while, still wordless, I got up and went out. I started to take a walk and then realized I had no energy, so I sat in the park a block from the Fairmont. I don't know how long I stayed there, ruminating on the bleakness of my future, and San Francisco's, and the labor movement's, when a woman in black, so shrouded and veiled she had to have come from a funeral herself if she wasn't hiding from the law, sat down beside me. Now what? I thought with annoyance.

"Why did you leave me?" a voice came from under the veil. "You left me all alone up there. Please don't leave me."

"Jesus," I said, turning to the veil, "I had no idea it was you."

"Let's have dinner in the room tonight," she said.

We walked a little, aimlessly following California Street a few blocks, then turning back to the hotel. For the first time, I felt I could have held Pammy's hand in public, but I did not. I ordered room service, and each of us picked at our food.

She fell asleep before I did. Though I scarcely knew it at the time, our lovemaking was that of an old married couple—this is what she wants, this is what he likes—each of us pleasing the other, then ourselves. I watched her sleep with the moon both lighting and shadowing her features. It was impossible to stop my mind from racing ahead. How would being back home change what was going on here? Would she still want me at all? What actually *was* going on here? Could I believe in it? How would we get back to Los Angeles in the morning? She whimpered once, as she had the night before, and I wanted to hold her and didn't want to wake her, so I did nothing. She whimpered again but stopped immediately. I saw the sky begin to lighten before I fell asleep. I dreamed of steak tartare, which gave me indigestion. When I finally awoke she was gone.

The note was on Fairmont stationery. Where had she found the six lilies it was clipped to? "I'm off, Sweet O," the note read. "If you'll pardon my quoting myself, I still can't find the good in goodbye. You are to me what spring showers are to the hungry earth, bringing up blossoms in all kinds of unplanned spaces. Be patient, my cherished. Love all ways, Your PM."

Nils Maynard, upstaging Largo Buchalter this time, had sent his plane for her. She was probably back in Los Angeles before I'd even had breakfast. As I left the city myself, the headline on the newspaper at the train station said, "Red Army Marches on San Francisco."

33

Bumblebee

Pammy was welcomed home venomously in Louella's column: "Good for Mossy Zangwill over at Jubilee if he refuses to reinstate the oh-so-holier-than-thou Palmyra Millevoix who is importing not merely her European elegance but also an alien ideology. Radio stations should stop playing her songs the way Zangwill, once her champion and then some, has suspended her from the picture she walked out on. My spies tell me he is threatening to cancel her contract. If she doesn't mend her ways, and fast, this non-citizen should be deported, and faster."

But Louella didn't run Jubilee. To my surprise Pammy plunged back into work at the studio, where Mossy immediately voided her suspension. He needed her; it was that simple. When I asked her why she was returning to the studio she said, "What good am I on the outside?" To the studio it was as if she'd had a fever that had receded and her temperature was now normal again. Mossy assured Pammy that the Mexican seamstresses had been given fifty percent raises with time and a half for overtime; he claimed he hadn't known how little they were being paid before.

Nils Maynard had replaced Wick Fairless, the director Pammy hated, with Nils Maynard, and a quick rewrite of the script had given her a far stronger character. *Love Is for Strangers* now had Pammy leaving her unfaithful husband and subsequently taking up with a horse breeder, who in the earlier version had been only a friend of the philandering husband's. Pammy's character had a baby by the ne'er-do-well husband, causing her mother, played by Ethel Barrymore at her haughtiest, to refuse to see her grandchild and break off all contact with her daughter. Things went swiftly on the set, Pammy's favorite, Stage Eight, which, she maintained, had the best acoustics on the lot.

I myself was put on the rewrite of a dud called *Firebrand*, their way of letting me know I was on probation. A young couple has bought their first home—the husband a fireman, the wife a bookkeeper in a clothing store. You know the rest: one evening the owner of the store, facing bankruptcy and assuming everyone has gone home, starts a fire to burn the store down so he can collect the insurance. The conscientious wife is still in the store going over sales records. By the time the fire trucks arrive the place is ablaze. The fireman fails to save his wife but does find evidence of arson. Brokenhearted, he tells the police who take forever to trace the fire to the owner. Meanwhile, the insurance company is tracking down all suspects and their investigator is a woman who, of course, falls for the fireman in his grief. Makes friends with his two adorable motherless youngsters. Nothing here but soapsuds, yet it was my back-in-the-fold assignment, and my fingers flew at the keys of my Royal, famished crows pecking for corn. The main change I made was to have the woman investigator be the daughter of the guilty store owner, which meant that eventually she'd have to choose between loyalty to her father and to the fireman who wants revenge. I was briskly replaced by the reliably arch Tutor Beedleman who didn't care about the romance but spruced up the plot so that the fireman had a criminal record of his own, a shady past he was trying to escape. And so on.

Besides being the ultimate company towns, Hollywood and Washington have one further attribute in common that keeps everyone in either place from relaxing. They're always trying to figure out what the rest of the country wants. More than anything else, it was the worry about whether his hunches would find audiences that kept Mossy as anti-union as he was. He wanted everyone on the lot to have the same vision he did: lines around the block in Schenectady. That left no time for labor disputes.

But Pammy had taken her secular vows, and San Francisco only confirmed them. Back at work on a picture, she hadn't forgotten the principles behind the dockworkers' strike. Anyone who was not an owner was by definition being exploited, from which it followed that owners were exploiters. Even if Mossy didn't entirely own Jubilee because of his need for the New York bankers, he was New York's West Coast proconsul and held a major portion of Jubilee stock. What Pammy wanted was to make Jubilee Pictures a model for the rest of Hollywood, a studio fully organized by unions.

She was hardly alone. Each craft had representatives who wanted the picture business to be part of the labor movement. Yeatsman a bit reluctantly led the writers—with the Screen Writers Guild still in its infancy, Mossy predictably supported their company union rivals, the Screen Playwrights. For all his bluster, Largo Buchalter was driving the interested directors. Set designers and decorators were restless. Cameramen were grumbling about overtime. Pammy was simply the most visible among the actors favoring a union. Like her sister Elise among the decorators, Pammy wanted to get all the crafts together, and after we returned from San Francisco she asked me who she ought to speak to among the carpenters.

To my eternal shame, I told her I'd heard that Hop Daigle, the jelly-eyed carpenter, had emerged as the leader among the set builders. She and Yeatsman had a private meeting with Daigle off the lot. They decided to hold a rally outside the Jubilee gates and announce plans to organize the studio. Then they had a second meeting with craft representatives—film editors, sound engineers, makeup artists, and stuntmen.

The day after the second meeting Willie Bioff, the labor fixer—racketeer, go-between, shakedown artist, they all fit—came to see Mossy again with, of course, Hop Daigle. I had no idea. When Elena Frye told me about this later, I knew I shouldered lasting responsibility and would never know how much. Daigle, whose jelly eye had turned whitish according to Elena, told them of the plans to organize Jubilee as essentially a union shop with many guilds representing the various crafts. Rumblings at the other studios were similar. It was primitive, hardly a threat to capitalist enterprise, nothing like the broad-based unions that were out to organize entire industries. But it was enough to make the Hollywood titans first shudder and then become furious. The rumor at Fox was that Darryl Zanuck threatened to mount a machine gun on a parapet above the studio gates and have anyone mowed down who marched outside with a picket sign.

Up north, Harry Bridges's creed was to find out what the rank and file, as he always called longshoremen, wanted to do and then help them do it, from the bottom up. Willie Bioff, as he'd done when Jubilee's sets were being trashed, would find out how much he could extort from the bosses, then pass as little of the boodle as possible to the workers, from the top down, keeping the rest for himself and his mob handlers. I doubt Bridges and Bioff ever met, but if they did they couldn't have understood one another's language. Elena Frye told me that Willie Bioff, smiling and joking throughout the meeting, had started at a hundred thousand dollars with Mossy, promising labor peace if his price was met, and had settled for thirty-five. Hop Daigle nodded his agreement, the jellied eye gone milky for the occasion, and Mossy quickly looked away.

The night before the rally at Jubilee I went to dinner at Pammy's house. Millie at last had a real dog, which she'd delightedly named Cordell. Cordell was beloved in different ways by each of his mistresses—Millie, Costanza, and Pammy. Millie asked me if I could write a screamplay about her and Cordell. The puppy, an Airedale terrier, could still barely stand so Millie carried it. She'd taken the name from her mother's jingle on the secretary of state, who the seven-year-old Millie hadn't heard of. She seldom sang it the same way twice. "I'm in love with Cordell Hull, He treats me nice though he's awfully dull." Sometimes, trying out a new word, Millie would do the second line as "But I have to admit he's indubitably dull," and in an irritable mood she'd sing, "When he's mean I want to bash his skull." Cordell the dog, unlike his stolid namesake, was as lively and jumpy as his puppy legs would let him be, but when he was swooped into Millie's arms he subsided into a quick cuddle.

Pammy and I scarcely had eye contact at dinner. In the way a precocious child can dominate an occasion, the conversation wound around Millie, Cordell, her school, or something she hoped to do. The three of us chewed our lamb chops in unison, each new subject announced by Millie, and we were not a family.

Before Costanza took her upstairs, Millie asked me for a story. I told her that in my story there would be a fairy godmother and a mean mother. "Oh good," she said, "a really mean mother." I set off, not knowing where I was headed, and had looked away from Millie to her mother when Millie asked me to describe the fairy godmother. "She was so pretty," I said, "that she looked like a sunny morning in a golden meadow. She had gossamer eyebrows below her wide forehead lined with all the thinking she did, and the eyebrows slanted down a little on the sides giving her hazel eyes perhaps a tiny glimmer of sadness, but it was only the sadness that there were too many more children to help than she had time to get to, so whenever she helped a child her eyes became a little less sad. At the tip of her nose her nostrils widened slightly giving her the look of wanting something she didn't quite have, or once had but didn't have anymore."

"A fairy godfather, right?" said Millie. "That's what she wanted." "Maybe," I said, "but maybe it was only she still had so much to do. Her smile was the other thing children always noticed because it was a little one-sided on the left where her lips turned up more than on the right. And again, this was because she hadn't quite helped enough children yet and when she finally finished helping all the children who needed her she was going to have a full smile on both sides of her mouth."

"Uncle Owen, what's gossamer eyebrows?"

"Oh, thin wispy little things, eyebrows you almost couldn't see because they were honey-colored and blended right in with her thoughtful forehead. Anyway, here's what happened—there was a little girl who had the meanest mother in the world." "That's impossible," Millie interrupted, warming to the tale, "my mother is the meanest mother because she won't let me stay up late and she spends too much time at the studio and isn't home for dinner enough and sometimes she stays away almost a week in San Francisco." "Well, okay, that's pretty mean, but this mother was even *named* Meanie. Mrs. Meanie.

The mean thing she did one night was to not let her daughter Lily have dessert, no dessert at all even though Lily had cleaned her plate, Brussels sprouts and bony fish which she hated, but Mrs. Meanie had promised Lily a special treat for dessert if she finished everything on her plate."

"Wait a minute, Lily is her name?" Millie said. "Why not Barbara or Genevieve?"

"She looked a little like you so her name sounds like yours, but she had an even meaner mother. Listen to what Mrs. Meanie did to Lily when Lily thought she was about to get dessert. Mrs. Meanie tied her daughter to a chair in the kitchen while she went and got ice cream, peppermint stick ice cream which was her daughter Lily's favorite."— "It's my favorite too Uncle Owen and you know it!" Millie squealed.— "But it was Lily's favorite and she loved chocolate cake with it, which Mrs. Meanie had baked specially because just the smell of it would drive Lily crazy."

"So she wasn't that mean after all. She gave Lily the dessert?"

"Of course not. Mrs. Meanie brought out the chocolate cake and peppermint stick ice cream and then she, Mrs. Meanie, proceeded to eat it very slowly, spoonful by delicious spoonful, right in front of Lily who was tied up begging for a bite. 'Please, please!' Lily said, 'just one little bite of the cake and ice cream.' But Mrs. Meanie looked at her and said so slowly that the word lasted a long time, 'Noooooooooooo.' Lily cried and was put to bed with no dessert, and that's when the fairy godmother with the gossamer eyebrows and ever so slightly one-sided smile came in her window carrying a huge slice of chocolate cake and four scoops of peppermint ice cream."

"Please," Pammy said, "could we hold it to two?" "No!" Millie said, "I want Lily to have four!" "Yes," I said, "it was four scoops because she had to have extra scoops to make up for all the times her mean mother Mrs. Meanie hadn't allowed her to eat any dessert at all. Her fairy godmother promised she'd be back whenever her mean mother was at her meanest. So Lily went to bed happy and slept soundly with the most disobediently adventurous dreams."

Millie gave me a first hug. I glimpsed the future.

When she had kissed Millie good night, Pammy told me about

Mossy's promise that the studio seamstresses would get fifty percent raises. "I congratulated one of them who brought a gown to my bungalow. She said the raises were twenty percent and not a penny extra for overtime. *Bâtard!* Power, power, power is all he craves! Everything else, every*one* else, is just useful. Power, that's the woman he loves."

Her face was like iron. I wondered if you could take a picture of such a face, of that mood.

I had never seen her so beautiful as when she gazed at Millie, nor so afflicted as when she described Mossy and the seamstresses. In San Francisco she had been in a rage at injustice; now the grievance was intensified by betrayal and lying. And by its source. But then the anger left her as suddenly as it had arrived and she looked, simply and guilelessly, as Mike Quin had described the marchers on Market Street, resolved. "It's done," she said, "or will be shortly."

It was time for me to go, past time. "Good luck tomorrow," I said, and she said I should come to her bungalow after the rally so we could make plans for the weekend. "You can tell by the hug from my little seductress that she wants you at Red Woods too, okay?" As I was leaving, kissless, almost out the door, she said, "Now give me, sweet Ownie, the TK." "TK?" I asked. "You know," she said, "the tooth kiss we accidentally had in my bungalow at the studio that first day."

First day? I thought driving home. She remembered. Touching. Yet how many men has Millie called Uncle? Not only wouldn't I ask, I didn't want to know. I'm here now, I told myself, and I'll stay here inside this enchantment until the weekend or the end of time, whichever comes first.

What came first was the end of time.

Word was passed at the studio that there would be an important labor rally at noon just outside the Jubilee lot. Someone had called the press, and since a movie star was promised, a couple of newsreel cameras were there. The carpenters quickly set up a makeshift platform—nothing more than a few sawhorses with some two-by-fours and sheets of plywood—on the public property side of the imposing wrought-iron studio gates that sported the J U B I L E E lettering sculpted into the iron. The gates were flanked by tall plaster pillars that curved above the wrought iron to form an arch. *L'Arc de Triomphe du Jubilee*, the writers called it when they were sure no spy was in earshot. The sound men had supplied an old-fashioned microphone, giving the occasion the look of a candidate's campaign during the World War. Elise Millevoix had her set decorators hide the sawhorses with patriotic bunting and, because it was a blazing day, they added a little canopy over the platform.

I've never been a good crowd estimator but it was busy out there. By the time the interested union advocates showed up, a group enlarged by Jubilee employees who didn't want commissary food and were filing out to local bars and burger joints, there must have been more than two hundred of us. A number of passersby attached themselves to the gathering. I stood near the front, as expectant as everyone else.

The rally began with a carpenter—not Hop Daigle, who was well back in the crowd—saying a crook was trying to buy off his men but it wasn't going to work this time. The next speaker, a sound engineer, said the primitive microphone had been used in a movie about Teddy Roosevelt and that TR would be proud of citizens standing up for their rights. He was heckled by a young man who looked like the body builders at Muscle Beach. This fellow, surrounded by friends who looked just like him—tan, brawny, half-brained—shouted that the speaker ought to shut up and be grateful he had a job in hard times. Yeatsman followed the sound engineer, and now the Muscle Beach contingent became rowdy and disruptive. Yeatsman tried to say that all he wanted was free speech, free exchanges of opinion, and the free rights of working people to assemble and decide what to charge for their labor. By the time he said that this was happening not only all over the country but around the world, the rowdies were drowning him out. "Ladies and gentlemen," he shouted, "we have some stooges here who have been sent to prevent us from having a peaceful meeting." When the newsreel cameras swung around to focus on the Muscle Beach guys, they quieted, and Yeatsman introduced Pammy.

Still in the evening gown she was wearing on the set that day, Pammy was helped onto the platform by Nils Maynard, who had come over from Stage Eight with her. "When I'm in front of a crowd," she began, "most of the time I prefer to sing."

"Please sing!" yelled a number of Jubilee people who knew and loved her. "Sing, Pammy, sing!" Most studio employees are ardent fans well before they're aware of labor complaints, even their own.

Pammy smiled her biggest smile, with even the side of her mouth that usually didn't grin widening in gratitude and, I thought, joy. "Yes sure, why don't we all sing every problem away," she said, mocking her trademark invitation. She shook her head. "I wish I could just sing, but today all of us have to declare very clearly something very important and serious to our great studio."

But the Muscle Beach rowdies took up the chant: "Sing, Pammy, sing!" Panning around to them, the newsreel cameras again silenced them.

"Some of us," Pammy went on, raising her voice, "are paid very well for what we do. That's undeniable. But many, many more are paid next to nothing. The seamstresses who sewed the evening gown I'm wearing in a movie that millions of people will pay to see, we hope"—she didn't pause for the laugh she got—"those women work up to twelve hours a day and earn less than thirty dollars a week. If we care about our work we can also care about our fellow workers and our mutual need to win the right to negotiate the terms of our employment. We all want to make pictures, and we want to make them for Jubilee. The time has come for us to raise our voices together, not in song but nevertheless in unison, to support union bargaining rights. These are the rights of all labor. What we must do now—"

She paused, and I saw her raise her arm to flick an insect off her forehead. I thought she was groping for the right word. But then I saw the insect was large enough to be a bee, and I hoped she hadn't been stung. The next instant I saw it must have been a bumblebee, huge. The instant after that she was down flat on the platform. I hadn't heard the shot.

By the time I leaped onto the platform Nils and Yeatsman, Elise and others were huddled over her. Someone produced a white hand towel, and the little jet from Pammy's forehead stained the towel blood bright, bright as life. Her eyes were open, staring at nothing, and after a few gasps, gulps for air, there was only her face, breathless, voiceless. Nils told me later I yelled at him, "Make it unhappen you son of a bitch, you're a fucking magician!" But all I remember is seeing what I saw and wanting a film to be running in reverse—the blood pouring back down into her forehead, the rest of us springing backward off the platform landing on our feet, her standing up as if pulled on puppet strings, the bumblebee flying away, and her finishing her sentence—"What we must do now is organize and confront Jubilee where the studio can feel it, in the cash register."

I see this again and again, a strip of film running backward to make the scene, the unthinkable, not occur. Go on, Nils, you sleight-of-hander, do it, transfuse her, you can do anything, you bleed for her, you're a bleeder anyway and a survivor, go ahead, you bleed. Please. All of us on the platform huddle in a circle forming an umbrella over her. We pull our heads away, no longer covering, smothering her, and she unfalls—she rises—as we resume our spots in the audience. Sometimes the bee flies off from that curved marvel of a forehead that was always a little worried, and she finishes speaking, in Swedish because it's English going through the Moviola backward, with its Scandinavian glottals and oomphs. Then she sings and I hear the song forward, "Oh, you can't scare me I'm stickin' to the union, I'm stickin' to the union … till the day I."

A blur. The screaming, men and women running, studio guards taking charge or trying to, pandemonium. Elise and I staying on the platform on either side of her. Inert Pammy. Sirens.

By the time the police arrived there was nothing much for them to do. They asked questions but there were no answers. Elise was about to go off in the ambulance with Pammy when my mind began to function. I said I'd call the house. Elise said Millie had to be gotten away before the hordes arrived. "We'll go see her later together," Elise said.

Inside the studio I found a phone. When Costanza answered at Pammy's house I was wheezing so hard I couldn't catch my breath enough to push out words. She hung up, and I fainted. I must have made a loud noise as I dropped because the next thing I knew Comfort O'Hollie was bringing me around with smelling salts. I heard her say to someone, "Our Pammy has fallen?" That brought me back to what was going on, and I realized I must have run to the writers building. "You've only been seconds out, poor dear," Comfort said. "Can you speak?"

I could. The wheezing had stopped. Comfort held my trembling hand as I called the house again. I told Costanza what had happened. Before she had a chance to moan I said she had to take Millie out of there, out to Red Woods where she'd have to play games with her and read and listen to records until I could get there with Elise. I said I'd send a studio car to take them. Costanza said she couldn't tell Millie, and I said she shouldn't try. All she had to do was keep Millie away from outsiders, from newspapers and above all from radios. "Hide every radio in the house at Red Woods. Tell Millie her mother is on location."

The Jubilee lot was in an uproar. Men and women who barely knew one another wept in each other's arms. Someone held a spontaneous prayer service in the commissary. The police demanded that no one leave Jubilee until they completed their preliminary investigation. They questioned everyone, and everyone knew nothing.

Theories shot around like electrons. A plainclothesman from the Los Angeles Police Department's infamous Red Squad had done it. A rejected lover had hired a hit man. The twin to that story was a jealous actress had wanted a bigger star eliminated. Willie Bioff could have set it up with the Muscle Beach hecklers because he had promised Mossy labor peace. Hop Daigle fired the shot, aiming with his one good eye, because he had been paid off by Willie Bioff to keep the Jubilee lot quiet. The Reds themselves had done it because they were hungry for a movie star martyr. Someone even said Mossy had told a prop man to fire a blank at Pammy just to scare everyone away from joining unions, but the prop man accidentally had a real bullet in his pistol.

Everyone had to wait at the studio while police swarmed into every office, every cutting room, all over the sound stages. Filming stopped. No one did any work.

Late afternoon, Mossy called me in. Elena told me not to comment on his appearance. I was about to learn the short trip from tragedy to farce. Mossy had a shiner, his right eye almost closed. Yeatsman told me later Mossy had been caught the evening before, while I was having dinner with Pammy and Millie. He was caught not by Esther Leah but by an angry husband, the powerful entertainment lawyer Edgar Globe, who had come home unexpectedly from Chicago to find Mossy with his wife, Francesca. Francesca yelled, "Oh Jesus" when she heard her husband come in the front door. Mossy grabbed his pants and ran for the back stairs in the Globes' Bel Air mansion. Like the cunning litigator he was, Edgar Globe anticipated his opponent's next move and forsook his front staircase, intercepting Mossy halfway down the back stairs.

"Edgar, you're my lawyer," Mossy had said, as if that squared things, was ethically exculpatory.

"Not anymore, shithead," Globe said, his fist crashing into Mossy's face.

Now Mossy gave me his visor squint, his black eye looking like a penlight trying to shine out of a dark tunnel. "I need you to do something for me," he said.

I was completely shattered, didn't know how to respond or if I could do anything for anyone. "I'm very upset," I said.

"Sure you are. We all are, numb and crazy at the same time. I'm heartbroken." He stopped and shook his head. "I'm a lot sadder than you may know, much sadder than I can show around here. But don't stay gloomy. When you write it, kid, which one day you will, she don't die."

"What are you talking about? She's dead, gone."

"In the picture, she's injured bad, very serious, legs gone maybe, and your hero has to take care of her the rest of her life. She's in a wheelchair, bravely rolling herself in and out of scenes. She can still write her songs, ect ect you get it."

The annoying *ect ect* habit, more than I could take that afternoon, always let a listener know the scene went on and on, you figure it out.

"I wouldn't dream of writing about her," I said.

"I'm telling ya in the picture she can still write her sweet songs, ect ect ect."

"Her song is gone."

"C'maaahn, kid," he said. "So you don't get the girl. You get the memories."

"The hell with you, Mossy. What did you want to see me about?"

He ignored the affront to his authority. "I'm telling you, in the picture she don't die." Mossy used his ungrammatical Bronxian lingo judiciously, in this case to get cozy with me, as if he sensed, or even knew (though I shuddered to think about it) that he and I now and forever shared something of inestimable value.

"Owen," he said, "I'll have to say a few words at the funeral. Today's Thursday and we'll do it here on the lot Saturday. Will you give me some help with this?"

I walked out of his office without bothering to say no.

On Friday I went to the studio but did no work. None of the writers did. I merely wanted to be around people who knew her but were not named Amos Zangwill, and I couldn't bring myself to make the drive out to Red Woods yet. Millie was there with Costanza, who was teaching her how to play the new game of Monopoly. She had the whole rest of her life to be motherless, I rationalized. Mossy ordered that filming continue on all sound stages except for the one where Pammy had been working, which was to be the site of her funeral.

Louella crowed her condescending condolence. "The shooting at Jubilee tragically cut short what should have been a long stellar career for Palmyra Millevoix. She had thrown herself back into her film *Love Is for Strangers* after the misadventure in San Francisco, reportedly inspiring her coworkers by giving her all until the mortal shot was fired. Poor Pammy, she thought she was bigger than the whole Hollywood system, and that was her fatal mistake. We all know what pride goeth before, and it did just that yesterday outside the Jubilee gates. We mourn the loss of her gifts if not her politics. One hates to say there's a moral to this tale, but let's hope the rest of our motion picture family, and we are a family, all stay with our assigned roles."

Under my door at home: MY DEEPEST SYMPATHIES STOP OVERWHELMED BY FURY AT FASCIST RUBOUT OF LOVELIEST PROGRESSIVE SOUL STOP NON ILLIGITAMUS CARBO-

RUNDUM STOP CARRY ON STOP QUIN. Switching to Latin no doubt when Western Union wouldn't let him say *bastards*.

Quick, emergency appointment with Pogo early Saturday before the funeral. Loss, pain, denial, fury, retreat to childhood. From an earlier appointment he already knew about San Francisco—the unexpected fulfillment of my love for Pammy as the waterfront battle raged—and that things had been more distant though still hopeful after my return home. He didn't mind seeing me on a Saturday morning, but he was unusually argumentative. Though he'd read about the horror at the studio gates, I described it anyway. "Did she want to die?" he challenged. "No!" I thundered, offended. "Then why get up in public with so much antagonism in the air, so many threats, right after what happened up north, the ecstasy of violence?"

"Ecstasy" was a strange word to use, I thought, but I let it go. "What happened in San Francisco," I said, "was already violent for a good two months before the police opened fire on the strikers. Courage was needed, and she had enough to give a talk in public." "A defiant talk," he said, "a very political talk in a time of vicious politics, a polarizing talk when the sides are poles apart. A mature adult knows dry leaves need only a tiny spark to set them ablaze." "Okay," I said, "but she didn't want to leave her daughter, her songwriting, even me, dammit, she didn't want to leave me."

He took a deep breath, having stepped away from being my analyst to advocating for the death instinct. "I'm not blaming her," he said, "I blame her killer of course. A terrible crime, an unfathomable loss. I'm telling you only that she may have had feelings of welcome concerning death itself. There is a ripeness that comes to fruit ready to drop off the tree. The song 'Born Blue,' risqué connotations combined with deep melancholy."

"She was working for some kind justice, campaigning for it."

"Yes, but she was also in open rebellion against neglectful parents—the Church, the studio, an unfair political climate, perhaps against the domination of men." It sounded to me as though he was trying to synthesize Marx and Freud; perhaps the endless uncivil war between the followers of each was being waged in Dr. Pogorzelski himself. "I can venture," he said, "that in the unconscious there are no accidents. I'm not telling you she wanted to die, only that what you do now with her death will probably be to re-order its meaning. To think of her murderer, for instance, as trying to deprive you of her. How is her death affecting you?"

"Awful. I feel awful," I said, indignant but also tearful. "I've never felt so besieged by, I don't know, the gods, fate. Abandoned."

"Abandoned? Again ...?"

"Yes, for Christ's sake."

"This is what I mean," he said. "You say she didn't want to die yet you feel abandoned by her. Another interpretation for the flower you dreamed of with the sick petals. Palmyra held the wilted flower as she vanished into the sea. You were already afraid of losing her when you didn't yet even have her. Perhaps in your unconscious she gave herself up for you in order to show you how to count for something, substituted her own death for yours."

"Have it your way." I stopped for a moment as I considered his drift, the concept of sacrifice. I found myself weeping. "But she did not goddamn intend to die," I blurted.

"I'm talking about the possibilities in your unconscious, a place where she has now joined all the dead, especially the prematurely dead."

Dry-eyed, I asked him about the unconscious itself, its meaning.

"What do you mean its meaning?" he said. "You know the unconscious is what we have either schooled ourselves to forget or not yet permitted through the doorway of awareness. Either way, this is repression."

"I know the conscious mind of Palmyra Millevoix doesn't exist any more. It's as dead as the rest of her."

"That's right," he said. "Of course."

"But what about the unconscious?" I asked. "If the unconscious isn't conscious, how do we know it dies too?"

"We don't know where the unconscious goes. Is it merely a function of the conscious mind that we haven't yet been granted access to, or is it a separate entity with its own independent existence? Are we finally dreaming, or are we being dreamed? Next time, Owen, see you next time. So sorry for your loss."

But something made me want to turn the tables on him. "Wait a minute," I said. "You're aggressive today. Her death bothers you. Are you angry yourself?"

"Goddamn right I am," Dr. Pogorzelski said.

Elise Millevoix had insisted that everything on Stage Eight be draped in white for her sister. "Death is not black," she told me. "It's everything bleached, it's the whitest of whiteness." The casket itself, placed on a raised floor of the set where Nils and Pammy had been shooting their picture, was covered in white silk with a blue fleur-de-lys on it. Pammy never claimed Frenchness in particular, but the prop department had already been given Yeatsman's adaptation of *Madame Bovary*, in which Pammy was to star, and they were confecting various Gallic emblems. "A fleur-de-lys is a hell of a lot better than a Red Star anyway," Yeatsman mumbled as we walked in together. The microphone was so close to the casket that the speakers could hardly escape the impression that they were being judged by its occupant. Finishing a medley of Millevoix songs, the Jubilee studio orchestra segued into the Third Brandenburg Concerto's first movement.

Wagons of flowers had been trucked to the studio by Obie Joyful from the Zangwills' lush hyperbole of a garden. Harry Bridges sent tulips and a thank-you note. From Washington President and Mrs. Roosevelt sent yellow roses and purple violets. From London Prime Minister Ramsay MacDonald sent red and white roses, and from Paris Andre Malraux, as if knowing what Elise Millevoix wanted for her sister, sent a bouquet of white lilies. Unaccountably, since their politics were so far from Pammy's, both William Randolph Hearst and Benito Mussolini had dispatched garlands to honor the fallen star. FDR's and Malraux's messages were notable, the former's mostly because it was from The White House. Goddard Minghoff read aloud from the tributes. "Mrs. Roosevelt and I will forever gratefully recall," the president (or his ghostwriter) said, "the melodic sweetness and captivating charm Palmyra Millevoix brought to a nation recovering hope in a time of unprecedented calamity." Malraux simply quoted himself, or his publishers did, in English: "The greatest mystery is not that we have been flung at random between the profusion of matter and the stars, but that within this prison we can draw from ourselves images powerful enough to deny our nothingness." To which the great author, in the midst of his own leftist period, added, "*Bon voyage, ma petite tourterelle engagée.*"

At least six hundred of Jubilee's contract employees crowded Stage Eight. Mossy was in the front row with Esther Leah, two people sitting next to each other looking as though they were on opposite sides of the country. Two hundred additional seats were set aside for honored guests, mostly from the Hollywood community. Jack Warner wasn't there—no sentimentalist, he would not give up a Saturday polo match—but Louie Mayer was never one to pass up an opportunity to shed righteous tears. Mervyn Gallant had wheedled his way past the guards, steering his Hispano Suiza onto the lot where Joey Jouet had worked until he was fired and, on his last day, bestowed his final act of kindness by fixing the old silent picture director's flat tire prior to pitching himself off the Santa Monica Pier. "A vocalist who'll be greatly missed," Gallant said to no one in particular as he entered Stage Eight, "only wish I could have used her myself." Hurd Dawn also came back to pay his respects to a woman he adored, and I was pleased to see him wearing the old cape that had made him look so majestic I had taken him for Amos Zangwill himself my first day on the lot. Hurd embraced Elise, enfolding her in his cape.

The musicians and composers contingent would have pleased Pammy. Duke Ellington was playing at the Cocoanut Grove, so he was there, as were Benny Goodman, Dorothy Field, Jack Teagarden, and Russ Columbo, who had less than two months to live before his own mysterious gunshot death. Columbo came in with his girlfriend Carole Lombard as all heads turned. They stayed turned while Irving Berlin and Cole Porter, both in town composing picture scores, walked in together.

Bravely, Teresa Blackburn gave the first eulogy. Sensibly, she addressed the casket. "Dear darling Pammy," she said, "what times we had, and should have had. I want to raise a child as you were raising Millie, and learn from you as I learned about my profession, and about personal life, and public life, and about love, from you. You were stolen from us so cruelly it is hard to see any divine hand behind the brutal act. Please help us to carry on in your spirit, your name, with your principles. Anything I ever do that's good will be because I knew you, dearest Pammy."

Prominent friends and colleagues briefly recalled the first time they had met Pammy, and how it was to work with her, and how they missed her. When it was Mossy's turn he walked to the microphone wearing large sunglasses to hide his black eye and perhaps the sting of remorse. Often he reminded me of a cannibal; today he was a defrocked bishop, shamed and using his sunglasses as an unsuccessful disguise. "What happened this week at Jubilee Pictures," he began, "is not only sad and terrible, it is beyond my understanding, beyond all meaning. This taking of Palmyra Millevoix hits all of us where we live most profoundly, and we live most profoundly in our hearts. What can we say or do as we begin to begin again, as we struggle to find any consolation, anything that will comfort us? I can't say I know the answer. I can say Palmyra Millevoix was passionate about her work. I believe she would want us to carry on with ours, and carry on we will."

Listening to Mossy, I wondered who he had dragooned into helping him with this. Maybe for once no one. Did he have any idea how mad she had been at him when she died? He might have. "It's no secret"—he said as I held my breath for a confession, which those around me seemed also to do—"that Pammy and Jubilee had a falling out recently. We wanted what we wanted, and she wanted what she wanted. But these were family quarrels, that's all, and she was working diligently and brilliantly on this very stage, almost finished with a new picture, until two days ago. The last time we spoke I offered her Grushenka in *The Brothers Karamazov*. She accepted eagerly. How wonderful she'd have been in that great role."

The assemblage sagged. Far from an acknowledgment of an affair or even of something as mundane as a new contract, this seemed a blatant lie, possibly made up on the spot. But was it? Who ever knew with Amos Zangwill? He wound up with a little couplet, stretching out every syllable, letting someone else express his feelings so he wouldn't have to reveal them in front of Esther Leah. Possibly he was trying to soothe the anger of the coffin's tenant, apologize to her. "'No more will linger down the days The flowing wonder of her ways.' I yield now to Jubilee's own Yancey Ballard, who tells me where to go when he feels I'm out of line, and who wrote Pammy one of the finest roles she ever had in *The Mill on the Floss*. Yancey talked me into letting the novel's unhappy ending stand, and he was right even though the picture sank without a trace. Sometimes, as we all know today to our sorrow, endings do have to be unhappy."

His cud chewed, his whole body slouching, Mossy returned to his seat.

Yeatsman was the final speaker. He stood silently, staring at the casket for a long moment, and I wasn't sure he could speak at all, he seemed so consumed with rage and grief. "If we are believers," he commenced, "it is hard not to impute to the Almighty a malign intent at such a time. How could he, if he even bothers to exist anymore, let this happen? How in the name of himself could he take her from us? Oh God."

Yancey heaved a sob, and I thought he couldn't continue, but after a pause he summoned his chivalry. "Music is as natural as breathing, as eloquent as prayer; it's how we praise creation, mourn, rejoice. Pammy's music is about delight, sadness, love, loss, sometimes all the emotions in the same room at the same moment. Her music now outlasts her, reminding us of what we had, what we lost."

He put his hand on the casket and patted the white silk covering it. "A studio head," Yancey said, now winding himself up, "and I'll be uncharacteristically charitable enough not to name him except to quiet your fears by revealing he has nothing to do with Jubilee, recently called Palmyra Millevoix a Red bitch. I'll tell you something. This Red bitch could sing. This Red bitch could write, and this Red bitch could act. This Red bitch could turn a braggart into a mouse, and this Red bitch could also turn a man into a giant, and she could turn him back into a cricket whose measly chirp, whose squeak, was that of a bully who had learned his lesson. A number of you out there know firsthand what I'm talking about." Some squirming was visible, and appreciative titters were heard.

"In this room," he continued, "on this sound stage she worked, in this town where we are all geniuses, each of us believing himself or herself to be in possession of more brilliance than the person in the next chair—go ahead, look around, you're better than any of the others, aren't you?—and at the same time assailed by doubts and even by the conviction that all we're doing is fooling our betters who will any day now spot us for the untalented impostors we truly are, which of us knows a star or a musician or a singer or a picture-maker who is not vain? As we pay our respects here to a woman who scorned and mocked vanity, we do well to remember that this occasion is only the frightened tithe we offer death, the wily thief lying in wait to rob all of us of everything we have."

Yeatsman finished as a hush fell over the usually noisy throng of egotists, now as silent as just before a take. "All of us are inflated with illusions," he said. "That is our sin. Pammy had no illusions. That, perhaps, was hers. She had been cured of illusions long before we knew her. Instead of conceit and selfishness, she shared her gifts, her talent for living and loving. She was our graceful swan, comely, elegant, her voice the voice of an angel with sex appeal, her song the song of gentle breezes through trees in leaf, of water playing over pebbles. Who can be here today and not complain with my own hero William Yeats of a fire in our heads? Enough. We can only hope with the Irish bard that our Pammy has found the other wild swans, where she may glide free

And walk among long dappled grass,
And pluck till time and times are done
The silver apples of the moon,
The golden apples of the sun."

Hollywood is no stranger to overdoing everything in its path. But that day, that sweltering noon in the last week of July 1934, the members of the Jubilee family did not perform the tears they shed. As for Mossy himself, he had to be helped from Stage Eight by Elena Frye and Esther Leah. His shiner, hidden behind the dark glasses, was weeping on its own, but I would give him credit for half his tears being genuine grief at the catastrophe he endured, or caused, or both.

The saying around town was that your first murder in Los Angeles was for free. Despite rumors that lived far longer than the victim, no promising suspects surfaced. No arrest was ever made.

The New York Times reported that the passing of Palmyra Millevoix set off a wave of public mourning not seen since the death of Rudolph Valentino eight years earlier. Millevoix fan clubs sponsored memorial services around the country. Some were even held in churches, but the liveliest were in theaters, the picture palaces she had filled with her larger-than-life self that was now also larger than death.

It turned out to be a killing week. In Vienna, Chancellor Engelbert Dollfuss was assassinated during a failed Nazi coup meant to take over Austria. Hitler had to wait another four years to march into Linz, his Austrian hometown, and on to Vienna. In Chicago, the bank robber, murderer, and hard times folk hero John Dillinger was killed by the FBI as he came out of a theater where he had just seen *Manhattan Melodrama* starring Clark Gable, Myrna Loy, and William Powell. Both men and women rushed to dip their handkerchiefs in Dillinger's blood for souvenirs of the bandit some believed was a Robin Hood of the Depression years.

I had to reach Millie before any radios or visitors did. Seven years were all Millie was granted to know her mother, and her mother was all she really knew. My nine years with my own mother suddenly felt opulent. I wondered if Millie had had time to build a little world of her own or if she was still so attached to her mother that this would be like the amputation of a vital organ. What could I do with her, feeling as aimless and neglected as I did? I knew I was at the end of my youth, but being only twenty-four I also knew I was at the beginning of something else, though I wouldn't have dignified it by calling it maturity. It was something larger than I was though I participated in it, something about Hollywood, about the Communists, about the country and our Great Depression, how they all fought one another yet also intersected.

A chilling possibility from the grogshop of my grief: if Pammy had lived would she have become infected by starshine, too burned even to mention me in her memoirs, sticking to fellow celebrities? Very well, I remained in love with a shadow that needed no substance. The shadow itself would reliably vanish, I already knew, like a ballerina twirling offstage, filling me with memory until the day when I become only a memory myself. So are we all, possessors of memories until we are vanished into the memories of others.

Elise Millevoix Jouet wasn't coming out to Red Woods with her own children until the next day. She held herself together until the funeral was over and then essentially collapsed into her twin griefs—for Pammy and, always, her guilt over the death of her husband, her conscience on the rack as if she'd been sentenced by Torquemada. She said she couldn't face Millie until I'd done the dirty work.

I kept my radio off as I set out because I didn't want to hear about the police following their leads, nor did I want to listen to Pammy's songs being played in the dirge of obituaries. This did no good because on a hot day the other cars had their windows down and their radios on. As I drove through the communities heading east, the Millevoix songs rang out until they seemed to be the air I was breathing. Some homes probably had radios on, but the persistence of certain songs suggested people were playing their favorite records on phonographs as they said goodbye. One house played "Dynamite," and I remembered when she and Jolson had sung together—"There's never an erosion, It's more like an explosion When Dinah makes me feel high as the sky; She's such dynamite that I love her, Maybe Dinah might love me too, For I'd love to be her lover And I know that I'd be true." Another house broadcast "Can Sara Wear a Pair 'A Dungarees"—"I'll ask it sweetly, I'll go down upon my knees: Hear my prayer, Mr. McDougall, I know you're kinda frugal, But could Sara wear a pair 'a dungarees?"

A large house in San Marino was blasting forth "I'll be brokenhearted 'till the next time we kiss,/ I'll be brokenhearted, It started when we parted, I'll be brokenhearted, like thiiiiiis." At a mansion half a mile away a loudspeaker had been installed on the lawn and was broadcasting "I can do anything except say goodbye Since the word by itself leaves a tear in my eye, So please don't ask if you don't want me to cry, I never have found where's the good in goodbye." Finally, a house was playing "Born Blue" and I was sure the trees themselves were drooping. It was a small home with a hedge around it in Azusa. "I'm born blue, blue, blue; That's me not you, you, you;

It's always been true … that I was born blue." Pammy herself knew her song fit its composer. For the girl of my dreams, there was never anything else she could be.

The song floated from homes on the afternoon wind. I heard "Born Blue" several more times—in Pomona, Claremont, finally in Upland itself as I approached San Antonio Heights, where Pammy lived. Lived on weekends. Had lived. "If you hear this song in a bar or a train, Put a nickel in the Wurlitzer and play it again." I comforted myself with the sad smile that Pammy's ghost must be tired of singing "Born Blue" by now.

Half a mile from the house was a roadblock. Eight or ten cars were pulled over to the side. The roadblock was manned not by police but by two uniformed guards. I recognized the familiar logo, a starburst with Jubilee Pictures inscribed below it. One of the guards approached me and I identified myself as a writer for the studio and a friend of the family needing to get through to the house to see Miss Millevoix's daughter. The guard addressed me as if he were reading a script written for a Marine officer. "Mr. Zangwill's orders were to keep everyone away until you were inside the property, sir," the guard said. "Fans are showing up for some kind of vigil and we were instructed not to let anyone through until you were with the daughter."

So Mossy was muscling in even now. He wasn't doing any harm. Still, I resented his hand in creating the roadblock. I'd shortly be with the daughter.

I approached the Red Woods grounds, fronted by its row of date palms interspersed with camphor trees, which secluded the house from the road. Pammy had invited me here for the weekend and now here I was. I smelled the pungent camphor before the house was visible, and when I saw the trees I began to be nervous. The palms and camphors, which made agreeable pairs when I'd seen them before, looked uneasy, mismatched today. When I turned into the circular driveway Costanza and Millie rushed out to the front porch of the rambling old ranch house that Pammy had restored. Millie was carrying her puppy, Cordell, with his enormous paws on his small quivering body. How was I going to do this? What could Millie know? Costanza had assured me radios had been put in closets all over the house so Millie would not hear any news at all, much less stations devoting their entire programming to her mother.

As I pulled up in front of the porch Costanza was already talking to me. She was like an overfilled balloon ready to burst. "Mr. Owen, thank God, I'm so glad, I don't know how long –" and she pointed to the edge of the driveway where, though I hadn't noticed as I drove in, a photographer was camped, waiting for a picture of Millie.

"Uncle Owen," Millie said, "what took you so long? We've been waiting for you all day. Will you tell me a story?"

Costanza had evidently continued to hold herself together since I'd last spoken to her on the phone. Now, as she saw me and knew what I had to tell Millie, her face was suddenly, though still silently, a stream of tears. I nodded at her and asked Millie to take me up to her room. Costanza ran to the kitchen and I heard her turn the water on in the sink to hide her bawling as I swept Millie into my arms and started to carry her up the stairs. "Oh, Uncle Owen, don't be silly," she said, "I can beat you upstairs any day." She ran and I followed. Behind me Cordell struggled stair by stair.

Millie's room had stars on the ceiling, a light shade of sky blue on the upper portion of the wall, a darker watery blue on the lower portion. On the wall was a large blown-up photograph of Pammy and Millie as they ran along a beach toward the camera. An eager pair, mirroring each other, all laughter, hair blown on their faces. We sat on Millie's bed, Cordell at her feet. For a moment each of us looked at the other, and I could hear the seconds of Millie's innocence ticking down. I took a deep breath and for some reason she did the same. "Millie honey," I said, "I have to say something I'd give the world not to tell you."

"Hush," she said as she reached up and put her small hand over my mouth. "Let's sing."

34

Aftermath

Confounding my certainties, the General Strike in San Francisco not only happened but more or less succeeded, "more or less" being the operative phrase. No weapons, no more furious demonstrations, no violence. For most, it was a cheerful mutiny. Harry Bridges and the other labor leaders knew they could not beat machine guns and bayonets. Their weapons were numbers. By the thousands, men and women all over San Francisco and Oakland simply left their jobs, a gesture of bravery, perhaps bravado, at a time when over twenty percent of the workforce had no jobs at all. At the final strike vote Bridges announced, "The ayes have it and the nos know it." In addition to the dockworkers, seventy-eight other unions joined the walkout. The General Strike was led by the Teamsters, who had earlier opposed it, and almost all factories and businesses in the Bay Area, even restaurants, were shut down. Some shops hung signs in their windows: "Closed Till the Boys Win." "We're Out as Long as You're Out."

The first woman ever to hold a Cabinet post, Secretary of Labor Frances Perkins, telegraphed President Roosevelt who, in that irony Bridges had aptly noted, was taking a cruise while the seamen and longshoremen were on strike. OFFICERS OF THE UNIONS, Perkins wired, HAVE BEEN SWEPT OFF THEIR FEET BY THE STRENGTH OF THE RANK AND FILE MOVEMENT STOP THERE IS

UNUSUAL MASS MOVEMENT UNUSUAL SOLIDARITY AND UNITY STOP THERE HAS BEEN RELATIVELY LITTLE DISORDER UNTIL THE POLICE WERE PUT ON THE DOCKS WITH ORDERS TO SHOOT IF NECESSARY STOP THE SITUATION IS SERIOUS BUT NOT YET HOPELESS STOP.

When Secretary of State Cordell Hull (of Pammy's jingle and Millie's puppy) and Attorney General Homer Cummings advised that the U.S. Army be mobilized to put down the strike, Perkins warned that it would be unwise for the Roosevelt administration to start shooting it out with working people, especially working people who were only exercising their rights. She said the General Strike was not led by the Communists, who were loudmouthed but not in control, any more than by the traditional union leaders, who had pretty much been discarded. For his part FDR counseled from shipboard that he'd like to see arbitration, which had already failed to win support from either side. "A lot of people completely lost their heads," he later recalled, "and telegraphed me that I should sail into San Francisco Bay, all flags flying and guns double-shotted, and end the strike." He did nothing. Perhaps more presidents should take more vacations; Roosevelt continued his cruise and let the conflict run its course.

The course, in the event, was a short one. With the Bay Area approaching a crisis as the basic provisions of food and gasoline were cut off, the mass walkout of over one hundred thousand men and women lasted only four hot July days. As the General Strike went into its second and third days, panic ruled the business districts. In contrast, Mike Quin wrote me gleefully, a holiday spirit prevailed in working-class neighborhoods. "Like the workers themselves," Quin said, "the owners know perfectly well no revolution is coming, but they use revolutionary rumors as a strategy to scare the middle class." He couldn't finish his thought without landing an uppercut to my jaw, to everyone in the picture business: "You show good people as well dressed and groomed and polite with clean shirts on, the better sort; rough features and soiled clothes are signs of the underworld and the lower classes, not people you'd want to associate with. Workers and people who look like workers, that's who the movies paint into crime scenes."

The Teamsters, who began the General Strike, broke it, leaving Longshoremen in the lurch, and then the Longshoremen went back to work, leaving the Seamen on dry land. Quickly, all the unions followed the Teamsters and returned to their jobs. The solidarity that Harry Bridges wanted vanished even from his own union (he had opposed going back to work), and it appeared, as San Francisco caught its breath again, that the owners had won.

Yet the strike changed the labor scene. The solidarity was gone, but the fear remained, and this time the fear belonged to the owners. If this happened once, they understood, it could happen again. At another mass meeting in Dreamland—one of many during the next few weeks—federal, municipal, and union officials were all shouted down when they urged settlements favoring the dock and shipowners. A chant of "We Want Bridges!" went up throughout the auditorium until Bridges took the stage and said all workers had nothing to lose by standing firm until their demands were met.

When the inevitable arbitration—proposed by FDR—was over, the longshoremen won almost everything they had struck for. Wages rose, hours declined, overtime pay became standard, working conditions improved. Most importantly, the company union on the docks was gone, and the International Longshoreman's Association became the sole bargaining entity for the dockworkers. Daily hiring was put under the nominal control of both the employers and the union, but since the dispatcher had to be from the union, only union members were dispatched. The power of the longshoremen, and the authority of Harry Bridges, remained solid for decades.

Defiantly, the longshoremen's newspaper printed a declaration: "Labor is prior to and independent of capital. Capital is only the fruit of labor, and could never have existed if labor had not first existed. Labor is the superior of capital, and deserves much the higher consideration." The foregoing is not, the newspaper went on to point out, an instruction from Moscow. It is a quotation from Abraham Lincoln.

Union fever was rising in Hollywood too. I joined the Screen Writers Guild, barely out of the larva stage, the precursor of the other talent guilds. At Jubilee, even the producers were talking about forming a guild until Yeatsman went to them and said, "You blind bats—what the hell do you think a studio is, or the Motion Picture Academy itself for Christ's sake, if not a producer's association?"

Mossy assigned Nils Matheus Maynard to direct the love story, if it was that, of Queen Victoria and Prince Albert. The executives reasoned that Nils's hemophilia would enhance his sensitivity to the bleeding disease that affected Victoria's own family. The studio also announced it would produce the biography of its fallen star. The picture was to be called *Crusading Angel* and would be written by Jamie McPhatter, Sylvia Solomon's bombastic heavy drinking former escort, who had never known Pammy but who had come up with the title. I vowed to sabotage this project and told myself it would be for Millie's sake. McPhatter was halfway through the first draft when one night I wrote him an anonymous memo that his pages reeked of maudlin insincerity masking his reactionary contempt for his subject. Whether because of my nastiness—I hadn't seen a word he'd written—or because Comfort O'Hollie purposely mangled his scenes as she typed them, McPhatter stayed drunk for the next week and then was taken off the script. The title was changed, fresh writers were put on the story, but the project was allowed to dwindle before anything serious was done about it. Who, for instance, would expose herself to the darts that would be aimed at any actress presuming to impersonate Pammy?

In the weeks following Pammy's death I could barely function. Memory was still too sharp a pain to allow the thought to surface that most people went their whole lives without knowing Palmyra Millevoix while I—and selected others I chose to ignore—had been brushed by the wand of a fairy godmother who granted the wish I had never dared to wish. And then snatched it away. I felt like a painter who contrived to put a singular wash over his canvas that would, years later, bring out the colors even more vividly than when he first applied them. Instead of fading, the pigments became stronger, burned more brightly, than they had even in the moment. The only lasting solace came to me decades later, after the war, with the relief that she had not had to endure the frightful Hollywood blacklist, the years of betrayal and ostracism and cowardice.

Love Is for Strangers, the picture Pammy was making when she died, was near enough to completion that Mossy wanted it released and knew Millevoix fans would flock to it. The principal scene that Pammy hadn't lived to film was the reunion with her mother when the latter is enduring her fatal illness. Pammy's entrance to the sickroom had already been shot. The rest of the scene plays in close-ups of Ethel Barrymore and medium shots of Pammy's stand-in from behind looking at Ethel, whose earlier hauteur has given way to apologetic humility. Pammy's lines were shortened to a simple, "It's all right, Mother, it's all right," played over the back of the stand-in's head. The words were borrowed from an earlier picture where she had been Marie Dressler's daughter and Marie had accidentally poisoned the family dog. Nils retrieved a shot from a third picture, a scene where Pammy had been about to kiss Trent Amberlyn and the shot had been over Trent's shoulder. Nils had this blown up to eliminate Trent and create a close-up of Pammy, then matted it into the room where Pammy was visiting Ethel. The way the shot emerges, instead of expectantly awaiting a kiss from the gay actor Pammy now looks eager for reconciliation with her mother. For the final shot of the scene, Ethel insists on getting out of bed and kneels to bury her head in the stand-in's lap, eternally sorry for having been such an antiquated fool. The scene, and the picture, ends when she raises her head and says to Pammy, "Now when can I see my grandchild?"

The slight solace that did come to me within months was a weak, bitter tea. I found myself at Jubilee one morning in the fall, the grim weeks of the Santa Ana wind when the dry air blasts everything in its path. Against the wind's moan, I was in Mossy's office with a clutch of others having a story conference. I had come to be soothed by these meetings, whose levity opposed my grief; I could say anything and get away with it without paying much attention because no one was paying much attention to me. Haunting the story conferences of other writers who were glad to have someone along to dodge barbs with, I was protected from being alone in my office with nothing to do, from direct images of Pammy and her laughter, the way she sounded, her half smile, and always the hole that sprung in her forehead. "Let's have Teresa pregnant then, already pregnant when she steps off the train even if we don't know it yet," Yeatsman was saying. "Then when she meets Trent, we know she's been through hell and he has to do some thinking himself. He's always too goddamned naïve if you ask me, with that knowing but basically ignorant grin. It's time Trent Amberlyn grew up."

A stunned silence. I'd only half-heard Yeatsman. Should I try to rescue him or was Mossy about to take up the idea? "Very funny, Yancey," Mossy at last chipped in mirthlessly. "The Hays Office let a woman unbenefitted by clergy just suddenly be knocked up, walk pregnant right into a movie? Let's be serious."

The sex scandals of the Twenties having hobbled Hollywood, the Hays Office was the rigid morals police. Yet Yancey was on the right track. I came to life, in my fashion. "No, no, the woman had a husband," I offered, "and the guy climbed on the top of the train to rescue a hobo who'd gotten stuck up there. It was their honeymoon. He fell off, widowing her within a week of their wedding. Now she can be pregnant."

"You're coming out of your coma," Mossy said. "Thanks, pal," Yeatsman said.

That's right, I thought. It's high time Trent Amberlyn grew up.

I was put to work on the screenplay of *Lorna Doone*, the English adventure tale of warring clans and ultimately triumphant romance. At last: I could write the story of a man who actually saves the woman he loves even though she does get shot. That buoyed me. It wasn't my story—in Hollywood you don't write your own story—but it was a reclamation project all the same.

I collect and recollect. Especially in Hollywood, memory is a function of myth, a product of whoever has the strongest fantasy of the moment, the most persistent dream. Dreams don't only matter; they are matter. In a climate of exaggeration, where within weeks we all come to believe our own superlatives, who could say which were, pardon me, *really true*, and which mere figments? What if I am the undetected guest at the banquet of life? Nothing more than a speck in a landscape by Watteau. A derivative figure with its uses in the painting, drawing the eye to significance, perspective, the vastness of everything else, how sublime it all is in comparison with the speck.

Yancey cheered me, or tried to, one day when he shot a question at me direct from Yeats, a query both soothing and unanswerable: "'Does the imagination dwell the most On a woman won or a woman lost?'"

He had me there.

Years later, when Yeatsman was questioned about Gloriana Flower's Party party, where he had contributed a thousand dollars, he refused to say anything to his inquisitors beyond a passage from his sage: "'O but we dreamed to mend Whatever mischief seemed To afflict mankind, but now That winds of winter blow Learn that we were crackpated when we dreamed.'" They cited him for contempt.

When he emerged from the blacklist, Yancey persevered in Hollywood. His later gloom—I wouldn't call it tragedy—was that his originals seldom got made and weren't very successful. His regret was that he neither went home, as he called it, to novels and plays nor did he become a director, which would have enabled him to guide his pages onto the screen. His adaptations continued to pay him handsomely, and he was too gracious to allow self-contempt, the occupational hazard of screenwriters, to leak out. He was still in good form on his eightieth birthday, quoting the master as always: "'Did all old men and women, rich and poor, Who trod upon these rocks or passed this door, Whether in public or in secret, rage As I do now against old age?'" When he was finally installed at Forest Lawn a few years back, a cheeky young writer, jealous of Yeatsman's status, said in the commissary after Yancey's sound stage memorial service that his headstone should bear the Yeats quote, "'The best lack all conviction.'" Mossy, no longer head of the studio but still its biggest stockholder and on hand that day for Yancey's service, had the writer fired on the spot.

Gloriana Flower's party took its toll on others as well. When political investigations strafed Hollywood Edward G. Robinson was accused, twenty years later, of having had the temerity or bad judgment to attend Gloriana's gathering. To this charge he replied both sheepishly and defiantly. He said he'd been naïve, on the one hand, and that on the other hand it was nobody's business but his own where he went and what he did. Sylvia Solomon, my obliging date at the party, put her own situation succinctly after being named by, of all people, Mitch Altschuler, perhaps the most passionate Communist any of us knew. "Why was I a Communist?" she repeated the Congressional investigator's question. "Well, since the Communists were the only people standing up for what I believed in against the terrifying inequality and prejudice and economic rapaciousness in America, it seemed silly not to be one of them." She was duly blacklisted. As for the two Communist recruiters at Gloriana's house, Greta Kimple and Mort Leech, they were *agents provocateurs*. When they finished seducing, in their curious way, new Party members, they shed their Red masks to reveal that their true faces were those of the FBI. They turned in everyone they'd ever turned, including Kimple's brother and Leech's wife, whom he promptly divorced. Then Greta Kimple and Mort Leech married.

When the inquisition came for me, small potatoes, I was a step ahead of it. I'd left Hollywood for Rome and buried myself in spaghetti Westerns until the storm blew over.

Hindsight, reputed to be twenty-twenty by social ophthalmologists, is actually muddied by everything that happened between the event and whatever present we choose for our judgment platform. The Communist functionaries Zinoviev and Kamenev, for instance, specified by Mitch Altschuler as Jews Stalin valued in his inner circle, were purged and executed in 1936. Mitch scoffed at the possibility that Hitler would kill all five hundred thousand Jews in Germany; Hitler, of course, was only clearing his throat when he reached the half million mark in dead Jews. Having named all the Red names he could think of for the House Un-American Activities Committee, Mitch managed to remain employed in Hollywood, but he lost his furious wife and most of his friends. "I saw the light when the Korean War started and I knew my own country was fighting the Communists," Mitch told the Committee, though in fact he had signed a protest against the war right after it began in 1950.

For labor racketeering and extortion Willie Bioff was eventually sentenced to ten years in prison. Alcatraz did not suit his Hollywood tastes, and he soon asked to testify against his former confederates. Five of them were convicted, and Bioff was paroled. A dozen years later, after moving to Arizona and changing his name to Bill Nelson, becoming friends with Barry Goldwater and going into business with the senator's nephew, Bioff started his pickup one morning and the explosion blew his body parts twenty-five feet from the wreckage. Hollywood treated its informers with the alternating current of professional rehabilitation and social ostracism; the mob's solution was simpler.

In San Francisco, the anniversary of Bloody Thursday was marked for many years by a memorial to martyrs when longshoremen stopped work in honor of Nick Bordoise and Howard Sperry. Harry Bridges became an institution. Mike Quin wrote his own account of the dockworkers' strike but died before it was published.

Time is a controlling force here, a character enacting its own will. No good reason exists for it to go forward always and not turn around the way other characters do, or even travel in a curve endlessly encircling itself. If time is arbitrary and indivisible, as physicists come closer each year to believing, Pammy is still singing and Yancey still quoting, or in another sphere they have not yet begun. Pammy will always be available melodically regardless of the state of recording technology. We may as easily find Mossy Zangwill dressing, conscientiously outfitting himself in front of his wife or a mistress as we might discover Achilles girding himself for battle. It is not purely a sadistic joke, though the slimeball means it that way, when my agent tells me it is part of Hollywood's doctrinal minutiae that my own future is behind me. So it has been always.

The time is coming when we will venture both into what we decide is the known past as well as the unknown future. Then we will know whether Palmyra Millevoix studied music formally—I never asked her—or just let it flow from her, whether she knew she was going to die, whether she loved me or merely flung her charms in my direction for the nonce to amuse herself.

Dr. Pogorzelski wondered if we are dreaming or dreamed. I knew the answer finally. We are encased within our own dream, dreamers and dreamed both. An actor is only someone performing in someone else's dream. When Pammy dies she is no longer dreaming but instantly becomes, forever, anyone else's dream. The dream within the dream, ect ect ect as Mossy would put it. You dream of a prince who dreams of a princess who dreams of a bear who dreams of a seal who dreams of a queen who dreams of you.

In the parallel universe where antimatter presides, there are no films but anti-films. These are the movies we writers write that never get made. I have my name on quite a few of these, some starring such luminaries as Spencer Tracy and Olivia de Havilland, others stocked with unknowns I thought would be right for my screenplays. There are even anti-movies of movies that did get made but with other casts. *Casablanca* not with Bogart and Bergman but with the benign Fred MacMurray or earnest Ty Power and the no-nonsense Maureen O'Hara or Loretta Young. Can't you see MacMurray or Ronald Reagan or Robert Montgomery wrinkling their sincere brows to say "I was misinformed" when told the waters are nowhere near Casablanca, or later, "We'll always have Paris"? And Loretta Young, who would never acknowledge having had a love child (as they were called then) with Clark Gable in real life, how about her trying to say throatily, "I wish I didn't love you so much," or "Kiss me, kiss me as if it were the last time"? Tinny? Can we say Palmyra Millevoix continues to sing in this parallel universe, and does her unconscious exist there too? I don't believe in ghosts, but what exists exists.

Millie Millevoix moved in with her Aunt Elise and her cousins. I looked in on her and she was doing all right, a new school in the fall and her puppy Cordell embraced into the new family as its only male figure. Millie didn't ask me to tell stories anymore.

The police did detain a few suspects but only for questioning. They had no real evidence. Anyone could have done it. People have asked me whether Pammy would have been killed if she hadn't gone to San Francisco and been inspired, or fooled, or inoculated into believing the waterfront strike could be exported, transposed, down the coast to a Hollywood studio. Pammy was hardly ignorant of the differences between dockworkers and filmmakers. She was excited by the possibilities of steering Hollywood, such a company town, toward a condition where the distribution of wealth and power was more equitable. She would, I imagine, have cheered the breakup of the old studio system that took place after the war, and she would also, I further imagine, have been appalled at the power that fell, as a result of the breakup, into the hands of prima-donna actors and autocratic directors. But I don't know. Perhaps she'd have become a prima donna herself.

The course of Palmyra Millevoix, viewed from the twinkling interval when left was right and right was wrong, or from the year she served in the blood bank during the First World War until she made tourniquets for the San Francisco strikers and mounted the platform outside Jubilee Pictures, has the arc and thrust of an appointed curve. If she could speak to us from her crypt at Forest Lawn, I have no doubt she would say, "What happened to me signifies nothing, only destiny. We make our choices and our choices, in their sweet turn, make us. Someone please watch over Millie."

Years later a French director trying his luck in Hollywood told me he had glimpsed Pammy once, in solitude, in the early Twenties, on a promenade outside a dance at Cap d'Antibes. The Eden-Roc, vanilla cream marble, and the lordly look of statuary, facing off against the shadowy Mediterranean. He said she was smiling to herself and there was a small roar from the sea as she walked slowly toward the balustrade and the hotel glided backward. He didn't dare disturb her. I see her present in his wistful sketch, the way she inhabited her diaphanous ballgown, in heartbreaking profile, looking out over the terraced gardens leading down to the blue, dark water, spinning her web whether anyone watched or not, everything yet to come.

Author's Note

My primary source for this novel was growing up in Hollywood, the son of screenwriters, in the decades following Owen Jant's coming of age in the 1930s. The time before my time drew me to itself like a Venus flytrap I couldn't escape, a black hole I desperately wanted to shine some light into. Additionally, my shelves hold more than sixty books on one or another aspect of motion pictures, the Great Depression, the San Francisco dockworkers' strike, the American Communist Party, popular songs, magic, and hemophilia.

A few books seemed to become, along with my own background, part of my DNA. *An Empire of Their Own: How the Jews Invented Hollywood* by Neal Gabler, and *City of Nets: A Portrait of Hollywood in the 1940s* by Otto Friedrich are both enriching. Though my imagination flew back to the 1930s, specifically a few heady months in 1934, Friedrich couldn't resist taking informative backward glances to see what went on earlier that made the Forties what they became. Likewise, Gabler's superb portrait of Hollywood was not restricted to what Jews themselves contributed.

The Bancroft Library at the University of California, Berkeley contains almost numberless oral histories and accounts of the dockworkers' strike in San Francisco. The two books I found particularly helpful are *Workers on the Waterfront: Seamen, Longshoremen, and Unionism in the 1930s* by Bruce Nelson, and *The Big Strike* by Mike Quin, published after his death. I was using it for research when one day Quin marched right out of his own book and into my story.

One fictional character in *Girl of My Dreams* is also not original. Bruno Leonard, the professor from New York who harangues the faithful at Gloriana Flower's party, was first a character in *The Unpossessed* by Tess Slesinger, a novel published in 1934. My justification for this is I think it's okay to steal from your own mother.

Acknowledgments

Authors traditionally thank immediate family members last. Get the better half into this even if it feels like an afterthought. I prefer first coming first. Without the critical eye, perseverance, advice, and patience of my wife, Alicia Anstead, a writer and editor herself, this novel would not exist in anything like its present form. My daughter, Tonia Davis, a studio executive, pored over an early draft as if she were Sherlock Holmes sleuthing a misdeed. While she may not have solved the crime, she certainly humbled the criminal.

I am grateful to others who read versions or portions of the novel. Sally Arteseros provided useful editorial help on an early draft. Additionally, Dr. Henry Kandler, Andrea Pitzer, John Mankiewicz, Jeffrey Lewis, Professor Christie McDonald, and Elizabeth Murphy all gave beneficial advice, criticism, and suggestions.

Laura Starrett has copy-edited with an admirable attentiveness to detail.

I very much appreciate Open Road's having become the highway for *Girl of My Dreams*.

My agent, Julia Lord, has seen this novel through many drafts and revisions; she has my lasting gratitude along with my hopes that her other authors don't take so long.

About the Author

Peter Davis is an acclaimed author and filmmaker whose writing has won praise from Graham Greene, John Irving, Robert Stone, and William Styron. He covered the war in Iraq for the *Nation* and was a contributing editor for *Esquire*. He spent eighteen months traveling among the poorest Americans for *If You Came This Way*, the title of which is from a poem by T. S. Eliot. Davis's films have won many prizes, and he received an Academy Award for his documentary on the Vietnam War, *Hearts and Minds*.

CPSIA information can be obtained at www.ICGtesting.com
Printed in the USA
BVOW05s1752040615

402954BV00003B/3/P